THE LUCKY SIX

Other works by Gordon Cooper

Watkins Glen Tour Guide

THE LUCKY SIX

ILLUSTRATED & ANNOTATED

A NOVEL

BY

GORDON COOPER

PRESTON WOODS PUBLISHING CO.

LOS GATOS

2025

The Lucky Six
By Gordon Cooper

Preston Woods Publishing Company
Los Gatos, CA 95032 USA

10 9 8 7 6 5 4 3 2 1

Library of Congress Control Number: 2024900932

ISBN 978-0-9725571-8-4

In memory of my father,
John Allen "Jack" Cooper,
who always enjoyed a good story

Watkins Glen Cavern Cascade and The Grotto

CONTENTS

PREFACE   XI

GLINTING GOLD   1

I   A GOLDEN DEATH   3
II   GLENWOOD CEMETERY   11
III   34TH NORTH CAROLINA   19
IV   THE SHERIFF AND THE GENERAL   26
V   THE TOMBS   35
VI   THE LANTERN   45
VII   FRESH FISH   55
VIII   THE MADAM   59
IX   LEAVING NEW YORK   69
X   HICKORY NUT GAP   74
XI   PULLMAN PARLOR CAR   81
XII   LUXURY HOTELS   89
XIII   INTERVIEW AT LAKE VIEW   99
XIV   TEA WITH ABRAHAM 111
XV   ENGLISHMEN'S REMAINS   121
XVI   UNEXPECTED VISITOR   127
XVII   HOPE'S ART GALLERY   137

AMIDST SYLVAN GLENS   145

XVIII   THE BROWNSTONE   147
XIX   DEATH AND DESERTION   155
XX   FALLEN ANGEL   161
XXI   THE JEFFERSON MEETING   170
XXII   UP THE CHURCH TOWER   179
XXIII   FACING THE FIRING SQUAD   191
XXIV   PLAYING CROQUET   197
XXV   STEAM YACHT *ESTELLE*   207
XXVI   BATTLE OF THE WILDERNESS   218
XXVII   GLEN ELDRIDGE   225
XXVIII   KIDNAPPED   233
XXIX   OVERBOARD   244

XXX TRAIN TO HELL............................ 252
XXXI THE PINKERTON 260
XXXII HIGH WIRE ACT 274
XXXIII ELMIRA PRISON CAMP.................... 289
XXXIV CIRCUS MENAGERIE 299

BEWARE SECRETS HELD 307

XXXV THE LIST................................ 309
XXXVI SUDDEN DEATH........................... 312
XXXVII SOUTHBOUND 326
XXXVIII THE TATTOO 333
XXXIX CORNELL UNIVERSITY.................... 344
XL DISAPPOINTMENT 361
XLI THE JOURNAL 366
XLII CONFESSIONS........................... 380
XLIII GOLDEN DECEPTION 399
XLIV FALLEN MAN............................ 406
XLV CHEMUNG CANAL 421
XLVI ORTUS SOLIS 435
XLVII THE HIDEOUT 447
XLVIII PAST REVISITED 461
XLIX MELANCHOLY 470
L SOLDIER'S HEART 479
LI FREER'S OPERA HOUSE 490

SHADOWS DANCE 505

LII UNMASKED 506
LIII THE SURVIVOR.......................... 522
LIV BLOODY REUNION......................... 531
LV ANGEL OF DEATH 541
LVI A BEAUTIFUL FUNERAL.................... 546
LVII A GOLDEN OFFERING 566

HISTORICAL NOTES 569

ACKNOWLEDGMENTS 570

ABOUT THE AUTHOR 572

LIST OF ILLUSTRATIONS

1. APOLLO BELVEDERE AT GLEN ELDRIDGE 228
2. ART GALLERY 136
3. BATTLE OF FREDERICKSBURG 54
4. BATTLE OF THE WILDERNESS 220
5. BILLIARDS ROOM. 548
6. BLUE BEARD TABLEAU VIVANT 30
7. BROOKLYN BRIDGE TOWERS 146
8. CANAL BOAT AND MULES 430
9. CEMETERY AT NIGHT 6
10. CIRCUS COMING TO TOWN 280
11. CIRCUS ENTRANCE 308
12. CORNELL UNIVERSITY 352
13. CORNER OF FRANKLIN AND FOURTH, WATKINS, NY 110
14. ELEPHANT AND DROMEDARY. 298
15. ELMIRA PRISON CAMP 290
16. FIRST PRESBYTERIAN CHURCH, WATKINS. 180
17. FLOCKS OF WILD PIGEONS 100
18. GLEN MOUNTAIN HOUSES AND BRIDGE. 96
19. GLEN MOUNTAIN HOUSE, SOUTH AND NORTH 316
20. GLEN MOUNTAIN HOUSE SWISS CHALET. 162
21. HECTOR FALLS. 236
22. HICKORY-NUT GAP, CHIMNEY ROCK 78
23. HORSE DRAWN TROLLEY. 390
24. JEFFERSON HOUSE 174
25. LAKE SARATOGA 444
26. LAKE VIEW HOTEL 90
27. MALT HOUSE GROWING FLOOR 448
28. MONTOUR HOUSE, HAVANA, NY 266
29. MULE TRAIN 24
30. MULE TRAIN 24
31. NEW YORK CITY AND THE HUDSON RIVER 68
32. NEW YORK THEATER. 466
33. NIAGARA FALLS CAVE OF THE WINDS 544
34. NIGHT STORM 420

35. Overlooking Seneca Lake 410
36. Picking Cotton 114
37. Playing Croquet 198
38. Potomac River from Maryland 360
39. Pullman Parlor Car Interior 82
40. Railroad Disaster 258
41. Rebels In Prison 294
42. Return to the Brothel......................... 286
43. Roland and Mrs. Phelps........................ 372
44. Sailboat on Seneca Lake....................... 516
45. Sailing Before the Storm...................... 416
46. Sea Monster 250
47. Searching the Cave 124
48. Small Town Opera House....................... 496
49. Stock Exchange Doors Being Closed in 1873....... 214
50. Susquehanna River 328
51. Taughannock Falls............................ 346
52. The Livery................................... 398
53. Tombs City Prison, Interior 42
54. Tombs City Prison, Lower Manhattan 34
55. Trinity Church 528
56. War Between the States........................ 18
57. Watkins, Courthouse and Sheriff's Residence 382
58. Watkins Glen, Cavern Cascade and Long Stairs..... 142
59. Watkins Glen Cavern Cascade and The Grotto vi
60. Watkins Glen, Entrance........................ 166
61. Watkins Glen, Rainbow Falls 486
62. Watkins Glen, The Cathedral 568
63. Watkins, New York 2
64. Watkins, Steamship Landing and Train Station 206
65. Winter Camp................................. 190

PREFACE

In 2009, I wrote *Watkins Glen Tour Guide*, a history and travel book for the picturesque village my family moved to when I was three years old. As I researched and wrote that book, I was fascinated by the long forgotten historical details I uncovered—many existing now only as echoes of the past reflected in repurposed buildings, historical panels in the Glen, or the monthly journals from the Schuyler County Historical Society. I wanted to explore some of those stories in more detail.

This book is a work of fiction. The main characters and plot are all fictional. However, as much as possible, the world I have placed these characters in is based on the real world of 1874. Most locations are real, and some events and supporting players are as well.

Let me be clear, I did not write this book as a history lesson. My goal was to write an entertaining mystery/thriller that immerses you in a world that—as much as I can recreate—once existed. The illustrations are all original engravings from the late 1800s, although some have been modified to fit the narrative.

You shouldn't need additional knowledge to read this book, but for those who prefer a bit of backstory, here are some nuggets of information to provide more context.

Watkins Glen today is a tourist town at the end of Seneca Lake, the largest of the Finger Lakes, in upstate New York. It is known for its famous gorge, the many vineyards and wineries along Seneca Lake, and its rich auto-racing history. The roots of its life as a tourist destination began in 1863 when Morvalden Ells saw the potential of the 1.5-mile gorge that flows into the village. He built wooden walkways and stairs, advertised like crazy, and successfully opened "Watkins Glen" as a tourist attraction.

The village at the time was named Watkins after its late founder, Samuel Watkins. The gorge was named Watkins Glen. For years, visitors confused the village's name with the name of the gorge, so in 1927, the village of Watkins officially changed its name to Watkins Glen. The village's neighbor to the south, Montour Falls, also had a name change. It was called Havana until 1893.

I chose 1874 because it was the peak of a tourist boom in Watkins. By the 1870s, the United States was transforming into an industrial nation. The railroads that sprang up everywhere helped rapidly move raw materials and goods across the country and created an interconnected society. People were free to travel longer distances and were in search of exciting destinations. Watkins Glen became one of those destinations, and its charms were often compared to Mammoth Cave and Niagara Falls.

The American Civil War enters the story because of the overlooked part that Elmira, New York—only thirty miles south of Watkins Glen—played with its prisoner of war (POW) camp for Confederate soldiers. Elmira rivaled its southern counterpart, Andersonville, in prisoner deaths, but northern newspaper readers heard much more about the horrors of Andersonville than Elmira. As Winston Churchill famously said, "History is written by the victors."

The 1870s were difficult times for women and people of color. Despite advancements in the women's rights championed in nearby Seneca Falls, N.Y., women were still discouraged from working outside the home and often limited to low-paying jobs when they did. Women would not win the right to vote until the 19th Amendment passed in 1920. At the same time, freed slaves were trying to find their footing in a world biased against them. I tried to balance historical accuracy with respect for these groups. Whether I succeeded or failed in that attempt, I defer to your judgment as a reader.

With that, you have enough information to start your journey back to the late 1800s. Enjoy the adventure!

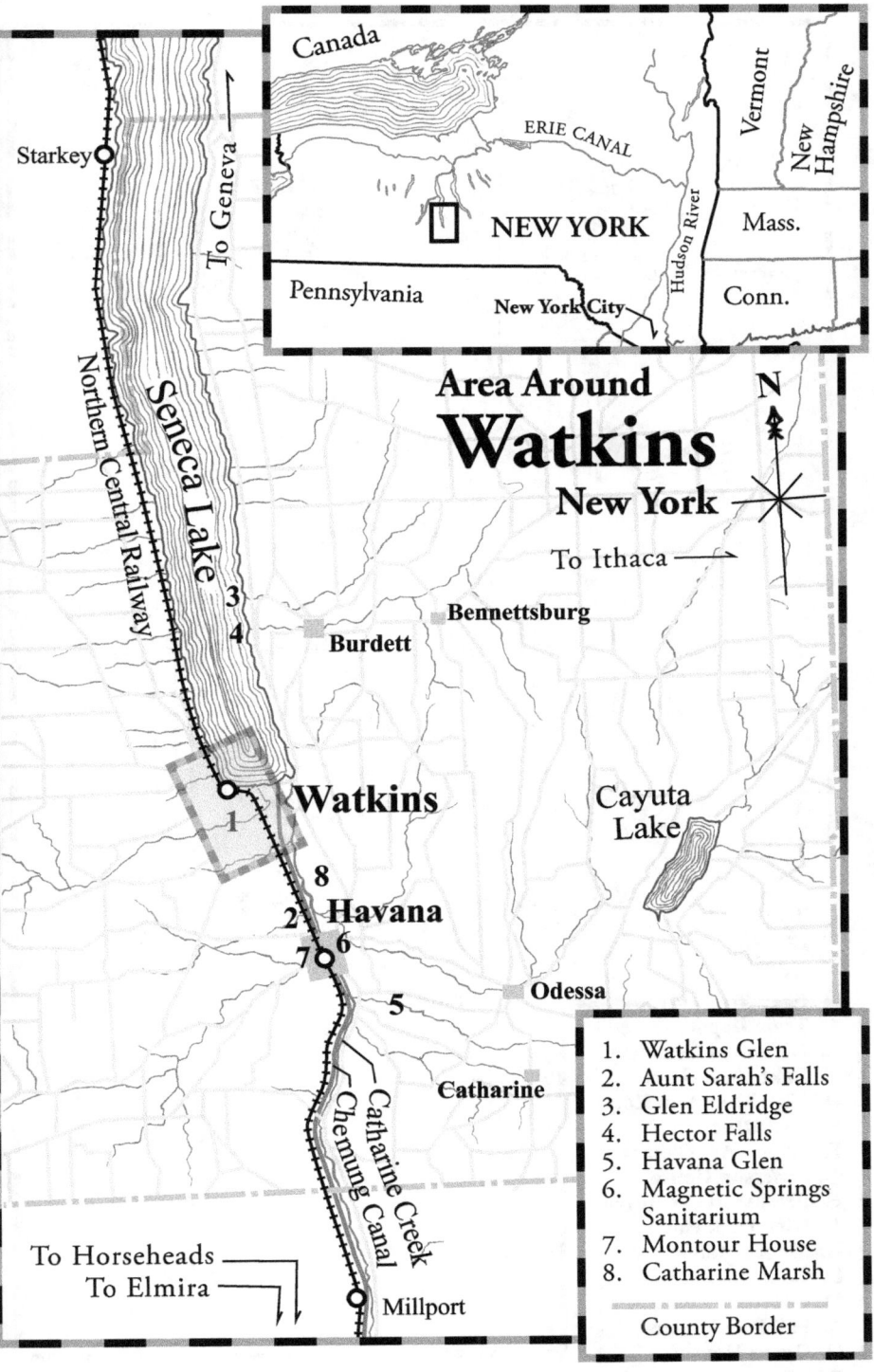

Canada

ERIE CANAL

Vermont

New Hampshire

NEW YORK

Mass.

Pennsylvania

New York City

Hudson River

Conn.

Starkey

To Geneva

Northern Central Railway

Seneca Lake

Area Around
Watkins
New York

N

To Ithaca

3
4

Burdett

Bennettsburg

Watkins

Cayuta
Lake

8

2   Havana
7   6

Odessa

5

Catharine

Catharine Creek
Chemung Canal

To Horseheads
To Elmira

Millport

1. Watkins Glen
2. Aunt Sarah's Falls
3. Glen Eldridge
4. Hector Falls
5. Havana Glen
6. Magnetic Springs
   Sanitarium
7. Montour House
8. Catharine Marsh

County Border

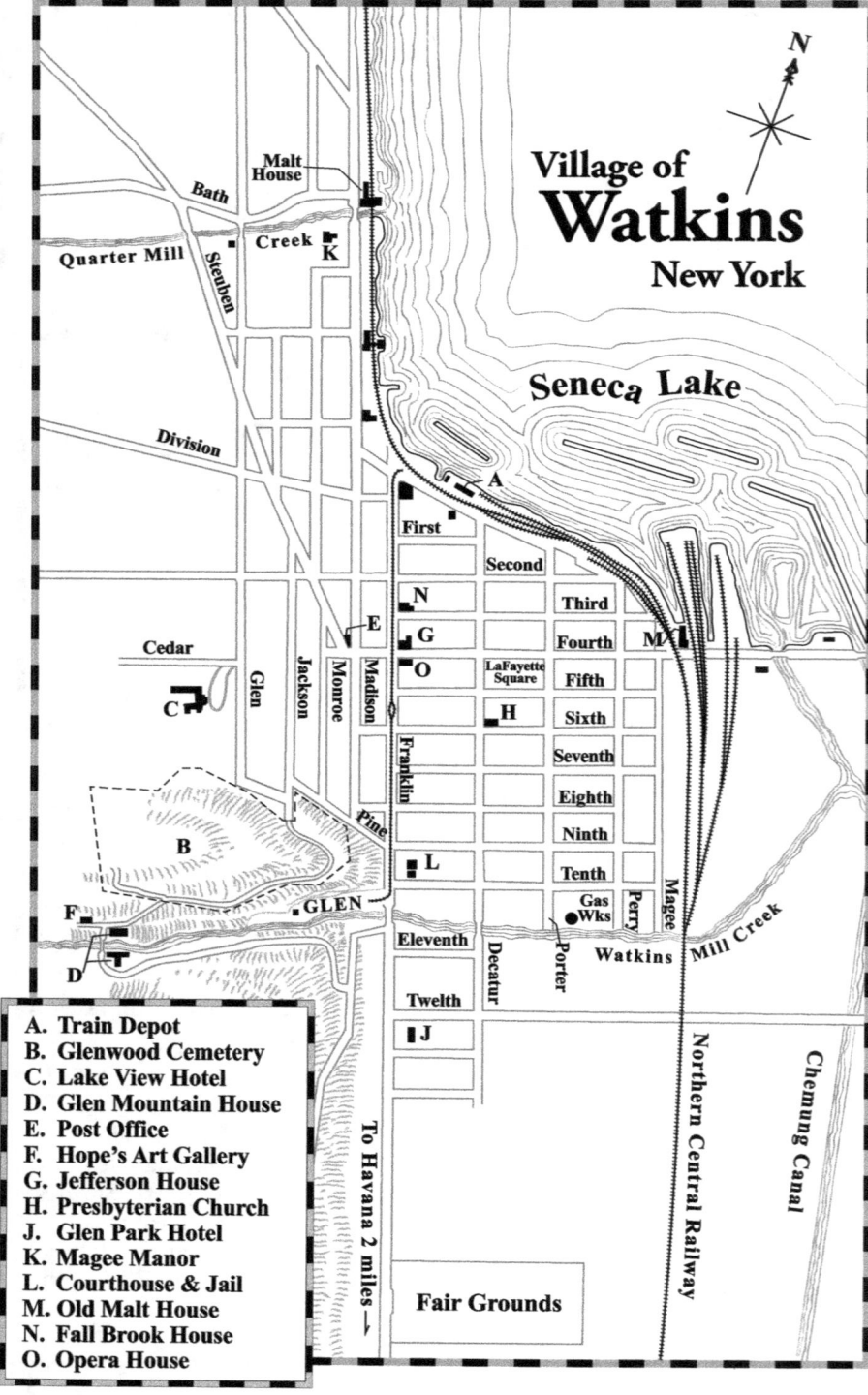

Village of **Watkins** New York

Seneca Lake

A. Train Depot
B. Glenwood Cemetery
C. Lake View Hotel
D. Glen Mountain House
E. Post Office
F. Hope's Art Gallery
G. Jefferson House
H. Presbyterian Church
J. Glen Park Hotel
K. Magee Manor
L. Courthouse & Jail
M. Old Malt House
N. Fall Brook House
O. Opera House

Fair Grounds

To Havana 2 miles →

Memories fade but ghosts reside,
In fields of war, where hope had died.
Lest glinting gold release its thrall,
Amidst sylvan glens and thundering falls,
Beware secrets held, dark and deep,
For shadows dance where dangers creep.

PART ONE

GLINTING GOLD

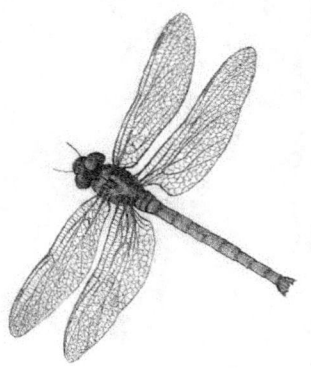

WATKINS, NEW YORK

CHAPTER I

A GOLDEN DEATH

Friday, July 10, 1874

ON an unseasonably warm and dry summer afternoon, Lewis Crawford stepped down from the Northern Central train in the small village of Watkins, New York, unaware that he would be dead before the next sunrise. Not yet forty, his legs cramped and his joints ached after the long journey. Had he known his end was near, he would have reboarded the train and hurried back south to die in the land of fragrant magnolia trees, warm peach cobbler, and humid summer days surrounded by a wife who loved him and an extended family that did not. Crawford journeyed to this northern village, determined to right an old wrong and desperate to reclaim a life that had been stolen from him. But determination and desperation can blind a man and obscure the subtle warning signs that his future would follow a different trajectory.

Crawford walked a few paces away from the train and stopped to orient himself. Men of various ages passed by wearing dark multipiece suits and silk top hats, felt bowlers, or straw boaters to block the summer sun. Women with long, colorful dresses and dainty hats gently herded their children ahead of them. Many passengers had arrived on holiday, choosing Watkins for its growing reputation as a summer destination.

Crawford looked north toward the shimmering blue waters of Seneca Lake, turning his back on the new arrivals crowding the depot. He grudgingly admitted the view was impressive. The smooth waters of the lake filled the valley—one to two miles wide—and stretched out to the north as far as the eye could see. Sloping hills, covered with a patchwork of distant farmland, rose hundreds of feet above the eastern and western shores, cradling the lake. The village of Watkins sat at the head of Seneca Lake, where the flat valley met the sloping western hill.

Crawford considered his options. Several hackmen called to offer rides to their affiliated hotels, but he ignored them. Any hotel that could afford its own carriages was too expensive for him.

A piercing whistle and a hiss of steam announced the departure of the train. The black locomotive pulled its load of passenger cars out of the station and up the lake's western shore toward distant Geneva. With the train gone, Crawford saw a water tower, a lumber yard, and the Northern Central House across from the station. The last looked like the cheap—if less than reputable—hotel that fit his needs and budget. He picked up his travel bag and headed for the hotel's entrance, pausing at the doorway to dust off his clothes.

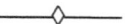

A dozen hours later, after 3 a.m., Crawford tiptoed across the empty main room of the Northern Central House. He ignored a drunkard asleep at one of the tables and eased out through the front door. Moving quickly, he disappeared into the darkness of the village streets.

Franklin Street, the main road through town, had gas lighting, but the side streets were dark and deserted. Crawford moved cautiously, sticking to the shadows as much as possible. He had no desire to bump into any night patrols. He traveled south away from the lake with only the faint glow of the crescent moon to illuminate his path. The meager light helped him avoid the deeper ruts in the dirt street that could turn an ankle. He wore his darkest suit—in truth, he only had two to choose from—and carried an unlit lantern and a shovel as the mysterious note had instructed him to. Tucked into his pants pocket was a six-shot Colt "Army" Model 1860 revolver he'd bought on his own initiative. After nine blocks, Crawford turned right on Ninth Street, which turned into Pine Street after crossing Franklin. Pine led him up a steep hill. After a few hundred yards of climbing and fighting to catch his breath, he turned left and found the entrance to Glenwood Cemetery.

The night was warm, and Crawford's exertion caused prickly

sweat to spread under his shirt collar, but a chill passed through him as he stared into the dark cemetery built on a lonely, wooded hillside rising above the town. The sliver of moonlight failed to penetrate the woods that lined the road into the cemetery, and Crawford's mind conjured images of wandering souls beckoning him ahead into darkness and eternal oblivion.

Looking back toward the village, Crawford saw a bright light in the heavens. The comet, with its straight and narrow tail of light, had appeared in the sky a few nights earlier in line with the polestar and below the Dipper. The Great Comet of 1874 the papers called it. Some saw a comet's arrival as the harbinger of misery to man.

Crawford withdrew a waterproof tin of matches from his pocket, extracted a match, and struck it. The flare of the match destroyed his night vision, but he lit and adjusted the lantern's wick until a welcome glow enveloped him. With shovel in one hand and lantern in the other, he willed himself forward through the cemetery entrance.

The dirt road wound left, then right, then left again, but always uphill. Crawford stopped to listen now and then on the unlikely chance that anyone else was out this late. At one point, he thought he heard footfalls behind him, but the sound drifted away, leaving only crickets and the wind passing through the trees.

As the road continued uphill, Crawford's lantern illuminated gravestones on either side of the path. His legs burned from the climb. He was annoyed that his lack of vigor forced him to take deep breaths to keep moving forward. He was of average height but had extra weight collecting around his waist caused by too little walking, too many carriage rides, and a less-than-healthy fondness for drinking. It didn't help that his head was still fuzzy from the whiskey—purchased to entertain himself until the called-out rendezvous time.

Crawford heard the distant sound of water trickling through a rocky glen. Off in the darkness to the south was the region's most famous gorge, Watkins Glen. Long ago, streams flowing into the valley carved deep gorges into the hillsides. Tourists on the train had raved about the Glen's wonders, but he'd ignored them. When the road began to level out, he knew he was nearing his destination.

CEMETERY AT NIGHT

Over the last three weeks, Crawford had received three anonymous notes in the mail—one every few days—that had cryptically
implied a trip north would change his fortunes. He pulled the third
note from his pocket and studied the final directions in the light of
his lantern.

By now, he was in the upper part of the cemetery. The gravestones appeared more frequently, but there were no other buildings nearby. Off to his left, through the woods, would be the Glen
Mountain House, a hotel on the gorge's edge. Somewhere ahead
and far off to his right was another grand hotel, the Lake View
Hotel. Raising the lantern as high overhead as possible, he moved
forward slowly until he found the fork in the road. The left fork led
down toward the gorge and the Glen Mountain House. He turned
right and walked another twenty or thirty yards before using the
lantern to scan the writing on nearby tombstones.

He searched for a specific name, but the frustratingly haphaz-
ard placement of the graves made his task more difficult. After
checking multiple groups of gravestones, he became discouraged.
Why set a meeting for the middle of a cemetery in the middle of the
night? Why tell him to bring a shovel? Now that he was here in the
dark cemetery, Crawford questioned the motivations of the mysterious note writer. He wondered—not for the first time—if he was
being set up. The soothing weight of the Colt pistol in his pocket
comforted him. He would not be someone's fool tonight.

As Crawford scanned the next row of graves, his lantern's light
fell across two midsized tombstones next to each other. The chis-
eled letters on the right gravestone held the name he was looking
for.

Sarah Anderson
beloved wife and mother
Born December 3, 1835
Died May 17, 1867

Crawford pulled out his pocket watch and checked the time
using the flickering light of the lantern. It was 3:46 in the morning.
Fourteen minutes until the arranged meeting time. The lantern lit
up twenty feet around him, but there was a wall of blackness just

outside the lantern's reach. During the war, a good sharpshooter could kill a man holding a lantern from a hundred yards away. Crawford doused the light and put the lamp on the other side of Sarah's gravestone out of sight in the long grass. He leaned the shovel against the grave and waited in the darkness as his eyes readjusted to the starlight.

He inhaled and listened for any changes to the night sounds. He heard nothing but the murmuring of a distant waterfall and the hum of insect wings. He spun around, making sure no one might sneak up on him. He looked up at the boundless sea of glittering stars overhead and then looked away as the sight made him feel small.

Four in the morning came and went. No one appeared. Crawford lit a match to check his watch. After another five minutes, he began to fidget. After fifteen minutes, his anxiety turned into anger. He would not give up after coming this far, but it was infuriating to be made to wait. Surely, the mysterious note writer wouldn't have brought him this far north on a lark.

Moments later, Crawford noticed a light in the distance moving like a fairy floating through the woods. It came from the direction of the gorge and the Glen Mountain House. *Finally*, Crawford thought. He breathed in deeply, then slowly released the air from his lungs.

The light came closer, and he could make out the outline of a man. The man's features were in shadow as the light reflected forward. Crawford tilted his body so the approaching figure would not see him remove the Colt from his pants pocket. He held it down by his side. His hands were clammy and sweaty.

The figure kept approaching, and still, the face was in shadow. When the man drew near, Crawford squinted from the light and raised his Colt, aiming for the center of the man's body. "That's far enough."

The figure stopped. The light remained in Crawford's eyes, blinding him.

"It's rude to point a gun at a man—unless you plan on shooting him."

Crawford's jaw dropped. That voice. The man raised the lantern higher, illuminating his own face.

"You," Crawford said.

"Point your gun somewhere else," the man demanded, annoyed.

"Why should I trust you?" Crawford said defensively. "It has been a long time." His mind flashed back to the last time they had seen each other.

The other man sighed. He transferred the lantern to his left hand and reached slowly with his right hand into his pocket.

"Careful," said Crawford. "I'd hate for you to give me a reason to cut this reunion short."

"That would be a shame," the other man said dryly, slowing his movements even more. He drew his hand from his pocket and held his closed fist to Crawford. As he opened his hand, a shining gold nugget sat in the center of his palm.

"You found the gold?!" Crawford cringed hearing desperation creeping into his voice. He steadied himself. "Is the gold buried in this grave? Is that why you had me bring a shovel?"

The man looked at him but stayed silent.

Crawford tore his eyes away from the gold nugget and looked the man up and down. "I don't see you carrying a shovel. If digging is involved, I can hold the gun while you do the sweat work."

"Can I trust you to split whatever we find fifty-fifty?" the man asked.

Crawford hesitated. Did he trust the man to honor such an agreement? He was glad he was the one holding the gun. He licked his lips. "You can trust me. Fifty-fifty."

The other man nodded and held out the gold nugget. "For you." The man was so close that Crawford smelled the alcohol on his breath. Crawford didn't lower the gun, but his full attention was on the nugget. The gold was mesmerizing. Crawford grabbed the nugget in his left hand and marveled at its weight. The other man raised the lantern and brought it closer for Crawford to examine the gold.

Years of regret and frustration faded as lantern light made the nugget glow.

"You deserve this," the other man said, and Crawford silently agreed. Crawford's brain was slow to realize the subtle change in the man's tone. His mind tried to scream a warning, but his body— slowed by alcohol and poor living—did not react fast enough to the danger. With a quick motion, the other man knocked Crawford's gun aside and then lunged forward.

Crawford registered a hard punch to his ribs. He didn't realize a long, slim dagger had been plunged into his heart. Crawford stared at the gold nugget as the man whispered into his ear. The man twisted the knife for maximum damage, then jerked the blade free. A small amount of blood sprayed from Crawford's body before his heart stopped pumping.

Crawford's eyes widened as his knees weakened and gave way. The other man helped him to a sitting position and then leaned him back against the nearest gravestone. Crawford opened his mouth to protest. "This is not right," he wanted to say, but he could not get the words out. His vision grew dark. The man stood over him, watching the light fade from his eyes.

Crawford's last thoughts were not of his wife becoming a widow or that he would never see the glory of a Southern sunset again. His last thought before darkness claimed him was *Don't drop the gold.*

Far above, the comet continued its journey across the night sky.

CHAPTER II

GLENWOOD CEMETERY

Saturday, July 11, 1874

A NNIE Anderson's legs propelled her through the entrance of Glenwood Cemetery above Watkins in the early morning light. The dew clung heavily to the long green grasses beside the empty road, forcing her to the center of the dirt track to avoid dampening her shoes. The ground was packed down from the passage of hundreds of wagon wheels over the years and the recent dry spell. Annie wrinkled her nose as she entered a lingering cloud of woodsmoke from breakfast cookfires. The smoke hung in the air, resisting the light breezes that caressed the hillside. Annie increased her pace. She was eager to rise above the smoke and reach the upper portions of the cemetery and the sweet summer smells of cut grass and blooming flowers.

A wood thrush chirped from the high branches of a nearby tree as Annie stifled an involuntary yawn. She had awakened as the first rays of sunshine peeked over the eastern hillside of the valley and, after dressing quickly, slipped out the door of the house in Watkins that she shared with her grandmother and two boarders. Her destination was the graves of her mother and father—gone eight years now. Walking helped organize her thoughts, and she had a lot on her mind. She had graduated from Elmira Female College a month earlier and was now living at home with no idea what to do next with her life.

As she walked, she reached up to tame the strands of long brown hair that had come loose from the hairpins holding everything in place. Annie was convinced she had too much hair, but long hair was fashionable these days, so she knew better than to complain.

Annie passed the first set of gravestones as the road turned back on itself and continued up the hill. She had been thirteen when her parents drowned in Seneca Lake in a boating accident. They had set out on a calm spring day when an unexpected storm blew across the lake, chasing away the sunshine and capsizing their sailboat. Neither made it to shore. Annie's last memory of her mother was watching her pack a picnic basket for the excursion while happily singing "Beautiful Dreamer"—forcing Annie forever to associate her mother with the line "Beautiful dreamer, out on the sea." Annie had been in class when her grandmother showed up to break the news. The whispers and alarmed looks her classmates cast in her direction as rumors of the tragedy spread were seared into her memory.

A part of Annie died with her parents that day. Her mother had raised her to think for herself. Her father treated her as the son he'd never been blessed with. By the time she was twelve, she was an expert with a rifle and a sewing machine. Her parents had convinced her that women were as smart and capable as men.

Annie's petite Scottish grandmother tried her best to raise her after the tragedy but was more traditional in her ways. Annie had always been shy, but now she withdrew into herself and became angry. Angry at God for taking her parents away. Angry at her parents for leaving her. Angry at the storm and the waves of Seneca Lake. Her grandmother withstood Annie's attitude for weeks until she'd had enough. She'd grabbed Annie by the shoulders and locked eyes with her. "I can't fix what angers you," she said to Annie. "Go to the cemetery and talk to your mother. Tell her how you feel. She will hear you from heaven." She spun Annie by the shoulders and pushed her toward the front door. Annie suspected her grandmother wanted a few minutes of peace away from her teenage granddaughter, but the advice changed Annie's life.

That first strenuous climb to the top of Glenwood Cemetery had drained her anger, and Annie had slumped down by her mother's gravestone and sat quietly until, slowly, she began pouring her heart out to the spirit of her dead mother. She'd left hours later feeling heard and unburdened for the first time since her parents' accident. Each Saturday since, Annie made the journey into the cemetery for one-sided conversations with her mother's spirit. The spirit of her father—a burly but quiet man in life—seemed content to listen.

The road turned back on itself again. Annie breathed deeply, happy to inhale fresher air above the persistent woodsmoke.

Even as a college graduate, there weren't many options available to Annie as a woman. The obvious choice was to find a man and get married, but that wasn't as easy as it sounded if one had standards. Two years ago, she had felt differently. A lovely man, eight years her senior, noticed Annie in church and courted her. She appreciated his kind, funny, and adventurous personality. Nana appreciated that he belonged to a wealthy local family. Just as Annie saw the hints of a pending proposal, things had gone tragically wrong. Her grandmother wanted Annie to allow herself to see new opportunities, but Annie wasn't ready to be courted again.

Last Sunday at church, Annie overheard her grandmother describing her as "a great catch for some lucky man" to a new acquaintance. Annie did not want to be someone's catch. She wanted to travel the world and have exciting adventures first. The world was large, yet Annie had never traveled more than fifty miles away from Watkins. Society did not expect a woman to want adventures or a successful career. Society expected a woman to find a man, marry him, have children, and support "his" successful career.

Despite her reluctance, Annie was courted by the church woman's nephew, Theodore. After a formal introduction, he'd escorted her two days ago to a party of amusements and games held by George and Emma Magee at their Madison Street mansion, called Glenfeld. Theodore, call me Ted, Sharpe was handsome and easy to talk to, and for a short time, Annie thought her grandmother had done her a favor. That was until Ted started talking about his expectations for his future wife. "Of course," he had said, "I expect my future wife to keep the house clean. If dust is left too long, it will turn into fleas."

Annie had blinked in confusion. She had no problem keeping a clean house, but dust did not turn into fleas. Spontaneous generation, a once-accepted scientific theory, claimed living creatures could spring from nonliving matter. Bread left in a dark corner for too long will turn into mice. Or mud into worms or tadpoles. In college, she had learned the theory was discredited. Annie had taken her studies seriously and thrived in classes. Elmira Female College was much more than a glorified finishing school for women. It offered a rigorous academic curriculum as challenging as the courses at men's colleges. Her favorite subjects had been chemistry, philosophy, and literature, with studies of French and German languages.

"I'm sorry," she'd said, as gently as possible. "Dust doesn't turn into fleas. Louis Pasteur disproved that theory in 1859."

Ted's smile faded, and Annie saw a shift in his eyes. "You should leave the thinking to the men in your life. Everyone knows dust leads to fleas." His arrogance and dismissiveness stunned her. Ted leaned closer and whispered in her ear, "Know your place," and then turned his back to her to start a conversation with Josephine Knapp, an attractive blonde Annie knew from school. The flush of embarrassment reddened Annie's face. She had to fight to unclench her fists. Not knowing what else to do, she stood up and excused herself.

Annie did not fault a person for being uneducated. But she did find fault in a person's contentment to stay that way. She thought of her mother's advice given when Annie was much younger. "People—especially men—will tell you things they expect you to believe. You're allowed to question anything and everything they say. Seek the truth for yourself." The truth, Annie decided, was that Ted was a fatheaded buffoon.

Annie's eyes darted around the sizable parlor filled with men in their best suits and women wearing flowing dresses. Annie did not do well in crowds. She rarely laughed or expressed much emotion in public, and people found the steely, determined gaze she'd developed after her parents' death to be off-putting. Men often thought she was unfriendly when she was simply reserved—and often bored—in typical social situations. Annie did have a kind smile when she chose to show it, but anyone who looked close enough could see the pain lurking behind her eyes.

Annie's night was saved by the appearance of one of her closest girlfriends, Jesse Hope. "Annie," Jesse's face burst into a grin when she spotted Annie. "It's so nice to see you out! And that dress.

It's tailored perfectly!" Annie knew—from the way men looked at her—that she wasn't unattractive. But a compliment on her sewing skills from a female friend made her glow.

The sun cleared the eastern hills as Annie continued her journey up Cemetery Hill. Its warmth created prickles of perspiration down the small of her back. She slowed her pace, still thinking about Ted and Josephine and the party. After Annie had said her goodbyes and slipped out the mansion's front door, she'd noticed Josephine and Ted in the shadows. As she hurried away, Josephine's voice floated out of the darkness. "I would never let dust collect in any house I lived in."

Annie paused and turned as she reached the point in her climb that offered the best views. The village of Watkins spread out below her, and Seneca Lake shimmered just beyond. Her hometown might be small—about 3,500 people living in a village twelve blocks long and six or seven blocks wide—but it was exciting from June through September as tens of thousands of tourists flocked to the area. New hotels had sprung up over the last few years, attracting a sophisticated crowd with money to spend as they enjoyed the lake and Watkins. The big-city tourists contrasted sharply with the small-town shop owners in the village and the rugged farmers outside it.

Was there a sophisticated traveler ready to whisk her away to a life of adventure? Annie sighed, feeling the weight of her grandmother's expectations pressing down on her. Why couldn't she whisk herself away? Instead, here she was, a college graduate with no job prospects, no marriage proposals, no adventures to look forward to, and no idea what came next.

Resuming her walk, Annie wondered if she should give up on men and embrace life as a spinster. She could become a teacher or open a dress shop. She'd learned to make her own clothes from an early age and was good at it. Her mother's Singer sewing machine became her most prized possession after her parents' death. But Watkins already had a dress and cloak maker. Annie could set up shop in another town, but she worried her grandmother couldn't live without her.

Annie reached the upper portion of the cemetery and passed

the turnout that led down through the trees to the Glen Mountain House, one of the newer hotels. She occasionally stopped for tea on the Glen Mountain House's wide porch overlooking the gorge. Her parents' graves were not far now.

As she neared her destination, an uneasy feeling came over her. Was it the unexpected stillness in the air? Annie stopped to glance around. No one else was in sight, but she no longer heard the sounds of birds or insects. The eerie silence unnerved her as she continued toward her parents' graves.

Annie noticed the boots first. Scuffed and worn and out of place. Then, she saw the top of a man's hat. She approached cautiously until she saw a man leaning back on her mother's gravestone. His head slumped forward, and his chin rested on his chest. His hat covered much of his face. A dragonfly, resting on her mother's gravestone, launched into the air as Annie approached. It flitted back and forth before disappearing into the nearby trees. Dragonflies always reminded Annie of her mother, who had loved them.

The man ignored her presence. Her trepidation turned to anger. Was he an inebriate sleeping off a night of hard drinking in the peaceful and quiet cemetery? Why had he chosen her mother's gravestone of all places? That made it even more insulting to Annie because her mother had been an ardent supporter of the temperance movement.

Annie stiffened her back and was prepared to give the man a piece of her mind. "Sir! Excuse me, sir!" As she stepped closer, the righteous indignation fled her body.

The man's utter stillness and the disturbing smells wafting on the breeze caused the hairs on the back of her neck to stand up. She shivered. Looking around, Annie saw no one in sight. She forced herself—curiosity fighting her better judgment—to move closer. When she got within a few feet of the man, she saw no movement in the man's chest. His head was down, but Annie could now see his unblinking eyes staring at his left hand—a hand closed into a fist.

Annie's hand flew to her mouth. Was he dead? Had he drunk himself to death?

From his hat and the cut of his three-piece suit, she knew he wasn't from the area. His suit was of quality material but of an older style. It was fraying at the cuffs, and the areas covering the man's knees and elbows were shiny with wear. The suit had been carefully mended in places. This man's fortunes had fallen, but he still had someone willing to mend his clothes lovingly.

A portion of a tattoo on the man's wrist peeked out from under his right sleeve, pushed up as if his hand had been extended. There was an old scar on his face, only partially hidden by his beard. Many men who survived the War Between the States had scars—some more conspicuous than others.

As Annie leaned closer, she smelled alcohol, urine, excrement, and something coppery. She leaned away, trying not to gag.

"Sir?" she said. Her voice came out small. She cleared her throat and spoke louder. "Sir? Can you hear me?" No reaction. She recoiled at the thought of reaching down to touch him to check for a pulse or to feel the warmth of his skin. Perhaps she could nudge him? Annie drew back her right foot and kicked the bottom of the man's boots. In her nervousness, she kicked harder than she intended to.

The man gave no visible reaction, but Annie's kick caused his jacket to fall open and dislodged what he'd been holding in his left hand. Annie's eyes widened at the sight of the gold nugget, but it was the bloody chest wound exposed by his now-open jacket that made Annie's skin crawl. This man wasn't just dead, someone killed him. Annie realized that the killer could be close and that she was in peril.

The morning light filled the cemetery with long shadows. Each tree and gravestone looked menacing, as if, at any moment, the killer would appear from his hiding place. Annie couldn't shake the feeling that someone was watching her. From behind her, she heard the sound of rustling branches.

WAR BETWEEN THE STATES

CHAPTER III

34TH NORTH CAROLINA

From the Journal of Private H. Thompson

April 16, 1862 – My father, Samuel Thompson, should've celebrat-ed his fiftieth birthday today, but he was the least lucky man I ever knew. His wife died, giving birth to his only son. Me. At least he never held it against me and did his best to raise me. We farmed a small plot of land near Asheville, North Carolina, until a horse threw him, breaking his arm. When an infection set in, the doctor amputated his arm. He'd survived the surgery but couldn't run a farm one-handed even after I dropped out of school at fourteen to help. We lost the farm and ended up in debt. A year later, pneumo-nia took him. Dead at forty-four. My father had rotten luck. I spent six years working as a farmhand for the Barnett family, trying to pay off my father's debts.

Also today, Jefferson Davis and his Confederate Conference passed the First Confederate Conscription Act. All white men be-tween the ages of eighteen and thirty-five are eligible to be drafted for three years of military service. A year into the war, and I guess our leaders have realized this conflict won't end as quickly as ev-eryone hoped.

May 15, 1862 – Got my Enfield rifle today. I'm now a proud mem-ber of the 34th North Carolina Infantry Regiment. I did not volun-teer. The draft passed over me, but old man Barnett's worthless son hadn't been so lucky. The Conscription Act allowed the well-to-do to hire someone to take their place, so old man Barnett offered to pay off the balance of my debt, $300, to let me die in battle on his son's behalf. I took his deal and joined the Army. I was tired of be-ing an underpaid farmhand. I planned to survive the war and start my life fresh.

June 9, 1862 – After a few weeks of marching, drilling, and weapons training, the Army decided my Enfield rifle and I were ready for combat. I hoped the Army in its wisdom is right. Most of the soldiers I trained with were young men between the ages of eighteen and twenty-one. I never thought being twenty-six would make me feel so old. We marched fifteen miles today.

June 11, 1862 – Made a new friend, Private Calvin Shoemaker. He'd been with the 34th since it formed last year in High Point, North Carolina. Tonight, he took me around to meet some of the ladies in this neighborhood. They treated us as Southern ladies know how to treat soldiers—with respect and something good to eat.

June 24, 1862 – Orders came down to draw two days' rations to pack in our haversacks. Private Shoemaker said we would be in a fight soon.

June 26, 1862 – We marched into battle at Mechanicsville with clean clothes, fresh faces, and a quick step. Our officers formed us in line of battle. When the enemy came into sight, we gave the rebel yell—a howling mix of hog calls and Indian war whoops meant to intimidate the enemy and bolster our confidence—and charged forward. I'm proud that my nerves held. I know now that I'm no coward.

June 30, 1862 – I survived several days of fighting for General Robert E. Lee's Army of Virginia. We pushed back McClellan and his Union Army, sparing Richmond, the capital of the Confederate States of America, but not without a cost. At Gaines' Mill, I lost my only friend. Private Shoemaker got three fingers shot off his hand and was sent to the rear.

After the battle ended, we marched away until our leaders called a halt. Soldiers dropped to the ground in exhaustion. I found the nearest tree and slumped against it, ignoring the dirt, sweat, and blood on my hands as I reached into my haversack for food. I found hardtack but couldn't eat another dry cracker with an empty canteen. Disappointed, I pulled off my wide-brimmed slouch hat to wipe my brow. It kept the sun off my neck better than the regulation cap. When I put it back on my head, I noticed a bullet hole in the cloth brim. I wiped my hand through my hair to make sure I wasn't bleeding without knowing it. That bullet passed through my hat and didn't leave a mark on me. Amazing luck. I was sitting on the ground with my finger poking through the hole when a tall soldier dirtier than I was called out. I got to my feet when I saw the dual chevrons on his sleeves.

The corporal asked me about my hat. "That your hat, private?" I told him it was. "And that bullet hole? Did that happen while you were wearing it?"

I smiled at him. "Damnedest thing, isn't it?" He nodded as if I'd answered correctly and asked me if I was any good with my rifle. I was very good with my rifle and did not mind saying so. "I can hit an Appalachian cottontail mid-hop at six hundred yards."

I thought I was in trouble when he said, "Come with me, Private."

July 1, 1862 – Our division was held in reserve today. We could hear the sounds of battle. For several hours, we came under artillery fire. Several men were killed, but I came through unhurt, as did my four new friends. Corporal Taylor was in charge of a small team of sharpshooters. He had three privates—Frank, Buck, and Ace—who, like me, were in their mid-twenties. Frank had black hair and a bushy black beard. He looked like a cross between a man and a bear. He's taller than Taylor and twice as wide. Buck and Ace were about my size and could be twins except for their facial hair. Ace had a bushy beard, while Buck kept his mustache neatly trimmed.

Each member of Taylor's team had a story similar to my "bullet hole in the hat that I was wearing" story. A few weeks ago, Ace stepped on a diamondback rattlesnake, which immediately bit the soldier standing next to him. Buck had his hat shot off his head in battle. While on picket, Frank had just finished reloading his Enfield rifle when a Yankee soldier popped up twenty feet away and had him dead to rights—only to suffer a misfire. Frank shot the Yankee dead. Taylor had run out on the battlefield to retrieve a fallen battle flag and returned to find three bullet holes through his clothes but not a mark on him.

Luck may seem an odd thing to bond over, but soldiers needed faith in God or an ironclad belief in their own good fortune to run toward the bullets and cannonballs fired in their direction. Taylor and his men counted on luck to survive and were happy to sur-

round themselves with others who possessed it.

Taylor promised to get me assigned to his sharpshooter team as long as I passed the shooting test. I knew I would pass. For the first time since my father died, I belonged somewhere.

July 4, 1862 – We did not celebrate the country's Independence Day. We mourned our dead, readied our equipment for the next march, and did our best to distract ourselves from the horrors of war. We spent a lot of time cleaning our rifles. It is good to be lucky, but it is better to be lucky and prepared.

July 15, 1862 – I returned from washing my clothes in the creek and joined Taylor, Ace, Buck, and Frank around the fire. We ate a meal of salt pork, hard bread, and dried vegetables. Frank poured a hot cup of coffee into my tin mug. He didn't talk much, but he sure could make a good cup of coffee. Union soldiers received regular coffee rations, but us Rebels usually made do with boiled hickory root. I asked Frank where they got coffee. Buck, answering for Frank, told me I should thank the Yankee bastards willing to die on the battlefield so we could drink their coffee.

After the five of us settled into a comfortable silence around the fire embers, Ace asked Taylor to tell the new guy his story about the hidden gold waiting to be found in North Carolina. The other men smiled. They'd heard Taylor's Lost Gold story multiple times but didn't mind a retelling. I had learned quickly that soldiering consisted of moments of sheer terror on the battlefield, surrounded by long stretches of boredom. Anything that helped pass the time was appreciated. Besides, listening to stories in the dark was better than fighting off memories of injured or dead friends.

Ace whispered to me that Taylor's family was obsessed with finding gold. Taylor had descended from Cornish miners who'd brought their expertise from England to find their fortune in the Carolina gold rush. Years later, when news came of gold being found at Sutter's Mill in 1849, Taylor's father struck out alone for California to make his fortune—never to return.

Taylor waited until we quieted down, then looked me in the eye and told me there was hidden gold east of Asheville near Hickory Nut Gap. He had my attention. Who doesn't dream of finding buried treasure? Here's the story he told me that night:

According to legend, a group of five or six Englishmen owned a gold mine in western Carolina and were traveling with a mule train laden with gold heading east to the port in Charleston, where they would sail back to England with the gold. But things did not go as planned when the Englishmen tried to pass through the Hickory Nut Gap.

Back then, there were few, if any, settlers in the area. The Indian tribes used the Gap to travel from the mountains to the flatlands. The Cherokee and the Catawba tribes claimed the gorge as sacred ground—neutral land between the tribes. On the day the Englishmen reached the Gap, they must've been dreaming about how rich the gold would make them because they weren't vigilant. They drove their mules through the Gap and right into the path of a surprised tribe of Indians.

The Englishmen were on sacred Indian ground, so the tribe attacked. The Englishmen defended themselves, but they had been unprepared for battle and were getting the worst of things. They couldn't escape, so they searched for shelter and found a cave near Round Top Mountain. Even with the relative safety of the cave, the Englishmen died one by one until only one was left alive. That last man knew he was going to die unless he found a way to escape. Against all odds, he was still alive come sundown, when the Indians stopped their attack. This last Englishman left the gold behind to save his life and snuck out alone in the dead of night. A week later, exhausted and starving, he stumbled into Charleston, where he boarded the first ship back to England.

When he reached England, he organized a search party to return to America and recover the gold. But fate intervened. On the night before his return voyage, he mysteriously lost his eyesight. Just went blind. Instead of making the trip himself, he dictated a map—as best as he could recall—to a member of the return party to show where the gold was hidden. But even though the search party scoured the mountains near the Gap, they found no gold.

Taylor sat back to let his tale sink in. I knew about North Caro-

MULE TRAIN

lina's gold rush in the early 1800s and had grown up in western North Carolina, so was familiar with the Hickory Nut Gap. It was a fourteen-mile pass through the mountains about halfway between Asheville and Rutherfordton. "That would be a large area to search," I said, thinking out loud.

Taylor smiled. He'd been saving the best for last. He withdrew an oilskin pouch from his haversack and extracted a small piece of parchment. "I have a copy of the Englishman's map," he said. Taylor's father made a duplicate from a man who claimed to have inherited the original map the Englishmen dictated. Taylor was proud of the map. To me it looked like a series of arbitrary lines, so I had little confidence that the map would lead us to the gold—if the gold really existed. But the story of the missing gold—waiting for us to find—became one of our favorite ways to pass the time as the months of military service dragged on. We speculated on where to look, boasted about how we would've been able to beat back the Indians and not needed to hide in a cave, and imagined what each of us would do with our share of the gold. I knew exactly what I would do if I had money.

August 5, 1862 – We had marched to Gordonsville where our regiment was placed under the command of Major General "Stonewall" Jackson. Rumors had come and gone all month, but this time Taylor cautioned us to be ready for battle. We checked our equipment, cleaned our rifles, and ensured our powder was dry. When I had a few minutes alone with Taylor, I asked him the question that had been nagging at me. "If gold was hidden in Hickory Nut Gap," I asked, "wouldn't someone have found it by now?"

Taylor paused and looked into the evening sky as the blues turned yellow and orange. "Men have searched for years," he said. "But no one has ever claimed they found it. That doesn't mean it is still there, but I feel it's waiting for us to find it." I asked him how we could succeed where others had failed. He shrugged and smiled. "Who knows," he said. "Maybe all we need is a bit of luck."

CHAPTER IV

THE SHERIFF AND THE GENERAL

Saturday, July 11, 1874

A NNIE spun around to prevent someone from sneaking up on her. She saw no movement in the trees and heard no further rustling but couldn't shake the feeling of being watched. She shivered at the thought. Rising fear urged her legs to take flight—to run away from this dead body and the cemetery as fast as she could.

She fought down the panic and considered her options. She could flee downhill back the way she'd come, but it was the longest path to other people and safety. The Glen Mountain House was close, but the dirt road to the hotel was narrow and cut into the steep hill leading down through the woods. If the killer waited in that direction, there would be no path to escape. Her last choice was to continue in the opposite direction of the Glen Mountain House, traveling over the hill to a trail through the woods that would take her to the Lake View Hotel. Annie's stomach knotted as she imagined a killer lurking behind one of the gravestones or in the woods.

Her imagination decided for her. She pulled up her skirts, turned, and sprinted downhill, back the way she had come.

Annie ran a long way before her sprint down the hill slowed to a steady trot and then into a fast walk. The feeling that someone was staring at her faded as she descended Cemetery Hill. The shock and fear of finding a man killed gave way to intense curiosity. Murder wasn't a common occurrence in her hometown. Who was this man? Who killed him? Why was he propped up on her mother's grave?

Annie reached the cemetery entrance without seeing another person. This road had been, until recently, cluttered with hackmen, milkmen, butchers, or other tradesmen eager to do business with the Glen Mountain House. When that hotel—with buildings on both sides of the gorge and a beautiful new arched bridge connecting them—built a new road on the opposite side of the gorge, the village restricted the use of Cemetery Hill to visiting the cemetery. Leave the dead in peace was the general feeling.

Annie would have forgiven a friendly merchant for breaking those rules and coming up the road this morning, but none came.

Outside the cemetery, Annie headed for the first house she saw and walked up the path to the front door. She paused momentarily to ensure her hair wasn't a complete mess and thumped loudly on the door.

After a few minutes, a blurry-eyed man opened the door in pants and a shirt while pulling his suspenders over his shoulders. He was thin but rugged, and neither young nor old. He looked unenthusiastic about the prospect of an early morning visitor.

"There's a dead body in Glenwood," Annie blurted out. The man stared at her blankly. Of course, there were a lot of dead bodies in Glenwood. "No, I mean a newly dead body." Annie was flustered. She took a breath and started again. "I'm Annie Anderson. I found a man's body in Glenwood. I think he was murdered."

The man's eyes went wide, and he introduced himself as Mr. Wilber before excusing himself to rouse his two sons. He instructed the older one to run into town to fetch the sheriff and ask him to meet us at the cemetery entrance. His younger son helped the man harness a beautiful chestnut mare named Dolly to a carriage. When they finished, Wilber leaned down and whispered in his younger son's ear. The boy ran into the house and returned with a revolver which he carefully handed to his father.

Mr. Wilber nodded to his son and turned to Annie. "Just in case," he said.

He helped Annie into a well-maintained two-wheeled carriage with no top. Until recently, only the well-to-do could afford a personal carriage, but now, mass manufacturing made personal ownership more common. Wilber snapped the reins and guided his horse to the cemetery entrance, where they sat in wait for the sheriff.

It did not take long before two beautiful black stallions effortlessly pulled a well-appointed four-wheeled buggy up the steep hill. Given the early hour, Annie was surprised by how quickly the sheriff, John Swartwood, arrived. The carriage held two occupants while a third man, Annie recognized Deputy Cole, followed on horseback. Annie also recognized the buggy, and her heart sank as Sheriff Swartwood pulled alongside Wilber's modest carriage. The buggy did not belong to the sheriff but to the man sitting next to him, General George J. Magee.

"Good morning, Miss Anderson," Sheriff Swartwood said. Lean and humorless, the sheriff carried an air of self-importance that made him annoying to all except his closest friends. He was a man who got right down to business. "Tell us why we are here."

Annie ignored George Magee and focused on the sheriff. She told him about the dead man she had thought drunk and the knife wound in the man's chest. The sheriff asked one or two more questions and then nodded to Deputy Cole, who spurred on his horse and led the carriages up the hill.

Annie was relieved to have armed men with her on the return trip and wondered how long it would take them to catch the killer. A murder would be a front-page story in the next edition of the *Watkins Review*, the village's local paper. Annie decided she didn't want to be known as "that girl who found the body." Maybe the reporter could call her an unnamed source when interviewed.

Their carriages passed the Glen Mountain House turnout, and the sheriff looked back at Annie with a questioning look. She helpfully pointed in the direction of her parents' gravestones not fifty yards from the turnout. The sheriff pulled Magee's carriage parallel to the graves and climbed down. As she exited Mr. Wilber's carriage, the sheriff looked at her oddly.

"This is the place?" he asked.

Annie looked to her parents graves. The body was gone.

"He was right there!" she said, pointing to where she'd last seen the dead man. "He was leaning against my mother's gravestone." Had she made a mistake? Her face flushed from embarrassment at the thought, but she remembered how the man smelled and was sure he had been dead. She looked around, but the body was gone.

Someone or something had clearly disturbed the grass in front of her mother's grave, so the sheriff and the deputy examined the nearby area. Deputy Cole found drops of blood, but there were no other obvious signs that a dead body had been there less than an hour earlier. It had been a long time since the last rain, and the ground, hardened by a long spell of hot, dry weather, revealed no obvious footprints or other tracks.

"There isn't much blood," the sheriff said. He looked at Annie with an expression she couldn't read. "Are you sure he'd been stabbed?"

Annie nodded. "Right here," she said, pointing to her left ribcage.

"Found this, sir," Deputy Cole said, holding a lantern. "It was in the long grass behind the gravestone."

"Do you recognize this?" the sheriff asked Annie.

She shook her head.

"It looks new," the deputy said.

"They sell those lanterns down at Treman & Son's hardware store," said Mr. Wilber, standing by his horse.

The sheriff leaned forward and gave Deputy Cole additional instructions. The deputy set the lantern down and left to search a wider area.

General George Magee chose that moment to step down from his carriage. The sheriff started introductions, but the general waved him off. "I have known Miss Anderson for a long time. Good to see you again, Annie," he said, taking her hand. He was tall, broad, and well-dressed with an air of confidence that rich, successful men carried. He had inherited tens of millions of dollars from his late father, John Magee, and controlling interest in the Fall Brook Coal Company, headquartered in Watkins.

Annie was convinced George Magee did not like her and that he was only being polite. Despite their history, he rarely went out of his way to converse with her these days. As he held her hand, she had a disturbing vision of that same hand holding a sharp-edged weapon. The evening's entertainment at the Magee's party two nights earlier had consisted of *tableau vivant*—French for "living paintings"—intermixed with charades. For each tableau vivant that his wife, Emma, had convinced him to participate in—the assassination of Julius Caesar, Shakespeare's Romeo and Juliet, and Blue-

BLUE BEARD TABLEAU VIVANT

beard—he had brandished a long knife or sword in his hand.

It had been his wife, Emma, who had insisted that Annie participate with six other women in the tableau recreating a poem about
Bluebeard and his curious wife, Fatima. Emma, dressed in flowing
silk and holding a large wooden key, played Fatima. George, as
Bluebeard, wore a turban and a cerulean blue beard while holding
an evil-looking scimitar. The crowd cheered as Emma opened the
door of the forbidden closet to reveal the heads of his seven previous wives hanging by their hair from a rope stretched across the
room. Annie did her best to stay still and look dead with her head
poked through the hole in the white muslin fabric and her hair tied
to the rope above her. The party guests had applauded the performance as Emma cowered in fear while George held his scimitar
high, preparing to collect the head of his latest victim.

"Is there anything you haven't told us yet?" George asked,
looking at her curiously. When Annie shook her head, he nodded.
"I think we can all agree that the most important thing is your
safety. No telling what might have happened to you in an isolated
place with a drunken man." He turned to the sheriff. "I appreciate
your diligent work, John. What is your professional assessment?"

Deputy Cole returned from his search and gave a negative
shake in response to the sheriff's inquiring look.

Sheriff Swartwood looked at Annie and then back to George
Magee. "There is no body, and there are no signs of a struggle," he
said. "If the man were dead, we'd have seen a lot more blood left
behind. Whoever it was didn't lose enough blood to kill him. The
evidence tells me an injured drunk took a nap on a random gravestone, sobered up, and then walked away."

The general nodded in agreement. "Well, I'm glad this was a
false alarm. A murder here in the village would be poor publicity
ahead of September's rowing regatta."

Besides his job running Fall Brook Coal Company, Magee was
the board president of the Watkins and Seneca Lake Rowing and
Regatta Association. The village expected ten thousand visitors at
its first annual regatta in two months' time.

Annie wanted to tell Sheriff Swartwood and General Magee
what they could do with their regatta, but good manners forced

her to bite her tongue. Still, she refused to be dismissed so easily. "I don't know where the body is now, but it was right there." She pointed back to her mother's grave. "The man had been stabbed. He wasn't moving."

"But he is not here now," the sheriff said.

"I know a dead body when I see one!"

"Now, young lady," the sheriff said with growing impatience, "have you seen many dead bodies?"

The image of her drowned parents lying cold and pale in their caskets flashed into her mind. Tears began streaming down her face despite her efforts to choke them off. All the men became uncomfortable and looked elsewhere, making Annie even more frustrated. She knew they disregarded her story because they believed she was a naïve, emotional woman. That man on her mother's grave hadn't stumbled off under his own power. Dead men do not walk away.

George offered her a handkerchief, which she accepted despite her anger.

Sheriff Swartwood held up his hands. "I will order some men to search the area further. If the man you saw was seriously hurt, he couldn't have stumbled far. I'll also check with doctors' offices to see if anyone has sought treatment for a chest wound." He paused and gave Annie a look meant to convey the authority of his position. "We can all agree that, until a body is found, it would be irresponsible to spread rumors about a murder in the cemetery."

With a tip of their hats, the sheriff and the general climbed into the general's buggy and headed down the hill with the deputy trailing behind. Mr. Wilber respectfully waited by his carriage until Annie regained her composure. She looked back at her parents' graves. Sarah and Edward Anderson. Gone too soon. "I miss you both," Annie whispered, her words floating in the morning breeze, turning and swirling away across the treetops.

Mr. Wilber helped her back into his carriage and dropped her off in front of her house.

"Mr. Wilber," Annie said, fighting back her frustration, "I'm very sorry to have disrupted your Saturday morning." He waved it off as if it was no bother, but then paused before departing.

"There wouldn't be much blood if the knife hit the heart," he said. "The heart can't push blood out of the body if it stops pumping." Wilber looked at her. "Just sayin'." He tipped his hat to her and turned for home.

Annie picked up a small branch that had fallen in the road and tossed it into the tall grass. How dare the sheriff and the general ignore her opinion because she was a woman. How dare they put the success of the regatta above justice for a dead man. Annie wanted to know why the dead man was in the cemetery, who killed him, and, most importantly, why his body was left on her mother's grave. If the sheriff had no interest in figuring out what happened in the cemetery, Annie would do it herself.

She moved toward the door, then hesitated. Was she brave enough to solve a murder? Annie's mother had been fond of quoting Elizabeth Cady Stanton, a leader in the women's rights movement from nearby Seneca Falls. Her mother's favorite Stanton quote was, "The best protection any woman can have is courage." Annie would find the courage, and she would do as her mother always encouraged her to do. She would question everything and seek the truth. Annie squared her shoulders. She would seek the truth about the man in the cemetery despite the risk.

Annie walked through the front door of her house carrying the dead man's lantern that she had picked up from where the deputy had left it in the cemetery.

Tombs City Prison, Lower Manhattan

CHAPTER V

THE TOMBS

Saturday, July 11, 1874

THE prisoner callin himself Bradford Whitey entered the yard of The Tombs detention center in lower Manhattan looking for a small man with a hooked nose and a handlebar mustache. The Tombs was a temporary stop for criminals while they waited for trial and sentencing, which could take months. Convicted criminals got shipped out to the Blackwell Island penitentiary on the East River or Sing Sing State Prison farther up the Hudson.

An unlucky few, convicted of murder and unable to pay lawyers for lengthy appeals, ended their stay in this yard compliments of the hangman's noose.

Despite the warm, sunny weather, the yard was not crowded. Only prisoners with the means to "incentivize" the guards for the privilege had regular access to this outdoor space. Bradford did not have money to spare, but he did know an influential man eager for him to make the acquaintance of one Thomas Pickens, recently arrested on suspicion of counterfeiting.

Bradford spotted Pickens easily enough. Today was Pickens's first full day in prison. A small man whose prison uniform hung loosely on him, Pickens had taken up a defensive position near one of the corners rather than enjoying an opportunity to stretch his legs in the sunshine. Pickens stood with his back against the wall, posture erect, attempting to project confidence and not look small and vulnerable. His graying handlebar mustache, meticulously maintained until his arrest, had developed a depressing droop. His head pivoted left and right, looking for danger. Bradford could see the fear in his eyes—fear that Bradford could put to his own use.

Bradford's height was above average, and his broad shoulders and thin waist gave the impression of a collegiate athlete instead of the brawler that he'd become. To appear less threatening, he slouched his shoulders and hunched his body, then he set out on a leisurely, counterclockwise stroll along the edges of the yard, allowing him to approach Pickens from the side in a nonthreatening manner. As he neared Pickens's location, Bradford looked up as if startled to find the older man in front of him. When Pickens made eye contact, Bradford smiled and said in a surprised voice, "Pickens? Mister Thomas Pickens? Why, fancy meeting you here! Mind if I join you?" Without waiting for permission, Bradford chose a spot on the wall a few paces from Pickens and leaned back as if he didn't have a care in the world.

It is hard for those with manners—when asked politely—to turn down a reasonable request. Pickens was no different. He didn't want to appear rude, but he was still cautious. "Do I know you?"

"Oh, well now." Bradford let his smile grow wider. "Where are my manners? You, sir, are quite famous in certain circles, but you would have no reason to know me." Bradford leaned forward and extended his hand. "Bradford Whitey. A pleasure to make your acquaintance."

Pickens hesitated, but only for a moment. Propelled by decorum, he reached out and shook Bradford's hand. Bradford, his youthful face working in his favor, had brown hair that had grown longer than the current fashion, and although in his early twenties, he had failed in his attempts to grow a mustache and beard. Many men underestimated him, to their misfortune.

Bradford settled back into his leaning position. This was the first time he had had the sun on his face since arriving at The Tombs. Pickens could not bear the silence.

"You said you've heard of me?"

"Yes, indeed," Bradford said. "I know you are an exceptional engraver. A true artist, in fact, at creating nearly flawless plates for printing counterfeit hundred-dollar bills. I heard you produced almost one hundred thousand dollars' worth of phony bills over the last seven years before the cops caught you two days ago. Is that true?"

Pickens did his best to look indignant. "I assure you that is just a scurrilous rumor. I'm a legitimate businessman who ran the presses at one of the premier printing houses in the city." Pickens's defense of his character would have carried more weight before jail when he had been an impeccably dressed gentleman. Now he was just another man in a prisoner's uniform.

Bradford laughed and held up his hands as if surrendering. "All right, save your arguments for the trial. I'm not asking for a confession." He paused for a moment before looking straight at Pickens. "But I assure you I'm well-informed. I know you are a master at creating counterfeit plates."

Pickens opened his mouth to protest again, but Bradford cut him off.

"Mister Pickens, walk with me, will you? All this standing around is wasting an opportunity to exercise our legs." Pickens hesitated, then joined Bradford as he continued his counterclockwise stroll around the yard.

"Why do you think," Bradford continued as they walked, "that you and I are both out here in the yard on this beautiful sunny day?" Pickens's brow furrowed at the change in subject. "I'll tell you why. The people you worked for contacted the people that I work for. They set up this opportunity for you and me to be in the same place at the same time."

"I don't understand."

"You didn't ask me what I'm in prison for."

Pickens looked confused but shrugged and asked, "What are you in prison for?"

"The coppers arrested me two days ago. Allegedly, I got paid to kill a detective over in Brooklyn who was asking too many questions. MacGregor was his name. They found his body in a private room in his favorite restaurant, face down in a plate of steamed oysters." Bradford looked off in the distance as if remembering something. "I deny any involvement, of course," he continued. "Luckily for me, the key witness has disappeared, and with no one to testify against me, my employers will provide the judge with the right financial incentives. I'll be out of here tomorrow. That gives me just enough time to take care of one very important job." Bradford turned to look at Pickens.

"Are you..." The blood drained from Pickens's face and his body stiffened. "Are you here to kill me?" He hissed out the words as his eyes darted back and forth, looking for a way out.

"Mister Pickens, relax," Bradford said in a calming voice. "Nothing is going to happen here in the yard. Now, let us keep walking. We are just two acquaintances enjoying the sunshine."

Bradley grabbed Pickens by the arm to keep him walking.

"The truth is that your employer wants to make sure you never get the chance to provide evidence against them."

"I would never do that!"

Bradford shrugged. "They aren't willing to take that chance."

Pickens tried to regain his composure but was on the edge of a full-blown panic attack. His hands started shaking, so he shoved them in his pockets. Bradford did his best to appear nonthreatening as they walked along in silence.

Pickens looked up at Bradley. "Why are you telling me this?"

"Let me ask you a question, Mister Pickens. Do you want to die?"

"Of course not!" The words came out louder than Pickens intended.

"Well," Bradford said, bringing the conversation back to a whisper and forcing Pickens to lean closer to listen. "I ask because you will probably get twelve years for the counterfeiting conviction. Maybe more with the Secret Service cracking down on counterfeiters. They might choose to make an example of you. You're not a young man, no offense, and being a counterfeiter in a prison full of murderers and thieves... well, let us just say those would be hard years in a place like Blackwell Island." Bradford looked sympathetically at Pickens as they completed a lap of the yard. "If you wanted a way out, I could make it quick and painless. You might not even feel it."

Pickens shook his head back and forth with such vigorous denial that his body quaked.

"All right, all right!" Bradford said. "I'll take that look on your face as a no. And honestly, I'm glad to see some fight in you." Bradford looked up to make sure no one else was paying attention to them. "I like you, Pickens. Normally, when I take a job, I see it through to the end no matter what. It's a matter of principle. But I have been thinking about a career change, and this is as good a time as any. That's why I have decided not to kill you. Besides, it's damn unprofessional of your employers to pay you to do a job—a job done extremely well from what I have heard—and then turn on you through no fault of your own."

Pickens, looking cautiously relieved, nodded enthusiastically. "That is... that is good news."

Bradford offered a sad smile. "Well, yes and no."

"What do you mean?"

"Well, I'm not going to kill you. But I'm not the only one who was hired to do the job."

"What!?" Pickens looked panic-stricken again.

"A new inmate arrived this morning. It was a man I recognized. His name is Johan Nilsson. A Swede. Easy to spot because of his bald head and tattoos. He is a mean bastard, and unfortunately for you, he and I share a profession. To be honest, I'm not a fan of his work because, well, let me just say his approach is much less subtle than mine." Bradford looked over at Pickens as they walked. "His work is messy, but he does get results."

"You can't know for sure he's here for me, can you?"

"Well, without being obvious, look over to the doorway by the cell block entrance."

Pickens looked over to see a brute with a bald head and tattoos staring at him from across the courtyard.

The blood drained from Pickens's face.

"He's been staring at us from the moment I walked over to you."

Pickens struggled to catch his breath. It was his first full day in jail, and already two men had plans to kill him. It was just too much. "I could talk to the warden!" he blurted out.

"Yes, you could, but I would deny everything. Innocent until proven guilty." Bradford let a small smile flash across his face. "Or."

"Or what?"

"Well, as I said, I'm no fan of Nilsson. He works for a rival outfit, and he and I have crossed paths before. You could pay me to kill him. Get him before he gets you."

Bradford thought Pickens would need a little time to work through the moral dilemma of paying money to end another man's life, but the small man didn't hesitate. "You would do that?"

Bradford took Pickens by an elbow and steered him to a deserted part of the yard. "If, allegedly, I got paid to kill a nosy detective in his favorite restaurant with a chef's knife... well, that's business. But the key part of that story? I got paid. I don't kill people for fun. Yes, I can take care of Nilsson for you." He paused. "If you have the money to pay for my services." Bradford let this last statement hang in the air.

Pickens was silent for a moment, then he said, "I have money."

Bradford gave the slightest of nods. "Three thousand dollars."

"What?" Pickens hissed, horrified. "That's got to be ten or twenty times what it costs to hire someone on the outside. I'm not paying that much!"

Bradford shrugged. "Look, Pickens, I'm taking all the risk. You'd be hiring me to take out one of the biggest, meanest killers around with little time for planning. Isn't your life worth three thousand?"

Pickens hesitated as if weighing the value of his life. "Yes," he said, "but how do I know everything you've told me isn't a lie? Maybe Nilsson is here to kill you, and you're making this all up."

"Excellent point," said Bradford. He stopped walking. Their most recent lap around the yard had brought them to within twenty yards of the entrance where Nilsson waited staring. Bradford paused for a moment until he noticed the guards were not paying attention. "Stay here for a moment."

Pickens watched Bradford move away. Nilsson's eyes followed Bradford, and Pickens grinned in vindication. For five seconds. Then, an evil smile appeared on Nilsson's face, and he turned his full attention to Pickens and began walking directly toward him. Pickens's mouth opened, but no sound came out, and a cold chill ran through his body. He stumbled and fell backward in his haste to escape the approaching Swede.

Nilsson was almost on him when Bradford stepped between them. Bradford had lost his slouch and looked relaxed and dangerous at the same time. Pickens didn't think Bradford could win a direct confrontation against the larger Nilsson, but maybe he would slow the Swede down long enough for the guards to intervene.

Nilsson stopped and stared at Pickens on the ground and then at Bradford. He sneered at them before moving away as if nothing had happened.

Bradford reached down and helped Pickens to his feet. "He'll wait until I'm gone tomorrow. But he will try again. Good luck finding someone else to solve this problem for you."

"I'll pay you five hundred dollars," said Pickens.

"Negotiating for your life? I'm impressed. The price is still three thousand, or I'll wish you a good evening and walk away again."

Pickens gritted his teeth. "Will you take two thousand? That's all I have. I can pay you two thousand dollars to kill Nilsson."

Bradford rubbed his chin. "Closer. Anything else to offer?"

"What do you mean?"

"My current employer won't be happy that I left unfinished business here, so I'll need to disappear. I also need to change my occupation. I'll need a new job."

Pickens looked back to where Nilsson stood staring at him. "Are you sure you can kill him?"

Bradford shrugged and smiled at Pickens. "I'm an optimist."

Pickens looked down. His fingers played with his drooping mustache, trying to revive it. "Someone is recruiting for a big job upstate. They wanted me a week ago and offered a lot of money, but I turned it down," he said. "I don't like leaving the city. Although if I had left town, I wouldn't have been nabbed by the cops, and I would never have met you."

"And here I thought we were getting along so well."

Pickens sighed. "This is information I'd normally guard with my life," he said, "but my life doesn't seem worth as much as it did yesterday. I suppose I have to thank you for not killing me yourself."

"You are welcome. A well-paid job out of the city might be just what I need."

"You don't have my skills," Pickens said, "but maybe they can

Tombs City Prison, Interior

make use of your other talents."

Bradford held out his hand. "Two thousand dollars, and you share your contact for the job and put in a good word for me. Deal?"

Seeing no other option, Pickens shook Bradford's hand and then leaned in and whispered the name of the contact and the meeting location he had been given. Bradford did not know where Watkins, New York, was, but he was sure he could find his way there.

"Now," Bradford said, turning serious, "when we get back to our cells, I'll bribe one of the guards, who will bring you a pencil and a sheet of paper. Write down where I can find the money and return the note to the guard. If I'm satisfied, Nilsson will no longer be a threat when you wake up." Bradford saw Pickens hesitate. "If you double-cross me, let me remind you that I kill people for a living."

Bradford smiled again, but there was no humor on his face. Pickens nodded.

"And your two thousand dollars better be real, not counterfeit."

"It's real."

Bradford looked around the yard. The afternoon shadows had grown longer. "They'll call us back inside soon," he said. "Make sure you stay next to me and away from Nilsson. You'll be safe enough tonight once you're back in your cell."

They stood quietly for a few minutes, then Bradford turned to Pickens. "Can I offer you some advice?"

Pickens looked up at him. "What?"

"By tomorrow, neither Nilsson nor I will be a risk to you. But there's nothing to stop your former employer from hiring someone else. If they're not showing you loyalty, consider whether you owe any loyalty to them." Bradford paused as if it pained him to make his final suggestion. "Turning state's evidence might be the only way to save your life."

One of the guards blew a whistle, signaling the end of yard time.

Bradford and Pickens crossed the courtyard and followed the rest of the inmates, who were funneling through the doorway. Nilsson watched them but didn't try to approach. As they neared their cells, Bradford nodded at Pickens and was gone.

The afternoon light filtered through the high chink in the wall of Pickens's small, bare cell. His living space included a bed with two thin blankets and a straw pillow, a small table, and not much more. An hour passed before Pickens heard a swift knock on his cell door. The heavy door had a square aperture in it, and Pickens looked up to see two sheets of paper and a pencil push through the opening. "Make it quick," came the voice of one of the guards.

Pickens used the small table to write out directions to where Bradford would find the money and hastily scribbled the second note that Bradford had requested. He folded the papers several times and passed them back with the pencil to the waiting guard.

Lying on his bed and staring at the ceiling, Pickens convinced himself he had made a mistake giving away the money. What was to stop Bradford from coming for him in the night and killing him anyway? Or taking off with the money and leaving Pickens to be torn apart by Nilsson in the morning? Pickens spent long hours praying that Bradford and Nilsson would kill each other, leaving him safe with all his money. In the middle of the night, he dropped into a fitful sleep.

In the early morning, a loud commotion woke Pickens. He looked through the small opening in his door to see multiple guards converging on a cell just out of his view. A rumor started spreading around the jail about a prisoner's suicide. As Pickens lay in bed wondering what this all meant, he overheard two guards talking in low voices outside his cell door.

"Suicide, my ass. I don't believe it. If that big Swede really committed suicide, how did he stab himself in the middle of his own back?"

CHAPTER VI

THE LANTERN

Saturday, July 11, 1874

A NNIE'S stomach cared little that she was still angry at the sheriff and George Magee for dismissing her observations and opinion. Instead, it growled in happy anticipation as she opened the door of her family home and the smell of bacon and fresh biscuits greeted her. Annie's stomach won this round. She would eat first and then come up with a plan to solve the mystery of the dead man in the cemetery.

"Annie?" Her grandmother called out from the dining room. "Breakfast will be ready in ten minutes." Saturday breakfast was the only meal Nana cooked anymore. Their live-in cook and housekeeper prepared all the other meals but was away visiting family in Scotland. Mrs. Phelps, a widow and fellow parishioner from the church, filled in while Mrs. Casey was away. Even with the extra help, there was no end to the chores that Annie helped her grandmother with around the house and in the garden. Annie dreamed of traveling, but how could she leave her grandmother alone?

She set the lantern down by the front door. "Nana, I'll be back down as soon as I change." She turned and hurried up the stairs. Her walking outfit wouldn't do for breakfast.

Their house was more prominent than most in town. Her parents had built it after they married and had hoped their love would fill the multiple bedrooms with a large family, but in the end, they had been blessed with only one child. Annie stepped into her bedroom and closed the door behind her. She poured water from a large pitcher into the bowl on her dresser and dipped a towel into the water. The moist cloth cooled and refreshed her face and neck. Annie turned to her armoire and considered her clothing options.

Since Annie was in a hurry, she slipped into a more casual morning dress with long sleeves and high neckline. She tamed her hair as best as she could, hurried back downstairs, and forced a smile onto her face as she walked into the dining room. Her grandmother was already seated, as were her grandmother's two boarders. They had waited for her before starting their meal.

"Good morning!" Annie said with a brightness she didn't feel. She sat in her usual chair and bowed her head as her grandmother said grace. Annie paused two heartbeats after hearing "amen," then attacked her food in as ladylike a way as possible.

"I'm used to Annie being up early," her grandmother said, turning to the two men at the table, "but I was surprised you both were up and out early this morning."

After her parents' deaths, Annie's grandmother had decided the big house needed more life in it, so she opened their home to boarders. Keeping boarders and lodgers was a common source of income for widows. Luckily, two rooms were rented by two men who'd been close friends of her parents. They had doted on Annie as she grew up. Their presence, attention, and guidance had softened the blow of her parents' tragic deaths, making it easy for Annie to think of them as her uncles.

"I had some errands to run," Glendon Robinson said. He was the more stoic of the two and a more conservative dresser, favoring black top hats and frock coats. He looked serious, but when he got a mischievous twinkle in his eye, Annie knew he was about to say something that would make her laugh out loud.

"And I was out for a morning walk," said Roland Smith, flashing a grin in Annie's direction. "I wanted to follow Annie's example and get more exercise." Roland was leaner than Glendon and the more fashionable dresser, choosing colorful striped shirts, a shorter tailored jacket, and a rounded bowler worn with a rakish tilt. Where Glendon had a well-trimmed beard, Roland had long hair and a well-trimmed mustache that he took great pride in. Glendon was quietly funny. Roland was just fun. Roland turned strangers into friends and could belt out a song, dance a jig, or announce the start of an adventure into the woods at a moment's notice. Both men insisted that Annie call them by their first names.

Annie blissfully ate a buttered biscuit while ignoring her grandmother's stare. Her grandmother had an uncanny ability to tell when things were amiss. Annie did her best not to look guilty of hiding something, which only made her look more guilty.

"Annie."

"Yes, Nana."

"Is everything all right, dear?"

"Of course," said Annie. She sighed, knowing her grandmother would not let it end there.

Saturday breakfast was normally Annie's favorite meal of the week. It was the one meal where her makeshift family lingered around the table exchanging the latest news, gossip, and opinions. Annie loved this family time but knew what she was about to say would spoil the meal.

She faced her family and took a deep breath. "I found a dead body on Mother's grave this morning, but now it has disappeared, and no one believes me that a dead body was there in the first place."

Annie registered the stunned looks from around the table. Her grandmother's mouth dropped open, Roland's eyes widened, and Glendon's face was etched with concern. Nana recovered the quickest. "You had better start at the beginning, dear."

Annie shared everything that had happened since leaving the house that morning, including the gold nugget that fell from the man's hand, his obvious stab wound, and Annie's unfortunate run-in with the sheriff and George Magee. She finished by mentioning the lantern that she had brought home. Her family supplied the appropriate "oohs" and "aahs" as she told her story. She didn't share her vow to uncover the identity of the dead man and his killer.

As silence settled around the table. Annie found her mind racing ahead. "Has gold ever been found in Watkins?" she asked—wondering if the gold nugget might have been mined near Watkins, although a gold rush bringing hordes of prospectors to the village was more terrifying than exciting.

"No dear," said Nana. "There is a silly legend that someone hid treasure in a little niche in the rock face behind Aunt Sarah's Falls."

Annie was fond of the small falls on the road to Havana, named long ago after an old Indian woman who'd lived nearby.

"We don't have the geology for gold," said Roland. "But then again, gold is often discovered in rivers, and many of the glens have recently been explored more thoroughly for tourism."

As Glendon lifted a jam-covered biscuit to his mouth, a large portion broke off and landed jam-side down on his trouser leg. He groaned. Annie ran to get him a wet cloth. When she returned, he thanked her and then looked at her cautiously. "Annie, the man in the cemetery, are you absolutely sure—"

"Please stop," said Annie. "I know you don't think I'm an idiot who can't tell a dead body from a drunk." She stared at Glendon and Roland accusingly. They now needed to answer for all men.

Roland shifted in his seat uneasily. "Annie, sometimes it is difficult to tell with the newly deceased. I've heard a cemetery in Ohio uses a string to connect newly buried coffins with a bell in case a person is unintentionally buried alive."

"Oh, my," Nana said, not appreciating all this talk of death and cemeteries after the nice meal she had just served.

"If there was a body—" Glendon stopped when he saw the look on Annie's face. "I mean, OK, so there was a body with a stab wound." He paused again and then abandoned that line of thought. "Well, we are all just glad that you're safe."

Roland and Nana nodded in agreement. The meal was quiet after that. There would be no lingering to share the latest gossip today. As soon as it was reasonably polite to do so, Annie jumped up to clear the table. "Nana," she said after she'd finished. "I have some errands to run in town this morning."

"Not so fast, young lady. There are more strawberries than we can eat this year, and you promised to help me prepare and can my strawberry jam this morning. And there are floors to scrub and rugs to beat."

Annie should have seen that coming.

Glendon cleared his throat again. "I'd be happy to accompany Annie into town this afternoon."

Anna wanted to leave immediately but nodded and followed her grandmother downstairs to the kitchen.

———◇———

Several hours later, Glendon and Annie descended the front steps on their way into town. She wore a sky-blue dress, slim in the front but with fabric-covered wire hoops creating a structure in the back to provide "fullness." Bustles were the height of fashion and quite unavoidable if one wanted to present oneself as a proper lady. Annie accessorized her look with the lantern from the cemetery.

"Another warm day," Glendon said as they reached the street. He carried a hickory cane more for style than necessity and wore his favorite top hat. A gentleman would be equally unwilling to appear in the street without shoes or stockings as with his head bare.

As they descended Fourth Street, Annie took Glendon's arm with her free hand for stability.

The town founder, Dr. Samuel Watkins, gave the east-west streets numbers and the north-south streets the names of famous people. Franklin Street—named after Benjamin Franklin—served as the dividing line between the part of town on the valley floor with streets named after War of 1812 naval heroes Decatur, Porter, and Perry and the part of town climbing the western hill with streets named after former presidents Madison, Monroe, and Jackson.

As Watkins's prosperity grew, beautiful three-story red brick buildings began replacing the older two-story wooden structures. Annie's favorite building was the opera house at the corner of Fourth Street and Franklin. Made of gray stone, it stood out from the red brick buildings. Seeing the opera house reminded Annie that she needed to work on a dress to donate to the Firehouse Charity Auction in three weeks.

When they reached the wooden sidewalks on Franklin Street, Glendon paused and turned to Annie. "OK, out with it. What are you scheming?" He knew her well enough to know she had some plan in mind.

Annie stiffened her back. "I'm going to figure out who the dead man in the cemetery was," she said. "And I want to know why he was killed and left on Mother's grave."

Glendon squinted his eyes, looking as if he had a headache coming on. "That is a horrible and potentially dangerous plan."

"Maybe," Annie said, with more defiance in her voice than she intended. "Probably. But I won't be talked out of it."

Glendon sighed, removed his top hat, and wiped his forehead with a handkerchief. "I reminded of a story your mother told me once from when you were eleven. She said one of your neighbors started beating his horse with a switch because it refused to pull his wagon, and you threw yourself between the helpless creature and your neighbor. You refused to move even after the man threatened to beat you with the switch."

"I remember the neighbor yelling, 'Young girls should know their place,'" Annie said. "That's when my father came outside."

"And still you refused to move," Glendon said. "Your father ended up buying the horse from your neighbor." Glendon shook his head as Annie smiled at the memory. "What I know," he said, "is that when you see an injustice and set your mind on the righteous path, you refuse to be turned from it."

"I also remember," Annie said, "that the horse was lame. That's why she couldn't pull the wagon. After she healed, my father sold her to a kinder owner and pocketed a nice profit."

"Not every story has a happy ending," Glendon said. Annie opened her mouth to speak, but Glendon waved his hand, conceding defeat. "Tell me, then, where are we going?"

"To Treman & Son's," Annie said without hesitation.

It was a short walk to the hardware store. Glendon opened the door, then stepped back to let Annie enter first. Polished hardwood floors stretched to the back of the store, which was much deeper than wide. Well-stocked display cases and wooden shelves ran down both sides of the store, offering cutlery, nails, and other hardware. In the center were displays of cooking stoves, wheel rakes, and grain cradles.

Annie breathed in deeply. The smell reminded her of her father. Whenever he walked into a hardware store, he took a deep breath and said, "Smells like possibilities!" Then he'd wink at Annie and ask her to help him find whatever he needed for his latest project.

Glendon closed the door behind them as the store owner stepped forward to greet them. Mr. Treman nodded to Annie but addressed Glendon. "Mr. Robinson, so nice to see you. What can I help you with today?"

"Good afternoon, Mister Treman," said Glendon. "Can I trouble you to answer a few questions about this lantern that Miss Anderson found?"

Annie held up the lantern.

"That is a model we sell," said Treman, confused.

"I found this," Annie said, "and am hoping to identify the owner. Have you sold many lanterns like this one recently?"

Treman knew Glendon as a good customer and a well-known man in town, so he was willing to be helpful. "Just yesterday, a very disagreeable man came in to buy that lantern model and a shovel. The man didn't like our prices and said so, but I assured him they were very competitive."

"Could you describe him, please?" Annie asked.

Treman scratched his head and considered her question. "He had dark hair and a beard," he said. "And a scar." Treman pointed to his own face just below the corner of his mouth. "From his Southern accent, I could tell he wasn't from around these parts."

Annie tried to hide her excitement. "Did he leave his name, by any chance?"

Treman shook his head. "He paid in cash and left the store." Treman had little else to offer, so Annie and Glendon thanked him and exited his store.

The summer sun beat down on them from above, sending them in search of a shady spot nearby. Tourists outnumbered the locals on the crowded sidewalks, and a steady stream of carriages passed by on Franklin Street, kicking up dust. The smell of horse manure drifted by on hot breezes.

"I did not see a shovel near my mother's grave," Annie said. "You don't think he planned to..." She could not finish the thought.

"There could have been many reasons he needed a shovel," said Glendon. And then, after a few more moments, "I think it is good news you did not see a shovel in the cemetery." She nodded and let the thought go.

"All right, what do we know?" Annie spoke more to herself than to Glendon. "The man was from out of town and could have arrived by train, steamer, or stagecoach."

"Or he could have walked in," said Glendon. "Any of those would be hard to check."

Annie agreed, a bit frustrated.

"Tell me again," Glendon said, "what you remember about what the dead man had with him."

Annie tried to picture the scene in her mind. "Besides the knife wound and unblinking eyes," she involuntarily shivered, "he had on a charcoal suit, a white shirt, and a black hat." His clothing wasn't much help. Watkins had a lot of visitors who were not from around the area, so his outfit wouldn't have drawn much attention. "There was the gold nugget that fell out of his hand. The lantern was behind Mother's gravestone. That is all I remember."

"It doesn't sound like he had much with him," said Glendon thoughtfully.

Annie thought about it some more. All he had was a lantern and a gold nugget. He was from far away and didn't have much with him. "He didn't have a travel bag or a steamer trunk!" Annie said excitedly. "He would've traveled with some type of luggage. And if he came from far away, he would have needed a place to stay. That is where his luggage is. If we can find his hotel room, we might find his name!"

Glendon smiled. "But what if he was visiting family or friends? Then there is no hotel room to find."

"I will assume," said Annie, thinking it through, "that if he was visiting family or friends, they would have reported him missing, and the sheriff would have known about it by now."

"Unless it was his family that killed him," said Glendon, "and then buried him in their backyard."

"You are not helping!" Annie laughed and elbowed him in the side.

Glendon let out an exaggerated grunt and smiled at her. "All right. Let's assume he was on his own and got a hotel room. Now what? There are a lot of hotels and rooms to rent in this village. Or he could have walked in from Havana. That's only three miles south of here."

Annie closed her eyes to think. She remembered that the man's charcoal suit had been mended. Of course! It was obvious. Clothes were a symbol of status. "His clothes were mended. A wealthy person would've just bought a new suit. We can rule out the most expensive hotels."

Glendon looked at her with pride.

"That rules out Lake View, the Glen Mountain House, the Glen Park Hotel, and probably the Jefferson," Annie said. "Shall we start from the bottom?"

Glendon shrugged and pointed. "The Northern Central House is just a block away."

Battle of Fredericksburg

CHAPTER VII

FRESH FISH

From the Journal of Private H. Thompson

October 15, 1862 – Private Eddie Pierson joined the 34th Infantry Regiment after the Battle of Sharpsburg. He arrived a naïve, baby-faced eighteen-year-old recruit, and our group wanted nothing to do with him. As sharpshooters, we considered ourselves better than the average soldier. Sharpshooters received the best arms and enjoyed a level of independence other squads wished for. We messed and quartered together. We did everything together. Only death or disability could break us apart.

We were also savvy veterans, having survived battles at Cedar Mountain, Second Manassas, Harpers Ferry, and Sharpsburg. In each battle, Robert E. Lee's Army of Northern Virginia pushed the Union Army back. We should have been winning the war, but we lost Confederate soldiers faster than we could replace them while the North seemed to have an endless supply of bodies.

Our group of five, enjoying a combination of luck and skill, had gotten through all the skirmishes without a scratch. We were reluctant to let anyone else into our group, especially someone as young and green as Private Pierson, but he refused to go away. Instead of hanging out with soldiers his age, he kept showing up around our campfire. We called him "Fresh Fish" and shooed him away when he stuck around too long. But he kept returning, undeterred and usually bearing some offering like water for our canteens or a fresh kill for dinner. He was an excellent shot with the rifle, better than me if I had to admit it, and had great skill bagging the occasional shoat pig or rabbit, which we were always happy to accept.

November 22, 1862 – We got orders to march toward Fredericksburg, Virginia. The Union Army usually ran home for the winter,

*but this year, they had stayed. Private Pierson marched along be-
side us, annoying me with his positive attitude. By then, we had
shortened his nickname to "Fish." At the end of the day's march, I
sat by the fire writing in my journal when Fish walked up. When I
had time, I wrote down my thoughts and drew pictures of things I'd
seen and wanted to remember. When I was young, my father had
looked over my shoulder and claimed I was a regular "Harper's
Weekly," a weekly newspaper out of the North famous for its wood-
engraved illustrations. My real first name was Hugh, but I had
been called Harper for as long as I could remember.*

*Fish asked if he could sit with me, and since he looked so lone-
ly, I took pity on him and asked what was on his mind. Well, Fish
sure could talk. As I sat quietly drawing, he talked about his family
and their farm in western North Carolina. He told me his father
had passed away before the war started and how his mama kept the
family together and worked as hard on the farm as any man ever
could. How his two older brothers had run off to join the fighting
when the war started and now served in the western campaigns.
How his baby sister was the apple of everyone's eye and was just
the sweetest, most adorable child that'd ever been born. And finally, how it had broken his mama's heart when he got drafted and
sent to join the Army of Northern Virginia.*

*I realized as Fish talked—and he was still talking non-stop,
telling me all the names he and his brothers had given to the animals in their barn—why Fish liked our company. He wanted to be
around us because we must remind him of his older brothers.*

I tolerated Fish's presence a lot more after that.

*December 3, 1862 – We arrived near Fredericksburg after march-
ing through cold and miserable weather for twelve days straight.*

*December 15, 1862 – From the high ground behind Fredericks-
burg, we watched the Yankees build a pontoon bridge under sniper
fire and then cross the Rappahannock River to reach us. We were
miserably cold and exposed to the elements and not allowed to
build fires. When the Union forces attacked, they did so with almost
twice our numbers, but our Rebel units held well-fortified positions, including some lovely stone walls to shoot from behind. The
34th North Carolina Regiment caught a lot of fire from the advanc-*

ing enemy. We stood in our lines and returned fired, beating them back again and again. Many of those bluebellies died trying to cross that open ground and climb the hills to reach our positions.

Out of the corner of my eye, I noticed Fish hit every Yankee he aimed for. His shooting rivaled Ace's. When Fish tried to change positions to get a better angle on the enemy, he slipped in the mud and fell flat on his back. The instant he fell, the person standing directly behind him took a bullet to the shoulder. Taylor and Buck had also seen it happen. Fish had our kind of luck.

After stopping the last Union advance of the day, we had a cold night ahead of us. As we huddled, shivering in our defensive positions, Frank pointed to the northern sky. "Aurora borealis," he said quietly. Shimmering bands of color quietly danced over the frozen fields of death. It was a good omen. We complimented Fish on his excellent shooting and his better luck. Fish was one of us. We were now the Lucky Six.

December 25, 1862 – This was a hard Christmas for our unit. Our victory at Fredericksburg had boosted everyone's spirits and reinforced our belief that General Lee's army couldn't lose the war, but none of us were happy to be in the field in late December. We facing bitter cold and constant rain and snow with barely adequate shelter. We'd been forced to stuff leaves into our tents for added warmth and to form beds.

It was so cold that when Fish went down to the stream to wash up, he returned with his hair frozen and sticking out at all angles. He had to stand by the fire for a long time to thaw it out. The rest of us were huddled around the fire, good-naturedly teasing Fish, when Taylor surprised us with a splendid cake one of the local Southern ladies had baked for him. Frank added to the surprise by producing coffee he'd saved for the holiday. It wasn't much of a Christmas, but we were thankful for simple pleasures.

By the firelight, Buck called for the Lost Gold story. Fish sat in rapt attention as Taylor spun his tale of the Englishmen and their mules laden with gold and the unrelenting attack of the Indians. At the end of the story, as he'd done with me, Taylor pulled out his precious map to share with Fish. Where I saw random squiggly lines, dismissing the map's value, Fish stared at it for a long time. The rest of us grew quiet as we watched him concentrate. Taylor asked

Fish what he was thinking.

Fish looked up with a strange expression on his face. "I grew up near Hickory Nut Gap. My pa used to take me huntin' there." Taylor got excited and asked if he recognized anything on the map. Fish said, "I think... maybe?"

Now, perhaps Fish just wanted to fit in with the group and was saying what we wanted to hear, but we all wanted to believe his knowledge of the area was the missing piece we needed to find the gold. In our minds, it was no longer if we found the gold but when.

Our talk of gold became an obsession, but it would be a long wait until all six of us would get the chance to travel back to western North Carolina to begin the search.

CHAPTER VIII

THE MADAM

Saturday, July 11, 1874

IT was a short walk from Treman's hardware store to the Northern Central House across from the train depot. Annie considered what questions to ask the proprietor about the dead man while considering a list of other hotels and boardinghouses to try if this one failed to turn up any clues. She'd been so preoccupied with her thoughts that she didn't notice Glendon had fallen behind. Annie stood by the door to the Northern Central House and realized he was no longer by her side. Glendon had stopped ten paces away. He stared at the building with a look of distaste, perhaps just now remembering it was his job to protect both Annie's person and her reputation.

The Northern Central House had been a perfectly lovely hotel a few years earlier—it had even offered wedding services to vacationers. But with new ownership in 1872, the reputation and the clientele had taken a significant drop in respectability. This hotel now included a saloon and was known locally as a house of ill repute.

"This is where the shooting took place last year." Glendon gestured to where he was standing. A year earlier, a married man named Morgan had taken a liking to one of the working women and tried to prevent two other men from entering the hotel and sampling her charms for themselves. A fight broke out, and Morgan pulled out a revolver and shot the two men—one in the arm, the other in his eye socket. Miraculously, both survived. The second man—despite having a bullet lodged near his brain—went back to work as a boatman on a canal boat. A few months later, the boatman dropped dead when the bullet finally finished its intended job. Morgan was arrested and put on trial but was later found not guilty of the shooting by reason of self-defense. He promptly abandoned his wife and fled to the West.

Annie gave Glendon a questioning look. He shrugged. "I don't want your reputation to be tarnished by being seen near this place."

"Right," Annie said, looking around. "Then we'd better get inside before anyone sees us." She smiled at Glendon and entered the building, leaving him no choice but to follow.

Annie's eyes adjusted to the dark interior, revealing a lobby that was a mixture of saloon and parlor. It was early on a Saturday, so the place wasn't crowded. Several men played cards while young women kept them company. The fragrances of the working women mingled with the men's tobacco smoke.

Annie had never been to a brothel before. She was fascinated to see something she had only heard rumors about. As she walked deeper into the lobby, some men tilted their heads down to avoid being recognized while one or two stared at her boldly. She ignored them and turned toward the bar. A large man wearing a small hat stood watch with his arms crossed, eyeing both the doorway and the interior. Annie guessed he was employed to control unruly clients and perhaps disobedient women.

As Glendon joined Annie, a tall, broad, middle-aged woman approached them from across the room. She was packed into a flowing maroon dress in the latest style with a corset tight enough to risk pushing her breasts out of her dress. Since Watkins was a small town, everyone knew Maggie Woodruff ran the Northern Central House. Annie had read that brothels were often run by an older prostitute whose beauty had faded, but she didn't know if that held true in Miss Woodruff's case. Annie could only guess her age because her makeup had been expertly applied. She was making the best of what she had.

"Mrs. Woodruff? I'm Annie Anderson."

"Everyone calls me 'Big Mag,' so you might as well too." The madam nodded to Glendon with a smile before turning back to Annie. "Looking for a job?"

Annie blushed. "No, thank you."

"A pity," said Big Mag as she looked Annie up and down before turning her attention to Glendon. "Nice to see you again, Glendon."

Annie was taken aback at the madam's familiarity with her uncle but assumed Glendon had plenty of reasons to know Big Mag besides the obvious one that Annie tried to push from her mind.

"Big Mag," Glendon said, tilting his head.

"I'm looking for a man," Annie said quietly so as not to be overheard by those in the parlor.

Big Mag chuckled and grinned. "We get lots of men here, Miss Anderson."

Annie's blush deepened. "I mean, I'm looking for a specific man. In his late thirties or early forties. Southern accent. Full beard hiding a scar on the left side. His suit worn but mended."

"Why?"

"Why am I looking for him?"

Big Mag nodded, then stared at Annie, waiting for an answer.

Annie was sure that a glint of recognition had flashed across Big Mag's face when Annie mentioned the man's accent and scar. Big Mag knew something. Annie cleared her throat and decided on a version of the truth. "I saw him in the cemetery, and he looked injured."

"Are you the type of young lady who saves injured animals and rescues baby birds fallen from the nest?" Big Mag said with both humor and disdain.

"I thought he might have been staying here," Annie said.

Big Mag considered Annie's words, then a dismissive look settled on her face. "Our guests value discretion," she said, looking back toward the parlor, growing tired of their conversation, and having more important things to do. "There is no man here who matches that description. Good luck with your search."

Big Mag began to walk away, but Annie wasn't ready to give up. She reached out and touched Big Mag's arm. "Can we speak privately?"

The older woman's eyes flashed with displeasure. Annie removed her hand immediately. It was poor etiquette to touch a woman. Before Annie could express her regrets, Glendon spoke quietly. "We will make it worth your while."

Big Mag looked at Glendon for a moment, then nodded. She glanced casually about the room to make sure all was calm, and no one was paying them too much attention. Big Mag made eye contact with the big man by the bar, passing along some wordless message, then she gave Annie and Glendon a subtle "follow me" nod and led them away from the parlor to a small office.

As the door closed behind them, Annie rushed her words. "Big Mag, let me be honest. I know the man I'm looking for is not here because, based on the condition I saw him in, he is never coming back. I want to find out who he is so his next of kin can be notified that he won't be returning." She paused for a heartbeat. "Will you help me?"

Big Mag considered this new information. "Is the sheriff involved?"

"He didn't believe what I told him because I'm a woman."

Big Mag scoffed, having had her own experiences with men underestimating her abilities. "I may have some information on a Southern gentleman who arrived on the northbound train yesterday." Annie looked at her expectantly. "But I'm a businesswoman…" Annie was waiting for Big Mag to get to the point, but Glendon was already handing a crisp green bill across to Big Mag, who smiled and tucked it into her dress close to her heart. Annie realized that appealing to Big Mag's goodwill was a waste of everyone's time. Everything was a transaction.

Big Mag turned to Annie. "Middle-aged? Southern? Scar here?" she asked, pointing to her left cheek. Annie nodded as Big Mag continued. "Your man came in right off the train yesterday afternoon. Clearly from the South based on his accent. If I had to guess, I'd say more mountain southern like Kentucky or Tennessee than coastal like Georgia. He paid for one night, but he said he might stay longer." She paused. "He left in the middle of the night last night and hasn't returned."

"He won't be back," said Annie. "Is there any chance he gave you his name?"

"Overnight guests are required to sign the registration book, but I can't guarantee they use their real names."

"What name did he use?" Annie asked.

"The name he wrote in the book was Harper Thompson."

Annie was pleased. A name got her halfway to her goal. "You

said you were expecting him to return. Is that because he left belongings in his room?"

"He did."

Annie waited, but Big Mag had more patience. Annie spoke first. "May we see his room?"

Big Mag smiled and turned to Glendon, who handed over two more bills without being asked. "I always enjoy doing business with you, Mister Robinson," she said as she led them out of the room.

Annie looked at Glendon with wide eyes and an expression that asked, 'What have you been up to?' Glendon was flustered. "It's not what you—" But Annie held up both hands in the universal gesture for "stop, I don't want to know." She shook her head but spared him with a smile before turning to follow Big Mag out the door. They climbed the stairs to the second floor, and when they reached a room in the middle of the corridor, Big Mag extracted a set of keys from within the fabric of her dress and opened the door. She stepped aside to let them in.

As Annie and Glendon entered the room, Big Mag hovered in the hallway. "You won't mind if I watch from here," she said, leaning against the door frame. It was not a question.

The room was small, with a bed on one side and a dresser on the other. A pitcher and washbasin sat on the dresser, both half-filled with water. At the foot of the bed was an empty chamber pot. There was no sign that anyone had returned to the room.

Annie checked the dresser drawers. They were empty. Glendon looked under the bed. He pulled out a travel bag.

"Anything of value you find," said Big Mag from the doorway, "I will take and apply to his room bill."

Glendon grabbed the bottom of the travel bag and dumped its meager contents onto the bed. There were wool socks and undergarments, a second suit carefully folded yet still wrinkled, a small wooden case, and a Bible. The small case was wrapped in cloth. Glendon picked it and opened it. The empty case smelled of gun oil.

"There was no gun at the cemetery," Annie said. She picked up the suit jacket. The seamstress in her admired the repair work. She checked all the pockets, but they were empty. She was disappointed not to find the man's name stitched into the suit, but she did find a tailor's label sewn to the inside of the jacket.

R.M. Robinson
Fashionable Tailor
Rutherfordton, NC

"Relative of yours?" Annie asked as she showed the label to Glendon.

"Very funny."

She turned to Big Mag. "Do you think he could have been from North Carolina?"

Big Mag paused, replaying the accent in her head, then shrugged. "It's possible."

Annie now had a name, Harper Thompson, and hopefully a location. She was pleased with her progress.

The last thing to examine was the Bible. Many families used their Bibles to track family births, marriages, and deaths, but this Bible was small and likely for traveling. There were no names written inside. All this Bible had to offer was a picture of an attractive woman and two scraps of paper. The picture had been taken in a studio, but there was no studio name on the print. From the style of the hoop dress the woman was wearing, Annie guessed the photo was about ten years old. The name Sadie was carefully lettered on the back of the print. Sadie was smiling and happy in her photo. *This was the woman who mended the dead man's suits,* Annie thought to herself.

Annie unfolded the first scrap of paper and read the cryptic handwritten message before handing the paper to Glendon.

What we lost in Hickory Nut Gap is in New York.
Pack for a long trip. More to follow.

She'd never heard of Hickory Nut Gap. She unfolded the second piece of paper.

Arrive in Watkins, New York, by the seventeenth of July.
Say goodbye to your poor life.

Annie shivered as she realized the double meaning of the second line. "What did you find?" Big Mag asked as Annie and Glendon studied the notes.

"A couple of personal notes and this photo," said Annie, flashing the photo at Big Mag. Annie made a show of flipping through the Bible to prove nothing else was hidden inside. Glendon handed Annie the notes, which she refolded and slid back into the Bible.

Annie turned to Big Mag. "What will you do with this stuff?"

"From what you tell me—and I believe you even if the sheriff didn't—our Southerner is not coming back. So, I'll get whatever value I can from selling his belongings and throw away the rest."

"I'd like to take this picture and the Bible and return them to his wife," said Annie. She was guessing that the dead man was married. She didn't remember seeing a wedding ring, but few married men wore them. Glendon handed one more bill to Big Mag to preempt any negotiations. She folded it and put it with the others.

Annie and Glendon stepped into the hallway as Big Mag locked the door and then led them back down the wooden staircase.

Something nagged at the back of Annie's brain. As she reached the bottom of the stairs, it came to her. "Big Mag," she said, "when I saw Mister Harper, I smelled alcohol. Did he buy it here?" If not, Annie thought, the man might have met his killer at another saloon before visiting the cemetery together, giving her another potential clue to follow.

"Are you trying to get me into trouble?" Big Mag said as they entered the parlor. "The temperance movement has swayed our town fathers, and now liquor licenses are no longer being renewed. Watkins is becoming a dry town." Big Mag glared at Annie, but it turned into a grin. "Of course," she said, "if a customer buys other services, nothing prevents me from providing free drinks." She winked at Annie.

Standing with her back to the room, Annie opened her mouth to respond when she was yanked off her feet and dragged backward. A large farmer, smelling of spitting tobacco and stale body odor, pulled her onto his lap. "How about some free samples before I decide to spend my money on you?" The man said, pulling her in for a kiss.

Annie pushed against his chest. "Let me go!" she said, horrified.

She looked toward the big man with the small hat, but he hadn't moved. Suddenly, she was lifted off the farmer's lap. His dirty fingernails scratched her arms as she was pulled away. Glendon raised her into the air, steadied her, and then gently set her down behind him. The farmer stood up, furious, and stared Glendon down.

"Who do you think you are, Mister Fancy?" The farmer spit out his words. "My money is as good as yours in this place. She's too young for you anyway." The farmer was taller, wider, and younger than Glendon. Annie feared for her uncle and herself.

"You have made a mistake," Glendon said, not backing down. His voice was firm. "We are leaving."

Glendon started to turn away from the farmer, but the man didn't take kindly to being dismissed. The larger man roared and stepped toward Glendon, swinging a fat fist at his head.

Annie opened her mouth to shout a warning, but before any sound came out, Glendon weathered a glancing blow from the farmer and landed two quick punches into the farmer's soft middle, knocking the air out of him. Then, as the man doubled over, Glendon slammed the farmer's head onto the nearest table. Blood burst forth from a split lip and a busted nose, and the farmer crumbled to the floor in a heap.

Glendon leaned down and whispered in the farmer's ear, "Remember, you started this."

The burst of aggression from Glendon had been so quick and brutally efficient that the entire room went quiet. Glendon turned toward Big Mag and handed her a much larger bill than before. "For the cleanup."

Big Mag tucked the money away and looked to the big man with the small hat. "Kenneth?" She tilted her head from Kenneth toward the fallen farmer. The big man lumbered into action. Big Mag turned to Annie. "This is your fault for confusing my customers. This isn't a place for you. Don't come back."

Glendon took Annie by the elbow, guiding her across the room and out the front door. As they exited the Northern Central House, Annie realized that after all these years, perhaps she didn't know her "uncle" as well as she thought.

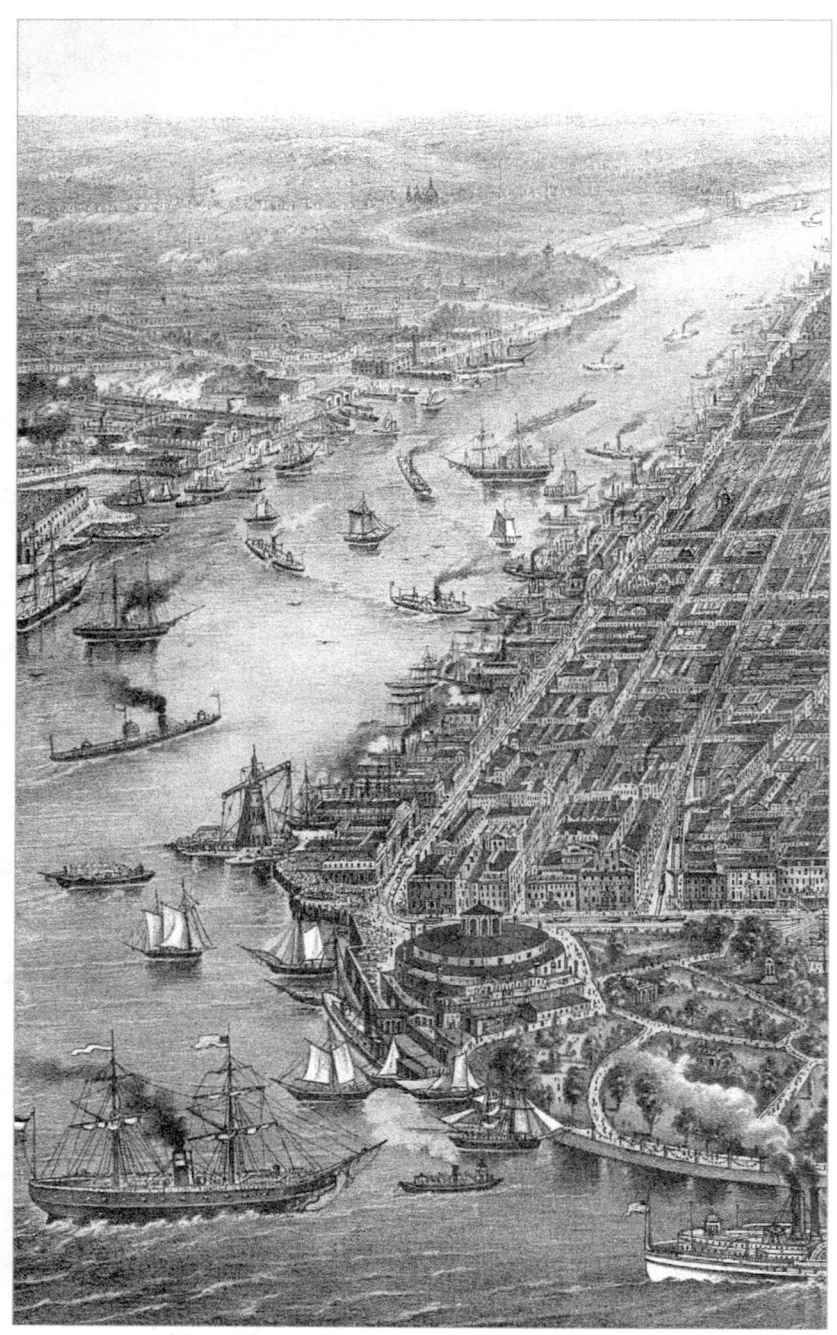

New York City and the Hudson River

CHAPTER IX

LEAVING NEW YORK

Sunday, July 12, 1874

A WELL-DRESSED gentleman calling himself Bradley Webster bought a ticket on the Erie Railway from New York City to Watkins late on the morning of July 12. He bore little resemblance to the man who had been released from The Tombs detention center the night before. A new suit, fashionable and understated, a fresh shave, and a large amount of money in his pocket had worked an impressive transformation.

The first thing Bradford had done after walking out of The Tombs last night was to liberate the stashed money Pickens owed him for his services. Pickens's apartment had been thoroughly searched after his arrest, but he'd hidden his money in the back of a picture frame at his mistress's rented room on the East Side. Bradford found her building and paid a young boy to knock on her door and whisper that the police were coming to question her. After she ran out of the building, Bradford was in and out in five minutes with money in hand.

His next stop was the riskiest, and while he chastised himself for being sentimental, he still returned to his shabby one-room rental near the garment district. Inside, under the floorboards by the bed, he had hidden a pocket watch his father had given him. The watch was worn, a bit scratched, and prone to stopping, but when it did work, it kept immaculate time.

Bradford stayed in the shadows and then climbed up the fire escape and through the window. He'd paid his rent through the end of the week, so the apartment hadn't been rented again yet. He gave himself three minutes to get in and out, but took a few extra seconds to grab a knife he had left behind before leaving for prison.

Securing the watch in his vest pocket, he tucked his knife into his left boot and climbed out the window and down a drainpipe.

Bradford reached the pavement, pleased he had gotten out cleanly. His self-congratulation didn't last long. As he exited the alley behind his building, three men in the darkness turned in his direction. They were half a block away and had been watching the front of the building. From his quick glance, they were lean and muscular and dressed like men who didn't mind getting their hands dirty. Bradford Whitey had made more than his share of enemies who would be happy to do him harm. There was no reason to stick around and give them the opportunity.

Bradford walked away quickly but not urgently. He didn't want his pursuers to know that he had spotted them. As he approached the end of the block, he increased his speed, and as he turned the corner, he started sprinting. Moments later, shouts from his pursuers rose behind him as they reached the end of the block and saw him pulling away. The shouting was replaced by the thumping of their feet as they chased after him.

There were not enough people out at this time of night for Bradford to lose his pursuers in a crowd. He noticed a passing hansom cab and veered toward the fast, two-wheeled carriage without slowing down. He dodged a four-in-hand coach speeding by, then leaped into the cab and shoved too much money up through the trapdoor in the roof toward the driver.

"To the Grand Central Depot, quick as you can!" Bradford didn't have to fake the urgency in his voice. He wasn't dressed like a man who could afford to take cabs, but money talked, and the driver and horse surged into traffic quick enough to throw Bradford back in his seat. He turned around to see his three pursuers cursing as they faded in the distance.

When the cab arrived at the Grand Central Depot, home to the Hudson, New Haven, and Harlem railroads, Bradford paid the driver, walked in one door, passed through the station, and then walked out the door on the opposite side. He jumped into another cab and told the driver to take him south to Broadway Avenue. He looked back but could see no pursuit. The shops were closed, but he requested the cab pull over when he saw a reasonable boardinghouse. Bradford used his new money to pay for a room that offered hot baths.

At first light, Bradford was waiting outside a clothier shop as the owner arrived. Since Pickens had moved in a world where impeccably tailored clothes mattered, Bradley Webster needed to dress like a man from those same social circles. Thanks to Pickens's money, he could now afford to dress the part. Bradford admired his new outfit, then threw everything from his old life—except his knife and his father's watch—into the trash before walking out of the clothier's shop.

After a stop at a reputable barber for a haircut and a shave, Bradford Whitey, the man who'd spent time in prison, disappeared, and his new identity as Bradley Webster was born. Bradley hadn't worked out his new story yet, but he would present himself as a respectable young gentleman willing to apprentice in the illicit world of counterfeiting. It was not the first time Bradford had reinvented himself.

Bradley took a final cab ride to the Chambers Street Ferry Terminal on the Lower West Side. With no bridges over the Hudson River from Manhattan, travelers on the Erie Railway needed to cross the river via steam ferry to connect with their westbound trains in Jersey City. Bradley merged into a large throng of men, women, and children shuffling toward the ferry. On board, he found a spot on the back deck that gave him the best view of the city.

The city of New York was a contradiction. It was full of marvels—national banks that financed railroads, telegraphs, and mining projects around the country, the booming garment district, shopping stores multiple stories high with their own steam elevators, and soon the New York and Brooklyn Bridge, the world's longest suspension bridge. For those with money, the city was magical. Outside the affluent areas, the streets were beds of uneven cobblestones caked with mud and manure and, too often, the rotting carcasses of horses. Immigrants were crammed into squalid, overcrowded tenements infested with crime and diseases like cholera, typhoid, and consumption. It was a hard place for those less fortunate.

After surviving ten years with those less fortunate, Bradley watched from the ferry deck as the city and his life as Bradford Whitey faded from view. He would not miss either. A sudden vision of Detective Mac MacGregor dead in the restaurant intruded on Bradley's memories, but he shook the thought away.

Bradley wrinkled his nose as warm summer breezes brought the smell of rotting fish and subtle hints of sewage. He wouldn't miss those odors either. He turned and made his way to the front of the ferry to watch the Erie Railway's Pavonia Terminal, with its brightly colored three-story tower, growing closer. As the ferry docked, he followed the crowds onto the shore of Jersey City. It was a short walk to the terminal, where twelve train tracks waited to whisk passengers on to new destinations.

The sea of people that moved toward the terminal began to blend into another large crowd maneuvering in the opposite direction to board the ferry for its return trip. Bradley looked down to check the time on his pocket watch. Distracted, he bumped into a large man in a tweed jacket and a brown felt derby hat coming from the train terminal. As Bradley bounced off the man and moved past, he turned sideways to tip his cap in apology.

The eyes of the other man grew wide in recognition.

"You!" the man spat the word out in disgust.

Of all the rotten coincidences, thought Bradley.

Declan O'Donnell's face was turning red with rage as he grabbed Bradley's jacket. "Fergus!" Declan called to an even bigger Irishman nearby. "It's that bastard, Brady Wheelan!"

Bradley rolled his eyes at his miserable luck. Both O'Donnell brothers in the same place!? He couldn't blame them for being angry, even if they didn't know the whole story. But now wasn't the time to explain himself.

Without hesitation, Bradley grabbed Declan's wrist and twisted it, eliciting a howl of pain. The Irishman's grip loosened enough for Bradley to pull free. He pushed Declan backward toward his brother, forcing both off balance, then turned and ran through the crowd to escape pursuers for the second time in two days.

He headed straight for the terminal and to the first cop he saw. "Officer, those men just tried to steal my watch!" He pointed back to the two angry Irishmen pushing through the crowd.

Bradley was dressed like a gentleman, while the O'Donnell brothers were dressed like the hooligans they were. The cop blew his whistle and stepped toward the brothers with his billy club raised giving Bradley time to slide through the terminal doors. He looked back long enough to see the O'Donnell brothers reversing direction. They were no friends of the coppers.

Bradley hurried through the station until he found the correct track for his train to Elmira. Seeing no sign of pursuit, he climbed into the first car and made his way past fellow travelers until he arrived at the right train carriage. He didn't relax until the train pulled away from the station.

CHAPTER X

HICKORY NUT GAP

From the Journal of Private H. Thompson

July 1, 1863 – In the Pennsylvania countryside, outside of Gettys-burg, General Lee's Army of Northern Virginia took the battle to the enemy. The 34th North Carolina and four other infantry regi-ments charged into enemy musket fire while under a deadly artil-lery barrage. Every officer in our brigade except two were killed, as were many enlisted men.

July 3, 1863 – What was left our the brigade charged up Cem-etery Hill following General Pickett's division, trying to break the Union center. When the dust settled, the 34th had been crushed. Despite the shocking losses, the Lucky Six emerged miraculously unscathed.

December 31, 1863 – The Lucky Six passed a quiet New Year's Eve at our winter quarters at the Orange Courthouse in Virginia between Richmond and Washington, DC. For the first time in a year or two, we'd received coffee, sugar, and dried apples with our rations.

Our luck had not failed us in the losses at Gettysburg and Fall-ing Waters or later skirmishes at Bristoe Station and Mine Run. The six of us escaped harm each time. As our company licked its wounds and rebuilt for next year's campaigns, new recruits be-gan showing up to replace the men killed, disabled, or captured. I should be thankful for more "fresh fish," but many of these new soldiers were in their forties with no soldiering experience and no obvious enthusiasm to improve their combat skills. This didn't give me confidence for the battles ahead in 1864.

March 2, 1864 – The Lucky Six did our best to stay warm through the long, cold winter. Our hut was made of logs stacked two-to-three feet high and topped with a canvas tent. We added a chimney and did what we could to stay comfortable.

Taylor, recently promoted to sergeant, stepped into the hut as we guessed how the war might end. Buck thought it would end when the Yankees got tired of sending their men to die and called a truce. Ace declared it would come down to a Democrat beating Lincoln in the elections in November and ending the war. Frank was quiet as always, but Fish couldn't stop talking about how he was ready to head north and kill all those damn Yankees so he could go home to his farm and hug his mother and sister. I believed the generals would go on fighting until all able-bodied men dead were left for dead on the battlefield.

We turned to Taylor and noticed the solemn look on his face. "Gentlemen, we've got new orders," he said. We all groaned, expecting a long march into freezing weather and cannon fire. Taylor stared at us, trying to keep a straight face and enjoying the moment before finally shouting, "Furlough! I got all of us an eighteen-day furlough. At the same time. We leave tomorrow."

We all started whooping, hollering, jumping up and down, and slapping each other on the back. None of us had not been home or seen our families in two years. Amid the celebration, Buck suggested we use some of our furlough to look for the gold. Taylor never admitted a search was part of his motivation for the group furlough, but I saw a flash of relief cross his face at Buck's suggestion. The group agreed to visit our families first and then use the last three days of the furlough to venture into the Hickory Nut Gap in search of the hidden gold.

With my father long dead, I had no home to go back to, but I sat back, happily enjoying everyone's enthusiasm for a family visit. Fish noticed me sitting alone and dropped down beside me. "You probably got lots to do, but I know my ma and sister would be thrilled to have you come to our farm for a visit. Ma makes the best meat pies." He made a contented humming sound at the thought of his mother's pies. "Besides," he added, "you tell great stories, and we can always use an extra set of hands around the farm."

Never knowing my own mother, the thought of Mrs. Pierson

baking a meat pie for me overwhelmed my imagination. I had a sudden need to scratch an itch just below my eye and then discreetly wipe the moisture away with my jacket. Clearing my throat, I said, "I need to stop in Asheville for a few days to check on things, but if it is all right with your mother, I'd love to visit after that."

Fish flashed me a big smile and clapped me on the back as he got up. "You won't regret it!"

March 7, 1864 – I knocked on the door when I arrived at the Pierson family farm in Rutherfordton, North Carolina, several days later, as agreed. The rest of the Lucky Six would meet at Fish's farm on the fourteenth day of our furlough to begin our search for the gold. Having no reason to go to Asheville, I had killed time in Rutherfordton to give Fish a few days to enjoy his family reunion without distractions.

Fish was excited to see me and enthusiastically introduced me to his mother, Mrs. Abigail Pierson, and his young sister, Libbie. Mrs. Pierson was a striking woman in her late thirties. Libby was eight years old, having been in the womb when their father passed. Sadly, news had come that Fish's two older brothers had died in the war. Jeb took a bullet to the chest in Vicksburg, Mississippi—some would say a noble death—while poor Rufus died from dysentery somewhere in Tennessee. Neither man's body returned home. Mrs. Pierson and Libbie did their best to work the farm and got what help they could from neighbors, but the property was in sad disrepair.

Fish gave me a tour of their farm, and afterward, I insisted on earning my meals by helping with chores. He and I got busy mending fences and replacing rotten boards in the barn, then cutting cords of firewood to get the women through the winter. Doing hard but productive work during the day and spending the evenings enjoying a delicious meal and good company was heaven on earth after two straight years of battling boredom, the elements, and the Union Army.

March 16, 1864 – Frank, Ace, and Buck arrived at the Pierson Farm early in the morning and enjoyed the breakfast Fish's mother prepared. Taylor had arrived yesterday from Morganton in a buckboard wagon pulled by two horses hired from a livery stable. After years of talking about it, we were all excited to start the search for gold.

By midmorning, we said our goodbyes to Fish's family. Fish's mom hugged her son for as long as he let her, then she released him, wiped her tears, and told him to return safely to her. We loaded up the wagon and headed toward Hickory Nut Gap. We had two full days to search for the gold before we needed to hurry back to Morganton, return the horses and wagon, and take a series of trains back to the Orange Courthouse in Virginia.

It was cool during the day and would drop near freezing after dark. We wore a mixture of our uniforms and personal clothing to keep warm. Taylor said cold weather worked in our favor. "With all the leaves off the trees, it will be easier to spot caves to search."

We traveled along Hickory Nut Gap until we came near Round Top Mountain, overlooking the gap between the granite mountain bluffs rising on either side of us. The sun dipped below the hills. Opposite the river, we saw Chimney Rock—an isolated monolith that rose from the mountainside and reached toward the sky like the circular turret of a fantastical castle. Within its view, we set up camp just off the road, pulling the horses and wagon out of sight before building a fire. By the time we finished our meal, the night had grown dark. Outside the edge of the fire, it was pitch black.

As we settled around the fire, Buck and Ace argued about who would have killed more Indians back when Indians were something to worry about here in the Carolinas. Wanting to change the subject, Taylor brought up one of our favorite topics. "What will you do with your share of the gold?"

Fish blurted out his plan to buy himself all the rock candy he could eat. He had a sweet tooth and gave the same answer every time the question was asked. "And then I'll buy Mama a big house somewhere nice with lots of flowers around it and maybe a lake to look at. And I'll hire some servants to help her so she doesn't have to work so hard."

Buck planned to move to Richmond after the Yankees gave up and went back north. He was convinced a lot of money could be made there. Since it took money to make money, he planned to use the gold to become the richest man in all the Confederacy.

Ace said he'd buy a big plot of land outside of Asheville where

HICKORY-NUT GAP, CHIMNEY ROCK

he could build a mansion and raise a family. We all nodded, having heard this before. Land ownership was something rich men aspired to. Then, Ace added something new. "And I'll send each of you a telegram every week—I won't even care about the word count— just to tell you how great my life is."

Buck laughed and said that after Ace went broke buying all those telegrams, he'd come to Asheville and buy Ace's property at a discount. There were groans and more laughter.

When Fish asked me what I would do with my share, he caught me mid-thought. I was ashamed to say aloud that I'd been think- ing of the love of my life. Instead, I told him I didn't realize what a handsome woman his mother was, so I'd use my gold to court her and become his stepfather. And then, while he was caring for the farm, she and I could travel the world.

Fish blushed. He had come into the group naïve and easy to wind up, but a year and a half of hanging with this lot meant he'd learned to give as good as he got. I could see the gleam in his eyes as he glanced at me sideways. "That is mighty charitable of you, Harper," he said slowly, a big smile forming. "I reckon I can learn to call you step-pappy. And since you'll be taking care of my mama, I will be free to use my money to turn myself into a gentleman and find myself a proper lady to raise the next generation of Piersons!"

The Lucky Six hooted and hurrahed.

"All the boys will be strong like me," Fish said, "and all the girls will be beautiful like their mother." He leaned back and brought his hand up to rub his chin while nodding, imagining how much fun he would have making a dozen new Piersons.

I glanced toward Frank, who until then had quietly been whit- tling on a piece of wood and listening to the rest of us. Taylor asked him if he had anything to share. Taylor was always careful to phrase questions so Frank could reply with a nod or a grunt. Frank had never offered an answer to what he would do with the gold before. Usually, he just shook his head. He surprised us this time. "I have what I need," he said with a shrug.

Buck said, "If you aren't going to buy your own house, Frank, we'll expect you to take turns visiting ours!" Frank grinned and nodded.

Then it was Taylor's turn. "I don't think I'll spend any of the gold right away," he said. We looked at him, expecting more. "For a while, I think I'll be happy just knowing we found it and that any of us can buy anything we want. That will make me damn happy." Fish wondered if Taylor was putting us on and asked if he really wouldn't buy anything. "Oh, I will eventually," said Taylor. "But I'll tell you something that I will do for sure. I will carry a gold nugget everywhere I go, and every time I put my hand in my pocket, I will remember the six of us here tonight."

Four of us said, "Hear, hear" or "Amen to that," while Frank let out an agreeable grunt. With that, we were left with our own thoughts of riches and glorious futures. Fish volunteered to take the first watch. The rest of us wrapped ourselves in our blankets and drifted off to sleep one by one.

Two weeks of furlough and thoughts of gold had dulled our survival skills. We fell asleep, not realizing we had been followed.

CHAPTER XI

PULLMAN PARLOR CAR

Sunday, July 12, 1874

WHEN you spend most of your life scratching and scrambling to survive, being thrust into a world of luxury can be a shock. *A very welcome shock*, Bradley thought as he sat in the comfortable, upholstered armchair, which swiveled, allowing him a view of the scenery passing outside his first-class train car's wide windows. Bradley had been on his share of trains before but never on anything as luxurious as this. From his comfortable chair, he admired the carved walnut paneling, polished brass fittings, beveled French mirrors, and elegant carpets of the train car. Tassels and fringe were everywhere. As the train headed west and north, the click-clack of the wheels passing over the rails seemed quieter and the occasional steam whistle more muted.

"A Pullman parlor car," said the well-dressed businessman sitting nearby, "there's nothing finer." The man had noticed Bradley staring in appreciation at his surroundings. "Your first time on one?"

"It's obvious, I suppose," Bradley said with a smile. He extended his hand to his new acquaintance. "Bradley Webster."

"Fredriksson," the man said. He was middle-aged with receding salt-and-pepper hair and round spectacles, which he occasionally had to push back up his nose. Fredriksson shook Bradley's hand. "I'm in the steel business."

The train car was full of well-dressed men and women. Bradley realized they must be looking at him and seeing someone who belonged among them. If they only knew! Bradley saw an invaluable opportunity to gather information from men he couldn't normally approach. He knew that men—especially successful men—were

Pullman Parlor Car Interior

happy to talk about themselves and their businesses if given a small amount of encouragement.

"A pleasure to meet you, Mister Fredriksson. I wonder if I could trouble you for some advice?" Bradley waited until he got an agreeing nod from Mr. Fredriksson. "I have recently come into my inheritance and have some investment decisions to make. I wonder if you might share your opinion on the steel business and whether I should consider investing in it?"

Fredriksson looked Bradley up and down recalibrating his initial appraisal. Bradley was no longer just a young man in nice clothes. He was a young gentleman with money to spend. Of course, Fredriksson thought investing in the steel business was an excellent idea. He talked about ore smelting, the Bessemer process, and the importance of the Pennsylvania coal mines to the making of steel. Fredriksson droned on so much about his work that Bradley breathed a sigh of relief when the man exited the train at Port Jervis.

Over the next few hours, Bradley struck up conversations with a furniture manufacturer, a maker of steam engines, and a man in the oil business. Each enthusiastically talked up his own industry, encouraged Bradley to invest, and offered his card. Each time, Bradley listened intently, absorbing a bit of each man's business expertise as well as their mannerisms and pattern of speech. Then he would thank them and pocket their card.

In Binghamton, another man came aboard who caught Bradley's interest. This man had an easy way about him but was clearly prosperous based on his understated yet expensive suit. The man looked worldly but not so old as to have lost his vigor and enthusiasm for work. After reciting his conversation starter, Bradley learned that the man, Harry Goldstein, worked in the banking industry.

"Yes, banking can be a great investment," Goldstein said, encouragingly. "Many markets are still growing and require investments, which means bank loans. But of course, you cannot trust just any bank as not all are robust or deserve your money. A lot of large banks went bankrupt last year."

Bradley hadn't paid too much attention to the worries of rich men while living in New York, but even he had heard of last year's financial panic triggered by over-investment and speculation in the railroad markets. Building a railroad cost a lot of money and was slow to bring a return. When the money supplies got tight, many railway companies went bankrupt and took with them banks that had heavily invested in building railroads.

"So, your bank is one of the smart ones?"

Goldstein laughed. "I certainly hope so."

Bradley nodded and then steered the conversation toward the subject of his upcoming job interview. "Tell me, though, don't counterfeiters make investing in even healthy banks a risky proposition?"

The rich man nodded as if this was a common concern. "Well, counterfeiters have been a problem in the past. You may be too young to remember, but before the war, every bank issued its own money. All those private banknotes provided great opportunities for counterfeiters." The banker shook his head, recalling banking's dark days. "It was almost impossible to know which notes were real or counterfeit. In fact, back in the 1840s, places like Ohio were littered with counterfeiters."

"Ohio? I would've thought New York, Philadelphia, or Boston had more counterfeiting."

"Those cities have their fair share, but rural areas provide perfect hideouts for the printers of counterfeit money. They only need to be close to major cities to have convenient markets so their passers can spread the fake money around."

"Passers?"

"Yes, passers 'shove the queer' as they call it, passing the fake money off as real money."

"Forgers don't distribute their own counterfeit money?"

Goldstein shrugged. "Different skill, I suppose. Or forgers don't want the risk of being caught with counterfeit money. The forgers sell their fake money to passers or confidence tricksters who distribute it. Women make great passers, by the way. I guess they appear more honest to gullible men."

"So," Bradley said, trying to absorb what he learned, "the forgers set up shop in some rural area and figure out how to make credible engraving plates to print their counterfeit money and then sell it to the passers?"

"Yes," said Goldstein, "although it's also about getting the right paper and dye, forging credible signatures, and knowing how to run the printing presses."

"Isn't all this a problem still?"

"Well, this is just my opinion," said Goldstein thoughtfully, "but I can think of three reasons why there is a lot less to worry about now than there was before the war." Bradley gave him an encouraging look. "First, the government started issuing greenbacks—our first national currency—during the war. Everyone knows what the bills should look like now, so it is harder for counterfeiters to pass off their fakes. Second, a limited number of companies are authorized to print money for the government, and those supplies are tightly controlled, making it harder for forgers to get the right paper and dye. Third, the United States Secret Service—set up as the war ended—is getting really good at tracking down and stopping the counterfeiters before they get away with it for too long."

"So, no need to worry about counterfeiters?"

"Well, there will always be some low-level counterfeiting, but fraudulent money is fairly easy to find because it is rarely perfect. Forgers trip up on the paper or the ink, or perhaps the engraving is just a bit off. If the U.S. government takes over the printing of currency, which is being discussed, it will get even harder for the counterfeiters. Yes, I think the time of counterfeiting on a large scale is coming to an end."

If counterfeit money was fairly easy to spot, then it was a risk to carrying it around. Bradley wondered if that was how Pickens got caught. As the train pulled into Elmira, Bradley thanked the banker for his insights, took the man's offered card, and prepared to disembark.

The city of Elmira, with its 16,000 inhabitants, served as a transportation hub for the Southern Tier of New York. Bradley had to wait for his connection to a Northern Central train that would take him along the banks of the Chemung Canal past Horseheads, Pine Valley, Millport, and Havana to Watkins at the southern end of Seneca Lake. The summer sun sat low in the sky. At least luck was on his side, and he didn't have to wait long before boarding his northbound train.

The passenger car was only one-third full, giving Bradley plenty of seating choices. His traveling companions included a man in work clothes, a pair of older women clearly excited as they chatted away loudly about seeing Niagara Falls for the first time, and an older, travel-weary man in the last row who had fallen asleep sitting up. Near the front of the car was a family traveling together. Bradley chose a seat several rows behind and across from the family of four. The woman sat next to the window with a two or three years old child on her lap. The boy stood on her legs as she held him steady. The boy's father cradled a baby dressed in pink. The father looked awkward as if he hadn't had a lot of practice holding his daughter, but he smiled and made cooing noises at her. They weren't a family of great means as there was no nurse or nanny with them, but they seemed to be a loving family.

Bradley watched without staring. People had an uncanny ability to detect eyes that lingered too long, so Bradley used his peripheral vision. The mother began gently bouncing her son on her lap. The boy giggled as the train rolled along and, at times, let out an infectious, bubbling laugh—the kind that only pure happiness produced. Bradley remembered his own mother bouncing his brother on her lap when he was young. Thinking of his mother made his heart ache.

"Sir, would you be so kind? I could use your assistance."

The voice came from across the aisle where an older woman smiled hopefully at him. She had gotten on at the Horseheads stop. *Odd name—Horseheads*—he thought. He smiled back at the woman, turning on his charm.

"Bradley Webster at your service, ma'am."

He understood quickly that her handbag had gotten stuck under her seat, so he reached down and dislodged it for her.

She thanked him. "Are you traveling far?" she asked politely.

"I have a job prospect in Watkins and am just heading that way now. And you?"

"I'm traveling to Havana to get treatment for my rheumatoid arthritis at the Magnetic Springs Sanitarium." She held up her deformed left hand and looked at it in dismay. "I'm hoping they can improve my hands. I would very much enjoy sewing again. But if that is too much to ask, then perhaps just being able to garden would be lovely."

Bradley had no opinion on magnetic and sulfur springs, but he knew they were all the rage with advertisements claiming that chemicals in the water had curative powers. He wished her the best of success.

As the ticket collector passed through the car, Bradley noticed a newspaper folded over on the seat next to the elderly lady. "Ma'am, is that today's *New York Times*?"

"Yes, something to read while I'm waiting my turn for the baths," she said. He had just done her a favor, but he could tell she struggled between her desire to appear generous and her desire to keep the paper to read later.

"I don't want to take it, but if you don't mind, I'd like to check the lost and found section. It will only take a moment."

"Of course," she said, relieved his interest was temporary.

Bradley flipped through the pages until he found a small section on the bottom of page six. There was only one entry in Lost and Found. A man named Houbert was offering a twenty-five-dollar reward for a lost gray bloodhound. Bradley handed the paper back to the old woman.

She smiled politely and then her curiosity got the better of her. "Have you lost something?"

Bradley nodded. "A long time ago."

When it was clear he wouldn't elaborate, she turned away to enjoy the view out her window. He settled back into his own seat. They passed through Pine Valley, leaving only three more stops—Millport, Havana, and then Watkins—before he'd need to disembarked. It had been a long day of train travel, and Bradley made a mental note to book an express train if he had to make the trip again. He went back to watching the young family in his peripheral vision. The mother was now feeding their baby from a glass feeding bottle as the father entertained their son with a toy.

At Millport, a man got on and lingered at the front of the train car as if deciding which seat to take. Bradley recognized the look in the man's eyes and noticed he wasn't carrying a bag, which left both hands free. Bradley watched as the man timed his movements, starting down the aisle as the young father stood up to retrieve the toy his son dropped. The father grabbed the toy and stood triumphantly as the man reached him, causing them to bounce into each other. The new man grunted an "excuse me" before continuing down the aisle toward Bradley.

Bradley sighed. He shouldn't get involved but stood up casually as the man approached. He stepped into the aisle as the man reached him, creating a second collision of bodies..

"Oh, beg your pardon, my good man," Bradley said cheerfully.

The man hissed. "Watch where you are going," he said under his breath before continuing to the end of the car and out the door toward the next car.

Bradley watched him leave and then approached the family. He made a big show of bending down as if finding something on the floor, even though he already had the father's wallet palmed in his hand. He stood up and held out the money-filled wallet to the father. "Did you drop this by any chance?"

The man's eyes went wide as he patted the breast pocket of his suit, which is where he had last known his wallet to be.

"Oh, Robert," the wife said. "That has all our money for our vacation. That would have been a catastrophe!"

Robert was chagrined but gratefully accepted his wallet back.

"It could happen to anyone," said Bradley. The little boy was looking at him, so Bradley made a silly face, trying to get a laugh. The boy shyly hid his face in his mother's dress. "Enjoy your vacation," Bradley said, tipping his hat as he departed.

Bradley passed through the cabin in the opposite direction the pickpocket had traveled. When he was between cars, he pulled out a second wallet. Six dollars, a picture of a scantily clad woman, and the pickpocket's train ticket. "Amateur," said Bradley as he pocketed the money and threw the rest from the train.

CHAPTER XII

Luxury Hotels

Monday, July 13, 1874

THE Lake View Hotel was a quarter of a mile from the center of the village and three hundred feet above lake level. Annie held tightly onto Roland's arm for stability as they climbed uphill. Light breezes brought the sounds of chirping birds in search of morning worms. As Annie and Roland reached the new carriage road, the hotel rose in front of them. The brick building stood four stories high, towering over the landscape and giving guests an unrivaled view of the village and the southern part of Seneca Lake. The hotel advertised large and airy rooms with the latest amenities, including gas lights and running water with hot and cold baths, but for the steep price of $3.50 per night.

Annie noticed the hotel staff arriving for their workday and sweat-covered horses pulling delivery wagons up the steep incline from the village to make early morning deliveries. Glancing toward the rising sun, Annie was pleased that they had arrived at the same time of day as when she found the body in the cemetery two days earlier.

"Are you ready to tell me why we're here?" Roland asked. He wore his usual brown suit, appropriately the color of rich earth since Roland loved being outdoors and working with his hands. His bright striped shirt provided a colorful contrast to the suit. While his clothes were impeccably tailored, he wore polished but dusty, and well-broken-in boots.

Annie smoothed out her peacock green walking dress that she had chosen because it gave her confidence. "I am certain—well, pretty certain—that after I left the body in the cemetery Saturday morning, no one else exited the way I had through the main en-

LAKE VIEW HOTEL

trance. That means—assuming the killer didn't try carrying a body through the woods, he had to use the paths that exit by the Lake View Hotel or the Glen Mountain House on either side of the cemetery. I need your help to find witnesses who saw what happened on Saturday."

Annie worried Roland would tell her she was being foolish, but he just smiled and nodded. "A fine day for a quest!" Roland had always been the most entertained by her adventures and occasional misadventures, and she loved him for it. "So," he clarified, "I should ask everyone who was here Saturday morning if they saw a dead body being dragged out of the cemetery?"

"Shhh! No mention of dead bodies!" Annie was ready to clamp her hand over his mouth when he chuckled. "Very funny," she said. "Better to ask about unusual wagons or anyone carrying a heavy package." No point in ruffling the feathers of the sheriff or the richest man in town by mentioning dead bodies before their precious regatta.

Roland nodded and headed inside to talk to the staff while Annie approached the men outside. She talked with the wagon drivers, several landscapers, and the men preparing the horses and carriages to pick up guests at the train station. Quite a few had been working Saturday morning, but none had been near the cemetery or remembered seeing anything unusual. One man in particular—a sturdy man with a grizzled beard and dirt under his fingernails—said he would swear on his wife's grave that no one had come out of the path leading from the cemetery carrying anything larger than a parasol from sunrise to at least nine in the morning. He had been on duty the whole time.

Annie was pleased. It seemed likely that the body had been removed by way of the Glen Mountain House on the other side of the cemetery. She walked up the front stairs to look for Roland and found him deep in conversation with a sharp-dressed colored man near the main entrance.

"Annie!" Roland was pleased to see her. "Let me introduce you to Stephen Newby. Mister Newby is one of the barbers who work for this fine establishment."

"Pleased to meet you, sir," she said.

"The pleasure is mine," said Mr. Newby. He was a handsome man in his early thirties and sharply dressed in a crisp work uniform. He kept his curly hair short.

"I asked him about Saturday morning," Roland said.

Annie looked at Mr. Newby hopefully.

"You're worried about an injured man?" asked Mr. Newby. Annie nodded.

"I didn't see anyone coming or going from the cemetery Saturday morning," said Mr. Newby, "but...." He hesitated momentarily, perhaps wondering too late if he should have kept his mouth shut. "Well, my uncle Abraham Adams is visiting us for the summer, and he likes to walk up the hill with me when I come in for work. He often returns home through the cemetery and the Glen. He loves walking through the Glen. He was with me on Saturday morning, so perhaps he noticed something that might help you?"

"Oh, I would love to speak with him," said Annie.

Mr. Newby nodded, charmed by her enthusiasm. "I don't know his plans today, but I know where he'll be at four in the afternoon tomorrow." He smiled a bit self-consciously. "My mother loves to arrange get-togethers around afternoon tea on my days off." After another pause, he added, "It's the Canadian influence." Afternoon tea was common in parts of the British Empire. "You're welcome to join us. My mother would love someone new to talk to, and Uncle Abraham never misses afternoon tea. He can't get enough of my mother's finger sandwiches."

"If it's not an inconvenience, it'd be a pleasure to come to afternoon tea, Mister Newby," Annie said.

"Not at all." Newby provided Annie with his address, then excused himself to hurry back inside to start his shift.

"Progress!" Annie smiled as she grabbed Roland's arm. She looked back toward the lake one more time to appreciate the view. Several vessels steamed down Seneca Lake as it stretched north toward Geneva, forty miles away. Closer in, a bright red kite knifed through the deepening blue of the summer sky.

The roads and walks in Glenwood Cemetery were wide, with many grand trees and the occasional evergreen to add charm to the grounds. "Did Glendon say anything to you before he left?" Annie asked Roland as they started across the cemetery.

Annie hadn't seen Glendon since he escorted her from the Northern Central House Saturday afternoon. He had avoided her attempts at conversation as he'd walked her home, then quickly left, making vague comments about catching up on work. He hadn't joined the family at church on Sunday, and Annie learned from her grandmother yesterday afternoon that Glendon had left town for business in New York City. This wasn't unusual. His job often required him to travel for days or weeks, but Annie blamed herself for this absence. Watkins was a small town, and Glendon was well known. Rumors of his fight with a farmer at the local brothel were sure to spread around town. It didn't matter that he acted in self-defense and to protect her honor. Why was a reputable man at a brothel in the first place? It would be difficult to imagine which would hurt him more, the damage to his reputation or the damage to his business.

"No, I haven't talked to him, but you know how he gets when he is busy with work." Roland seemed unworried, which made Annie feel better. She had shared with Roland the details of her brothel adventure, including the two notes Glendon and Annie had found in the dead man's Bible. At least their visit to Big Mag's establishment was productive. Her fledgling detective work had uncovered the name and hometown of the dead man from the cemetery, and she planned to visit the Western Union office later in the day to send a telegram to Sadie Thompson, the assumed wife of Harper Thompson of Rutherfordton, North Carolina.

They had to cross the width of the cemetery before reaching Annie's parents' gravestones, closer to the Glen Mountain House hotel and the famous gorge. The location was peaceful and quiet, with the murmuring of the waters of the nearby glen adding to the tranquility. There was no evidence now of the dead body that had disappeared two days earlier.

Roland stared down, looking uncomfortable. He shifted his weight from one foot to the other. "I really should visit more often," he said, more to himself than to Annie. He'd been the best of friends with Annie's father, Edward. Roland leaned down, pulled at the long grass, and swept away stray leaves from her father's grave. When his eyes started watering, Annie turned away to give him a moment.

She wanted to look anywhere except at her parents' graves anyway as the vision of the dead body against her mother's headstone was too fresh. The sun felt warmer, and Annie started to worry she was running out of time to find the right people to talk to at the Glen Mountain House. She turned to look toward the road leading through the woods and down to the gorge. What she saw made her breath catch in her lungs, and her entire body freeze.

Not thirty paces away, a giant man with black hair and a black grizzled beard looked out from the woods, his body partly in shadow. He stared directly at her—his eyes boring into hers. Eyes that did not blink. A chill ran over Annie's body. She was afraid to look away. Was this the killer of the missing man? She tried to call for Roland, but his name stuck in her throat.

Annie tore her eyes away and looked back at Roland. She uttered his name with such a strained voice that he jumped to her side with a pistol in each hand. Even though she had been looking right at Roland, she couldn't have recounted how the pistols had gotten into his hands so quickly. She pointed toward the woods, and as she turned back, the woods were empty.

"There was a man," she said. "A giant man! He was right there!"

Roland started forward. "Stay close," he said as his eyes searched for any movement in the woods. Annie, following only a few steps behind, directed Roland to the spot where the man had been standing.

"Here?" he asked. She nodded, and Roland spent several minutes scanning the area. "No sign of anyone," he said as his two pistols disappeared under his jacket. "Did he threaten you in any way?"

Annie admitted that all the man had done was stare at her.

Roland nodded. "It may be nothing. Maybe a vagrant or another drunk. But I don't like coincidences."

They remained vigilant as they headed to the Glen Mountain House. The road down to the hotel had been cut into a steep slope, with a wall of vegetation and dirt on the right and a precipitous drop-off toward the gorge on the left. Annie and Roland kept to the center of the road and swiveled their eyes forward and backward, looking for any movement. They saw none.

A few hundred yards later, the road descended until it reached the upper lip of the gorge and an iron bow bridge that spanned the deep ravine. On their left was the original Glen Mountain House—built in a Swiss chalet style—perched on the near side of the gorge almost hundred feet above the stream. Across the gorge on the southern side was a new addition to the Glen Mountain House, opened this season to support up to 150 more guests.

Annie looked to her right at James Hope's Art Gallery and residence nestled against the hillside. Beyond the art gallery, trails led down into the upper part of the Glen. Annie ruled out that direction as an option for the killer. Jesse Hope and her family would never be involved in a murder, and trying to carry a body down into the upper gorge made little sense. There were no obvious places to hide a body in the narrow and well-visited Glen.

Annie and Roland started with the northern building, asking everyone they encountered if they had seen anything suspicious two days earlier. Few had been around Saturday, and those who had said there had been a flurry of activity that morning—a lot of people and luggage and supplies moving about—because a large group had been checking out and getting rides to the village.

The bridge, with wooden planks wide enough for a carriage, brought them to the southern side where they got the same story from those they met. Annie was frustrated. Too many people moving around meant too many possibilities. Roland looked at her sympathetically. "What do you want to do?"

"Can you give me a few minutes?" she said, not ready to give up. Roland nodded, and Annie moved toward the southern building. She opened the door to the hotel office and stepped into the lobby where several staff members were working. Ownership of the hotel had changed over the winter, so the staff was newly hired for the season. Annie recognized one of the clerks.

She stepped up to the counter. "Mister Nichols?"

"Oh, hello," he said. Annie saw the recognition in his eyes. "You attend the Presbyterian church in town, don't you?"

"I do, yes," said Annie.

GLEN MOUNTAIN HOUSES AND BRIDGE

"I never forget a face." Nichols was tall but rounded his shoulders to appear less so. He wore a crisply starched white shirt under his dark suit. He had a pleasant smile, but he struggled to maintain eye contact. His eyes lingered a few seconds too long on places that made Annie uncomfortable.

"Mister Nichols, I'm sorry to bother you, but could you help me?"

"If I can," he said, finally looking in her eyes.

"Can you show me who was registered here over the weekend? On Saturday morning, I met someone who I think stayed here, but don't recall his name." That was a lie, but Annie wanted to see if there were any guests from the South. "Perhaps seeing your list of guests would help me remember?"

Mr. Nichols smiled. "That would be easy. We publish our list of guests in the paper every now and then." He leaned forward. "It's good advertising, given the quality of visitors we get." He waved her over to the end of the counter and pulled out the registration book. Opening it up, he flipped back a few pages and turned it around for her. "The list of registrations for the weekend starts here," he said, pointing. "I'll warn you that it was a busy weekend. One hundred and fifty registered guests."

Annie thanked him and quickly scanned the list. It included an Episcopal bishop from Delaware, the president of Swarthmore College, a celebrated photographer, several Army officers, representatives from the Northern Central Railroad, businessmen in jewelry, cottage furniture, publishing, and locomotive engines, and families visiting from Washington, DC, Newark, Tioga, Syracuse, Websterport, and Denver City. There was even an entry for a man from South America. None of it meant anything to her, although she noticed that a large party from Kentucky had departed on Saturday.

"Mister Nichols, did everyone from the Kentucky group check out as planned?"

He gave her an odd look. "I assure you, we did not lose any of our guests over the weekend."

Annie didn't know what to do with the information. Kentucky was not near Rutherfordton, North Carolina. "Did anything odd happen at all on Saturday morning?" she asked.

Mr. Nichols assured her that it had been a normal day as far as the hotel was concerned.

Annie thanked him and stepped outside to find Roland patiently waiting.

She shook her head, temporarily defeated. She was now convinced the killer had used the commotion created by the large party checking out to move the dead man's body out of the cemetery, across the iron bridge, and down the new road into town. But she didn't know how, and so far, she had no way to prove it.

"I find," said Roland, "that no matter how bad the day is, it can be improved with ice cream. Let me buy us some, and then you can send your telegram from Western Union." As Roland arranged for a carriage to take them down the hill into town, Annie looked about. Her eyes passed over a one-armed man standing by the hotel entrance, smoking a thin cigar and looking toward the iron bridge. Annie paid him no attention, but as soon as she and Roland climbed into their carriage and it started to pull away, the man stubbed out his cigar and rushed to the next available hack to follow them down the hill.

CHAPTER XIII

INTERVIEW AT LAKE VIEW

Monday, July 13, 1874

B RADLEY woke up naked, his body tangled in crisp, clean sheets. Early morning daylight streamed in through large windows. Mercifully, his night had been free of the usual nightmares, and he had slept like the dead. It took him a few moments to get his bearings. After his late-night arrival, he had taken the first available carriage from the train station to the Lake View Hotel, paid for his room, and fell fast asleep.

In The Tombs, Pickens told him to contact Mr. Alistair Sinclair at the Lake View Hotel in Watkins to discuss the possibility of a lucrative job. With Pickens arrested for his part in a different counterfeiting ring, it wasn't hard to guess the nature of the job. Bradley's task now was to find and persuade an unknown man to hire him for an illegal job he wasn't qualified for based on the most tenuous of references. Bradley shrugged to himself. He had faced worse odds before.

Climbing from bed, Bradley walked across the room and peeked out the windows. He'd have to buy himself a nightshirt for sleeping. He appreciated the hotel's luxury and the views in the morning light. No wonder the room was so expensive. Bradley searched for a washbasin and towel to freshen up. What he found instead was hot and cold running water. What a marvel! He played with the water faucets longer than he would care to admit before drying off and pulling his one suit from the armoire. He spot-cleaned a dirt stain on his pant leg and then dressed. If he wanted to be recognized as a man of means, he needed more than one set of clothes. First things first. Get the job. Then he would buy a new wardrobe.

It was too early for breakfast, so Bradley walked across the lob-

Flocks of Wild Pigeons

by and out the main entrance into the early morning sunshine. He'd sat for too long on the train yesterday, so a quick walk to stretch his legs was just what he needed. Descending the hotel's front steps, he inhaled the clear morning air. Woodlands and cultivated fields stretched for miles on both sides of the valley and Seneca Lake.

A bright red kite sliced through his line of sight, dancing in the morning breezes. Bradley's eyes followed the string down to a young boy in the center of the clearing made by the semicircle of the carriage road. Standing nearby was a young woman who, from her attire, was likely the nanny.

Bradley remembered the last time he'd flown his favorite blue kite. He had barely gotten the kite into the air when a great cloud of wild pigeons swept over the horizon. The vast flocks—a mile in breadth and tens of miles long—arrived with a roar as if distant thunder rolled toward him. The sky had grown dark, and Bradley watched in amazement as waves of birds sped over his head. Given his home life at the time, he'd wished to fly away with those flocks.

Bradley watched the boy's kite for a few moments and was about to move on when the wind died down. Despite the boy's best efforts, the kite tumbled from the sky and disappeared into the upper branches of a large tree by the side of the road. Bradley strolled down the hill toward the boy, the nanny, and the tree. He got there in time to hear the nanny's Irish lilt.

"Master Henry! Sorry, but you won't be climbin' that grand tree," she said firmly. "If you land on your head, I'll lose my job. C'mere now so we can find someone to recover that kite for you."

Master Henry was reluctant to give up on his kite so easily. "Just a moment, please, Nanny Kate," he said as he stared up into the tree. The boy was checking for a climbing path to reach his stuck kite. A boy from a well-to-do family, as the presence of the nanny proved, who wasn't whining about his lost kite and demanding others cater to his wants? Bradley admired the self-assurance of a budding man of action.

Walking over to the boy, Bradley squatted down until he was at eye level with him. Then he followed the boy's gaze into the tree. "Is it high up?" he asked.

Henry looked at Bradley. "Yes, very high."

"Is it a good kite? Worthy of the risk?"

"It's a very good kite," said Henry with confidence.

Bradley nodded. "Right, then." He stood up but leaned toward Henry and said in a lowered voice. "Mind if I give it a try?"

"Would you?" Henry's eyes lit up.

"Oh, sir," said Nanny Kate hovering close by. "We can get the staff to help. A gentleman like yerself shouldn't...."

Bradley stopped her with a smile and an upraised hand. "I shall enjoy the challenge." He handed his hat and coat to the nanny and easily pulled himself up, disappearing into the canopy. A bit of rustling followed, and moments later, Bradley called down. "Master Henry, pull on the string!"

Henry reeled in the string and found nothing attached to the other end. He and Nanny Kate looked up as Bradley dropped from the lower branches with the kite safely in his hand. He had used the knife from his boot to cut the string from the kite to free it. He quickly reconnected the string to the kite and tucked his knife away.

"This is a very sturdy kite," Bradley said to Henry as he handed it over. "You were right to want it back." Bradley smiled and then said in a quieter voice, "I do think you might have reached it yourself, given the chance."

Henry smiled at that. "You're a great tree climber," the boy said.

"I climbed many trees when I was younger," Bradley admitted.

Nanny Kate looked relieved they'd gotten the kite back. "Very kind of ye, sir," she said. "May I ask your name?"

"Bradley Webster at your service, ma'am." He gave a half bow.

"Thank you, Bradley," said Henry with a smile.

"That is 'Thank you, Mister Webster'," said Nanny Kate, reasserting her authority. "Now, we must get back and find your sister," she said. With a wave goodbye, Nanny Kate marched Master Henry, kite in hand, toward the hotel's front steps.

Bradley placed his hat back on his head and made two loops around the hotel to stretch his legs and get his bearings. He admired the hotel and grounds and nodded to the other early morning walkers. Out of habit, his mind identified entrance and exit points should he ever need to sneak in or depart quickly. Satisfied with his walk, Bradley headed inside to try the hotel's breakfast.

The hotel was nicely furnished, and the staff was professional and accommodating. The dining room was crowded with groups of men, women, and families. The low buzz of happy conversations filled the space. Delicious smells drifted out from the kitchen. Bradley's stomach growled loudly as he was shown to his table. His stomach was not disappointed with the offerings of beefsteak and pork, lake trout, eggs, fried potatoes, hotcakes with maple syrup, coffee, tea, and all manner of fresh fruit and pastries. Bradley hadn't eaten much the day before on the train. He made up for it now.

Eventually, he pushed his empty plate away and sighed contentedly. How easy it was to get used to—and feel entitled to— good food, well-tailored clothes, and money to spare in his pocket. He enjoyed the feeling of a full belly but hoped he never took what life brought him for granted. He had survived on very little for many years and being blessed with enough always tasted sweeter to a person who has known want.

Bradley looked about the room and caught the eye of one of the attendants. He waved the man over. "Could you tell me who the hotel manager is?"

"Was something wrong with breakfast, sir?"

"No, no, not at all. Fabulous. I was just curious who was running such a lovely hotel."

"Oh, well then, that would be the manager, Mr. H.S. Smith."

"Very good. And, uh, the owner of this fine establishment?"

"That would be Judge George Freer, sir." The server leaned in and added proudly, "the second-wealthiest man in the village."

"Ah, well, both are to be complimented!"

"Thank you, sir. Will there be anything else?"

"Do you know anyone by the name of Alistair Sinclair?"

"No sir, but if he is a guest, I'm sure the front desk can help you."

Bradley thanked the man, settled his bill, then stood up and brushed off any stray crumbs before heading toward the front desk. With the air of a wealthy man whose time was important, he told the clerk he was meeting with Mr. Alistair Sinclair and invited the man to direct him to Mr. Sinclair's room. The clerk gave him the room number and offered to have a porter take him up right away, but Bradley made a show of looking at his pocket watch and announcing he would find his own way when it was time.

Bradley strolled across the lobby and sat in one of the comfortable waiting chairs to think. Given the time, he would have spent several days observing Mr. Alistair Sinclair to learn his habits, identify his acquaintances, and determine when Sinclair would be alone and approachable. Time wasn't on Bradley's side. He could not risk losing the job because Sinclair found other men to fill any vacancies on his counterfeiting crew. Bradley's alternate plan was the direct approach. He had been accused of impatience in the past, but things had always worked out for him—so far. He stood up, climbed to the top floor, found the right room, and knocked confidently on the door.

The door opened inward, revealing a broad man with a giant mustache, wearing a loose sack suit and a bowler hat. About what a walrus would look like if you put him in fancy clothes. The man blocked the doorway, looking Bradley up and down. "What do you want?"

"I'm here to see Mister Alistair Sinclair about a job."

The man blocked his way a moment longer, then opened the door wider, allowing Bradley to see a tall, dashing man standing on the far side of the spacious room. The dashing man nodded to Walrus Mustache, who shrugged. "This way," he said, turning his back to Bradley and leading him into the room. Bradley had taken enough steps to clear the door when an unseen assailant—hidden behind the door—grabbed him from behind and pushed him against the closest wall. The point of a long knife pressed into the skin under Bradley's chin.

"This is not your lucky day," his assailant said.

Bradley held his head very still. The position of the knife under his jaw made talking a risky proposition. The man facing him was about his age, fancily dressed, and had a blond goatee. His eyes were cold.

"What are you doing, Vance?"

The rich baritone voice must belong to Alistair Sinclair. "Release him," Sinclair said with authority—although Bradley also detected a touch of weariness in the man's voice. Perhaps it was not the first time Vance had overreacted.

"Mister Sinclair," Vance said, keeping the knife in place. "It is my job to keep you safe and to handle any problems. This man looks like he could be a problem."

A drop of blood slid down Bradley's neck. He wondered if word of his conversation with Pickens had made it to Sinclair's team or if this was how they treated all their visitors.

The blond man increased the pressure of the knife. "I'm sure Mister Sinclair has no interest in hiring a man so easily caught unaware."

Walrus Mustache cleared his throat. "Vance," he whispered, "look down."

Annoyance flashed across Vance's face. Bradley decided that was the perfect moment to cock the revolver he held in his right hand. A revolver pointing at Vance's heart.

Vance's eyes widened. With exaggerated slowness, he pulled the knife away from Bradley's throat and backed away. He kept his hands up.

"Shall we call this one a draw?" said Bradley, smiling broadly.

"Isn't that your pistol, Vance?" Walrus Mustache said, keeping his voice low so Sinclair wouldn't hear. Bradley had indeed found the Colt revolver under Vance's jacket. Pickpocketing was a skill he had kept very sharp. Holding the gun on Vance a bit longer than necessary, Bradley put more space between them and then expertly removed the bullets from the revolver, dropped them into his jacket pocket, and threw the empty gun back to Vance, who glared at him. Bradley now knew three things about Vance. He was impulsive, favored knives even when he had a loaded gun in his pocket, and Bradley had made an enemy of him. So be it.

"Mister Sinclair," said Bradley, turning toward the one man in the room who mattered. "I have come from New York City at the suggestion of Mister Thomas Pickens. I'm no threat, but I would like to discuss employment opportunities with you."

Sinclair's eyes gave nothing away, but they held no animosity.

He had an athletic physique and was a few inches taller than Bradley. His tailored clothes hinted at European influences, but he wore no unnecessary adornments—not even a watch chain could be seen on his waistcoat. His own light brown hair and beard were short, trimmed regularly. He looked exactly the way Bradley expected a rich man vacationing at a luxury hotel to look—except for the ugly scar running from Sinclair's right eyebrow down to his chin that hinted at violence in his past. Bradley also noticed a tightness around the man's eyes and wondered what kind of pressure he was under.

Sinclair turned to Vance and Walrus Mustache. "Leave us."

Vance stood his ground. "I don't think that's a good idea."

Anger flashed in Sinclair's eyes. He stared down Vance before turning to Bradley. "Mister Webster. Are you here to start trouble?" he asked impatiently.

"I'm not."

Sinclair looked back at the other two men. "Out!"

As soon as the door closed behind them, Sinclair walked over to a nearby dresser with an obvious limp and retrieved a half-empty glass of whiskey. Sinclair drained the amber liquid in one gulp and then turned back toward Bradley. The man weighed and measured Bradley with his eyes.

"I don't know you," he said.

"My family is in the steel business," Bradley said, feeling confident he could repeat some of what Mr. Fredriksson shared on the train. "But I'm looking for a different career." Bradley pulled a letter out of his jacket pocket and stepped forward, offering it to Sinclair. He watched Sinclair read it, knowing what it said.

> *The bearer of these few lines, Mr. Bradley Webster, has my full confidence. Please give him serious consideration for the job at hand. Sincerely, Mr. Thomas Pickens*

"Rather short for a letter of introduction," Sinclair said as he pocketed the note. "Do you have the same skills as Mister Pickens?"

"No," Bradley admitted. "I don't."

"That is a shame," said Sinclair. "I already have an impulsive young man who is good with weapons," Sinclair gestured to where Vance had been standing, and Bradley saw a flash of humor in the man's eyes. Sinclair's face grew serious again, and he paused as if thinking it over. Finally, he shook his head. "I don't see how I can use you."

Bradley opened his mouth to plead his case when the door burst open. A beautiful woman with a regal posture strolled in, followed by tumbling flashes of color and noise. The two towheaded children rushed forward toward Sinclair. Their nanny, the last to enter, closed the door.

The worry lines softened on Sinclair's face as he bent down and hugged his children.

"Father," said his daughter. "Why can't we go to Saratoga Springs like last year? Like we do every summer?"

Her brother started talking before she could finish. "I like it here, Father! Mother said I can play under a waterfall tomorrow. Will you come with us?"

Bradley recognized the boy's voice as the two children registered his presence and turned in his direction. "Bradley!" called out Henry excitedly. "Father, Bradley is an expert tree climber. He saved my kite."

Sinclair was surprised and amused as Henry told his kite story. When Henry finished, the boy smiled at Bradley and then quickly frowned. His face turned serious. "Mister Bradley, you're bleeding."

Bradley pulled out a handkerchief and wiped away the drops of blood that had rolled down his neck and onto his collar. "It's just a scratch."

Sinclair's wife swooped into action. "Nanny Kate, take the children to their room. I'll be along shortly."

Sinclair squatted down to his children's level and hugged them. "Hannah, next year we can go to Saratoga Springs. There are plenty of exciting things to see in Watkins. And Henry, of course, I want to play under a waterfall with you!"

Nanny Kate ushered the smiling children out of the room. Mrs. Sinclair waited for the door to close, then turned in Bradley's direction. "And you are?"

Mr. Sinclair spoke first. "My dear, this is Bradley Webster. He was seeking a job, but now he is leaving. Mister Webster, this is my wife, Elizabeth Sinclair."

"It is a pleasure to meet you, Mrs. Sinclair," Bradley said. She held out her hand to shake his. Her hands were warm and soft, but her handshake was firm. Her beauty reminded Bradley of a museum painting—stunning colors, exquisite details, and priced beyond the reach of mere mortals. When she released his hand, Bradley turned to Mr. Sinclair hoping to plead his case, but Mrs. Sinclair was not done with him.

"What are your skills, Mister Webster?" she asked.

Bradley paused for a second, looking back and forth between husband and wife. Then he answered truthfully. "I protect what needs to be protected. I find things that need to be found. And I'm very skilled at removing problems. Permanently if needed."

"But are you loyal?"

She asked a direct question, so he offered an honest answer. "I'm loyal to whoever is paying me."

Elizabeth stared at him with her piercing green eyes as if judging him. Like Sinclair, she had an excellent poker face. Then, to Bradley's surprise, she spoke loudly with a clear, melodic voice:

O Captain! my Captain! our fearful trip is done

She stared at Bradley, expecting a response. He blinked. Once. Twice. Then, almost as a reflex, he completed the next two lines of Whitman's poem.

The ship has weather'd every rack, the prize we sought is won,
The port is near, the bells I hear, the people all exulting

Mrs. Sinclair nodded and then leaned in close to her husband. The two whispered back and forth until he frowned, and she smiled. "I'll leave you to your discussion," she said to her husband. "Good day, Mister Webster." As she left the room, she took some of the light with her.

Sinclair watched the door close, then turned back to Bradley. He cleared his throat. "I may have a job for you after all."

———◇———

Bradley stepped down from his carriage in front of the Western Union telegraph office on the east side of Franklin Street, between the Fall Brook and Jefferson Houses. A telegram was the fastest way to send a message long distance, and Bradley needed to send two telegrams back to New York City. He tipped the carriage driver well then crossed the wooden walkway and pulled open the door of the telegraph office. Bradley stepped back, holding the door open, as an attractive young woman in a beautiful peacock green dress exited the shop. She smiled and gave him a polite "thank you" before returning to her conversation with the middle-aged gentleman following her out.

Bradley entered the shop and grabbed two telegraph blanks. The first message, to one of the few close friends left in the city, was easy to write. The second required more finesse. He considered what to say, then filled out the form and handed it to the clerk. The man checked the addresses and calculated the word count to determine payment required. Bradley handed over the right amount in coins and asked how soon the messages would be sent.

"Within the hour," the clerk said.

Bradley tipped his hat and exited the store, almost bumping into Walrus Mustache as the large man entered. "Excuse me," Bradley said. "I didn't catch your name earlier."

The larger man looked at him. "I didn't offer it earlier," he said, disappearing into the shop and leaving Bradley holding the door. Bradley chuckled as he closed the door. Fair enough, he would refer to the man as the Walrus. Bradley hummed to himself as he set off to find a men's clothing store.

CORNER OF FRANKLIN AND FOURTH, WATKINS, NY

CHAPTER XIV

TEA WITH ABRAHAM

Tuesday, July 14, 1874

A NNIE arrived at Mr. Newby's house at the appointed time, neither too early nor too late. Roland had dropped her off by carriage and promised to return in one hour to collect her. That should be more than enough time to talk to Stephen Newby's uncle, Abraham Adams.

The Newby family rented a house on Magee Street on the opposite side of town, nearest the train tracks. The home was small, but the yard was well-tended. Annie paused momentarily before approaching, considering the questions she hoped to ask Abraham about what he might have seen Saturday morning. She hoped for a clue that could help find Harper Thompson's missing body. She would like to have more information when Sadie Thompson from Rutherfordton, North Carolina, replied to the telegram Annie had sent.

Earlier in the day, Annie had visited the sheriff to check on his progress. He assured her that no one with knife wounds had sought treatment from a town doctor recently. When Annie asked if any bodies had been found, the sheriff's eyes lost their friendliness, and he wished her a good day.

Annie took a deep breath as approached the Newbys' front door. Social situations where she knew no one made her anxious. The house windows were open to take advantage of any cooling breezes, and the sound of loud voices and laughter could be heard within. Out of habit, Annie reached up to make sure her hair wasn't misbehaving, then knocked loudly. She heard footsteps approaching. As the door swung open, Stephen Newby greeted her with a smile.

"Welcome, Miss Anderson! My mother will be very pleased you chose to join us."

"I brought this as a thank-you for your invitation." Annie held up a fresh huckleberry and raspberry pie that Nana had helped bake earlier in the day. Both berries were now in peak season. At an early age, Annie learned that showing up empty-handed when answering an invitation was poor manners.

Mr. Newby gratefully accepted the pie and ushered Annie inside ahead of him. As she crossed the threshold, everyone turned to look at the new arrival. Apparently, she was the only white person who had accepted the invitation to tea. The room became quiet and heat rushed up Annie's neck and cheeks. Several heartbeats passed before Mr. Newby's mother saved her from death by social awkwardness.

"You must be Miss Annie Anderson!" Mrs. Newby's voice filled the hushed room as she stepped forward to take Annie by the hand and pull her farther inside the house. "Stephen mentioned you might be coming. Welcome, welcome, welcome," she said with a sincerity that put Annie at ease. The cheerful murmur of conversations resumed. "I'm Stephen's mother, Esther."

"Lovely to meet you, Mrs. Newby," said Annie. Mrs. Newby had an open face and a mischievous twinkle in her eye.

"Oh, my dear, call me Esther!" she said brightly. Esther still held Annie's hand and used their connection to turn Annie so she could admire her cream- and olive-colored dress. "Look how lovely you are!" said Esther. "The green matches the hazel of your eyes."

Esther guided Annie around the room and introduced her to the other guests. Everyone was cheerfully wearing their Sunday best and seemed pleased to meet her. Annie smiled and tried to commit each person's name to memory. Esther's good friend Phyllis Green worked as a housekeeper, but today, she watched her granddaughter, six-year-old Catharine Phinney. Thomas Jefferson and his wife Mary were both in their fifties. He was a laborer, and she cleaned houses. Emma Strong was in her seventies and had worked for a local miller. John Berry, another barber, was one of Stephen's co-workers at the hotel.

"Abraham is not here yet," said Stephen as he arrived with a tray bearing cups of tea for Annie and Esther. "We expect him shortly." Annie was disappointed, but with an hour to fill until Roland returned, she would make the best of it.

Esther thanked Stephen and left Annie to circulate around the room. Annie chatted pleasantly with Phyllis Green and Mary Jefferson until Esther returned and encouraged Annie to join her on one of the sofas in the sitting room. "There's food to go with your tea if you're hungry," she said. The table before her held several plates offering pastries and finger sandwiches. Ham with mustard. Egg salad. Fruit jam. Annie reached for one of the ham sandwiches and nibbled on the corner. It was delicious. Her attempts to be dainty failed as she finished the rest of the small sandwich with large bites.

Fighting the urge to reach for another sandwich, Annie turned toward Esther. "What a lovely tea," she said. "Do you do this often?"

"Once or twice a month. I quite enjoy feeling 'afternoonified' by having tea with close friends. Something I picked up when I lived in Toronto. When my son has a day off during the week, I make an event out of it."

"Were you born in Canada?"

"No. Few colored folks are from that far north. Abraham and I were born in North Carolina."

"What brought you to Watkins?"

Esther smiled. "Now, that's a long story. But if you really are interested, I can tell you the quick version." Esther reached for a sandwich.

"I'd love to hear it." A story would fill in the time before Abraham arrived, sparing Annie from unnecessary small talk.

Esther took a small bite of her sandwich. "Well, Abraham and I were born to slave parents on a tobacco plantation." There was no shame in Esther's voice. If anything, she carried a sense of pride at having endured her upbringing.

"My mother bore eight children. Abraham was the youngest, and I was one year older. But we never lived all together as a family." Esther's eyes drifted away into the distant past for a moment before returning to focus on Annie. "Some slaveholders kept

PICKING COTTON

families together. Most didn't try. Perhaps the cruelest part about slavery was the tearin' apart of colored families. Our 'owner' sold my pa and my oldest two brothers to a cotton plantation in Georgia while our mother was carryin' Abraham. The master gave us no warning. Although why would he, since we were property to him? But it broke my ma's heart. By the time Abraham was twelve, only three of us were left on the plantation. Me, Ma, and Abraham. The rest were gone. Spread throughout the South. Then, that horrible day came. They took Abraham away. Sold 'im to a horse trainer in Virginia. They didn't even let the poor boy say goodbye to his mother." Esther paused to quietly sip her tea.

"I'm so sorry."

"Nothing for you to be sorry about, but I 'preciate the thought. Have another sandwich, dear." Esther smiled as Annie reached forward to try the egg salad. Tasty but not as delicious as the ham. As Annie chewed, she tried to imagine being sold out of state, away from her parents, never to see them again. It was unspeakably depressing.

"That was the point my Ma ran out of tears," said Esther. "I remember she turned to me—I was thirteen by then—and said, 'Esther, you are my last baby. Before I die, I'll see you living as a free woman. We owe it to Pa and your siblings.' Ma had heard rumors a local Quaker family helped slaves escape. We didn't know it then, but they were part of the Underground Railroad. You've heard of it?"

Annie nodded. "When I was a little girl, I imagined a great train traveling through an underground tunnel bringing slaves north to freedom."

Esther chuckled. "I wish that had been true. Each 'station' was the house of a brave family risking their lives to help us poor slaves find our way to freedom. My mother and I waited until past midnight on a Saturday. That was the night of the week our master drank himself stupid. We took what little we owned and snuck through the darkness to the Quaker's house. I thought my heart was going to jump out of my chest, I was so scared. We didn't know whether they'd help us or send us back to be beaten or killed or worse. I didn't 'preciate until years later how brave Ma was that night."

Esther's friend Phyllis joined them on the couch. She didn't interrupt but sat quietly, sipping her tea.

"The Quaker family hid us in the bottom of a wagon and started us on our journey north that night. We got taken from station to station, mostly after dark. Sometimes a station was a hidden room in a house or barn, sometimes in a school or a church. Everyone was kind to us. They gave us food, and some gave us warmer clothes. We kept going until we reached Canada and freedom."

"That's amazing," Annie said, not knowing what else to say.

"My mother passed away a few years later," said Esther. "She never saw her other children again. After that, I did my best to live my life to honor her and my siblings. Because of her, I grew up in Toronto as a free woman, married a free man, and had free children. We didn't come back to the States until poor Mister Lincoln issued his proclamation."

Phyllis leaned over and patted Esther on the knee. "We are so glad you came to Watkins."

Esther patted Phyllis's hand in return. "I came to Watkins because of the Underground Railroad station in Burdett, a few miles up the lake. That family told us how beautiful the area was, and since I was born on a farm, I appreciated living in a small town. So here we are."

"How did you find Abraham?"

"He found me after the war ended. He'd been taught to read and write—not many slaves could do that. Owners were afraid that if us negros learned to read and write we were more likely to rebel. Probably true. So, they made a law against it. Anyway, Abraham kept posting 'Information Wanted' notices until he found me and two of our sisters. They live in Philadelphia now. But he never found our father or other sister or brothers. And he never found any trace of his wife or daughter."

Before Annie could ask another question, little Catharine ran over to Phyllis to ask if she could play outside. "Yes but stay in the yard!" The rest of the women had taken seats, leaving the men to stand on the other side of the room to enjoy own topics of conversation.

"Enough about me," said Esther. "Abraham is late. As a punishment, he might miss out on these finger sandwiches he loves so much. But that gives us time to hear your story. Tell us about yourself. I see you aren't married yet, but I imagine a beautiful, talented girl like yourself must have her pick of suitors."

Annie sighed, realizing she was now the center of attention. Where to begin? "Well, I was almost engaged once."

"Almost?"

"I thought he was about to propose, but... he died. Unexpectedly."

"Oh, heavens," said Esther. The other women offered condolences. Without mentioning his full name, Annie talked of John's kindness. The way he'd listened to her. The small gifts he brought her from his trips abroad. Her confidence that he was preparing to propose. That horrible day, the news had come of his passing.

"We both got ill," Annie said. "I recovered, but his family and I were shocked when his health took a turn for the worse. He died in April of last year from congestion of the lungs. He was only twenty-eight."

After a moment of respectful silence, Esther took her hand. "It is right to mourn him. But it is also right to move on. You are young. You are alive. You have a long life ahead of you, and I know you will find your way."

Annie's eyes started to water. Esther's kindness made her long for her late mother's wisdom. When Annie was ten, she asked her mother how old she had to be to get married. "Oh, Annie dear," her mother had said. "You are young. Let's save our money and then travel around the world and have adventures together. After that, when you are old enough, you can decide when to be married."

Annie heard several shouts of "Abraham!" as the front door burst open.

"Am I late?" Abraham asked as he stepped inside. "One of the mares at Wickham's farm had a hoof infection," he said, offering his excuse. "I hope you saved me a few finger sandwiches!" His nice suit, wrinkled from a hard day's work, accented his muscular frame. The smoothness of his deep mahogany skin made him look much younger than his sister, but the gray creeping into his curly black hair at his temples said otherwise. He seemed relaxed as he greeted each guest with a bright smile.

Esther stood and hugged her brother and then turned to Annie to make an introduction. Recognition flashed across Abraham's face before he forced it into a neutral expression. Annie watched the energy flow out of Abraham as he confronted the stranger in his sister's house.

"Abraham, this is Miss Annie Anderson," Esther said. "Stephen mentioned she would be coming by to ask you a few questions?"

"Nice to meet you, Miss Anderson," he said. There was nothing genial about his greeting.

"Likewise," Annie said, suddenly feeling warm. Had Abraham recognized her from the cemetery?

"Perhaps, Miss Anderson," Abraham said, forcing a smile on his face, "we should talk outside where it is quieter?" Without waiting for her, he stepped back out the front door.

Esther opened her mouth to protest, but Annie simply thanked her for the wonderful hospitality and the finger sandwiches and excused herself as she followed Abraham outside.

Abraham stood at the end of the walk by the street. "What questions do you have?" he said as she approached.

Annie cleared her throat and looked around. She felt exposed and uncomfortable. But to seek the truth, she had to ask questions.

"I was in Glenwood Cemetery Saturday morning," Annie said, choosing her words carefully. "I saw an injured man. I went for help, but he was gone when I returned. I worry something bad might have happened to him." Her voice trailed off. Abraham's face was unreadable. "Your nephew told me you walk to work with him and sometimes return through the cemetery. I wondered if you might have seen anything...."

"And you think I had something to do with a disappearing white man?"

"No," she stammered. *Not until this very moment,* she thought to herself. "I hoped you might have seen where he went."

He stared at her long enough that the silence made her uncomfortable. Finally, he sighed. "I didn't see anything that could help you. I'm sorry you wasted the trip." Abraham left her there and went back inside. Annie had been dismissed.

"Is Abraham mad?"

The small voice came from the corner of the house. Annie turned to see young Catharine staring at her.

"Perhaps he is tired from a long day," Annie said.

Catharine thought about that. "I like Abraham. He tells the best stories, but I wouldn't want him mad at me."

"I'm sure he is not mad at you," said Annie. "What kind of stories does he tell?"

"His horse stories are the best. I like those." Catharine took a couple of steps closer. "But my favorite is him telling 'bout escaping the mean slave owner."

"How exciting," Annie said. "How did he get away?"

"Abraham hit the bad man so hard he didn't get up again."

Someone called out "Catharine" from inside the house.

"I've got to go," the girl said. She went back inside, leaving Annie alone on the sidewalk.

Well, that didn't go as planned, Annie thought. She was disappointed not to learn more but wanted to get away from Abraham as quickly as possible. She didn't want to wait twenty minutes for Roland to arrive, so Annie began walking back toward the center of Watkins. She was four blocks from Franklin Street and a few more blocks from the business district where Roland and Glendon kept an office. Annie looked back once, but no one followed her from the Newby house.

The sun was sweltering even this late in the afternoon. Annie started to sweat immediately and regretted not bringing along a parasol. As she walked, she considered the fate of Harper Thompson. Annie was sure Abraham had seen her in the cemetery that morning and, if he'd seen her, he might have also seen the body. Abraham was a former slave who struck his master to escape, and Harper Thompson had been a Southerner. Could it be as simple as that? Perhaps Harper had said something hateful to Abraham after an accidental meeting, and Abraham took offense. The thought of Abraham hiding in the cemetery bushes, waiting for her to leave so he could dispose of the body, gave Annie shivers despite the heat.

Annie was lost in her thoughts and didn't notice the horse-drawn carriage until it pulled beside her. She looked up to see that the driver was a handsome man about her age. "Awfully hot afternoon to be out walking," he said. "Can I offer you a ride, miss?"

The man's blue eyes were inviting. He wasn't a local but one of the many well-off vacationers who visited in the summer. Maybe this was the sophisticated man Annie had been waiting for, ready to whisk her away on a life of adventure. She would have welcomed a ride up the hill, but she needed to stop at Roland's office—only a block away now—to save him from making the trip to Abraham's house.

Annie looked toward Franklin Street. "Kind of you to offer, sir, but I'm arriving at my destination."

"Perhaps I could insist?" he said. "As an act of chivalry in this heat?"

Before Annie could reply, she heard her name being called from across the street. She turned and recognized Mrs. Phelps, the attractive widow helping Nana with the cooking while the family's housekeeper was away. "Everything all right, Annie?" Mrs. Phelps asked while staring at the man in the carriage suspiciously.

"Everything is fine, thank you, Mrs. Phelps." Annie turned back toward the carriage as it pulled away. A moment later, the man with blue eyes and a blond goatee disappeared around the corner.

CHAPTER XV

ENGLISHMEN'S REMAINS

From the Journal of Private H. Thompson

March 24, 1864 – Taylor and Fish huddled around the parchment map while the rest of us broke camp and hitched the horses up to the wagon. It was cold enough that we could see our breath as we exhaled. We ate a simple breakfast of salted pork and dried bread. We were all anxious to get started.

Soaring granite cliffs rose steeply along both sides of the Hickory Nut Gap Road, stretching up to broad ridgetops. Waterfalls tumbled back to the forest that surrounded the river. The Englishman's story was vague enough, and the terrain was so vast and wild that it was no surprise that the gold had never been found. Fish's interpretation of the map suggested the best place to search for the gold was where a gully descended from a hilltop close to the river. There were a lot of gullies near the river.

We worked along the road and checked every place that even remotely resembled a location on the map. Since our rented wagon couldn't travel far off the road, we agreed that two of us would watch the horses and wagon while the other two joined Taylor and Fish in the search for our golden cave. We did our best to keep the wagon out of sight at each new search location. We didn't want anyone to stop and ask us questions about our purpose in the Gap.

As the morning passed into midday, we developed a rhythm. We would ride the wagon along the road until Fish, consulting the map, pointed up the hill. Then, four searchers marched into the woods, and two stayed behind on guard duty. Each time, the searchers returned with a shrug, and we continued down the dirt road. If Taylor was frustrated with the effort, he wasn't showing it.

Being on the search team was exciting, but I didn't mind guarding the horses and wagon. It allowed me time to admire the undis-

turbed forest rising on either side of the road up to granite cliffs
that touched the sky. The air was still. The tranquility of the place
was disturbed only by distant bird calls and the bubbling of the
stream working its way over rocks.

Ace, on guard duty with me, said, "Damn beautiful country out
here." I agreed with him. As I looked around, taking in the scenery,
I wondered which direction I would've run if suddenly attacked
by Indians. A thought occurred to me, and I asked Ace to see if
he would come to the same conclusion. He looked around. "De-
pends on what direction the attack came from," he said. He looked
forward and back along the road. "The road is the best way to
escape, but the mules would've been slow, saddled with the weight
of all that gold. If they didn't want to leave the gold behind...." We
looked at each other and smiled. Who would? He pointed across
the stream. "In the summer, when the water is low, I would've tried
to escape that way."

When our search party returned empty-handed, Ace and I
suggested crossing the creek to Taylor and Fish. I could see Fish
thinking. He said, "I know a place on the other side of the river to
check."

After a meal of bean soup and salted meat, Fish led us back up
the road the way we'd come. He paused now and then and stared
into the woods, looking for something he recognized. Finally, he
stopped. "We cross here," he said and pointed into the woods.

It was Buck and Frank's turn to stay with the wagon, so Ace,
Taylor, and I followed Fish across the stream. The water was cold,
and our boots got soaked. Reaching the far side, we shook off the
water and climbed up the bank. Fish led us through the woods until he found a wide gully that led uphill. On our right, the ground
rose until it turned into a granite cliff. The cliff face was broken
in places with large cracks running up and down, but all were too
narrow for a man to squeeze through.

We climbed further following the bottom of the cliff face until
Fish stopped and pointed. "That cave might be big enough," he
said, pleased with himself. "Pa took me huntin' in this area when
I was eleven." His smile faltered for a second at the thought of his
late father.

The jagged entrance in the rock face wouldn't have been obvi-

ous to the casual passerby had they not been looking for it. Taylor stepped forward to examine the cave entrance. He disappeared into the blackness and emerged with a grin a few moments later. It indeed was large enough for a man to enter. Maybe big enough for a mule laden with gold as well.

"Well done, Fish!" said Taylor. "This is the best cave we've found so far."

Taylor extracted a small tin case from the inside pocket of his jacket, and from the case, he pulled out a friction match. It had been my turn to carry the bag with our wooden torches. Taylor, making sure he was out of the wind, struck his match and lit a torch, which flared to life. We used two torches to start with. Taylor carried one, and I carried the other.

"Stay close," Taylor said as he disappeared through the entrance. One by one, we followed him through the opening—Fish after Taylor, then Ace. I was the rear guard. I hesitated, staring at the dark entrance as a damp and musty smell drifted out. Sweat broke out over my body as I imagined the tunnel walls collapsing in on me. I closed my eyes, took a deep breath, and then forced myself forward. As we moved deeper away from daylight, I tried not to think about the mountain of granite suspended above our heads.

The flickering light from my torch showed a dark entrance extending into the mountain. The walls were smooth as if the entire mountain had been sliced and split apart at this spot. The ground was a jumble of rocks to be carefully scrambled over. Taylor called out from ahead that it was wider inside.

He waited for us at the opening of a larger chamber. We could stand up easily there. The floor was still rocky, but the rocks were flatter. The walls were smooth, although cut at odd angles. This chamber was as wide as a dozen men, but our combined torches couldn't tell us how deep the cave ran.

I imagined what it must have been like for the Englishmen trapped in a cave like this with desperate or dying companions and panicked mules, knowing that Indians waited outside to kill them. If we had expected a pile of gold to be waiting for us in the middle of the cave, we were disappointed.

Taylor and I held our torches high while we fanned out and moved deeper into the cave. The flickering light creating ee-

SEARCHING THE CAVE

rie shadows on the wall. We should have brought oil lanterns, I thought. After thirty feet, the chamber narrowed until our progress stopped at a rock wall. Taylor raised his torch over his head. We had found nothing.

As Taylor examined the back wall, I held up my torch and looked toward the entrance. Part of the cave floor—near the side wall—was not as flat but more a jumbled pile of rocks. I had failed to notice any difference on the way in. Taylor joined me. "Whatcha thinkin'?" he asked. "Rockfall, maybe?" He stepped closer to get a better look. "Let's try movin' some of the rocks."

Taylor and I handed our torches to Ace and Fish and carefully moved some of the rocks to the side. After moving a dozen medium-sized rocks, I froze. There are moments when you think your mind is playing tricks on you. I blinked, struggling to process what I was seeing. I got Taylor's attention and pointed toward the ground where I had uncovered the bones of a human hand.

Taylor, unable to hide the excitement in his voice, called for Fish and Ace to bring the torches closer. We moved a few more rocks, and with the extra light, there was no doubt that we had found the remains of a man. We propped up our torches, and all four of us started furiously moving rocks on the cavern's edge. We uncovered one skeleton and then two. There was no sign of mule bones, but several men had met their Maker in this cave. We kept moving rocks and digging until Ace exposed what looked like the corner of a leather satchel.

We were convinced we had found the remains of the Englishmen who had failed to escape the Indians. Five or six Englishmen could have been driving a dozen mules through Hickory Nut Gap. The gold would have been carried in leather satchels on one side of each animal and counterbalanced by heavy boxes on the other.

With Fish holding the lantern high, Taylor and Ace freed the satchel from the rocks, and Taylor looked at each of us with a smile before loosening the straps and peering inside. He reached into the bag, pulled out one shiny gold nugget, and held it high. For a moment, the air was sucked out of our bodies, and we stared in silence... before spontaneously whooping and hollering.

"We found it, we found it, we found it!" Fish yelled as he jumped up and down.

Ace and I were yelling excitedly, and Taylor just stared at the shining gold in his hand with a smile that was as bright as the gold. Either the rockfall or the last Englishman had buried the dead bodies and the gold all those years ago. Their mules had either been released or taken by the Indians.

We passed around the nugget, each taking a turn feeling its weight and staring at its glow.

Taylor told Fish to run down to the wagon and send Frank and Buck back up. We needed their help to carry the gold down. Fish could feed and water the horses and stay with the wagon so we could leave as soon as we got the gold down.

Fish grabbed his torch and hurried off. Taylor, Ace, and I kept moving rocks and digging. By the time Frank and Buck arrived, we had found another skeleton and two more satchels. We celebrated again with Frank and Buck, then returned to excavating the rest of the treasure. It was grim work unburying skeletons, but we all focused on the treasure. In the end, we recovered seven leather satchels, each filled with gold.

We placed the satchels in a row on the edge of the cave near the entrance and pulled out handkerchiefs to wipe the sweat and rock dust from our faces. Our smiles never wavered, even as our second set of torches started failing. Finding this cave had changed our lives' trajectory. Brothers united by luck in battle and now in golden triumph.

The sound of boots scrambling over loose rocks came from the cave entrance. We all turned to look—thinking Fish had returned. It wasn't Fish. Two men we'd never seen pushed into the larger chamber. Their pistols were pointing directly at us, and their faces could not hide their sneers of satisfaction.

CHAPTER XVI

UNEXPECTED VISITOR

Tuesday, July 14, 1874

A NNIE reached the brick building on Franklin Street where Roland kept an office, opened the door on the side of the building, and climbed the wooden stairs to the second floor. Roland's office was small but had a large window with a lovely view overlooking the street. Annie's favorite pair of leather buttoned ankle boots made muted click-clack sounds on the hardwood floor as she walked toward the front of the building.

The door to Roland's office was ajar, so Annie peeked inside, not wanting to disturb him if he was hard at work. Roland looked up. "Annie!" he said, surprised at her arrival. Roland reached for his pocket watch but relaxed when he realized he hadn't lost track of time. "You are back early. Is everything all right?"

"I left early, and I didn't want you to go looking for me."

"No problem," he said. "Give me a few minutes, and I'll walk you home. I'll have just enough time before my meeting to present this proposal."

Annie looked at the large drawing spread across the table in the center of the office. "Is this your bid for the Magee landscaping job?"

"Yes, it is," Roland said, with pride in his voice. He was bidding for a large contract to work for George and Emma Magee. The Magees had finished remodeling their mansion, Glenfeld, and now looked to update the ten acres of manicured grounds surrounding their house. Roland's proposal included a large, landscaped garden and a sizable greenhouse. Annie admired his drawing skills.

Both her uncles were successful business owners with several employees each. Glendon was a trader who bought merchandise in the city and sold it to stores around the region, while Roland had a landscaping and gardening business that served affluent clients in cities up to an hour away—Elmira, Ithaca, Bath, and Geneva. Both were successful enough that they could have moved out of Nana's boarding rooms long ago. When each had bought a parcel of land with views of the lake—Glendon on the east side and Roland on the west—Annie worried one or both might move out. She was grateful that both had stayed to be there for her as she grew up.

Annie wanted to tell Roland the details of her encounter with Abraham and share her concerns that he might have been involved in Harper Thompson's death but felt a pang of guilt noticing how focused he was on his work.

"Finish your proposal," Annie said. "I'm a big girl. I can walk myself home."

Roland hesitated. "Glendon and I agreed you shouldn't travel alone with a killer on the loose."

Annie knew her uncles meant well, but she didn't need anyone else to make decisions about what she should or should not do. "Plenty of people are about, and it is only a few blocks up the hill. I'll be fine," Annie said. "I appreciate you worrying about me."

"Are you sure?" Roland stole a glance at the unfinished plans on his table.

"Of course. And I promise not to take any detours through the cemetery on the way home."

Annie patted him on the shoulder and stepped back out into the hallway to leave him with his proposal. Roland called out as she started to pull the door closed. "Please tell Nana I won't be home for dinner tonight."

Moments later, Annie was back on the street, feeling the sun on her face and the prickly heat on her skin. The horses and horse-drawn carriages kicked up clouds of dirt as they passed by. Watkins was overdue for a cleansing rainstorm.

Annie stood on the wooden sidewalk and watched the faces of the men and women walking by. In the quiet months from late fall to mid-spring, Watkins reclaimed its status as a small town. In the off-season, Annie could recognize almost everyone she passed on the street. But now, with the summer-pleasure season underway, unfamiliar faces crowded the village. Unfamiliar faces that could include a murderer.

Annie walked briskly along Franklin Street and then turned up Fourth Street toward home. As she started across Madison, she passed the new post office, dubbed the flat-iron building for its odd shape. The front was wide enough for an entrance door, and then the building fanned out into a triangle to fill its oddly shaped lot on the slope of a hill.

As Annie reached the opposite sidewalk, a movement off to her right made her turn her head. The large man with his wild black beard stepped out from the far end of the building—only forty feet away—and stared at her. It was the same man who stared at her from the shadows in the cemetery. Annie's momentum and her strong legs carried her past the edge of the flat-iron building, blocking the man from her view. Fighting off a feeling of dread, Annie kept moving forward. Her shortest path to safety was back toward Franklin Street, but Annie couldn't bear the thought of turning around and seeing the man approaching. Instead, she picked up her skirts and ran uphill toward the safety of home. She looked back once, expecting to see him rounding the corner of the building in pursuit, but he didn't appear. She ran until she reached her front door, then she slipped inside, locked the door behind her, and leaned against the wall, taking deep breaths to force the anxiety from her body.

Annie had just started to relax when she had a horrifying thought. If the man had followed her from a distance, he now knew where she lived. Before she could process this new fear, Nana's voice called out.

"Annie? We have company. Come join us in the parlor."

Annie composed herself before pushing open the mahogany pocket doors and stepping into the parlor. The parlor, reserved for entertaining guests, also served as the repository of her family's treasured possessions. Annie loved the parlor's wooden paneling, ornate fireplace, heavily patterned wallpaper, and the many green plants giving the room life.

Nana, glowing in the gentle rays of sunlight streaming in from the window, sat upright in one of the smaller armless chairs pre-

ferred by women with large skirts. Partially in shadow, in the large
throne-like chair favored by her late father, sat Abraham Adams.

Annie froze.

Abraham cleared his throat, but Nana spoke first. "Come sit,
Annie. Mister Adams tells me you spoke earlier. He said he had
urgent information that could not wait. Of course, that must be the
case for someone to show up unannounced and uninvited."

If Annie hadn't been suddenly fearful of Abraham's intentions, she would have smiled at Nana's not-so-subtle rebuke of their
guest. It was bad manners for a stranger to show up unexpectedly.
It was even more unusual for an unexpected visitor to be a lone
colored man.

Annie chose the chair farthest from Abraham. He might have
killed Harper Thompson in the cemetery. Were they in danger?
Was he here to keep her quiet? Annie refused to let her imagination
get the best of her. She steeled her nerves and looked their guest in
the eyes. "It is a surprise to see you again so soon, Mister Adams."

"I want to make sure there were no misunderstandings based
on our previous conversation," he said. "Or, based on what you
might have heard from young Catharine."

"We had never met, but you recognized me at your sister's
house. You must have seen me in the cemetery, if you saw me, you
were there when the body disappeared. And now you are here."

Abraham sighed. "Miss Anderson, I'm not a threat to you."

"And if we asked you to leave?" Annie wanted information but
was worried about her grandmother. Annie would have preferred to
have this conversation when Glendon or Roland were in the house.

"I won't leave until I've said what I came to say. Then I'll go,
and you never have to see me again."

"Did you kill Harper Thompson?" The words escaped Annie's
mouth before she could pull them back.

"Annie!" Nana thought it rude to accuse a guest, even an uninvited one, of murder. It was also not prudent.

"I don't know who that is," Abraham said.

"Did you kill the man in the cemetery?"

"No, I did not." Abraham's voice was calm and matter of fact.
He did not seem defensive or deceitful in any way. "Do you think I

killed him because I'm colored?"

"No. But he was a Southerner, and you are a former slave. And you tell stories to little girls about beating a Southern white man."

Abraham, hat in hand, worked his fingers around the brim of his hat. "You shouldn't believe tales told by six-year-old girls," he said. "And I didn't know the man in the cemetery was a Southerner."

"So, you did see something!"

Abraham went quiet for a moment. "I came to tell you that I had nothing to do with what happened in the cemetery, and if you tell anyone otherwise, it will put my life and my family's lives in danger."

"What?" Annie was confused. "If you saw something, you have to tell the sheriff. If we both come forward, he will have to believe us!"

"I can't do that!" The force of Abraham's response surprised Annie. "You think I should tell the sheriff that I saw a dead body in the cemetery?"

"Yes."

"Forgive me for saying so, but you are being naïve, Miss Anderson. If I tell the sheriff I was in the cemetery and they find a body, who is the first person the sheriff will suspect of the murder?"

"But...." Annie's words faltered. "But... this isn't the South."

Abraham sighed again. "You have a lot to learn about the way of the world."

Annie opened her mouth to protest, but Nana stopped her. "He is right, dear. It is not fair, and it is not how things should be, but it is true. If something bad happened in the cemetery as you believe it did, it does Mister Adams no good to draw attention to his presence there."

Abraham looked at her grandmother with appreciation. "Please call me Abraham, Mrs. Sullivan."

Nana stood up. "Since we have established that you are not a killer, Abraham, may I offer you some pie?"

"I would love some pie."

"Good," said Nana. "I haven't started making dinner yet, and I'm feeling peckish."

Annie's grandmother prided herself on being a good host.

"Miss Anderson," Abraham said, "what's the man in the cemetery to you?"

"No one, but... Someone killed him, and the men who run this town are doing nothing about it." Her words had come out more forceful than she intended. "And his body was on my mother's grave. It feels personal."

"That could be a coincidence."

"My mother's grave?" Annie said. "I hope so."

The ticking of the grandfather clock filled the silence until Abraham cleared his throat and changed the subject. "My sister took a liking to you."

Annie blinked at the change in direction of their conversation. "She is a lovely woman. I enjoyed her afternoon tea. Until you arrived."

Abraham chuckled. "That's fair," he said. "I was rude, and I apologize. Esther told me you enjoyed the finger sandwiches."

Annie regretted not asking Esther for the secret to making those little ham sandwiches so tasty, but she wasn't ready to give up on learning what Abraham knew. "Abraham," she said. "Why should I believe you? And why did you tell Catharine a story about beating up a white man?"

Nana returned carrying a tray with three slices of huckleberry and raspberry pie on their good china with three forks, three linen napkins, and three empty glasses. "I did not have time to make tea," she said. "But, under the circumstances, perhaps our guest will join me for a bit of good Scotch whisky?"

Nana stepped over to a wooden cabinet and pulled out her late husband's favorite whisky. She splashed a large amount into her own glass.

"It would be rude to let you drink alone, Mrs. Sullivan." Abraham held up his glass.

Nana laughed and poured an equally large dollop of whisky into her guest's glass. "In that case, Abraham," she said, "you may call me Johanna." Nana turned to Annie, but Annie shook her head. Nana sat down, placing the bottle next to her glass.

"Since you are staying for pie," Annie said, looking at Abraham, "can you tell us how you escaped the South?"

"I'd prefer not to. It happened a long time ago. " Abraham took a bite of the pie and chewed slowly before swallowing.

"How about the short version?" Nana asked. "Since you still have pie on your plate."

Abraham glanced at his pie accusingly as if he'd been tricked, then sighed. "The short version, then. I was born a slave on a tobacco farm in North Carolina. When I was twelve, my owner sold me to a horse breeder in Virginia." He paused, took a large bite of pie, and washed it down with whisky. "I was luckier than most slaves. My new master taught me to read and write, and as I got older, I started to take over the running of his horse farm."

Nana had cut him a large slice of pie, but he was making short work of it.

"I married another slave, Evaline, who worked in the main house, and we had a daughter. Born a slave, of course. When our daughter was thirteen, our old master died, and all his property—including my family—was inherited by his only son. The son didn't know anything about horses. I don't think he cared. He wouldn't listen to any advice from me. I was just a slave to him. So it didn't take long for the business to suffer." Abraham drained his whisky glass and stared into space for a moment. "Then one day, my wife and daughter disappeared. He'd sold them to raise money. He refused to tell me where they'd gone."

Nana topped off Abraham's glass.

"I made up my mind then and there to escape or die trying. That night, I stole a horse and rode to freedom."

Abraham pushed his empty plate away from him. He ignored the rest of the whisky.

"And the part where you hit your master so hard, he didn't get up again?" Annie asked.

"I may have knocked down my new owner while stealing his horse," Abraham admitted.

"Did you kill him?"

"No," Abraham said, looking visibly uncomfortable. "I admit, I wasn't sure at the time, but I found out later he survived. He's hard to kill... like a cockroach."

Annie thought about everything Abraham had said. Losing your spouse and only child would be devastating. But... how could she be sure any of it was true? He seemed sincere, but sounding sincere is also the gift of good liars. Annie thought to herself, *Question everything.* If she asked detailed questions, she could decide if he was answering from memory or making up answers on the fly.

"What was the name of the horse?" she asked.

Abraham had an amused look on his face. "The horse I rode to freedom? Shadow. My daughter named him when he was born."

"What happened to Shadow when you gained your freedom?"

"I sold him to a farmer in Pennsylvania for one hundred dollars. He was worth twice that, but I was in no position to haggle. I used that money for food, clothes, and a train ticket north."

"Annie," Nana said, trying to interrupt. "That's enough."

"What did you see in the cemetery last Saturday?"

Abraham looked at her defiantly. "I saw you kick the foot of a man on the ground, and I thought to myself, I don't need to get involved in white people's problems. So, I left as quietly as possible. I made sure no one saw me."

"Annie, I said that's enough," Nana said, raising her voice. Annie nodded, while Abraham stood up. He thanked them for the pie and the whisky and saw himself out.

Annie watched from the window as Abraham reached the street and disappeared. It felt late, but the summer sun still lingered above the horizon.

"Annie?" Nana put a hand on Annie's arm. "You have to stop," she said.

"What?"

"Stop asking all these questions. Stop playing detective. If Abraham had been the killer, we could both be dead by now. I'm an old woman, but you have your whole life ahead of you."

"Nana, I'm sorry." Annie would never forgive herself if she caused her grandmother harm. "I wanted to know what happened to that man's body."

"Blame it on the wee folk." Nana said, raising her glass to her lips. "The wee folk can make a body disappear."

The wee folk? Once Nana started talking about fairies, it was a sure sign she'd had too much to drink. Time for bed or at least a nap.

Nana let Annie guide her to the back parlor. Annie draped a light blanket over her grandmother as she curled up on her favorite settee.

"Annie," Nana said, yawning. Her grandmother often needed a sleeping elixir to fall asleep at night, but when she drank, sleep came easily. "Promise me you'll stop all this nonsense and find a good man. You can make a difference in the world after you get married. Join a charity or a women's organization. They will appreciate a smart woman like you." Annie waited, but Nana closed her eyes without saying more.

"Rest, Nana."

Annie cleaned up the pie plates and glasses left in the parlor and took them downstairs to the kitchen. She put together a small plate of bread, cheese, and fruit for her dinner. "I can't make you that promise, Nana," Annie said into the silence. As she ate, she considered Abraham's story. She didn't believe he told the whole truth about what he had seen in the cemetery. If he hadn't seen what happened to the body, he would not have been so shocked to see her at his sister's house.

Annie sighed. She gathered another plate to bring to her grandmother in case she woke before morning. Nana was right about one thing. Annie had put both their lives at risk tonight. She needed to be a lot more careful moving forward.

ART GALLERY

CHAPTER XVII

HOPE'S ART GALLERY

Thursday July 16, 1874

B RADLEY stepped down from his rented carriage, walked past the southern Glen Mountain House, and bought an admission ticket to access the famous Watkins Glen and Hope's Art Gallery. He had worked for the Sinclairs for three days and already had a day off. But he wasn't happy. The job Alistair Sinclair offered him was tutoring the twins, Henry and Hannah, during the family vacation in Watkins. Two dollars a day was a reasonable salary. It became a generous offer when Sinclair added room and board at the Lake View Hotel. Still, Bradley had assumed the mentoring role was a cover for some other illegal activity—like counterfeiting—and had readily accepted it. But now he was confused.

He had joined the Sinclair family on their excursions for the first two days. On Tuesday, they visited Havana Glen, a smaller gorge in the next town over, which capitalized on the popularity of its more famous cousin in Watkins. Henry and his sister did get to play under a waterfall. Soaked to the bone, their smiles lasted until bedtime. On Wednesday, Mrs. Sinclair arranged a round-trip steamboat ride to Geneva, forty miles away at the far end of Seneca Lake. Although the Sinclairs had a dozen servants back in the city, only Nanny Kate traveled with them to Watkins. Their nanny came along on every outing, as did either Vance or the Walrus, but never both. Neither Vance nor the Walrus had been on the family's payroll in the city.

Bradley wasn't particularly useful on either trip. Once or twice, Mrs. Sinclair called on him to entertain the twins with a story. He had not come to Watkins to be a children's tutor and felt his talents were wasted. He had several ideas on how to prove himself an asset to Mr. Sinclair. Finding a local engraver—to replace the skills Sinclair sought in Thomas Pickens—could be his way into the gang.

It was only midmorning, but the summer heat had been stifling on the ride to the Glen Mountain House. Bradley paused crossing the iron bridge, feeling the cool air rising from the gorge below. Standing on the edge of the Glen, the temperature was more agreeable.

Inquiries about artists in the village led him to Hope's Art Gallery near the northern Glen Mountain House. Capt. James Hope had been a portrait artist working in Montreal and New York City before moving to Watkins and building a home for his family inside the Glen with a studio and gallery attached. Apparently, Hope planned to spend his retirement painting the wonders of the Glen and selling those paintings to visitors who paid to visit his gallery.

Entering the gallery, Bradley noticed a handful of other tourists appreciating Hope's artwork. He scanned the small crowd for threats and noted alternate exits should he need one. It took him a moment to stop and appreciate the walls of the art gallery filled with a superb collection of a hundred oil paintings and sketches of prominent scenes from Watkins Glen, New England, and other parts of the country. James Hope was an artist with impressive talent.

On the gallery's far side, the artist talked with a visitor in front of a large painting titled *Rainbow Falls*. Bradley kept an eye on Hope—waiting for an opening to approach—while appreciating the man's artwork. There were scenes from other locations, but Bradley enjoyed the paintings from Watkins Glen with titles like *Gem of the Forest*, *Sylvan Dell*, *Crystal Creek*, and *The Basin*. Bradley slowly moved counterclockwise around the room, each new painting bringing him closer to where Hope stood in deep conversation.

As Bradley moved again, he found himself in front of a painting much different from those featuring waterfalls and rocky cliffs. The painter's view in this large canvas was from a hill looking down onto a huge army encampment. A sea of white army tents filled the valley floor, and from the right side of the painting, a line of cavalry climbed the hill toward a lone officer on horseback. Bradley glanced at the title, *Army of the Potomac*. He would have known without looking that it was the Union Army. The painting drew him in. As he stared into the line of soldiers, fragments of sounds and visions came to him unbidden. He heard thumping in his ears, and his body flushed with heat, causing sweat to break out on his brow and across his body. Bradley tried to draw in a breath to calm himself, but breathing became difficult. A great fear consumed him as his hands started to tremble, and his vision darkened and narrowed. His legs weakened, and he was at risk of collapsing to the ground when someone placed a calming hand on his shoulder.

A soothing voice reached his ears. "You're safe. All is well. You're safe. All is well." The voice repeated the words while taking deep breaths between each sentence. Bradley concentrated on breathing, trying to match the man's rhythmic breaths. After a few minutes, his tunnel vision subsided, and the tremors in his body faded away. He was covered in sweat and had to blink a few times to remember where he was.

The gallery was empty except for James Hope, who stood beside him with concerned eyes. The artist patted him on the back. "All right, then?"

Bradley nodded.

"I asked everyone to step out for a moment," Hope explained. "Take your time. I've seen these types of episodes before, but..." and here he paused. "You look much too young to have served."

Bradley was embarrassed but nodded his head at the implied question. He cleared his throat as he looked up at Hope. "I was a drummer."

"You must have been very young."

"I was twelve when I ran away to join my uncle's unit."

"I served with the 2nd Vermont Regiment," Hope said. "I know of many soldiers who have struggled with nightmares, vivid flashbacks, and sometimes deep anger."

Bradley stiffened. Soldiers who admitted such weaknesses were, at best, pitied or, worse, locked up in an asylum. "I appreciate what you did for me, but I'm fine now," Bradley said, even if it was only partially true. If he was honest, he was more broken than fine, but he wiped the sweat from his brow and pushed the negative thoughts away. "If you don't mind, I came here today to discuss possible business opportunities with you."

Hope looked at him for a moment, concern still etched on his face, then he nodded, encouraging Bradley to continue.

Bradley cleared his throat. "I represent a rich businessman from New York looking to commission some artwork. You have amazing paintings, but I wonder if you do engraving work? Or perhaps you could recommend someone else locally?"

"I'm a painter," said Hope. "I'm sorry, but I have no interest in engraving."

"Someone said your son is also an artist?"

"He is a photographer." Hope laughed gently to himself. "A photographer who tells me that painting is the past, and eventually, no one will want to buy paintings because perfect reproductions will be available on glass plates. He might be right, but I hope I'm long gone when that happens." Hope thought for a moment. "You can skip Gates and Crum as they are both focused on photography as well. You could try Frank Loomis. He is a talented artist, but I doubt he's much of an engraver. Sorry, no one else comes to mind."

Bradley thanked Hope and was reaching out to shake the artist's hand when a side door opened and two young women stepped into the gallery. Hope's eyes lit up when he saw them. He turned to Bradley. "Will you excuse me for a moment?"

Hope stepped over to the women, allowing Bradley to listen discreetly from a few paces away. The slightly older woman came up and hugged Hope. She wore a pale brown housedress but carried a lovely plum-colored evening dress in her arms. "Father, look at this beautiful dress Annie created for me to wear to the next Glen Park Hotel Hop!" The second woman blushed slightly at the compliment. "Plum is this year's most popular color," Hope's daughter said as she held the dress in front of her.

"Jesse, it's beautiful!" Hope said. "If there are any intelligent men at the dance, your dance card will be full all evening."

His daughter grinned. "I prefer intelligent men but won't mind dancing with a few handsome idiots either." Captain Hope chuckled and turned to acknowledge his daughter's friend. "Lovely to see you, Annie."

"Wonderful to see you, as well, Mister Hope."

Bradley looked at Annie. She was about his age—perhaps a year younger—with wavy hair of golden brown and bright eyes more green than brown. He remembered those eyes from outside the Western Union office. Annie wore a pleasant smile that made her face thoughtful and kind but also a bit sad around the eyes. Her plum-colored walking dress, less frilly than Jesse's new ball gown, fit her perfectly. Bradley watched her adjust her hat and realized she was staring back at him. He looked away.

Captain Hope came to his rescue a second time. "Ah, this young man and I were just discussing local artists."

Annie looked at Bradley and back at Hope. "Oh, I'm sorry if we are interrupting."

Bradley shook his head. "No, no, not at all. We had just finished our discussion."

Annie smiled politely at Bradley, then turned to Hope and his daughter Jesse. "I'll see you both at church this Sunday. I'm off to walk the Glen to escape this heat." Jesse and Annie hugged, and then Annie stepped out the gallery door.

Bradley watched Annie leave and then looked toward Hope. "Captain Hope, thank you again for your assistance." He tipped his hat and followed Annie out the door. He almost collided with the visitors waiting to return to the gallery. He held the door open long enough to let them enter and then walked down the stairs in time to see a flash of plum-colored fabric enter the Swiss Chalet's lower veranda.

He stood for a moment near the iron bridge, watching other people moving about alone or in small groups, and considered his options. He saw something that made him decide he was not done with Miss Annie Anderson. Bradley hurried toward the Swiss Chalet in pursuit.

Tourists and hotel guests crowded the Swiss Chalet's lower veranda. Visitors jostled against one another to find seats for the noon meal. It was a popular location with views a hundred feet above the ravine. Bradley pushed through the crowd quickly, looking for Annie's dress. He lost time deciding if she would have gone to the upper veranda to eat or out the opposite door toward the lower glen.

WATKINS GLEN, CAVERN CASCADE AND LONG STAIRS

Guessing, he crossed the length of the porch and out the other side just in time to see a plum-colored dress start down the stairs leading to the gorge trail some distance ahead.

Bradley moved quickly to reach the stairs. He had lost sight of her, but he thought he could catch her if he hurried. Surprisingly, few people were on this part of the trail, as many had already returned to the hotel for lunch. Bradley took the stairs two at a time. He focused on the trail ahead and for any sign of Annie's plum-colored dress. He smiled to himself when he saw her looking out over the gorge below.

The proprietors of Watkins Glen made yearly improvements to its pathways, staircases, railings, and bridges to ensure visitors could safely enjoy the views offered from the gorge's dizzying heights. It was quite a surprise then when, just after noon, a scream of terror shattered the tranquility of the Glen, horrifying all who heard it as it echoed off the rocky walls of the gorge.

Bradley glanced over the railing at the broken, lifeless figure a hundred feet below him wearing a plum-colored dress. She had fallen without making a sound. The scream came from a witness to the woman's impact. Bradley turned and hurried back up the trail.

PART TWO

AMIDST SYLVAN GLENS

Brooklyn Bridge Towers

CHAPTER XVIII

THE BROWNSTONE

Spring 1874

THE South Ferry carried Sanna Virsunen away from Manhattan, dropping her at Atlantic Avenue in Brooklyn Heights. As the sun hugged the horizon, cool breezes chased away the warmth of the city's first sunny day of spring, and Sanna was glad for the long sleeves on her maid's uniform. As she walked away from the dock, her eyes followed the eastbound rail lines which could take her into central Long Island or northeast toward far away Boston. She sighed and turned north, heading up Furman Street. A less pleasant fate than sightseeing on Long Island awaited her this evening, and it was only a short stroll away.

Large brick buildings crowded both sides of Furman Street, and the breeze carried the salty, fishy stench of the East River to her nostrils. She caught glimpses of workers loading or unloading tall sailing ships along the docks on her left. Far in the distance, one of the towers of the unfinished Brooklyn Bridge rose above the neighborhoods like an exaggeratedly large church wall with its dual lancet windows staring across the river toward its twin in Manhattan.

After a few blocks, Sanna hiked up her uniform skirt to protect its hem and waited for a gap in the steady traffic of wagons and carriages on Furman Street. When her moment came, she dashed out, only to snag her toe halfway across on a rut in the packed dirt. Her athleticism kept her on her feet, thus narrowly avoiding the hooves of a sorrel mare racing by under the whip of an impatient businessman in a buggy. Sanna reached the far sidewalk and paused to calm her breathing before continuing away from the waterfront into the nearest neighborhood.

The streets were cleaner here than in Manhattan. She didn't

see abandoned piles of trash or dead animals, and even the smell of urine—left behind by drunks or the homeless—was conspicuously absent. This must have been a respectable neighborhood of businessmen who worked in the city by day and took the ferry home at night to their families. Respectable? She scoffed. There was nothing respectable about her job this evening.

When Sanna reached the address that she had memorized, gas streetlights lit the block, compliments of the lamplighter passing through. Sanna faced a row of four-story brownstone townhouses. The occupant of the second brownstone, R.B. Featherstone, awaited her arrival. An industrialist on the rise, Featherstone had a sterling reputation. He owned multiple properties in Manhattan and a sizable portion of the city's import and export business.

Sanna passed through the opening in the waist-high cast-iron fence and climbed the dozen stone steps up to an arched doorway leading to the second or parlor level. As she raised her hand to knock, the door swung open. A swarthy man in a wrinkled suit looked out and appraised her with dark eyes. From inside, another male voice called out. "Is that her?"

"Who else would it be?" the first man said with a gravelly voice. He kept his eyes on her—checking her up and down—while avoiding eye contact. "You're one of Stella's girls, aren't you?"

Sanna nodded.

The second man peered around the doorway and mumbled under his breath, "She doesn't look like a whore."

The door opened wider, and the first man ushered her inside. "That is the point of making her wear a servant's uniform, right? Neighbors talk."

"Yeah, I guess so." The second man was not the brains of the operation.

"The boss isn't some idiot who would let a loose woman appear on his doorstep while his family was away." He looked toward Sanna. "No offense."

She didn't reply, and the heavy door swung closed behind her. There was no retreating now. She smoothed out the white apron she wore over her black skirt and black bodice. Her uniform was neither provocative nor alluring. She dressed per the instructions she had received. She wore the dark skirt and long sleeves of a working-class maid with a white apron and mobcap to complete the look.

Standing next to the two men in the brownstone's entranceway, Sanna felt claustrophobic. The second man was younger and taller. He stared at her lustfully, and she knew he was imagining what she might look like without her uniform on. She took a half step backward to gain distance from him and the sting of body odor that stuck to his suit.

"Take her to the parlor." The swarthy man turned his back on Sanna as he spoke to the younger man in a lowered voice. "The boss will come along when he is ready and will not want anyone to disturb him. I'll be back with the carriage an hour before dawn. She must be out of the house before the sun rises." He cast a pitying look in Sanna's direction, then glanced down at his shoes and back to the younger man. "If I were you, I would lock up and wait downstairs." He adjusted his hat and ignored Sanna as he opened the front door just wide enough to slip through.

The younger man closed and locked the heavy door. Now that he was in charge, he puffed out his chest and turned back to Sanna. He looked her up and down. "Maybe another day you and I—"

"We shouldn't keep Mister Featherstone waiting," she cut him off.

He frowned, but Sanna stood calmly waiting for him to escort her to the parlor. The man's pockmarked face and missing tooth were his most interesting features. She almost felt sorry for him. Except for his body odor. There was no excuse for that.

"This way," the man said, leading her to a set of double doors off the main hallway. He opened the doors, and she walked into a tastefully appointed parlor. "Wait here," he said, closing the doors behind her and leaving her alone.

Sanna stood in the middle of the room, admiring the lofty ceilings, decorative moldings, and expensive furnishings. A feminine hand had styled this cozy space. Mrs. Featherstone made effective use of her husband's money. A fire glowed in the ornate fireplace making the room too warm. Sanna unbuttoned her bodice and then her blouse, exposing the corset below. The black fabric of her corset, reinforced with whalebones for support, contrasted with her pale Scandinavian skin.

She massaged the palm of each hand with the opposite thumb, a ritual that calmed her nerves. Behind her, the sliding double doors to the rear parlor opened, and a large, middle-aged man stepped out.

Featherstone wore no jacket or vest, and the top buttons of his starched white shirt were open, exposing dark chest hair. He strode confidently toward Sanna—the smell of whiskey proceeding him into the room. Ruggedly handsome, he wore a wolfish grin as he stared at her with the sharp, confident eyes of a man who always got what he wanted. Sanna was taller than the average woman, but Featherstone towered over her.

"You're young," he said. This pleased him. He looked down at her open dress and frowned. "I paid a lot of money for a virgin. Are you?"

She nodded, her stomach churning at the thought of his touch.

"Better not lie to me," he said, a glint of menace in his voice. "I'll know myself soon enough."

"I'm not lying," she said softly, and his wolfish grin grew.

"Come with me."

It made a significant difference where he took her. She didn't want to be trapped in the basement or to have other men in the room with them. She expected he would lead her to one of the upstairs bedrooms. Instead, he nodded toward the rear parlor. He let her pass in front of him and then followed behind her. As she crossed the threshold into the rear parlor, the hairs on the back of her neck rose. The parlor carpets gave way to empty hardwood floors. Someone had cleared out the rear parlor, leaving only a lone sofa in the center of the room. With the blinds drawn and the windows closed, Sanna knew no one would hear her from this room. She turned back toward Featherstone. "Are you sure—"

His broad hand slapped her across her face, knocking her to the floor. "Do as you're told."

She rolled away from him and let out a small cry. "Please don't hurt me," she said. Several of Stella's girls had returned from a Featherstone visit covered in bruises. More than one had returned seriously injured.

Featherstone laughed.

Sanna spit blood onto the hardwood floors. His slap had cut the inside of her cheek. She turned her head and looked back at him. He slid his suspenders off his broad shoulders and then reached for the buttons of his trousers. Whiskey or the excitement of pending sexual conquest flushed his face. Sanna could see her fate in his eyes. He meant to beat her and rape her and then throw away what remained.

As Sanna lay on the floor, she smiled. Dimples formed at the corners of her mouth.

Her smile had disappeared by the time Featherstone reached down, grabbed her by the hair, and yanked her to her feet. As he pulled her close, she retrieved a narrow blade from the lining of her corset and slashed him across his forearm. He howled and immediately released his grip on her hair. She dropped to the floor, stepped away, and forced a scared look on her face. She held the blade with two shaking hands as if to ward him off.

Rage filled Featherstone's face. He looked at the cut on his arm and then back at Sanna. "You'll pay for that." Seeing a frightened target, he marched forward to grab the knife from her. "Give me that."

Sanna pivoted away easily—the empty room working in her favor—then lashed out several times with her knife. Her arm was a snake, and her blade its fangs. None of the cuts were deep, but they enraged Featherstone. Twice her size and eyes filled with hate, he lowered his head and charged. She sidestepped as he barreled forward and slipped below his outstretched arms. She left deeper cuts on his legs. He tried to turn quickly, but Sanna was quicker. She lunged forward and punched the knuckles of her right hand deep into his throat. He clutched at his neck while choking and gasping for air. The rage in his eyes turned to fear.

Sanna smiled at him.

"Guard!" Featherstone yelled, but the blow to his neck had done its damage. His mild croak evaporated before crossing the parlor. Featherstone wiped the blood from a cut to his forehead and stared at Sanna's blade. He realized he was fighting for his life.

Sanna followed his eyes in their frantic search for an escape route. "Guard!" He tried again, his voice louder this time.

When Featherstone turned for the parlor door, Sanna lunged forward, swept his legs out from under him, and jumped on his back. Her extra weight and the cuts to his legs propelled him face first onto the floor. Sanna used her thighs to straddle him and pin his arms down while she pulled off her apron and twisted it around his neck. Featherstone bucked and thrashed, but she held on until his eyes bulged and his body fell still. She waited another thirty seconds and loosened the apron. The man wasn't dead yet. She quickly cut the apron into strips and bound his hands behind him. She'd started to bind his legs when a voice echoed from outside the parlor.

"Sir? Sir? Is everything all right?"

The night guard must have heard the commotion and disobeyed orders not to disturb his boss. Sanna did not curse. She simply adjusted to the situation. Stuffing the mobcap into Featherstone's mouth to silence him, she jumped up and slid the rear parlor doors closed. She listened as the outer parlor doors opened, and a moment later, furtive steps crossed the room. She had no desire to kill the guard but would if she had to.

With unfortunate timing, Featherstone spluttered back to consciousness and let out a loud groan.

The night guard rushed forward and threw open the rear parlor doors. "Hey—" The man had enough time to register Featherstone's bloodied and tied-up body before a flick of Sanna's wrist sent her knife flying into the guard's throat. She pulled a second knife out of her corset and stepped toward him. The man staggered backward, made a gurgling sound, and collapsed onto the ground. She shook her head. The man was not innocent, but he had not been on her list. Even worse, he was bleeding all over the carpet in the parlor.

Sanna returned to Featherstone. His eyes were bulging as he stared up at her. He lashed out, trying to kick her off her feet but only earned a deep cut in his leg from her knife. He grunted in pain as she pulled out the blade and stepped back. She kept her distance as Featherstone shook his head and spit the mobcap from his mouth. "I can pay you," he said. "Triple whatever you've been offered to get to me."

"I'm not for sale."

His eyes narrowed. "What do you want then?"

"I want you to feel as helpless as the women you've hurt," Sanna said. "But the main reason I'm here is to deliver a message from my employer. You made a mistake when you rejected his offer to buy the factory on the Lower East Side central to your smuggling ring. A lucrative crime for a 'respectable' businessman."

"We can work out a deal," Featherstone said, raising his voice. "Tell your boss it was just a misunderstanding."

Sanna shook her head slowly. "A deal has already been made with your partner who will own a controlling share of the business after your death." Featherstone's face had become deathly pale. Her last strike—surgically delivered—had opened an artery in his leg. Featherstone was already dead. He just did not know it yet. "I did not come to make a deal with you." She leaned down to whisper in his ear. "The Butzemann does not forgive or forget."

Featherstone's eyes widened, but the fight had left his body with most of his blood. Sanna waited another few minutes to be sure he was dead. "You've beaten your last prostitute," she said as she reached down and dipped Featherstone's finger in his own blood and drew the letter *B* on the floor.

Sanna could have killed him instantly when he yanked her off the floor, but men like Featherstone did not deserve an easy death. Even if it increased her risk. Besides, her instructions were clear. Reach Featherstone where he felt the safest and make sure he suffered. Mission accomplished. The swarthy guard would return before dawn and later talk about what he found. The Butzemann legend would grow.

Sanna retrieved her knife from the night guard's throat, holding her breath as she leaned down. The man really did stink. She cleaned both knives and returned them to their hiding places in her corset. The mobcap and pieces of apron went into the parlor fireplace, which flared to life before settling back to a warm glow.

Sanna did not think the swarthy man had gotten a good look at her. Even if there was a search, she was neither a maid nor one of Stella's girls. No one would find her. With the white mobcap and apron gone, Sanna's all-black outfit blended perfectly with the darkest shadows. She slid open the rear parlor window, dropped onto the garden patio, and disappeared into the night.

CHAPTER XIX

DEATH AND DESERTION

From the Journal of Private H. Thompson

March 24, 1864 – Taylor, Buck, Ace, Frank, and I stared at the two men pointing guns at us while torchlight flickered on the cave walls.

"Raise y'all's hands where I can see 'em," the older man said with a raspy voice. His white beard was stained from years of spitting tobacco juice. His partner was young. Younger than Fish, if I had to guess. Neither wore a uniform. One was too old, and the other was too young for military service.

We raised our hands over our heads. Our own guns were leaning against the side of the cave or stowed in our bags. We had not been expecting trouble or company. If they pulled the trigger, it would be nearly impossible to miss from this short distance. My brain distractedly wondered about cave walls and ricochets. I noticed both men had steady hands.

The older man tilted his head toward his partner. "Looks like we found us some deserters, Clem." Taylor told him we were not deserters. "Y'all're wearin' uniforms," the man said, "but I don't see any Rebel units nearby or any Yankee soldiers y'all should be killing."

The older man did not believe we were soldiers on furlough. He spit tobacco juice on the cave floor and then wiped away the string of spittle clinging to his beard with his left sleeve while never taking his eyes off us. I asked if they were members of the home guard. The duties of the home guard were to protect strategic points like bridges or depots, aid in repelling any Union invasions, and capture deserters. Home guards rarely wore uniforms.

"Damn right," the younger man said. "We followed all'a y'all from Rutherfordton."

"Hush up, Clem," the older man said. But he smirked when he noticed the surprise on our faces. "The way I see it," he said, "y'all started in Rutherfordton dressed to get back to your units. Maybe put on a good show for your families, huh? But then, Clem and I saw you headin' west steada east. That was damn suspicious. Then we watched y'all spend the day searchin' for a cave to hide in so y'all couldn't be found." He pointed to the leather satchels. "Looks like y'all have stored up supplies which'll let you keep your heads down for a time in this hidey-hole of yours. Clem! Check those satchels."

Ace was closest to me. I saw his hands twitch in the cave's dim light as Clem stepped toward the satchels. I had no doubt Ace had a pistol somewhere on his body and, for a moment, thought he might risk reaching for it. It would have been suicide. We could do nothing to stop Clem from leaning down and opening the closest satchel. "Jesus, Mary, and Joseph!" Clem blurted out. When the older man asked what Clem found, the younger man did not hesitate. "Gold, Walt. A whole damn bag of gold!"

Walt didn't turn, but his eyes narrowed, and he licked his lips. "Are ya sure?" Clem bit into one of the nuggets and held it up to see the small dent his teeth had made. Clem was sure. The cave went quiet. I could see Walt working through this new information.

"It's our job to find deserters, and we found us some tryin' to hide stolen gold," Walt said. "There'll be a big ole reward in it for us when we return with y'all and this gold to the nearest unit..." his voice trailed off. "You know, Clem, what if these here deserters were to try and escape? If they tried to get the drop on us, we'd have every right to shoot them. It would be you and I exercisin' our right to defend ourselves."

I did not like the new look that settled onto Walt's face. As if it was occurring to him, he could claim a few of those satchels as his reward before turning the rest in. The only obstacle to his plan—the men who knew how many satchels there were to begin with—was standing in front of him. Taylor saw the same look on Walt's face. "You won't be able to kill all of us," Taylor said. He spoke quietly, but we heard his unspoken message. Be ready.

Walt pulled out a second pistol. He pointed one at Taylor and the other at me. Clem's pistol was aimed at Frank. "To be honest,"

Walt said, "I like our chances."

Time slowed down. None of us had been trained to wait around to be killed. Each of us prepared to throw ourselves forward, trusting our luck that hitting a moving body in the dim light would be harder. Walt and Clem were at least ten feet away. Even if some of us died, we were confident we would take one or both intruders with us. My body tensed in anticipation. I was disappointed to die without ever meeting my child.

As Walt straightened his arms to aim, a voice came from behind him. "I wouldn't do that if I were you." Walt and Clem froze. No one moved. No one breathed.

Walt forced a chuckle. He tried to keep his voice friendly, but I could see his eye twitching. "Well, now," he said, addressing the voice. "Let's not do anythin' stupid. We got reinforcements comin'. This can get all sorted out when they get here." He paused, licking his dry lips. "Why don't you come into the light, and we can all talk this out like civilized—"

As the last word left his mouth, Walt made a lightning-fast move—impressive for his age—dropping, spinning, and shooting at the space behind him. Two guns went off simultaneously, their echoes booming through the cave. Walt's shot went wide and ricocheted harmlessly out of the cave entrance. Fish's bullet hit Walt dead center. Walt's mouth opened as if he wanted to say something, but no last words emerged, and he collapsed to the ground. Before his body landed, a third shot blasted through the cave. Clem had frozen at the sound of gunfire, giving Ace the time needed to draw and fire. A third eye bloomed on Clem's forehead, and he pitched forward onto the cave floor.

The air was acrid with spent gunpowder. We were momentarily speechless until Frank, of all people, broke the silence. "It was them or us."

We appreciated that it was them and not one of us on the cold, hard rocks, but none of us were happy. Killing was not foreign to us, but we were not accustomed to shooting fellow Carolinians. Taylor reached down to check each man for a pulse. They were dead, which made what came next easier. He turned to Fish and nodded his approval. "Good timing," Taylor said.

Fish stepped into the cave. "I thought I saw something through the woods after Buck and Frank crossed the stream," said Fish. "I tied off the horses and wagon and went to check it out. Came along just in time to see these two sneakin' into the cave. I followed 'em real quiet." Taylor asked if Fish had seen any other home guard nearby, but he had not.

Taylor said, "We can't take the chance that they were alone. We can't be caught carrying gold that we can't explain. It would be confiscated and might lead back to this cave and the bodies. We've gotta leave the gold behind." None of us liked the idea, and we all said so. The killing was in self-defense, after all. Taylor switched to his sergeant's voice. "We can't risk moving the gold. We're leaving without it. Fish didn't see anyone else close, so nobody knows about this cave. The gold will be safe here."

Buck and Ace were angry. I was, too, although my anger was directed at the two dead men who ruined our moment of triumph. Frank wore his normal neutral expression. Taylor looked at the five of us. "Let's make a pact right now," he said. "This gold is our gold. The Lucky Six found it when no one else could. We'll all survive this war, and when it's over, we'll meet back up at Fish's farm and claim this gold together. No one'll remember these two by then, and we won't have to tell anyone where the gold came from."

No one argued. Taylor sent Fish back to the wagon to get the horses ready to move. There wasn't much daylight left. The rest of us buried the two fresh bodies with the remains of the Englishmen and the satchels of gold back under the rocks. It wasn't long before we exited the cave, each looking back one last time at our reburied treasure and derailed dreams.

I heard Ace sigh as he muttered, "The Lord gave, and the Lord hath taken away." The sun was already out of sight behind the trees when we emerged into the fading light. Sunset was close. We crossed the stream and rejoined Fish, who sat in the wagon's driver seat. Taylor stacked a few rocks to mark the location we needed to cross the creek. I tried to memorize the landmarks. As we climbed aboard, Fish started the horses off. No one else was in sight. Moments later, we were on the way to Morganton, fifty miles to the northeast.

After the sun went down, we traveled by moonlight, determined to get as far as possible from the bodies in the cave. No one slept.

In the darkness, Fish stared blankly into space. I worried he was dwelling on the shooting, so I told him it had been an impressive shot back in the cave. "Aw, wasn't nothing. I couldn't miss at that range." I also said I was impressed that he made sure that none of us were in his line of fire in case the bullet passed through Walt, Fish laughed. "Who says I did that?" He was too good with guns and too good a shot to do otherwise, but it got all of us smiling.

Buck complimented Ace on his fast draw. "A real gunslinger," said Buck, patting his friend on the back. We reached the edge of Morganton in the middle of the night and pulled the wagon off the road into a clearing. We tied the horses and wrapped ourselves in blankets for a few hours of sleep.

March 25, 1864 – After returning the horses and wagon to the livery, we caught the first train out from the train depot east of Morganton. As the train rocked and click-clacked its way east, we each retreated into our own thoughts. I spent my time scribbling notes on scraps of paper for the memoirs I hoped to write when the war ended. Leaving the gold behind was a setback. Finding it in the first place reinforced how lucky we were. I hadn't been this elated since I was sixteen and standing optimistically before my true love's father to ask his permission for her hand in marriage. A happy life was within reach.

Fish asked Buck how much money he reckon'd each of us would get for our share of gold. Buck scratched his head, mumbled about gold prices and pounds to ounces, and then rolled his eyes toward the sky as he did rough calculations in his head. After a few minutes, Buck looked at Fish and smiled. "Assuming each satchel's like the first... I'd guess each is worth about sixty thousand dollars."

Fish let out a low whistle. With land prices at four dollars an acre, Fish could buy a nice house on two hundred acres of land for about two thousand dollars and have plenty of money left over for rock candy.

In Salisbury, we changed trains and took the North Piedmont line to Danville, Virginia. There, we switched to the Richmond-Danville Railroad. As the train left the Danville station, I heard Buck lean close to Taylor and ask what would happen if some of us didn't survive the war. A shiver ran down my spine. Just asking the question courted bad luck. Taylor was quiet for a moment, then shrugged. "We split things among the survivors."

Sitting next to Fish, I could tell by the look on his face that he had also heard Taylor's reply. It was a sobering consideration. We reached our winter quarters later that evening. I was stiff and exhausted from the journey. We had been gone only two weeks, but tonight, military life felt foreign. It would take several days to settle back into the routine.

As I lay in the darkness that night, I wondered if it would have been better to find the gold after the war had ended. Before our trip to Hickory Nut Gap, we didn't think much about the future. We lived each day, trusting each other and hoping our luck would hold. Now? Thoughts of riches waiting for our return weighed heavily on the Lucky Six.

A sound woke me up in the middle of the night. I yawned and looked around. There was just enough moonlight to see Fish awake and working something in his hands, rubbing it like a worry stone. When I sat up, he was startled and quickly hid the gold nugget under his blanket. "I didn't mean to take it," he said, sheepishly. "I put it in my pocket when Taylor sent me to the wagon. The first time. I forgot it was there."

I told him to keep it hidden. It was too late to put it back now. I started to fall back asleep when Fish's hushed whisper floated across the darkness. He asked me how long I thought the war would last. "Feels like it will go on forever," I said, then rolled over and fell fast asleep.

I wish now that I could relive that moment. I'd slap myself awake and tell myself to pay attention. That this moment mattered. But instead, I gave Fish the worst answer possible and left him alone with his thoughts in the darkness. In the morning, Fish's bed was empty. He was gone. Deserted in the night.

CHAPTER XX

FALLEN ANGEL

Thursday, July 16, 1874

A NNIE had exited Hope's Art Gallery and descended the handful of stairs to the trail. She considered which direction into the gorge she would take. The right path led to the upper two-thirds of the Glen. She enjoyed exploring the Cathedral, the Triple Cascades, and Rainbow Falls, but it was lunchtime and Annie's stomach rumbled gently. She turned left toward the Glen Mountain House's Swiss Chalet and the lower section of the Glen.

Hotel guests and tourists filled the veranda of the Swiss Chalet. Annie, unwilling to fight for an open seat, decided to skip lunch on the veranda and descend through the lower third of the Glen. Her thoughts turned to the ice cream she could buy at the lower entrance as a treat, and she licked her lips.

In the last ten years, Watkins Glen had become one of the most popular summer resorts in the United States, drawing tens of thousands of visitors annually from all over the country. Annie loved the Glen but disliked the number of visitors it attracted in the summer. She crossed the first-floor veranda—nimbly maneuvering through the crowd—and headed down the opposite stairs. Reaching the trail, she walked along shaded by an emerald canopy of stately trees.

The trail led along the northern cliffs over an inaccessible portion of the gorge. Watkins Glen is a natural gorge carved into the western hillside above the village of Watkins. An unassuming stream, starting miles away and hundreds of feet above the valley floor, tumbled over cascades, around rocks, in and out of circular pools, and through deep, narrow caverns until it emerged from between rocky cliffs onto the level valley floor. To walk the Glen

Glen Mountain House Swiss Chalet

was to follow the path of the stream back up into the hillside. Man-made stairways, pathways, and bridges were added only ten years ago to make this hidden world accessible to visitors for the small fee of fifty cents per person or fifteen cents for a child under fifteen.

Annie was glad she'd worn her plum-colored walking dress and her most comfortable boots. The pathways and wooden stairways of the Glen were no place for white skirts, thin shoes, or delicate fabrics. The mistake a lot of first-time visitors made was not real-izing that getting dripped on and a little muddy were part of the ex-perience. As she got farther away from the Glen Mountain House, the crowds thinned until Annie was alone on the trail.

Despite her best efforts, Annie wasn't any closer to solving the mystery of the dead man on her mother's grave. She had done her best not to draw attention to her efforts, but she had pestered the sheriff for updates, interviewed more people at the Glen Mountain House, and checked daily at the Western Union office for a reply from Sadie Thompson, the dead man's wife. Lots of activity with nothing to show for it.

When Annie got frustrated, she threw herself into sewing. It calmed her and gave her time to think. She had made Jesse Hope's dress as a favor and had been thrilled with her friend's enthusiastic reaction. Jesse insisted on paying Annie and declared the dress was worth three times the amount Annie was willing to accept.

Annie had already started designing her next dress, destined for the Firehouse Charity Auction. Not for the first time, Annie fantasized about moving to a big city and setting up her own dress-making shop. Her parents had spent a lot of their money to build the family home, but surely there was some money left for Annie's in-heritance. She wouldn't need a lot. Just enough to buy some fabric and supplies and rent a shop for a few months until she got on her feet. Annie resolved to ask her grandmother about her inheritance as soon as the time was right.

The trail brought Annie to the top of Long Staircase, a steep set of wooden stairs that descended fifty feet from the northern cliffs into the first section of the Glen. The bottom of the staircase ended just past the top of a fifty-foot waterfall called Cavern Cascade. Annie was always excited to descend into the gorge—it offered a cool respite from the sweltering summer weather and this lower section, named Glen Alpha, had some of the Glen's most scenic views. Annie leaned forward to see if the stairs were clear as another woman, not much older than herself, climbed up from the Glen and stepped off the top of the stairs.

Annie smiled at the woman who was catching her breath after the climb. It was no easy pull up the long flight of stairs. The woman smiled back and turned to admire the view. "Amazing, isn't it?"

Annie smiled. "It certainly is."

The woman looked back down the stairs. "My friends haven't started the climb yet, so you're welcome to go ahead if you like." The stairs were empty, so Annie stepped out onto the top step. She turned back to say something else to the woman, but as she did so, her heel caught, causing her balance to shift slightly backward. Annie's heart leaped into her throat and time froze for her as she felt the sickening pull of the abyss. A steadying hand reached out and grabbed one of Annie's flailing arms.

"Thank you!" was all Annie could manage.

"Are you all right?" the woman said, visibly concerned.

"I am now," said Annie. "Thank you."

"I'm just glad I was here to help," said the woman. She looked at Annie with kind eyes.

"I just wanted to say," said Annie, clinging tightly to the railing for support, "that I love your dress!"

"Oh, thank you," said the woman. "She looked down at her dress and laughed. My mother made it for me. And I love your dress too. I guess plum really is this season's popular color."

Annie said goodbye and left her new friend staring at the view with her back to the trail. Annie descended with caution, spooked by her near brush with disaster. As she reached the bottom step, she found several men and women waiting to climb the Long Staircase. She excused herself and moved out of their way. A moment later, Annie heard an oddly loud thump, followed immediately by an anguished scream that froze her blood. While everyone around her was shouting and pointing down into the gorge, Annie looked up, hoping to see her new friend where she had left her. Instead, she saw the face of the man she had just met at Hope's Art Gallery, staring down into the gorge. A second later, the face disappeared.

Ruth Van Etten had fallen ninety-five feet into the gorge. Although a doctor was called for immediately, it was obvious the woman had died instantly. Annie looked down into the gorge to see the woman's head bent at an unnatural angle and her body, wrapped in her plum-colored dress, half in and half out of a shallow pool at the bottom of the gorge. Ruth's blood seeped into the stream. Annie couldn't bear to look any longer.

Annie stayed nearby in case she could be of service. She comforted several of the dead woman's friends. The group, from Auburn, New York, had traveled down Seneca Lake by steamer that morning and arrived at the Glen on this beautiful sunny day in the best of spirits.

When Sheriff Swartwood arrived, Annie approached him to offer her description of events, but he waved her away. She again felt the sting of disrespect. She stiffened her back, determined not to let her frustration show. In the sheriff's defense, the owner of the Glen had also just arrived and was demanding the sheriff's attention. Annie watched as several of the town's prominent men huddled together to decide on the official version of events. They carefully examined the upper portion of the trail and would later determine that the woman had lost her footing and slipped below the railing. An unforeseen calamity but no fault of the owners of the Glen.

It took a long time to remove Ruth's lifeless body from the bottom of the gorge.

When it was clear no one was interested in Annie's account of events, she slipped away from the scene and descended through the Glen. She was numb to the sounds of waterfalls, to the glistening sunbeams penetrating the shadows, and to the cool and fresh breezes on her cheeks. She climbed down the long wooden entrance stairs and into the entrance amphitheater, ignoring the looks on the faces of visitors blocked from entering. Word of a death in the Glen was spreading. Annie walked past the towering cliffs and passed the entrance to the Glen Bazaar. Any appetite she had for ice cream had disappeared.

Watkins Glen, Entrance

"Miss Anderson?"

Annie turned, startled to see she had just walked by Abraham as he stood holding the reins of a lovely palomino mare hitched to a small wagon. His dark skin glistened with sweat. He removed his hat and wiped his brow with a red handkerchief. The hat's leather band was stained with sweat.

"Oh, Mister Adams," she said. "I didn't see you." She had meant to stop by to see Esther but didn't want to run into Abraham again. Now she couldn't avoid him.

"Are you all right, Miss Anderson?"

Annie assumed he had heard of Ruth's death and had seen Annie come down the entrance stairs. She opened her mouth to give a dismissive answer, but something about Abraham's face gave her pause. He had done a poor job hiding his displeasure and annoyance the first two times they met. Now, his face projected a sense of concern. Concern for her?

"I met the woman who died," Annie found herself saying. "She was very kind."

Abraham nodded but said nothing—offering her silence in case she had more to say. She didn't. No one expected death on such a beautiful sunny day. As she thought of Ruth's life ending so abruptly, Annie's eyes began to water. Abraham shuffled his feet and then cleared his throat. In his rich baritone, he recited a verse from memory.

> *"Kindness is the only service that will stand the storm*
> *of life and not wash out. It will wear well and will be*
> *remembered long after the prism of politeness or the*
> *complexion of courtesy has faded away."*

Annie blinked. She turned toward Abraham and tilted her head. "That is not a Bible verse. Keats? Longfellow?"

Abraham shook his head. "Abraham Lincoln."

Annie smiled. "It's lovely."

"Forgive me for saying so, Miss Anderson, but you look out of sorts. My sister, Esther, would not forgive me if I didn't offer you a ride home." He used his hat to fan the flies away from his horse's face. "Goldie here loves to stretch her legs, and for the price of a

carrot, she can get us to where you want to go before you even realize we've left." Abraham held up a carrot and smiled.

His horse had a gold coat, white mane, and large, intelligent
eyes. "She's beautiful," Annie said, approaching slowly and strok-
ing Goldie's shoulder.

"She's a Tennessee walking horse," Abraham said, "but between you and me, I think she has some thoroughbred in her."

Annie was sorry not to have a treat to offer Goldie. She turned
back to Abraham. "I appreciate the offer," she said, "but I could use
the walk to clear my head." Annie was ready to believe Abraham
had not killed the man in the cemetery, but she wasn't ready to trust
him.

Abraham nodded and climbed into his wagon. With a tip of his
hat and a quick flip of the reins, he departed in a rolling cloud of
dust.

Annie watched him go and then looked back toward the Glen's
rocky entrance. Ruth's death had not been the first in the Glen. Last
summer, a woman died when an overhanging rock detached and
crashed down on a party of ladies and gentlemen walking in the
upper sections. But something about today's death felt personal.
Annie couldn't believe that Ruth had accidentally slipped under the
railing after saving Annie from falling. The fates were not that cruel. And why had that man from Hope's Art Gallery—the man who
peered over the edge and then disappeared—not come forward? He
must have seen what happened to Ruth. Was he responsible for her
fall? Annie felt a sudden sinking feeling in the pit of her stomach.
He must have followed her from the art gallery. Had he mistaken
the woman from behind, dressed in a similar plum-colored dress,
for Annie?

Annie had a moment of shocking clarity. What if someone was
trying to kill her? Had she asked too many questions, or did the
killer believe she had seen something incriminating in the cemetery? If that was true, Annie's investigation cost Ruth Van Etten
her life.

Annie approached the nearest hackman and paid for a carriage
ride home. It was too dangerous for her to walk alone now, even in
the daylight.

As she leaned back in her hired carriage, she failed to notice the wagon following at a discreet distance, pulled by a horse with a gold coat and white mane.

CHAPTER XXI

THE JEFFERSON MEETING

Saturday, July 18, 1874

TWO days had passed since the tragic death in the Glen. The news spread rapidly, casting a somber mood over villagers and vacationers. Town gossips spent their energy arguing whether the falling death had been an unfortunate accident that could not be foreseen or a preventable tragedy caused by a glen that was not as safe for visitors as its promoters claimed. Hearing that town officials ruled the woman's death an accident came as a surprise to Bradley, but he avoided conversations on the topic. He was in a foul mood of his own. His nightmares had returned after the episode at Hope's Art Gallery and sleep came with great difficulty.

Bradley dodged an omnibus pulled by a team of four horses as he crossed Franklin to reach the Western Union office. He brushed the road dirt off his pant legs and stepped inside. The telegraph office provided no respite from the afternoon heat. The muggy, close interior caused drops of sweat to roll down Bradley's temples and across his cheek. To make matters worse, the smell of dirt, sweat, and body odor from the other customers was so potent he could almost taste it. Bradley was fastidious about his own personal hygiene. He removed his hat to fan his face.

There was only one worker servicing customers in the telegraph office, and the line moved slowly. Bradley debated returning later but was growing frustrated at the lack of responses to his previous telegraphs, so he resigned himself to waiting so he could send follow-up telegrams.

At least his job with the Sinclair family had been a pleasant distraction. On Friday, they visited the newly opened Height's Mammoth Museum, near the entrance of the Glen, where the twins marveled at the large variety of native and foreign beasts, birds, reptiles, shells, relics, and other curiosities. This morning, the family went for a swim and a picnic. Mrs. Sinclair told Bradley to take the rest of the day off as the twins were tired, and the family planned to relax at the hotel for the rest of the day.

As Bradley approached the front of the line, the Western Union man looked up and noticed him. Bradley had dropped in every day since he had sent the original telegrams, and each time, the man had greeted him with a disappointing headshake. Today, the man smiled at Bradley and waved him over. Bradley ignored the grumbling from the men still ahead of him.

"This came for you, sir."

Finally! Bradley thought to himself. He thanked the man as he took the folded message and slid it into his jacket pocket. He would read it in the sunshine and fresh air.

Bradley walked along the wooden sidewalks toward the train station, where he knew he could find a shady spot to read his telegram. He liked this small village. It was cleaner and less crowded than the city, and it was full of energy and life. He liked smiling at the people he passed. Getting a return smile always improved his mood. But his smile faltered when an attractive woman approached wearing a plum dress. Thoughts of the broken body at the bottom of the Glen filled his mind. The woman, a stranger, hesitated when she caught Bradley staring at her. He muttered "good day" and gave her plenty of room to pass.

He tried to increase his pace only to get stuck behind two old men, grumbling about the prolonged hot spell the village was enduring.

"We need us a good creek-raising rainstorm," the first man said to his friend. They shuffled along, leaving footprints in the fine layers of dirt on the sidewalk deposited from dust clouds kicked up by passing wagons.

Bradley stepped into the street and lengthened his stride to move ahead of the old men. He turned right onto First Street and soon arrived at the train station and the large shade tree nearby. He reached into his jacket pocket and pulled out the Western Union telegram. The telegraph worker had transcribed the dots and dashes into a handwritten message on one of the standard blank forms.

THE WESTERN UNION TELEGRAPH COMPANY
Dated *July 18*_____1874
Received at *Watkins, N.Y.*
To *Bradley Webster*
*More information needed. Sending Otto Fuchs for update.
Noon, July 21, Montour House, Havana.*

Bradley crumpled the telegram in frustration. This was not the answer he was expecting. Who was Otto Fuchs? And was he coming to help him or condemn him? Bradley had little to show for his efforts since he sent the original telegram. His attempt to find an engraver had turned up no promising leads. Instead of being a trusted member of the counterfeiting ring, he was an overpaid male nanny for a rich family. What update could he offer Fuchs?

He sat under the tree and allowed himself a few minutes to stew in frustration and self-doubt. Joining the counterfeiting ring was his key to success, and he had nothing to show for his efforts. Bradley needed to change his tactics. As an idea formed in his mind, he stood, dusted himself off, and headed back toward the shops on Franklin Street. He needed a change of clothes and, time permitting, a quick stop at the butcher shop.

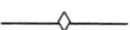

The oranges and reds in the western sky faded into purple as Alistair Sinclair's carriage deposited him in front of the Jefferson House on the corner of Franklin and Fourth Street. A lamplighter, igniting the gas streetlamps as he worked his way down Franklin Street, stepped aside as Sinclair walked by with a slight limp. The hotel had entrances on both Franklin Street and Fourth Street, but Sinclair chose the Franklin Street entrance. He walked up the stairs and disappeared inside the large, three-story brick-and-stone structure.

The man who entered the Jefferson behind Sinclair walked hunched over with a limp of his own, wore thick glasses, sported an unkept handlebar mustache and longer hair, and wore a workingman's suit that was a size too large for his frame. Bradley had considered adding an eye patch but rejected the idea as excessive and impractical. Sinclair did not see Bradley jump out of a following carriage close on his heels, but he would not have recognized him if he had. Bradley's mother would not have recognized him. He had spent the afternoon making sure of it.

After the War Between the States ended, Bradley found himself alone in New York City, barely a teenager, and with no money to his name. He had been forced to live on the streets, and, to survive, had fallen in with a group of youths who taught him to pick the pockets of arrogant, rich businessmen. A year later, Bradley had been lucky to find work at a vaudeville and burlesque theater. It wasn't glamorous work, but he had a curious mind and took the opportunity to learn everything he could about stage makeup and costumes. Knowledge that he was now putting to good use.

Earlier in the day, Elizabeth Sinclair had let slip that Alistair had an engagement this evening. For a week, Sinclair had played the part of a rich man on vacation. Bradley hoped this was an opportunity to finally learn the details of the "big job" Pickens claimed he had been offered. If Bradley was lucky, Sinclair's engagement would be a meeting with his counterfeiting crew.

Bradley entered the Jefferson House in time to see Sinclair escorted across the lobby toward the dining area. This hotel was the oldest in the village. Bradley had heard it had been around since the 1830s, and he was thankful that gas lighting had yet to be installed. He had confidence in his disguise, but the dimmer oil lighting helped when in a crowded space.

Sinclair entered a private room off the dining area where he settled in for dinner. Bradley found a table with an unobstructed view of the private room but began to worry this was a waste of time. Why hold a secret meeting for your illegal enterprise in the middle of one of the busiest hotels in the village? It didn't make sense. The thought had barely crossed his mind when Bradley recognized the next two men to enter the dining area. He was careful not to look directly at Vance or the Walrus as they walked past within a few feet of him and entered the private room.

This was more promising.

Bradley ordered a light meal as he waited and watched. Over

JEFFERSON HOUSE

the next ten minutes, three more men entered the private room, joining Sinclair, Vance, and the Walrus. The first had thinning silvery hair and a stylish mustache but with clothes straining to contain his portly figure. He carried himself like the self-important headmaster of a boys' school. He reminded Bradley of an overfed version of Thomas Pickens. The last two arrivals were in their thirties with light brown hair and trim beards. They looked alike enough for Bradley to guess they were brothers.

The brothers shut the door behind them, blocking Bradley's view. He would learn nothing new by staring at a closed door, so he had a choice to make. If he moved, he might miss any late arrivals or early departures, but he couldn't see or hear anything with the doors closed. He waited a few more minutes to finish his food, dropped some coins on the table to cover the meal, and departed Jefferson House via the Fourth Street exit. Reaching the street, he turned left and left again to enter the alley. The streetlights did not penetrate the shadowy passageway, forcing Bradley to move slowly until his eyes adjusted. He counted windows and positioned himself below the open window of Sinclair's private dining room.

Voices drifted out but were carried away on the evening breezes before Bradley could make out the words. He looked around to ensure he was alone in the alley, then jumped up and grabbed the stone windowsill a few feet above his head. He lifted his body upwards, trying not to expose himself to those inside.

"—next week." Bradley could hear Sinclair's voice. "Bill, that will be your responsibility. Now, what about the ink?"

"It's ready." An unknown voice.

"It's ready? But is it perfect, Bill?"

"It is ready for us to continue, and it's perfect."

"It had better be," Sinclair said. "Otherwise, we will miss the deadline. That's all, then. Enjoy your dinners."

Bradley was preparing to drop down when he heard Vance's voice. "What about Bradley Webster?"

Bradley froze and strained to listen.

"What about him?" Sinclair asked. "He is not a part of this."

"He's a problem," Vance said. "He is asking too many questions."

Bradley couldn't be sure, but he thought he heard Sinclair sigh. "When the time comes," Sinclair's voice was clear, "I'll let you deal with the problem."

Vance wasn't done. "I don't understand why you hir—"

A hand yanked on Bradley's pant leg with enough force to break his grip on the windowsill. He landed hard on his heels, then lost his balance and pitched backward. Instead of landing hard on his back, Bradley curved his spine and turned his fall into a backward roll. He had enough momentum to throw his legs over his head and land back on his feet. As he rolled, his mind registered that it was not a policeman who had accosted him. Policemen in the city were unpredictable, and unless you knew the copper was one of the good ones, running was always the best option.

"What are you doing out here!"

This man was just an overly concerned citizen. Bradley began coughing uncontrollably while slowly backing away from the open window. He did not want the men in the private room to check on the disturbance outside their window.

"You can't lurk outside other in people's windows!"

Bradley continued to back away while coughing loudly into a handkerchief he'd pulled from his pants pocket. The man followed, berating him. As they neared the entrance to the alley, Bradley stopped coughing and pulled the handkerchief away from his mouth. It was covered in blood. The man saw the blood, registered the baggy suit and Bradley's pale complexion, and came to the obvious conclusion that Bradley was dying from consumption. Before the man could react, Bradley reversed his retreat and stepped closer to his antagonist.

"Meant no harm, sir," Bradley said in a shaky voice. "Was just hopin' someone'd throw me down some food." Bradley had moved uncomfortably close to the man. "Perhaps you could help me, sir? Spare a coin for a poor dyin' man?"

The man's angry and impatient expression turned into one of horror as Bradley waved the bloody handkerchief near the man's face. The man stepped backward, sputtering. "Just get out of here!"

"Right, sir. Right away."

Bradley turned, stepped out of the alley, and dashed across

Fourth Street. He walked along the stone wall of the Freer Opera House until he found a darkened doorway to disappear into. Sinclair's team should be exiting the Jefferson House soon enough, and Bradley wanted to see what direction each member headed.

Bradley carefully rolled up the bloodstained handkerchief as he waited and tucked it back into his pocket. The pig's blood he'd bought from the butcher had worked better than he'd hoped. He had learned that trick from a beggar in the Bowery who faked a bloody handkerchief to drum up sympathy and increase donations.

The silver-haired counterfeiter was the first to exit the Jefferson House. He crossed Franklin and headed south away from the lake. The brothers followed a few moments later, but they turned north. Sinclair stepped out next. He lit a pipe and stood on the corner waiting. There was no sign of Vance or the Walrus, but they might be enjoying the hotel's bar and billiards room.

A minute later, Sinclair's carriage driver pulled alongside the Fourth Street entrance facing west. Sinclair climbed in. If the carriage continued west on Fourth Street, Bradley would know Sinclair was heading back to the Lake View, and then Bradley could try to catch up with the portly headmaster. Sinclair's carriage turned right on Franklin and then right again, heading east on Third Street. Bradley considered his options, then started running east on Fourth Street. He needed to reach the next intersection in time to see which way Sinclair's carriage turned. He needn't have hurried as the carriage turned right, coming back toward him. Bradley ducked his head as the carriage reached Fourth Street again and turned left. The driver immediately pulled over adjacent to Lafayette Square, a village park that filled the block. Sinclair stepped down from his carriage and entered the park. *An odd location for a meeting on a dark night*, thought Bradley.

The park had two paths that crossed diagonally from the corners. In the middle was a small bandstand. Trees filled the space, and Bradley lost sight of Sinclair in the darkness.

Bradley stayed off the path but moved as quickly as he could in the darkness. When he saw two dark figures standing near the bandstand, he dropped to his stomach in the shadows to watch. He was too far away to make out what they were saying, but from appearances, Sinclair was having a lively conversation with an acquaintance a few inches shorter than he was.

The conversation ended abruptly. Sinclair returned as he had entered, and the shadowy man exited on the opposite side of the park. Bradley was forced to lie still to avoid revealing his presence, giving him no chance to follow either man. After Sinclair's carriage pulled away, Bradley picked himself up and began the long walk back to the Lake View. He wouldn't find a carriage to hire this late, and the walk would give him plenty of time to think.

When Bradley reached his hotel room, he slipped out of his clothes to wash up and then slipped into his new night shirt. He spent a few minutes stretching tired muscles, then, with a yawn, reached out and pulled back the bedsheets. That is when he saw the envelope on his pillow. Bradley opened the envelope, unfolded the paper, and read the note.

Someone had carefully written *Jacub Jagusiak, Cornell University.* Below were three more words hastily scrawled. *Trust no one.*

CHAPTER XXII

Up The Church Tower

Sunday, July 19, 1874

A NNIE and Glendon climbed the steps of the First Presbyterian Church on Sixth and Decatur in Watkins, entered the brick building's vestibule, and ran the gauntlet of church elders welcoming them to morning service. The vestibule, a room as wide as the church but easily crossed in a few strides, served as a coatroom and as a buffer from the outside weather. Maneuvering through the crowd, they left the vestibule behind and entered the large auditorium-like chapel.

Annie hadn't planned to attend today's service, but she had been subtly dropping hints that her grandmother was overdue to call on her friend Beatrice in Bath. Thinking it was her own idea, Nana had left yesterday and would not return until the charity fundraiser for the fire department in over a week's time. One condition of Nana leaving for Bath was Annie's promise to put a quarter into the offering plate in her absence.

Today was only the second time Annie had left the house since the death in the Glen. To her pleasant surprise, Glendon had arrived home late last night from his extended business trip, and she was happy to have his company. It also gave Annie peace of mind to know Roland waited outside. He never came into the church. Roland joked it was too late to save his soul, much to Nana's constant lament and hand-wringing.

Glendon ushered Annie to their usual seats and joined her on the long wooden church pew.

The First Presbyterian Church was a large church for a small town. The chapel, designed for 750 worshippers, was two stories tall and over one hundred feet long. Annie admired the sunlight

First Presbyterian Church, Watkins

streaming in through the six tall, ornamental stained-glass windows on either side of the building. The church was built with Watkins's future growth in mind.

Annie leaned into Glendon and whispered, "How was your business trip?"

He kept his eyes forward. "Not as productive as I had hoped. How is your investigation going?"

"I've hit a dead end," Annie said. Glendon looked relieved at her answer.

She wanted to ask him more questions, but Reverend Howe, the First Presbyterian's pastor, clasped his hands together and called out from the pulpit, "Let us pray." Reverend Howe's voice reverberated throughout the chapel.

Annie set her purse down next to her and settled in for the hour-long service. Her grandmother coped with the death of her daughter, Annie's mother, by leaning harder into religion and finding comfort in divine providence. For Annie, her parents' death had severely damaged her faith. She struggled to worship a God who heartlessly made her an orphan. If she hadn't lost her way, she could have taken comfort in God's protection, but that protection hadn't saved her parents. She embraced the phrase, "God helps those who help themselves."

Yesterday, after her grandmother left for Bath, Annie asked Roland to drive her to James Hope's art studio. Annie wanted to know more about the man she'd seen in his gallery—the man whose face had looked down on Ruth Van Etten's mangled body. Unfortunately, Mr. Hope had no information to share. The young man had been looking for an engraver but hadn't offered his name or returned since.

"Can I offer you some fatherly advice?" Hope had said, rubbing his beard. "Men who have gone through what that young man has gone through... they can be unpredictable. They can be dangerous to themselves... or others."

When she returned home, she searched her house until she found her father's derringer pocket pistol in a wooden box tucked in the back of an old armoire. Her father had taught her how to clean, load, and fire revolvers and rifles before she'd turned twelve. She remembered the comfortable feel of the derringer's curved wooden handle, the ringing in her ears after she'd pulled the trigger, and the sulfurous smell of gunpowder. Her father had said, "Small things can still pack powerful punches." A gun as small as her hand was the perfect defensive weapon to conceal in a man's coat pocket or a lady's purse.

Last night, Annie had burned through two candles sewing a pocket into the folds of the dress she now wore. The pistol fit perfectly. Annie almost felt guilty sitting in church with a loaded gun hidden in her dress, but—if someone was really trying to kill her—she was determined not to go quietly.

When the ushers passed the offering plate down her pew, Annie dropped in Nana's quarter and one of her own. Glendon generously put in a new one-dollar greenback. After the last hymn, Reverend Howe kept the congregation standing as the music faded away. He held up his hand while reciting a final prayer and then released the congregation. With the service complete, the socializing began. Mrs. Phelps, who had cooked them breakfast that morning, came over and struck up a conversation with Glendon. Mrs. Phelps had married young but lost her husband in the war. Despite her personal tragedy, she had a contagious passion for life. She dressed demurely, but the effort failed to hide her ample charms.

As Annie politely greeted those around her, she felt a tap on her shoulder.

"Miss Anderson. Annie?"

She turned and took a half second to recognize Mr. Nichols, the clerk from the Glen Mountain House. The use of her first name was a touch too familiar, and the look in his eyes made her worry that he was about to ask her on a chaperoned outing. She opted for a polite but not an encouragingly polite tone. "Hello, Mister Nichols, how are you?"

"I'm well, thank you," he said. His eyes darted left and right, and he lowered his voice conspiratorially as he leaned toward her. "Do you remember asking me if anything odd had happened at the Glen Mountain House?"

"Yes."

"Well, a family from Chicago arrived on the eleventh and had planned to stay through the summer. But after the unfortunate accident in the Glen—" He trailed off, and Annie nodded to encourage him to continue. "Well, they decided to depart early and asked us to return their travel trunks to them. We store empty trunks in the back halls of the Swiss Chalet. Well, when we checked, one of the dome-top steamer trunks had vanished. That's never happened before."

The body in the cemetery disappeared on the morning of July 12, the day after this family had arrived from Chicago. A steamer trunk was the perfect size to move a dead man.

Nichols smiled at her. "I'd say that's odd. Maybe a steamer trunk thief is on the loose here in Watkins!" He was overly excited at the prospect.

"That is very odd," Annie agreed, trying to contain her own excitement at this new clue.

"Oh, Annie?" Mrs. Phelps's interruption gave Annie a polite excuse to disengage from Mr. Nichols. He was a nice man, and she appreciated the information, but she didn't want to encourage any romantic interest in her. Mr. Nichols paused—he had hoped to extend the conversation—then nodded. "Perhaps we can discuss it more at the church social," he said before walking away.

Annie turned to Mrs. Phelps, who was standing next to Glendon. Annie told her she looked extremely lovely in her dark gray dress.

"That's so kind," said Mrs. Phelps. "Annie, I'm having a problem with my water pump at my house, and Glendon has offered to get it running again. Would you mind if I stole him away for a bit? He's so very handy."

Annie smiled. She liked Mrs. Phelps and secretly wished Glendon would stop working so hard and realize the widow Phelps would be a perfect companion for him. "Of course, keep him as long as you like," Annie said.

Glendon blushed as Mrs. Phelps grinned.

Annie paused near her pew to keep her distance from Mr. Nichols. As the crowd thinned, Annie saw Emma Magee approaching. Emma's four children were at the back of the church with George, who stood next to another family that Annie did not recognize.

There was a time when Annie happily sat with the Magee family at church, but those days were gone. Still, she liked Emma.

"Annie," Emma said, smiling warmly, "it is so good to see you. I told George the other day that we don't see enough of you."

"Emma, you look stunning. I love your earrings." Annie knew Emma's understated earrings cost a minor fortune.

Emma smiled at the compliment. "Now, I know this is last minute, but George and I want you to join us on an excursion tomorrow on that new steamer, the *Estelle*. I hear it's very lovely and there will be plenty of people to mingle with and plenty of food to eat. You could also pack your own picnic basket if you like. We leave the docks at ten in the morning. Please say you will come!"

This unexpected invitation caught Annie off guard. She no longer moved in the same social circles as the Magees. She had only gone to the Magees' charades and *tableau vivant* party as Ted Sharp's guest. Annie was tired of hiding in her house but not enough to accept a social invitation when someone might be trying to kill her. When Emma smiled at her in anticipation, Annie sighed. "Yes, of course," she said. "So nice of you to consider me."

"Wonderful! George and I miss your company. I can't wait to catch up tomorrow." She gave Annie's hands a squeeze then turned to rejoin her husband.

Annie slumped onto a pew, already regretting her acceptance.

She felt a dull ache in her heart. Had she married George's younger brother, John, she would have been a permanent member of the family and Emma's sister-in-law. Annie would have liked to have a sister. Now she was just—someone they used to know. It had been a long time since the Magees had asked Annie to join them socially. Annie was convinced George blamed her for his brother's death.

Annie looked over to the pew she had been sitting in when John first approached her. She knew this church only existed because their father, also named John Magee, had donated $50,000 for its construction. When the richest man in town wants a grand church, he gets one. It was sad when John Sr. died in 1868 before the grand opening, but workers had rushed to finish construction in time for his funeral.

Annie pushed the melancholy thoughts away and stood. The rest of the congregation had descended to the large church basement for the start of the church social. Annie was the last person left in the sanctuary. Roland would be starting to worry. As she stood and turned to the entrance, Annie's eye caught movement up in the gallery—a second-floor seating area above the vestibule. The giant man with black hair and a black grizzled beard stared down at her.

Annie froze.

As the man watched her, the frustration and anxiety of the last few days bubbled up and something inside her snapped. Annie rushed toward the church entrance. The gallery's only stairs were at the vestibule's far end. Annie dashed through the vestibule doors and turned right without slowing down. She reached the bottom steps of the stairway just as the threatening stranger reached the top step. They both stopped. Annie looked at the man's face. His expression was neutral, but she detected a hint of curiosity. Surprised perhaps that she had run toward him instead of away from him. He started to open his mouth, but she spoke first.

"Why are you following me!" Annie yelled. "Why were you in the cemetery?"

The stranger stared at her for a few seconds, then stepped forward. They were completely alone. If he reached the bottom, Annie would be at his mercy. Without thinking, she tucked her purse under her arm and grabbed her father's derringer from within her dress. She pointed it up the stairs at the man's chest. His eyes widened. He took two steps backward, then turned and disappeared back into the gallery.

Annie ran up the stairs, holding the gun and her purse in one hand and lifting her dress with the other. She took in gulps of air as she reached the top landing but kept moving forward toward the open doorway and into the gallery. Her heart thumped in her chest. The architect had designed the gallery for eight pews, two wide and four deep, with a tiered floor ensuring each row could see over the previous. She set her purse down on the first pew to free her hands for the derringer. Sunlight streamed through three beautiful stained-glass windows behind the last row of pews. There was no place for a big man to hide, but Annie carefully checked each row of pews.

On the opposite end of the gallery, Annie came to a door that was ajar. She hesitated. The stranger must have gone through that door, but what if he was waiting for her on the other side? The pistol in her hand gave her confidence—and scared her at the same time. She approached the door and kicked it, then jumped back, holding the gun ready. The door thumped open. No one was in sight.

Annie stepped through the doorway and realized she was now in the church's bell tower. This sixteen-foot by sixteen-foot room was the ringing room. A rope rose from the floor and passed through a hole in the high ceiling above her. The only light came from an arched window across from the door. Below the window, a wooden stairway climbed up to the left, turned at the corner, and continued to the landing above her.

The room was eerily silent.

"I only want to talk," Annie called out. She heard a thump above her and then more silence. As she crossed the room and started up the narrow stairs, she held the gun in a death grip in front of her.

When she reached the next level of the tower, Annie found herself in an unfinished brick room with high walls. The rope from below continued up through the room into another hole in the high ceiling. Except for the rope, the room held two wooden ladders. The shorter ladder leaned against the right wall below a large rectangular opening. Annie climbed the four rungs and cautiously peered into the hole. In the darkness, she could see the beams, joists, and rafters holding up the church's peaked roof. There was enough light to see that the large space was undisturbed. Sweat broke out along her forehead from the blast of heat trapped below the roof. Annie climbed back down and turned to the larger ladder leaning on the opposite wall. It led to a closed trapdoor in the ceiling above her. There was nowhere else the stranger could have gone. He had trapped himself in the bell chamber eighty or ninety feet above the street.

"I just want to talk," she called out again.

Muffled thumping came from above, and she could hear furtive footsteps. Had she trapped a murderer? He looked large enough and strong enough to stuff Harper Thompson's body into the missing steamer trunk and then drag it back to the Glen Mountain House. The dry spell had made the cemetery ground hard enough to prevent noticeable tracks from being left behind. Annie wondered if he was working with the man from the Glen.

Annie knew climbing the ladder and sticking her head through the trapdoor posed a significant risk for her. If she went for help, she would have to descend to the church basement, giving the man plenty of time to escape. The energy drained from her body. *I could just go home*, she thought to herself. *Pretend that no one is trying to kill me.*

Annie looked up at the trapdoor. What would she do if, after climbing up, he attacked her? Would she be able to pull the trigger to save her life? Could she shoot a man dead inside a church? She shifted the pistol to her left hand and used her dress to wipe the sweat off her palm.

"I don't want to hurt you!" she called out, shifting the pistol back to her shooting hand.

Silence.

Stay and get answers, or leave and live for another day? The temptation to run to safety pulled at her. But who did she want to be? She took a deep breath, exhaling slowly, already knowing the answer. She didn't want to be a person who spent the rest of her life afraid. Annie wanted to be a person who got answers. Steadying her nerves, she began climbing the ladder. She would only pull the trigger if he forced her to.

"I'm coming up," Annie announced. She wouldn't surprise him, so she hoped to calm him with her voice. "I noticed you in the cemetery last week. Did you know my mother?"

Annie reached the top of the ladder—her head just below the trapdoor. She paused and listened. Her ears strained, but she could hear nothing. She inhaled deeply and then pushed hard on the trapdoor with her left hand. It thumped open. Annie kept her body below the opening while trying to peer into the bell chamber. "Can we talk?" No answer. She held the pistol in her hand as she slowly pushed with her legs until her head and shoulders cleared the floor level. There was no sign of the stranger. The bell chamber was empty.

Annie looked down to make sure he hadn't somehow gotten behind her. Had she missed him? She couldn't have. She pulled herself up into the bell chamber, struggling briefly when her bustle and wide skirt caught on the edge of the opening. There was no place to hide in the bell tower. The man had disappeared.

Annie walked around the church bell. Each wall of the bell chamber held a pair of arched windows. Summer sunshine leaked through the shutters covering each window, but Annie noticed that more light came in through one of the windows that faced back toward the church's roof. Inspecting it, she saw that the shutters had been pried open. Annie pulled the shutter aside and looked down. Her mouth dropped open. Far below her, the black-bearded stranger was picking his way across the church's slate roof. The church's Romanesque architecture had given him enough hand-holds to climb down twenty feet from the bell chamber to the roof.

"Hey," Annie yelled. The man looked back briefly but offered no reply. He continued along the roof's edge, looking for a way down. Even the lowest part of the roof was thirty or forty feet above the ground. If jumping didn't kill him, it would easily break a leg. The height of the roof prevented his escape.

Annie could only watch and wait. He looked back at her as he reached the far corner of the roof. She was about to call out again when he stepped off the roof's edge and disappeared. Annie's hand flew to her mouth. Had he just jumped to his death?

Annie scrambled back down through the trapdoor, climbed down the ladder, and sped down the bell tower stairs. She crossed the gallery, grabbing her purse as she passed, and reached the top of the staircase. As she descended to the vestibule, she tucked the gun back into her dress pocket and pushed through the front doors. She nearly collided with Roland, who had come looking for her. "Follow me," she called over her shoulder as she kept moving. She reached the sidewalk, turned right, and rounded the corner of the building. She ran along the northern wall of the church, expect-ing to see another dead body or at least a broken one. Instead, she found scaffolding left by workers who had been doing maintenance on the projecting corners of the roof. The stranger had dropped onto the scaffolding, climbed to the ground, and disappeared before Annie arrived.

She stopped and reached into her dress pocket to feel the comforting weight of her pistol. Were there now two men who wanted her dead?

WINTER CAMP

CHAPTER XXIII

FACING THE FIRING SQUAD

From the Journal of Private H. Thompson

April 7, 1864 – Our days started and ended with the sound of military drummers. In between, each day was filled with drilling, marching, weapons cleaning, inspections, camp upkeep, and more drilling. Occasionally, we got guard duty. This afternoon, we gathered firewood.

I watched Frank roll his broad shoulders, lift his ax, and swing it effortlessly. The thunk, thunk of his blows echoed through the woods as Ace, Buck, and I gathered the loose firewood he generated. We all worried about Fish's desertion but had no choice but to settle back into camp life.

Fish hadn't been the only soldier to disappear from camp without permission during the chilly winter months. A few had had enough of frostbitten toes. Some were losing faith that the South would eventually win this war. Others just ached for their families back home. I knew Fish was in the last category, but Buck had a different opinion. Buck was convinced that Fish would steal the gold for himself. As we started back to camp with our firewood, Buck argued, "Fish has all the time in the world to get back to that cave, take those satchels, and disappear a rich man."

Ace spoke up. "If Fish does recover the gold, it will be to protect it for us."

I was convinced Fish's desertion had little to do with the gold. "Seeing his mother and sister alone and struggling on the farm was too much for Fish," I said. "Especially with his brothers dead. Fish will be working on the farm, ignoring the gold."

Frank, as usual, kept his opinion to himself.

As we returned to camp, the smoky haze from hundreds of campfires hung over our makeshift city of white canvas tents and wooden huts. The thick smoke assaulted our eyes and noses. Camp life was dismal. Many men were sick, food was scarce, and water quality was questionable. We made the most of each other's company in the cramped log huts that sheltered us through the winter.

"Y'all are being naïve if you think Fish isn't goin' to take the gold," Buck said.

I was tired of Buck's lack of faith in Fish's intentions. "Buck, do you think he'd steal the gold because that is what you would do? Take the money and cheat the rest of us?" The words came out harsher than intended, and I immediately regretted saying them. Buck's face turned red. He glared at me and opened his mouth to reply but restrained himself. He turned and stomped off on his own. Frank looked disappointed and just shook his head. Fighting among ourselves would help no one. He followed after Buck.

Ace offered me a halfhearted smile and clapped me on the back. "Well, ya ain't wrong."

April 18, 1864 – I saw the first buds of spring on the trees and shrubs around camp today. We all welcomed warmer weather even if it meant our winter rest from battle was ending. Growing rumors circulated about moving camp, but no orders had come down. Today was warmer than most, and the sunshine gave me a burst of optimism. "Today is going to be a great day," I announced as the drummers called us to formation midmorning. I was wrong.

Taylor's sergeant duties had kept him busy, and we hadn't seen much of him. I tried to catch his eye as I found my place in the formation, but he looked straight ahead. We marched a short distance to an open field. In the distance, a red-tailed hawk floated lazily on the breeze. Across the field but in clear view of the division stood three men. I could hear hushed whispers. "Deserters." Across the field, the three men each stood next to a stake. I heard Ace's groan the same moment I saw Fish. The wayward member of the Lucky Six was the third man on our right. Fish stood in a dirty uniform before the division, looking small and unwell. Wherever he had been hiding before capture, he had not been eating well. He had lost so much weight that his baggy uniform made him look like a young boy dressed up as a soldier.

Fish's eyes found me across the distance, and he offered a brave smile.

In the past, captured and convicted deserters received a flogging or—in some cases—had the letter "D" branded on their hip. Too many lashes during a flogging could be life-threatening—Confederate rules allowed for up to thirty-nine—but Fish was young, and I was confident he would survive either punishment. At least he was safe and would rejoin our unit after he recovered. And then I noticed what rested behind each man as a sergeant tied the deserter to their stakes.

My heart dropped in my chest. I stole a glance at Taylor, who continued to stare straight ahead.

Behind each man was a wooden coffin, and next to each coffin, a hole dug into the dirt. There'd be no flogging today. I would learn the details later, but a squad of twelve soldiers and one officer formed before each condemned man. The officer gave each member of the squad a rifle. Eleven contained powder and lead ball. One only powder. None of the men knew which rifle wasn't loaded.

Fish did not break eye contact with the rest of the Lucky Six until an officer blindfolded him. The officer returned to stand behind his men and began calling out the commands.

"Ready." This was all happening too fast. "Aim." I silently screamed to the heavens, begging God to spare Fish. "Fire." God was not listening. The eerie calm shattered, and three bodies slumped against their stakes. They died instantly. As the echoes from the shots faded away with the clouds of smoke from the gunpowder, our leaders marched the division forward past the dead men so that every soldier could witness a deserter's fate.

Last summer, Fish had convinced the Lucky Six to get matching tattoos. Only Frank had abstained. Fish had thought up the design idea and asked me to draw a picture as a reference for the traveling tattoo artist. The tattooist charged us a week's wages each. We all chose different locations for our tattoos. Fish proudly chose his left chest—over his heart—for his tattoo.

Eight lead balls passed through Fish and his Lucky Six tattoo. The Lucky Six's good fortune died with Fish that day.

April 23, 1864 – Taylor lost his sergeant stripes. He never shared the details, but I'm convinced he had fought so hard to spare Fish's life that the command demoted Taylor back to corporal for not accepting their decision. Too many desertions meant an example had to be made, and Fish had been in the wrong place at the wrong time.

The five surviving members of the Lucky Six continued to soldier on with the utmost military professionalism, but internally, we all grieved. I grieved for the loss of Fish, and I grieved for the loss of our unfounded belief that we were invincible. That our luck was an armor that protected us during this grueling, unforgiving war.

On Saturday, after final formation, we decided to head to the Georgia brigade's area for a friendly poker game to blow off some steam. As Ace, Buck, and Frank prepared to leave, Taylor pulled me aside to ask for my help. I told the others I would find them in an hour or two.

Taylor was apologetic. "I have to collect Fish's belongings and return them to his mother," he said. "You were closest to him—"

Of course I agreed to help. I led Taylor to Fish's sleeping area. It had been untouched since his desertion. Taylor let me do the sorting. He pulled out a harmonica from his jacket pocket and played softly, distractedly. I recognized "Dixie and the Bonnie Blue Flag" as I collected Fish's worldly possessions.

Fish had owned a tin cup for coffee and a metal plate with a knife, a fork, and a spoon. He had one small frying pan and an old canteen. There were several letters from his mother and sister wrapped in twine. On the top of the wooden stockade by his bed, I pulled out the dime novel Fish had been reading when we left on furlough—Nathan Todd; or, The Fate of the Sioux' Captive. Fish had been wearing most of the clothes he owned when executed, but I found an extra set of flannel long johns and two pairs of wool socks his mother had knitted for him.

Taylor told me to keep the socks. "His mother would want them to go to someone who needed them."

I carefully packed the rest of Fish's belongings. Everything he owned that was worth keeping fit inside his haversack. When the job was done, Taylor and I sat in silence. I thought he wanted to say something, but when he didn't, I cleared my throat. "Taylor, Fish's death wasn't your fault." He looked at me with a sad smile. I know he blamed himself for dragging us all to Hickory Nut Gap in search of the gold. I blamed myself for not doing a better job listening to Fish that last night he was in camp. "In the end," I said, "Fish made the decision to leave."

Taylor reached deep into his trouser pockets and pulled out an object. He held it in his closed fist. "I talked to Fish the night before the execution," Taylor said. "He hadn't gotten more than three miles from camp. He had been hiding in a hayloft when they captured him. And then he gave me this." Taylor opened his hand, palm upward, and revealed a gold nugget. "He had been hiding this in the toe of his boot. He said he was sorry for taking it out of the cave."

It was the gold nugget I had seen in Fish's hand the night he ran away. I told Taylor to keep it in memory of Fish. "When this war is over," I said, "we can reunite it with the rest of the gold." Taylor smiled for the first time that night. He tucked the gold nugget back into his jacket pocket, and we sat together, telling Fish stories until Buck burst into the tent, yelling that Frank had gone berserk.

Taylor quickly got the story out of Buck. After Ace, Buck, and Frank found some Georgia boys to play poker with, Frank started in on the whiskey as the first hand was dealt. He had taken four or five pulls from the bottle when one of those stupid goober-grabbers mouthed off. Said deserters deserved getting iron balls through the heart. Frank sucker-punched the man, knocking him out like he was swatting a fly. Then the man's friends jumped in. Frank had the whole lot unconscious on the ground before Ace or Buck could even stand up. Now Frank refused to leave, insisting he couldn't take their money until after he'd won it fairly. "He is just sitting in their hut," Buck said, "shuffling his deck of cards and waiting for them to wake up."

Taylor and I raced after Buck as he led us through rows of tents until we arrived out of breath at the Georgia brigade area. I had never seen Frank drink before. Ace met us near the door of a four-man hut. "He's inside," Ace said. "I can't get him out." Taylor ducked to enter the hut while Ace, Buck, and I followed behind.

Frank registered our presence with a slight shift of his eyes in the dimly lit interior. It felt like we were entering a bear's den without knowing how hungry the bear was. Frank continued shuffling cards and ignoring the unconscious men on the floor. I was relieved that each of them was still breathing.

"Have you come to join our poker game?" Frank said. This was not the gentle giant I had known for the last few years. Frank's *eyes were black and lifeless. And he had already said more words in the last few seconds than I had heard him utter in the last month.*

Taylor realized the potential for dire consequences—especially if more Georgia infantrymen appeared. "Frank," Taylor said. "It's time to leave." Taylor reached out to grab Frank's arm to help him to his feet. Frank threw a punch at Taylor's face, shocking us. Taylor tried to spin away, but the punch caught him on the chin, and his knees buckled. To his credit, he did not go down. Taylor responded with a punch that snapped Frank's head back. I thought all hell was about to break loose, but to my surprise, Frank reached up, felt his chin, and then turned to face Taylor as if seeing him for the first time. Taylor again told Frank it was time to leave. Frank nodded. Without another word, he followed us out of the hut and back to our camp.

CHAPTER XXIV

PLAYING CROQUET

Sunday, July 19, 1874

THE red wooden ball rolled across the manicured lawn and clunked against the side of an iron hoop set in the ground. Henry groaned. "Aww... I missed." He looked up to the puffy white clouds and the perfect blue sky and let out a heartfelt swearword under his breath. It was perfectly articulated for a sailor surrounded by his shipmates, but not appropriate for an eight-year-old playing croquet with his family.

Bradley covered his mouth to stifle a laugh. Elizabeth wasn't pleased with her son.

"Henry!" she yelled.

Henry's eyes widened as he realized that the fury and disappointment in his mother's voice meant he had miscalculated his word choice.

Elizabeth bent down and spoke firmly and menacingly inches away from Henry's face. "Where did you hear that word!?"

Henry looked to Bradley and then at the Walrus, but neither man wanted any part of Elizabeth Sinclair's righteous indignation. Even Nanny Kate had backed away, straining to recall if she had ever accidentally let that word slip out of her mouth while watching the twins. Henry was on his own for this one. He finally met his mother's gaze and offered a meek reply. "From father?"

Elizabeth's body stiffened slightly. "Well, that is a conversation we will have this evening. Now, you are a young gentleman, and I expect you to behave like one."

"Yes, Mother."

Elizabeth straightened his cap and brushed imaginary lint off his jacket. "Make sure you follow through next time you strike the

PLAYING CROQUET

ball," she said quietly. "It will go straighter for you."

"My turn!" called out Hannah. Henry's twin sister confidently swung her wooden mallet, sending her blue ball into his red one, earning her two bonus strokes. Henry groaned. Bradley turned away to hide his smile, knowing the boy's new swear word was still dangling on the tip of his tongue.

A family game of croquet had been Elizabeth's idea, but Alistair Sinclair had begged off at the last minute, claiming he had work to do. After lunch, the rest of the family had set out across the cemetery and down through Watkins Glen to the Glen Bazaar's Croquet Grounds at the Glen's lower entrance.

Bradley's job required him to join Elizabeth and the twins, but he looked forward to tracking Alistair again after hours. Last night's eavesdropping had been a success, confirming the existence of the counterfeiting ring.

When it was Elizabeth's turn to swing her croquet mallet, she did so with the style and finesse expected of a wealthy socialite. She also cleared multiple hoops to the applause of several bystanders who had gathered to watch from the edges of the field. Elizabeth motioned for Nanny Kate to take the next turn.

Bradley wondered how much Elizabeth Sinclair knew about her husband's activities. She seemed much too intelligent to be a naïve spouse. But it wasn't uncommon for husbands to keep even the most intelligent of wives in the dark about the family's finances. After all, Elizabeth would have her hands full in New York, running the household, managing the servants, raising the children, planning and attending galas, and, no doubt, participating in multiple charitable causes. Bradley wondered if she had been the source of last night's note.

"Your turn," said Henry, tugging on Bradley's sleeve to get his attention.

"What?" Bradley pretended to be startled. "What game are we playing again? Ground billiards, is it?" He pretended his croquet mallet was a billiards cue and poked the air in front of him several times.

"Croquet!" Henry laughed but then became serious. "And the women are winning."

Bradley nodded in understanding at the dire circumstances the men now found themselves in. "I'll do my best."

Bradley cleared two hoops, earning a nod from Elizabeth. He tipped his hat to her in return. When he was Henry's age, he had played a lot of croquet with his mother and brother. Luckily, he hadn't lost all his skills with a croquet mallet.

As Bradley stepped aside for the next player, he sensed someone watching him. He spun around in a circle. There were groups of people nearby, but no one looked suspicious.

The Walrus was the last to take a turn. Bradley had been surprised when the big man agreed to play. Vance or the Walrus attended every family outing—watching silently but never participating. Both spent too much time watching the family and too little time scanning for external threats to be good bodyguards. Something had thawed in the Walrus's standoffishness. Something that became obvious when the man stole a glance in Nanny Kate's direction before swinging his mallet. The Walrus had taken a liking to the nanny! Bradley smiled to himself and wondered if this new information could help him. Perhaps the Walrus would prove to be the weak link in the counterfeiting gang.

Bradley considered what he knew. The counterfeiters had found a way to acquire the perfect ink for printing, but they still needed the plates and the right paper. Fiber paper used for currency was nearly impossible to reproduce outside government-contracted printing houses. The gang also needed industrial printing presses. Setting up a professional printing operation would require space and privacy. Bradley needed to find either the silver-haired counterfeiter or one of the brothers from last night to tail. If Bradley could find the gang's hideout, he could wait until they printed up batches of counterfeit money. Then, with some boldness, he could see his way to a successful outcome even without joining the gang.

The Walrus's mallet strike sent his ball careening away from any of the wire hoops.

Nanny Kate stifled a laugh with her hand. "A bit awkward, that one," she said under her breath with a touch of sympathy in her voice.

Elizabeth won the croquet match, but she made sure everyone

enjoyed the outing. After returning the balls and mallets, Elizabeth gathered their group on the edge of the croquet lawn. "Who wants pastries?" she asked.

The twins jumped up and down, shouting in unison. "I do, I do."

"Excellent," Elizabeth said. "The Glen Park Hotel has a pastry chef up from New York, and it is only a few blocks away. I believe we have all earned refreshments."

They walked in pairs toward the luxury hotel. The twins first, followed by Nanny Kate and the Walrus. That left Bradley with Elizabeth. She unfolded a delicate parasol to shade herself from the sun. Bradley offered her his arm as they crossed Franklin Street, which she accepted.

"You surprised me with your croquet skills," she said.

Bradley laughed. "I was still no match for you." As they reached the far sidewalk, he guided her to his left, placing himself between Elizabeth and the street. It was a gentlemanly act he had done without thinking. To his surprise, she reached for his arm again as they continued walking.

"You're a man of surprising talents for one so young."

Blood rushed to his cheeks, and he was at a loss for words. They walked in comfortable silence for a block before Bradley trusted his voice. "If I may ask, why did Mister Sinclair hire me? Your twins are lovely, but your husband would find me very useful in his other business ventures."

"Bradley, Alistair wasn't the one who hired you. I did." Elizabeth laughed softly, but there was no humor in the sound. She gripped his arm tighter. "My husband has his own distractions at the moment."

"I'm not sure I understand," Bradley said. He noticed her intimate use of his first name.

"I could tell you I hired you for your kite retrieval skills," she said. "Henry couldn't stop talking about how you climbed that tree, and I find children and animals to be good judges of character. Or I could tell you that knowing the Walt Whitman poem convinced me you were educated. But neither is the reason. Do you remember what you told me about your loyalty?"

"That I'm loyal to whoever is paying me."

Elizabeth smiled but squeezed his arm tighter and stared into his eyes as if extracting a promise. "When the time comes, remember that I'm the one who is paying you, and I'll be counting on your loyalty." She let go of his arm and raised her voice. "Ah, here we are, the Glen Park Hotel. Time for pastries." Elizabeth stepped ahead quickly to catch up with her children in front of the hotel.

The spot on his arm she'd been holding turned cold in her absence.

The Glen Park Hotel was a four-story brick building that stretched the length of the block between Twelfth and Thirteenth Streets. Like the Lake View, it catered to wealthy vacationers and attracted them with a restaurant, laundry, barroom, barber shop, pastry shop, and its own magnetic springs spa.

"Let's stay together, children," Elizabeth said as she guided them through flower-filled landscaping, past a fountain, and up the stairs and into the hotel. Bradley hadn't been inside many fancy hotels, but the word elegant came to mind.

Elizabeth requested an introduction with the pastry chef, and proceeded to ask him questions about his craft while listening with wide-eyed enthusiasm to his answers and adding a few subtle touches to his arm. It did not take Elizabeth long to charm the entire hotel staff and make best friends with the pastry chef. Soon, delicious pastries arrived with tea and coffee for the adults and lemonade for the children. The twins happily munched on jelly-filled pastries as Elizabeth chatted animatedly with her new friend about life in the city. Bradley stared in her direction without staring at her. She was a rare beauty, but he most admired her joy of life that came out in moments like these. Alistair was a lucky man.

Bradley was replaying their earlier conversation in his mind when he heard a startling sound directly behind him. He turned slightly. The odd sound was the Walrus laughing at something Nanny Kate had said. Bradley had no idea the man had a sense of humor.

An hour later, Bradley was in front of the hotel with the Walrus waiting by a carriage as the women took the twins to the water closet. Hoping to capitalize on the Walrus's good mood, Bradley tried to strike up a conversation.

"It was a lovely afternoon, wasn't it?"

The Walrus offered only a noncommittal grunt.

"The nanny is a lovely woman," Bradley offered. The Walrus ignored him. "I thought she enjoyed your conversation." Something hopeful flashed across the Walrus's face but disappeared quickly as the man eyed Bradley suspiciously.

"Who are you really," the Walrus said.

"What do you mean?"

"You dress like a gentleman, but you're something else. I never met a gentleman who could get the drop on Vance as you did."

Before Bradley could respond, he noticed the women and children descending the front stairs of the hotel.

"Watch out for that one," said the Walrus, following Bradley's eyes.

Bradley turned toward the Walrus, surprised. "What?"

"I see the way you look at her."

For the second time that day, blood rushed to Bradley's cheeks. The Walrus was talking about Elizabeth.

"Last night, when Vance and I came back from dinner and drinks, I saw her sneaking back into the hotel. No proper lady should be out alone that late at night. Rumors are she prefers younger men, so maybe you have a chance."

Bradley had no reply.

The Walrus shook his head. "But you can't trust her." He looked at Bradley and then looked away. "You can't trust anyone."

The words startled Bradley. They were very close to what had been written on the note left in his room. *Trust no one.* Bradley waited for him to say more, but Walrus's face drifted back to its neutral, slightly vacant expression.

It was a quick carriage ride from the Glen Park Hotel across town and up the hill to Lake View.

Bradley helped Elizabeth down from the carriage. With barely a nod in his direction, she walked toward the hotel's entrance. At the last moment, she turned back to him. "Tomorrow," she said, "we have a picnic excursion scheduled, so be ready to leave at nine. Henry tells me you promised him a story about river pirates. Nothing too frightening, please."

"Of course," he said. "Will Mister Sinclair be joining us?"

Elizabeth smiled politely but ignored his question. She disappeared with her children and Nanny Kate into the hotel.

With Alistair nowhere to be found, Bradley discreetly followed the Walrus as the man walked back down to Franklin Street. The Walrus stopped at the Jefferson House for dinner and moved to the billiard room for drinks. When Bradley realized the big man was not leaving or meeting anyone else, he left the Jefferson and walked toward the lake.

Bradley stood on the shore as the sun went down, considering his next move. If Alistair did not attend tomorrow's family excursion, it would be another day wasted playing babysitter to the twins. He had to find a path into the counterfeiting ring or a way to find the counterfeiter's hideout. He would give it one more day, then resign from his job with Elizabeth and devote his time to following Alistair Sinclair.

As the last colors of sunset faded from the western sky, Bradley again felt the odd sensation of being watched. He spun around, but the shadows had grown long. Too many places for someone to hide. He kept his senses on alert as he trudged back up the hill to the Lake View. The hotel was quiet as he slipped through the front door and along the gaslit corridors. As Bradley neared his room, he almost bumped into Nanny Kate, heading in the opposite direction. She nodded but said nothing.

Bradley reached his room and locked the door behind him. He turned up the wick in the room's gas lantern before looking toward his bed. Another envelope waited for him. If Elizabeth had been out last night, she could not have left yesterday's envelope.

The envelope held two pieces of paper. The first was a newspaper clipping from an article dated a year earlier.

Fire at the National Bank Note Company
Washington — The investigation into the fire at the National Bank Note Company has served to strengthen suspicions that it was the work of arsonists who wished to steal either partially finished notes or the peculiar blank paper which is very difficult for counterfeiters to obtain. From

the ashes and cinders sent to Washington by the company to square their insurance claim, it is impossible to determine whether any paper is missing or not. But it is not impossible that considerable quantities of it have fallen into improper hands.

Someone wanted Bradley to know that the counterfeiters had already obtained the perfect paper source for their operation. Bradley was intrigued. He held the second piece of paper up to the light. The handwriting was the same as the day before, but the message was more ominous.

You are being watched.

WATKINS, STEAMSHIP LANDING AND TRAIN STATION

CHAPTER XXV

Steam Yacht *Estelle*

Monday, July 20, 1874

ANNIE gazed out on the blue waters of Seneca Lake as the sun warmed her face and chased away the last of the morning mist. It was a beautiful day for a steamboat excursion. The steamboat landing where she stood was just past the train station, making it convenient for travelers needing to arrange connections. Annie set her picnic basket at her feet and turned to Roland, who had escorted her to the water's edge.

"Thank you for the ride and the company."

"My pleasure." Roland looked stylish in his flat straw boater hat and impeccable brown suit. He had a rare ability to look fashionable and relaxed on any occasion. Annie had felt bad asking for the ride. It was hardly worth hitching the horse to the carriage for such a short trip, but Roland reassured her that he had other errands to run.

"Oh," Annie said, "I wanted to ask. Any word on your bid for George Magee's landscaping job?"

Roland shook his head but grinned at her. "No word yet, but I like my chances. It helps that the Magees like you. It makes me look good by association."

Annie wanted it to be true but gave Roland a skeptical look. "Emma is friendly, but George barely tolerates me. You will have to count on being good at your job!"

Roland laughed. "Miss Anderson, I think you underestimate yourself."

Annie glanced back toward the train station. "George and Emma should be here any minute. If you get the timing right, you can bump into them as they arrive."

"I can't possibly leave you," he said. "Plus, I don't want to appear too eager." Roland glanced back toward the station and the street. "I'm eager, of course, but I don't want to appear that way."

"Go!" Annie said. "If you can walk past them and wish them a good day, they'll be forced to think about you and your bid." When Roland hesitated, Annie grabbed his shoulders and pointed him back toward the street. "I insist!"

Roland bowed deeply to her as if accepting a curtain call at the theater. "Your wish is my command. I'll be waiting here when your ship returns. In the meantime, enjoy your excursion." Roland turned and walked off with a jaunty step. He never failed to make her smile.

Annie looked around. Many people lingered near the train station and on the nearby street, so she had chosen a spot to wait for Emma Magee away from the crowds. The incident yesterday at church had given her a boost in confidence. She had made a giant man risk his life to run away from her. As she looked around, her confidence began to erode as she realized that someone with nefarious intentions could be watching her from some hidden location. She suddenly felt exposed. There were at least two men in town who might want her dead. She was glad she'd added pockets to all her dresses, as she reached for the comfort of her derringer.

Why would someone want to kill her? Was she getting close to finding the killer? She didn't feel like she'd made much progress. She hadn't even gotten a reply from her telegram to Rutherfordton and Sadie Thompson.

Frustrated, Annie turned her mind toward her new favorite mental exercise—thinking of ways someone might try to kill her. A knife would be the thing to watch out for in a crowd. Best to stay out of crowds. Poison could be avoided if she refused to eat anything she hadn't prepared. Hence the basket she carried. A gun was always a problem, but she resolved not to be out in the open any more than she had to. She didn't think being choked in public was likely. Annie needed to avoid being alone with a strange man with strong hands. As she considered how to avoid poisoned arrows, she noticed a one-armed man approaching.

One-armed men, often survivors from the war, were not uncommon, but this one looked vaguely familiar. Something about how he had pinned his empty right sleeve to the shoulder of his jacket. Annie, standing off by herself, realized he was headed right for her. When he had gotten uncomfortably close, she held her palm outward and yelled, "Stop!" It took willpower not to draw the pistol from her dress pocket.

The man stopped ten feet away and looked about nervously. He leaned forward as if he had clandestine information to share with her. "That man you were talking to," the stranger said. "What is his name?"

"Do I know you, sir?" she replied coolly. It was poor etiquette to approach an unfamiliar lady and initiate a conversation.

"The man you were talking to. What is his NAME?"

"I don't understand, what—"

"WHAT IS HIS NAME?" The man's face contorted in anger, forcing Annie to take a step backward.

"Roland?" The name flew out of her mouth unbidden—involuntarily thrust forward to shield her from the stranger's aggression. She regretted saying Roland's name immediately.

"Roland. Roland," the man repeated, with a disturbing new gleam in his eyes. He looked at Annie, then spat on the ground in front of her. "He is not who you think he is." The one-armed man turned and walked away as fast as he had arrived.

How strange, Annie thought. And unsettling. She considered following the man and demanding an explanation, but as a rule, she avoided crazy, threatening, and volatile people who might cause her harm. She hoped it was a case of mistaken identity but would tell Roland at her first opportunity. As the man disappeared from her view, Annie caught sight of Emma and George Magee.

The village's wealthiest couple strolled arm-in-arm down the path to the steamboat landing. There was no sign of their four children—they must be home with their nanny. Emma looked more relaxed than usual. Annie picked up her picnic basket and walked toward her hosts.

A grin spread across Emma's face when she saw Annie. "Oh, I'm so glad you made it. I was just saying to George what a beautiful day it will be out on the lake."

"Thank you again for inviting me." Annie offered a graceful inclination of her head to George, who nodded and offered a half-hearted tip of his hat. He quickly excused himself to mingle with the other guests. Emma grabbed Annie's arm and led her toward the steam yacht *Estelle*, anchored at the water's edge.

Emma told Annie they expected fifty ladies and gentlemen for today's four-hour excursion. Many were employees or business associates of George's company, the Fall Brook Coal Company, headquartered in Watkins. The day's itinerary included a steamboat ride up the lake's western shore to view the ravines and glens north of Watkins and then across the lake and back down the eastern shore. At Glen Eldridge, they would enjoy a picnic lunch and then explore the stairs and walkways of this newly developed glen.

Emma paused by the boat ramp. "Will you keep me company as I welcome the guests on board?"

Guests slowly made their way to the steamer as its boiler hissed impatiently, anxious to be away and slicing through the water.

The *Estelle* had had her maiden voyage two months earlier. At seventy-six feet in length, the steamer accommodated several hundred passengers on summer excursions, but it was still less than half the size of the Seneca Lake Steam Navigation Company's other vessels, the *Onondaga*, and the *Schuyler*. Those larger steamers ferried cargo and passengers to Geneva and back six times a day, crossing from one side of the lake to the other to take on and put off passengers at each steamer landing.

Emma made small talk with each new arrival, but Annie noticed her friend continually glanced back toward the street.

"Are you waiting for someone in particular?" Annie asked.

To Annie's surprise, Emma blushed. "Now, Annie, please don't be upset with me. You know I adore you. I was so happy to see you when you came to the house for charades." Emma was now staring toward the street and smiling.

Annie followed Emma's eyes, and her heart sank. *Emma, Emma, Emma, what have you done?* Annie watched as a tall, broad man with handsome features approached them. He had the confident swagger of a young man who had seen early success in life or had grown up with money. His movements were almost feline. A stalking lion, hungry for a lone gazelle.

Emma whispered to Annie. "He is new to George's company but appears very promising. He has just moved to the area, so I thought...."

"I can't believe you didn't warn—"

"Mister Hastings," Emma greeted the new arrival. "So glad you could join us!"

"Mrs. Magee, so lovely to see you again."

Emma turned to Annie. "Miss Annie Anderson, may I introduce Mister Allen Hastings."

"A pleasure to meet you," the man said as he tipped his hat. He looked Annie up and down and then turned to his hostess. "Mrs. Magee, you were true to your word. She is as beautiful as you said she would be."

Annie blushed at Hastings's compliment but was horrified to realize her invitation came only so she could serve as a potential paramour for one of George's new employees.

"Annie grew up right here in Watkins," Emma said. "She can tell you all about the area."

Annie wanted to run away, but her new acquaintance extended his arm to her. "Shall we board and enjoy the view from the upper deck?" He grinned at her as she took his arm. Annie had to admit his teeth were magnificent.

As they boarded the steamer, Annie looked back. More guests had lined up to board the steamer. Farther away by the train station, Annie noticed Abraham standing beside his horse, Goldie. He was looking her way. Annie raised her hand in greeting as she stepped onto the steamer, but Mr. Hastings's broad figure blocked her view before she could see if Abraham waved in return.

An hour into their journey, Mr. Hastings had established himself as an impressive specimen of a man. He told Annie about his childhood in Maryland, where he had been born to loving parents and, as the eldest son, would one day inherit the family's lucrative quill pen business. His most satisfying accomplishment came as a Yale varsity rower when his side beat Harvard in the 1865 Yale-Harvard Regatta. He attributed the victory to teamwork and a willingness never to quit. He volunteered with orphans when time permitted, he loved animals, and the Fall Brook Coal Company had just hired him as their youngest executive. When he adjusted his new straw boater hat, Annie noticed how his muscles strained against the fabric of his expensive three-piece suit.

When Hastings mentioned that—with his new job—he had everything he needed in life except the right person to share it with, a single young lady might have gone weak in the knees. After all, he had given Annie his full attention for an hour to the exclusion of everyone else on the ship. He clearly had some interest in her. What he had not done, Annie noticed, was ask her a single question about herself the entire time they talked.

Annie attempted to point out the scenery as they passed— Coal Point, Rock Stream, Big Stream—but gave up when Hastings showed more interest in talking about himself than sightseeing.

Emma finally showed up, mercifully rescuing Annie from another story about Hastings's college years. By then, the *Estelle* had crossed over to the eastern shore and started its journey south toward Glen Eldridge.

"Mister Hastings," said Emma, "Mister Magee requests your company in the gentlemen's cabin. He is holding a cigar for you."

Hastings turned to Annie, grabbed her hand, and kissed it while maintaining eye contact. "Please take good care of Miss Anderson while I'm gone."

Emma waited for Hastings to leave before pulling her over to the port railing away from other guests. "Tell me, tell me," Emma said excitedly, grabbing Annie by the shoulders. "What do you think?"

Annie prided herself on her honesty, but in this case, she chose not to hurt her friend's feelings. "He seems very nice," she said, which wasn't a total lie.

"I knew you would like him," Emma said, basking in the results of her matchmaking skills. Annie held a smile on her face for as long as she could.

"Perhaps we have time for a tour of the *Estelle*?" Annie said, changing the subject.

"Of course! Let us start in the ladies' cabin so we can freshen up. Do you want to set your basket somewhere?"

"I don't mind carrying it."

They maneuvered through the crowd and down the stairs to the lower deck, where separate gentlemen's and ladies' cabins could be found. The ladies' cabin impressed Annie with its finely upholstered sofas and native black walnut furnishings. A beautiful vase of flowers adorned the center table.

"This reminds me of a Pullman parlor car," Emma said, looking around. Annie, who had never ridden in one, nodded.

A tall, elegant woman with piercing blue eyes approached them. Ever the seamstress, Annie noticed the quality fabrics and the precise tailoring of the woman's dress. A dress that would have been right at home on the cover of the latest French fashion magazines. The woman's bodice, snuggly fitted to her hips, had a daringly open neckline trimmed with ruffles and lace to preserve modesty.

Emma reached out to the woman and embraced her.

"Elizabeth," said Emma. "I'd like to introduce you to Annie Anderson. Annie, this is Mrs. Elizabeth Sinclair. Elizabeth and I have known each other since we were your age."

"Pleased to meet you." Annie recognized Mrs. Sinclair as the woman at the back of the church with her family yesterday, standing next to George Magee.

"Emma, did you notice what my children were doing?"

"I just saw them on the lower deck with your nanny," Emma said. "They'd gotten tired of looking at the shore and were playing a clapping game."

"Lovely," said Elizabeth. "They will get into mischief if not kept occupied. I have a few more minutes, then. Will you join me?" Elizabeth led them to an empty sofa, where she and Emma fell into the comfortable conversation of old friends. Annie contributed where she could, but as the talk turned to husbands and children and household finances, Annie had little to offer, and her attention drifted.

Annie considered her current situation. Unless she wanted to be the killer's next victim, she had to solve the mystery of why someone chose her mother's grave as Harper Thompson's final resting place. Thanks to Mr. Nichols's information, Annie knew

STOCK EXCHANGE DOORS BEING CLOSED IN 1873

the killer stole a steamer trunk to move the dead body after she had run for help. Perhaps using a handcart from the Glen Mountain House. A lot of guests were checking out that morning, so the killer would have been able to get away with the trunk in the confusion. But who had Harper Thompson come to Watkins to meet? Why was he killed and why did he have a gold nugget in his hand? Annie also wondered where the man's body was now and why someone wanted to harm her. Finding all those answers suddenly felt daunting.

"If George has his way," Emma said, "we will have another railroad along the western shore of Seneca Lake in a few years." Emma explained that the Fall Brook Coal Company planned to ship their Pennsylvania coal to Syracuse by railroad instead of canal barge. Canals had the misfortune of freezing over during the New York winters.

"As I'm sure you know," Emma said to Elizabeth, "raising the funds to build a railroad has become difficult after last year's stock market crash."

Annie felt the need for fresh air. "Excuse me, Mrs. Sinclair," she said. "If you'd like, I'll happily check on your children."

"I'm sure they are safe with their nanny, but it's lovely of you to offer," Elizabeth said before falling back into conversation with Emma.

Annie remembered Elizabeth's children at the back of the church standing next to George Magee and their parents. They were blond and about eight or nine years old. There were few families on the trip, so they should be easy to find. Annie searched the lower deck. She saw blond hair, but it belonged to Josephine Knapp, her former friend. When Josephine looked up, Annie nodded politely. Josephine's father worked for the Fall Brook Coal Company.

Annie climbed the stairs to the crowded upper deck. The smell of smoke, belching out of the steamer's tall smokestack, became more noticeable as she moved toward the ship's rear. She found Henry and Hannah standing near the back railing and smiling as they watched a man acting out a story. He had his back to Annie, so she could not hear his voice as he waved his arms pretending to fight imaginary enemies. Annie inched closer until she found a spot along the railing where she pretended to enjoy the scenery while eavesdropping.

"—and then the gang, a choice collection of ruffians, stole a sloop and raised the Jolly Roger flag up the mast. They sailed up and down the Hudson River—from New York City all the way to Poughkeepsie and even Albany—doing pirate things."

"What are pirate things?" Henry interrupted.

"Well," the man hesitated for a moment. "Well, these river pirates stole money and jewelry from mansions. They kidnapped people and held them until the families paid ransom. And they used their sailboat to silently swoop in on other boats and board them to steal all the loot. They even made men walk the plank."

"Did they drown?" Hannah said, eyes big with concern.

"Oh, well, no. I'm sure they had nice swims to shore," the man said. Hannah was relieved.

Annie hadn't seen the man's face but noticed that his fashionable clothing looked newly purchased. He was tall, although not as tall as Hastings. He looked more like a college athlete than Hastings had. There was something familiar about him.

"And their leader's name was Sadie, the Goat."

"Their leader was a goat?" Henry asked, confused.

"Their leader was a woman who had the nickname 'the Goat.'"

"Bradley, why did they call her a goat?" Hannah asked.

"I'm glad you asked!" the man said. "They called her 'the Goat' because when she saw a rich man that she wanted to rob, she would duck her head and butt him in the stomach." The man made a bleating sound and pretended to butt the children with his head which made them giggle uncontrollably.

Their giggling was contagious and caused a small laugh to escape Annie's lips before she could cover her mouth. Hannah noticed Annie laughing and grinned at her. Bradley followed Hannah's eyes and turned around.

Annie locked eyes with Bradley. Her blood ran cold. It had been his face Annie saw at the top of the Glen after Ruth Van Etten plunged to her death.

Annie saw Bradley's eyes widen. *He knows I'm not dead now,* she realized. Bradley's shocked expression suddenly turned into a look of anger. Annie shuddered and reached into her dress pocket but hesitated when she heard another man's voice in her ear.

"Hello, Miss Anderson, we meet again."

Backed against the boat's railing, Annie had little room to maneuver, but she turned toward this new voice. It was the man with the blond goatee who had offered her a ride in his carriage. The new man stepped between Annie and Bradley. He looked concerned when he noticed the panic in Annie's eyes. "I'm sorry if I startled you. My name is Maurice Vance, and I work with Mrs. Sinclair's husband, Alistair. I heard you asked for a tour of the ship, and I wanted to volunteer my services."

Before Annie could reply, a large muscular body casually brushed Mr. Vance aside and took Annie by the arm. "There you are, Miss Anderson," said Allen Hastings. His breath smelled of cigars and whiskey. She offered no resistance as Hastings whisked her away toward the front of the Estelle. She could feel the other men's eyes watching her as she and Hastings walked away.

CHAPTER XXVI

BATTLE OF THE WILDERNESS

From the Journal of Private H. Thompson

May 1, 1864 – Rumors had been flying for weeks that hard fighting was ahead. When the generals' wives began leaving their winter quarters, we knew another battle was in our near future.

Frank had managed to avoid a formal court-martial after his drunken altercation with the Georgia soldiers, but he still suffered consequences. The first sergeant kept a list of recent offenders and assigned them unpleasant tasks as they came up. Frank spent many additional hours digging or filling up latrines, burying dead horses, and cleaning up after the company cooks. He shouldered his punishment without complaint. I never even saw him look tired. If anything, the extra work made him stronger.

I spent the evening sorting through my possessions by the light of a candle. I judged each item as to whether it deserved to be carried into battle. More than once, I glanced at Fish's abandoned bedroll. Going to battle without him—were we now the Lucky Five?—felt wrong.

May 4, 1864 – Our marching orders came this morning. Last night, the Union Army broke camp and crossed the Rapidan River using pontoon bridges. For five months, the Union Army's winter headquarters lay a mere twenty miles away across the shallow Rapidan from Lee's Army of Northern Virginia. Lookouts reported the blue-bellies headed east, trying to flank us. We broke camp and headed in the same direction to cut them off near Chancellorsville.

The veterans in our regiment had learned—from experience—to carry the bare minimum. The new recruits had overpacked and could be seen falling out of ranks to lighten their load. After the first few miles, abandoned items—extra blankets and clothes, over-

coats, tents—littered the side of the road.

May 5, 1864 – By midday, we were twenty-five miles from Orange Courthouse, traveling along the Orange Plank Road toward Chancellorsville and entering the Wilderness—seventy square miles of dense woods and thickets. It was a perfect spring day in Virginia with crystal clear skies. The trees surrounding us were bursting with light green leaves. I walked next to Frank. Ace and Buck marched just ahead of us. Taylor followed behind. After so many years together, I could pick out the other members of the Lucky Six from a great distance just by the way they walked. Taylor walked stiffly but with confidence. Buck walked with purpose and a slight side-to-side wobble. Ace had his own swagger. Frank, well, he was just impossible to miss because of his size. Fish, when he was alive, had bounced more than he walked through life.

Several new recruits flinched when they heard the first boom of distant cannon fire. We marched deeper into the Wilderness as the sounds of battle drifted out of the dark forest to our left. The enemy was nearby. Even as a veteran, I had to fight back feelings of paranoia. To a man, we would rather face the enemy in battle than wonder and worry about where old Billy Yank was hiding. We continued east along the Orange Plank Road until orders came to spread out.

Both sides of the road were heavily forested with impenetrable undergrowth. "At least we won't have to worry about Union artillery in there," Taylor said. The lack of visibility neutralized the Union's greater numbers of men and artillery.

Officers ordered our regiment into the dense forest to the right of the plank road. We pushed through the shrubbery, maneuvered around scrubby oaks and low-limbed, haggard pines, stepped over old logs, and tried not to trip on the grapevines that grabbed for our boots. An annoying pebble had worked its way into my right boot, but I could not afford to stop and remove it. We moved forward as quietly as possible, feeling for the enemy. All talking stopped. Attackers who moved blindly and noisily became easy targets for concealed defenders.

When the first shots rang out, our officers ordered the sharpshooters to the front. With British-made Enfield rifles, sharpshooters—the best shots in the brigade—can kill men five hundred yards

Battle of the Wilderness

away. The average soldier was lucky to kill a man at fifty yards. The restricted visibility worked against us today. Sight lines were less than fifty yards. Our regiment formed in line, advancing toward the enemy with a full-throated rebel yell.

Attacks and counterattacks raged through the woods until dusk. When the gloom of night descended, the chatter of gunfire trailed off. After a few moments of silence, I heard the chirping of whippoorwills echo through the woods, mixing with the moans of the wounded. We'd fought to a bloody stalemate, holding position against a larger opposing force. Neither side had gained an advantage, but the casualty rate had been high for both Rebels and Yankees.

I collapsed where I had been fighting, prepared to sleep with my rifle at the ready. Our brigade stretched out in ragged lines sprawled through the woods. When I was sure there would be no more attacks coming, I yanked off my boot and removed that damn pebble. Ace, on my left, rolled onto his back and pulled food out of his haversack. He whispered quietly in the darkness, asking if I had any water. I shared what I had in my canteen.

We were silent for a time. Then Ace cleared his throat. "Harper," he said. "I got a letter from my girl before we left." I knew he'd left a sweetheart behind when the war started. "She's pregnant. I'm going to be a father."

I was shocked but congratulated him. He'd been busy during our furlough.

"She wanted to get married while I was home," he said, "but I left early to join the search for the gold. 'Course, I didn't know I'd gotten her pregnant." When he next spoke, it sounded like he was sending a prayer to the heavens. "I hope this war ends before she has the baby. I hope I live to marry her and make her an honest woman."

I thought he'd be a great father and told him so.

"Do you really think so?"

"Why not?"

"Yeah." Ace laughed softly. "Why not?"

I put my boot back on and lay in darkness, thinking of the past. "Ace," I said. "I want to tell you something."

"I won't stop you."

"Ten years ago... when I was sixteen... I met the love of my life. It was summertime and we were inseparable. Soon enough, we were sneaking off together to be alone. We couldn't keep our hands off each other, and by autumn, she was pregnant." Ace let out a low whistle but waited for me to continue. "I loved her. I went to her father for his approval to marry her."

"And?"

"Well, he didn't say no... He said hell no." Years later, the rejection still stung. "Said I wasn't good enough for his daughter. He saw a worthless farmhand with no family and no prospects, and from that moment on, he told me to stay away from his daughter. Two days later, her family moved back North, where they had relatives. I found out later they married her off to an older man."

Ace shook his head but said nothing.

"A year later, I got a letter from her. She wanted me to know our baby was healthy but told me we could never see each other again. Out of respect for her husband." The tightness returned to my chest, remembering the first time I'd read those words. "I think her parents made her say those things. After we return to that cave and claim our gold, I intend to find her and convince her to run away with me. I know she still loves me."

"How do you know?"

I reached into my haversack and pulled out a small gold picture frame wrapped in oilcloth. I gently unwrapped the oilcloth to show Ace. "She sent me this picture ten years ago to remember her by. And she named our child after my father."

May 6, 1864 – The Union attack came at dawn, catching us by surprise. An overwhelming number of Yankees rushed through the woods toward us. Our lines crumbled. I heard Taylor call for us to fall back as he fired another shot. Many soldiers along our line had already turned tail and ran, but we backed away, firing as fast as we could.

Our Confederate side was headed for a crushing defeat until Lieutenant General James Longstreet's First Corps surged down Plank Road, providing fresh Confederate troops and reinspiring those already in the battle. Our officers reformed our lines, and we fought through the morning. By noon, the Confederate Army was on the offensive, crushing the Union left flank. Our momentum might have carried the day, but word came that Longstreet had fallen, and the offensive lost steam.

General Lee called for another Confederate attack in the late afternoon, and the battle raged until nightfall. By the time we fell back, our regiment was scattered throughout the forest. Despite the confusion, the five of us—the Lucky Six survivors—stayed together throughout the battle.

We were the only Confederate soldiers in sight as we retreated through a hellscape. The woods were saturated in blood. Thousands lay dead on both sides. The moans and cries of the wounded echoed across the battlefield. As we dodged the last of the Union gunfire, we had to maneuver around small fires sparked to life from the many rifles shot in dry underbrush.

When we finally stopped to catch our breath and get our bearings, Frank looked back and then turned to the rest of us. "Taylor?" he asked. We looked around, but there were only four of us now.

"He was right behind me when we crossed the last ridge," Buck said.

The four of us looked back at the way we had come. Darkness had descended, and the glow of spreading fires began filling the woods. We all knew the rules. It was strictly forbidden for anyone other than the ambulance corps to remove the dead or wounded from the field of battle. Even if wounded friends cried out for water or, worse, for someone to kill them and end their pain. Wounded soldiers stuck between the lines were often left to die or become prisoners.

I didn't care. I was determined to go back for Taylor.

Buck spoke first. "He's probably dead already," he said, refusing to look me in the eyes.

"But he might not be," I said. Buck had made his position clear. I looked at Ace and remembered that he was deathly afraid of fire. I turned to Frank. "Frank, are you with me?"

Frank nodded. I turned to Ace and Buck. "Stay here. Wait for us. We will be back."

Ace grabbed me by the shoulder. "I won't leave without you," he said.

Frank and I ran back through the woods. The fire had spread and was raging around us. We crossed the ridge and pushed our way through the forest looking for Taylor. Frank spotted him first. Taylor, his left pant leg soaked in blood, had propped himself up against a shattered, bullet-riddled tree trunk. His face was blackened by gunpowder and smoke. He held his cocked rifle by his side and his ramrod in his hand. His eyes had been on the approaching fire. His intentions were clear. He would shoot himself before allowing the fire to burn him alive.

When we reached him, he looked at us first in confusion and then in naked relief. I grabbed his rifle and equipment while Frank got him to his feet. We half-carried and half-dragged Taylor across the ridge and then rushed back to Buck and Ace as the crackling fires chased after us.

Ace was true to his word. He and Buck stayed where we left them. When we came into sight, they ran to help support Taylor. Disoriented by the darkness and the smoke, the five of us ran from the growing inferno. We crashed through the underbrush, fighting exhaustion as we tried to reach safety. As we broke into a clearing, we found ourselves free from the fires but surrounded by Union soldiers. We had run the wrong way.

We laid down our rifles, too tired and too outnumbered to put up a fight. We were now prisoners of war.

CHAPTER XXVII

GLEN ELDRIDGE

Monday, July 20, 1874

HENRY threw the rock as hard as he could then watched it disappear into Seneca Lake's calm waters. Only two skips. "Good sidearm throw," Bradley said, "but remember to flick your wrist and give it more spin as you release." He handed Henry another flat stone. This one had a bit more weight to it. Henry held it in his hand to get a feel for it, then let it fly. They counted the skips together.

"One, two, three, four, FIVE!"

"That was my best one yet!" Henry said, beaming.

Henry had been the first to eat his fill of the Glen Eldridge picnic lunch that included ham, buttered biscuits, fresh fruit, and, for the thirsty, ice water, lemonade, or pure grape juice. Unlike his sister, who sat quietly enjoying her biscuits, Henry was full of pent-up energy after two hours on the steamer.

"Mom, can I go exploring by the shore?" he asked for the third time.

Elizabeth was engaged in a lively debate with a group of guests on the shortcomings of the Grant administration and which Western territory would become the country's 38th state. Most argued for Colorado, but the Dakota Territory had several supporters thanks to the recent discovery of gold in the Black Hills. Alistair had other commitments and had not joined the day's excursion.

Bradley noticed Nanny Kate sigh and push aside her unfinished lunch. He had eaten enough, so he stood up quickly. "I'll take Henry," he said. Nanny Kate mouthed a quiet "thank you" that he acknowledged with a nod. Even though Bradley was exhausted—recurring nightmares had ruined last night's sleep—a walk in the sunshine seemed infinitely more desirable today than idle small talk with upper-class strangers.

"Don't let him get wet!" Elizabeth called out as Bradley and Henry walked away from the picnic area. He and Henry wandered Glen Eldridge's shoreline looking for minnows in the shallows and other interesting creatures among the rocks before trying their hands at skipping stones.

After his five-skip triumph, Henry searched for more flat stones while Bradley gazed out from Glen Eldridge Point. The green swath of distant shoreline—over a mile or two away—separated the dark blues of the undulating lake from the cerulean blues of a cloudless sky. Bradley breathed in the summer air. Gentle waves lapped at his bare feet. He and Henry had removed their boots and rolled up their pants before wading into the cool waters. Bradley exhaled slowly, trying to release tension from his body.

Hearing the crunch of footsteps on the beach behind him, he turned to see Hannah, watching them skeptically from the shore. Bradley offered an encouraging smile. "Do you want to give it a try?" he said. "I can help you find a good skipping rock."

"No thank you. Mother doesn't want me to get my dress wet." Her voice betrayed her disappointment. Bradley could tell she absolutely wanted to dip her feet into the lake and skip stones, but he had no idea how to keep the hem of her dress out of the water. Hitching up a dress was more complicated than rolling up pant legs. Hannah settled for helping her brother count his skips.

Beyond Hannah, Bradley could see that most guests still lingered over their picnic lunches and showed no urgency for the next event—exploring Glen Eldridge's considerable ravine. Bradley's eyes drifted over to Miss Annie Anderson.

When the *Estelle* arrived at Glen Eldridge, Bradley had watched from the upper deck as the excursion party disembarked onto the dock and made their way toward the picnic grounds. Carrying her picnic basket, Miss Anderson had been one of the first women to step off the steamer. The muscular man who had escorted her away from Bradley and Vance remained beside her. Bradley wondered if the man was a suitor or maybe even her fiancé. He didn't know anything about Miss Anderson except that she was friends with

James Hope's daughter, that she looked amazing in a plum-colored dress, and that she should be dead.

Bradley turned back to Hannah. "How about you and I try skipping stones from dry land?"

Glen Eldridge Point, originally called Board Point, served industrious settlers seeking to move their grain and lumber to distant markets. These large triangular points of land jutted into the lake at the mouth of each stream. The land expanded as bits of rock and earth cascaded downstream and settled in the lake. Recently, a developer purchased Glen Eldridge Point and had been hard at work turning the site into a destination for wealthy summer vacationers. In addition to the large dock, the developer had constructed pathways and wooden stairs to make the gorge more accessible. Near the picnic grounds, a concession stand sold refreshments.

"Bradley, will you tell us another story about river pirates?" Hannah asked.

"And Sadie the Goat?" Henry added.

The twins had grown bored of skipping stones.

Bradley hesitated. The rest of his stories about Sadie and her gang of river pirates contained both cruelty and murder.

"How about instead you guess which Greek god that is out in the water?" Bradley said. He pointed to a life-sized metal statue standing on a stone pedestal just offshore, positioned to welcome visitors to Glen Eldridge. The statue was naked except for sandals, a robe over his shoulders, and a strategically placed fig leaf. The statue's left arm extended out, and, in that hand, someone had placed a nautical flag.

Henry started naming every Greek male god he knew. "Zeus, Hades, Ares, Apollo, Pos—"

"Stop," said Bradley. "Nice try. One guess at a time."

"Zeus," Henry said.

"Good guess, but Zeus statues always have a beard."

"Poseidon?" Hannah guessed.

"God of the sea. Excellent thought. But no. Poseidon would have a beard and a trident."

"Ares?" Henry guessed.

Apollo Belvedere at Glen Eldridge

"No, but another good guess. Hannah?"

"Apollo?"

"Very good!" said Bradley.

"Aww," Henry groaned. "I said Apollo first."

"Can you name Apollo's powers?"

"Archery!" Henry yelled.

"Music!" Hannah yelled at the same time.

Bradley was impressed. "You're both right. Did you know he was a twin like you two? He had a twin sister, Artemis."

"Henry and Hannah!" All three turned to see Nanny Kate walking toward them. "Everyone is leavin' to climb into that grand glen. Sorry, but ye 'ave to come now or ye'll be left behind."

Bradley looked back. The last stragglers were leaving the nearly deserted picnic ground and heading along the creek toward a wooden staircase that climbed up into the rocky gorge. Most of the stairs and the glen beyond lay hidden behind vegetation. Hannah ran over to Nanny Kate while Bradley and Henry dried their feet. Bradley kneeled to help Henry into his boots.

"Hurry, please!" Henry said. "I don't want to miss it!"

Bradley tied Henry's laces and straightened the boy's pant legs before sending him after his sister and the nanny.

"Thank you, Bradley!" Henry yelled over his shoulder as he sprinted away. Bradley had to admit he was growing fond of the twins. But just as quickly as the thought came to him, he pushed it away. This would all end soon—and it would not end well for everyone involved.

Bradley picked up his boots and started walking toward the wooden stairs. He noticed that Miss Anderson and her escort had reached the first staircase just ahead of the twins and the nanny. No one remained in the picnic area. Bradley's eyes swept the beach, looking for Vance. His rival had made himself inconspicuous since the ship docked.

After reaching the stairs, Bradley sat on the second step to put on his boots. He was in no hurry. The sound of voices drifted down the stairs. Trees and bushes blocked his view of the landing above him, so he crept a few stairs closer until he could see Miss Anderson and her escort, but knew that they could not see him.

"We should catch up to George and Emma," she said. "I hear there's a lovely waterfall ahead."

"I just wanted to enjoy a moment alone with you." Her escort stood close to her. The man glanced around quickly to make sure they were alone and then swept Miss Anderson into a tight embrace and kissed her deeply.

Bradley paused for a heartbeat. Quite indecent and scandalous for her reputation, should someone find them kissing so brazenly in public. Not wanting to confront the couple, Bradley retreated down the stairs and headed for the shore. Maybe she was engaged after all, although he had not seen a ring on her finger. He wondered again about her reaction to him earlier. Had she seen his face in the Glen when he looked over the edge at the fallen woman? That seemed the only explanation for her look of shock and fear at seeing him on the *Estelle*.

Bradley hadn't gone twenty paces when Miss Anderson hurried down the stairs alone. They noticed each other at the same time and locked eyes for the second time that day. Bradley registered her flushed face before she turned and hurried toward the concession stand. He watched her disappear into the building, and then—still carrying his boots—headed back to the water's edge. He could afford to bide his time. He would wait to see what she did next.

With one eye on the concession stand, Bradley considered his next steps regarding the counterfeiting ring. He wondered if following Sinclair was his best option or if following Vance or the Walrus made more sense. Although he did have another clue—the name written on the note left in his room. *Jacub Jagusiak, Cornell University.* Bradley had asked around and knew that Cornell University was in Ithaca only thirty-five miles away. With no direct train connection, that journey could take half a day. Whoever had left him the article on the stolen banknote papers must have thought the Cornell clue important. Bradley needed to find a way to reach Ithaca and seek out Mr. Jagusiak to find out what he knew.

Bradley was determined to quit his job at the end of the day, but in the little time he had had to interact with Elizabeth today, he had suggested she consider a day trip to Ithaca. The family had already visited every waterfall near Watkins, but there were more to ex-

plore in nearby Ithaca. She thanked him for the suggestion but reminded him that tomorrow, The Great New York and New Orleans
Zoological and Equestrian Exposition was coming to Watkins. The
twins were extremely excited about the parade of animals it was
bringing.

As Bradley stared at the water, lost in thought, a dragonfly zig-
zagged in front of him and then flew away. His eyes tracked the
dragonfly's path in the direction of the concession stand. He was
shocked to see Vance leading Miss Anderson away from the building and onto the dock.

"What are you up to, Vance?"

A second, smaller steam yacht, partially hidden from view by
the *Estelle*, rested on the opposite side of the dock. Not quite half
the *Estelle*'s length, this new yacht likely belonged to some rich
vacationer who steamed up the Hudson River from New York City
and then across the Erie Canal and down the Cayuga-Seneca Canal
to Seneca Lake. Steam billowed from the tall smokestack in the
center of the boat. A blue-and-white canopy ran the length of the
vessel to provide shade. A small cabin, built in the center of the
boat, must house the steam engine.

Bradley watched Vance and Miss Anderson continue out onto
the dock. When Vance turned back to make sure no one was watching them, Bradley could see the smirk on his face—the same smirk
Vance wore when crushing small animals under his boot. Bradley started walking quickly toward the dock with his boots still in
his hands. When Vance and Miss Anderson reached the steamer,
Vance offered her a steadying hand as they stepped onto the boat
and disappeared in the shadows under the canopy. A few seconds
later, Vance jumped back onto the dock and started untying the
mooring lines. Seeing this, Bradley started running.

As Bradley reached the start of the dock, Vance disappeared
back on board. There was no sign of Miss Anderson. More steam
and smoke puffed and hissed from the smokestack as the steamer prepared to push off. Bradley dropped his boots and sprinted
along the dock—his bare feet thumping on the wooden planks. The
steam yacht pulled away slowly but picked up speed as it ran parallel to and a few feet off the dock. Bradley knew he was running

out of both time and dock. Summoning one last burst of speed, he launched himself into the air, hoping to catch the yacht's stern. He flew over the water, arms extended, fingers grasping. His fingertips grazed the ship's stern but found nothing to grip onto, and he crashed face first into the water.

CHAPTER XXVIII

KIDNAPPED

Monday, July 20, 1874

A NNIE realized she had made a horrible mistake the moment she stepped onto the boat.

She had stayed close to Allen Hastings since arriving at Glen Eldridge, hoping to use him as a shield against threats from Bradley or anyone else. Hastings might be a bore—he had so many stories about himself—but Annie counted on him to be a gentleman and her protector if needed.

Annie's plan worked until they started climbing the stairs to see Glen Eldridge's waterfalls. Hastings moved slowly, and they found themselves the last to leave the picnic area except for the Sinclair twins, their nanny, and Bradley.

The twins hurried past Annie and Hastings while climbing the first set of stairs.

"Excuse me," Henry said as he ran by.

His sister, Hannah, was close behind. "Nanny said not to run," she yelled as she ran after her brother.

The nanny reached the first landing just behind Annie and Hastings. "Beg yer pardon," she said as she maneuvered around Hastings. "I said no runnin'!" she yelled, lengthening her stride, trying to keep pace with the twins.

"Let's give them a head start up the next stairs," Hastings said, pausing to look around.

Annie wanted to keep moving and suggested they catch up with George and Emma. She worried that Bradley could be nearby. She looked down the stairs but saw no sign of him.

"We should catch up to George and Emma," she said. "I hear there's a lovely waterfall ahead."

"I just wanted to enjoy a moment alone with you."

Annie had been so busy avoiding Bradley that she didn't recognize the danger standing next to her until Hastings pulled her into his arms and kissed her hard on the lips. Shocked, Annie tried to push him away, but he held her tight, pressing his body against her. A feeling of helplessness and shame came over her as it had when the farmer yanked her off her feet at Big Mag's. Glendon would not be able to save her this time. When Hastings's hand wandered toward her breasts, Annie's shame turned into anger. She reached up into her hat, grabbed a hatpin, and stabbed Hastings in the thigh.

Hastings howled as she pulled away, but he quickly covered his mouth to avoid drawing unwanted attention. He plucked the hatpin out of his thigh and threw it into the bushes. The veins in his neck bulged, his pupils narrowed, and his face turned a mottled red.

"How dare you!" Annie shouted, backing away from him and pulling out a second hatpin for defense. For a moment, Annie feared for her life as Hastings's eyes went black. At that moment, a dragonfly passed in front of Hastings's vision. He swatted at it, but it disappeared into the trees. When Hastings turned back to Annie, he had gotten his anger under control.

"Come now," he said, dusting off his jacket sleeve as if he didn't have a care in the world. "You've wanted me to kiss you all day. You're making a fuss over nothing."

"You're mistaken, sir," Annie said. "And you have embarrassed us both."

"We clearly have different opinions on what just happened. It was just a friendly exchange." His voice turned cold. "If you say otherwise, I'll make sure every person on this excursion knows you forced yourself on me, and that I was the one who rejected you. It will be your word against mine."

It was a horrible but effective threat, as many would believe a prominent man's version of events. Annie realized how practiced his words sounded. "I'm not the first woman you've done this to, am I?"

Hastings stiffened and glared at her. "Say anything, and I'll ruin your reputation." Without another word, he stomped off up the trail, leaving her alone on the landing.

Annie let out an impressive swear word. She looked up the trail but could not bear the thought of being near Hastings or facing the Magees after Hastings whispered lies in their ears. She turned and started down the stairs. At the bottom, she locked eyes with the one person she had hoped to avoid all afternoon. Bradley stood not twenty paces away. Could her luck get any worse? He looked surprised to see her. She turned quickly and hurried toward the concession stand, hoping he would not follow. When she arrived, a lovely, older woman saw her distraught face and immediately ushered her inside the small building.

Annie sat on a wooden crate out of sight with her head in her hands.

When the woman left to get more ice, Annie decided to stop feeling sorry for herself. She stood up and reached into her dress pocket for the comforting weight of her pistol. She didn't need Hastings. She would defend herself if needed.

Annie stepped out of the concession stand and almost pulled her gun out when she saw Maurice Vance, the man with the blond goatee, walking over to her with a concerned look on his face.

"There you are!" he said. "Mrs. Magee sent me to find you." He seemed distressed.

"What's wrong?"

"Henry Sinclair fell off the stairs. He hit his head and is in a bad way. I've offered to take the family back to Watkins on our steam yacht, and Mrs. Magee suggested we bring you to guide Mrs. Sinclair to the best doctor when we get there."

Vance talked fast while urgently motioning toward the dock. A steamboat would be the fastest and smoothest way to return to Watkins.

Annie let Vance guide her toward the smaller steam yacht moored across from the *Estelle*. She was happy to have a reason to leave Hastings behind and avoid Bradley. She considered which doctor could best treat Henry as they reached the steamer. Vance offered his arm to help her on board.

When Annie stepped onto the boat, the hairs on the back of her neck stood on end, and a rush of panic surged through her body. There was no one else on board. She immediately spun around and

Hector Falls

reached for her pistol when Vance struck her hard across the face, knocking her to the floor. He grabbed her hair and dragged her into the cabin in the middle of the boat. He tossed her in, kicking at her feet so he could close the door. Annie heard a key turn in the lock.

She lay on the ground, stunned by the blow.

The steamer moved forward, gathering speed. The cabin contained the ship's steam engine. Its throbbing filled her ears, but Annie strained to listen. She thought she could make out the muted roar of Hector Falls, a 165-foot cascade just south of Glen Eldridge at Hector Point—meaning Vance was heading south toward Watkins.

Annie sat up. She wiggled her jaw. It was painful but not broken. She got to her feet and tried the door to be sure, but it would not open. The windowless cabin smelled of oil and soot. Annie held her pistol in front of her. She listened, and she waited.

Why had Vance kidnapped her? Was he working with Bradley? They both worked for the Sinclairs. Was Alistair Sinclair responsible for the dead man in the cemetery?

Sooner than expected, the boat's momentum slowed. The sound of the engines trailed off, and Annie heard footsteps outside the cabin. She prepared herself.

The key turned in the lock. Vance opened the door, holding a knife in his hand. His eyes widened when he saw Annie's pistol pointing at his chest. He immediately took a step backward.

"The little honeybee has a stinger," Vance said calmly. Too calmly. He backed away toward the bow of the boat. He put his knife away and spread his hands in the air.

Annie stepped out of the cabin and followed him. The ship's bow pointed toward Coal Point north of Watkins, but Vance had taken her to the middle of the lake. No other boats were nearby.

"What was your plan?" Annie held her gun as steadily as possible.

He shrugged. "Hit you on the head and throw you into the water. Maybe have a little fun with you first."

The blood drained from her face. He could have been talking about train schedules for all the emotion he showed about ending her life. "Why do you want to kill me?"

"It's not what I want. It's just what needs to happen."

"I-I don't understand."

"Someone is willing to pay me a lot of money to make your death look like an accident."

Annie shook her head. "This is a mistake," she said. "I didn't see anything in the cemetery."

Vance looked confused, which surprised Annie. Did he have no idea about what had happened in the cemetery?

"When I get hired," Vance said, "my employer expects quick results. You have been making me look bad."

"I hope you aren't expecting an apology."

"So far, you have been lucky. I would have talked you into my carriage last week if that busybody hadn't passed by."

"I'm not feeling very lucky."

"You were lucky that two of you wore the same dress in the Glen. Well, lucky for you. Not so lucky for the other girl."

"You killed the woman in the Glen?"

"It should have been you," he said with a smile that did not reach his eyes. "In a way, it is your fault that she is dead. Imagine my surprise when I learned it wasn't you. And then you showed up on the *Estelle*."

Annie was not naïve. Vance answered her questions only because he did not expect her to live long enough to tell anyone else. He was stalling. Waiting, perhaps, for her to make a mistake that allowed him to regain the advantage.

"How did you know I would get on this boat? What if I wasn't alone?"

Vance shrugged. "I can be persuasive. And if you had stayed with your large gentleman, I would have invited you both for a private cruise," he said. "Then he would jump in to save you when you accidentally fell overboard. A heroic but futile gesture resulting in two more tragic drownings."

"Lucky for me, I have this gun," she said.

The boat had been rocking back and forth. At first, Annie thought the wind was picking up, but now she realized Vance had been shifting his weight back and forth, causing the boat to roll left and right. It was initially subtle, but now Annie had to brace against the cabin to steady herself.

Vance smirked at her. "You aren't going to shoot me." He stepped forward, pushing down hard with his right leg, rocking the boat even more. He had no problem keeping his balance.

"Stay where you are," Annie said. She raised her gun slightly and tried to keep it on target. The rolling boat made aiming difficult.

"I have a job to do," Vance said. He stared into her eyes as he took another step forward.

The explosion of gunpowder and the burst of smoke surprised Annie, even though she had intentionally pulled the trigger. As the acrid cloud dissipated with the lake breeze, Vance stood before her with a shocked expression. He looked down at his shoulder and saw a trickle of blood. Annie groaned. Her bullet had only grazed him.

"You had one shot," Vance said. His face turned hard as he pulled his knife back out. "Too bad, honeybees only sting once, and then they die." He stepped toward her.

"Good afternoon, Miss Anderson." The voice came from her left. "Forgive me for saying so, but you keep questionable company. Hello, Vance."

Vance stopped. His face twisted with anger. Annie turned to see Bradley coming around the cabin from the back of the boat. He was soaking wet.

"How the hell did you get here?" Vance asked.

"Rude of you not to invite me along for the ride, Vance. But when you threw off the mooring lines, you let them trail behind the boat. I managed to hang on while you dragged me out to this lovely spot." He looked over at Annie. "Sorry that I couldn't join the party sooner." He winked at her.

Annie didn't know how to react. Even if Bradley hadn't killed Ruth Van Etten, he worked with Vance.

"It's a big lake," Vance said. "Plenty of room for an extra body at the bottom."

Bradley shook his head and took a step closer to Vance. "I'm saving you from making a mistake," he said, lowering his voice. "Change of plans. The boss wants her alive now."

"I don't care what Sinclair says. And I don't believe you."

Bradley smiled at Vance. "You and I both know," he said, "that Sinclair is not the only man in charge."

Vance's eyes narrowed.

"Miss Anderson has some information that he needs," Bradley said. "If you kill her and she takes what she knows to the grave, be sure to tell him it was your screw up."

Annie had no idea what Bradley was talking about, but she noticed that as he talked—calmly and confidently—he was moving closer to Vance. Neither man seemed affected by the motion of the boat.

"You're lying," Vance said. "I'm going to kill her and make it look like an accident."

Bradley had placed himself directly between Annie and Vance. She would have run if there had been anywhere to go. She thought about locking herself back in the cabin, but Vance had pocketed the key.

"You can always kill her later if I'm wrong," Bradley said with a smile. He now stood directly in front of Vance.

"And I'm telling you—"

Annie was shocked at Bradley's speed as he lunged forward and grabbed Vance's knife hand. Vance reacted quickly but not fast enough to snatch his hand back. Instead, Vance threw his weight forward, straining to bury the blade in Bradley's midsection. Bradley held on, shifting his weight to avoid the blow. As the two men grappled over the knife, they lost their footing and fell hard to the deck.

Annie stood motionless, watching.

Bradley and Vance wrestled their way across the deck, battling soundlessly. While Bradley kept both hands on Vance's knife arm, Vance reached into his jacket with his free hand. As Bradley knocked the knife out of Vance's hand—sending it skittering across the deck toward Annie—Vance pulled a revolver out of his jacket. Bradley headbutted Vance and grabbed the hand holding the revolver.

"Get the knife!" Bradley yelled at Annie. Both men had a grip on the revolver.

Annie snapped out of her trance. She tucked her empty pistol back in her dress pocket and was about to step forward and grab the knife when Vance's revolver swung in her direction. Her eyes widened, and she ducked down as the gun went off and blasted a hole in the cabin wall behind where she had been standing.

"Never mind!" Bradley called out.

Annie retreated around the edge of the cabin and then ran to the back of the boat, searching for a weapon. With little to choose from, she grabbed one of the folding wooden chairs near the stern. Another gunshot echoed through the air.

Chair in hand, Annie peeked around the corner of the cabin. The two men had gotten to their feet but still fought over the gun between them. Bradley noticed Annie first and pivoted, turning Vance's back to her. Annie lifted the folding chair with two hands and brought it down hard on Vance. He dropped to his knees but kept a hand on the pistol. Bradley, failing to wrestle the gun away, gained enough control to pull the hammer back and fire it four times in rapid succession, emptying the six-shooter into the deck. The wood splintered from the barrage of bullets.

Vance roared in frustration and threw a punch that caught Bradley in the face. Vance wrenched the empty revolver free from his stunned opponent and hit Bradley across the head, dropping him to all fours. As Bradley tried to reach his feet, Vance grabbed the chair from Annie's hands and broke it over Bradley, who collapsed face down on the deck. Bright red blood spread across the wooden deck boards.

When Vance grabbed the chair, Annie had gone for the knife. She held it in front of her as she backed against the cabin.

Vance, catching his breath, just laughed at her. He slowly reached down, lifted his pant leg, and pulled out another gun. A one-shot derringer like the one she had used. "I've had enough of you," he said. He raised the gun.

"Stop!" she yelled as if words could protect her from Vance's bullet. As Vance pointed his gun at her heart, Annie realized how much she wanted to live. Her body clenched involuntarily, anticipating the bullet.

The gunshot rang in her ears, but she felt nothing.

As Vance pulled the trigger, his body was knocked hard to

the side, causing him to crash against the ship's gunwale. Bradley stood in front of Annie, bleeding from the cut to his head and holding the ship's anchor.

"Are you all right?" he asked.

She nodded her head. He had just saved her life. Bradley gave her a small smile and turned toward Vance.

As Vance straightened up, Bradley and the anchor crashed into him, sending both men overboard to disappear under Seneca's cold waters. The anchor's rope spooled out after them.

Annie rushed to the side. She could see two bodies thrashing just below the surface. They came up for air once. As they fought against the anchor's weight, Bradley looped the rope around Vance's neck. Vance threw punches at Bradley. They went under again. When Bradley surfaced, he yelled, "Cut the rope," before an unseen force dragged him violently back under the water.

The knife in Annie's hand was extremely sharp and made short work of the anchor rope. After she cut the rope, one end disappeared over the side into the now still water. Annie held her breath.

It was only seconds but felt like long minutes before Bradley resurfaced, gasping for air. Blood still flowed from his head wound. He looked exhausted. He could barely keep his head above the water. Annie saw no sign of Vance.

Annie locked eyes with Bradley. The look on his face was one of resignation.

She turned to search the boat for some way to help him. She found two life-preserver rings and rushed back to the side.

"Here, grab this!" She threw the first ring near Bradley, who was drifting away from the boat. He raised his arm, attempting to swim toward it but had no energy to reach the ring. It floated away. Bradley was going to drown, Annie realized, and all she could do was watch.

Annie hesitated—the thought of her parents drowning in the lake leaped to her mind. All those nightmares from her teenage years came back to her. She spun around, searching the lake, but no boats were nearby. No help was coming. A breeze from the south created wavelets whose crests sparkled in the sunlight.

Bradley had saved her life. He was also the only lead she had to figure out who was trying to kill her. Annie grabbed the second life-preserver ring and jumped into the water.

CHAPTER XXIX

OVERBOARD

Monday, July 20, 1874

GRAVITY plunged Annie's body below the surface of the shockingly cool lake waters. Even in the summer, the sun struggled to penetrate far into Seneca Lake's six-hundred-foot depths. Thoughts of her parents' last moments came unbidden as the cold and darkness enveloped her. With her death grip on the life-preserver ring, Annie surged back to the surface into the sunshine and warmth. She shook the water out of her eyes and breathed deeply to steady her nerves before spinning around to search for Bradley.

Bradley's brown hair bobbed up and down twenty feet away. He was barely keeping his head above the water. Annie tried to kick her way over to him, but her boots, built for style, provided no traction in the water. She turned to her side and used her free arm to scoop at the water and propel herself toward him. Her feet kicked weakly behind her.

Annie was within arm's reach of Bradley when he slipped below the surface. "No!" she shouted to herself. She didn't want her jump into the lake to be for nothing. Annie spun around in the water to reach down for him, but as she did, he resurfaced, sputtering and coughing up water. He was not ready to die just yet. As Bradley flailed his arms, she shoved the life-preserver ring in his direction. He instinctively grabbed onto it and tugged it into his chest, pulling Annie closer to him. Only then did he notice her in the water beside him. His half-focused eyes stared at her in confusion.

"You're going to be all right," she said. It was the first thing that came to her mind. She forced herself to smile as she kicked her feet and paddled her arms to keep herself upright. She hoped she sounded convincing for both their sakes.

Bradley shook his head back and forth, and his focus returned. He stared into her eyes momentarily and then smiled as he recognized her. "A lovely day for a swim, Miss Anderson," he said weakly and coughed from the effort. She laughed despite herself. The cut on his head continued to ooze blood but only slowly now.

With effort, Annie managed to get the life-preserver ring over Bradley's head and his arms through it. He laid his head on his arms and closed his eyes.

Annie looked about, feeling alone as they floated together. This part of the lake was almost two miles wide, and they were in the middle. Far away, she could see Hector Falls but couldn't hear its gentle roar. The steam yacht continued to drift away from them. Annie noticed for the first time the neatly lettered name, *Bonnie Lynn*, on its side. Even if she could get them to the boat, Annie knew she would not have the strength to pull Bradley or herself back on board. No other boats were near them. The breeze blew west and north, pushing them away from Watkins and the Glen Eldridge side of the lake toward the less developed western shore. As the wind picked up, the waves began cresting higher.

It was futile to fight against the wind and the current.

Annie held on to the outside of the life-preserver ring and looked in the direction the wind was taking them. "We're going to have to swim to shore," she told an unconscious Bradley.

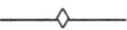

Eight years earlier, thirteen-year-old Annie had sat with her face pressed against a rain-streaked window in the front parlor of her house. It was a chilly day in May, and her cheek began to feel numb. She prayed for the feeling to spread to her entire body, because then maybe the hole in her heart would not hurt so damn much. She had watched her parents' coffins being lowered into the ground the day before, and she still couldn't believe they were truly gone.

Nana had tried to coax Annie away from the window an hour earlier but gave up when someone came calling. Annie assumed it was more neighbors offering condolences while they silently thanked God that death had chosen the Andersons and hadn'vert darkened their own doorstep.

Through the window, the village below was covered in a gray mist. To her left, the dark waters of Seneca Lake churned from the rain, unconcerned with Annie's loss.

Annie felt anger welling up inside her. Anger at the lake for its ambivalence. Anger at God for taking her parents. Anger at her parents for leaving her. They had drowned because their sailboat sank in a sudden storm and neither knew how to swim. Annie knew that many people couldn't swim. Her father once told her that even sailors who crossed the ocean did not bother to learn. If they fell overboard or their ship sank, it was more merciful to drown quickly than prolong the inevitable.

As Annie looked out at the lake, her anger drove her to a decision. "Seneca Lake is not the ocean," she told herself. She stood up and warmed her cheek with her hands. She would not repeat her parents' mistake. She straightened her dress and then marched to the parlor where her grandmother talked with a visitor. Annie pushed the door open and stepped inside.

"I want to learn how to swim," she announced.

Glendon Robinson turned to Annie in surprise. Sitting next to him, her grandmother turned away from Annie and brought a handkerchief to her eyes. Was she crying? Annie opened her mouth to repeat what she had said but hesitated. She had intruded on a private conversation. She suddenly wanted to flee the room but felt rooted to the floor.

Glendon smiled kindly as he turned toward her. "Hello, Annie," he said. Nana would not take on boarders for another week or two so Annie only knew Glendon as her parents' friend.

"Excuse me, Mister Robinson. Grandmother," Annie said in a lowered voice. "I'm sorry to interrupt."

"It's all right," Glendon said. They both glanced at Nana who was still dabbing her eyes. "It is a difficult time for everyone," he said, looking back at Annie. "Why do you want to learn how to swim?"

Annie stared at the floor but realized that Glendon was giving her his full attention. He was listening instead of yelling at her for interrupting. She raised her head and looked him in the eyes. "If I ever fall overboard, I want to be able to swim to shore."

Glendon's smile chased some of the sadness from his eyes. "Then I'll teach you how to swim," he said without hesitation.

Nana started to protest—swimming was not an activity for proper young ladies—but Glendon had already begun to plan.

"Cayuta Lake will be the best place to learn," he said. "It is smaller and warmer than Seneca, and I know the family that owns all the land surrounding it. I'm sure they will be accommodating, given the circumstances." Cayuta Lake, only two miles long, was in the hills between Seneca Lake and Cayuga Lake. "Your father's friend, Roland Smith, has a canoe," Glendon added. "That will come in handy. He'll help if we ask."

Not long after, Nana took on both Glendon and Roland as boarders. And so began Annie's swimming lessons and the start of a new family. Every weekend that summer, Nana, Glendon, and Roland took Annie across the valley and up the opposite hill to Cayuta Lake which was ten miles from Seneca Lake and twenty miles from Cayuga Lake. Nana packed a picnic basket, Roland paddled around in his canoe, and Glendon did his best to teach Annie how to swim.

Annie's first lesson had been a disaster. She wore her mother's wool bathing dress—tightly pinned to fit her more girlish figure— along with bloomer-like trousers for under the dress. Head-to-toe wool might maintain privacy and modesty but it got very heavy when wet.

"Are bathing dresses designed to drown women?" Annie asked. She was annoyed, frustrated, and tired of accidentally swallowing lake water. But she was determined to endure.

"Stubborn like her mother," Nana had said so many times that Annie wore the comment as a badge of pride.

After that first miserable attempt, Annie pulled out her mother's Singer sewing machine and began experimenting with different fabrics. If she were going to learn how to swim, Annie would need a better swimming outfit. This restarted her love of sewing and made Annie feel closer to her mother.

With each swimming lesson and each iteration of her swimming outfit, Annie gained more confidence in the water. Those summer days were some of her fondest memories of growing up. Glendon was a comforting presence at her side. Roland smiled from his canoe, always keeping just within reach if needed. And her grandmother could always be counted on to say, at least once every trip, "You do know that the fastest way to cross a lake is to stay in the boat?"

On the very last day of summer, Annie and Glendon swam the width of Cayuta Lake and stood triumphantly in knee-deep water on the far shore. Roland clapped his hands in approval from the canoe and offered to ferry them back across. Annie had just grinned and asked Glendon if he was ready to swim back.

Annie smiled at the memory as she pulled Bradley through the waves. She kept his face out of the water and hoped that he was not dying on her. Seneca Lake was much larger and colder than Cayuta Lake, but the water felt warmer now than when she had first jumped in. Either her body had just adjusted to the temperature, or she had warmed from the exertion.

Swimming was much harder fully clothed. Annie's water-logged boots, skirts, and corset dragged her down. She had already let her hat drift away. She paused to wriggle out of her overskirt and bustle. The skirt sank quickly, pulled down by her father's derringer that was in her dress pocket. Next, she removed her blouse but could do nothing about her corset. Reluctantly, Annie reached down to untie the laces of her boots. She exhausted herself from the effort but finally kicked her boots off one at a time. As they sank into the depths, she looked resentfully at Bradley. *I just gave up my favorite pair of boots for you,* she thought. *You'd better be worth it.*

Annie caught sight of the afternoon steamboat making its way north from Watkins toward Hector Point. It was on the wrong side of the lake and too far away to see her or offer any assistance. Next, she heard the whistle of the Northern Express train heading away from Watkins up the western shore. Annie continued swimming in the direction the wind pushed them—diagonal to the shore. Bradley drifted in and out of consciousness.

When Annie was younger, she had heard old-timers share stories about a sea serpent living in the lake. Some said the lake was bottomless, and the creature could come and go at will from far-off places. When her parents died, Annie imagined the sea serpent was to blame. It must have knocked over their sailboat and dragged them to the depths. The sea monster became a convenient target for her anger as she mourned. Annie hated the lake and its lake beast. As she grew older, she learned that monsters weren't hidden in lakes—they walked among us. Men like Maurice Vance. If the sea creature existed and surfaced next to her, Annie would politely ask it for a ride to shore.

In the distance, the remains of an old mill sat on a point of land jutting out into the lake. That would be her target, she decided as she steered toward the outcropping. The early settlers had taken advantage of almost every available stream to power one mill or another. As settlers cut and cleared the heavy forests, many streams dried up in the summer months, making the mills obsolete. Newer mills, like Frost's Grist Mill on Franklin Street, built just two years ago, relied on steam power, created from burning wood or coal. Seeing the ruins of an old mill, Annie hoped there was a road to follow that would lead to help.

When Annie's feet finally touched down in the shallow water, her body flooded with relief and an amazing sense of satisfaction and accomplishment. Bradley would have died if she hadn't jumped in. He still might, but not from any lack of effort on her part.

She dragged his unconscious body half out of the water and collapsed beside him. Rolling over, she looked into the blue sky and let the sun warm her skin. She was exhausted, someone wanted her dead, and she had no idea how far she would have to walk barefoot while half dressed in soaking wet clothes, but at that moment, she took a deep breath and laughed aloud, feeling more alive than she had in a long time.

After a short rest, Annie got to her feet and considered her options. She would have to leave Bradley in the warmth of the sunshine as she went for help. She was struggling to pull him Further up the beach when she heard the approaching clatter of a horse's galloping hooves. Annie felt exposed and suddenly afraid. There

SEA MONSTER

was nowhere to run or hide, and she had dropped her only means of defense—Vance's knife—on the *Bonnie Lynn*. She could run back into the water and hope whoever approached did not know how to swim, but that would mean leaving Bradley behind.

Annie stood her ground and waited. As the horse and rider came into view, Annie's mouth dropped open. The horseman drew rein and let his horse trot up to within a few feet of her.

"How did you find me?" she asked.

CHAPTER XXX

TRAIN TO HELL

From the Journal of Private H. Thompson

May 6, 1864 – Last night, our Yankee captors ran us double quick from the front lines into Union territory. Frank had gotten a field dressing on Taylor's wounded leg, and we took turns carrying him along two at a time. He bore the pain stoically. The bleeding had slowed, but we could only hope that his leg escaped amputation.

As the Yankees hurried us deeper behind Union lines, the number of reinforcements and equipment the Union Army had available shocked me. They had three to four times the resources our Confederate officers commanded. I was both proud that our soldiers and fearless leader, Robert E. Lee, had held our own against such tremendous odds and disheartened that the final result now seemed inevitable. The North had too many men, while the South struggled to replace losses with capable soldiers. Any faith I had that our Confederate side could win the war died that day.

Our Yankee guards stopped us in front of a wooden corral with three hundred other captured Confederate prisoners inside.

A Union officer noticed Taylor's injury and barked out a command to a nearby sergeant. Two members of the Union Ambulance Corps showed up and loaded Taylor onto a stretcher. We had no time for goodbyes. None of us wanted to believe that that might be the last time we'd ever see him.

Frank, Buck, Ace, and I remained penned up as prisoners in the rear of the Union Army through the night. Buck and Ace whispered quietly between themselves, talking of escape, but I was ambivalent. I had signed up to clear my debt, and I had done that. I was no longer willing to risk sacrificing myself for a lost cause.

May 18, 1864 – We arrived at Point Lookout prisoner of war camp after days of marching. Our captors had taken us east, past the Chancellorsville battlefield, around Fredericksburg, and into Maryland, and then down to the extreme tip of a long, low, and barren peninsula where the broad Potomac River met the western shore of Chesapeake Bay. We passed through the camp gates to find forty acres of flat space—mostly sandy ground without shrubs or trees—filled with prisoner tents and surrounded by a fifteen-foot-high fence with elevated walkways for Union soldiers to patrol the camp's perimeter.

All the prisoners lived in tents. Long parallel "streets" of tents ran east to west inside the camp, each row housing a thousand or more prisoners. On our first day, the four of us set out to explore our surroundings. We found the long buildings used for cookhouses, but we only received food rations twice a day. We had already missed dinner and were starving. In the dozen days since our capture, we had only received food on half the days. Some days, we were lucky to get light bread or crackers. Our clothes hung loose on our bodies.

With no food available, we headed to the other end of camp, up against the Chesapeake Bay. Ace had never seen the ocean, so he walked toward the fence to see if there was a crack or knot in the wood to look through. The guards' elevated walkway ran along the opposite side of the fence. They had clear visibility into the stockade perimeter, but prisoners only saw the upper portion of their bodies. I noticed for the first time that the guards on the fence were colored soldiers.

As Ace approached, the nearest guard called down from his position on the walkway. "Stay away from the fence." Although we all knew and worked with slaves, only Buck's family owned any. None of us had ever received a direct order from a colored man. Personally, I respected any man holding a rifle, regardless of the color of his skin.

Ace looked up into the negro's eyes. Whatever he saw caused him to nod and take two steps backward. Buck, however, couldn't leave well enough alone. He stepped forward and began yelling at the negro holding a rifle. "Who do you think you are, boy?" Buck said, his face turning red. "Y'all aren't free. Y'all're just slaves in a state of insurrection. Y'all'll be put back in your places when we win this war."

The guard's answer was to swivel his rifle in Buck's direction. "Get away from the fence," he repeated. Buck stared defiantly, ignoring his peril, while Frank and I stepped forward and grabbed him by the shoulder. I whispered, "Today is not your day to die," as we dragged him away. I nodded to the guard as we left. "Sorry, friend, we'll be on our way."

"I'm not ya friend," he said. "The bottom rail is on top now."

July 2, 1864 – Taylor was the one who brought us together. His absence weighed heavily on all of us. I spent less and less time with Ace, Buck, or Frank as the days dragged on, although the hidden gold remained the connection that prevented the remaining members of the Lucky Six from drifting too far apart.

Our captors allowed access to an area on the beach to bathe, wash clothes, and find additional food, such as clams, lobsters, and fish. With the summer sun warming my body and a soft breeze in my face, I turned my back on the prison walls and pretended to be somewhere else while staring at the tall ships in the distance sailing up or down the Chesapeake Bay. I was surprised to find Frank standing next to me, staring out into the bay, trying to see what I was seeing. When I turned to welcome him, he had a huge grin on his face. "Taylor's here," he said.

Frank led me to a tent deep in the middle of the camp where we found Taylor talking with Ace and Buck. I was relieved to see both his legs attached to his body. Taylor looked weary and thin, but the smile on his face was genuine. We clasped hands, and he told us how a Union doctor removed the shrapnel from his leg and sewed him back up. Once they were sure he hadn't gotten an infection, he requested to be shipped to Point Lookout. "I still have a limp," he admitted, "but I can finally walk without crutches."

That night, it was like old times. The five of us ate together, supplementing our food rations with a crab I'd caught that morning and food that Ace had won gambling. Hungry Confederates often used their bread, crackers, or meat as poker bids, and Ace had become a master of separating men from their food. Our captors did not allow us any money for fear we would bribe the sentinels and make our escape, so crackers and tobacco had become the unofficial currency at Point Lookout.

As we sat comfortably together out of earshot of others, Buck revisited our favorite topic. "After we get home and I get my share of gold from that Hickory Nut cave, I'm gonna find me a beautiful Southern bride and build her a plantation with a hundred slaves to serve us as a marriage present. But if we lose this war," he said with a disturbing light in his eyes and his voice growing louder, "I'm going to raise a militia and keep the fight going. I refuse to live in a world where colored men pretend to be my equal."

Buck's fervor surprised me. None of us wanted to share following his rant. After an awkward silence, Taylor cleared his throat. "The war's not over yet, Buck." He accepted a tobacco-filled pipe from Frank and puffed momentarily in thought. "I had a lot of time to think while lying in that Union hospital," he said. He blew two smoke rings into the air and watched them drift upward into nothingness. "When we recover the gold, I'll make sure my family in North Carolina is taken care of, but then I'm going to California to find out what happened to my father." He smiled at each of us. "Y'all are welcome to come visit."

Back in my tent that night, I realized I had forgotten to ask Taylor what had happened to Fish's gold nugget. The guards had searched us multiple times, so I could only assume some lucky Union soldier now had it in his pocket.

July 13, 1864 – We left Point Lookout for a newly opened prisoner of war camp in Elmira, New York. Point Lookout, built for 10,000 prisoners, had swelled to around 15,000 Rebels, so the Yankees began sending groups of prisoners farther north. We joined hundreds of other prisoners loading on a steamer that traveled up the Atlantic Coast to New Jersey. The guards assigned Taylor to a different prisoner company, but luck kept us together as both companies were making the trip. I enjoyed the fresh air and ocean views on the steamer, but many of our fellow prisoners got seasick. I had never seen Frank look so woeful—or so green—before.

July 15, 1864 – We landed on the Jersey shore in the early morning and were immediately transferred to railroad cars. Over eight hundred Confederate prisoners and over a hundred Union guards filled the train's eighteen boxcars. Taylor, assigned to a different prisoner company, loaded into a boxcar near the front of the train.

Ace, Buck, Frank, and I climbed into our assigned boxcar in the middle of the train. There were three Union guards at each door. One of the guards told us it would take half a day to travel the two hundred and seventy-three miles to Elmira.

The first part of the trip was uneventful. The locals treated us well when we pulled into stations, especially during a stop in Goshen, New York, where the ladies brought us eatables, and the men gave us tobacco. As the train pulled out of Port Jarvis, I noticed Ace and Buck whispering to each other. Ace waved Frank and me over so Buck could share his plan. When the train slowed for a curve, he wanted to rush the guards, push them out the door, and then jump after them. "We'll be long gone by the time they stop the train to look for us," Buck said.

In a hushed whisper, I pointed out the flaws in his plan. "It's daylight," I said, "and the train will still be traveling at twenty or thirty miles an hour. We won't get away if we break our legs. And if we jump now, we'd be leaving Taylor behind."

"Taylor couldn't make the trip south anyway," Buck said. "Not with his limp. We'll save him his share of gold, but we're going now. You can either come with us or stay on the train."

I placed myself between Buck and the nearest boxcar door. I tried to appeal to Ace and Frank, but they wouldn't look at me. I was the only one willing to wait out the war. I had no desire to escape and go back to the front lines. Buck sneered and called me a coward. I shrugged. "It's a matter of principle," I said, "If we can't all go, none of us should go."

We all felt the train entering a curve. I could read in Buck's eyes that he meant to jump. He rocked backward and brought his hands up, preparing to shove me out of his way. His hands started forward, but they never connected. A tremendous bang echoed in our ears, and we were all propelled into the air.

Time and gravity lost their meaning. Our train car tilted on its side, then rolled, and we tumbled with it. Horrendous screeching and groaning and the sound of wood splintering assaulted our ears. Although it was a mere ten seconds, it felt like an hour passed before our boxcar lurched to a halt on its side. An eerie silence descended as every man in our boxcar lay stunned.

The quiet did not last long. Cries of the wounded and dying

rose all around us. Men moaned or shrieked in agony. I could hear some praying.

I lay for a moment, checking my body for the worst. Except for bruising, everything seemed to be working. I got to my feet and started helping others up. It was then that I noticed smoke starting to fill the boxcar. Desperate to get off the train, we stepped out into a scene of horror.

Buck, Ace, and Frank stood beside me, staring at the wreckage. Our train had crashed head on into a coal train, traveling in the opposite direction on the single railway track. It was the result of a catastrophic error. Miraculously, none of us received serious injuries. I could see in Buck's eyes that he still wanted to run, but many of the Union soldiers had been in the last car of the train and had the fewest injuries. They'd already formed a loose perimeter around the crash site.

Ace asked, "Where's Taylor?" We rushed forward toward the front of the train. The crash had pushed the two locomotives high into the air—giants grappling with each other even in their death throes. The massive floor timbers of the engine tenders had snapped like matchsticks. Our train's engineer was pinned by cordwood against the boilerplate—slowly being scalded to death. He was beyond saving, but I admired the dying man who used his last words to warn others away in case the boiler exploded.

The wooden boxcars near the front of our train had collapsed into one another, crushing the occupants, hurling some through windows, or pitching them onto the track. The front car now filled a space of less than six feet. The two cars behind it were almost as badly wrecked. Arms, legs, and mangled bodies were visible everywhere. Some had been impaled on iron rods and splintered beams.

This was worse than anything we had seen on the battlefield.

None of us knew for sure which car Taylor had been in. We moved through the wreckage, calling Taylor's name and looking for any sign of him. We did our best to avoid the puddles of blood as we searched. The unrelenting stench of death intensified as we moved closer to the front of the train. Multiple bodies had somersaulted from the wreck and lay in odd positions along the tracks. We checked them all, but none of them were Taylor.

Citizens from the nearby towns of Shohola and Barryville be-

RAILROAD DISASTER

gan showing up to help where they could. We had run out of time to search as the Union guards began rounding up the prisoners. Taylor had either escaped, or the collision had mangled his body beyond recognition. When we heard a groan from Ace, the remaining Lucky Six members turned toward him. Ace stood amid the wreckage, holding up a bloody jacket. We all recognized it as Taylor's.

CHAPTER XXXI

THE PINKERTON

Tuesday, July 21, 1874

B RADLEY regained consciousness, surprised to be waking up in a strange place naked again. He was glad to be alive, but his whole body ached, and his head throbbed. He sat up, befuddled, and struggled to get his bearings. The last thing he remembered was falling into the water. Now, he was in an unfamiliar bedroom with no memory of how he'd gotten there. Drapes kept the room dark except for a small gap that allowed daylight in. Dust particles, defying gravity, floated restlessly in the narrow beam of sunlight.

He reached up, gingerly probing his hairline, and found a fresh dressing. That someone had bandaged his head wound was a good sign. He tried to swing his legs out of the bed but found his right ankle secured to the bedframe by iron shackles. That was not a good sign.

"Awake at last."

The voice came from behind him and to the left. Bradley twisted his body to see a man twirling a pistol in a comfortable armchair. The man, wearing a brown suit and a striped shirt, smiled at him politely but without warmth.

Bradley cleared his throat. "You have me at a disadvantage, sir," Bradley said. "There appears to be a misunderstanding, so if you bring the key to these shackles—and my pants—I will gladly compensate you for any inconvenience and be on my way."

The man laughed. Without another word, he stood, tucked his gun into his jacket, and left the room.

A few minutes later, the door opened, and Miss Annie Anderson stepped in carrying a bowl of soup. She looked at Bradley and smiled.

Bradley's heart skipped a beat. Seeing her face brought a flood of memories. Jumping for the steamer. Grasping the rope and being dragged through the water. Vance with a knife. Vance with a gun. Fighting Vance in the water. Annie in the water. Wait, how did Annie get into the water?

The man with the twirling gun followed behind Annie. He carried a pile of clothes that looked encouragingly familiar to Bradley. Annie set the soup bowl on a marble-top dresser on the far side of the room. She took the clothes from the man's hands and set them down beside the soup. "Thank you, Roland," she said. "Will you give us a few minutes?"

Roland looked at her in surprise. After several hushed whispers back and forth, Annie smiled and patted his arm. He did not look happy, but he nodded.

"Thank you for worrying," she said. "I'll be fine. Will you be all right?"

Roland shook his head and laughed. "Sure, sure. I'll be as happy as a dead pig in the sunshine. Please be careful." He stepped back out of the room and closed the door behind him.

The smell of the soup drifted over to Bradley's nose, causing his stomach to knot up. He was suddenly starving. Annie pulled a chair over to the bed and sat just out of his reach.

"You'll have to forgive me for not standing as you entered the room." He shook his right leg, rattling the leg shackles. His movement caused the bedsheet to drop to his waist. Bradley registered the flush spreading up Annie's neck as she turned away. It was improper for a single lady to be alone with a man, much less a naked one. She must have a strong reason to talk privately. He pulled the sheet back up to his neck.

"The shackles were Roland's idea," Annie said. "He didn't want a strange man in our house who might get up and shoot us in our own beds. You wouldn't have shot us in our sleep, would you, Mister—?"

"Webster. Bradley Webster," he said. "Of course not. If I wanted to kill you, I wouldn't have shot you. Rude to bother the neighbors with multiple gunshots. I would have used a knife. It's much quieter." From the look on Annie's face, she was trying to decide if he was joking. He laughed. "No, Miss Anderson, I wouldn't hurt you. If I promise to behave, will you release me and let me put my clothes back on?"

"Sorry, Roland has the key. I'll call him back in after you answer my questions."

"I have some questions of my own," he said. "Like how I got here."

"All right," Annie said. "You're not going anywhere, so you ask your questions first, and then I'll ask mine."

Bradley's stomach growled. "And the soup?"

"That is your reward for answering truthfully. It was extremely hot when I brought it in but ask your questions quickly unless you want to eat cold soup."

"You drive a hard bargain. All right. My first question is, how did I get here?"

"What do you remember?"

"I remember the fight on the boat and going into the water. And—Maurice Vance?"

Annie paused, looking Bradley in the eyes. "At the bottom of Seneca Lake."

"Good," Bradley said. "I was worried that I had only imagined that part."

"You killed a man," Annie said with a hushed voice. "Doesn't that bother you?" It was clear that it had been bothering Annie.

"I saw Vance following you that day you left Hope's gallery. I could tell Vance was up to something, so I followed him. I was only twenty feet away when he approached the woman in the plum-colored dress. She stood facing away, admiring the view, and never saw him. I thought it was you. Vance didn't hesitate. He lifted her up and over the railing, then turned and headed back the way he had come in one motion. I'll never forget the smirk on his face when he passed me. I rushed to the edge to see if anything could be done...." Bradley's voice trailed off.

"Why didn't you tell the sheriff?" Annie said. "If you had, Vance would have been in jail and not trying to kill me."

"Would he have?" Bradley asked. "It would have been Vance's word against mine, and I haven't always had the best relationship with law enforcement. In fact, if the police ask, I was never on the *Bonnie Lynn*."

"In the Glen, I saw you when you looked over," Annie said. "I thought you had might have been the one—"

Bradley nodded. "Exactly. I would have been the one in jail. Vance killed that woman in the Glen thinking it was you. Yesterday, when he tried again, it was him or us. I have no regrets." He studied her lovely face. "And you shouldn't either."

Annie stood and crossed her arms, hugging herself. She paced across the room. Bradley's attention drifted toward the soup. His mouth watered from the aroma. Annie turned back to him. "Why did you risk your life to save mine?"

"It was the right thing to do?" From the look on her face, this didn't satisfy her. He tried again. "I saw Vance come up behind you on the *Estelle*. It made me furious knowing what happened in the Glen. When I saw the smirk on his face as he guided you to that other steam yacht—well, I knew how it would end if I did nothing."

Annie shivered. "You saved my life."

"You're welcome. But, Miss Anderson, how did you get me out of the water?"

"Please, call me Annie," she said. "I jumped in with the second life preserver and pulled you to shore."

Bradley, dumbfounded, said, "You jumped in—for me. Why?"

"I couldn't watch you drown," Annie said. "And I wanted answers. You told Vance on the boat that the boss wants me alive. Who were you talking about? Who is the boss? Sinclair?" She leaned forward in her chair.

"I was bluffing," Bradley said. "Well, I was guessing that Sinclair is working with someone else. Vance didn't correct me, so I'm confident someone else is involved, but I don't know who or how."

Annie took a deep breath. "Vance told me that someone was paying him a lot of money to kill me and that I was making him look bad to his employer."

Bradley wondered how she could be a threat to the counterfeiting ring. "A couple of nights ago," he said, "I secretly followed Sinclair to the Jefferson House and then to that park a block away."

"Lafayette Park?"

"I guess so. Sinclair met someone there. They might be working together, or maybe Sinclair works for someone else. It was dark, and I couldn't see who it was."

Bradley watched Annie's face as she tilted her head, squinted her eyes, and wrinkled her nose in thought. It made her even more attractive. "Sinclair is the key to solving the mystery," she said. When she caught him staring, she smiled self-consciously. "You're lucky Sinclair didn't see you at the Jefferson."

"Oh, I wore a disguise."

"Really?"

"I dressed like an old man with consumption. Baggy clothes. Glasses. A fake beard. You would be surprised at how many people ignore the old, the poor, or the infirm. I might as well have been invisible."

Annie stood up again and walked over to the curtains. She flung them open, allowing sunlight to flood the room.

"You still haven't told me how I got here," Bradley said.

"A man named Abraham found us." Annie returned to the chair. She pulled it closer to the bed. "He helped me get you back to my house. For a while, I wasn't sure you were going to survive. You took a nasty blow to the head. Abraham sent Doctor Bennett over to bandage your head."

"Is he a good doctor?"

"Excellent. But he is also the town coroner, so no matter how things turned out, you were in good hands."

Bradley laughed out loud. "Good planning on your part." His head ached when he laughed. The brightness of the sunshine in the room finally registered in Bradley's brain. "How long have I been here?"

"Eighteen hours."

He let out a low whistle. "Wait, what time is it?"

"Almost eleven o'clock Wednesday morning."

Bradley had a noon appointment in Havana. "I apologize, Annie, but can we finish this conversation later? I have a previous engagement."

"Nice try. You agreed to answer my questions, and I have many more to ask."

Bradley nodded his head slowly. "Fair enough, but before we continue, could I bother you for a glass of water?"

"Of course," Annie said. She stood up and headed to the door.

"Oh," Bradley thought of one more question to ask. "Where is Roland from?"

Annie thought about it. "Honestly, I don't know. Why?"

"The only place I've heard that expression about dead pigs and sunshine was in Georgia."

Annie shrugged. "He says it all the time."

As soon as Annie shut the door, Bradley sprang up from the bed. With his right leg shackled to the bedframe, he had to hop on his left foot and stretch to reach the lone hatpin he had seen on the marble-top dresser. He bent the hatpin and used it to open his shackles. Freed from the bed, Bradley grabbed his clothes and ran to the window. It slid open quietly, and he threw the clothes out. He was on the second floor and would have to hang down and then drop to the ground. Running back across the room, he tried a spoonful of soup. He groaned quietly. It was delicious. He ran back to the window and climbed out.

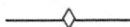

An hour later, Bradley entered the Montour House on the corner of Main and Montour Streets in Havana. The three-story brick building occupied a prominent place in town. The train line ran just across Montour Street and the Chemung Canal, running parallel to the train line, was half a block farther. A few blocks west at the end of Main Street, Havana's 156-foot waterfall tumbled down the western hillside.

The Montour House was a first-class public house, and Bradley appreciated the lofty ceilings and elegant furnishing as he was escorted to the dining area. He scanned the room with telegram in hand for someone who might match the name Otto Fuchs. A crowd of diners filled the space, but Bradley spotted a lone man sitting by one of the unused fireplaces reading *The New York Times*. He wore a middle-class suit with a brown grid pattern that matched his thinning brown hair. The man had waxed the ends of his bushy mustache to fine points. With a leather satchel leaned against his

Montour House, Havana, NY

chair, the man looked like a professor, not that Bradley had ever attended university.

"Mister Otto Fuchs?"

The man looked up at Bradley. "You are late." The vertical lines between his brows deepened when he frowned.

"I had to make sure I wasn't followed."

"Excuses," Fuchs tsk-tsked in his precise German accent. "You are not starting well. Sit down."

Bradley sat in the chair opposite Fuchs. It was lucky he'd managed to arrive at all. After dropping down from Annie's window, he'd scrambled into his clothes and returned to the Lake View Hotel barefoot. He refreshed himself quickly in his room, donned his second pair of boots, and dashed off a quick note to Elizabeth Sinclair apologizing for his hasty departure from Glen Eldridge. He promised to meet up with the Sinclair family in the afternoon and dropped the note at the front desk before requesting transportation to Havana.

The hotel clerk rattled off several options to travel the three miles between villages. The Northern Central Railway only took seven minutes, but the next train wasn't until 1:41 p.m. There was also the horse-drawn Watkins and Havana street trolley, and a line of eighteen-person stages pulled by four-horse teams. The clerk volunteered to check the schedules and pricing, but Bradley decided to throw money at his problem and hired a carriage from the hotel's livery.

Marshland filled most of the valley between Watkins and Havana, so the main road ran at the foot of the western hill. As they reached Havana, Bradley instructed the carriage driver to drop him off several blocks short of the Montour House. He spent the next twenty minutes taking side streets and doubling back on himself to ensure no one had followed him. After his last twenty-four hours, Bradley considered it a minor miracle that he was only five minutes late to meet Fuchs.

Fuchs looked him up and down, taking Bradley's measure. "Your head? What happened?"

Bradley touched the bandage above his left temple. "I slipped on wet rocks and fell near the lake," he said. "It's nothing." It was too risky to admit he'd killed Vance even in self-defense.

Fuchs stared at him for a moment and then nodded. "Why are we here?" he asked. "Why would the Secret Service request a Pinkerton detective to meet with you?"

The Pinkertons provided various detective services including tracking down fugitives. For a few seconds, Bradley found himself fighting off an unreasonable fear that Fuchs had arrived to take him back to The Tombs prison. But he shook off the thought. Fuchs did not know about Bradford Whitey and was here to meet Bradley Webster, the upstanding citizen. And Bradley had sent the telegram with a plan in mind.

"You saw my telegram?" Bradley asked.

"You sent a telegram to the U.S. Secret Service office in New York City claiming you had uncovered a counterfeit ring in Watkins. I'm sure you're aware that the Pinkertons specialize in train robbers and counterfeiting. Your contact reached out to me because I have caught my share of counterfeiters. I arrived from New York this morning to meet you here as a favor."

"Thank you."

"The favor is to the Secret Service, not to you."

Bradley started to speak, but Fuchs cut him off.

"Who are you really, Mister Webster?"

"Does it matter who I am or what my background is if I'm able to expose a counterfeiting ring?"

Fuchs considered this. "Perhaps not. But convince me I'm not wasting my time."

Bradley's stomach interrupted, rumbling loudly. "I haven't eaten since yesterday. Would you mind if we ordered first?"

Fuchs smiled for the first time. "Food is an excellent idea." He motioned to a nearby waitress who came over to take their order. Bradley chose roast beef with new potatoes and string beans. Fuchs ordered the baked fish.

The waitress, her graying hair pinned in a bun, complimented them on their choices and flashed a quick, bright smile as she left to put in their orders. Fuchs turned to Bradley. "The teeth are a great ornament to the face, are they not? And of unquestionable value."

Bradley grinned and nodded. "Mine will be valuable as I sink them into that roast beef." He looked around the room at the other diners while considering Otto Fuchs. He cleared his throat. "Herr Fuchs," he said. "Forgive me for being direct, but why should I trust you are who you say you are?"

Fuchs nodded. "We Germans appreciate directness." He reached into his jacket pocket and pulled out a gold-colored badge and handed it to Bradley. Raised letters spelling out *PINKERTON NATIONAL DETECTIVE AGENT* filled the center of the badge. Below were the words *New York*, and at the top of the badge was the "all-seeing eye" and the Pinkerton motto, *We Never Sleep*.

Bradley nodded and handed the badge back to Fuchs. "I've never met a Pinkerton before."

Fuchs tucked the badge back into his jacket. "I'm honored to be the first. Now, tell me about this counterfeiting ring."

Bradley explained how he received information from Thomas Pickens, a known counterfeiter, that led him to Watkins and Alistair Sinclair. He explained how he got his job with the Sinclairs but had yet to penetrate the counterfeiting ring. He mentioned his undercover visit to the Jefferson that exposed at least five members of the gang. Bradley was finishing a summary of what he knew about each member of the gang—Vance, the Walrus, the portly, silver-haired man, and a man named Bill and his brother—when the food arrived.

They remained silent as the waitress deposited their meals and left, then Otto waved at Bradley to continue his story, but Bradley could not withstand the smell of the roast beef. "To shorten a long story," he said, "the gang has the perfect paper and the perfect ink and a sense of urgency. They also have some connection to a steamer named the *Bonnie Lynn*. I need help exposing them before it's too late." Bradley attacked his roast beef. The only parts of the story he'd left out were The Tombs, any mention of Annie Anderson, and his involvement in Vance's death.

Otto swallowed his last bite of fish, fastidiously wiped the corners of his mouth with his linen napkin, and then set the napkin on his plate. "Before I comment," Fuchs said, "tell me what is in this for you, Mister Webster. You're not a Pinkerton or the Secret Service. You're not law enforcement. You have the table manners of a gentleman, but your eyes continually scan the room for threats, suggesting you have spent time in ungentlemanly pursuits. You are an oddity. Why pursue a counterfeiting ring?" Otto caught Bradley chewing a large mouthful of roast beef.

There were several answers to Fuchs's question, but Bradley gulped down his food and offered the one he thought Fuchs might be expecting. "I'd expect a reward for stopping a counterfeiting ring." Bradley said, taking a few more bites of his food before continuing. "And recognition for my part in the matter might get me a job with a detective agency—despite my inexperience. Perhaps you would put in a good word with Mister Pinkerton or the Secret Service?" Bradley smiled at Fuchs and then looked down at his plate, disappointed that he had finished his roast beef.

"I admire ambition," Fuchs said. "Even when it's unreasonably optimistic."

Bradley opened his mouth to respond, but Fuchs held up his hand silencing him.

"It is not impossible to imagine Alistair Sinclair forming a counterfeiting ring," Fuchs began. "Little was known about him before he met his wife ten years ago. The story of how they met is well known. She was vacationing in the Alps, and he was convalescing at a sanatorium in Switzerland. They married quickly and are members of New York's high society." Fuchs paused and looked about the room before leaning forward and lowering his voice. "There are rumors that Sinclair overinvested in railroad stocks only to lose most of his investment in last year's financial crisis."

"Then I could be right—"

Fuchs held his hand up once more. "It is not impossible, but it is very unlikely. Elizabeth is the youngest daughter of one of the richest families in New York City. She might be rebellious and impulsive but asking her father for money would be much easier than starting an illegal enterprise."

Bradley frowned. "Isn't it true that rich people run counterfeiting networks? They're the only ones who can afford all the equipment."

"True," Fuchs said, "but now let us consider your evidence.

When Thomas Pickens told you about a job offer in New York, did he say it was an illegal job?"

Bradley thought back to their conversation. "It was implied."

"So, you don't know for sure. Pickens, before his arrest, was a respected member of society. It would not be unusual for him to receive legitimate job offers related to his skill set."

"But what about the 'perfect ink'?"

Fuchs sighed as if explaining what was obvious to him was a chore. "There is a sense of urgency. There is ink. It must be perfect. For all you know, Sinclair and his staff are printing invitations for Mrs. Sinclair's next ball, dinner party, or charitable event." Fuchs motioned for the waitress and requested two coffees and the check. When he turned back to Bradley, he shook his head in disappointment. "You have no evidence. You have no proof. You are wasting your time and mine. You should go back to New York City, Mister Webster."

Bradley sat stunned. Anger and embarrassment rose inside him.

Fuchs assessed Bradley's reaction. "I'm German," Fuchs said. "Perhaps my words are too direct."

A new, younger waitress arrived and carefully placed mugs of hot coffee in front of them. Bradley noticed her looking at him, so he glanced up and smiled despite the sting of Fuchs's words. The waitress's long blonde hair shielded part of her face, but Bradley saw dimples dancing at the corners of her full lips.

Bradley thanked her for the coffee and waited until she left before turning back to Fuchs. "Can't we have someone interrogate Thomas Pickens? I know he meant the job in Watkins was an illegal one."

Fuchs blew on his coffee. "Mister Pickens has disappeared. No one knows where he is."

"He was in prison!"

"And now he is missing."

Bradley felt his opportunity slipping away. Returning to the city and poverty was not an option. He pulled out the newspaper clipping on the fire and possible paper theft at the National Bank Note Company. "I have this."

Fuchs took the clipping and read it. "Interesting. By itself, this is just an article clipped out of the newspaper."

"Someone left this in my room with a note. I don't know who it was from, but I'm convinced there is a counterfeiting ring and that someone is working undercover and sharing information with me."

Fuchs finally looked interested. "Someone working on the inside could have valuable information for us. Any idea who left the note?"

Bradley considered it. "No, not yet, but I can find out."

Fuchs motioned to the younger waitress who was hovering nearby. "I would like two sugars, please." He turned back to Bradley. "You have my attention now. If it is true that you have uncovered a counterfeiting ring, we need to know how far along they are in making their fake money. Once the printed counterfeit bills leave Watkins, there will be no way to recover them and no reward for you. You understand?"

Bradley nodded as the waitress arrived with two sugar cubes for Fuchs's coffee. She turned to Bradley. "And you, sir?"

"No, thank you," Bradley said. She seemed almost disappointed in his answer. As she reached for his empty plate, she bumped his coffee mug, spilling the hot brown liquid across the table.

She looked horrified. "I'm so sorry, sir!" She cleaned up what she could and then rushed away to fetch another towel and more coffee for Bradley.

"One more thing," Bradley said. "There is someone else involved. I saw Sinclair meet with another man in Lafayette Park late at night. I think it might have been the Butzemann."

"The Butzemann?" The name surprised Fuchs. "Most people think he is a myth."

"I'm not one of them," Bradley said.

"Would you recognize that person if you saw him again?"

"No, it was too dark."

Fuchs nodded. "Then it could have been anyone." Fuchs leaned across the table. "In counterfeiting cases, local law enforcement is often paid to look the other way and therefore cannot be trusted. If you want to be involved—if you want to have any chance at a reward—you will report to me only and do as I say. Are we clear?"

Bradley agreed with some reluctance.

Fuchs nodded. "I will investigate Sinclair's business dealings. You stay close to Alistair and Elizabeth. It is Pinkerton's cardinal principle that it is impossible for the human mind to retain a secret. Everyone must have a vent for their feelings and will select some-one to whom they can confide. Someone to whom they can unbur-den themselves. Try to be that person for the Sinclairs. And try to find out who is working undercover. You don't yet know if that per-son is helping you or setting you up for some trap. I will leave now. You stay and finish your coffee so no one sees us depart together."

"How do I contact you again?"

"You don't. I will contact you again soon." Fuchs gathered his leather satchel and walked out of the restaurant.

This was not the outcome Bradley had expected when he sent the telegram, but he was willing to let a Pinkerton order him around if it got him closer to penetrating the counterfeiting ring and find-ing the Butzemann. With or without Fuchs's help, Bradley would not quit until he fulfilled the promise he made to himself before leaving New York.

Bradley was considering which of the delicious pies he would order and enjoy with his coffee when he realized that Otto Fuchs had stuck him with the bill.

CHAPTER XXXII

HIGH WIRE ACT

Tuesday, July 21, 1874

A NNIE sat on the edge of her parents' old bed eating cold soup as Roland entered the room. He looked around, confused. "Did Mister Webster pick the lock on the leg irons and climb out of a second-story window naked?"

"Mm-hmm."

She heard Roland chuckle as he picked up the leg irons and the bent hatpin. "Impressive. Not a set of skills I would have expected from someone who looked like he could be playing baseball for an Ivy League university."

Annie pouted. She was counting on Bradley's information to help uncover the man who killed the Southerner in the cemetery and whoever was now trying to kill her. By fleeing, Bradley became another complication on her path to finding the truth. Her head turned at the sound of the front door opening and closing. A few seconds later, Glendon yelled up the stairs. "Annie?"

"Coming!" she called out.

A flash of silver under the bed caught her attention as she stood. She reached down and picked up a pocket watch with the initials *B.W.* etched into the case. Bradley Webster? She slid the watch into her dress pocket and started down the stairs.

Glendon hadn't arrived alone.

"Miss Anderson." Sheriff Swartwood stood next to Glendon with his hat in his hands, pale and stiff as always. "I have a few questions for you."

"Of course, Sheriff." Annie looked at Glendon—what had he already told the sheriff, she wondered? She offered the sheriff her friendliest smile. "If you wouldn't mind waiting in the parlor, I'll bring in some cold lemonade, and you can ask me anything you like."

"If it's all the same, Miss Anderson, my questions won't take long, and I'm not thirsty."

Annie hesitated. Every instinct compelled her to defer to his will. Instead, she did something she would have never dared do a few days ago—keep an important male visitor waiting. "I'm thirsty even if you are not, so please excuse me for a few minutes." She walked through the dining room and ran down the stairs to the kitchen, relieved that Glendon followed her.

"What does he know?" Annie whispered as she banged the cabinets a little louder than necessary to mask their conversation.

"We arrived separately," Glendon said. "Whatever he knows, he did not hear from me."

"Good. That is good." Annie poured lemonade into three glasses and offered one to Glendon.

He accepted it with a smile. "Oh, this just came for you by messenger." He held the telegram out to Annie. Excited, she thanked Glendon and shoved it in her dress pocket beside Bradley's watch.

Annie and Glendon returned to the front entrance, where the sheriff waited. He was checking his pocket watch and looking impatient. Roland had come downstairs—as Annie knew he would—so she handed him the third glass of lemonade. She took a deep sip from her own glass and daintily wiped her lips with a handkerchief before turning to the sheriff. "You said you had questions?"

"George Magee and his wife reported you missing from an outing to Glen Eldridge yesterday," he said. "They asked me to check on your well-being." The sheriff's eyes settled on Annie's bruised left cheek. Vance's slap had left its mark.

"I appreciate the concern, Sheriff, but I already sent a note to George and Emma last night to apologize for my sudden departure yesterday. I started to feel unwell and needed to get home." Feeling "unwell" was a polite way of acknowledging a woman's monthly cycle, and that usually stopped men from asking for details.

"I see," the sheriff said. "You felt unwell. How did you return home?" He was not thrown off his line of questions that easily.

"Is that important?" Annie asked. "Surely you have a busy day with the circus in town."

The sheriff looked over to Glendon and Roland, standing be-hind Annie, then back to her. "There is another person missing from yesterday's excursion. A man named Maurice Vance. I was hoping you might have seen him."

Annie considered her options. Old Annie would have told the sheriff everything, but her confidence that he was looking out for her best interests was slipping. She decided not to admit her or Bradley's involvement in Vance's death, but she might have been seen on Vance's ship so she had to say something. She took a deep breath. "As I said, I felt 'unwell' and needed to leave the picnic suddenly. A man employed by Alistair Sinclair, who introduced himself as Maurice Vance, offered to bring me back to Watkins on the steamer *Bonnie Lynn*. I accepted his offer, but—"

The sheriff leaned forward at this information. "So, you will-ingly climbed aboard the missing man's boat?"

"He only presented himself as a gentleman," Annie said. "And he gave me the impression that others would be traveling with us, but he was lying. When I stepped on the boat, no one else was on board."

"And?"

"Mister Vance struck me across the face," Annie reached up to gently touch her bruised cheek, "and then took me out to the middle of the lake." Her eyes watered involuntarily at the memory.

The sheriff hadn't expected this. The house grew still. Nana's grandfather clock in the parlor began chiming the hour. As the tones faded, the sheriff cleared his throat. "What happened in the middle of the lake?"

"He made advances." Annie straightened her back and held her head high. "Of course, I fought him off, but he was stronger than I was." She paused to stare at the sheriff. He did not meet her eyes. "I took the only option available to spare my virtue. I grabbed a life preserver and threw myself overboard. I did not see him again once I landed in the water."

Both Roland and Glendon had reached out to put a hand on her shoulder. The sheriff processed this new information. "These are serious allegations. Why didn't you come forward immediately?"

"And be the talk of the town? I hoped to preserve my dignity."

The sheriff looked skeptical, but they both knew the attempted assault would be a juicy morsel for small-town gossip if word got out. "Is there anyone else who could confirm your story?"

"We were the only two people on board the *Bonnie Lynn* when it pulled away from the Glen Eldridge dock." That was true.

The sheriff nodded, then addressed Roland and Glendon. "Two fishermen found the *Bonnie Lynn* floating in the middle of the lake yesterday afternoon and towed it back to Watkins. There was no sign of Maurice Vance. I searched the boat this morning and found a significant amount of blood near the bow and multiple gunshots in the wood deck."

"Sounds like he got what he deserved," Roland said under his breath.

The sheriff turned back to Annie. "Can you explain any of those things?"

"What I can explain is that when Mister Vance attacked me, I was lucky to escape overboard with my honor and my life. And I was lucky to reach shore." Annie did not hide her irritation with the sheriff's question.

"When you find Mister Vance," Glendon said, "I expect you will arrest him on assault charges."

"Yes, although we will have to hear his side of the story," the sheriff said. "That is if Mister Vance is still alive." The sheriff put his hat on and looked at Annie. "If Vance fell overboard for some reason—well, bodies tend to float back to the surface after a few days." Annie wondered if the sheriff knew more than he was admitting. "One last question, Miss Anderson. After you reached shore, how did you get back home?"

"Abraham Adams—a local horse trainer—saw me climb out of the lake and gave me a ride back to town in his wagon," Annie said. "I'm sure he will confirm that fact." Annie did not want the sheriff to ask how Abraham just happened to find her on a remote part of the lake, so she kept talking. "Sheriff, I have a question for you. What progress have you made finding the missing body from the cemetery?"

She could see annoyance flash across the sheriff's face. "The drunk that sobered up and walked away? There is no body, so there is nothing to follow up on." The sheriff stepped toward the door but turned back to look at Annie. "If you want an investigation, find me a body."

Glendon closed the door after the sheriff's departure and then turned to Annie. "Why didn't you tell the sheriff that someone is trying to kill you?"

Annie did not know herself. "There is something about the sheriff I don't trust."

Glendon turned to Roland for support, but Roland shrugged. "I didn't vote for him."

"Annie," Glendon said, "this is serious. Your life is in danger."

"I know," she said. "And it scares me."

"Then let's leave," Glendon said. "You've always wanted to travel. We can be on a train tomorrow for New York City and on a ship sailing for Europe within a few days. We can go wherever you want. You've always wanted to see Paris. We can go around the world if you want. See elephants in Africa and tigers in India. Let me take you out of Watkins and away from whoever is after you."

Annie's eyes widened in amazement. Her parents had spent all their money building this house and after they died, Nana had never let Annie travel far. Now, here was the offer of a lifetime. Why not? Why not leave Watkins and the threat to her life behind? She could explore the world as she always wanted to. And yet—if she left now, could she ever come home again and not be looking over her shoulder? She sighed, realizing she already knew the answer. She took Glendon's hand. "You taught me growing up that I cannot run from my problems," she said. "I need to find out who killed the man in the cemetery and who is trying to kill me. If I don't, I'll never feel safe anywhere."

Annie watched a range of emotions flash across Glendon's face, then his shoulders slumped. "I'm worried we can't protect you here," he said. He looked at Roland.

"I support whatever decision Annie makes," Roland said. "And we both know that when her mind is made up, there is no changing it."

"Stubborn like her mother," Glendon said with a wistful smile.

"Just promise that you will consider the idea?" He donned his hat, not waiting for her reply. "I'm going to look at Mister Vance's boat myself to see if there are any clues the sheriff missed. Then, I'll find out who Vance worked for and see what he has to say for himself." He left as abruptly as the sheriff had.

Roland turned to Annie. "You started something, and I trust you to figure out how to finish it." Annie hugged him. His support meant the world to her.

Annie remembered the telegram that Glendon had handed her. She reached into her pocket, removed the telegram, and read the message. She cursed under her breath and turned to Roland. "How do you feel about going to a parade?"

A surge of visitors flowed into Watkins to see The Great New York and New Orleans Zoological and Equestrian Exposition. The show had been traveling around the country on its second annual tour and had arrived in Watkins in the middle of the night. Two trains pulling sixty freight cars brought all the machinery and the extensive menagerie of animals that made up this circus. Workers had started setting up the tents at the Watkins Fairgrounds on Franklin Street beyond the Glen Park Hotel and 14th Street.

Annie led Roland into town and toward the train station. They jostled their way through the crowd which had formed to watch the circus's parade when it passed through at noon. A parade helped the circus attract publicity and paying customers. It also led the crowds toward the fairgrounds for the 1:00 p.m. circus. A second show was scheduled for 7:00 p.m.

"Annie." Roland looked around nervously. "It would be safer to watch the parade from my office." She knew he was worried about protecting her in the tight crowd, but she had chosen their spot carefully. Braving the multitudes was a calculated risk. Most of the spectators pressed in around her were from farming families who had traveled long distances in their wagons to come down into town for the parade and the show.

A hurrah went up just after noon as the parade kicked off with a large music wagon pulled by fourteen dromedaries—one-humped

Circus Coming to Town

domesticated camels. Next came twenty equestrians dressed as huntsmen and mounted on impressive steeds. The riders, dressed for an English foxhunt, were also performers in the upcoming show. The next eye-catching wagon contained a lion tamer standing inside a cage full of lions for all to view.

Annie enjoyed the parade but kept one eye on the crowd. As she scanned back and forth, she noticed several friendly faces. Mr. Charles Frost, across the street, stood in front of his Schuyler Marble Works. Dr. Bennett, the town coroner and proprietor of the Drug & Medicine Store of Bennett & Hurd, tipped his hat to her as he walked by. Annie waved to her friend Kat Auble, who owned the town's cloak and dressmaking shop. Annie did not yet see the face she was looking for.

A long line of colorful wagons—each carrying its own den of live animals—passed by the onlookers and headed for the fairgrounds. Annie particularly liked the tigers, kangaroos, gorillas, and the gnu or wild horned horse.

As Annie scanned the spectators on the opposite side of the street, she noticed an angry face staring directly at her. She grabbed Roland's arm and pointed just as Zingra and his den of serpents blocked their view. The snake charmer stood inside his plate-glass cage as the reptiles coiled around and about him. When his wagon passed, the one-armed man had disappeared.

A Parisian steam calliope pulled by ten horses served as the grand finale for the parade. High-pressure steam pumped through the numerous large whistles made the calliope's music loud enough to drown out the crowd noise. As the "Battle Hymn of the Republic" blasted out, the crowd began moving along with the calliope south toward the fairgrounds. Annie finally found the one face she had been seeking. Big Mag had joined the crowd heading south toward the fairgrounds. Annie smiled.

"Just as I had hoped," she said. "Big Mag is going to see the Walk for Life with most of the town."

"The what?"

"The Walk for Life. The 'wonderful ascension feat'? It was advertised in the newspaper. Right before the first show, a woman walks up a single wire from the ground to the top of the circus tent two hundred feet off the ground." Annie shivered involuntarily at the thought. She was afraid of heights.

"Then what?"

"Then she comes back down, I guess."

"Okay. Where are we going instead?" Annie grabbed Roland by the arm and set off in the opposite direction. Crossing the street near the train station, they swerved to avoid the fresh camel dung in their path.

Annie pulled out the telegram as they walked. "The telegram confirmed there is no one named Harper or Sadie Thompson in Rutherfordton, North Carolina. Either our dead Southerner used a fake name in Big Mag's registry, or I got the location wrong."

The crowds disappeared as they reached the Northern Central House.

"I smelled alcohol on the dead man that day in the cemetery," Annie said, "so I know the Southerner had been drinking. Big Mag told Glendon and me that Watkins outlawed liquor sales, but she could include alcohol if guests paid for services. What service would our Southerner pay for at a brothel?"

"A shoeshine?" Roland said and then laughed at his own joke.

"Is that what they're calling it these days?" Annie said, laughing with him. "No, we have to find the woman he visited with. If I am lucky, she'll have information to help us figure out who he was and why someone killed him."

Annie looked about, ensuring no one was watching them, then led the way into the dimly lit and perfumed confines of the Northern Central House. Only three people occupied the large space. A drunk with his head down on a table, a bored woman who looked up briefly before returning to her nail filing, and Kenneth, standing in his usual position and still wearing a hat too small for his head.

Big Mag told Annie not to return, so Annie approached Kenneth holding out a gold quarter eagle coin—a day's salary for a skilled worker. "Do you remember the Southerner who came in almost two weeks ago?" He looked at her, then nodded. "I would like to talk to the girl he spent time with. I only want information, but I'll pay her for it."

Kenneth held out his hand and allowed Annie to place the coin in his palm. He hefted it twice as if weighing it, then slid it into his pocket. Without a word, he left the room.

Annie looked at Roland, who shrugged. They had no choice but to wait. Annie estimated it would take Big Mag a minimum of forty-five minutes to walk to the fairgrounds, see the Walk for Life, and then return.

Kenneth reentered the room and returned to his usual position. He gave Annie a slight nod and held out his hand. She stared at it for a moment before realizing he wanted more money. She pulled out a stack of dollar bills she had earned from her sewing projects and placed them into Kenneth's hand one at a time. When she paused, he looked at her with his hand still extended. Annie wasn't in a position to negotiate, so she kept placing bills into his hand until he finally nodded and closed his fist. The money disappeared into his pocket, and then he held up two fingers, then one, then three.

Annie blinked. "Room two one three?" she asked. Kenneth gave an almost imperceptible nod of his head. "Thank you," Annie said. She headed for the stairs she and Glendon had used during her last visit.

Roland tried to follow, but Kenneth extended an arm blocking his path.

"Uh, Annie?" Roland called after her.

Annie turned to see Roland peering around Kenneth. "I'll be all right," she said, patting her dress pocket. Roland had gifted her a replacement for the derringer she'd lost in the lake. "I'll be back soon."

She climbed the stairs and went down the hall to room 213. She was excited for the new lead and knocked confidently on the door. A muted voice came from within. "Come in."

Annie opened the door and stepped into the room. An attractive dark-haired woman not much older than herself greeted her with a smile. Annie blushed and fought the urge to run from the room. The woman was naked and floating in a large bathtub.

"Come in and shut the door," the woman said. Annie quietly closed the door. When she turned back, she looked anywhere except at the woman's naked body. In addition to the tub, the room had a comfortable bed, a mirror on the wall, and a dresser supporting an arrangement of bone-handled brushes, American and French perfume bottles, lotion, and tooth-wash bottles, and several glass syringes for personal hygiene.

"You aren't what I was expecting," the woman said, playing with the water in the tub. "I haven't kissed many women, but since you paid full price for my time, I guess I don't mind."

Annie's blush deepened as she realized Kenneth had made her pay for "services" for the hour. "No, I just wanted to ask you some questions."

"Oh." The woman crossed her arms over her breasts and smiled at Annie. "It's your money. However you want to spend your time is fine with me."

Annie wasn't sure what to do next. "Should I wait outside while you finish your bath?"

"No, I'm just soaking. Do you mind asking your questions while I enjoy the warm water while it lasts?" She didn't wait for an answer. "What's your name?"

"Annie."

"Hello Annie, I'm Désirée."

"That's a pretty name." Annie did not know where to look. She settled for keeping eye contact. The woman did not look like a Désirée. "Is that your real name?"

The woman laughed. "No," she said. "No, it's not. My real name is Jeanne. I don't tell the men that, and they never ask. So, what are your questions, Annie?"

"I know a man with a Southern accent booked a room here two weeks ago. He spent time with you, and I'm hoping you could tell me more about him."

"If I betray confidences, my customers will stop visitin' me. Why is it important to you?"

Annie looked into Jeanne's eyes and gave her an honest answer. "I think something bad happened to him, but no one believes me. I'm trying to prove that the men who doubted me are wrong."

Jeanne stirred the water in the tub. "I remember your Southerner well," she said. "I was supposed to have the day off, but he wanted a black girl," Jeanne said. "Or at least a mulatto. I'm only quadroon, but I'm as exotic as it gets in Watkins in my line of work, so Big Mag sent him to me. He arrived at my door with a devilish grin and a bottle of whiskey in his hand."

Jeanne had dark hair, dark eyes, and slightly darker skin, but Annie couldn't have picked out any features that signaled her one-quarter negro heritage. Jeanne was just a beautiful woman. "You could easily pass for white," Annie said. Before emancipation, the one-drop rule meant any amount of African ancestry—even one drop of colored blood—made a person black and at risk of enslavement.

"So why admit I have negro blood?" Jeanne said. "Well, we are all free now, and, to many men, I'm forbidden fruit. It's good for my business. You'd be surprised at how many gentlemen ask for me."

"Like the Southerner?"

"Yeah, like the Southerner. He and I sat on my bed awhile, talking and drinking. He shared his whiskey, which not all men do, so I liked him well enough. 'Course drinking changes a man." Jeanne's face clouded over. "We were talking when he grabbed me and pushed me down." Jeanne looked up at Annie. "He tore at my clothes, pinned my hands over my head with one hand, and started to choke me with his other. I thought he was going to kill me—"

Jeanne's eyes watered. Annie grabbed a handkerchief off the dresser and walked over to Jeanne.

"Thank you," Jeanne said, wiping her eyes before continuing. "And then, he just deflated. In every sense of the word. He started telling me how much he loved his wife. He said things had been hard, but his luck was turning. I held him and let him cry and talk about his wife. I kept the drink away from him after that."

"Did he ever tell you his real name?" Annie asked.

"He told me that when his wife, Sadie, agreed to marry him and become Mrs. Lewis Crawford, it was the happiest day of his life."

Lewis Crawford, not Harper Thompson, the name he had written in Big Mag's guest book. Annie was excited but wondered why he had put a fake name in the registry and why that name. She thought of another question for Jeanne. "Did you see his tattoo?"

"On his forearm? The snake?"

RETURN TO THE BROTHEL

"Yes! Is there any chance you could draw it for me?"

"I could try. The bathwater is getting cold anyway."

Annie handed Jeanne a towel and then turned around to give her privacy. Jeanne dried off and then wrapped herself in a lacy robe. After some digging, Jeanne found paper and a pencil buried in a dresser drawer. She bit her lip as she sketched a picture of a rattlesnake forming the number six. When she was satisfied with the result, she handed the drawing to Annie.

"You're very talented," Annie said. And she meant it. "Did Lewis Crawford say anything else about himself?"

"No. We both fell asleep, but I heard him get up in the middle of the night. He turned off the gaslight and left. He didn't come back even though he'd paid for the whole night."

Annie got what she came for and wanted to leave before Big Mag returned. She thanked Jeanne and started to open the door but turned back. "Can I ask you one last question?"

"Why do I work here?"

"Yes. I don't mean any offense."

"It's all right. I ask myself the same question all the time, but working at a brothel has benefits—a roof over my head and money in my pocket. And honestly? My husband used to beat me and take advantage whenever he felt like it. He got violent when he had been drinking, and he was always drinking, so I left him and came here. Now I get paid when I open my legs."

Annie returned to the lobby to find the lone woman trying to chat with Roland. He looked relieved to see Annie. She filled him in on what she had learned as he escorted her out into the sunshine. "His real name was Lewis Crawford, and he had this tattoo on his forearm." Annie showed Roland the drawing of the snake forming the number six. Roland took the paper from her and studied it.

The look on his face surprised her. He stared at the image so long that Annie wondered if he had seen this tattoo before. He returned the paper to her but stayed silent as they returned to the house.

"Annie," Roland said after delivering her safely home, "I have to go talk to somebody about this." He appeared agitated. His natural affability had faded away. "Please stay home with the door locked. I'll be back in no time at all." He left before she could protest.

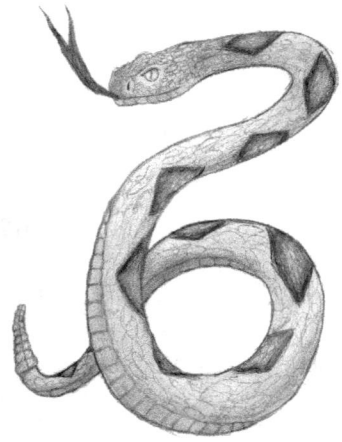

Annie wandered around the empty house. Glendon hadn't returned, and Roland had left her alone. Annie pouted in silence for twenty minutes, then decided she could not sit around and wait for others to solve her problems. She headed upstairs to her trusted Singer sewing machine. She had an idea.

CHAPTER XXXIII

ELMIRA PRISON CAMP

From the Journal of Private H. Thompson

August 27, 1864 – Frank caught my eye as I sat in the grass writing in my journal. I gave him a nod and then stood up and dusted myself off. My turn was drawing near. I carefully packed my ink pen, ink, and journal pages. I vowed to put as many of our experiences on paper as possible now that my direct participation in the war had ended. Paper was hard to come by, and what paper could be found was often of low quality, but Ace had gifted me a gorgeous leather-bound journal. He would not tell me where it came from— or whether he had traded for or stolen it—but did suggest that I not let any Union officers see it in my possession.

I wanted to avoid what came next, but knew I couldn't. The warmth from the sun felt good, but I knew it wouldn't last. Cool breezes were moving in as September approached.

Frank led me away from the Elmira Prison Camp's whitewashed perimeter wall. I looked back at the three locals staring down at me and waved. One lifted his hand in a halfhearted response. Some enthusiast businessmen had erected two observation platforms with chairs and binoculars outside the camp and across the street. For a mere ten cents, visitors could pay to watch us going about our day. Some prisoners were furious at being gawked at and made lewd gestures in the direction of the onlookers, which no doubt reinforced the North's already low opinion of Confederate soldiers. Most of us ignored the spectators. Personally, I found their presence entertaining. Daily life in the camp was dull, so I enjoyed watching the watchers.

The prison camp in Elmira had a lot in common with Point Lookout. Both had high fences manned by Union sentries, insufficient food, and questionable housing in crowded tents with few

Elmira Prison Camp

comforts. I missed my view of Chesapeake Bay. Here, the camp was about a mile and a half west of the Elmira city center on the northern shore of the Chemung River. Prisoner's quarters—some barracks but mostly tents—filled up about half the space of the camp closest to the street and the observatories. Then came several cookhouses where our meager rations were prepared. Beyond the cookhouses was a large, narrow pond stretching the length of our enclosure. Extending over the water were our prison privies. Beyond the pond was more fence, and then the river where prisoners were taken to bathe.

Ten thousand men filled a camp designed for half that many, but Frank's broad frame cleared a path through groups of prisoners, making him easy to follow. I had remained close with Ace and Frank, but my relationship with Buck was cool at best. None of us had gotten over the loss of Taylor or could agree on whether he had escaped or died during the train crash.

Frank and I maneuvered through the sea of white tents. As we neared our destination, I could see his head swivel left and right, keeping an eye out for guards. He pulled back the flap on one of the tents in the second row on the north side, and I ducked down and entered. Frank leaned in, put a small pouch filled with dirt in his pockets, and wandered off toward Foster's Pond.

"There you are, Harper," said Private Washington Traweek as he climbed out of the dirt hole in the middle of the tent. "We're making good progress." He handed me a dull pocketknife and a scratched metal spoon.

We'd first met Traweek in mid-August when his group of Alabama soldiers—members of the "Jeff Davis" artillery—arrived by train from Baltimore. We had been friendly—the Alabama boys had tents near ours—but that changed last night. Traweek had come to our tent in the evening and steered the conversation toward ideas for escape. Buck reacted with enthusiasm. "It's our duty to escape!" When Frank and Ace agreed, Traweek asked the four of us to meet with members of his unit. They made us place our right hand on the Bible and take a solemn oath not to divulge what we were about to hear under penalty of death. It was only then we learned about the tunnel.

It had been Traweek's idea to start digging an escape tunnel in an empty tent. His small group had already dug down six feet and had then started digging horizontally. The tunnel needed to travel sixty-eight feet to clear the perimeter fence to the north. Having no tools other than pocketknives and silverware, the artillerymen had made slow progress the first few days and realized they needed more help. That's where we came in. Digging was demanding work. Harder still with the poor food rations.

Today was my first time digging in the tunnel. Traweek had me take off my uniform and put it back on inside out. I did as he told me. "If we don't turn our clothes inside out while we dig," he said, "they start to turn the color of the dirt clay. We can't have the guards getting suspicious during roll calls."

The hole in the ground was a circle about three feet in diameter cut in the thick sod of grass that formed the floor of the tent. The artillerymen had cut the sod out into one piece, which now lay upside down next to the hole.

Dig for thirty minutes, and then someone else will come to take over. Place the loose dirt into these sacks as you go." He held up a cloth sack filled with about a quart of dirt. The sacks were cut from a man's shirt and crudely sewn. Traweek tucked a full sack into his pocket. "Every now and then, someone will come by and pick up a sack. We dump them in the pond when no one is looking. We only dig during the day. We can't carry the dirt away at night without drawing attention to ourselves. Any questions?"

I shook my head and forced a smile on my face. He wished me luck and tipped his hat, then disappeared through the tent flap.

I stared at the hole in the ground. I hadn't wanted to escape on the train, but each day in Elmira, the number of prisoners increased, the weather and the rations got worse, and more men were getting sick. I had no desire to spend the winter freezing and starving in New York, and I knew I could not trust Buck to share the gold if he got to it first.

I had never told the Lucky Six, but tight places terrified me. The thought of the tunnel collapsing around me filled my mind with dread. I struggled to muster the will to move. Would anyone notice if I failed to dig? Yes, they would wonder why the cloth sacks remained empty. I took a breath and conjured a vision of the woman I loved in my mind. This tunnel would get me to the gold, and the gold might bring me back to her. I tried to remember the feeling of having her in my arms. To be able to hold her again—for that, I *would challenge death itself.*

Spoon and pocketknife in hand, I climbed into the hole.

Aug 31, 1864 – Ace and I walked toward the shore of Foster's Pond. He'd managed to wash most of the bloodstains from Taylor's large Confederate overcoat. Despite the heat, he wore it to carry multiple bags of dirt from the tunnel. Prisoners had to make do with whatever they had for clothing. Camp authorities burned any donated clothes not gray in color to avoid mistaking rebel prisoners for Union soldiers or civilians.

We walked along the pond's edge, discreetly shaking out the contents of the bags, then left quickly. The pond, once a pleasant little body of water, had turned into a cesspool. It had become the "bathroom" for ten thousand prisoners. Sanitary conditions in the camp were deteriorating daily, and diarrhea was becoming widespread. Men were dying from it. The prisoners started calling the camp Hellmira.

"I heard from the guards that Grant and his Union troops are laying siege to Petersburg," I said as we maneuvered around several barefoot prisoners sitting listlessly on the ground. We got little information from the outside world, but the guards often bragged about Union Army successes.

"Robert E. Lee's boys will push them back north soon enough," Ace said, but without conviction. Sunken cheeks and hollow eyes from poor rations had aged his normally handsome features. He looked small in Taylor's old jacket. "I heard that Sherman is moving against Atlanta," he said.

I asked him why he suddenly cared about Georgia. He pulled a letter out of his jacket. "From my fiancée," he said. "When her family learned she was pregnant, they sent her away to live with an aunt in Georgia."

"Ace, I'm sorry."

"I should have married her instead of leaving to look for the gold." He stared away in the distance, then turned to face me. "When we escape, I'm going to Georgia to marry her before she has our child."

We continued along the perimeter fence. I counted the months. If they conceived in February, his fiancée would give birth in mid-November. Not much more than two months. Ace was running out

Rebels In Prison

of time.

September 15, 1864 – We awoke to learn there had been a failed tunnel escape last night. We had weeks of work left on our own tunnel, but we all understood that the guards would search relentlessly now until they had uncovered all other tunnels. As the day wore on, guards began detaining prisoners for questioning. Prisoners began to point fingers to save themselves. It was a tense afternoon for the rest of our group of tunnel diggers.

We got wind that the Yankees were organizing an inspection of all tents tomorrow. There was a general panic among our group, but we were determined to save our tunnel. We shut down digging efforts, and one of the artillerymen stole pieces of plank from the sidewalk to place three feet below the surface of our tunnel entrance. We filled the hole with dirt and placed the circle of sod over the hole, packing it down to leave no signs of our tunneling efforts.

Yankee guards roused us from our tents early the next morning. We'd done such a thorough job of hiding our tunnel that the guards complimented the artillerymen on the cleanliness of the tent. By the end of the day, camp authorities had uncovered and shut down twenty-eight other tunnels.

September 29, 1864 – The Yankee suspicions have died down, so we started our digging efforts again.

September was a very cold month. Worse than any winter I had experienced in the South. I longed to feel the comforts of home. More soldiers were getting sick, and the death count continued to rise. Buck had gotten sick but recovered from whatever ailed him. Now, Ace lay in our tent with a fever and a headache. For the second day in a row, I took his turn in the tunnel to give him extra rest.

Climbing into that hole hadn't gotten easier for me. The closer we got to the perimeter fence, the farther underground I had to crawl to dig. My fears made it torturous. At least it was warmer in the tunnel, but all that digging built up a sweat that made me colder when I returned to the surface.

I scattered my last bag of dirt in the pond and then headed back toward my own tent. No onlookers looked down from the empty observation towers. Maybe it was the deteriorating weather, or perhaps the onlookers finally realized the brutal reality of what they were pay-

ing to see.

From far above, I heard plaintive honking. A flock of geese in V formation passed overhead on their way south. I craned my neck to watch them until they disappeared beyond the hills south of camp. I did not spend time envying their freedom or imagine I could fly south with them to the warmth of the Carolinas. I only wished I'd had my Enfield rifle and some ball and powder. I could have shot several out of the sky and gotten them to land inside the camp perimeter. I was so damn hungry.

As I walked past one of the barracks, I saw a rat scurrying for cover while two prisoners from Virginia chased after it. Rat meat had become a thriving business here in camp. The five cents for a killed and dressed rat was more than most prisoners could afford. Some prisoners traded rats for tobacco or haircuts. I was hungry enough to be tempted, but so far, only Frank in our group had added that delicacy to his diet.

Frank and Buck were waiting for me when I returned to our tents. The looks on their faces worried me. A range of possibilities flew through my brain. I looked around. Ace was gone. "Someone told the guards he was sick," Buck said. "They came by to check on him. Once they saw the rash, they took him away to the hospital on the other side of Foster's Pond. He's in isolation. They think it might be smallpox."

October 6, 1864 – We hadn't heard from Ace since the guards took him away. The Hellmira doctors isolated those with contagious diseases, attempting to slow the spread of disease through the prisoner population. Smallpox was deadly, but I was less worried for myself. The Army had vaccinated me at the start of the war.

Traweek was sympathetic but unyielding when I asked to delay our escape until Ace's recovery. The tunnel was ready and there would be no second chances. Hesitation meant failure. "I'm sorry about Ace," Traweek told me. "With or without him, we go tonight."

Frank, Buck, and I had avoided talking about escaping without Ace, but we couldn't delay the conversation any longer. We had to make a decision. I took a deep breath, preparing to argue on Ace's behalf—we all go, or none of us go—when Buck surprised me.

"We can't leave without Ace," Buck said. His face looked pained as he said the words aloud. I looked to Frank, who nodded. It was

decided. We would stay. For a moment, I mourned the loss of our escape. We would have a miserable winter at Hellmira, but it was the right decision. When we left this camp, the Lucky Six survivors would leave together.

Buck kicked the toe of his boot into the dirt. "I know a prisoner that takes supplies to the isolation ward," he said. "I'll see if he can get us word on how Ace is doing." After Buck left, I searched out Traweek and told him of our decision. He said if we changed our minds, the plan was to go in the middle of the night, around 3:00 a.m.

Frank and I played cards while we waited for Buck's return. Buck arrived long after the sun had set. His face was pale, and he looked distraught. Frank and I stood to meet him. "Ace is dead," he said. "Smallpox killed him."

Frank looked stricken. I was speechless. Ace's child would never know its father. We sat in silence, lost in our memories of Ace. Our days as fighting members of the 34th seemed a lifetime ago. When my thoughts turned to my true love, I cleared my throat. "Traweek said to be ready at three a.m. if we changed our minds."

We had no reason to remain behind.

At 3:00 a.m., Traweek crawled through the tunnel first. We would be the last of the ten escapees. If the first men through were discovered, we would all end up in isolation. When it was our turn, Buck ducked into the tent with the tunnel and dropped into the hole. Then Frank. It had to be a tight fit for Frank, and yet I was the one afraid of getting stuck. I slipped into the tent, tucking my oil-clothe-wrapped journal under my shirt before I lowered myself into the dark hole. The dirt under my hands felt like freedom. I crawled forward with my eyes closed, relieved it was a one-way trip. I bumped my head at the end of the tunnel and looked up surprised. Frank reached down and pulled me out. The other escapees had already disappeared into the darkness. We stood alone on the streets of Elmira.

The first hints of sunrise appeared in the east as Buck, Frank, and I headed to the river. We waded across and climbed up the hills beyond. Looking back, I could see inside the prison walls. We could hear distant yelling as guards discovered our tunnel exit. A search party was forming.

They were coming after us.

ELEPHANT AND DROMEDARY

CHAPTER XXXIV

Circus Menagerie

Tuesday, July 21, 1874

A S the sun dipped lower in the sky, Hannah and Henry weaved their way through the crowds at the Watkins Fairgrounds with wide eyes. They had seen circuses before, but there was always excitement around discovering something new. After speaking with Otto Fuchs, Bradley decided not to resign his job with the Sinclairs. He apologized to Mrs. Sinclair for disappearing from Glen Eldridge the day before. When the twins asked about the bandage on his head, he told them he was embarrassed that slippery lake rocks caused him to fall and cut his head and that he'd left Glen Eldridge to find a doctor in Watkins to get patched up.

The twins had forty minutes to search the small city of exhibition tents before the evening show began under the big top—an immense oblong tent. There were as many tents to choose from as wagons in the parade, and Henry and Hannah seemed determined to visit them all. Bradley and Nanny Kate followed close behind the twins while Elizabeth waited in line for the tickets. The Walrus had wandered off alone. Alistair, called away for work, was absent again. No one asked about Vance.

The smell of fresh, warm pies temporarily overpowered the scent of wood shavings and the faint reek of animal manure as the group passed several food vendors. Henry skipped around a man selling slices of watermelon and yelled over his shoulder that he would "be back later." The twins explored a large tent with Hannah's favorite animal, an elephant. Hannah waved hello while the creature stared back with placid eyes, then the twins raced off to the reptile tent to see Zingra and his serpents.

As Nanny Kate hurried to catch up, Bradley heard her mutter,

"I should never 'ave helped 'em learn to walk."

Bradley paused at the entrance of the reptile tent and looked behind him. He had an unsettling feeling that they were being watched. Casually scanning the crowd without appearing to do so, he noticed a pickpocket stalking the circusgoers but ignored the man. Not his problem tonight. No one else looked suspicious, but the feeling did not leave him.

Zingra's serpents didn't hold the twins' attention long. Hannah came barreling out of the tent, squealing while Henry followed, pretending his arms had turned into wiggling snakes as he chased his sister. They both ran on ahead. Nanny Kate, looking harried, struggled to keep up. Bradley reached for his pocket watch, remembering he had lost it the day before. It made him ill to think that his father's watch was now at the bottom of Seneca Lake with Maurice Vance.

Hannah's voice called out from ahead. "We found him! We found the sea lion!"

One of the circus's star attractions this season was Neptune, a monstrous Alaskan sea lion exhibited in a mammoth holding tank filled with forty barrels of seawater. The only living sea lion outside the Pacific Ocean if you believed the barker's spiel. Here was something new. Here was something the twins had never seen before. While everyone by now had seen lions, tigers, elephants, and all nature of African and Asian beasts, very few had ever seen a genuine sea lion from the West Coast.

Inside Neptune's tent, the twins wiggled to the front and pressed their small faces against the sea creature's glass cage. Nanny Kate was content to stop inside the tent entrance and catch her breath, leaving Bradley to move through the throngs of viewers to stay close to the twins. Bradley paused as the feeling of being watched intensified. He kept his eyes on the twins and tried to use his peripheral vision to catch someone staring at him. He was about to turn around when he heard a familiar voice at his side.

"If you were a gentleman, you would have done me the courtesy of saying goodbye before you climbed out my window."

Bradley was startled but tried not to show it. Standing at his side was an older woman wearing a dark-hued working-class dress mended more than once. She had graying hair tucked into a simple bonnet. Bradley looked closely and noticed that she had removed the lenses to her glasses.

"And if I were a more intelligent man, Annie, I would have escaped from your lovely jail with that delicious bowl of soup."

"Miss Anderson to you," Annie said, still annoyed.

Bradley met Annie's eyes and then went back to watching the twins. "You look spectacular, Miss Anderson." An odd compliment, given that she looked much heavier and older than when he last saw her, but she acknowledged his praise with a smile. "How did you get your hair so gray?" he asked.

"I brushed in some white face powder and then used sticky hair product to keep it there. You were right. Dressing as an older woman has made me invisible. I've been following you since the twins arrived."

"You missed me that much? I'm charmed." Not noticing her following left him humbled and impressed.

"You owe me answers. I sacrificed my favorite boots to save your life."

"As a gentleman, you have my word that I'll make it up to you."

"Are you?"

"Am I what?"

"Are you a gentleman?"

Bradley caught her looking at him with curiosity and a vulnerability that made him understand it was an important question. He hesitated for a moment. "For you," he said. "I could be." He wanted it to be true.

She leaned toward him and said in a low voice, "I'll forgive you for my lost boots if you help me find out who is trying to kill me." She forced a smile onto her face. "I want to be free to step outside as myself without fearing for my life—" Annie stopped talking when she heard Bradley's intake of breath. "What is it?" she asked.

Bradley had been listening to Annie while scanning the crowd out of habit. He'd been surprised to see one of the counterfeiters from the Jefferson meeting. The short, heavy-set man with silver hair stood a dozen feet from the twins.

"Annie," Bradley said, lowering his voice, "do you see the

shorter, portly man with the silver hair about six people to the right of the twins?"

"The one with the pretentious mustache?"

"Yes. He is part of a counterfeiting ring."

"Counterfeiting? You do have a lot of questions to answer."

"He might know who Sinclair is working with. The person who was giving Vance orders."

"The person who wants me dead?"

"Could be," Bradley said. "I want to try something. Will you help?"

Annie nodded.

Bradley leaned closer and whispered in her ear. "Count to ten, go over and ask him for the time, and then return to this spot." Bradley set out through the crowd, synchronizing his movements with Annie. He reached the silver-haired man as Annie started talking to him. As the man consulted his pocket watch, Bradley stumbled into him, apologized, and then quickly moved away.

Annie met Bradley back where they had started. "What did we just do?" she asked.

"I was hoping to get his wallet, but I only managed to find this." Bradley surreptitiously showed Annie a metal key with the number 207 attached.

"I'm quite sure pickpocketing isn't in the gentlemen's etiquette guide," Annie said.

Bradley ignored her comment. "I don't know who he is or where he is staying, but if I can follow him back to his hotel room, I can use this key to search his room. Maybe that will help us figure out what is going on."

"I can do it," Annie said.

"What?"

"I know what hotel this key goes to, because I've lived in this town my whole life. I can search his room now while you and the twins enjoy the circus."

Near the glass cage, the twins started losing interest in Neptune. Bradley was running out of time. "It's too dangerous."

Annie's eyes flashed with anger. "More dangerous than waiting around to be killed?"

She had a point. Since he had to stay with the twins, was it worth the risk? He handed the key to her. "What hotel?"

"This is a Glen Mountain House room key." Annie pushed the key into her pocket. "Meet me after the circus, and I'll tell you what I found—after you answer my questions. You know where I live." As Annie turned to leave, she leaned closer to him. "I'm not the only person following you tonight." Annie left before he could reply.

The twins grabbed his hand a moment later and led him to Nanny Kate. "We want watermelon before the show starts!" they said in unison. Their small group headed back toward the main tent and the watermelon vendor. There was a long line.

Nanny Kate checked her own watch. "Your mother is expecting us. We don't have time to wait," she said. The twins groaned.

"If you take the twins to Mrs. Sinclair," Bradley said, "I'll wait in line for watermelon."

"Are ye sure?"

Bradley, who was very hungry himself, nodded and watched Nanny Kate and the twins disappear into the crowd. All around him, gaslight fixtures bloomed to life, pushing back the growing darkness. Bradley was fourth in line for watermelon when someone whispered in his ear. "Don't turn around."

He recognized the voice, but it still took willpower to keep facing forward.

"I have looked into this *Bonnie Lynn*," Otto Fuchs said, leaning in close enough that Bradley could smell his breath. "I believe that you have stumbled on more than you realize. You might be correct about the Butzemann's involvement."

The city's lower classes and ne'er-do-wells in New York City had been whispering that name in fear and reverence since the war ended. In a city full of gangs—the Charlton Street Gang, the Bowery Boys, the Daybreak Boys, the Whyos—the Butzemann was an oddity. He never used the same crew twice and did not control any region of the city or favor a particular type of crime—like river pirating. He would appear, make a lot of money by stealing, robbing, or embezzling, and then disappear again. No one knew who he was, what he looked like, or if he was a real person instead of a story told late at night to scare criminals and lawmen alike.

"You don't think he's a myth?" Bradley asked.

"Oh, he is real," Fuchs said. "The Pinkertons have been trying to identify and bring him to justice for years. This steamship was registered to a company believed to be associated with his crimes. And now you have connected Alistair Sinclair to that steamship."

If the Butzemann set up this counterfeiting ring, no one was safe. No one willingly worked for the Butzemann because anyone who got close enough to see his face disappeared—their bodies never found. No one knew they worked for the Butzemann until it was too late. Bradley whispered over his shoulder. "What should we do next?"

"Let me worry about the Butzemann," Otto whispered. "You focus on the other counterfeiters and your mysterious source. Have you learned anything?"

"I have a lead on one of the counterfeiters. The man with the silver hair and mustache. I know where to find him. Tomorrow, I'll follow him to see if he leads me to the counterfeiters' secret printing location."

"Good work," Otto said. Bradley appreciated the compliment. "Keep your wits about you. You know of the Butzemann's reputation. The closer the counterfeiters get to their goal, the sooner the Butzemann will start to clean up loose ends."

A chill ran through Bradley as he realized he was near enough to the counterfeiters to be considered a loose end. Before he could reply, it was his turn to order. He bought six slices of watermelon, then casually turned around. Otto was gone.

Bradley walked through the crowds, lost in his own thoughts. When he reached the main tent, he saw Nanny Kate standing beside Elizabeth and Hannah. Both Elizabeth and Nanny Kate turned to Bradley and said at the same time, "Where's Henry?"

Bradley was confused. "What?" He looked to Nanny Kate. "He was with you." Bradley saw a look of fear rising on the women's faces.

"He ran back to help you carry the watermelon," Elizabeth said.

"I never saw him."

"He promised to run right to you," Elizabeth said. He could

hear the rising panic in her voice.

By now, gaslights brilliantly illuminated the fairgrounds, turning night into day. Bradley had taken a straight path from the watermelon vendor. He would not have missed Henry. The boy had disappeared.

PART THREE

Beware secrets Held

Circus Entrance

CHAPTER XXXV

THE LIST

Tuesday, July 21, 1874

S ANNA watched Elizabeth Sinclair and her Irish nanny talking to
Bradley Webster near the main entrance to The Great New
York and New Orleans Zoological and Equestrian Exposition. Sanna had no interest in the women. She had been following Bradley
for over a week now and was curious why he wasn't dead yet.

He was younger than her typical target. Handsome, she had to
admit. Bradley was a man who looked good in his tailored clothes
and exuded an air of confidence that men born to privilege carried.
But Sanna knew he was not a rich gentleman looking to spend his
father's money. She wondered why he was pretending to be.

Bradley had obvious street skills. He hadn't spotted her yet,
but she could tell he knew someone was watching. He had almost
caught her once or twice, but she had managed to blend into the
background each time. The closest he came was at the croquet field.
Bradley had turned so quickly that he forced Sanna to lean away
and kiss the man standing next to her. The stranger had been surprised but willing. She avoided Bradley's detection, but it had taken
her an hour to get the stranger to leave her alone afterward. Sanna
had also been close to Bradley in the art gallery. She had made
friends with a young girl who was there with her parents. The girl
had loved Sanna's red hair. That was one of Sanna's favorite wigs.
Sanna had watched Bradley staring at the military painting when
he had some sort of episode. What was he carrying around inside
him? To Sanna, that made him more interesting. When the gallery
owner ushered everyone out to give him the privacy to compose
himself, Sanna was forced to leave with the rest.

Bradley intrigued her. That is why she risked exposing her face at the Montour House. She wanted to see him up close. When she brought him coffee, she noticed that he had kind eyes. She had not expected that. Kind eyes and a nice smile. Sanna pushed that thought out of her mind. If Bradley Webster was on her list, he earned what was coming. Why her boss hadn't given her the signal to end Bradley's life was a mystery, but it would just be a matter of time. Bradley was a murderer, after all.

Something we have in common, she thought.

Sanna watched the crowds around the circus's main tent. She waited to find someone leaving, then positioned herself so the man blocked Bradley's view of her as she headed toward the exit. Now that Bradley had seen her face, she could not risk him recognizing her—at least not until his time had come.

Bradley would have to wait. She had other tasks, including a new addition to her list. Miss Annie Anderson. Sanna had killed women before, but they were older. She'd never killed anyone near her age. Would it matter? No reason that it should. The woman must be on her list for a reason.

Sanna left the fairgrounds and went in search of a carriage. With each target, she received specific instructions. For Miss Anderson, she had been given the leeway to kill in any manner she saw fit, but the body had to be found and had to be recognizable. There could be no doubt that Miss Anderson had perished. That ruled out, say, burning Miss Anderson's house to the ground while she was inside. No matter, Sanna disliked using fire. Light one building on fire, and half the town burned down before you knew it. Sanna avoided involving innocent victims who were not on her list. She wasn't that cold-blooded.

Sanna found a driver, and after some haggling, handed over a few coins before climbing into the carriage. Her employer had made it clear that Annie Anderson had to be dead no later than Tuesday, July 28. That gave Sanna one week to study her prey and choose the right moment and method. She would need that time because Annie had protection. A man named Roland Smith accompanied her wherever she went. Roland was a problem. Sanna let her hands drift to where her knives lay hidden in her corset. She would find a way. She always had in the past.

Sanna looked back at the fairgrounds as the driver started to pull away. She liked it here in Watkins. Maybe, after her list was clear, she could stay longer. No one knew her here. She closed her eyes and breathed deeply, smelling the conditioned leather in the carriage. Who was she kidding? She could dream, but a normal life wasn't her reality. Her employer did not let go easily.

CHAPTER XXXVI

SUDDEN DEATH

Tuesday, July 21, 1874

ELIZABETH commanded Nanny Kate to stay with Hannah and headed back toward the watermelon vendor. Her head pivoted left and right as she called her son's name with increasing desperation.

Henry could have ducked into one of the tents to see more animals, but Bradley had to consider the worst case. If someone had grabbed Henry, darkness waited outside the glow of the circus lights. A killer would drag Henry off into the marsh, which bounded the fairgrounds on three sides. In that case, Henry could be dead already. A kidnapper would take Henry immediately to Franklin Street and get him out of the area. Was Henry a loose end? Or a valuable chess piece?

Bradley turned to Nanny Kate. "I'm going to check the entrance."

He started running as soon as he was out of Nanny Kate and Hannah's sight. Bradley made no friends as he pushed through the crowd. He reached Franklin Street, where the wealthier patrons had left their drivers to wait with horses and carriages along the dirt street. Many drivers stood in small groups, smoking or exchanging stories. Bradley ran up to the first group he found.

"I'm looking for a blond boy about so tall," Bradley said, holding up his hand. "With one or more adults. Just left the fairgrounds." The drivers shrugged or shook their heads. Bradley looked left and then right. One way led back to Watkins, the other to Havana, several miles away. Bradley took a deep breath. He had to push aside his own rising panic and decide on a direction. He turned and raced along the line of carriages pointed toward Watkins. It was the direction he would have gone had he been the kidnapper since a carriage could disappear quickly onto one of Watkins's side streets. Bradley asked every driver he found, but no one had seen Henry. He was ready to rush back in the other direction but tried one more driver.

"Have you seen a blond boy—?" Before Bradley finished his sentence, the driver was nodding.

"Yeah, dodgy old guy was pulling a little blond boy along. It didn't seem right. They just got into that carriage," the driver said, pointing.

Bradley's heart dropped. That carriage was twenty yards away in the darkness, heading for Watkins. He sprinted toward the carriage, hoping not to break an ankle on the uneven dirt road before reaching it.

The carriage was an enclosed four-wheeled buggy with a driver on a bench in front of a cab that held two people. Even if Bradley could reach the back of the buggy, there were no handholds to grab. Reaching for the door on a moving carriage required jumping onto an extremely small footrest between two large wheels. Bradley's only chance to stop the carriage was to get to the driver.

He reached into his pants pocket and yelled out, "Driver! Driver! You dropped your coin purse." Bradley held his own coin purse up in the air and shook it, making the coins jangle.

A New York City hack would never have fallen for it, but Bradley hoped a local carriage driver would be more greedy than suspicious. "Driver," he yelled again as he pumped his arms and willed his legs for more speed. "You dropped your coin purse." The carriage slowed down.

The driver looked back in the darkness from his perch as Bradley came up beside the carriage. He held the coin purse in the air as he gasped for breath. Bradley shook the coin purse again. "I found this on the road," he said breathlessly. "It must be yours." Behind the driver, the carriage shades were down, making it impossible to know who was inside.

The driver seemed skeptical. Bradley shook the coin purse again. The sound of so many coins rubbing together produced a musical sound, and a greedy look crept into the man's eyes. "I can't keep it," Bradley said. "It is a matter of principle. I'll let you decide what to do with it."

"Thank you," the driver said, and Bradley knew he had him.

Bradley motioned that he would toss the leather coin purse up to the driver but then said, "Probably best if I hand it up." He kept talking as he stepped closer to keep the driver distracted. "There is a lot of money in there. I'm sure you would have missed it. I'm glad it got back to the right place." As the driver reached out, Bradley grabbed the man's wrist and pulled him from the carriage, dropping him on the dirt road, narrowly missing a pile of fresh horse manure. The fall knocked the wind out of the driver, so Bradley had the man's full attention as he pinned him to the ground. In a quiet voice, Bradley asked, "Is there a boy in that carriage?"

The driver's eyes widened. He nodded. Bradley took a coin out of the coin purse and pressed it into the man's hand. "Leave. Now. And don't be so greedy next time."

The driver disappeared into the darkness as Bradley heard a thumping from inside the carriage. "Driver—what is the holdup?"

Bradley stepped around to the side of the carriage and flung the door open. He was thinking emotionally, not strategically, and it almost cost him his life. The silver-haired counterfeiter sat in the cab with one arm draped possessively around Henry. In the man's other hand was a pistol pointed at Bradley's head. An evil smile twisted the older man's face as he pulled the trigger. Bradley owed his life to Henry, who pushed against the counterfeiter as the door opened, throwing off the man's aim. Bradley leaped forward, not letting the man get off a second shot. He smelled whiskey on the man's breath as he grabbed the gun in one hand and punched the man in the face with his other. The man's nose exploded, sending blood everywhere. Bradley threw two more punches before he could stop himself. He wrenched the gun away and pulled Henry out of the carriage.

Henry kept a brave face until Bradley got him out of the carriage and standing beside him. Henry clung to Bradley and started sobbing, so Bradley picked the boy up and carried him to the side of the road. Bradley had intended to go back and interrogate the counterfeiter at gunpoint, but the old man was quick. He scrambled out of the cab and into the driver's seat of the carriage. Before Bradley could stop him, the man flicked the reins and raced down the road.

Bradley watched him go, then knelt in front of Henry. "Are you hurt?" he asked. Henry shook his head and wiped his eyes. Bradley straightened Henry's jacket. "What made you go with him?"

"He told me he was taking me to my father. That it was important and that my father needed me." Henry's lips quivered. "I think he was lying."

"He was lying, but you are safe now. And you were very brave," Bradley said. "You saved my life when you pushed his arm." Some of the fear left Henry. "Let's get back to your mom," Bradley said, taking Henry's hand as they walked toward the bright lights of the circus.

Almost everyone else had entered the big tent for the show, leaving Nanny Kate, Hannah, and Elizabeth standing outside looking anxious and forlorn. Their heads whipped around as Henry ran toward them, yelling, "Mother!" Elizabeth Sinclair pulled both her children into a giant hug. As Bradley followed Henry, Nanny Kate mouthed "thank you" to him, her own eyes glistening.

Bradley's hand hurt, but he felt relieved and lucky. Had he been five seconds slower, Henry might have been lost forever.

Surprisingly, Henry was the first to recover. He let go of his mother and said hopefully, "Mother, can we still see the circus?"

Elizabeth laughed through her tears. She took a deep breath and let it out slowly. She glanced toward Hannah, who nodded her head enthusiastically. Elizabeth looked back at Henry. "Of course," she said.

Elizabeth pulled Bradley aside as Nanny Kate ushered the children into the main tent.

"Did someone try to take my son?" she quietly asked Bradley, her blue eyes flaring with righteous anger.

"The man got away. But I know where to find him."

Elizabeth's face hardened. "Find him. And then make sure he never has a chance to come near my children again."

Bradley nodded, adjusted his hat, and turned back toward the road.

GLEN MOUNTAIN HOUSE, SOUTH AND NORTH

———◇———

The door to room 207 at the Glen Mountain House swung open without a sound. Annie stepped in from the hallway, then closed and locked the door behind her. She slid the key into her dress pocket, where it clicked against her new derringer.

Annie felt her way across the darkened room to close the curtains. The room was on the second floor, but night had fallen, and Annie did not want anyone to notice the gaslight, which she lit and turned to its lowest setting. She stood in the middle of the room, taking deep breaths, trying to calm her thumping heartbeat. Her body vibrated with excitement and nervousness that had been building since she had taken the key from Bradley. It was impulsive, but she desperately wanted to make something happen instead of waiting for something to happen to her. Even if that meant illegally breaking into a strange man's hotel room to search for clues on who wanted her dead.

Annie looked around. "Now what?" she asked herself.

The room included a single bed against the wall with a desk and chair next to it. She could see an empty wastebasket, half hidden, under the desk. On the opposite wall was an armoire and a dresser with a pitcher and washbasin. A mirror hung over the dresser. There were a few toiletries on the dresser but little else to indicate the room had an occupant. Annie smelled polished wood and clean linens—the hotel's housekeepers had done their job well. "What am I looking for?" Annie said in a hushed whisper. She caught herself. "Why am I talking to myself?" She answered her own question. "Because I'm scared."

Annie reached into her pocket. The curved wood and cold metal of the pistol gave her courage.

She started her search with the desk. In the drawer, she found hotel stationery, but it was blank. She moved over to the dresser. She ignored the toiletries and searched the drawers. One had a half-empty bottle of whiskey. From the few clothes she found, Annie knew the owner was of modest means but had expensive tastes. The armoire told the same story. There was only one extra suit, but it was expensive. The pockets were empty. The name *H.L. Smythe* was handwritten on the jacket label. So that was the silver-haired man's name. The armoire also held one extra pair of boots. The man had small feet. Annie moved over to the bed. She found nothing under the mattress or under the bed. She climbed onto the bed to see if anything was on top of the armoire. She had to bounce twice on the bed to get high enough.

Annie heard footsteps in the hallway and froze. The sound was coming closer. The room she had broken into was at the end of the corridor, so if Smythe returned early, he would corner her in the room. Surely, it was too soon. She listened with growing anxiety until the footsteps stopped. Down the hall, a door opened and then closed. Annie started to breathe again.

She climbed down from the bed and stood in the center of the room, frustrated. She tucked the fake glasses that she still wore into her dress pocket, where they clinked against the key and her small pistol. "What did you expect?" she asked herself. "A written confession from Lewis Crawford's killer? That would be nice." She shook her head. "Stop talking to yourself!"

Annie looked over to the mirror on the wall. She saw a stranger staring back at her, which made her happy. She had put a lot of work into her disguise and was enormously proud of it. No one had recognized her at the circus, although she had walked past several acquaintances from church. Abraham had stared at her briefly before moving on. Hopefully, Mrs. Casey, the family cook and housekeeper, would forgive the transgressions she had committed against the woman's favorite dress and spare reading glasses. Annie thought of Bradley, and her smile grew wider. When he told her she looked spectacular, she knew he was complimenting her disguise. Men had called Annie pretty and occasionally beautiful. They praised her wifely skills like sewing, cooking, and cleaning. Bradley recognized her talents for a skill that he valued in himself.

Unbidden thoughts of Bradley's eyes came to mind. She liked the way he looked at her. "Stop distracting yourself!"

Annie restarted her search, determined to dig deeper. She ran her hands over the bed to make sure nothing was under the sheets. She looked behind the mirror. She checked for loose floorboards and along the wall for secret hiding places. She checked each dresser drawer for a false bottom or anything attached to the underside.

She moved to the dresser, where she checked the pockets of all the clothes. She reopened the armoire. She had already checked the jacket pockets but moved her hand along the garment, searching for anything concealed in a hidden pocket. She felt something crunch under her hand when she reached the bottom right corner of the jacket. She peered into the jacket's front pocket again. It was empty, but she saw a hole she had missed the first time. She reached inside the pocket and pulled out a piece of paper that had pushed through the hole. She made out the words *Ortus Solis* and the number 17510 in the dim light. Latin had been a required part of her curriculum at Elmira Female College. *Ortus solis* meant sunrise or the rising of the sun. Annie carefully placed the paper into her dress pocket.

She spent a few more minutes looking in other places but started to feel silly when the boots did not have fake heels and tapping the desk legs showed they were not hollow.

After Bradley had mentioned a counterfeiting ring, Annie had expected to find lots of money in the room—although she would not have been able to tell the difference between real and fake bills. She wondered what a counterfeiting ring had to do with the dead Southerner in the cemetery. Did the Southerner work for the counterfeiters? A rival organization, perhaps? Is that why someone killed him? Was Smythe behind all this? Too many questions and too few answers.

Annie turned off the gaslight and opened the curtains. It was time to leave. She reached into her pocket for the key when she heard multiple footsteps in the hall. A couple returning to their room from dinner, perhaps? She would have to wait for them to reach their room so she could step into the hall without being seen. The footsteps grew closer, and Annie's heart leaped into her throat as she realized that her luck had run out. The footsteps stopped outside her door. A hand rattled the doorknob. She heard voices.

"Thank you for letting me in."

Annie's eyes widened as a person on the other side of the door inserted a key into the lock. She looked around in a panic. She would never make it out the window in time. She heard the key turning as she turned off the gas light and dove under the bed and wiggled herself out of sight. The door swung open on well-oiled hinges.

"I must have dropped my own key when I was attacked in my carriage."

"I'm afraid there will be an extra charge to replace your key."

"Surely, you can make an exception given the circumstances."

"I will talk to the manager, sir. And I'll send up the extra towels that you requested."

Smythe grumbled a thank-you, and the door closed. A moment later, the gaslight sprang to life, illuminating the room. From her vantage point, Annie could only see the man's shoes. She watched as he walked over to the armoire—he must have hung up his jacket—and then back to the bed. Annie held her breath. Does he know I'm here? The man sat down violently on his bed, and Annie stifled a cry when the mattress pressed down dangerously close to her head. The man grunted as he removed his boots and dropped them, one after the other, next to Annie's head. She almost gave herself away a second time as she silently gagged from the smell.

The man swung his legs onto the bed and lay down directly above Annie. She lay beneath him, trying not to breathe.

For a few panicked seconds, she feared she would be stuck under the man's bed all night, but she reassured herself. She would only have to wait until he fell asleep, and then she could silently creep out the door. As she lay on the floor, her hand was in her dress pocket, gripping her pistol. Why did she have to wait? If she rolled out from under the bed fast enough, she could catch him by surprise and point the gun at him. Then she could ask him who he worked for and what he knew. She was not Annie Anderson tonight, so he might not even recognize her later. Emboldened by her plan, she slid Mrs. Casey's reading glasses back on her face and prepared to wiggle out.

A knock came on the door.

Smythe groaned at the interruption and got to his feet. Annie heard the door open and assumed the extra towels had arrived. "What do you want?" Smythe did not sound pleased to see whoever was on the other side of the door.

The newcomer made no reply. Annie could hear only muffled

sounds. A grunt. A low groan. She looked to see two sets of dusty black shoes moving into the room. Smythe stumbled backward and then crashed to the floor. He landed only inches away from Annie's position under the bed. His unblinking, lifeless eyes stared directly at her. Annie shoved her fist into her mouth and bit down hard enough to draw blood. She gripped her pistol tighter.

The counterfeiter's portly body blocked Annie's view, but she heard a soft click as the door to the room closed and footsteps receded down the hall. She was alone in the room with a dead body.

To get out from under the bed, Annie had to push Smythe's body out of her way. He had dried blood on his face and a fresh knife wound in his chest. She jumped to her feet and headed straight to the door. She put her key in the lock and gave it a half turn. Pistol or no pistol, she didn't want to risk running into the killer in the hallway. Hopefully, the extra key in the lock would make it harder for the killer to reenter the room. Annie ran to the window. It slid open easily, and she scrambled onto the roof of the first floor's porch. She turned and closed the curtains behind her and pulled the window shut.

Annie had to get away before the killer returned without drawing attention to herself. She needed to get off this porch roof before anyone spotted her. The roof extended the length of the building and was about six feet wide. This side of the hotel enjoyed views of the Glen. Annie—afraid of heights—was glad the darkness hid the almost hundred-foot drop into the gorge.

She started crawling along the roof toward the opposite side of the porch for a shorter drop to the ground. A fluttering near her ear startled her, and she raised her hands for protection. The large moth bounced off her and flew away into the darkness unperturbed. With her hands up, Annie began slipping. Terror gripped her, and she lay flat to stop her slide. She didn't move until her breathing returned to normal. She wished she could fly off the roof like the moth, but her only choice was to continue forward.

Annie inched along until she had crossed the length of the porch and reached the edge. She peered over and saw a ten-foot drop to the ground. She rolled onto her stomach and lowered herself over the ledge. When half her body hung over the side, she began to slide again and grabbed frantically at the roof edge. She hung fully extended from the roof, afraid to let go. Suddenly, strong arms wrapped around her legs.

Panicked, she kicked out and heard a muffled "oof" as she lost her grip.

"I've got you," Bradley said, holding her firmly around her thighs. She stopped struggling, and he loosened his grip to let her slide down his body until her feet touched the ground. She found herself in his arms, looking up into his eyes. She mumbled a thank-you as she pushed away from him and straightened her dress. No one else was in sight.

"Taking the stairs too easy for you?" Bradley asked. He was smiling at her, which pleased and annoyed her at the same time.

"Your counterfeiter is dead," Annie said in a harsh whisper.

Bradley's face turned serious, and he pulled her back into the shadows under the porch. "What happened? Are you hurt?"

Annie explained how H.L. Smythe returned sooner than ex-pected, forcing her to hide under the bed. After a knock on the door, a dead Smythe landed inches from her with a bloodied face and vacant eyes.

"Are you—"

"Am I sure he's dead?" She cut him off as anger flared inside her. "If you don't believe I can recognize a dead body, feel free to check for yourself."

Bradley shook his head. "I believed you the first time," he said. "I was asking, 'Are you able to identify the murderer?'"

"Oh," Annie said. She shook her head. "Dusty black shoes. That was all I saw."

Bradley nodded. "We need to get you out of here. The murderer might not recognize you, but we can't risk that."

Annie shook her head. "I'm going to get the sheriff and tell him another murder has been committed. He will have to believe me this time."

"How are you going to explain being dressed as your cleaning lady and witnessing the murder from under the dead man's bed?"

"I—" Annie knew he had a point.

Bradley looked at her with concern. "I have a general distrust of the police."

Annie started to open her mouth to speak but closed it just as quickly. Could the sheriff be involved? She felt tired. She wanted to be home with Glendon and Roland, where she felt safe. They could advise her what to do next. She had been near too much death in the last two weeks, and her nerves were fraying.

"Take me home," she said.

Bradley extended his arm. Annie took it, and he guided them around the building toward where the hacks dropped off guests. "If we are lucky, the carriage that brought me here is still waiting," Bradley said in a low voice. Gaslights illuminated the walkways, but the glow did not extend far from the buildings.

Bradley stopped suddenly and pulled Annie back around the edge of the building.

"What?"

"The Walrus!"

"Who?"

"Well, I don't know his real name. He worked with Vance."

Annie involuntarily squeezed Bradley's arm tighter. "Let me see," she said. Bradley moved aside, and Annie peered around the corner. She saw a wide man with a bowler hat and a large mustache standing beside a black carriage. The walrus description fit him well. "He's waiting for someone."

"Or looking for someone," Bradley said. "Last time I saw him, he was at the circus. It's possible he followed me."

Annie thought about it. She was in disguise and had a gun in her pocket. She and Bradley could march over to this walrus man and demand answers. Then again, what if he had a larger gun and was much more willing to use it? Bad plan. Especially since Annie did not know how much she could count on Bradley. She sighed. Live to fight another day, she told herself. She grabbed Bradley's hand and led him back to the Glen side of the building.

"Where are we going?" Bradley asked.

Annie noticed an older couple exiting the building, so she lengthened her strides to intersect their path. She was pleased that Bradley followed her lead.

"Lovely evening isn't it," Annie said as they neared the other couple. "Would you mind if we walked with you? We have not been to the north side yet." As Annie hoped, the other couple was on their way across the iron bridge to the Swiss Chalet and were happy to walk with them. If anyone watched the bridge, it would appear the two couples were together.

As the group reached the Swiss Chalet, Annie said goodbye to their new friends. She felt pleased with herself until the other woman looked back and said, "I hope you and your son enjoy your stay here in Watkins."

Her gray hair had fooled them. She could hear Bradley chuckle beside her. She elbowed him in the side, making him laugh louder.

Annie led Bradley up the dark road behind the Swiss Chalet toward Glenwood Cemetery, which they could cross and exit by the Lake View Hotel. The waxing moon barely penetrated the woods, forcing them to move slowly.

Annie held Bradley's arm tightly as they crossed the uneven ground. She would never have taken this road alone at night. She focused on the path ahead while Bradley repeatedly looked back to ensure no one was following them. They were halfway to the cemetery when she felt his body stiffen. "There's someone trailing us," he whispered in her ear.

They picked up the pace. The road continued upward. To their left was a hillside too steep to climb, and to their right, a steep drop. It was a poor location for a confrontation with an unknown assailant. They needed to get to the cemetery before their pursuer reached them.

"He's getting closer," Bradley said as they neared the entrance to the cemetery. Annie risked a glance back. Whoever was behind them was little more than a dark shadow on the road. She looked forward again. A looming figure appeared twenty yards ahead of them, startling Annie. She immediately recognized the outline of the bearlike man with black hair and grizzled beard.

Bradley pulled Annie back and put his body between her and the newcomer. Both Annie and Bradley were reaching for their guns when a shot rang out. The large man in front of them staggered and crashed into the dark underbrush on the right of the road. His body started sliding down the steep incline.

Whoever followed them had a rifle. Bradley grabbed Annie's arm. "Time to run!"

CHAPTER XXXVII

SOUTHBOUND

From the Journal of Private H. Thompson

October 7, 1864 – On the first day of our escape, we traveled eight miles, constantly looking over our shoulders, expecting to see El-mira Prison Camp guards on our heels. We crossed into Penn-sylvania and followed the Harrisburg and Pennsylvania Railroad south through the mountains. We never saw any pursuit, nor did we see any of the other escapees. That first night, we found a barn where we holed up in relative comfort in a hayloft. The smell of the straw and its scratchiness against my skin made me feel more alive than I had in months.

October 8, 1864 – We snuck out of the barn at daybreak and con-tinued south. Frank stole a chicken, and when we got far enough down the railroad, we took a chance and built a fire with some matches he had in a glass bottle. I never tasted a chicken so deli-cious. With renewed strength, we continued south. Hundreds of miles through enemy territory lay ahead of us, and then we had to find a way to cross battle lines without getting shot by either side.

Buck was surprised the camp hadn't turned the dogs loose on us. He looked backward and then scanned the way ahead, ready to dive into the brush if anyone appeared. I was happy to take all the good luck we could get. I said maybe they were busy chasing the other escapees.

"Better them than us," Buck said. It was one of the few things he and I had agreed on in months.

October 10, 1864 – By the fourth day, the rail line led us to a large river. I later learned it was the west branch of the Susquehanna River near Websterport. This was good luck. Traveling by river

*would be the fastest way south. I envisioned floating all the way
to the Chesapeake Bay. We avoided populated areas and followed
the river as it flowed south. Buck helped me keep an eye out for a
boat while Frank remained quiet. We did not realize how much of
a problem we were about to have.*

*We came across a small skiff, and seeing no one to stop us, we
commandeered it. Although I got my feet wet pushing us out into
the river, I was elated to be heading downstream. I sat in the bow
while Buck took a turn on the oars. Frank sat glumly in the back.
My exhilaration did not last long. A few miles downstream, we began to hear what sounded like a storm approaching. As we got
closer, we realized it was the roar of waterfalls over a factory dam.
The dam, several feet high, created a reservoir that funneled water
through a race channel to a mill waterwheel. Any extra water ran
over the top of the dam. Buck pulled hard on the oars. Going over
the dam would surely sink us. "I'm going to try for the race channel," he shouted.*

*Frank had been mumbling to himself, but I could not make out
what he'd said. I asked him what the problem was. He was as white
as a sheet. His only reply was more mumbling. Buck, busy pulling
hard on the oars to get us to the race, hollered in Frank's direction.
"Speak up, man!"*

*"Can't swim," Frank said in a loud voice. Shit. Buck, fighting the
currents, yelled at Frank to just hold on. Buck saved us that day. He
managed to get our skiff into the race barely wide enough for us to
squeeze past the waterwheel, and then we floated back out into the
river below the dam. Buck sat on the skiff's wooden bench, covered in
sweat despite the chilly weather. I was impressed, and I told him so. I
might dislike the man, but I can give credit where it is due.*

*Frank had had enough. He was agitated and wanted out of the
boat. I worried he would panic and tip us into the water. I looked
toward Buck, who nodded in silent agreement and started pulling
for shore. We left the skiff on the riverbank, knowing we would not
return to the river. We headed into the mountains, where we rested
until dark.*

*October 12, 1864 – We traveled at night to avoid running into
Northerners who could tell immediately from our ragged gray uniforms we did not belong in this part of the country. On good days,*

Susquehanna River

we managed ten to fifteen miles. Our bodies adjusted to walking long distances again. I can thank the Confederate Army for training us for that task. When the weather was bad, we found somewhere to lie low and stay warm. We stole food and supplies when we could. We stole spare horse blankets to keep from freezing. I always felt guilty taking from civilians, but Buck scoffed at me. He took immense pleasure in stealing from Northerners. "They'd kill us if they got the chance," he said.

Some folks in the North supported the Confederate cause, or at least remained neutral enough to be kind to soldiers. But it was hard to tell who would feed you and who would shoot at you. I could not decide which would be the worst fate—getting shot or getting sent back to Hellmira.

When we came across small settlements, our first thought was to look for food to steal. Once, we found a remote house and took a position nearby as the night ended. When the inhabitants left in the morning, we went in to see what we could use. I found two suits that would fit me and Buck nicely. Frank would have to continue to wrap himself in horse blankets. In the bedroom dresser, I found an old pistol. There was no ball or powder, but I put the pistol in my pocket in case it came in handy later. Frank got us milk from the family cow. Buck found the root cellar under the house and stole apples. When Buck started to smash and destroy the remaining food, I stepped in.

"Destroying their food is cruel, and worse, it's stupid," I said. "It will only make the locals more eager to hunt us down." Buck sneered at me and called me a Yankee sympathizer. We would've come to blows if Frank hadn't separated us.

By midday, snow started falling, worsening our already foul moods.

October 17, 1864 – Now that I had a suit to wear, I practiced my Northern accent so I could approach farmhouses and ask for food or permission to sleep in the barn. Buck refused to "talk like a damn Yankee." As my confidence grew, I would stop at isolated houses and ask for directions and extra food while Buck remained on the road, and Frank hid in the woods. Getting directions allowed us to steer south and west to avoid the more populated Yankee cities of Baltimore and Washington, DC. We hoped to cross through the enemy's front lines near Harper's Ferry.

October 22, 1864 – This morning, we crossed into Maryland and stole a horse and wagon that helped get us south of Hagerstown. When the horse went lame, we left him near a farm and moved back into the mountains. An icy rain started falling, making the three of us miserable. We came across a cabin in the woods with smoke curling out of its chimney. We watched from a distance as a colored man stepped outside to collect an armload of firewood and then went back inside.

Buck suggested I use my Yankee accent to get us some food and permission to bed down in their barn. When I started forward, Buck kept pace with me. "I'm gonna watch you. Maybe I'll learn something," he said.

The old negro opened the door to my knock. It was getting late, so he was cautious. I did my best to appear nonthreatening. "Sorry to disturb you," I said. "We are coming from Pennsylvania and heading to Harper's Ferry, but we are a bit off track. Would you mind if we slept in your barn to avoid the rain? And we'd be much obliged if you had any food to spare." The negro looked us up and down. He wanted us off his property, but the worsening weather and his Christian generosity made him hesitate. That proved his undoing.

Buck pulled out the old pistol I had found days ago and forced the man back inside the cabin. I knew Buck had no powder or ball for the pistol, but the old man did not. Buck waved to Frank to join us, and the old man's eyes widened when he saw Frank's Confederate uniform. Buck shut the door after we all stepped inside. The cabin was cozy, with a roaring fire in the hearth and the smell of hot stew in the air. My stomach rumbled in anticipation.

A slender colored woman in her late teens or early twenties came out of a back room. She took in the scene and turned to run, but Buck stopped her with his words. "I'll shoot him between the eyes," Buck said. The young woman stopped and stared at Buck. He asked if there was anyone else inside. The woman shook her head. "Well then," Buck said, "we'll be accepting your generosity for the evenin'. Not to worry, though, as we plan to be gone by mornin'. If y'all behave, y'all got nothin' to fear."

Frank tied up the old man and the young woman. I could not tell if they were related and did not ask. The old man had ebony skin, while the young woman's skin was more copper-brown. Frank found the pot of stew, and we fell upon it like rabid dogs. With full stomachs, we searched the cabin for anything we could use. I found little, but Buck whistled and held up a near-full bottle of bourbon whiskey. "How 'bout that," Buck said. "It says 'distilled in Kentucky.' Very charitable to provide us a bit of Southern hospitality." Buck took a swig from the bottle and handed it to Frank, who tossed back his own healthy gulp. Frank offered the bottle to me, but I shook my head. Frank shrugged and helped himself to another gulp.

Buck walked over and sat next to Frank. They continued to drink the bourbon. Buck said, "For old times' sake, let's play that game of ours. What'll you do with your gold share? 'Cause I've been thinkin' 'bout my answer."

"Don't want any gold," Frank blurted out. "Never did." Both Buck and I looked over in surprise. Frank took another swig of bourbon, and I grew concerned about how quickly the amber liquid was disappearing from the clear glass bottle.

"Well, then, Frank," Buck said, "I'll take your share and invest it for you case you change your mind. That'll make two-thirds to me and one-third to Harper." Buck looked at me—daring me to challenge him. "Harper here is going to waste his share trying to buy back his girl's affections from her Yankee husband." Buck accepted the bottle from Frank and took another shot of whiskey. "Tell me the truth, Harper. How much is it gonna hurt to find out she's fat and ugly after birthin' ten more Yankee babies? I bet she's forgotten all about you."

My greatest fear was that she had forgotten about me, but I refused to let Buck know his words struck their target. I told him that at least I had a girl that loved me once. Buck gave me a dirty look. "With all that gold," he said, "I expect to have my pick of beautiful Southern belles who believe in our cause. If we lose this war, I will use my share to start an insurrection." There was a new, disturbing light in his eyes.

I ignored Buck after that. Frank, unsteady on his feet, stood up and stretched. He found a spot near the fire to curl up and fell asleep. Buck claimed the bed in the back and disappeared. One at a time, I let the old man and the young woman relieve themselves and then tied them up again near the fire.

I woke up to a strange sound in the middle of the night. The fire had died down, so I tossed in another log. With the surge of firelight, I realized the young woman wasn't where I had left her. I ran to the back room to wake Buck. If she had gone for help, we needed to leave immediately.

I found Buck on top of the young woman. His body weight pinned her down, and he was struggling to pull her clothes off. I could see her exposed shoulder and bare legs. The empty bottle of bourbon stood on the floor by the bed. The woman saw me first. Her almond-brown eyes pleaded one moment and then went dull the next as she assumed I had come in to take the next turn. Horrified, I charged over and pulled Buck off her. "What the hell you doin', Buck?"

"She's just a runaway slave," he said, his words slurring. He shoved me hard, and I fell backward against the cabin wall. When Buck turned back to the girl, he saw the bourbon bottle in her hand. Before he could react, she broke the end of the bottle against the bed and swung what remained at his face. Buck howled as the broken glass connected. Blood and bits of his face went flying. He staggered out of the room, leaving a trail of blood. I was about to follow him when I saw the young woman drop the broken bottle and dig under the bed. When she pulled out a shotgun, I cursed and jumped forward to wrestle it from her grasp.

"Stop," I yelled as I pulled the weapon away from her. I checked for shells in the chamber and then pushed her toward the main room. Buck had a cloth pressed to his face, trying to stop the bleeding. He would end up with significant scars, but he would live. When he saw her, he screamed and stepped forward but froze when I pointed the shotgun at him. I told him I was leaving and taking the man and the girl with me.

At my direction, the young woman untied the old man. I sent him out to the barn to hitch their horse and wagon. The girl grabbed clothes and blankets, and we backed our way out the door. Frank had woken up and stared at me glassy-eyed. Buck screamed that I was a negro lover and that he would kill me the next time he saw me.

I turned back. "You brought this on yourself," I told him. "If you and Frank make it over to the Confederate side, meet me in Morganton, and we'll finish this."

CHAPTER XXXVIII

THE TATTOO

Tuesday, July 21, 1874

BEFORE the echo of the gunshot faded, Annie and Bradley ran into the dark cemetery, out of sight of the shooter. They had a fifty-yard head start before the shadowy figure reached the cemetery entrance and shot at them as they ran. Trying to hide was a poor option, and since their pistols were no match for a rifle, their best chance to survive was to cross the cemetery fast enough to get out of sight. They headed uphill, running side by side. The moonlight was brighter out of the woods, allowing them to move faster but also benefitting the shooter. At least they both wore dark clothing. Annie and Bradley weaved around gravestones, taking the shortest path to the Lake View Hotel entrance. As they ran, Annie noticed the blinking of fireflies. The evening dew from the long grass soaked into her boots. Somewhere in the distance, a dog barked.

Annie considered it a minor miracle when they reached the treelined path to Lake View without getting shot in the back. Hidden by the vegetation, they stopped to listen for pursuit but heard nothing except the buzz of winged insects and the chirping of crickets. They continued down the path until they reached the dirt road and, in unspoken agreement, headed along darkened streets until Annie's house came into view. Annie, realizing she still held Bradley's hand, released her grip.

The house stood dark and lifeless on the quiet street. Annie hoped to find it well lit with Roland and Glendon inside anxiously awaiting her return. She wanted to hand the burden of what to do next over to her uncles. The grown-ups would know what to do. Now, Annie was alone with a man she barely knew and forced to be the grown-up and make her own decisions.

WWhen they reached the front door, Bradley insisted on searching the house. They entered the darkness with pistols drawn and bolted the door behind them. Moving quietly, they checked each room on the main floor and the basement before moving on to the second floor. Annie let him check every room except her own, which she insisted on doing herself while he waited in the hallway. She searched the few hiding places in her room, then self-consciously hid the undergarments she had left out before stepping back into the hallway.

"All clear?"

Annie nodded and looked at Bradley standing next to her in the hallway, bathed in the warm glow of the lantern. They were alone in her house at night outside her bedroom. She looked into his eyes. He had his hat in his hand, and Annie saw one brown wavy curl stuck to his forehead near his bandaged wound. Annie resisted the urge to reach up and free the curl. Why did she keep wanting to touch him? Should she ask him to leave?

"I can stay for a while," Bradley said. "Until Roland or Glendon returns if you like. I know I still owe you answers."

Annie wanted him to stay. She wanted that very much.

He smiled at her. "As long as your gentleman friend wouldn't mind you keeping company with a stranger."

"What?"

"Your suitor from Glen Eldridge," Bradley said. "Large man. Full of himself. You two seemed close at the picnic."

Annie's face clouded over. "Hastings? The man who assaulted me at Glen Eldridge? The man I had to stab in the leg with a hatpin to get him to let me go? I don't think he is worried about me, and I don't give a damn about his opinion."

A shadow crossed Bradley's face.

"I'm going into my room to change," Annie said abruptly. Thoughts of Hastings had given her a headache. She wanted to get out of her housekeeper's dress and wipe away the sheen of perspiration that covered her body. "I trust you can behave yourself until I return." She left without waiting for an answer and closed the door of her room.

"Of course," she heard Bradley say through the door. The

sound of his footsteps receded down the hallway.

Annie locked her bedroom door and walked over to her dresser. She poured water from the pitcher into the washbasin and then stripped down and scrubbed her face and body with a wet cloth. Refreshed, she took a deep breath, forcing the tension from her body. She wondered if any of her neighbors had noticed her entering the house alone with a man. Her reputation would suffer if word got out. At least she had been in disguise. She agonized momentarily about what to put on before settling on a house dress with long sleeves and a high neckline. She spent a few extra minutes managing her unruly hair.

As Annie descended the stairs, the smell of food and a faint odor of woodsmoke reached her nose and caused her stomach to rumble embarrassingly. She hadn't eaten dinner nor realized how hungry she was until that moment. She found Bradley cooking eggs in Nana's favorite cast-iron skillet in the basement kitchen. He had emptied the cookstove's ash box and lit a new fire in the firebox. The wood made popping sounds as it burned down. Nana's kettle, ever present in the back center of the stove, sent steam into the air.

Bradley smiled when she entered the kitchen. "I hope you don't mind," he said.

"No, I'm famished!" she said, gathering fruit, cheese, and the heel of a loaf of bread to add to their meal. They split everything equally on two plates and went upstairs to the dining room.

Annie took a bite of the scrambled eggs and groaned. They were delicious. "Where did you learn to cook?" she asked.

He shrugged. "Not everyone has a housekeeper preparing their meals."

At first, she thought he was criticizing her upbringing, but no malice showed on his face. What surprised Annie was that Bradley dressed and acted like a man who grew up with servants but also cooked his own meals.

"I'm sorry for what Hastings did," Bradley said. "If I'd known..." He seemed to want to say more, but paused. "I would have enjoyed seeing the look on his face when you stabbed him in the leg," he said, smiling. "Hastings seems like the kind of man who leaves his hat on in the theater."

Annie laughed and then ate another forkful of eggs. When her plate was empty, she pushed it away and surreptitiously rubbed her belly. "Who do you think was shooting at us tonight?" she asked.

Bradley shrugged. "Thinking about it now, I'm not sure they were. You had on a disguise, so why shoot at you? And we were too close for a good marksman to miss, even in the dark. Is it possible they were aiming for the big man all along? Maybe the shooter was protecting us."

Annie hadn't considered that possibility and suddenly wondered if the shadowy figure had been Glendon or Roland. But why wouldn't they have come home by now? Or called out to her when she ran. Too many questions. "Okay," she said. "You owe me answers. Tell me about the counterfeiting ring first. Whoever Vance was working for is the man who wants me dead."

Bradley started from the beginning. "A couple of weeks ago, I met a man in New York City named Pickens who had just been arrested for making counterfeit currency plates. He's an engraver. He told me Alistair Sinclair had offered him a job here in Watkins, so I came here hoping Sinclair would hire me as a member of the counterfeiting ring."

"Why would you want to do that?"

"To expose them from the inside."

"Are you some kind of detective?"

Bradley hesitated. "Not exactly." She could tell there was more to the story, but she let it go. "Alistair Sinclair refused to hire me—I wasn't an engraver—but Elizabeth Sinclair offered me a job tutoring the twins. I wonder now if she wanted protection from Vance. Anyway, I took the job to stay close to Alistair Sinclair who is the leader of the counterfeiting ring. Vance and the Walrus provided protection. Smythe and two men who look like brothers—one named Bill—are probably doing the actual counterfeiting work. I know they have the ink and the paper, but I don't know where they are doing the printing or if they have the engraved currency plates yet."

"I still don't understand what all that has to do with me," Annie said. "What is the connection to the man in the cemetery, and why do they want to kill me?"

"There is something else," Bradley said. Saving his life had earned her his trust. "I'm working with a Pinkerton detective named Otto Fuchs. We think either Sinclair or his unknown partner is a criminal called the Butzemann. According to the rumors, the Butzemann works with a new, unsuspecting crew on lucrative crimes, and then, when the job is over, anyone who might recognize his face mysteriously disappears."

Annie shivered despite the warmth in the house. "Like the body of the Southerner in the cemetery disappeared?"

"Maybe," Bradley said. "Maybe the Butzemann killed the man and thinks you saw him. And now wants to do the same to you."

"I didn't see anything," Annie said with exasperation.

"He only has to think you did," Bradley said. "Fuchs also thinks local law enforcement might be on the Butzemann's payroll. Another reason not to trust the sheriff."

"Where is Sinclair now? He still is the key to all this."

"I haven't seen him in a few days," Bradley said, "but his family is still in town. The Walrus is easy to find, but I'm unsure what he knows. With Smythe dead, I have to find the two brothers so I can follow them back to the counterfeiter's hideout. Once we have physical proof, Detective Fuchs can bring in the Pinkerton Agency or the Secret Service. If we can tie the counterfeit money or equipment to Sinclair and his silent partner, they will go to jail, and you will be safe."

Annie thought about it for a few minutes. "So, the dead Southerner may have been involved with the counterfeiting ring, and it may have only been a coincidence someone left his body on my mother's grave. I may have accidentally gotten the attention of a mysterious crime boss who makes people disappear. And our best plan—other than not dying—is to find Sinclair and get him to talk or find the two brothers and follow them to their counterfeit printing location. Does that sum it up?"

"And one more thing," Bradley said. "Someone on the inside has been leaving me notes." He pulled out the article about the stolen paper and the note naming Jacub Jagusiak and Cornell University. He handed them to Annie.

"Where does Jacub Jagusiak fit in?"

"No idea. I'm looking for an excuse to go to Ithaca to meet with him. He might know something that will help us."

Annie nodded and then remembered the paper she found in the hotel room. She pulled it out of her pocket. "This is the only clue I found in the dead man's room." She handed it to Bradley.

"*Ortus solis* one, seven, five, one, zero. It's cryptic," he said. "Any thoughts?"

"Well, *ortus solis* means sunrise or rising sun in Latin. I have no idea about the numbers."

"You can read Latin?" Bradley asked. "Impressive. 'Course now, you're showing off."

Annie laughed and punched him in the arm. "Get used to it," she said. He winced as if truly injured and grinned. She looked back at the note. "Sunrise might refer to a time," she said. "When was sunrise this morning? About four forty-five a.m.? Rising sun could have something to do with Japan, the 'land of the rising sun.' But these are just wild guesses." Annie hadn't heard that anyone from Japan was in town.

"I can't think of any images on greenbacks that depict a sun— rising or otherwise. Not sure how this clue is related to counterfeiting."

Annie thought of one more clue she had. "I'll be right back." She ran up to her room and returned with Jeanne's drawing of the snake tattoo. She handed it to Bradley. "This was on the Southerner's forearm. Have you ever seen a tattoo like this before? Maybe on one of the counterfeiters?"

Bradley looked at the drawing carefully. "No, but I'll keep an eye out for it." He set the drawing back down on the table and looked at Annie. "I don't know why someone wants to kill you, but we will figure it out."

Annie liked the sound of "we," but was less confident. "Why do you think so?"

"Well, I'm an optimist," he said. "And I know you are smart, so with our two brains working together, there is nothing we can't figure out."

Annie thought of herself as a realist but appreciated his attempts at making her feel better. Looking at his face, she noticed how handsome he was—not for the first time. Something about his eyes and the way he looked at her. But how much could she really trust him?

Annie noticed several dark spots on Bradley's neck. She stood up and leaned over him. "I think you have some dirt—" When she wiped the largest spot, it smeared red. It was not dirt. "Did you get cut?"

"What?" Bradley reached up to rub his neck. His fingers came away streaked red. "It's not my blood."

Annie felt lightheaded. She looked down at Bradley's shoes. He was wearing dusty black boots. Bradley had known the man's room number from the key he had pickpocketed. Bradley finding her dangling from the porch had been no coincidence.

"Annie, are you—"

She reached into her pocket and pulled out her derringer as she backed away from him. "Whose blood is it, Bradley?" His hesitation was all she needed to confirm her suspicion. "YOU killed Smythe!"

"What are you talking about?"

Annie cleared her throat. She pointed the gun at Bradley's heart. "You killed that man in the hotel. That is why you were outside when I came off the porch. You must have just come down the stairs." Hastings and Vance had pretended to be something they were not. They both fooled Annie. Now Bradley?

Bradley raised his hands slowly and looked at her with bemusement. She didn't see anything funny about the situation. "Annie, it wasn't me," he said. "I was never in that man's room."

"I don't believe you."

"Why would I kill him before finding out who is trying to kill you?" he said. Annie remained unconvinced. Bradley kept his hands in the air. "Okay. Selfishly," he said, "I wouldn't have killed him before I learned everything he knew about the counterfeiting ring. Tell me again what you saw in the hotel room when Smythe got stabbed."

Keeping the gun pointed at Bradley, Annie licked her lips. "I was trapped under the bed and there was a knock on the door," she said. "I heard a scuffle and a groan, and then Smythe fell to the floor. His face had dried blood around his nose, and his dead eyes stared at me. Then the killer left."

Bradley stopped her. "That dried blood was from me punching him in the face when I found him in a carriage outside the circus. He had kidnapped Henry."

"What!?"

"After you left with the key, Henry disappeared. I ran to the road and found Smythe in a carriage with his arm around a terrified Henry. I punched the man in the face one or three times before pulling Henry out. That is how his blood got on me. I would have punched him again, but he got away."

Annie lowered the gun slightly. "Is Henry all right?"

"I think so," Bradley said. "When I returned him to Mrs. Sinclair, he wanted to watch the circus. Amazing kid." Bradley shook his head in appreciation of the boy's resilience. "Then I realized Smythe might return to his hotel room, so I hired the first available hackman and raced to the Glen Mountain House to warn you. I had just arrived when I saw your legs dangling from the porch."

Annie lowered her derringer and slumped into a chair. "I'm sorry," she said. "Just promise me you're not a murderer."

"I promise you, I haven't killed anyone since drowning Vance."

Annie laughed despite herself. "Close enough." She put the gun back into her pocket. Trusting people was hard for her. At least Bradley didn't want her dead. "It is getting late," she said. The house was quiet. Annie wished she had Nana, Roland, and Glendon next to her. She looked at Bradley.

"Do you want me to stay?" He said it quietly. Annie wondered if he was a mind reader.

Yes, she thought. "No," she said. "I'll lock and barricade the door after you leave."

"Is there a shotgun in the house?" he asked. Annie led him to Glendon's shotgun and a supply of shotgun shells. "A bit more firepower than your derringer," Bradley said as he loaded the weapon and handed it back to her. Annie accepted the shotgun, feeling the weight in her hands. Bradley saw discomfort on her face. "Do you want me to explain how to fire a shotgun?"

Annie thanked him but shook her head. She knew how to shoot, load, and clean most weapons. Shotguns reminded her of hunting trips with her father. Her discomfort came from imagining what would happen to those memories if she ever had to pull the trigger of a shotgun to end a person's life.

She walked Bradley to the door, where he wished her a good night before disappearing into the darkness and leaving her alone in the house. Annie wedged a chair under each exterior door's doorknobs to prevent anyone from entering unannounced.

She lay awake for a long time with the shotgun and derringer by her side before sleep claimed her.

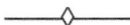

Annie dreamed of a swirling windstorm battering her house and of a tree branch knock, knock, knocking on the wall of her bedroom. She opened her eyes slowly. It was early morning. There was no windstorm, but the knocking persisted. Her sleepy brain took a few seconds to remember she had blocked the doors, and the knocking must have been coming from someone who wanted to get in. Hoping Glendon or Roland had returned, Annie jumped out of bed, grabbed the shotgun as she threw on a robe, and ran downstairs. Before opening the door, she peeked through a window and saw a concerned Mrs. Phelps waiting outside. Disappointed, Annie set the shotgun aside and opened the door.

"Annie?" Mrs. Phelps could see the worry on Annie's face. "Are you all right? What is going on?"

Annie ushered Mrs. Phelps inside, then quickly locked and barricaded the door behind them. "I'm glad you are here," she said. "Neither Roland nor Glendon came home last night. And I think someone might be following me." While Glendon came and went at odd hours, it was rare for Roland to stay out all night.

"Oh dear. Shall I fetch the sheriff?"

"No," Annie said. "But can we talk over breakfast? I have some questions I need to ask you."

"Of course," Mrs. Phelps said. Annie helped her prepare a breakfast of oatmeal and fresh fruit. As they sat down together, Mrs. Phelps looked at Annie expectantly. "What did you want to talk about?"

"I'm worried about Roland," Annie said. "It's not like him to be gone all night without a word. A few days ago, a man with one arm approached me and said Roland was not who he pretended to be. I don't remember much about Roland before my parents' death. What can you tell me?"

Mrs. Phelps played with her oatmeal before answering. "Well, I've lived here all my life," she said. "Your mother moved here with her parents right before she and your father married. You know they got married in the Presbyterian church. The old one before Mister Magee paid to build the new one. Neither Roland nor Glendon lived here back then."

"Oh," Annie said, disappointed.

"Both Glendon and Roland knew your parents before any of them moved to Watkins. You know your father's family is from Rochester, so I assumed he and Roland knew each other growing up. I remember hearing that your father and Roland had been the best of friends—inseparable—until they had a falling out right before your father married your mother. The first time I met Roland was around the time of your parents' death. He had just moved to town."

"What caused their falling out?"

"It is not my place to guess," Mrs. Phelps said in a way that convinced Annie she knew exactly what it was about.

None of this made sense to Annie. "Do you know if Roland Smith is his real name?"

"That's an odd question. Why wouldn't it be?" Mrs. Phelps asked.

Annie shrugged. She finished her oatmeal and took a bite from a plump, juicy strawberry. When she reached for a linen napkin to wipe her mouth, she saw the drawing of the snake tattoo still on the table from last night. She picked it up.

Mrs. Phelps stared at the drawing before quickly looking away.

Annie held up the drawing in front of Mrs. Phelps. "Have you seen this tattoo before?"

Mrs. Phelps barely glanced at it. "Oh, I can't be sure."

Mrs. Phelps was a lovely woman and a horrible liar. "Amelia," Annie said, using Mrs. Phelps's first name. "This might be a matter of life and death. Do you recognize this tattoo?"

Amelia Phelps looked concerned. "Death? Has something happened to Glendon?"

Annie thought she had not heard correctly. *Glendon?* "Why—" Annie's voice trailed off. She suddenly inhaled and then struggled to breathe. Goosebumps formed on her arms as a sinking feeling began growing in the pit of her stomach. She stared at Amelia Phelps, realizing who the woman would have seen undressed.

Mrs. Phelps turned bright red. "I'm sorry. It's not my place—I shouldn't—"

Annie grasped Mrs. Phelps's arm. "Where did you see this tattoo?" Annie needed to hear her say it.

Mrs. Phelps looked frightened by Annie's intensity. Annie waited. Mrs. Phelps's eyes darted around the room like a cornered animal. There was no escape for her. She sighed and answered in a quiet voice. "Glendon has this tattoo on his left thigh." She turned even redder.

Annie sat back in shock. Glendon had the same tattoo as the dead Southerner?

A knock came on the door. Mrs. Phelps jumped up while Annie sat dumbfounded, her world crumbling around her. Suddenly, nothing made sense.

Mrs. Phelps returned with a concerned look on her face. George Magee had followed her in and now stood by her side.

Annie looked up.

"Hello, Annie," George said. The look on his face caused Annie's heart to sink. "I have bad news. Roland's been shot."

CHAPTER XXXIX

CORNELL UNIVERSITY

Wednesday, July 22, 1874

THE steam train chugged out of the depot, heading north along Seneca Lake's western shore. The ride offered lovely views of the lake and surrounding countryside. Fishermen rowed flat-bottomed dories in search of trout and bass under a cloudless blue sky, while closer in, several yachts and sloops stood idle as wealthy vacationers finished their leisurely breakfasts at local hotels. Henry and Hannah sat quietly on the bench in front of Bradley, staring out the train's windows, while Elizabeth and Nanny Kate talked quietly on the opposite side of the train. The Walrus sulked somewhere in the back of the train.

Last night, Elizabeth had surprised Bradley as he returned to the Lake View Hotel from Annie's house. Before he could climb the entrance stairs, Elizabeth appeared out of the darkness, claimed his arm, and said, "Walk with me." Her warm hands steered him down a moonlit walking path. Her body gave off subtle odors of floral and citrus.

When they were far enough away from potential eavesdroppers, she stopped and turned toward him. "Thank you for bringing Henry back to me. I'm in your debt."

His hand still hurt from punching Smythe. "I did the job you hired me to do, ma'am."

"Call me Elizabeth," she said, "when we are alone." She stood very close to him. Her hand rested on his arm, connecting them. He wondered where her husband might be. "And the man who took my son?" she asked.

Bradley understood what she really wanted to know. "He'll never bother your children again," he said, even though the credit for facilitating Smythe's passage to the next world belonged else-where.

Elizabeth bit her lip, perhaps wanting to know more, but she gently nodded her head and nudged him back into motion down the path. "I have decided to take the twins and return to New York," she said. "The city can be unbearable in the summer, and Henry and Hannah will be disappointed to leave, but we need a change of scenery. This was supposed to be a family vacation, but Alistair has been so busy. And after almost losing Henry...."

Elizabeth was telling Bradley he was about to lose his job.

"I want you to come with us," she said, to his shock. "You have been wonderful with Henry and Hannah. I want you to continue working for me."

Bradley was temporarily speechless. He couldn't leave Wat-kins until he'd accomplished what he came to do, but it felt good to be wanted. Perhaps there was an alternative. "Could I make a suggestion?" he asked.

"Please do."

"Spend a few days in Ithaca first. It will give you a change of scenery, and there will be more there for the twins to enjoy." Ithaca was only thirty-five miles away at the end of neighboring Cayuga Lake. "After a couple days, you can decide if you want to continue to New York or perhaps return to Watkins."

Elizabeth had squeezed his arm in the darkness. "I like your compromise," she said. "Besides, someone told me recently about the many waterfalls to explore there."

Staring out the train window, Bradley saw Hector Falls and Glen Eldridge on the far side of the lake which made him think of Annie. He couldn't shake the feeling that he was abandoning her but had to seize the opportunity to travel to Ithaca to find Jacub Jagusiak at Cornell University. Before he left, he scribbled Annie a note explaining his sudden departure and left it for the hotel staff to deliver.

By midmorning, their train reached Geneva on the northern end of Seneca Lake. After a short transfer, they headed southeast on the Ithaca and Geneva Railroad. This wasn't the most direct path, but the Lake View staff had assured Elizabeth that this was

Taughannock Falls

the most attractive summer route between Watkins and Ithaca and much preferable to a bumpy stagecoach ride over the hill.

When the twins grew bored with the scenery, Bradley asked them what their favorite part of the circus had been.

"The trapeze acts and the clowns," Henry said.

"I liked the horses with the female riders," Hannah said. "And the performing dogs."

"And the monkeys!" Henry added.

When the train reached the Taughannock Falls stop ten miles north of Ithaca, Elizabeth hurried everyone off. "We have a new waterfall to visit, thanks to Bradley," she said with a smile. A porter tended to their luggage while Elizabeth paid for a carriage to the Taughannock House, a hotel that overlooked the chasm into which the towering 215-foot Taughannock Falls plunged. Cliffs rose another hundred feet above the waterfall on either side of the stream.

The Taughannock House served a delicious meal, fortifying them for their exploration of the gorge and waterfall. They navigated rugged paths and a series of wooden stairways hewn into the rock to reach the lower ravine. "It's fifty feet higher than Niagara Falls," Henry said excitedly, as they stood near the bottom of the falls and looked up. Bradley had never been to Niagara Falls, but took Henry's word for it.

Bradley watched Henry and Hannah as they laughed and played along the trail. Henry did not seem to show any obvious effects from his abduction, but Bradley noticed the boy no longer strayed far from his mother. Bradley started back up the trail when he heard footsteps approaching from behind.

He turned as the Walrus stomped to within a few feet of him. The big man got right to the point. He leaned in close enough for Bradley to smell his breath. "Where is Vance?" he huffed.

Bradley took his time answering. "Why would I know?"

"You and Vance disappeared on the same day, then you turn up with bruises and a cut on your forehead."

Bradley shrugged. "Life is full of coincidences."

The big man leaned closer. "I have made inquiries about you back in the city," he said. "I'll find out who you are, and when I do...."

The Walrus was letting his anger get the better of him, and Bradley wondered how far he could push the man. Better to force a confrontation now than to let the brute sneak up on him later. "I'm sure Vance deserved whatever happened to him," Bradley said, staring at the Walrus.

The Walrus's nostrils flared, and he rolled his shoulders. Bradley centered his weight on the balls of his feet, prepared to react to whatever move the Walrus made.

"Come now, boys," Elizabeth said, coming up the trail and stepping between them. She grabbed Bradley by the arm and whisked him away. "You can argue on your own time. We must head back now or miss the next train."

After their steam train pulled into the Ithaca station, a short carriage ride brought them to the city's center and the newly rebuilt Ithaca Hotel on the corner of Aurora Street and East State Street. Ithaca, at the head of Cayuga Lake, was larger than Watkins. Wetlands dominated the shoreline, so the city's downtown sat farther away from the lake on higher ground near a bend in Six Mile Creek.

Elizabeth checked in and then sent the twins to their room with Nanny Kate. When the Walrus left to smoke a cigar, Elizabeth pulled Bradley aside.

"You are free for the rest of the day," she said, handing him his own room key. "The kids are tired, so a quiet afternoon and evening would be good for all of us."

Bradley thanked her. "You have wonderful children," he said.

Elizabeth grinned. "A parent's favorite compliment."

Bradley smiled back. "May I ask you a personal question?" he said, hoping he wasn't pushing his luck. Elizabeth tilted her head. She nodded. "Did your husband get his injuries in the war?"

Surprise flashed across Elizabeth's face—not the type of personal question she had anticipated. She looked away as if recalling a memory and then looked back at Bradley. "My husband has never been willing to talk about what happened," she said. "We focus on the future, although... there are some days he gets a haunted look in his eyes." Elizabeth placed a hand on Bradley's arm. "I have seen that same haunted look in your eyes. You remind me of a younger version of him."

She left Bradley standing in the middle of the hotel lobby.

Bradley dropped off his travel bag, splashed cool water on his face, then headed back to the lobby. After a quick visit to the front desk, he stepped outside and headed down East State Street into the city's crowded main shopping area. He moved slowly, glancing into shop windows, tipping his hat at ladies passing by, and acting like he had all the time in the world. As he crossed Tioga Street, he saw what he had been waiting for—the Walrus tailing him.

Bradley stepped into a hatter and furrier shop. He could see the Walrus taking up a viewing position outside. Bradley took his time. He tried on several hats and settled on a nice brown bowler, which he paid for and had packaged in a hatbox. On the counter was an old edition of *The New York Times*, and, out of habit, he checked the Lost and Found section. A pair of gold eyeglasses had been lost on the west side of the city below Canal Street. A liberal reward was offered to the finder. Bradley sighed and placed the paper back on the counter. He stepped out of the store with his new purchase ten minutes after entering.

Next, he crossed the street and stepped into a dry goods store. Out of the corner of his eye, he saw the Walrus reposition himself. Bradley browsed the bolts of cloth, the linens, drapes, and towels. He bought a few items but still had time to spare. He wished he had his father's watch to count the ten minutes. To kill time, he asked the clerk for a pen and pencil and wrote a note, which he handed back to the clerk.

"I saw a Western Union Telegraph Office near the hotel. Here is an extra dollar if you'll send this telegram for me." Bradley still hadn't gotten a reply to his first telegram sent to his friend in the city, so he would try again. The clerk might have wondered why Bradley could not send it himself but happily took the money. Bradley headed back into the street ten minutes after entering the store.

Bradley continued down the street until he reached H. M. Straussman's merchant tailor and clothier's shop, claiming the finest stock of ready-made clothing in Ithaca. *Perfect*, Bradley thought. He stepped inside and bought a brown suit that matched his new hat. For ready-made, the suit fit him well enough. He could always get it tailored later. The clerk offered to deliver his purchase to the hotel for him, but Bradley smiled and asked to have them wrapped for hand carrying. For the third time, he left the store after ten minutes carrying a bundle of packages.

When Bradley stepped into the fourth shop near the end of the block, the Walrus lazily took up a vantage point and prepared to wait ten minutes. Bradley moved to the back of the store, out of sight of the street, and offered a generous sum to the shopkeeper to deliver all his packages to his room at the Ithaca Hotel. As soon as the shopkeeper agreed, Bradley—ignoring the horrified looks of the shopkeeper and several other customers—stripped out of his black suit, folded it quickly, and put on his new brown suit and hat. Bradley stepped out the door two minutes after entering with a newly purchased cane. He hunched over, kept his head down, and limped slowly until he rounded the corner onto Cayuga Street with the Walrus none the wiser.

As soon as he was out of the Walrus's sight, Bradley straightened up and headed to the carriage he had arranged with the hotel to be waiting at this location. He jumped in. "Take me to Cornell University."

The driver snapped the reins, setting his pair of horses into motion. They crossed over Seneca Street and turned right onto Buffalo Street. Bradley counted three large churches in the first three blocks.

The driver spat a long string of tobacco juice from the carriage onto the dirt street. "You plan on attending?"

"Me? No, just looking for someone. Is it a good university?"

"Godless den of heathens, so they say," he said, laughing as if he disagreed.

"Excuse me?" Bradley said.

"Cornell. The university doesn't embrace the holy spirit like them other universities. Nonsectarian they call it. But more people means more business, so no complaints from me."

"If I needed to find a specific student," Bradley asked, "where would I look?"

"Cascadilla Place."

"What's that?"

"Enormous building on the hill up ahead. Supposed to be a sanatorium for water cures, but the university took it over for student housing."

The driver whipped his horses as they slowed on the steep incline. Before long, Buffalo Street ended, and a left turn on Eddy Street brought them to Cascadilla Place. The driver tugged on the reins and brought the carriage to a halt. Bradley handed the man several coins and stepped down.

"If you can't find who you're looking for here," the driver said, "there's a wooden bridge upstream that will get you across the gorge. Keep heading uphill, and you'll find the new buildings they put up in Ezra Cornell's old cow pasture." The old man rubbed his chin. "Good luck, though. Commencement was first of July. Not so many students around now." The man steered his carriage back down the hill.

Bradley looked at the six-story stone behemoth rising on the hill before him. Behind Cascadilla Place, he saw a deep treelined gorge. Cornell University looked to be a lovely place. Bradley wondered how his life might have turned out if not for his stepfather. He could have been one of these students. When his thoughts drifted to memories of his mother, he shook his head to chase them away and looked for men about his own age who could be students.

It took several tries, but Bradley found a young man who had heard of Jacub Jagusiak. "I haven't seen Jacub since spring," the man said, "but I know his roommate works in the chemistry building on the main campus." Bradley asked for the roommate's name and directions to the chemistry building and then headed up the road behind Cascadilla Place to the wooden bridge that crossed over a series of cascades. Below the bridge, the stream dropped down a series of small rocky ledges on its way to Cayuga Lake.

Bradley followed the dirt road uphill until he reached a large, expansive field. Five new buildings transformed Ezra Cornell's cow pasture into a university. The three stone buildings, Morrill Hall, McGraw Hall, and White Hall, stretched along the brow of the hill to his left, overlooking the city of Ithaca and Cayuga Lake. Bradley crossed the field toward a large wooden building across from Mc-

CORNELL UNIVERSITY

Graw that housed the chemistry lab. The Shops, the student who gave him directions called it. Bradley pulled off his hat and wiped the sweat from his brow caused by the warm sun and long walk. Then he stepped into the building like he belonged there—bluffing with confidence. No one questioned him. He stopped one student to ask for directions and found his way into a small chemistry lab where a thin young man sat at a wooden desk, puzzling over a stack of notes.

"David Offenberger?"

The man looked up, surprised at the interruption. "Can I help you?"

Bradley offered his sincerest smile. "I hope so," he said. "I'm looking for your roommate, Jacub Jagusiak."

David's face transformed from curious to panicked. Fear flooded his eyes, and he stood up and staggered backward. His head pivoted left and right, looking for an escape route.

"Whoa, whoa," Bradley held up his empty hands, palm out. "I'm not here to hurt you!" David continued backward, and Bradley feared the man was about to flee. His voice took on a harder tone. "If you try to run, I will catch you and cannot promise it will be painless."

David froze in place. "Please don't hurt me," he said.

Bradley pointed David back to the seat he had just vacated, then pulled up another chair and sat down. "I'm not here to hurt anyone. I just want to talk to your roommate. Where can I find Jacub?"

David licked his lips and inhaled and exhaled slowly. "I haven't seen him since March twenty-seventh."

"That's quite specific. What happened on March twenty-seventh?"

David's eyes darted around the room, still wanting to escape.

Bradley's hand grabbed David's forearm. "The sooner you tell me, the sooner I leave you alone."

"We had a balloonist on campus," David said, staring at Bradley's hand. "That's how I remember. Donaldson was the guy's name. He had a thousand-foot rope attached to the balloon to let it out and then draw it back down. Jacub was supposed to meet me there. We were both excited to go up in the balloon... but he never showed up. No one has seen him since."

Bradley rubbed his chin. "Tell me what happened on the days before Jacub disappeared. Was he acting strange in any way?"

David looked down. "A few weeks before he disappeared, a large man showed up asking for Jacub. Like you did today. Jacub told me later that a relative had died, and the man came to take him to the funeral. Jacub was gone a couple of days."

"And when he returned?"

"He came back excited. Which I thought was odd. And he had money to spend. Jacub's family could barely pay for his classes, and he always had a chip on his shoulder about it. I figured his distant relative dying meant some kinda inheritance. Everything was great for a couple of weeks, and then Jacub started acting paranoid. Never wanted to go out or be alone...."

"Go on."

"The day before he disappeared, another man came around, asking for Jacub. This guy was thinner and meaner than the first guy."

"What was Jacub studying here at Cornell? Was he an artist? An engraver, perhaps?"

David shook his head. "No, he studied chemistry like me. We met in class. We became friends. Me being Jewish didn't bother him."

Bradley did not understand how chemistry connected with a counterfeiting ring. "What was Jacub working on?"

"Electrochemistry. Galvanoplasty," David said. He noticed the blank look on Bradley's face. "Have you heard of electrotyping?"

"Explain it to me."

"It's a wet chemical process that uses electricity to remove the copper atoms from a copper sulfate solution to form a thin shell of copper onto a wax mold."

"Assume I know nothing about chemistry."

"Right, umm... Well, electrotyping creates an exact copy of any woodcut or engraved steel or copperplate."

Bradley's mouth dropped open. "An exact copy?"

"Yeah," David said. "Jacub had remarkable results with several different metals. With electrotyping, he could make an exact copy of almost any engraved plate."

Bradley stifled a groan. Everything he assumed was wrong. Sinclair did not need an engraver. He had somehow gotten Jacub Jagusiak to use his electrotyping skills to create an exact copy of at least one set of currency printing plates before March 27 when Jagusiak disappeared. Why offer Pickens a job in July then? A memory tickled Bradley's brain. When he accused Pickens of being an engraver during their Tombs meeting, what had Pickens said? Something about "running the presses at one of the premier printing houses." Sinclair did not want Pickens's skills as an engraver. He wanted Pickens to run the printing presses. *I'm an idiot*, Bradley thought to himself.

He turned back to David. "Where did Jacub go for that family funeral? New York or the District of Columbia?"

"DC. How did you know?"

To make an exact copy of an official greenback printing plate, Jacub needed access to an original. That meant bribing or blackmailing an employee from either the American Bank Note Company in New York or the newly formed Bureau of Engraving and Printing in DC. Bradley ignored David's question. He let go of the man's arm and stood to leave. "You've been very helpful."

Bradley headed for the door and stepped back out into the summer heat. The afternoon sun drifted closer to the western hills across the valley. He did not see any carriages to hire, so he decided to walk to the Ithaca Hotel. He started downhill in the direction of the wooden bridge with a lot to think about.

Sinclair's counterfeiting crew had exact replicas of an official currency plate since the end of March or early April at the latest. The perfect printing paper disappeared in a mysterious fire over a year earlier, according to the article his mysterious benefactor had left for him. Sinclair's man claimed to have the perfect ink during their dinner at the Jefferson House. All they needed was an expert to run the presses. Is that the role they wanted Pickens for? Or had they found other knowledgeable men to run the presses? Had they been working for months or were they just getting started?

If they had started months ago and copied a high-value denomination plate, Sinclair's team could be sitting on millions of dollars of near perfect counterfeit money.

Bradley crossed over the bridge and turned right, following the road along the gorge. He passed Cascadilla Place and continued down the trail through the woods. The tree canopy blocked the worst of the day's heat. Bradley had let his assumptions take him in the wrong direction. Now, he worried he was running out of time. If Fuchs was correct—if Sinclair was the Butzemann—the process of tying up loose ends could have started with Smythe and maybe Annie's dead Southerner in the cemetery. Was Annie another loose end?

Bradley's preoccupation almost cost him his life. As he walked down the wooded path, the slightest sound triggered a survival instinct deep within. He pitched himself forward as the blow came to the back of his head. His reflexes helped him roll with the punch, deflecting much of the power behind it, but he still landed in the dirt in a daze. The ground was a horrible place to be in a fight, so Bradley did the only thing he could do. He played possum and waited. If his attacker had planned to shoot him, he would have already done so.

Through half-closed eyes, Bradley watched the Walrus step toward him and reach down. At the last possible moment, Bradley kicked out and caught the Walrus between the legs. Not very sporting, but on the streets of New York there are no rules when fighting for your life. The Walrus howled and fell to the side.

Bradley jumped to his feet and placed the knife he carried in his boot against the Walrus's neck before the man composed himself. The Walrus's eyes went wide, and he stayed very still. Of course, the Walrus knew about Jacub Jagusiak and would have guessed that's where Bradley might go. All the Walrus had to do was wait for the right moment to ambush him. Bradley was lucky to still be breathing.

"Since we have this quality time together," Bradley said. "I have a few questions for you." He pressed the knife a bit deeper into the Walrus's neck, making sure he had the man's full attention.

"Were you the man who took Jacub Jagusiak to Washington DC?"

The Walrus shot daggers out his eyes at Bradley but answered the question. "Yes."

"Did you bribe a worker at the Bureau of Printing and Engraving to get a copy of a plate?"

"A drunkard with gambling debts who owed the wrong people too much money."

"What denomination plate did Jacub Jagusiak copy?"

The Walrus did not want to answer, forcing Bradley to press the knife tighter against the big man's throat. "One hundred and five-hundred-dollar bills."

Bradley whistled. "Impressive choice. You are doing great so far. Is Jacub Jagusiak dead?"

"I didn't kill him."

"Vance? It sounds like a job that he would enjoy doing."

Bradley could tell from the Walrus's face that he had guessed correctly. "Why? Why kill him?"

"He tried to blackmail us for more money. He got greedy."

"Who is behind the counterfeiting ring."

"Sinclair."

"Anyone else?"

Another hesitation. "No."

Bradley could not tell for sure, but that sounded like a lie. Before he could ask another question, a voice spoke behind him. "What's going on here?" A university student had come down the trail.

Bradley pulled the knife away before the student saw it. The Walrus did not hesitate. With a hard backward swing of his elbow, he caught Bradley between the legs and sprinted down the path, leaving Bradley groaning and trying to compose himself. *I guess I deserved that one*, he thought to himself.

The student remained on the path with a confused look on his face. "That guy just tried to steal my wallet," Bradley said. Since Bradley looked like a student and the Walrus like a man who would steal your wallet, it was a believable lie. "I don't recommend following him down the path."

The student nodded his head vigorously and headed in the opposite direction. Bradley took his own advice and followed the student until they reached Cascadilla Place. From there, it was a leisurely stroll down Buffalo Street to return to the Ithaca Hotel. Bradley took his time. The sun lay on top of the western hills, and the sky had turned from blue to yellow to orange by the time he reached the hotel's front entrance.

Bradley's ego ached from the realization he had made so many mistakes in his attempts to join the counterfeiting ring, and his body hurt thanks to the Walrus. He pushed through the doors of the Ithaca Hotel with a cool bath and a soft bed on his mind.

"Where is my wife!"

Bradley stopped a few steps inside the lobby. A furious Alistair Sinclair stood beside the Walrus, who wore a smug grin.

"I have been here an hour," Sinclair said, "and Nanny Kate admitted both you and my wife have been unaccounted for all afternoon. Did you think you could sneak my wife away to a hotel in Ithaca and that I would not find out?"

The Walrus's grin grew wider, and it was clear he had been whispering lies into Sinclair's ear.

"I'm not sure what he told you—"

"Stop. All I want to know is where my wife is." Sinclair's height and scars gave him an intimidating look. His eyes held barely contained rage.

Bradley was not afraid of a fight and had little patience for false accusations. If he'd had a revolver, he would have drawn it and demanded that Sinclair tell him where the counterfeit money was and explain why someone was trying to kill Annie. He'd buy one in the morning. For now, he knew he was on extremely dangerous ground. The rich—especially the ultra-rich—had a way of getting law enforcement on their side. If Bradley wanted to stay out of jail, he needed to tread carefully.

"I'll ask you one last time," Sinclair said. "Where. Is. My. Wife."

"I'm right here, dear," Elizabeth said, appearing in the doorway behind Bradley. Sinclair's anger softened as his wife moved past Bradley and gave Alistair a peck on the cheek.

Sinclair turned back to Bradley. "Hiring you was a mistake," he said. "We no longer require your services. Leave this hotel immediately, and I expect you to depart the Lake View before noon tomorrow. Your final wages will be waiting there at the front desk."

Bradley looked at Elizabeth, but she offered no encouragement so he didn't argue. "Will you be all right, Mrs. Sinclair?" he asked.

"Yes, thank you," she said in a subdued voice. "And I'll say goodbye to Henry and Hannah for you." She didn't meet his eyes.

Bradley could only nod. He left the lobby and returned to his room to retrieve his travel bag and the purchases delivered there from his shopping spree. Bradley exited the Ithaca Hotel by a side door and searched for transportation. He had a long way to go if he hoped to return to Watkins by morning.

Potomac River from Maryland

CHAPTER XL

Disappointment

From the Journal of Private H. Thompson

October 28, 1864 – Three weeks after our escape, I arrived at the train depot just east of Morganton, North Carolina. Only six months earlier, the Lucky Six boarded a train here, returning to our winter camp after finding the gold. A lifetime ago, when the Lucky Six had a bright future. When a man approached me and asked if I was Harper Thompson, I nodded and handed him my bag. I had telegraphed ahead to arrange a carriage to transport me to the nearest boardinghouse.

After escaping the cabin, the old man and the young woman had taken me six miles down the dark road to another farm. As the sun rose, the old man handed me off to a friend who agreed to take me ten more miles. When the old man thanked me for saving the girl's dignity, I handed him back the shotgun and apologized. "Not all Southerners are like Buck," I said.

After another day's walk, I arrived at the Potomac River. I climbed down from the hills, avoiding the small bands of roving Union soldiers, and found a log to cling to as I floated across. Wet and exhausted, I climbed out on the West Virginia side and moved south through the woods, looking for a barn to hold up in. I did not see the middle-aged man until he stepped out from behind a tree and pointed his hunting rifle at me. "Who goes there!"

I could not believe I had come all that way just to be recaptured. I considered running away or trying to grab the man's gun. Better to die than go back, but I had never been the suicidal type. When the man asked me if I was a Rebel or a Yankee, I replied, "Which answer will get me a warm meal?"

The man laughed. "You sound like you're from the South. That's good enough for me." He lowered the gun. "Come on in out

*of the cold." Surprised, I followed him a short distance to his large
and inviting home.*

*My new friend was a Copperhead, a Southern sympathizer liv-
ing in the North. He had no sons but introduced me to his wife and
two lovely daughters. They cleaned me up, put me in new clothes—
one of the daughters had lost her husband in the war—and fed
me several delicious meals. In return, I regaled them with stories
of fighting for Robert E. Lee's Army of Northern Virginia, the
hardships of prisoner-of-war camps, and my daring escape from
Hellmira. I didn't mention Frank or Buck.*

*The next morning, after a good night's sleep in a real bed and
a breakfast of eggs, fried pork strips, and flapjacks, I had expected
to continue my journey on foot. My benefactor insisted on carrying
me south in his carriage until we reached a train station that would
get me to North Carolina. When he dropped me off, he gifted me a
travel bag full of his dead son-in-law's clothes and then reached
into his pocket and gave me a handful of silver and gold coins.
Enough to see me to my destination and then some. I thanked him
profusely. "After what you have been through," he said, "it's the
least I can do. Don't let anyone trade you for Confederate money,"
my benefactor said, "it's worthless these days."*

*As I settled into my room in Morganton, I wondered how many
days I would need to wait for Buck and Frank. There was a risk
they could go straight to Rutherfordton via stagecoach, but that
would take much longer than a train. I would wait for one week,
not a day more.*

*October 31, 1864 – Buck and Frank showed up on the fourth day. I
had waited for every train arrival, so I was at the depot to welcome
them as they stepped down from their train. Frank smiled when
he saw me. Buck—his chin and left cheek covered in bandages—
scowled. His frown deepened when he noticed the newly acquired
revolver I wore on my belt. I was relieved that he did not appear to
have one of his own. I stepped forward and offered them my hand.
"We started this together," I said. "We should finish this together."*

*Frank shook my hand willingly. Buck grasped it and tried to
pull me toward him. "How do I know," he hissed," you haven't
already gone for the gold?"*

"You don't," I said. "But I telegraphed the boardinghouse the

day before I arrived from Statesville. And the owner has seen me every day since then." I pulled my hand back. "I didn't want to spend the rest of my life looking over my shoulder, wondering when you'd find me."

Buck nodded. "Damn right," he said. I didn't care if he checked with the boardinghouse owner. I had not left the depot area since checking into the hotel.

"We can go our separate ways when this is over," I said. "For tonight, I have rooms at the boardinghouse, and I've arranged for horses and a wagon to be standing by. They'll be ready for us at sunrise."

November 1, 1864 – We set out at dawn for Hickory Nut Gap and our hidden cave. Buck and Frank rode in the wagon, while I followed behind on a chestnut mare that I had traded two new suits and some gold coins for. I named her Bertha. She was older and slow, but surefooted and even-tempered. Thanks to my benefactor's generosity, I had saddlebags filled with food and supplies, and the large canvas on the back of the wagon covered shovels and lanterns.

We rode in silence. Frank never talked, and Buck and I had nothing to say to each other. The day was cold, but not as cold as when we had traveled the same route back in February.

When we got close, we all searched for the rocks Taylor had stacked to mark the location to leave the road. There were no rocks, but Frank simply said, "Here," when we reached the right location. He jumped off the wagon. He was right, of course. No one was willing to stay with the horses and wagon, so we unhitched the team and set up a picket line between two trees. We tied the horses to that rope and hid the wagon as best as possible.

I did not want to risk turning my back on Buck. My overactive imagination envisioned a whack on the side of my head from his shovel. He must have felt the same way about me because we ended up walking side by side across the stream and up into the woods. Frank took the lead and guided us unerringly to the cave entrance. It looked undisturbed.

Buck went in first, followed by Frank. My fear of tight spaces hadn't left me, but I knew what lay ahead, so it was easier than the first time. We set up our lanterns and started digging immediately.

I could see the mounds where we had buried the two home guards. We knew exactly where the gold should have been. Except, the gold wasn't there. Just a sunken area where it used to be. The gold was gone.

I swore loudly. Cursed the heavens. I had little chance of winning back my true love without the gold. I threw my shovel down and turned to Frank and Buck. In the dancing light of the lanterns, I saw the revolver Buck held in his hand. Clever, I thought. He had managed to acquire one in the middle of the night.

Frank looked at Buck with concern in his eyes. Buck stared at me. "I wanna know where the damn gold is!" he yelled.

"Me too!" I yelled back. "I haven't left Morganton since I arrived. You must've checked with the manager. Do y'all think I would be foolish enough to be here right now if I had taken it?"

I saw the hesitation in Buck's eyes. "If you didn't take it, who the hell did?"

"Who the hell knows!" I paced around. Kicked a small rock. "Fish couldn't have had time, but he could have told someone. Or the home guard could have come looking for their friends and found this cave." I stopped pacing and stared at Buck defiantly. Frank stepped between us, forcing Buck to lower his gun. With no alternatives, we searched the cave one last time to convince ourselves that the gold was really gone. It was.

"Let's get to Fish's house," Buck said. "Maybe he got word to his mother before he got captured."

As we left the cave, Frank held up a finger, asking us to wait, and then disappeared back into the darkness of the entrance. He backed his way out a few minutes later—his body shielding us from what he had been sprinkling on the ground. I noticed the large bag he had been carrying on his back was gone. Frank pulled out his pipe and lit it with a match. Then he leaned down and used the match to light the trail of black powder leading into the cave entrance. "Best stand back," he said.

Buck and I dove for cover, and a giant "whoomph" collapsed the entrance, sealing the cave. After we stood up and dusted ourselves off, Buck and I turned toward Frank. He shrugged. "It's a tomb. May the dead rest in peace."

We hitched up the wagon and made our way to Rutherfordton

and Fish's family farm. We found it abandoned. The neighbor told us that with all her sons dead, Mrs. Pierson could not keep up with the farm, and the bank took it over. Last they heard, she and her daughter had gone to Tennessee to live with distant family members.

Frank, Buck, and I stood in front of the Piersons' empty farmhouse. The wind whistled through the trees. The sun was sinking in the sky. It was over. If she had had money, she wouldn't have given up the farm. Buck cursed. Frank shrugged—never caring about getting rich.

When I asked Frank what he would do next, he said, "Visit my family." I nodded, wishing that I had a family waiting for my return. I looked at Buck. He spit in the dirt, then touched the bandages on his face. He needed to find a good doctor to tend to his wounded face.

Frank promised to get the horses and wagon back to the livery in Morganton. I gave them both food from my saddlebag for the trip and watched them load onto the wagon. I would miss Frank, but if I never saw Buck again it would be too soon. Just before they pulled out, Buck turned back to me.

"Taylor could've survived the crash," he said. "He's the only other person who knew where the gold was."

"If it was Taylor, he's long gone," I said.

"I'm going to find him," Buck said. "I will never give up looking for the gold. Someone has it." He turned away, and I watched them head north.

I sat on my horse in the middle of the empty farm. The Lucky Six's luck had run out. Our story was over. I will finish this journal entry and, with it, finish my life as a Southerner. I had considered my options. There was only one. I would head north to find the love of my life and our daughter.

CHAPTER XLI

THE JOURNAL

Wednesday, July 22, 1874

A T sunrise, the Magee mansion caretaker, a solid, dependable man weathered by a life outdoors, found Roland lying, bloody and near death, beside a lilac bush in the middle of George Magee's property. Roland had been shot once in the chest. The caretaker managed to carry an unconscious Roland to his small cottage west of the main residence and then jumped on his horse to rouse Dr. Bennett. Several doctors did business in town, but Bennett was young—not yet thirty—and trained in the newest surgical techniques at Geneva Medical College at the other end of the lake.

The caretaker's choice prolonged Roland's life. Dr. Bennett immediately had the caretaker move Roland to the kitchen table and performed surgery to stop the bleeding and remove the bullet. Roland remained in critical condition and had not regained consciousness, but the immediate crisis had passed.

Annie jumped out of George's carriage before it stopped and rushed into the caretaker's house. "Where is he?" she asked, fighting back tears. George followed her in.

Dr. Bennett greeted them in the front room. "Roland is alive, Annie," he said with a sympathetic look. "I have done what I could, but it is in God's hands now. He will need rest and someone to watch over him."

Roland lay nestled in the caretaker's bed. His face was pale, and his breathing strained and ragged. Annie knelt beside him as tears rolled down her face. "I'm sorry, I'm sorry, I'm sorry," she whispered. If she hadn't tried to find Lewis Crawford's killer, Roland might still be home and safe with her.

George pulled Dr. Bennett aside. "How bad is it?"

"Only time will tell," the doctor said. "If Roland can regain consciousness and fight off any infection around the wound, there is a strong chance he will pull through." Dr. Bennett hesitated. "But you should know... with that much blood loss, it's possible that even if he wakes up, he might be... permanently damaged." The doctor promised to return in the evening to change Roland's bandages and then left to visit other patients.

Annie took Roland's cold hand in hers. A memory came unbidden from Roland's early days as a boarder in their house. He had invited Annie on one of his nature walks. They traveled through the woods and then across a flowering pasture to a still pond to watch hummingbirds. There were cows in the pasture, and Annie noticed the cows stared at her when she walked by. When a few of the cows started to follow her, she grew afraid. Roland smiled at the time and said, "They are curious. You are something new for them to look at." He held out his hand to her, and when she took it, she felt warmth, strength, and safety. Now Annie tried to will those feelings back into Roland.

She leaned toward him and whispered in his ear. "Fight this. Fight and come back to us."

Annie stood and wiped away her tears. She was angry now. Someone was responsible for shooting Roland. Someone had a lot to answer for. When Annie asked to speak to George, the caretaker volunteered to watch over Roland for a time. George Magee guided Annie back to the front room.

"George, why was Roland on your property last night?" Annie asked. "Did he come to meet you?"

"No, Annie. It's a mystery to me," George said, pacing around the small room. "I haven't seen Roland since our paths crossed near the train station before the Glen Eldridge excursion. Doctor Bennett was already operating before I'd even heard Roland had been shot on my property." George rubbed his hands together and looked toward the other room. "I asked my staff, but no one heard or saw anything unusual last night."

Annie had more questions, but a knock on the door spared George further interrogation. The door swung open, revealing Sheriff Swartwood and one of his deputies on the front step. "Ah,

Miss Anderson," the sheriff said with his crooked smile. "Just the person I was hoping to find."

George used the interruption as an opportunity to leave. "I have a full business calendar today," he said, "but Magee Manor's resources will be at Roland's disposal, and Emma will be by soon to check on you." George donned his hat and left Annie with the sheriff. Annie watched him leave, wondering if George still believed that his younger brother died because he caught Annie's cold. If so, George might be the one person in Watkins with a real reason to want her dead.

"My condolences," the sheriff said to Annie after George departed. "How is Roland now?"

"Holding on."

The sheriff nodded. "We are starting the investigation into what happened," the sheriff said, "and I have several questions to ask you."

Annie wanted to be doing anything besides feeling sorry for herself and Roland. "Take me to where Roland was shot," she said, "and I'll answer any questions that I can." The sheriff stared at her for a few heartbeats. Annie thought he would refuse, but he nodded and gestured with his arm for her to follow.

The sheriff and the deputy led Annie across Glen Avenue and down the path toward the main residence. They stopped near a lilac bush backed by a stand of pine trees. "Here is where the caretaker found Roland."

Annie looked around. Further down the path, she could see the tower of Magee Manor rising above the trees. In the opposite direction, Annie saw the roof of the caretaker's house. This spot was remote but not as isolated as she would have thought. There was a trampled portion of the underbrush at her feet. She could see where Roland's blood had soaked into the ground. Flies buzzed around the spot, turning Annie's stomach. Why would Roland be here in the middle of the night? Was he on his way to ask George about the tattoo? Had someone ambushed him, or was he with someone who turned on him?

"Didn't anyone hear the gunshot," Annie asked.

"We are still checking with the neighbors," the sheriff said. "If someone doesn't come forward, it will difficult to determine the time of the shooting. It could have happened between sunset when the caretaker retired for the evening and sunrise. When did you last see Roland?"

"After lunch yesterday," Annie said. "He dropped me off at our house and said he had errands to run. He told me that he would see me soon." Emotions rose inside her, but she fought them back. She didn't want to cry in front of the sheriff again. So much had happened since she'd last seen Roland. The circus, Smythe's killing at Glen Mountain House, the shooting of the bear-sized man, and her escape with Bradley across the cemetery.

"Would Roland have any reason to do himself harm?"

Annie was startled by the question. "What? No... Why would you... You think he shot himself?"

"Roland's gun was found beside him with one bullet missing."

Annie balled up her fists. "There is no way Roland shot himself!" Her eyes flared.

Sheriff Swartwood held up his hand. "Fine," he said. "Do you know anyone who would want to harm Roland?"

A vision of Bradley leaving her house last night popped into her head. He was the only man she knew who had killed before. It would have been a short trip from her house to Magee Manor.... Annie shook away the suspicion. "There was a one-armed man that had been following Roland and saying odd things. I don't know who he is or why he was interested, but he did not seem... stable."

The sheriff asked her to describe this one-armed man, then promised to investigate the lead. Annie noticed a distinct lack of enthusiasm.

"What?" she asked.

"Well," the sheriff said, choosing his words carefully, "if Roland didn't shoot himself... well... it's common knowledge that Roland was very good with his revolvers."

"Fastest draw I've ever seen," offered the deputy. "I can't see someone getting the drop on Roland."

"Makes me wonder," the sheriff said, "if whoever shot him wasn't someone he trusted." The sheriff looked at her meaningfully. "Do you know where we can find Glendon?"

Annie couldn't believe what the sheriff was suggesting. But she hesitated before answering. Roland went looking to talk to someone about the snake tattoo. Thanks to Mrs. Phelps, Annie knew that Glendon had that tattoo on his thigh. Did Roland know and confront Glendon?

"I wish I knew," Annie said. "I haven't seen Glendon since yesterday either."

"Where were you last night?"

"Home," Annie lied. "Waiting for Roland and Glendon to return."

"The truth will come out," the sheriff said, and for a moment Annie thought he was accusing her of lying. "Word will spread quickly about Roland's injuries," the sheriff continued. "I'm asking everyone involved to honor General Magee's wishes to call this an accidental shooting on his property until we know the full details. We don't want unnecessary panic."

"You mean we wouldn't want poor publicity ahead of September's rowing regatta," Annie said under her breath.

"What did you say?"

"You kept the news about a body in Glenwood Cemetery a secret," Annie said, her voice coming out louder than she expected. "Roland might have been shot by the same person who stabbed the man in the cemetery!"

"There is no reason to suspect a connection between your cemetery drunk and Roland."

"What about the bodies at the Glen Mountain House?" Annie said. "Are you going to keep those a secret, too?"

The sheriff's eyes narrowed. "We had reports of gunshots last night near the Glen Mountain House—someone illegally hunting at night perhaps—but there are no dead bodies. What do you know that you're not telling me?"

The sheriff's voice had taken on a menacing tone that surprised Annie. "Nothing," she said quickly, looking away from his stare. She had said too much and had already lied about being at home all night. She wondered if the sheriff was covering up the murders because of the regatta? Or had this Butzemann that Bradley had told her about already cleaned up the loose ends? "I'm just angry and worried about Roland," Annie said to deflect the sheriff's question. "In fact, please excuse me, Sheriff. I must get back to watch over him."

Annie climbed the dirt path back to the caretaker's house and spent several hours by Roland's side. Emma Magee dropped in to offer her condolences but did not stay long, giving Annie plenty of time to get lost in her own thoughts.

She focused on Roland's chest rising and falling. "Where did you go after you left me?" she asked her unconscious uncle. "Who did this to you?" As Annie looked down at Roland, she wondered if he also had the snake tattoo on his body. Could Glendon and Roland belong to some secret organization? Annie couldn't imagine disturbing him to search his body. Maybe the doctor had noticed a tattoo when he operated. Annie would have to remember to ask him.

The sheriff was wasting his time suggesting Glendon shot Roland. Annie refused to believe it even with Glendon's deception about his tattoo. Glendon must have known that the Southerner was Lewis Crawford all along. Could Glendon have killed Crawford in the cemetery? Is that why he wouldn't admit to knowing him? Annie was horrified at the possibility.

If not Glendon, then who shot Roland?

Annie wished she could talk to Bradley. She surprised herself with the thought and wondered what Bradley was doing at that moment.

At midday, Mrs. Phelps arrived to watch Roland and to bring Annie a late lunch. Annie devoured the meal as politely as possible and was checking her dress for crumbs when Mrs. Phelps told her members of the Presbyterian church had volunteered to take shifts sitting with Roland for the rest of the day and through the night to give Annie a chance to rest.

Annie had been confused. "But Roland never goes to church."

"No, dear, but you do. They are doing it for you and your family."

Tears welled up in Annie's eyes at the show of support. "Thank you," she said.

"Oh, and I almost forgot." Mrs. Phelps pulled out a note and

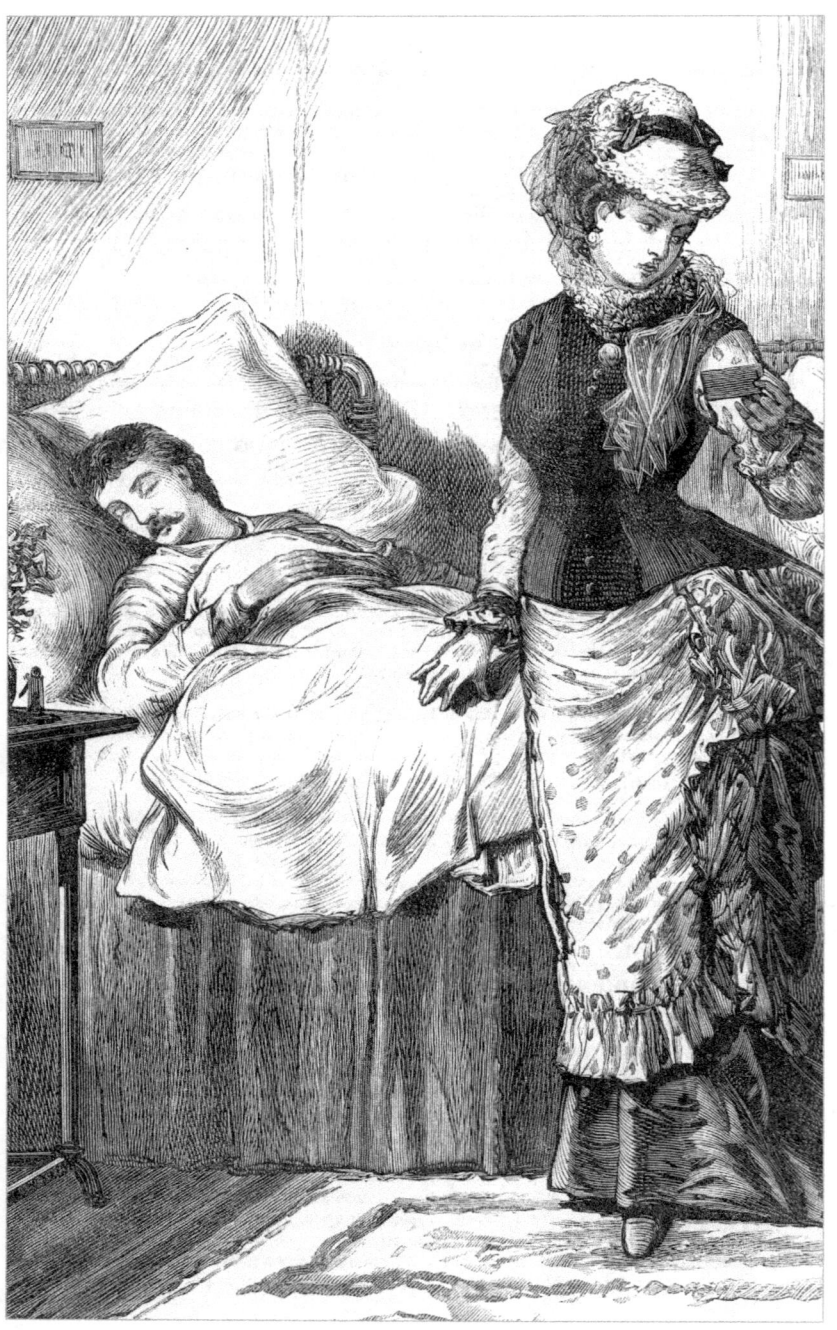

ROLAND AND MRS. PHELPS

read the front. "This came from the Lake View Hotel." She handed the card to Annie, who opened it.

It was from Bradley. He would be in Ithaca for at least a day and probably longer. "Thank you, Amelia," Annie said.

Mrs. Phelps looked concerned. "Is it bad news?"

"No," Annie said, which was a lie. It meant that with Glendon missing, Roland shot, and Bradley and Nana away, Annie was truly alone. She headed to the door of the caregiver's cottage but then turned back to Mrs. Phelps. "Do you have any idea where Glendon might be?" she asked.

Mrs. Phelps looked away. "No, I don't," she said.

Annie did not believe her.

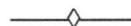

Annie knocked on the front door of the small house on Magee Street. Street. She had come seeking answers, but she also had few other safe places to turn. The caretaker had driven her there in a carriage after Annie decided to test George's offer of complete support. Walking alone would have put her at the mercy of whoever was trying to kill her.

When Esther Newby opened the door and saw Annie standing on her doorstep, her face lit up. "Oh, dear, so lovely to see you. Come in, come in."

Annie stepped across the threshold and felt safe for the first time since Roland left her. Esther guided her to the sofa and forced her to sit. "Would you prefer tea, coffee, or lemonade?" Esther asked.

"Please don't go to any trouble for me," Annie said.

"Oh, it's no trouble," Esther said. "I was thirsty myself."

Annie smiled. "Then tea would be lovely."

A few minutes later, Esther returned carrying a tray with two steaming cups of tea and a small jar of sugar. Her lavender house-dress complemented her dark skin tones.

"I love your dress," Annie said.

"Aren't you sweet," Esther said, looking down at her dress. "This is one of my favorites." When they were both settled on the sofa with tea in hand, Esther turned to Annie. "From the look on

your face," she said, "all is not as it should be. If you came to talk,
you've come to the right place."

Annie cleared her throat. "Can I ask if you know why Abraham
has been following me?"

Esther patted Annie on her knee. "I'm afraid that's my fault,
Annie," she said. Annie looked confused. "I had a feeling, my dear,
after your last visit that you needed help. I made Abraham promise
to keep an eye on you and help if he could. And I'm glad I did because he told me about that incident on the boat."

"I was shocked that he found me after I swam to shore."

"He used his spyglass to watch from above Glen Eldridge,"
Esther said. "He saw that man lead you onto the boat and strike
you down." Esther shook her head. "My brother was horrified. He
knew there was no way to get to you on that boat, so he watched
and he waited, and prayed too. When he saw you go overboard and
start drifting, he jumped on his Goldie and rushed around the lake,
guessing where you would wash up."

"But why?"

"Why?"

"Why would he do that for me? I accused him of murder when
he came to my house."

"Oh, never you mind that," she said. "He understood you were
looking for answers and that you suspected him because he'd been
in the cemetery. And not 'cause of the color of his skin." Esther
grew quiet for a moment. "Annie," she said, "did Abraham tell you
about his wife and daughter?"

"Yes, he did. How horrible it must have been to lose them both."

"Did he mention his daughter's name?"

Annie's eyes drifted up toward the ceiling trying to recall. "No,
I don't think he did."

"Abraham and his wife named their daughter Annabelle, but
they called her Annie for short. Her name was Annie. If she is still
alive, she would be just a few years older than you are now."

When Abraham came home an hour later, he was surprised to
find Annie in the house. She stood up to greet him but resisted the

urge to hug him. "Thank you," she said, "for looking out for me."

"Come join us, Abraham," Esther said. "We've been making small talk until you arrived. I've been waiting for Annie to tell us what's happening, and I promised we'd help however we could."

Abraham sat down on the chair facing the couch and waited for Annie as she took a deep breath. She started her story from the moment she saw Crawford's body on her mother's grave. She talked with little interruption and continued until she reached the part where someone shot Roland, and Annie made the decision to come to their house. Annie left nothing out.

When she'd finished, Esther patted Annie's knee again. "You poor dear," she said. "That's a heavy load to carry on your slim shoulders."

Abraham sat deep in thought, rubbing the graying stubble on his chin. Annie waited to hear what he had to say.

"How much do you trust Bradley?" Abraham asked.

Annie hesitated. How much did she trust Bradley? "He saved me from Vance and has had several opportunities to kill me since," Annie said. "I'm still alive, but he has his own agenda. I just don't know what it is. So, I don't know if I can fully trust him."

Abraham nodded, accepting her answer. "How can we help?" he asked.

Annie thought about it. The key was getting to Alistair Sinclair, but she didn't see how that was possible. If Bradley was chasing down his Jacub Jagusiak clue, that left finding the counterfeiters' location here in Watkins. "The counterfeiters have their printing presses set up somewhere nearby," she said. "If we can find the location, we can get the police to arrest everyone involved. Hopefully, that includes the person who murdered Crawford in the cemetery. The person who is trying to kill me."

"It would be a steep task to search every sawmill, grist mill, cider mill, or tannery in the county," Abraham said. "Or every large barn, for that matter. If this printing press is heavy, the counterfeiters would have sent it by train or boat. But all the mills are along the waterways or close to the train line, so that doesn't rule any out."

Annie furrowed her brow. "If we can't find their hideout, maybe we can find the last two counterfeiters and follow them until they lead us to their printing location. Bradley thinks they're brothers—one named Bill. I don't suppose that helps at all?"

Esther got a big grin on her face. "I think I can help you there, dear. You know that many of the housecleaners in town are negro. As are the barbers. White people talk as if us colored folk aren't even in the room, so we hear all the best gossip. Let me step over to my good friend Phyllis Green's house. She knows everyone in town, so she will know anyone with a brother named Bill."

After Esther left, Abraham cautioned Annie that she could be gone for hours once she got involved in a juicy gossip session. But Esther came back twenty minutes later with a triumphant look on her face.

"Bill Ballard is the man you are looking for," Esther said. "Phyllis is sure of it. The Ballard brothers live on Porter Street in a rented house."

Annie jumped up, ready to head out the door.

Abraham stopped her. "If the counterfeiters are the ones trying to kill you," he said. "It's probably not the best idea to show up at their front door and make it easy for them."

Annie opened her mouth to argue but sat back down.

"Let me go," Abraham said. "I'll knock on the door and ask if they have any paying work for a negro. That'll give me a reason to confirm they're home. Then we can find a way to follow them in the morning."

Annie hated being left behind, but there was no point in taking the risk of going herself without a disguise.

Abraham hitched up Goldie to the wagon and left, while Annie helped Esther prepare dinner. The afternoon was still warm, so they prepared a light dinner without warming up the stove. Annie's thought's drifted as they worked. She was excited to find the Ballard brothers. She was even more excited not to feel alone.

Abraham returned in time for dinner but the look on his face was anything but triumphant. "I'm sorry, Annie," he said. "I talked to their landlord. The Ballard brothers paid up and cleared out a few days ago. She didn't expect them to return."

"Did she have any idea where they might have gone?"

"No, but she did say one of the brothers worked as the night watchman for the Malthouse."

"The new one up the lake, or the old one on Fourth Street?"

"The one on Fourth Street," Abraham said. "I drove over and talked to the foreman. He cursed when I mentioned Ballard's name. Said the man hadn't turned up for the last few days. He was bent out of shape that he had to scramble to find a replacement."

Annie wondered if a night watchman's job could be connected to the counterfeiting operation in any way. "Abraham, is there any chance the Malthouse could be used as a secret printing location?"

"I don't see how. It's a working malthouse with more than a dozen men on the growing floors. Can't imagine there is any place to hide. Maybe before or after the growing season?"

Annie thanked Abraham while doing her best to hide her disappointment. Another dead end.

There was no offer to have Annie spend the night. It would have been socially awkward for both sides, so Abraham loaded Annie into his wagon and took her back to her house. He searched the interior with his shotgun at the ready, but its space was empty and undisturbed. Abraham promised to return in the morning and then bid her goodnight. Annie barricaded herself in again and sat at the kitchen table with her head in her hands.

She let herself wallow in self-pity for at least three minutes. Then she took three deep breaths and stood up. She was NOT going to lie down and die. Or wait for someone to kill her. The counterfeiters might be a dead end, but she had mysteries to solve closer to home.

Annie marched upstairs and entered Roland's bedroom. She had always respected her uncles' privacy, but they had kept secrets, and now lives were at stake. Annie looked about Roland's room. It was meticulously clean and organized. She started her search with his desk and then moved over to the dresser. Searching Smythe's hotel room had been good practice. Annie searched for an hour, but the only thing she found of interest was a photograph and a faded newspaper clipping from Georgia preserved in the pages of a Walt Whitman book of poetry. The photo showed two young men on the threshold of adulthood, standing close and grinning. Annie had never seen a picture of her father that young—before he'd grown his beard. Roland, standing next to him, had barely aged. The article detailed a bank robbery that left one man dead. A group of masked thieves got away with several bank bags of cash.

Annie moved to Glendon's room. It was organized but much more cluttered than Roland's had been. She stood in the middle, considering where to start, and noticed the old curtains over the windows. Curtains she'd sewn for Glendon years earlier when he first moved in. She and Glendon had picked out the fabric together, and she did the best she could using her mother's Singer sewing machine. She'd been proud of her work at the time, but as her skills improved, Annie begged Glendon to let her sew him replacements. He only smiled and said they brought him happy memories.

Annie methodically searched through Glendon's room. It took her much longer than it should have because she continued to find memories from her childhood. Little drawings she had made were preserved in cigar boxes. In one dresser drawer, she found a small bag of marbles she had played with relentlessly as a child and then lost interest in. She'd just assumed she'd lost them. Glendon had tucked a studio photo of her taken when she was ten into a book of children's stories that she remembered her mother reading to her at bedtime.

Annie put each little treasure aside and continued her search. She found books by many of her favorite authors—Charles Dickens, Mark Twain, Victor Hugo, Mary Shelley—as she worked her way through Glendon's bookshelves. Annie paused her search when she found a worn leather notebook tucked behind a small vase on a high shelf. As she pulled the notebook off the shelf, a photo of her mother dropped out. Her mother stared into the camera lens with a bright smile on her face. She was young, beautiful, and oblivious to her fate. Annie flipped through the journal pages filled with Glendon's handwriting. She sat on the floor and began reading.

From the Journal of Private H. Thompson

April 16, 1862 – My father, Samuel Thompson, should've celebrated his fiftieth birthday today, but he was the least lucky man I ever knew.

CHAPTER XLII

CONFESSIONS

Thursday, July 23, 1874

B RADLEY exited the John H. Newman store in Watkins with a
package wrapped in brown paper and secured with twine.
He adjusted his hat to block the midmorning light, then turned and
walked along the wooden sidewalks heading toward Annie's house.

Last night, he'd found a hackman with fast horses willing to
cross the dark hills from Ithaca to Watkins for an inflated price.
Bradley managed a few hours of sleep at the Lake View Hotel before he had to carry his belongings to the front desk and check out.
The front desk clerk handed him an envelope with his name on it,
containing his final salary payment from the Sinclairs. The amount
was generous. He walked down the hill and decided on a room at
the Jefferson House because he liked the food, and it was the hotel
closest to Annie's house.

Bradley, with his package tucked under his arm, climbed the
hill and the stairs to Annie's house. He knocked on the door, feeling guilty that he had been away for a full day, leaving Annie alone
while someone wanted her dead. No sounds came from within the
house. He knocked again and listened, but no footsteps approached.
Bradley began to worry. He had expected to find her safely barricaded in her house, but when he peered through a window, there
were no signs of life inside. Maybe expecting her to stay home was
too optimistic, given her personality. Annie had proven not to be a
"wait around to be saved" type of woman.

Bradley couldn't walk away without knowing. He'd simply
break in and make sure she wasn't inside and injured. Nonchalantly, he shifted the package from his left hand to his right and looked
to see if any neighbors were paying attention. He was choosing

which window to break when the sound of an approaching horse and wagon made him turn. A palomino mare kicked up a cloud of dust as it pulled the wagon toward him. Bradley's shoulders relaxed as he made eye contact with Annie. She sat beside a weathered colored man who drove the wagon. Bradley shifted the package back to his left arm, smiled, and waved.

The look on Annie's face when she saw Bradley—a smile that started at the corner of her lips and spread across her face until her eyes sparkled—caught his breath. A man could slay dragons and move mountains if he knew such a smile awaited his return.

The man drew in the reins and pulled up beside Bradley.

"Welcome back," Annie said. "We have a lot to talk about."

"Nice to see you again," the colored man said.

"I don't think we've—"

"Abraham rescued us after our swim in the lake," Annie explained. "Without him, I'd probably still be trying to drag you up the shore." A gentle laugh escaped her lips but faded quickly. Bradley could tell something was bothering her.

He turned to Abraham and extended his hand. "I'm in your debt, it seems."

"Jump on up, son," Abraham said, shaking Bradley's hand but waving off any obligation. "We have places to go."

Bradley climbed up as Abraham started Goldie in motion. Annie turned in her seat to look at Bradley, her face solemn. "Someone shot Roland two nights ago on George Magee's property."

"I'm so sorry." Bradley set his package down at his feet. A vision of Roland twirling his gun popped into Bradley's mind. "How bad...?"

"Alive but unconscious," Annie said. "The doctor told me it could go either way." Annie tilted her head toward Abraham. "We just visited him, but there's been no change since yesterday. Abraham and his sister, Esther, have volunteered to help where they can. They know about the dead man in the cemetery and the counterfeiting ring, so you can speak freely."

"Does the sheriff know who pulled the trigger?" Bradley asked. He saw no obvious connection between Roland's shooting and the counterfeiting ring, but there was a lot they didn't know.

WATKINS, COURTHOUSE AND SHERIFF'S RESIDENCE

Annie shook her head. "Not that we've heard, but he sent a deputy to request my presence at his office immediately. That's where we are heading. I'm hoping for news."

"The sheriff doesn't usually work that fast," Abraham said skeptically as the wagon merged into the flow of carriages and farm wagons on Franklin Street. At least the dust wasn't as bad today—the water wagon had come through with its massive wooden tank and sprayed the road, packing down the dirt. The town did its best to minimize the dust clouds infiltrating homes and businesses along Franklin Street.

"What did you learn in Ithaca?" Annie asked.

Bradley told Annie and Abraham about Jacub Jagusiak and his chemistry skills. "He created the perfect printing plates for one hundred and five-hundred-dollar bills. And when he got greedy, Vance killed him."

"That means the counterfeiting ring has paper, ink, and printing plates," Annie said. "What else do they need?"

"Printing presses and someone skilled enough to run them," said Bradley. "I'm pretty sure that's the role Sinclair wanted Pickens for. I hope that means we still have time."

Abraham pulled the wagon over in front of the courthouse and jail. The county buildings occupied the block between Ninth and Tenth Streets opposite the entrance to Watkins Glen. Bradley stepped down. He was reaching out to help Annie when he paused. "Annie, are you sure this is safe?"

Annie looked around nervously. "Did you see something?"

Bradley shook his head. "No, but you were unreachable in your house. Shooting Roland forced you out into the open. Maybe that was the shooter's intention. Is there any chance this invitation to the sheriff's office is a trap? Who told you to come here?"

"Deputy Cole," Annie said. She looked around, but there were few people nearby. "I have to know what the sheriff knows," she said, climbing down from the wagon.

Bradley took the newly purchased revolver out of his pocket and checked that it was loaded and ready. Abraham came around the wagon and leaned toward Bradley. "Protect her," Abraham said. "I'll keep watch out here until you return."

Bradley pocketed his revolver and followed Annie. The center of the block was dominated by the town courthouse, one of the tallest buildings in Watkins with its white tower topped with a bell-shaped roof. The sheriff's office, an attractive two-story brick residence with a whitewashed porch as wide as the building, sat to the right of the courthouse. "Nice benefit of the job," Bradley said.

"The sheriff lives in the front, but there are eight stone-lined jail cells in the back," Annie said. They crossed the porch and stepped inside, where Deputy Cole met them. Bradley watched for malicious intent, but Deputy Cole greeted them politely and then escorted them to the sheriff's office.

As Annie entered the room, she let out a large gasp. Bradley's hand reached for his revolver. "What is he doing here?" Annie said indignantly, pointing to a one-armed man. "Is he under arrest for shooting Roland? He should be locked up."

The sheriff ignored Annie and looked at Bradley. "Who are you?"

Leaving the revolver in his pocket, Bradley leaned forward. "Bradley Webster, a friend of the family," he said. The sheriff ignored Bradley's outstretched hand.

"Roland ain't who you think he is," the one-armed man sneered at Annie.

"Did you shoot Roland?" she asked.

The one-armed man tried to intimidate her with his stare. When that didn't work, he shook his head. "Nah, but I wasn't afraid of him."

"Read this, Miss Anderson." The sheriff handed Annie a large piece of paper. Bradley leaned close, and they read it together.

WANTED
One Thousand Dollars Reward!
WILLIAM ROLAND SMITH.

A reward of One Thousand Dollars will be paid for the arrest and delivery to Fulton County Sheriff, of WILLIAM ROLAND SMITH, who was under sentence for MURDER of Abel Murray, and who made his escape from jail on the evening of the 28th May, 1866.

$1,000.00 will be paid on delivery.

The flier included a description of the prisoner at the time of his escape. "William Roland Smith is about five feet eight inches in height, has a thin build, light brown hair, large gray or blue eyes, and a light brown beard." To Bradley, it was an accurate description of Roland minus the beard.

"This must be a mistake," Annie said, her voice quivering.

The one-armed man gloated. "I'm a bounty hunter. Was waitin' for the right moment to apprehend Roland into custody."

Bradley doubted Roland would have given the man that chance. "If you didn't shoot Roland, who did?"

"We can't rule out a self-inflicted injury," the sheriff said. "If Roland knew his true identity had been discovered—"

"There is no chance—" Annie started to raise her voice.

"Listen to me!" the sheriff said, raising his own voice. "Roland is a fugitive. If he survives, this man takes him back to Georgia to face justice."

"What? You can't—"

The one-armed man grinned.

The sheriff looked at Annie. "If Roland dies from his wound, Miss Anderson, you can bury him here as you see fit." The one-armed man's face dropped.

"I need him alive to collect the bounty," the one-armed man said. "He's the reason I lost my arm. He deserves to face justice." Bradley had no doubt it was the thousand-dollar reward and not justice the one-armed man cared about.

"If he dies," the sheriff replied, "God will exact justice. Your poster does not say 'dead or alive,' so you have a thousand reasons to pray for Roland's speedy recovery."

Bradley watched Annie set the flier down. In either scenario, she would lose Roland from her life. "Sheriff, please don't do this," Annie said. "You know Roland."

"My hands are tied," the sheriff said. He turned to the one-armed man. "You can leave now." Bradley and Annie stepped aside, making plenty of room for the man to exit the office. The sheriff waited until they were alone and then looked at Annie. "There is something else...."

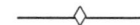

"I don't believe it." Annie stomped out of the sheriff's residence, eyes brimming with tears. "I refuse to believe it." Bradley handed her his handkerchief so she could blot the tears from her eyes. "I can't believe either Roland or Glendon could be murderers. There must be a reasonable explanation."

Bradley watched her mind working. He admired how she could endure a wave of emotions crashing over her and then, moments later, devise clearheaded plans to move forward.

Annie took a deep breath, then looked up at Bradley. "I need to hide Roland from the sheriff," she said. "Whatever he did in the past, he's not that person anymore. And then I need to find Glendon before the sheriff does."

Abraham waited where they had left him. Bradley surveyed their path for threats. As they walked toward Abraham's wagon, a carriage approached. Bradley was surprised to see Otto Fuchs at the reins. Bradley tilted his head toward Annie and said under his breath, "That's Fuchs, the Pinkerton."

Fuchs pulled up next to them. "Get in," he said. There was just enough room in the carriage for them to squeeze in.

Bradley leaned forward to climb in, but Annie stood her ground. "No." Fuchs looked at her in surprise. "I don't know you," Annie said, "and we already have a driver and wagon."

"I forget my manners," Fuchs said. He hopped out of his carriage, slung his leather satchel over his shoulder, and came around to bow slightly in front of Annie. He had on the same suit he wore when Bradley first met him. "Miss Anderson, allow me to introduce myself. I am Otto Fuchs, of the New York office of the Pinkerton Detective Agency."

"*Guten morgen, Herr Fuchs,*" Annie said. "How did you know my name?" Out of the corner of her eye, she saw Abraham pulling his wagon next to Fuchs's carriage.

"*Fraulein,*" Otto said, pulling out his badge. "I'm a detective. It is my job to know things. And good morning to you as well. *Sprechen sie Deutsch?*"

"*Ich spreche etwas Deutsch,*" Annie said.

"Well, speaking some German is better than none." Fuchs turned to Bradley. "You are outmatched with this one," Fuchs said, pointing to Annie. "If you were as educated as your friend, we could have this conversation in German. A pity. Now, I have important information to discuss with both of you, but I prefer not to linger in such an insecure area. Especially so close to the Glen crowds." A horse-drawn trolley, bringing another load of vacationers from the train depot and steamboat landing, followed the curve of the street railway into the Glen entrance across the street.

"Perhaps, Miss Anderson," Fuchs said, "you could suggest an alternative location for us to speak more privately."

Bradley watched Annie's face as she considered Fuchs's question. "Meet us at the corner of Decatur Street and Twelfth Street in ten minutes," Annie said. "Will that be private enough for you?"

"It will have to do," Fuchs said. He tipped his hat and climbed back into his carriage.

"Why there?" Bradley asked as he helped Annie into Abraham's wagon.

"It's on the edge of town but near the Glen Park Hotel, so not far away from other people. With Glendon missing and Roland shot, you two are the only men in town I trust are not trying to kill me." She had meant it partially in jest, but her words landed heavily as she felt the truth in what she had said.

Abraham used the Decatur Street bridge to cross Mill Creek. The smell of urine, feces, and decay assaulted them as they passed Richardson's Tannery on the corner of Eleventh Street. Bradley spit out the wagon's side to get the foul taste out of his mouth. Abraham crossed over Twelfth Street and pulled over. There were two or three houses nearby, but for the most part, this was where the town ended. Bradley could see Twelfth Street stretching east across the marsh to the far hill, and to the south, he could see the now-empty fairgrounds.

It took several minutes for Fuchs to arrive from the opposite direction. He pulled his carriage up beside them and did not waste time with pleasantries. He addressed Bradley. "I trust I may speak freely in front of Miss Anderson?"

Bradley nodded. Fuchs ignored Abraham.

"Very good, Mister Webster. Have you uncovered the identity of your note writer?"

Bradley shook his head. "Not yet, but I have discovered that the counterfeiters paid a Cornell college student to use electrotyping to create perfect currency plates of one hundred and five-hundred-dollar bills."

"Interesting," Fuchs said, smoothing his mustache with his fingers. "Will this student come forward as a witness?"

Bradley shook his head. "He's dead."

"I see," Fuchs said. "Difficult then to ask him questions. How about the counterfeiters' location? Were you able to follow your silver-haired man as planned?"

"Someone killed him before we could talk to him," Annie said.

Fuchs looked from Annie to Bradley. "Unfortunate coincidences seem to follow you both," he said. He shook his head. "What else have you learned?"

Annie spoke first. "We know the other counterfeiters are the Ballard brothers," Annie said. "But they cleared out of their boardinghouse a few days ago." Bradley was surprised to hear the information but impressed that Annie had made progress while he was away.

Otto rubbed his mustache again. "We learn that the counterfeiters had printing plates for months. We learn all the witnesses have died or left town. Very disappointing. However," Fuchs continued, "I have found some information. The Pinkerton office in New York has tracked down the registration for the *Bonnie Lynn* steamship. The ship was registered to a company owned by a man Miss Anderson knows well. A man named Glendon Robinson."

Annie gasped.

"Yes, Miss Anderson," Fuchs said. "I know he is a boarder at your residence. It is so, yes?"

"Yes, but——"

Fuchs cut her off. "Let me ask you a question, Miss Anderson. Does Glendon Robinson make regular trips to New York City?"

Annie opened her mouth and closed it again. Bradley saw the look of distress on her face. "That doesn't prove anything," she said. "Could your sources be wrong? I can't believe Glendon owns the boat that Vance was piloting when he tried to kill me."

"No source is infallible, Miss Anderson. But I think the chance of a mistake is small."

"Glendon is a good person," Annie said. "He is not a criminal."

"How long have you known Mister Robinson?" Otto asked.

"Long enough to know," Annie said. "And I found his journal from the war. He has always been a man of high character."

"Tell me about this journal," Fuchs said.

Bradley looked at Annie. This was something else she hadn't shared with him.

"He kept a journal during the war. His name was Harper Thompson then. He belonged to a team of Confederate sharpshooters that called themselves the Lucky Six. So lucky that they found hidden gold in North Carolina while on a furlough—although they had to leave it behind. They agreed to meet after the war to split it evenly."

"And did they?" Fuchs asked.

"Did they what?"

"Did they survive the war and split the gold?"

"No," Annie said. "Three of them died during the war. One was shot for desertion. A second died in a train accident. And the third died of smallpox in a prisoner of war camp. The other three returned home after the war, but the gold had disappeared."

"I see," Fuchs said. "Let me ask you something, Miss Anderson. Do you believe everything you read?"

"I don't understand," Annie said.

"Is it possible that you or someone else was meant to find the journal? A journal that says Harper Thompson is a good man who did NOT find the gold. But... what if he authored a fictional story? What if Harper Thompson killed the other three members of this Lucky Six so he would get a bigger share of the gold?"

Annie stared at Fuchs.

"I'm merely pointing out," Fuchs said, "that the journal may not be reliable information. What happened to the other two members of the Lucky Six?"

Annie sighed. "Someone stabbed Lewis Crawford in the cem-

HORSE DRAWN TROLLEY

etery two weeks ago. In the journal, he's called Buck. I think the other one—his name was Frank—died two nights ago near the Glen Mountain House."

"Miss Anderson," Fuchs said carefully, "if that is true, then the only surviving member of the Lucky Six is Glendon Robinson." Otto turned to Bradley. "Perhaps it is not Sinclair who is the Butzemann. We have a man, Robinson, who uses a false name. He owns a steamship used by one of the counterfeiters. He does regular business in New York. He may have killed five members of his sharpshooter unit for their share of the gold." Otto rubbed his chin. "The gold is an interesting angle. Counterfeiters sell their fake money to pushers for one-tenth of the face value. Perhaps Robinson is the pusher using his remaining gold to buy Sinclair's counterfeit money. Is it possible that Robinson was the man you saw meeting Sinclair in LaFayette Square?"

"No," Annie said, cutting in before Bradley could reply. "Glendon would never hire Vance to harm me!"

"You may be right, Miss Anderson," Fuchs said. "Perhaps he only wanted you out of his way, and Vance took things too far. Did Robinson try to scare you or encourage you to leave town?" Annie stared off into the distance, not answering.

Bradley felt the noon heat on his shoulders. The day was relentlessly bright, but dark clouds were gathering on the horizon.

Otto removed his hat, wiped the sweat from his brow, and placed it back on his head. "Miss Anderson," he said, "where is Glendon Robinson now?"

Before Annie could answer, a bullet exploded into the side of the wagon. Bradley was in motion before the echo of the gunshot reached them. He dragged Annie backward and down onto the wagon bed, where he shielded her with his body. Abraham snapped the reins, and Goldie leaped away as a second shot rang out. Otto Fuchs was cursing and racing in the opposite direction with a pistol drawn.

———◊———

Goldie sped down Decatur Street and took the turn onto Thirteenth Street, so quickly the outside wagon wheels left the ground.

It took Abraham a full block to rein her in. "Are either of you hit?" he asked.

"No," Bradley said.

"You can get off me now," Annie said. He rolled off Annie and helped her to sit up. She climbed into the front seat beside Abraham. "Take me home," she said. "I need to get inside. It was a mistake to come out in public without a disguise."

"Did Otto get away?" Bradley asked.

"I think so," Abraham said, looking over his shoulder. "The shot came from the direction of the marsh, but no way to know where exactly. And no way to tell who the target was."

Their wagon headed north on Franklin Street, maneuvering around carriages, pedestrians, and the horse-drawn trolley following the rail lines in the center of the street. Bradley scanned the crowd for danger, but no one looked at them twice. As they turned left on Fourth Street, Annie turned back to Bradley. "There's something else from the journal... if what is written is true... then Glendon is my real father. That's why I know he would never hurt me."

Bradley had known too many children in the city harmed in one way or another by their father but did not disagree with her. After the one-armed man left the sheriff's office, the sheriff told Annie a witness had come forward claiming to have seen Glendon with Roland on Magee's property. The sheriff was searching for Glendon to question him on the shooting and did little to hide his belief that Glendon was the likely shooter.

Abraham pulled the wagon in front of Annie's home. The front door was ajar. Bradley jumped down and helped Annie out of the carriage. As they stepped inside, muted thumping sounds came from the direction of the basement kitchen. Without hesitating, Annie pulled her derringer out of her pocket and marched toward the basement with a look of fierce determination. Bradley rushed to catch up as Annie descended the stairs. Seconds later, a scream came from within the kitchen.

"Samantha Ann Anderson!" Nana said, clutching her hands across her chest.

"Nana!?" Annie rushed forward and hugged her grandmother as Bradley reached the bottom of the stairs.

"I was killing a few Indian-meal moths," Nana said, "when you scared me half to death!" Nana wore her cooking apron, and Bradley could see the beads of sweat on her brow from working near the hot stove. Having the kitchen in the basement helped control the temperature, but it still got uncomfortable with the stove lit.

"I'm sorry," Annie said. She released her grandmother and stepped back. "I did not expect you home until tomorrow."

"Oh, Annie," Nana said, "I came home as soon as I got the telegram from Mrs. Phelps about Roland. I—" Nana paused when she looked over Annie's shoulder to see Bradley standing behind her. "Who do we have here?"

"Bradley Webster." Bradley said, extending his hand to Annie's grandmother. "It is a pleasure to meet you, ma'am."

Nana accepted his hand but held it with both of hers. She seemed to be admiring Bradley's well-tailored suit before turning to Annie. "Tell me you have a new suitor!" Hope blossomed in Nana's voice.

Annie blushed. "Nana, no! He's a friend. We have been helping each other. And Abraham is outside as well. Probably looking after his horse."

Nana turned back to Bradley. "Mister Webster, what are your intentions with my granddaughter?" It was Bradley's turn to blush.

"Nana!" Annie pleaded. "Please let him go."

"Fine," Nana said. She released Bradley's hand. "But since my granddaughter says you are helpful, please fetch an armful of firewood from the side of the house. I need more wood for the cookstove."

Annie mouthed "sorry" to Bradley, but he just shrugged and smiled. As he turned away, he saw Nana pull Annie closer and whisper, "Tell me what is going on—"

Bradley returned with a load of firewood in his arms. Annie's grandmother thanked him and stuffed a few logs into the cookstove's firebox. She opened the oven and put her hand in to gauge the temperature. "Not hot enough yet," she muttered, then stood up and adjusted several of the cookstove's dampers. Bradley saw two mincemeat pies on the sideboard, waiting to go in.

"Nana," Annie said, "the sheriff showed me a wanted poster.

He said Roland is a wanted murderer in Georgia. It can't be true, can it?"

"Ridiculous," Nana said, brushing flour off her apron. "Roland confessed to me once that he had 'made mistakes' in his past," Nana said. "But murder? He's not capable of murder." She took a sip from a fine-bone china teacup.

Annie stood quietly for a moment, then looked at her grand-mother. "Is Glendon my real father?"

Nana choked on her tea and bent over in a violent coughing fit. Her face had gone white.

"I found Glendon's journal," Annie said. "It says he and my mother fell in love when they were sixteen, and she got pregnant. But you and grandfather brought her north to marry my father. Is any of that true?"

Nana looked wide-eyed and glanced quickly at Bradley as if to say this wasn't a conversation for a stranger's ears, but when she saw the resolve on Annie's face, she sighed. Nana bent down and rubbed her knees. "There is a storm coming. I can feel it in my—"

"Nana!"

"Okay, okay." Nana took a large gulp from her teacup. Bradley noticed the open bottle of sherry on the table and realized why he hadn't been offered any tea. Nana checked the stove's temperature again and slid the two meat pies inside. "Let's talk upstairs," she said, grabbing the bottle of sherry and her teacup.

When they reached the dining room, Bradley whispered in An-nie's ear. "Should I leave?"

She touched his arm and looked into his eyes. "Please stay."

Nana slumped into a chair. Noticing that her tea was gone, she poured more sherry into her cup. She looked at Annie and then looked away as she started talking. "I did not want you to find out this way," she said, "but, yes, my dear, Glendon is your real father."

"All these years—"

Nana held up her hand. "Glendon was Harper Thompson back then," she said. "He and your mother were young when they fell in love. When Sarah told us she was pregnant, your grandfather was so angry... Oh, Annie. It would have been a scandal! Harper was a farmhand from poor circumstances. What life would they have had down there in North Carolina? Your grandfather had a friend in Rochester whose nephew needed a wife."

"What are you saying?"

"I'm saying that your father, Edward, married your mother even though he knew she carried another man's child."

"My father who wasn't my real father...."

"Annie," Nana said, "I know this must be very hard for you, but regardless of how you came into creation, never forget that Edward Anderson loved you as his own. He was the one who raised you and gave you a wonderful childhood. He will always be your father."

Annie sat silently for a moment. Then she wiped the moisture from her eyes. "What happened next?"

"After the war ended, Glendon Robinson showed up in Watkins. I didn't recognize him as Harper Thompson, but your mother did. Harper—Glendon—had come into some money and wanted your mother and you to run away with him. He wanted the family he felt had been stolen from him."

"But my mother loved my father and said no?"

"Annie, your mother learned to love your father—over time—but what she had with Glendon was... it was special. Just the way they looked at each other and made each other laugh. I didn't understand back then. Your mother wanted to run away with Glendon. Sarah knew it would break Edward's heart, but she hoped it would allow him to return to his own true love. The three of you reached the train station before Sarah changed her mind."

"Why? Why did she?"

"She stayed because of you."

"Me?"

"You were ten, then. Your mother told you she was taking you on an adventure. You were excited, but when the train arrived, you started to cry—worried your father would miss the train. Sarah realized then that she could never take you away from the man you knew as your father. Sarah loved Glendon, but she loved you more."

Bradley saw Annie's eyes well up. She pulled out his handkerchief, which she had kept in a pocket in her dress, to catch the teardrops.

"Did Glendon—" Annie's voice caught. "Did he blame me?"

"No, dear. Glendon was upset but stayed in town to be as close as possible to you both."

"So after my parents died... he moved in to be closer to me?"

"Yes," Nana said, "but there was another reason." Nana found her teacup empty again. "Do you remember the day we buried your parents? You walked in as Glendon and I talked in the parlor?" Annie nodded. "Your father's family disowned him years earlier, and all the money he had saved had gone into building this house. Your parents were penniless when they died. Glendon saved us from a life of destitution when he bought the house and—for appearances—let me pretend to be the owner while he moved in as a boarder. Not even Roland knew about the arrangement. All the money for this house, our food, your sewing supplies, and your college tuition... it all came from Glendon."

"Why didn't you tell me?" Annie said. "You should have told me when I got older."

Nana paused before answering. She sighed. "I never told you because your mother made Glendon and me promise not to."

"What! Why?"

"Because your mother never wanted you to question your love for Edward."

Annie stood, walked over to her grandmother, and wrapped her arms around her. Nana leaned into her granddaughter.

"If Glendon is my real father," Annie said, "then everything else in the journal must be true."

"I don't know, dear," Nana said. "I didn't know that it existed until you told me. I only know that Glendon loves you and would never do anything to harm you."

Bradley cleared his throat. "Annie," he said, "you told Fuchs that none of the Lucky Six ended up with the gold. If that's true, how did Glendon have the money to buy this house and pay all the bills?"

"I don't know." Annie shrugged. "But I can't believe he had anything to do with the counterfeiters or the dead Southerner in the cemetery."

Abraham appeared in the living room doorway. He held the package Bradley had left in the wagon. "I apologize for eavesdropping," he said, "but Miss Anderson, there is something you need to know."

"What is it, Abraham?" Annie said.

Abraham looked uncertain. He found a spot on the cluttered sideboard to set down the package he'd been holding. "I haven't been completely honest...."

"Abraham?"

"You know that I saw you in the cemetery that morning."

"Yes."

"I was watching from the bushes—I had stepped in to pick some blackberries—then I saw you run off down the hill. Thing is...."

"You saw something, didn't you?" Annie said. "Abraham, please tell me."

"After you left, a man appeared with a cart and one of those big steamer trunks. He used a blanket to roll up the body, then stuffed it into the trunk. He pushed that cart back down the hill toward the Glen Mountain House."

"Did you recognize the man?"

"Not at the time, but I've seen him since."

"Who was it, Abraham?"

Abraham shuffled his feet. He looked away and then back at Annie. "It was Glendon Robinson. I saw Glendon Robinson put that body in the trunk and carry it away."

THE LIVERY

CHAPTER XLIII

GOLDEN DECEPTION

October 26, 1864 – Hugh "Harper" Thompson stood outside the entrance of the Western Union telegraph office in Statesville, North Carolina. With the help of his Copperhead benefactor, he was days ahead of Frank and Buck following their escape from Hellmira and the events in the negro's cabin. Did he have enough time?

Harper could not stand the thought of Buck funding hatred with his portion of the gold. And Frank had made it clear—days ago and around every fire that the Lucky Six discussed the gold— that he had no interest in his portion. Was it worth the risk? Harper kicked a loose pebble off the wooden walkway, where it skipped and rolled into the dirt street. He imagined standing with Buck and Frank in an empty cave versus one filled with gold. Realizing his own life would be more at risk from Buck's greed if they found the gold together, it became an easy decision. Harper entered the telegraph office and wrote two telegrams, which he handed to the Western Union operator. The first telegram was to the boarding-house manager at the end of the train line near Morganton. The telegram requested that he be met when he arrived on the afternoon train. He paid the telegraph operator a significant amount for special services. "Send this in two days," he told the man.

The second telegram was to be sent immediately to a livery in Morganton requesting they ready a fast horse for his arrival later that evening. Harper would have two days. He hoped that would be enough time.

———◇———

At two in the morning, there were no lights on in Widow Pierson's farmhouse in Rutherfordton, but Harper smelled wood burning and noticed a small ribbon of smoke curling out of the chimney. Someone was inside. Not having the luxury of time, he knocked on

*the farmhouse door and continued knocking until it swung open.
His effort was rewarded with a shotgun pointed at his head.*

*Hours earlier, Harper had arrived at the last stop on the
western extension of the North Carolina Railroad six miles from
Morganton. He'd worn a dark suit and kept his head down so no
one would recognize him when he returned in two days. A jolting
ride on a crowded stagecoach took him into Morganton and the
town livery, where he haggled over the price of an even-tempered
chestnut mare that he'd taken a liking to. Horse and saddle cost
him several gold coins and two of the new suits his benefactor had
given him. As the sun hung low in the sky, he'd set out for Rutherfordton. A good horse could travel ten miles an hour on a flat, hard
road. Thirty-five miles to reach the Pierson's farm along unfamiliar
mountain roads with scant moonlight had taken him half the night.*

"Harper?"

*He'd changed since she'd last seen him, so he was surprised
Fish's mother recognized him with his unruly beard, gaunt appearance, and dusty suit. Prison life had taken its toll on him.*

*Abigail Pierson ushered him inside and locked the door be-
hind him. She pushed him along the dimly lit interior until they
reached the fireplace, which she stoked with fresh wood. A warm
glow lit her face as the heat began to loosen Harper's stiff body.
"What are you doing here, Harper?" He had written to her once
after Fish's death to tell her how bravely her son had met his fate.
He blamed himself for being unable to prevent what had happened.
She had written back to tell him she was glad her son had such
good friends—and hadn't faced death alone—and she encouraged
Harper not to fault himself. Still, the guilt lingered, and he never
wrote again. Now, he stood in front of her, needing her help.*

"It is a long story, Mrs. Pierson," he said.

"Please call me Abigail."

*"It's a long story, Abigail, and I know it's extremely late. But
before I explain, let me ask you one question." She nodded, but he
could tell her patience was limited. "How are you and your daughter doing?" Having lost her husband and all three of her sons, it
would be difficult to keep the farm going on her own.*

*Abigail Pierson visibly sagged at the question. Her eyes welled
with tears, and she looked around the room, unwilling to meet his*

gaze. He stayed silent. She gathered herself and stared back at him. "It's been a trying winter," she said with such force of spirit and defiance of fate that his heart went out to her.

Harper nodded. "I'm here to bring you a final gift from your son, but it will take two days of demanding work. Two days that will change both our lives." He explained his plan, and although she was shocked, she readily agreed. He went outside to put his horse up for the night in the barn. When he returned, Abigail had made him a bed near the fire and brought him some salted pork and a few crackers. They agreed to leave the house at sunrise. Tomorrow was going to be a long, exhausting day.

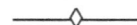

Harper, Abigail, and Libbie started their journey at sunrise in a wagon loaded with tools, hay, rope, and an oversized canvas. Harper's horse, Bertha, and the Pierson family horse, Chief, led the way. When she'd woken up, Libbie had been thrilled to see her brother Eddie's friend and refused to be left behind at the neighbor's house. Libbie never complained as they traveled seventeen miles along bumpy roads to reach the Chimney Rock area of Hickory Nut Gap.

As they neared their destination, Harper slowed the wagon. He started to doubt his memory when the stacked rocks Taylor had left behind appeared in the long grass, shockingly undisturbed. He stopped the wagon, handed Abigail the reins, and jumped out. Harper walked to the creek and stared across. Seven months had passed since he'd stood in this spot. Harper felt confident he could retrace his steps and find the cave. Thankfully, the water in the stream was low.

"Those clothes fit you well," Abigail said as he returned to the wagon. He appreciated her late husband's warm clothes and thanked her again. She tucked a strand of blonde hair behind her ear and smiled. For any age, Abigail Pierson was a beautiful woman.

"We have arrived," he said.

They pulled the wagon off the road. Abigail handed Libbie the rifle and asked her to watch the horses and wagon. Harper was reluctant to leave Libbie alone.

"I'm an excellent shot," Libbie said when she saw the worry on Harper's face.

"More importantly," Abigail added, "she won't hesitate to pull the trigger if necessary."

Abigail and Harper carried the shovels and lanterns across the creek and up the far side. Without much effort, Harper found the entrance to the cave and cleared away the vegetation. He ducked his head and entered with his lantern in front of him. Abigail followed close behind. The cave, smelling musty and earthy, looked undisturbed. It did not take long for Harper to dig out the first satchel. He pulled out a gold nugget, admired its cool weight, and offered it to Abigail. She waved him off. "I will appreciate this after the job is done."

Harper carried the first satchel out of the cave and dropped it to the ground. He was still weak from months in prison, and the satchels were too heavy for Abigail to carry herself. Abigail ran back to the wagon and returned with a hatchet. She solved their problem by cutting down a tree sapling of reasonable length, removing its branches, and sliding it through the top of the satchel. With one end on Harper's shoulder and the other on Abigail's, they managed to carry the first satchel out of the cave, down the hill, and across the creek. They placed each satchel on the hay. It was Libbie's job to hide it while Harper and Abigail returned for the next satchel. It took hours, and their breaks got longer as the bags piled up under the hay, but before the sun dropped out of the sky, Abigail and Harper had recovered all the gold from the cave.

Harper returned to the cave and spent a long time using tree branches to obscure their most recent footprints and any evidence of their visit. When next he returned, he'd need to convince Buck and Frank that no one had been in the cave in weeks or months. His life would depend on it.

With their two oil-burning lamps attached to the front of the wagon to light the way, they headed home to Rutherfordton. It did not take long for Libbie to wrap herself in a blanket and fell asleep in the hay, leaving Harper and Abigail in comfortable silence.

After a while, Abigail reached out and squeezed his hand. He looked over, surprised. "Thank you," she said. "I have been putting on a brave face, but... I didn't know how Libbie and I would *get through this winter."*

Harper smiled. *"Now half of all that gold is yours."*

"What was the original plan?" she asked.

"Well, each member of the Lucky Six was going to get a one-sixth share."

"And if someone didn't survive the war?"

"Taylor suggested splitting it among whoever was left," he said. He had been thinking about Taylor's comment with the benefit of time and distance. *"Honestly, I don't think Taylor imagined our luck running out and losing one of us... much less three."*

"Why aren't you sharing with Buck and Frank?"

Harper explained Buck's extreme views and Frank's lack of interest. She sat quietly for a while before speaking.

"One satchel is enough for Libbie and I to carry," she said. *"Keep the others. One will be more than enough to give us a comfortable life and to get Libbie into the best schools. Whatever I have left, I'll use to help others."*

"Are you sure?"

"Yes. One satchel is already life changing."

Harper considered what still had to happen for their plan to succeed. *"Are you ready for what's next?"* he asked. The next step was a crucial part of the plan but not without sacrifice.

"Do you mean am I ready to pack up everything of value that I own and leave the farm in the next twenty-four hours? I have been thinking about that. The farm was my husband's dream, not mine. I kept it after he died so one of my sons could take over one day. Libbie will miss her animal friends, but we will benefit from a fresh start. Are you sure it's necessary?"

"I don't think Buck will let this go. If there is any hint that you were involved, he will come looking for you. Looking for the gold. What Fish—I mean Eddie—wanted more than anything was to know you and his sister were safe and prospering. This is the safest way."

Harper remembered how the Pierson farm looked when he rode in last night. It would not take much to convince Buck and Frank that Mrs. Pierson had abandoned it weeks or months ago.

"I understand," Abigail said. *"I guess I can afford to buy anything I forget to take."* She laughed aloud. Something she had not

done enough of recently. She turned to Harper. "What about you?"

"I'll take my horse back to Morganton first thing in the morning and put him up in the livery for a day until I return and pretend to buy him again. I'll pay someone to drop me off at the train depot, where I'll find a spot out of sight until the late train arrives. If I time it perfectly, I can climb up on one side of the train pretending I had been on board all along, then step down on the other side of the train to meet the boardinghouse manager. He will be receiving a telegram tomorrow about my arrival. Then I wait for Buck and Frank to show up."

Four days later, Harper sat on his horse in the middle of the Pierson's empty farm. He watched as Frank and Buck disappeared on their way back to Morganton. He let out a slow breath. The Lucky Six's luck might have run out, but Harper had a little left working for him that day. He was unsure he had convinced Frank, but then Frank was Frank. He probably did not care. Harper had also been lucky that it had rained between when he and Abigail removed the gold and when he showed up at the cave with Buck and Frank. It helped hide their tracks.

Harper waited a few minutes longer to ensure Frank and Buck were gone, then he guided his horse to the neighbor's property. The neighbor, Mrs. Matheson, had done an impressive job convincing Buck and Frank that Abigail had lost the farm to the bank and disappeared with her daughter. In truth, they were waiting for Harper in Mrs. Matheson's guest room. The neighbor had even made up a family in Tennessee for Abigail and Libbie.

The next morning, Harper hitched the wagon to the horses while Abigail and Libbie said goodbye to the neighbors. As a thank-you, Abigail offered the Mathesons whatever they were willing to carry away from her farm—except the land and buildings, which the bank would reclaim.

Harper had planned to take the gold to Charleston and find a ship they could sail or steam north. He liked the thought of the gold completing the journey the Englishmen had started all those years earlier. But the Civil War raged in that part of the South, so Abigail convinced him to head to Charlotte, only seventy miles away. They could sell some of the gold there, and she was convinced she could get special papers—with extra incentive placed in the appropriate official's hands—allowing her to travel with her daughter and her "brother" to visit family members in New York.

"Will you stay in New York?" Harper asked her as their wagon headed to Charlotte.

"I have always wanted to visit Paris," Abigail said. "I think Libbie will love it there. And you?"

"I have some business in upstate New York," he said. A thought crossed his mind. "I suppose I need to change my name in case Buck comes looking for me one of these days. Any suggestions?"

"I've always liked the name Glendon," Abigail said. "You look like you could be a Glendon."

"I have an idea," Libbie said.

Harper smiled at her. "I would love to hear it."

"When I think of my brothers, I pretend they're still alive and on that island," Libbie said.

Harper looked at Abigail, who shrugged. "What island?"

"The one from Eddie's favorite book."

"The Swiss Family Robinson?"

"That's the one! I always liked that name."

Harper laughed. "That's an excellent suggestion, Libbie. Glendon Robinson, it is."

CHAPTER XLIV

FALLEN MAN

Thursday, July 23, 1874

A BLACK carriage pulled by two sturdy horses descended Steuben Street and paused briefly opposite the flat-iron building. Annie and Bradley stepped out from the shadows of the trees at the side of the road and jumped into the enclosed carriage. They'd snuck out the back door of Annie's house and crossed through the neighbors' yards to avoid unwanted detection. As Bradley closed the door behind them, Annie heard Abraham, sitting in the driver's seat, snap the reins and urge the horses into motion. The carriage smelled of leather, polished brass, and stale cigar smoke. The shades were drawn for privacy. Annie pulled at the edges of her shade to track their progress across Franklin Street as they headed west on Fourth Street toward the head of Seneca Lake.

After Abraham's confession, Annie had collapsed into a chair and held her head in her hands. Even if Abraham lied about what he saw in the cemetery, the sheriff and Otto Fuchs both had information incriminating Glendon. If she believed everything that she learned the last day, then Glendon was her real father, a counterfeiter, a murderer, a crime boss in New York City, and the man who shot Roland, who himself was an escaped murderer. It was too much to accept. It was too much to believe.

Annie had realized it WAS too much. She stood up and looked at the concerned faces around her. "I have to find Glendon," she said. She knew Glendon and Roland—maybe better than anyone else in the world. They were not cold-blooded killers. Someone was trying to kill her, and the two men who would protect her with their lives were now injured or in hiding—both accused of murder. It was too much of a coincidence.

"I don't believe he is a murderer," she said, "but only he can explain what is going on." Annie looked at Bradley and Abraham. She had only known each man for a few days, but she was still alive thanks to them. "I know it's unfair of me to ask," she said, thinking of the bullet hole in Abraham's wagon, "but will you help me look for him?"

"I'll help where I can," Abraham said. "My sister would insist on it, anyway."

Bradley ran a hand through his brown hair and then shrugged. "If Fuchs thinks Glendon is connected to Vance and the counterfeiters, I'd like to hear Glendon's side of the story. Count me in."

"We'll need to find him before the sheriff does," Abraham said.

"Annie," Nana said. "Glendon could be anywhere."

True. Glendon could be back in New York City, or heading west to the territories, or on his way to California. There were plenty of ways to disappear and not be found in North America. *No*, Annie thought, *that is what a guilty man would do.*

"I think he's still nearby," she said. "Could Mrs. Phelps be hiding him?"

"I doubt it," Nana said. "Too many people know about their relationship."

"What relationship?" Annie asked, surprised. "Why am I the last person to find out they're a couple?"

"Maybe it's because you like to say that marriage is domestic slavery for women," Nana said.

"Well, I just meant that for me," Annie said. She blushed when Bradley raised an eyebrow. She quickly changed the subject. "Nana, besides his office downtown, does Glendon have any other business properties?"

"No, the only other property he owns is the one overlooking the lake."

"I thought of that," Annie said, "but the sheriff would know to look there."

"Maybe not," Nana said. "Glendon bought the property in your mother's name long ago. When she died, it transferred into your name. There are no legal documents connecting him to that property."

"Then that's where we'll look first."

Abraham asked Annie to give him thirty minutes to return Goldie to her stable and exchange his wagon for a different carriage. "Whoever shot at us might be watching for Goldie and the wagon," Abraham said. A wealthy vacationer, called to Syracuse on business, had asked Abraham to watch over his horses and carriage for a few days.

Annie looked over to watch Bradley peering out the shade on his side of the carriage. He looked stylish with his jaunty bowler hat and perfectly tailored suit, but he remained a mystery. "Dark clouds coming this way," Bradley said. "We may get wet on this journey."

The farmers were desperate for a summer thunderstorm, but Annie hoped the rain would hold off long enough for them to find Glendon. Their carriage bounced over the set of railroad tracks marking the end of the residential area of Watkins. Next, they passed several factories and mills built along the head of the lake. First came Davis's original Malthouse, then the elevated rail lines that led to the Fall Brook Coal Company's trestle works. Elevating the railroad cars made loading the canal boats much easier. Next came the steam sawmill, the steam flour and grist mill, and then more coal company buildings. Annie peeked out as their carriage crossed the bridge over the Chemung Canal and continued east.

"Do I have this correct?" Bradley asked. "Harper Thompson was part of a six-man Confederate sharpshooter team that discovered hidden gold in North Carolina."

"Yes, they called themselves the Lucky Six," Annie said. She'd shared the details from Glendon's journal with Bradley while they'd waited for Abraham.

Bradley furrowed his brow. "Whoever shot at our wagon today could not have been a sharpshooter. The shooter was not that far away, and a trained marksman wouldn't miss from those distances. If it was a sharpshooter, they missed on purpose."

Abraham maneuvered the carriage through a hard left turn when Fourth Street ended at a cliff wall. The horses strained with the rising elevation as the carriage climbed up the eastern side of Seneca Lake heading north.

"What are you saying?"

"Maybe Fuchs was right. If Glendon is involved but not trying to kill you, he might have shot at us to scare you away for some reason."

Annie was silent. Could Glendon be involved? There was something else she remembered from the journal that was bothering her.

Abraham struggled to avoid the dirt road's potholes, ruts, and washouts. When they reached a fork in the road partway up the hill, he reined in the horses and brought the carriage to a halt. Bradley helped Annie down from the carriage and into the driver's seat next to Abraham. The right fork continued upward to Burdett and over the hills to Ithaca. The left fork led along the cliffs to Hector Falls and Glen Eldridge, two miles away. Glendon's property lay somewhere along the left fork. Annie had only been there once and did not remember the exact location.

It took time, but with three sets of eyes searching, they found a carefully concealed path leading off the road on their left side less than a mile from the intersection. Abraham got the horses and carriage off the road and out of sight while Bradley concealed the entrance again.

"No one will notice from a distance," Bradley said when he returned, "but if anyone is looking closely, they'll be able to tell that a carriage and two horses passed through the tall grass." To the southwest, the sky had grown darker, and the distant rumble of thunder warned of the approaching storm.

"I'll stay and keep an eye out," Abraham said. "I'm responsible for this rig and the horses."

Annie looked around. The shadows had grown longer. Tall grass and underbrush surrounded them, but she could see trees to the north. The land sloped gently back toward the lake, but only twenty yards away, the ground gave way to a cliff, dropping fifty to a hundred feet to the lake.

"Which way, Annie?" Bradley asked, offering his arm. Annie pointed toward the trees but let him go first to trailblaze a route. They picked their way forward until Bradley found the hint of a path—not much more than a deer trail—leading north. The woods were thick, and in no time, Abraham and the horses disappeared

Overlooking Seneca Lake

from sight.

"Bradley," Annie said as she moved forward, swatting away the flying insect that buzzed near her face. "What do you think of Abraham?"

She could see his shoulders shrug, perhaps surprised by the question. "Seems like a decent fellow. He rescued us after our swim in the lake. Has been helpful since. Why?"

Something Annie had read in the journal had been nagging at her. "In Glendon's journal, he wrote about a cabin in the woods in Maryland where an old negro and a young colored girl lived. One of the Lucky Six tried to rape the girl, but Glendon stopped him."

Bradley turned around. He glanced back in Abraham's direction, then focused on Annie. "And?"

"Abraham could be that man. He escaped slavery before the end of the war and could have been living in Maryland at the time. Maybe he tracked down Crawford or accidentally ran into him in Watkins. The colored man from the journal had a strong reason to want revenge, and we know Abraham was in the cemetery when the murder happened. Maybe Abraham is lying about Glendon moving the body."

"We should ask him." Thunder rumbled again in the distance. Bradley revised his answer. "But we should wait to ask him if he's a vengeful, lying murderer until after he gives us a ride back into town. I'd rather not walk back in the rain."

To their right and slightly ahead came the sound of a stick snapping in two. A second later, Annie heard a thrashing in the undergrowth as if a large body moved away from them. Her eyes widened, and she looked toward Bradley, who had crouched down instinctively. The lack of visibility made her feel claustrophobic.

Bradley stood up and reached for her hand. "Come with me." He pulled her along in the direction the sound had come from, but branches, thorns, and vines tugged at Annie's boots and walking dress, slowing her down. At times like these, Annie envied men their trousers. She concentrated on staying on her feet and avoiding tree branches snapping back into her face as Bradley pushed his way through the underbrush.

"Here," Bradley said as he came to a stop. They had reached

a trail formed in the woods from repeated use. Whatever creature had bolted through the woods had passed this way. Bradley
dropped to a knee to inspect the ground.

"Could it have been a deer?" Annie asked.

"Maybe," Bradley said, "but it's too dry to see any prints."

Annie wanted it to be Glendon, but why would he run? Whoever it was must have heard their voices. She reached into the pocket
of her dress to feel the comforting weight of her derringer. They
followed the new trail until it led them to a small clearing. In the
center was a large patch of the freshly overturned dirt. Annie's
stomach churned. It looked like a gravesite. Bradley gently guided
Annie by the elbow around the edge of the clearing. "We should
keep moving. We'll worry about whatever this is later."

The path led them closer to the cliff, from which they saw
glimpses of the lake through the trees. They followed the trail north
along the cliff until they arrived at a tent partially hidden by the
trees. Tall poles propped up white canvas shelter halves above a
waist-high log enclosure. Someone had patched the gaps between
logs with mud.

"It's a stockaded shelter tent," Bradley said. "I saw a lot of these
in the Army. This one has been here for a while."

Annie looked inside. "Someone has been here recently." A
bedroll lay on top of a gum blanket, and a dog-eared book lay on
top of the bedroll. A half-eaten tin of salmon sat on a flat rock.

"We disturbed someone's dinner," Bradley said.

Annie looked around. The view of the lake through the trees
looked familiar. She had been here once before. A vivid memory of a spring walk in the woods with Glendon popped into her
head. A year or two after her parents' deaths, she and Glendon had
traveled through sunshine-dappled woods along this narrow dirt
trail, muddy in spots from recent rains. Annie recalled the smell of
spring flowers and a ladybug landing on her sleeve.

Between trying to identify different bird calls, Glendon had
asked her about school. She'd told him her favorite subject was ge-
ography, and, no, there were no boys in the class that she liked.
"I'm never going to fall in love," she had said. Under her breath,
she'd added, "Because it hurts too much when you lose someone

you love." Annie didn't think Glendon heard her.

When they'd emerged from the shadowy woods into the sunshine on a wide cliff high above the waters of Seneca Lake, Glendon had looked at Annie with sympathetic eyes. "Everyone deserves true love. I think it is worth any risk." He'd smiled and then looked out over the lake. "I never get tired of this view," Glendon had said at the time.

Bradley cleared his throat, bringing Annie back to the present. "Are you all right?"

"Yes," Annie said. She pointed to the path that ran along the top of the cliffs. "We need to go that way."

The path led to a fallen log across a deep, dry streambed. With no branches to snag her dress here, Annie scrambled across effortlessly. She noticed the approving look on Bradley's face.

The trail continued along the top of the cliff. With the trees blocking her view of the cliff edge, Annie imagined it was just a walk in the woods. As they neared the opening that led to the wide cliff high above the lake, she tensed and grabbed Bradley's hand. Annie tried to fight the queasy feeling growing in her stomach knowing how high the cliff was ahead.

A man waited for them at the cliff's edge, facing the panoramic view over Seneca Lake and the hills beyond. The sun was setting, and the portions of the sky not blocked by dark clouds had turned a gorgeous orange-red. Flashes of light appeared in the clouds, and the booming of thunder drew closer. The storm was almost upon them.

Glendon turned around as they approached. "That's far enough," he said, pointing a Colt revolver at them. They stopped a dozen steps away. Annie let go of Bradley's hand, then wished she hadn't.

"Just the two of you?" Glendon asked.

"Abraham is watching the horses and carriage near the entrance," Annie said.

Glendon nodded and pocketed his revolver. He smiled at Annie. "I hoped you would find me here," he said. "You never stop amazing me."

Bradley took his own revolver out but kept it at his side.

"You must be Bradley," Glendon said. "Thank you for saving Annie's life on the *Bonnie Lynn*. You have nothing to fear from me, but both of your lives are in danger."

"Were you the one who took Crawford's body out of the cemetery?" Annie blurted out.

Glendon looked at her for long seconds, and then he sighed. "Yes."

A small sob escaped Annie. She wanted to find Glendon so he could tell her it had all been a mistake. That he wasn't a killer and not involved with the people trying to kill her. Was her whole life a lie?

"Annie," Glendon said, "please listen to me. We don't have much time. You have been followed even if you don't think you've been. It is just a matter of time before we have unwanted company. I'll answer as many questions as possible, but first, tell me, how is Roland?"

Annie wiped her eyes with Bradley's handkerchief, which she still carried. "Still unconscious," Annie said. "The doctor won't say it, but he worries Roland might never wake up."

"I'm so deeply sorry, Annie. I'm afraid it might be my fault."

"Did you shoot him?"

"No, of course not. But he was watching over you for me. Someone wants to get to me through you, and I'm afraid Roland got in their way."

More flashes of lightning came from across the lake, followed by booming thunder.

"How can I trust you?" Annie asked. "You've been lying to me my whole life."

"Annie, you know me. I would never lie to you."

"Are you my real father?"

Glendon's mouth hung open. No words came out.

"I found your journal," Annie said, her voice shaking with emotion. "I know all about the Lucky Six and your snake tattoo. I know about you and my mother. Nana confirmed it. You have been lying all this time."

"Annie—"

"Nana told me my mother made you both promise never to tell

me. Is that true?"

"Yes," Glendon said. "I have wanted to tell you a thousand times, but—I loved your mother. Even though it broke my heart, I honored her wish. Still, watching you grow up has been one of my greatest joys."

When Annie grew quiet, Bradley spoke up. "I have a question," he said, raising his revolver and pointing it at Glendon's chest. "Are you the Butzemann?"

Annie's eyes went wide, but Glendon was unbothered by Bradley's aggressive posture. "No, Bradley, I'm not."

Bradley hesitated, then lowered his weapon. "My second question is, if you never found the gold, how could you afford to buy Annie's parents' house after their death?"

"That is the one lie in my journal," Glendon said. "I did find the gold in that cave in North Carolina. I removed it with the help of Fish's—Eddie Pierson's—mother and sister. I gave them his share for helping. But for the Lucky Six, that gold is cursed. Nothing bad happened when I gave some away, but every time I spent it selfishly, bad luck has followed. Glendon's eyes watered as he turned to Annie. "The last time I spent any gold was when I bought your parents a sailboat. I blame myself for their deaths." He wiped at a tear rolling down his face.

Annie let out another sob. Her fear of heights kept her from moving closer to Glendon.

"How did you buy Annie's house, then?" Bradley asked.

"I was too afraid to touch the gold," Glendon said, "so I left the remaining six satchels sitting in the bank in Watkins. As it turns out, banks were eager to lend me money using that pile of gold as collateral. I used bank loans which I paid back long ago, to buy the house and start my business. The price of gold has dropped to pre-war levels, but what's in the bank is worth around two hundred thousand dollars." That represented a small fortune.

"Are you involved with the counterfeiting ring?"

"No."

"But you killed the Confederate in the cemetery?"

"Crawford? No, I moved Crawford's body, but someone else killed him." Glendon looked back down the path as if waiting for

Sailing Before the Storm

someone. "We are running out of time. Let me tell the story quickly."

Annie and Bradley remained quiet.

"I saw Buck—or Crawford—the day before he died. Fate put me on the sidewalk near Treman's hardware store just as Buck exited with a new lantern and shovel. He was twenty yards ahead of me, and I only saw the back of his head, but something about how he walked—a distant memory—made me pay attention. When he crossed the street, I realized it was Crawford. I knew he would only travel to Watkins to look for me and the gold, so I followed him to Big Mag's. I paid her a lot of money to let me sit undisturbed at a table in the shadows so I could keep an eye on Crawford." Glendon smiled at Annie. "That is why Big Mag said she enjoyed doing business with me. I paid her a lot of money to do nothing."

Annie shook her head. "You already knew about Crawford when we went to the brothel."

"Yes," Glendon admitted, "but you figured the details out without much help from me. Besides, getting into his room was your excellent idea. Anyway, I had fallen asleep at the table in the main room but woke up when Crawford came down the stairs in the middle of the night. I followed him across town and to the cemetery. He carried the lantern, the shovel, and a pistol, so I didn't get too close. He stopped near your mother's grave as if he was waiting for someone, so I tried to work through the woods to get close enough to hear their conversation. The second man showed up from the direction of the Glen Mountain House, but that man remained in the shadows. I saw Crawford drop to the ground, but I didn't know he was dead until the killer was long gone."

"Why not go to the sheriff?" Annie said.

"The killer left Buck's body on your mother's grave. When I saw the gold nugget in his hand, I knew someone was sending a message to me. Someone knows I have the gold. I don't trust the sheriff enough to tell him I'm a former Confederate soldier living in town using a fake name. I would have been the lead suspect in Crawford's death. I wanted to figure this out on my own, but now—Crawford's killer knows you are my real daughter. The members of the Lucky Six were the only ones who even knew I had a child.

Someone is trying to hurt you to punish me for that damn gold."

"Crawford is buried near your tent, isn't he?" Bradley asked.

"I should have weighed that steamer trunk down with rocks and thrown him in the lake, but—he was a friend once. I hoped that after I had it out with the real killer, I would find a way to ship Crawford's body back to his wife."

A lightning strike nearby made Annie jump. The storm had been passing south of their location, but now the wind blew the dark clouds and lightning in their direction. The last light of the day fought a losing battle against the darkness. Annie looked back through the shadowy woods, surprised to see points of light traveling through the forest like mischievous fairies.

The lights were the lanterns held by unknown men coming through the woods toward them. "They've found us," Glendon said. "I'm out of time." He locked eyes with Annie. "Annie, I have spent the last two weeks trying to figure out who killed Crawford and who is trying to kill you, but I've failed. Someone from the Lucky Six is still alive, or they shared information with someone who is now looking for the gold. Whoever it is has covered their tracks well."

Glendon reached into his pocket and pulled out the gold nugget. "Bradley," he said, "are you a superstitious man?"

"No, I believe we make our own luck."

Glendon tossed the nugget to Bradley, who caught it in his left hand. "This is the same gold nugget that my fellow sharpshooter, Fish, took from the cave and kept until the Army executed him. Corporal Taylor was the last man to have it before it showed up with Buck—Crawford—in the cemetery. If you two can figure out where it has been, you might figure out who the killer is. But be careful, it's cursed. It's only brought me bad luck."

Glendon turned and looked down toward the water. He was close to the edge.

"Keep her safe, Bradley," Glendon said, turning back toward them. "At least one of those men would take pleasure in killing Annie in front of me to make me suffer. If I'm gone, they may leave her alone. But they may not. Whatever you do, don't let anyone else take her away from you. Trust no one."

Annie looked toward the woods. The men were reaching the edge of the treeline. She could make out Sheriff Swartwood in the lead. All the men held lanterns and guns.

"Glendon—" Annie started to say, but he cut her off.

"Annie, I love you," he said. A gust of wind buffeted Glendon's words, forcing Annie to concentrate. "I have always loved you. I want you to know that everything I have will be passed on to you. You won't have to worry about money again. If you cannot figure out who the killer is, take the money and run. Live a long and happy life."

"What are you saying?"

The first, fat raindrops of the advancing storm crashed to the ground as the sheriff emerged from the woods, followed by his deputy, Leonard Cole, and then George Magee. Behind them came Otto Fuchs, and a thin man Annie did not recognize. Abraham was the last to emerge from the woods.

"Glendon Robinson, you're under arrest!" the sheriff boomed.

Annie looked into Glendon's eyes. He smiled at her with such sadness that Annie's heart dropped. She started to scream, "No..." as Glendon Robinson stepped off the cliff and disappeared into the darkness below.

NIGHT STORM

CHAPTER XLV

CHEMUNG CANAL

Friday, July 24, 1874

THE storm hit with a vengeance. For several hours, lightning crackled, thunder boomed, heavy rains flooded the glens, and fierce winds challenged the staunchest of trees. Then, as quickly as it arrived, the violence gave way to steady showers that continued into the next morning. By the time the rain faded away, it was late afternoon and the once dusty streets of Watkins had turned into a muddy soup. Tree branches littered the ground, and summer vacationers bemoaned their washed-out excursion plans, but the locals rejoiced. They stood in doorways and breathed in the freshness of their cleansed world. The rain brought a collective sigh of relief.

Bradley pulled out the town newspaper, the *Watkins Review*, and checked the Northern Central Railway timetables again. He had plenty of time to finish his dinner before the evening train departed. He set the paper down next to his half-eaten dinner. He enjoyed the Jefferson House but missed the chefs at the Lake View Hotel.

Bradley had also bought today's *New York Times*. He'd read about the weather-delayed Saratoga regatta race, murderous Indians in the Kansas Territory, and grasshoppers ravaging crops in southwestern Minnesota. He flipped the page to city news but saw no mention of Thomas Pickens's counterfeiting trial. The Lost and Found on page six held only one item. A boy had lost a check walking home, and a three-dollar reward was being offered. Bradley sighed and closed the paper. After ten years of searching, it was time to give up hope.

Bradley had not checked on Annie. He'd waited out the storm, then spent time looking for Otto Fuchs without success. He'd penned a note for Annie before dinner and put it in the hands of a local teenager for delivery. It would have to suffice. He was running out of time to find the counterfeiters, and Annie was safer locked in her house with her grandmother.

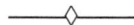

Last night, after Glendon threw himself from the cliff, Annie sprang forward only to fall to her knees. Her fear of heights and fear of what she might see kept her from looking over the edge. Bradley knelt beside her, placing his body between hers and those of the arriving men. He had no idea if Glendon was correct that the killer—or the killer's lackey—was one of the men who had arrived, but there was no reason to take chances. When George Magee rushed over to Annie, Bradley stepped in front of her, blocking the millionaire's path. "Your help is appreciated," Bradley said curtly, "but not necessary. I'll make sure Annie gets home safely." Magee opened his mouth to argue but got called away by the sheriff. Deputy Cole hovered nearby, watching Bradley while Abraham stayed in darkness at the edge of the woods.

The sheriff and George peered over the cliff edge into the void. "Nothing says guilty like committing suicide when you're about to get caught," the sheriff said, shaking his head and waving over Deputy Cole. There were discussions about sending men with boats and torches to search for Glendon's body, and then the raindrops began falling with enthusiasm. It would take an hour to backtrack and reach the spot below them. If Glendon had missed the rocks, he might have survived the one-hundred-foot drop, but a fall from that height could break a leg or knock a man unconscious. If that happened, Glendon would disappear beneath the waves, and it could take days before anyone found his body.

"An unexpected turn of events," Otto Fuchs said, tucking his 1849 Colt pocket revolver back into his jacket. He had stepped closer while the other men were preoccupied.

"Are you working with the sheriff now?" Bradley asked.

Fuchs shook his head. "No, but my driver and I have been following George Magee," he said. "He and the sheriff appear to be working together. They led us here. The question should be, how did they find you?"

Bradley helped Annie to her feet. "We have to go," he said. She nodded mutely.

Fuchs tipped his hat to Annie. "My condolences, *Fraulein*. We may never learn the truth now that Glendon Robinson and his Lucky Six are no more." Fuchs looked toward the cliff. "'What a tangled web we weave when first we practice to deceive.'"

Under her breath, Annie replied, *"Ich glaub ich spinne."*

Fuchs looked sadly at Annie. "I fear, *Fraulein*, that Glendon was *die spinne*, or the spider," he said, "and you are the fly left surrounded by his tangled webs."

The rain increased as Bradley led Annie over to Abraham, who unerringly navigated their way back through the woods. By the time they reached the carriage, all three were drenched. Annie climbed in and curled into a ball on the seat facing away from Bradley. Her body shook from uncontrollable crying or being soaked to the bone. Or both. Bradley couldn't tell. Whatever result Annie had hoped for in their search for Glendon, this hadn't been it.

Bradley felt useless on the ride back. He would have willingly wrapped his arms around Annie to comfort her or offer the warmth of his body, but Victorian propriety kept him rigid in his seat. Instead, he turned to look out the window.

Glendon, by denying any involvement with the counterfeiting ring, had proven to be a dead end for Bradley. Whether Glendon had lied or told the truth, Bradley had no leads left to follow. His only hope of success was to find the counterfeiter's hideout by following Alistair Sinclair or the Walrus after they returned from Ithaca or stumbling into one of the Ballard brothers. The only other clue he could follow was the cryptic *Ortus Solis 17510*, but he had not idea what it meant of it was relevant.

Lightning shattered the darkness several times a minute on the ride back to Watkins. As their carriage crossed the bridge over the Chemung Canal, another bright flash illuminated a canal boat's long, low body moored to a pier near the canal entrance. Bradley had a jarring thought. *Could it be that simple?*

When they arrived at the house, Nana greeted them at the door and, after hearing of Glendon's fall, wrapped Annie in her arms

and ushered her into the house. Annie paused to turn back to Bradley and Abraham.

"Thank you for helping me," she said. It looked like she wanted
to say more, but she turned and disappeared into the house. Bradley
listened as Annie's grandmother locked the door behind them, then
returned to the carriage.

Abraham dropped Bradley at the corner of Franklin Street and
Fourth Street and then disappeared with horses and carriage in the
rain and mist. Bradley watched Abraham leave but made no move
to cross the street and reach the dry comfort of the Jefferson House.
Instead, he reached into his pocket and wrapped his hand around
the gold nugget that Glendon had tossed to him. Perhaps this was a
sign that riches were coming his way. He turned up his collar and
headed east into the stormy night. He had a hunch to follow.

Last night's efforts had borne fruit, and it was time to take action. The late summer sun shone brightly as Bradley watched the
steam engine pull into the Watkins train depot. He maneuvered
around large puddles left by last night's storm and waited patiently
for the arriving passengers to step down. Out of habit, he reached
into his pocket for his father's watch but sighed, remembering its
loss. His hands found the gold nugget instead. Bradley carried a
bag with supplies over his right shoulder. The trip to Horseheads
would last almost an hour and then he had another long night ahead
of him.

The unsettling feeling that someone was watching him hadn't
returned since the circus, but Bradley remained vigilant. Healthy
paranoia had kept him alive those first years living on the streets in
New York City. Out of habit, he kept himself slightly apart from the
other passengers and scanned the crowds. He saw people waiting,
carriages arriving, and men loading and unloading items onto the
train. Nothing struck him as suspicious until, out of the corner of
his eye, he noticed a person pushing through the crowd and heading toward him. Bradley tensed, then relaxed. The teenager had his
head down to avoid the puddles, but Bradley recognized him as the
messenger he'd paid to deliver his note to Annie. The young man

wore a suit of cheap, dark material over a white shirt. Bradley was surprised at how happy he felt knowing Annie had sent a response. He was glad the messenger had caught him before he boarded the train.

The train conductor blew his whistle and called, "All aboard!" The crowd moved forward, jostling for position. Bradley saw something in the messenger's hands. At first, he thought it must be Annie's message, but as the teenager drew closer, Bradley realized it was a train ticket.

"Hey, mister, can you spare a dime?" The teenager stepped next to Bradley, holding out a hand. Then he tilted his head back and looked up.

Bradley's jaw dropped. "Annie?" he whispered. There was no mistaking her large, sparkling eyes, the gentle curve of her jaw, the wisps of long brown hair tucked into the teenager's large hat, or the cautious smile on her face.

She leaned toward him. "I got your message," she said.

"Annie, you should not be here. It is too dangerous."

A cloud passed over her face, and her smile faltered. "But I have a ticket," she said, and turned to board the train. She left Bradley no choice but to follow her. For a beautiful woman, she made a surprisingly credible teenage boy as long as she kept her hat on and her head down.

Bradley slid onto the bench beside her. They said nothing until the train lurched into motion, heading south. Looking out the window, he was surprised to see the attractive waitress from the Montour House watching their train leave the station. She had arrived seconds too late to board the train.

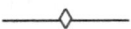

Sanna turned her back and left the depot as the train pulled away. She saw no point in chasing after Bradley and Annie Anderson. The next train would not pass through for hours and no horse and carriage would catch a steam locomotive with a head start.

Annie had fooled Sanna with the messenger's outfit, but Sanna was more impressed than angry. Sanna had been watching Annie's house, waiting for her target to make a mistake when the messenger arrived. He'd stayed inside longer than expected, but Sanna ignored him as he departed. It was luck that gave her a glimpse of the messenger still inside when the grandmother closed the curtains. Sanna hadn't thought Annie bold enough to disguise herself as a boy. She had rushed to catch up with Annie only to see her board the train with Bradley.

Annie won this round, but Sanna was patient. Time was growing short for Sanna to finish her mission and cross another name off her list, but it would only take one mistake—or a moment of inattention—for Annie Anderson to lose her life.

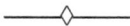

The rhythmic puffing of the steam engine and the clickety-clack of the train wheels helped obscure their conversation from eavesdroppers, as Annie spoke in hushed tones into Bradley's ear.

"Nana convinced Doctor Bennett to move Roland to our house," she said. "He was against it at first, but Nana wore him down. Argued it would be easier to watch over Roland in our home. We had to agree to let one of Sheriff Swartwood's deputies stay with us. They plan to arrest Roland and return him to Georgia as soon as he wakes up." Annie looked annoyed at the thought. "We know the deputy assigned—he comes from a good family—so for now, Nana and I are happy to have a man with a gun in the house."

As Annie talked, Bradley looked down at her slim hands held in her lap. She had used soot and dirt to make them look less lady-like.

"The sheriff came by today," Annie said, her voice tight. "The storm prevented his deputies from searching the lake last night, but there was no sign of Glendon after it passed." Annie paused. "But they found the steamer trunk and Crawford's body. The sheriff is keeping it quiet for now. He told me that the discovery confirms Glendon is a murderer and that it would be best for everyone—" Something caught in Annie's throat, but she fought through it. "Best for everyone if Glendon died in the fall. It would save the town a murder trial."

Bradley wanted to reach out to her, but he resisted the urge.

"The sheriff said it might take a few days for them to find Glendon's body."

This wasn't a surprise. Bradley thought to himself. Drowning victims often sank into the deep water only to resurface days later.

"Glendon is a really good swimmer," Annie said under her breath as if she read his thoughts. She turned her gaze to the window, fighting back tears.

Bradley gave her time to compose herself before asking, "How did you get out of the house?"

Annie turned from the window. "I'm supposed to finish the dress I'm donating for next week's charity auction," she said. "But I couldn't concentrate. I could not sit there waiting for Roland to wake up or to die. Or waiting for Glendon to be found alive... or dead. And then your note came saying you learned something about *ortus solis*." She grinned. "It's unsafe for Annie Anderson to leave the house, but I realized the delivery boy was about my size. I paid him a quarter eagle to borrow his clothes, hat, and boots. I got all my hair into the hat, and the clothes fit me well enough after I bound my...." Annie blushed and pointed toward her chest. Bradley willed himself not to look down. "His boots fit surprisingly well," Annie said. "Lucky for me, he has small feet."

"The kid gave up his clothes pretty quickly," Bradley said with a chuckle.

"He said for a quarter eagle, he would wear one of my dresses and spend the night scrubbing floors. Nana overheard him and put him right to work." Annie laughed. "Without the dress, thankfully. He is wearing one of Roland's old suits."

Bradley laughed with her. "And your grandmother? I'm surprised she let you leave."

"She hated the idea, but I'm an adult. She has to trust me to make my own decisions. Of course, I can't let something bad happen, or she might kill me herself."

The Montour House appeared outside his window as the train pulled into the next station. It had taken less than ten minutes to reach Havana. "You realize," he said, "that if someone discovers you gallivanting about dressed as a man, it will be a serious setback for your social standing in Watkins? Not to mention, you are alone and unchaperoned in the company of a single man."

Annie looked defiant. "I'm willing to take that risk. Besides, I can defend myself as needed." She reached into her pants pocket, where Bradley assumed she carried her derringer. "I'm quite enjoying trousers at the moment," she said.

They waited for the train to start in motion again, and then Annie unfolded a note from her pocket. She read it back to Bradley. "I figured out *ortus solis*. Heading to Horseheads. Will fill you in when I get back." Annie tucked the note back into her pocket. "Start talking, Mister Webster. What did you figure out?"

"When we came down the hill last night, I was thinking about *ortus solis* and what a silly phrase that was. Sunrise? Rising sun? Why would Smythe write down an arbitrary Latin expression? Then a flash of lightning as we passed the entrance to the canal made me realize—"

"*Ortus Solis* is the name of a boat!" Annie said, making the connection.

"Exactly what I thought," Bradley said. "So, I went back out last night, snuck into the toll collector's office in Watkins, and checked the logbook. Four days ago, a canal boat named the *Ortus Solis* paid the toll to enter the Chemung Canal from Seneca Lake."

"You broke into the toll collector's office?"

"I knocked, but no one was home," Bradley said sarcastically, "and I was in a hurry." When Annie looked at him skeptically, he admitted, "I was careful and left no traces. Except for wet footprints."

Annie moved on. "What about the numbers on Smythe's note? *Ortus Solis* one, seven, five, one, zero. Any ideas?"

"No," Bradley said, "they could mean anything. My best guess was a price of one hundred and seventy-five dollars and ten cents or seventeen thousand, five hundred ten dollars. But that doesn't get me anywhere. For all I know, it could be a random serial number."

"Now that we know *Ortus Solis* is a canal boat," Annie mused, "maybe it has something to do with the locks. There are forty-four locks over seventeen miles between Watkins and Horseheads." The locks—canal sections for raising or lowering the water levels— were placed irregularly along the canal wherever the elevation changed. Annie considered the possibilities. "Perhaps a location and time? Like lock seventeen at 5:10 p.m. Or lock one on July 5 at 10:00 a.m.?" Annie's brow furrowed in frustration. "We are just guessing." She turned her attention back to the canal boat. "If it takes two and a half or three days for a canal boat to travel from Watkins to Elmira or Corning, the *Ortus Solis* should be heading north to Watkins by now. Even if last night's storm slowed them down. Why are we going to Horseheads?"

"There is another toll collector's office in Horseheads," Bradley said. "I'll check there to see when the *Ortus Solis* passed through and then walk the towpath until I find the boat. It will be a long night." He looked at Annie. "You should take the return train from Horseheads back to Watkins."

Annie went quiet as she considered his plan.

Bradley glanced out the window. The railway, the canal, the creek, and the road from Watkins to Horseheads all ran parallel through the narrowing valley south of Havana. The creek, the only natural feature in the valley, meandered on the far side of the canal. When heavy rains filled the canal, workers diverted the extra water to the creek. Raging water now filled the creek and rushed north toward Seneca Lake. As the train pulled into Millport, Bradley saw canal boats moored along the canal out his window.

"Bradley," Annie said. "Do you trust me?"

"Why?"

"We should get off the train here," Annie announced, her voice filled with a quiet certainty. "I'm sure of it." She rose from her seat and waited for Bradley to join her.

Bradley hesitated, but only for a moment. When he stood, she rewarded him with a broad smile. They descended together from the train. They let the crowd move ahead of them and kept an eye out for anyone following them before crossing the street and heading downhill toward the canal.

Millport was a working-class town supporting six boatyards for canal boats, a tin shop, a shoe shop, a tannery, and a flour mill. Smaller than Watkins or Havana, Millport lay in a narrow valley between tall, deforested hills. The residents cut trees down in the winter, sawed them into lumber, then shipped the lumber to distant markets after the canal opened in the spring.

CANAL BOAT AND MULES

The number of canal boats moored for the night in Millport surprised Bradley. "Is that why we got off the train here?" Each boat, made of pine planks, had a name painted on the stern. They stretched sixty feet long and fifteen feet wide.

Annie nodded. "This section of canal between Millport and Havana has the most locks," she said. "It takes the longest for boats to get through, so this is the most likely place for the *Ortus Solis* to stop for the night, assuming it is on its way back to Seneca Lake."

Annie led Bradley to a bridge that crossed the canal. On the far side, they stood on the canal's towpath, and Bradley was relieved it offered solid footing after all the rain. Annie and Bradley searched the length of Millport, carefully checking the names of each canal boat moored for the night. None of them were the *Ortus Solis*.

Bradley hefted his bag onto his shoulder and considered their choices. They could search the seven miles south toward Horseheads or the six miles north to Havana and then Watkins. It was a coin toss to him. "What do you think?" he asked Annie.

She seemed pleased that he'd asked for her opinion. "If we go north toward Seneca Lake and we're wrong, we'll only lose a day in our search. If we go south to Horseheads and are wrong, the *Ortus Solis* reaches Seneca Lake, and we'll have lost our chance."

"Can't argue with that logic," he said. "North it is."

They walked quietly along the towpath through the shadows of the hills, heading toward Havana and Watkins. In fading daylight, the canal waters looked dark and ominous. They passed several canal boats moored against the bank for the night, often near the entrance to a lock. None of them were the *Ortus Solis*.

They passed many locks. At each one, the forty-two-foot-wide canal narrowed to the width of one canal boat. Once inside the ninety-foot-long lock, gates were opened or closed manually, and the water level was raised or lowered to match the next section of the canal. Each lock added a time-consuming delay on a canal boat's journey.

Bradley watched the last glow of sunset disappear from the sky as Annie broke the silence. "The Chemung Canal has been here twice as long as I've been alive," Annie said. "Hard to believe it could all be going away."

"What do you mean?"

"The railroads," Annie said. "The canal can't compete. If George Magee gets the funding for a second railway line to Watkins, he will stop transporting coal by canal barge. There are rumors that the canal might go bankrupt if that happens. Maintenance costs are too high because the canal builders gave the Irish laborers wood instead of stone for construction. Wood is cheaper but it leaks and decays over time. But the real problem is the canal doesn't open until May and then shuts down every winter, while railroads run all year and can move goods faster."

"You know a lot about the canal," Bradley said.

Annie hesitated. "Yes," she admitted. "I was courted by a man whose family was in the coal business. They did a lot of shipping through the canal and talked about it all the time."

Bradley had no response.

A half-full moon peeked through the overcast skies and offered enough light for them to walk comfortably and avoid stepping in the scattered piles of mule dung. The recent rains had rejuvenated the insect population, creating annoying buzzing around their ears, but bats swooped overhead, doing their best to gorge on the flying insects. Cricket chirps came from the long grasses, and now and then, Bradley could make out the bellowing of a bullfrog. A few miles along the towpath, Bradley called a halt and pulled his bag off his shoulder. He retrieved a battered, water-filled canteen that he offered to Annie. She accepted gratefully, took several gulps, and passed it back to Bradley.

They'd kept a brisk pace, and Annie had neither faltered nor complained. He returned the canteen to his bag. "Annie," he said, "Last night, Glendon wanted you to take his money and run. Have you considered it?"

She sighed. "I don't have access to Glendon's money, so leaving would be difficult. But yes, it has crossed my mind. First, I have to find a way to sneak Roland out of Watkins when he wakes up... if he wakes up. That will be the right time to disappear."

"And your grandmother?"

"She's happy in Watkins." Annie shrugged. "Besides, she has been trying to marry me off for years. If I'm on the run with Roland, I would no longer be her responsibility." Annie laughed, but there was sadness in her words. "I love the idea of travel, but I don't want it forced on me."

A lone canal boat—tied off to trees near the bank—came into view as the canal swung to the right, following the curve of the valley. Bradley had been enjoying Annie's company more than he was thinking about canal boats, so he was surprised to read the words *Ortus Solis* on the boat's stern as they got closer. Annie and Bradley looked at each other with wide eyes and then hurried back the way they'd come until out of earshot of the boat crew.

"I'd have been walking for days looking for this boat if it weren't for you," Bradley whispered. A feeble light glowed through the boat's aft cabin windows.

Annie's smile grew wider. "What is the plan?" she said, trying to contain her excitement.

"We want to know what cargo this boat carried for the counterfeiters and where they dropped it off," Bradley said. "The counterfeiters already have perfect plates, ink, and paper, so hopefully, the *Ortus Solis* just delivered a printing press. Worst case, they are picking up piles of finished counterfeit one hundred and five-hundred-dollar bills to take to the city."

"Canal boats would be a good way to spread counterfeit money around with all the cities along the Erie Canal," Annie said.

Bradley agreed as he reached into his bag and pulled out a glass bottle. "It's Friday night, and only an hour after sundown, so the crew should still be awake. The perfect time for a social call." He held up the bottle of whiskey. "This will get them talking."

"What about me? You wouldn't leave a defenseless lady alone in the dark, would you?"

Bradley chuckled softly. "Of course not, but I would temporarily leave a teenage boy with a derringer in his pocket who came along uninvited." When he saw Annie bite her lower lip nervously, his voice softened. "Annie, whoever is on board could be part of the counterfeiting ring. It would be safer to keep you hidden until I return—"

"Canal boat crews eat and sleep in the stern cabin," Annie said, ignoring him. "The mules or horses sleep in the bow, and the cargo is in between. After you start drinking with them, I could sneak on board and search for printing presses or piles of money." She looked into his eyes. "Please. Let me help."

A large brown curl had escaped the brim of her hat. Without thinking, Bradley reached out and tucked the curl back under. Annie's eyes widened, and Bradley froze. The gesture was more intimate than he'd intended—he might as well have caressed her cheek.

He pulled his hand back. Annie opened her mouth to speak, but Bradley—worried about what she might say—spoke first. "Okay," he said. "It could be helpful if you searched the cargo area. But promise me you will not approach until I have been inside for at least ten minutes. And stay away from the mules in the bow. If they sense you, they will make a racket and give you away."

Annie nodded. They agreed on a rendezvous point where they would meet in one hour, giving Bradley plenty of time to ply the crew with whiskey and learn what he could. He reached into his pocket and handed Annie a small brass match safe holding a dozen wooden matches. "You might need to light one or two during your search, but keep your body between the lit match and the aft cabin." He paused before adding, "Whatever you do, please be careful."

Bradley left Annie in the shadows. It was a good plan, but thirty minutes later, when it all went to hell, he blamed himself.

CHAPTER XLVI

Ortus Solis

Friday, July 24, 1874

A NNIE watched Bradley walking away, heading to the *Ortus Solis,* and felt the darkness closing in on her. It wasn't the night that she feared. The moon cast ominous shadows but gave her enough light to see her hands. She had made an impulsive decision to swap places with the young messenger, but she had also done it out of necessity. Alone and powerless in her house, she had struggled to keep the darkness of despair from growing within her. Roland near death. Glendon missing or dead. A mysterious enemy determined to end her life for unknown reasons. With Bradley by her side, Annie had managed to avoid the feelings of fear, anger, and doubt that had threatened to overwhelm her since returning from the cliffs. Now, she was alone again.

Annie focused on Bradley to keep her fears at bay. She watched him approach the *Ortus Solis* and called out to the crew.

"Silas, permission to come aboard!" he yelled, slurring his words.

Two men in their early thirties stuck their heads out. "There's no Silas here. Go on home with your drunken self."

"Isn't this the *Orlena?*" Bradley called out.

"This here's the *Ortus Solis.*"

Bradley cursed and held up the bottle, ensuring the men saw the label and could tell it was quality whiskey. "Silas promised dinner if I showed up with the good stuff. It seems I was misinformed about his location." Bradley peered into the cabin beyond the men. "Do I smell sausages?"

When Bradley disappeared into the aft cabin with the two crewmen, Annie pulled the messenger's dark coat around her, trying to cover the white shirt underneath. To say the suit's fabric was mediocre in quality would be generous. Annie remembered the messenger's limbs protruding from his sleeves and pant legs. He must have had a recent growth spurt and no money for new clothing. Annie preoccupied herself by mentally designing a new suit using better material to give the messenger as an added thank you... If she survived.

The valley was wider here, and the road and rail lines were farther away. The rumble of nearby Catharine Creek, swollen from the recent storm, drowned out all but the nearest night sounds. Respectable gentlemen and ladies did not frequent the canal, especially alone after dark. Canal men were known to be hard drinkers, which led to fighting, theft, and even murder.

After ten minutes, Annie looked left and right to ensure she was still alone, then moved out of the shadows as stealthily as possible. As she approached the *Ortus Solis*, her fears turned into nervous excitement. "You can do this," she whispered to herself.

The canal boat, moored against the wooden walls of the canal, had cabins at both ends and a large canvas tarp covering unseen cargo in between. Because it was a scow, the deck was only a foot higher than the shore. Annie moved to the boat's center, her nose wrinkling at the odor of the canal's stagnant water. She carefully swung her left leg up and gently transferred her weight to the deck to avoid alerting the men or mules on board.

That was much easier wearing pants, she thought to herself as she stood on deck.

Annie bent down and peered under the tarp. She reached for the match safe Bradley had given her, opened the hinged lid, and slid out a wooden match. Keeping her body between the match and the aft cabin, she used the striker on the bottom of the case to light it. Nothing but stacked lumber. She blew out the match and threw it in the canal, then felt her way along the tarp, moving toward the bow. She lit another match. More lumber. She climbed over the tarp to avoid getting any closer to the mules and headed toward the stern. Nothing but lumber. Could there be something hidden under all that wood? It didn't seem likely. Annie was disappointed she wouldn't have better news for Bradley when they rendezvoused.

The *Ortus Solis* carried nothing but a load of wood.

She now stood dangerously close to the aft cabin and considered retracing her steps when she heard Bradley laugh. She liked the sound of his laugh. Confident that Bradley was distracting the crew, she silently climbed over the tarp to the shoreside and began her slow-motion transition off the boat. Annie had one foot on deck and one foot on shore when a man climbed out of the aft cabin and stared directly at her.

The man's eyes went wide. He yelled, "Hey!" as Annie pushed hard off the boat and started running. The movement caused the man to lose his footing. He cursed loudly as he landed hard on the deck. Annie, heading for the dark shadows, heard the zip of a bullet pass over her head a fraction of a second before the crack of the firearm.

"Don't move!" the man yelled from the canal boat.

Annie froze in place, slowly raising her hands over her head.

"Paul, come on out here. We got ourselves a thief!"

Annie turned as Bradley and a second man climbed out of the cabin. Bradley held his whiskey bottle in one hand and a glass of amber liquid in the other.

"Luke," the second man said, "What the hell you shootin' at?" He saw Annie and cursed. "Another damn thief!"

Annie kept her head down so her features remained in shadow. She tried to think of the right words to get her out of this. She wondered if revealing that she was a woman would work for or against her.

Bradley spoke up, his words slightly slurred. "Why, that's just a boy," he told the two crew members. "Too small to keep. If he were a fish, you would have to throw him back in the lake."

"Can't let thieves go unpunished," Luke said. Annie didn't like having the man's gun pointed at her chest. She didn't want to test his aim from a dozen paces away.

"That's reasonable," Bradley said. He handed his whiskey glass to Paul. "I'll give him a thrashing, small fry or not." Bradley jumped to shore and walked toward Annie. When he got halfway to her, he started swearing loudly. The two crewmen looked confused. "This isn't a thief," Bradley yelled over his shoulder, "he's a spy." Bradley walked up to Annie and shocked her by grabbing her shoulders and giving her a good shake. "You spyin' on me, boy?"

Annie's eyes went wide in confusion.

"This here is my youngest brother," Bradley called out. "He must have been trying to sneak up on me. Did Ma send you? I can go drinking with friends if I choose to." With his back to the men, Bradley tried to signal Annie with his eyes. When that did not work, he whispered, "Bluff with confidence."

Annie's brain engaged. She pushed out with her arms to shove Bradley backward. "Darn right, Ma sent me," she shouted, using her best impression of a teenage male voice. "She knows you stole Pa's good whiskey. There's going to be hell to pay!"

Bradley winked at her and smiled encouragingly. He mouthed the word "gun," then turned away dismissively and walked back toward Luke and Paul. "Ignore my kin, fellas. Let's get back to drinking." Shielded by Bradley's body, Annie reached slowly into her pocket. He did not expect her to shoot anyone, did he?

Luke turned his gun toward Bradley. "You know, Paul, I'm beginnin' to think these two are working together to rob us."

Bradley laughed and held up the whiskey bottle. "Why, this whiskey is worth more than anything I could carry away from your boat, and I was happy to share it with you. But no hard feelings. I'll even let you keep the rest of the bottle for any inconvenience my brother caused." Bradley made sure Luke and Paul had their attention on the bottle, then tossed it underhanded toward Luke. The bottle arched high in the air. Luke took his eyes off Bradley and caught the bottle against his body. His grin of success disappeared when he saw Bradley's gun pointing between his eyes.

Annie pulled her gun out almost as quickly and stepped toward Paul.

"I wouldn't move if I were you," Bradley said. He plucked Luke's gun from his hand but left him with the whiskey bottle. Paul just shook his head. He ignored Annie's gun and drank the rest of the whiskey from Bradley's glass, still in his hand.

"What do you want?" Luke said, shifting his weight back and forth with nervous energy.

"We mean you no harm," Bradley said in a calming voice. Any

hint of slurred speech had disappeared. "And we are not trying to steal from you. The whiskey is my gift to you, if you answer one or two questions." Luke licked his lips. Paul nodded. "What did you pick up or deliver recently for a small, silver-haired British man named Smythe?"

Paul and Luke looked confused, then a light appeared in Paul's eyes. "Creepy older guy? Short and heavy with a pretentious mustache? Dressed fancy like he thought he was better than the rest of us?"

Bradley turned to Annie. She nodded. "That's the guy."

"Hell, yeah, I remember him," Luke said. Whether it was the promise of the alcohol or the gun pointing between his eyes, Luke was eager to talk. "The English guy had us deliver two crates back in May. Very particular about the details of the shipment. Real pain in the ass."

"May?" Bradley asked, confused.

"Mid-May, maybe?" Luke said. "He had us drop the crates at the back of the Malthouse, right off Seneca Lake. He had a few men with him, or we never would have gotten those crates off our ship."

"Any idea what was in the crates?" Bradley asked.

Luke and Paul shook their heads. "Manifest said spare parts," Paul offered. "Not that we believed it."

"Was it May seventeenth?" Annie asked, keeping her attention and her derringer on Paul.

"Sounds about right," Paul said.

"Maybe ten a.m.?" Annie asked.

"Ten p.m.," Luke said. "We got paid extra for a night delivery, so we knew not to get too curious about what was inside."

Bradley nodded in understanding. "Much obliged," he said as he emptied the bullets from Luke's gun and tossed them into the canal. He threw the gun into the bushes in the opposite direction and then motioned with his revolver for the two men to climb back on the *Ortus Solis*. After they shut the cabin door, Annie turned to Bradley.

"Now what?" she asked.

"Now we run!" He grabbed her hand and began sprinting down the towpath toward Havana.

———◇———

Annie and Bradley ran effortlessly in the moonlight. Running felt good to Annie—it helped burn away her dark fears and the nervous energy from a near-death experience. A half mile down the path, Bradley looked back and slowed to a fast walk. "We should be safe enough now," he said.

Annie caught her breath and looked at Bradley. "Did you just save my life again?"

She watched Bradley remove his hat and comb his fingers through his brown hair. "Probably," Bradley fit his hat back on his head and smiled at her. "That means I'm one up on you, not that I'm counting."

"I didn't know whether to run or talk my way out of it."

"Hard to outrun a bullet," Bradley said. "I learned a long time ago that people will believe anything you say—if you say it with enough confidence."

"Even when bluffing?"

"Especially when bluffing! You made an impressively annoying little brother, by the way!" She punched him lightly on the shoulder, and they both laughed. After a few more steps, he paused in the middle of the towpath, forcing Annie to stop and look at him. His face had turned serious. "I should never have let that canal man get by me when I knew you'd be searching the boat. It is my fault that Luke almost shot you. I'm sorry."

"Thank you," Annie said, "but I'm unharmed. And you did warn me that it could be dangerous."

Bradley still looked remorseful as they resumed their journey. "How did you know that the delivery was on May seventeenth?"

"The note in Smythe's jacket. *Ortus Solis* one, seven, five, one, zero. You reminded me Smythe was British. Europeans write their dates before their months. May seventeenth is five-seventeen to us but would have been seventeen-five to Smythe."

Bradley understood. "So, one, seven, five, one, zero was Smythe's shorthand for a seventeenth of May delivery at ten in the evening. Great detective work," he said to Annie, then shook his head with disappointment. "Assuming those crates held printing presses, the counterfeiters have had the presses and the perfect ink,

plates, and paper for months. We may be too late. Maybe the Ballard brothers left a few days ago because the work has finished."

They walked in silence down the quiet towpath, passing numerous locks but few canal boats. The ones they passed had darkened interiors, the occupants most likely asleep. Annie did not feel
tired, but the night was getting late, and they were still more than
a mile south of Havana.

"What I can't understand," Annie said, "is why deliver the
crates to the Malthouse? One of the Ballard brothers worked there
as a night watchman, which is too much of a coincidence. But
Abraham checked, and it's a working malthouse. There shouldn't
be any places to hide printing presses."

"We might as well sneak in and find out," Bradley said. "A
quick visit to look for the presses and collect any incriminating
evidence we find."

Bradley's use of the word "we" made Annie unreasonably happy. He could have told her to go home and gone without her. She
wasn't sure what it meant that she'd rather illegally break into a
malthouse in the middle of the night with him than be alone. "What
if we find something?" she asked. "What then? Do we take the evidence to Fuchs or the sheriff?"

"Maybe neither. We need to find the counterfeit money so it
can lead us to the person in charge. To Sinclair's silent partner who
is trying to kill you."

"Do you believe now that it's not Glendon?" Annie said, more
defensively than intended.

"If Glendon didn't kill the guy in the cemetery—"

"He didn't. He only moved the body to protect me."

"From what you said, whoever lured Crawford to the cemetery
knew about the gold. If not Glendon," Bradley said, "could another
member of the Lucky Six still be alive?"

Annie considered what Glendon had written in his journal.
"Fish died by firing squad, and the Army buried his body immediately."

"That seems pretty final to me," Bradley said.

"All they found of Taylor after the train accident was a bloody
jacket. No body," she said. "And Ace died of smallpox, but the sur-

viving Lucky Six escaped before seeing his body."

"We have two suspects, then," Bradley said.

"Three," Annie said. "Frank, the man who got shot in the Glen. The big guy. No one reported finding his body. We saw him fall, but he could have gotten away in the darkness. Wounded, but still alive."

"From his size, Frank could not have been the man I saw talking to Sinclair in Lafayette Park. Do you remember the descriptions of Taylor and Ace?"

Annie shook her head. "Only that Taylor was taller than the others. And fair-haired."

Bradley considered this. "Taylor was tall, fair-haired, and would have been injured in the train accident. Sinclair has scars and a permanent limp. He's not fair-haired, but his children are. Maybe it's not Sinclair's partner who is a member of the Lucky Six. Maybe it's Sinclair."

The canal and the rail lines ran right next to each other as they entered Havana. Annie and Bradley approached the Havana train depot, but no trains ran this late at night. They walked along deserted streets and passed dark homes. A few lamps glowed through windows at the Montour House.

With no other obvious choices, they continued on to Watkins on foot. Annie didn't mind. Being alone with Bradley felt intimate and comforting at the same time while distracting her from her reality.

They continued along the towpath, leaving Havana behind them. The silence was comfortable, but Annie wanted to know more about her companion. "Did you grow up in New York City?" she asked.

Her question floated away on the light breeze, and they walked in silence for so long after that Annie wondered if he had heard her at all or chose to ignore this intrusion into his personal life. Selfishly, she'd hoped the whiskey he drank might loosen his tongue.

"Would you like some cherries?" he asked.

He pulled his bag off his shoulder and, after a little digging, handed Annie a handful of the small, ripe, red fruit. As they walked along, Annie dropped each cherry pit at the side of the path while

Bradley spit his into the darkness.

"I grew up in Saratoga Springs," he said after his third cherry. "My father taught me to sail on Saratoga Lake when I was young."

"Your parents must miss you," she said.

Bradley winced in the darkness and grew quiet again. He popped another cherry in his mouth and chewed slowly. The road continued along the western hill, but the canal and railroad cut east, angling into the marsh. They stayed on the canal's towpath.

Bradley spit out another cherry pit and sighed in the darkness. "My father was an abolitionist," he said. "When the war started, he believed it was his duty to do what he could to help end slavery. He was one of the first men in Saratoga Springs to enlist. My mother cried when he left. He promised to write down his adventures and share the stories when he returned. Everyone thought the war would end in a few months... For my father, the war ended with his first battle. He died in the First Battle of Bull Run." Bradley looked up as if admiring how brilliantly the stars glittered in the night sky.

"Oh, Bradley," she said. "I'm sorry."

"A year after my father died, my mother was pressured into marrying his business partner. The man's wife died in childbirth, and he had young children who needed raising." Bradley's voice trailed off. "My mother was so busy tending to his children she never noticed that my new stepfather started hitting me. He said I brought the beatings on myself. That they would help turn me into a man."

"How old were you?"

"Eleven," Bradley said. "Then bruises appeared on my younger brother, so we ran away to my uncle's home. But my uncle had gone off to war as well, and my aunt couldn't feed both my brother and me. So... I left my brother there and headed south to join my uncle's unit as a drummer boy."

Annie crossed her arms as she walked, hugging herself. How horrible for Bradley and his brother. "What happened after the war?" Annie asked.

"My uncle died after I joined the battalion. After the war, I looked for my aunt and brother, but they had left with no forwarding address. I refused to return to Saratoga Springs, so I went to

LAKE SARATOGA

New York City and lived there on my own ever since."

Annie was speechless.

"More information than you wanted, I'm sure," Bradley said. He ate another cherry.

She reached out and clasped his hand. "I'm glad you told me. And I'm glad you are here with me now."

They lapsed into a comfortable silence. She hoped the feeling of her hand in his gave him as much comfort as it gave her. Annie looked out into the marsh to the right of the canal's towpath. Swampland occupied much of the land between Havana and Watkins. On the higher ground, gardens growing onions and celery flourished.

Around midnight, they reached the intersection of the canal towpath and Fourth Street in Watkins. Annie and Bradley turned left, heading toward town. After passing under the elevated rail lines of the Fall Brook Coal Company, they arrived at Frederick Davis's first Malthouse. Built in 1857, the large brick building sat between the road and the lake and was flanked by the Northern Central Railroad on its left and the Fall Brook Coal Company's trestleworks on its right. The tallest portion faced Fourth Street and towered seven or eight stories above them. A rectangular smokestack rose another four or five stories above the roof. The bulk of the building—five stories tall with a peaked roof and small windows—ran a couple hundred feet away from the road toward a short water channel providing access to the lake.

Bradley let out a low whistle. "It's going to take us a while to search that. We'll need a way in without being spotted by the night watchman." He turned to Annie. "Stay close," he whispered. Annie followed Bradley as he moved quickly to the left side of the building. There were no trees or shrubs to shield them from watching eyes, so they stayed close to the building in the moon's shadow. Crossing the length of the building, they reached the back corner close to the loading dock. Bradley peered his head around the corner and pulled it back quickly. "There is someone there," he whispered.

Annie peeked around the building to see a dark figure holding a lantern. The man stepped into the building and closed the door behind him. "He went inside," she said. She reached into her pocket to feel the comfort of her derringer.

"That was one of the Ballard brothers," Bradley said, grinning. "Come on." He moved quickly to the door the man had just entered. Bradley put his ear against it. Hearing nothing, he twisted the door handle. It turned, allowing the door to open a crack. As they slipped inside the building, the man with the light receded into the distance of the large building. Bradley reached out, grabbed Annie's hand, and led her into the darkness.

CHAPTER XLVII

THE HIDEOUT

Saturday, July 25, 1874

THE man's lantern bobbed up and down as he moved away from the entrance, leading Annie and Bradley deeper into the interior of the Malthouse. The only other illumination came from faint rays of moonlight passing through the building's small windows.

Bradley guided Annie around large storage tanks filled with water for soaking the barley. Or at least Bradley assumed that's what they were. In the darkness, it was difficult to tell. He tried to move quickly to keep the shadowy figure in sight but stopped abruptly when his foot landed on something unexpectedly soft. Annie bumped into his back as he considered unpleasant possibilities. Then he realized they must have crossed onto one of the Malthouse's growing floors. After soaking the barley to increase the grain's moisture content, workers spread it across growing floors and turned it regularly with large metal rakes or shovels until it germinated. Sprouting barley, six inches deep, filled much of the available floor space in a typical malthouse until it was time to send it to the kiln.

Bradley and Annie continued across the growing floor, their feet making shushing sounds. Aside from a slightly earthy, grassy scent, the barley below their feet did not give off much odor.

"He's gone," Annie whispered. The light ahead had winked out.

Bradley stopped again, worried that the Ballard brother had heard them following and snuffed out his light to ambush them in the dark. He listened to Annie breathing beside him. He could not tell if she was more nervous or excited, but he marveled at the feeling of her hand in his. She had not let go after he had reached for

Malt House Growing Floor

her entering the building. She had a lot of trust to follow him alone into this dark place when they both knew that someplace else— anyplace else—would be safer for her.

Faint thumping sounds came drifting through the large build-ing. "He's gone up the stairs," Annie whispered.

The levels above must contain more growing floors. They hadn't yet reached the far end of the building where the kilns dried freshly germinated grains or "green malt" giving the malt a lovely caramel or brown color. There was no good reason for the counter-feiters to operate printing presses near the kiln's heat.

They arrived at a flight of stairs and strained to listen, but the distant thumping sounds had stopped. As quietly as possible, they climbed to the second floor. The occasional creaky step caused Bradley to wince. Sound traveled far in the building's open spaces. The second level contained another dimly lit growing floor, but no signs of the man or his light. Bradley led Annie up the stairs to the third floor. More barley and more darkness. If the man had been here, he was gone now or had extinguished his light. On the fourth level, they stood in the darkness next to another thick carpet of barley. They heard and saw nothing.

Annie stood quietly next to him, still holding his hand. He gently pulled her closer. He could feel the heat of her body in the darkness. She wore no perfume, but the smell of her skin was in-toxicating. Even wearing the messenger's clothing, Annie smelled feminine, mysterious, and desirable. With a hint of cherries. Brad-ley's lips hovered dangerously close to her bare neck. He whispered in her ear, "Match?"

Annie let go of Bradley's hand and made rustling noises as she reached into her pocket and extracted the match safe he had given her near the *Ortus Solis*. She removed a wooden match and struck it once, twice, three times. The burst of light blinded him, and he cursed inwardly. He had been too distracted by thoughts of An-nie's smooth skin to remember to shield his eyes. He gave his head a small shake. He was fooling himself if he thought a woman like Annie would want anything to do with a man like Bradley once she knew his history.

Annie lifted the match over her head. Its feeble glow did not

extend far in the darkness, but they could see none of the barley
had been disturbed on the fourth floor. Annie turned and held the
match over the stairs leading to the attic. From the layer of dust on
the wooden steps, no one had passed that way recently. When the
flame reached her fingers, Annie extinguished it with two shakes
of her wrist and then dropped the remains of the wooden match to
the floor. She crushed it under her boot to ensure no spark endured.
Like everyone who lived in a town of wooden buildings, she feared
the flames taking hold and spreading.

Bradley and Annie descended the stairs to the third floor. He
looked away as she lit another match.

"There," Annie pointed.

A trail of footprints led through the barley heading back toward the lake end of the building. It could have been an old trail,
but workers with malt rakes turned the growing floors multiple
times a day. Someone created this trail after the workday's end. It
belonged to their quarry.

The match died out. Annie crushed the remains under her boot.

Treading carefully, they followed the faint trail through the
barley along the western wall of the Malthouse. When they approached the far wall, Annie lit another match. This wall was un-
broken except for one large door in front of them with the word
storage painted in crisp letters. Bradley tried the doorknob. It would
not open. He was prepared to pick the lock when Annie grabbed
his arm and pointed toward the ground. The trail of footsteps in
the barley turned before reaching the door and continued along the
wall. The man hadn't entered the storage room.

Bradley heard an exclamation from Annie as the match burned
her fingers, forcing her to drop the still lit match into the barley.
She stomped her foot in a panic to extinguish the flame and then
froze as the sound reverberated in the cavernous space. Neither
moved for a long minute. Then two. No unexpected noises came
from within the building. Bradley reached for Annie's hand again.
They followed the trail along the wall.

Two-thirds of the way across the building, the trail stopped
abruptly. Had the man doubled back using his own footprints?
They were not that far behind him. Bradley reached out and ran

his hands along the wall. He could find no latch or handle. He put his ear to the wall where the footsteps ended. Muffled sounds came from the other side. He repositioned himself and pressed his ear harder into the wooden wall, hoping to identify the noises. At that unlucky moment, one of the Ballard brothers pulled open the hidden door Bradley had been leaning on. Bradley lost his balance and fell into a well-lit room, knocking the Ballard brother over with him.

The man had been as surprised as Annie and Bradley.

As they fell, Bradley wrapped his arms around the man's waist and twisted to ensure Bradley landed on top. He heard a strangled *oof* as the air was knocked from the man's lungs. The man lay wheezing on the ground but managed to grab Bradley's jacket, preventing him from standing. A second Ballard brother stood beside one of two printing presses in the center of the room. Like his brother, he was in his late twenties, slim, and a few inches shorter than Bradley. The second brother jumped onto Bradley's back as the first hugged his leg. Bradley tried to reach his pistol, but the combined effort of the brothers toppled all three into a heap on the floor.

Bradley was stronger and more muscular, but it was two against one. The second brother got an arm around Bradley's neck while the first swung at his face. Bradley threw his head back, making the first man miss and striking the second man in the nose with a satisfying crunch. The second man howled while Bradley kicked the first in the ribs. It was a hard blow, and the man tried to crawl away toward the open doorway. Bradley grabbed him by the ankle and dragged him back. He could not see Annie but hoped she had fled for her safety. Bradley turned back to the second man to see the shadow of the large metal malt rake about to come down on his head.

"Stop."

Annie stepped into the room with her derringer pointing at the chest of the second brother. She had kept her wits and used her teenage male voice. The man let the malt rake drop to the floor and raised his hands. Blood covered the front of his shirt from his damaged nose. The first brother remained on the floor, holding his ribs.

They stared at Annie with dirty looks but made no effort to move.

Bradley stood up, dusted off his suit, and looked around. He was thrilled to see two printing presses occupying the center of the hidden room. He wasn't too late. They'd found the hideout! They'd found Sinclair's counterfeiting operation. A long table was set up along the wall, and several boxes of supplies were in the corner. Two cots with bedrolls were pushed against the far wall. The Ballard brothers were sleeping here while printing their perfect counterfeit hundred- and five-hundred-dollar bills. Carrying the presses up to the third floor must have taken a minor miracle, but if the brothers worked at night to avoid tipping off the malthouse workers, no one would ever think to search for them here.

Bradley stepped closer to the printing presses when he saw something that gave him a chill. In the shadows beyond the printing presses was a third cot and bedroll. The two brothers were not alone. Bradley spun back toward Annie just in time to see a third man lock the hammer back on his single-action revolver, pointing at Annie's head. From the man's features, it was obvious. There were three Ballard brothers.

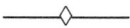

The cold gunmetal against Annie's temple triggered a sharp intake of breath. She held the air in her lungs, anticipating the bullet and the void that would follow. Her heart thumped so loudly that she wondered if Bradley could hear it from across the room. When a few seconds passed and death hadn't claimed her, Annie quietly blew the air out through her mouth. These men worked for whoever wanted to take her life, but they didn't recognize her in the messenger's clothes. The temporary reprieve was welcome, but she knew she was as good as dead if they figured out her real identity.

"Let the kid go," Bradley said nonchalantly. "I paid him a few coins to lead me to the Malthouse. That's all."

"Can't let him run for help." The third brother's voice came from behind Annie. "Your guns, please."

Annie lifted her arms higher, and the man plucked the derringer from her grasp and tucked it into a jacket pocket. Several oil lamps bathed the windowless room in a bright yellow glow. Annie looked at the two hand-operated printing presses and wondered if the factory owner knew about this secret room. If the owner was involved with the counterfeiting, maybe he was the person trying to kill her.

"Now, your gun," the man said to Bradley. His brothers pulled themselves together and stood within reach of Bradley to make sure he cooperated.

Annie looked toward Bradley and tried to read his expression. She saw shock, anger, and guilt pass across his handsome face. Then he offered her a determined smile, giving her strength, and turned defiant eyes toward the man holding the gun to her head.

The man recognized the look and sighed. He pulled his gun back a few inches so it no longer touched her skin. "No one has to die tonight," he said calmly.

Bradley hesitated, trying to judge the man's intentions, then relaxed and held his jacket open. The third brother handed his pistol to his closest brother and stepped forward to search Bradley's clothing. He pulled Bradley's new revolver out of his jacket and handed it to his other brother, who checked that it was loaded and pointed it back toward Bradley. Then, the man pulled a gold nugget from Bradley's pants pocket and let out a low whistle. "Pretty," he said.

"Keep it," Bradley told him. "It's brought nothing but bad luck."

The man considered the gold, appreciating the weight of it in his hand, then put the nugget back into Bradley's pocket. "I don't want your bad luck, and I don't want to give you any reason to follow us." He then searched Bradley's bag before turning to Annie.

She turned out her pockets before he reached her, but he still patted her down to make sure she had no hidden knives or guns. When he finished, he gave her an odd look before turning away.

"I know who you are," the man said.

Annie tensed, hearing the words, but realized he was looking at Bradley.

"Bradley Webster, isn't it," the man said. It wasn't a question. "Vance and Dewers warned us to be on the lookout for you. You have chosen dangerous men to make your enemies."

"You have me at a disadvantage," Bradley said. "Which Ballard brother are you?"

"Tom," the man said. "And that's Bill holding my gun. Looks like you might have broken George's nose. One more for your enemies list, I'm afraid."

"Self-defense," Bradley said with a shrug. "Say, is Dewers a large man? No sense of humor? Questionable hygiene and a mustache like a walrus?"

The corners of Tom Ballard's mouth turned upward. "That's about right," he said.

"Yeah, we're not friends. I call him the Walrus," Bradley said. "But you should be more worried about your own health and well-being. You're all working for a man who does not like loose ends when a job is finished."

"What does that mean?" George Ballard asked Bradley.

"I know you three work for Alistair Sinclair, but he also has a silent partner. Either Sinclair or his partner is the Butzemann."

The other two Ballard brothers looked confused, but Annie saw recognition in Tom's eyes.

"The Butzemann is a myth," Tom said. "A ghost story criminals tell at night to scare each other."

"What is he talking about?" Bill Ballard said, confused.

"What's a Butzemann?" George asked.

"You've had two months," Bradley said, "with those printing presses and your stolen boxes of official blank banknote paper. Two months means you had a lot of time to make perfect one hundred and five-hundred-dollar bills. You should be nearly done by now. That means the Butzemann has gotten what he wanted out of you. That is when he starts tying up loose ends. You three are loose ends." Bradley paused as he looked each brother in the eye. "You know that both Vance and Smythe are already dead?"

Bill's expression soured. George looked like he was going to be ill.

"Who are you," Tom asked, "and why are you here?" His voice had gained a hard edge.

"I came for the money and for the Butzemann," Bradley admitted.

Annie was surprised at Bradley's answer. A man with his own

agenda and a sign that she didn't know him as well as she thought.

"You're too late." Tom looked about the room as if he had lost something.

"What do you mean?" Bradley asked.

"I mean, you are too late. The money is gone." All three brothers were agitated. "We've been using this location since before the barley growing season started," Tom said. "Paid off the foreman of the Malthouse to let us build this secret room, and Bill got a job as the night watchman. That let us come and go after dark as we pleased. We look alike enough that in the dark, no one knew there were three of us. In the last two months, we've printed ten million dollars in one hundred and five-hundred-dollar bills. About once a week, Vance or Dewers showed up to take the finished bills away, promising we would get our percentage at the end." Tom started pacing as he talked. "Tonight, after the last malthouse workers went home, Dewers showed up. He told us he'd arranged for a special dinner at the Jefferson House for all our hard work. Said he would keep watch while we enjoyed our meal. The last pile of counterfeit bills and the printing plates were gone when we returned. So was Dewers."

Annie knew she should act like a disinterested teenage boy but couldn't help herself. "If you can't print any more money, why are you still here?"

Tom Ballard turned to look at her. "I want to convince Sinclair to let us keep printing money. I perfected the ink and figured out how to reproduce the fiber paper. If we had the plates, we could print money indefinitely—making everyone involved filthy rich."

"Or," Bradley said, "they will send someone to clean up this operation and everyone involved."

"When I opened the door, you attacked me," Bill Ballard said. "I thought you might be here to kill us." His grip on his brother's revolver tightened.

Bradley's laugh surprised everyone. "I fell into the room, and then you and your brother jumped me. You have nothing I want. We are no threat to you."

Tom Ballard sighed. He looked to his brothers and then nodded, coming to a decision. He turned to Annie and Bradley. "Would you agree that if I wanted to kill you, you would be dead already?"

Bradley and Annie nodded cautiously.

"Good," Tom said. "We are counterfeiters, not killers. Here is what is going to happen. Since I still don't trust you, we will tie the two of you to one of these printing presses. That will give us time to pack up everything of value and leave Watkins before sunrise. You are on your own after that. You may or may not be right about the Butzemann, but it is not worth risking our lives."

George had Annie and Bradley sit beside the nearest printing press and tied them to one of the press's cast-iron legs. As George stood up, Bradley asked a question that Annie had been wondering about herself. "Tom, if you and your brothers are so good at counterfeiting, where did Smythe fit in?"

"Smythe set up the printing presses after we hauled all the parts up here," Tom said. "He could run a press, but printing money is an art. You can't just slap ink on the plates. It takes a lot of skill to get everything exactly right. Smythe barely had the skills."

"Is that where Pickens came in?"

Tom Ballard seemed surprised at the mention of Thomas Pickens. He shrugged. "Smythe started drinking. He ruined a few sheets of paper, so I took over printing and let him focus on maintaining the presses when needed. Then he just stopped showing up altogether. I assumed he climbed into a whiskey bottle and drank himself to death. Vance wanted to bring in someone else, but my brothers and I had everything running smoothly by then. We didn't need Pickens."

The brothers ignored them after that and began packing everything in sight.

The excitement of almost dying multiple times that night finally caught up with Annie. She yawned and shook her head, trying to stay awake, but exhaustion washed over her. She leaned against Bradley and fought to keep her eyes open. As she drifted off to sleep, she heard his whisper in her ear. "I'll get you out of this."

She woke up several hours later with her head still on Bradley's shoulder. For an embarrassing moment, she worried that she had drooled on him in her sleep. She discreetly checked his shoulder, relieved to see it dry, then looked around. The room was empty except for the two printing presses, a small wooden crate with parts and tools for the printing presses, an abandoned table and chair, and Tom Ballard. A lone oil lamp burned in the corner.

"It's almost sunrise," Tom said. "We are leaving, but the workday will start here shortly. Yell loud enough, and the workers will hear you when they arrive to rake the barley."

"What if Dewers returns first?" Annie asked. From the expression on Tom's face, he didn't think that was his problem. "You aren't killers," she said, "but you might as well be if you leave us tied up for Dewers."

Tom cursed under his breath. He pulled his revolver out of his pocket as his brother George entered the room. "We're going to move them to the storage closet," Tom said. "Dewers won't bother checking there." George looked confused but nodded. He cut away the ropes and led Annie and Bradley at gunpoint onto the growing floor. The first glimmers of sunrise leaked through the eastern windows. Bill Ballard stood nearby with the malt rake, ready to follow them and remove all traces of their trail through the barley.

"Tie their hands in front of them," Tom told George. "Mister Webster is the resourceful type, and I'd like as much of a head start as possible."

"Tom," Bradley said, "Do you know who Sinclair's silent partner might be?"

Tom shook his head. "Never met anyone else involved besides Sinclair, Smythe, Vance, and Dewers."

When George finished tying the ropes, he opened the storage room door and handed Tom the key. Tom thanked him. "You and Bill get the wagon ready," Tom said to his brother. "Leave the rake, and I'll be right behind you."

Malthouse equipment filled the storage room from floor to ceiling, leaving almost no room for Bradley and Annie to stand. Tom shoved Bradley in first. Then Annie. Before he closed the door, he reached into his pocket and pulled out Annie's derringer. He took out the single bullet and then tucked it into her jacket. "A lady should have protection," he said. Before she could say thank you, he reached out and snatched the hat off her head. Her long brown hair dropped past her shoulders. "I thought so," he said triumphantly.

Bradley tried to shove himself forward to protect Annie, but Tom Ballard pushed him back.

"Relax," Tom said, "I already told you. I'm a counterfeiter, not a killer. Besides, I think you may be right about the Butzemann. Something odd about this job. Made no sense to use five-hundred-dollar plates when five-dollar bills are much easier to shove. A shame. Best work I've ever done." He tossed in Bradley's bag and then dropped Annie's hat near her feet. Without another word, he closed the storage door. They heard the lock turn in the keyhole and then muffled footsteps receded through the barley.

With little room to maneuver, Annie and Bradley pressed against each other awkwardly inside the pitch-black storage room. Bradley tried to shift his hands so they would not push into her hip. "I'm sorry," he muttered. Annie was unsure if he was apologizing for his hands or how the evening had turned out.

"At least we're still alive," she said.

"That's true," Bradley admitted. "Now, we just need to get out of here so we can stay that way." Bradley tried again to move his body. He lifted his bound hands, searching to find a comfortable position. He raised them over Annie's head, paused momentarily, and brought them down behind her back, trapping her in his embrace. Annie could feel the warmth of his chest against hers. She felt his breath on her cheek. She could feel his heart beating. *Can he feel mine beating faster?* she wondered to herself. She should be chastising him for being so forward, yet she felt safe and warm. She didn't mind waiting in this position for the workers to arrive.

Sunlight began squeezing under the door, allowing Annie to see the outlines of Bradley's face. She looked up and, as she did so, felt him pressing into her. He leaned forward. She felt the weight of his body pushing her against the door. She welcomed it and tilted her face upwards. He leaned forward a bit more, and she pushed up from her toes and pressed her lips against his. As he kissed her back and tightened his arms around her, a warm sensation flooded her entire body.

Suddenly, she heard a click from behind her, and the door popped open, breaking their connection. She stumbled backward and ducked out of his embrace. He had a stunned expression on his face. Annie looked down at his hands. He'd pulled out one of her hairpins and used it to pick the lock on the door. That is why he put his arms around her and leaned forward. He was not trying to kiss her at all.

"Annie?" Bradley stepped out of the storage room and reached for her with his bound hands. She stepped away, too mortified to even look at him.

"Nice work with the lock," Annie said, as if nothing had happened. "We'd better untie each other and get out of here."

Bradley hesitated, then nodded. "Here, let me help," he said. They made short work of the knots, and then Annie bent down to pick up her hat. After she shoved as much of her hair back into it as possible, she turned and practically ran for the stairs. Bradley grabbed his bag and hustled to catch up to her.

The sun had cleared the eastern hills as they stepped out onto Fourth Street. Industrious farmers passed by on wagons, but no malthouse workers had arrived yet. Annie could feel Bradley's eyes on her, but she refused to turn her head as they started walking down Fourth Street. They were less than a mile from her house. After a few minutes, Bradley spoke up. "Hey, can we—"

"Brady Wheelan!"

Annie and Bradley turned to see a carriage pulling up beside them with two large men inside. She turned to Bradley, who looked like a man who had accidentally sunk his whole foot into fresh horse manure.

"Are you kidding me?" he said to himself. "Of all the rotten luck, the O'Donnell brothers find me here?"

Declan O'Donnell stepped out of the carriage not twenty feet away. "We're going to beat your sorry ass and your friend's too," he said. Declan's brother, Fergus, came around to stand next to him.

Bradley turned to Annie. "Time to run!"

Annie raced off, heading down the railroad track. It would lead to the waterfront, where there might be places for them to hide. Her legs felt strong, and she was confident she and Bradley could outrun the larger men. She turned her head and realized that she ran alone. She looked back toward the street. Bradley had run toward the men to give her time to get away. Bradley got in a few good punches—giving better than he got—until his foot caught in a deep rut in the dirt road, allowing one of the brothers to tackle him to the ground. They punched him a few more times and threw him into the carriage.

Annie stood in shock, watching the carriage race down Franklin Street, carrying Bradley to an unknown fate. Annie touched her lips. She could still feel the warmth of Bradley's lips on hers.

CHAPTER XLVIII

Past Revisited

Saturday, July 25, 1874

BRADLEY recognized the awnings of the Fall Brook House on Third and Franklin as the O'Donnell brothers dragged him into the building. He could barely keep his head up. One of the brothers explained to the manager that Bradley had been drinking all night, and they were helping him to bed. Nothing to worry about.

They dragged him to a well-appointed room and tied Bradley to one of the chairs. The O'Donnells took turns hitting him until their hands got tired. Bradley spit blood onto the floor. He ran his tongue along his teeth and was happy they were still there, although one or two felt loose. Vain of him, but he hoped to keep his teeth. Given what the O'Donnells thought he was guilty of, he might have another body part to worry about.

At least Annie was safe.

"How did you find me?" Bradley asked, trying to get them talking.

Declan hit Bradley again in the stomach.

The blow knocked the air out of him, and he gasped for breath. Their punches had opened the wound on his forehead he'd gotten fighting Vance. Blood dripped into his eye.

Fergus was always the more talkative brother. "You sent a telegram from Ithaca to your friend with the tattoos," he said. "That telegram told us you were here in Watkins. It was just a matter of driving around until we found you."

Declan took a towel and wiped the blood from Bradley's face. "You can bring her in now."

Fergus stepped out, leaving Bradley alone with Declan. The

man was an Irish dockworker with thinning red hair. Fergus was part of a matching set, although his brown hair was fuller. They belonged to a large Irish-Catholic family.

"This is just a misunderstanding," Bradley said, looking at Declan. "Perhaps we can discuss it over a pint of ale? I'll be happy to buy, of course." Bradley remembered that Watkins was now a dry town. He could not catch a break.

"Shut up," Declan said, backhanding him.

A few minutes later, the hotel door swung open, and an attractive woman stepped in, holding a squirming toddler. Fergus followed behind and closed the door. "Declan," she said, "are you finally going to tell me what this is all—" She made eye contact with Bradley and gasped at his bloody, swollen face. All the while, she bounced her toddler up and down.

"Hello, Maud," Bradley said. "You look as beautiful as always." He tried for a smile, but his split lip made it difficult.

"Oh. Oh—" Maud looked at her brothers. "Please let him go. I don't want this." Her baby fidgeted in Maud's arms.

"We wanted you to see Brady's lying face one last time," Fergus said.

Declan looked at his sister and his little niece. His voice took on a sing-song tone to avoid upsetting the baby. "Brady needs to understand that no one messes with the O'Donnell family. He will apologize to you, and then you and little Fiona can go back to your room while Fergus and I make sure Brady here learns from his mistakes."

Bradley saw Maud's lower lip quivering. Her daughter, Fiona had her red hair. "Maud," he said. "I'm sorry." And he meant it, but not for the reasons her brothers thought.

Maud started crying. Her daughter Fiona, all pudgy folds and chubby cheeks, cried with her.

Fergus threw a punch that Bradley didn't see coming. His head snapped back, and he saw stars. Fergus hit harder than Declan. That one really hurt.

"That's for seducing and despoiling our sister and then abandoning her," Fergus said. He spit in Bradley's direction in disgust.

"Stop," Maud begged her brothers. "This isn't right." Maud

tried to grab Fergus's arm as he pulled back for another blow. Declan made cooing noises to calm Fiona.

There was a knock on the door.

"Go away," Declan yelled. "We're busy."

"I've brought the extra towels," a muffled voice said from the other side of the door.

"I didn't ask for any damn towels," Declan said. He looked at his brother, who shrugged. Neither brother had requested towels.

"Please, sir," the male voice said from the hallway. "I'll get in trouble if I don't deliver them."

Declan stepped toward the door. He used his large body to block the view of the room as he unlocked the door and turned the doorknob.

The door burst open, knocking Declan backward. Abraham Adams rushed in with Annie right behind him. Annie stepped forward and pointed her derringer directly into Declan's face. "Don't move," she said in a voice that sounded like she was begging for him to move and give her an excuse to shoot him. She looked wild in her messenger's clothes, with long brown hair spilling out of her hat. She was the most beautiful sight Bradley had ever seen.

Everyone in the room froze. Even the baby stopped crying... for three seconds. Then Fiona launched into a full-throated wail.

Annie took in the scene as Abraham closed the door behind them. She pointed to Fergus. "You. Untie him," she demanded.

Bradley was shocked and impressed that Annie had found him so quickly. He suddenly realized something that neither O'Donnell brother knew. There was no way Annie had time to find ammunition for her derringer. She was threatening these two men with an empty gun.

"Now, wait a minute," Declan said, not taking his eyes off the derringer. "We have no beef with you. But this man..." he said, pointing to Bradley. "This bastard took advantage of our sister and left her with child. Then just disappeared. He is not worth your time. Just leave us alone with him."

Bradley saw the gun in Annie's hands waver a tiny bit.

Maud cleared her throat. "Declan. Fergus. Just stop. You can't kill him. He's—"

"The father of your baby!" Declan said.

Annie's gun wavered a bit more.

"Fiona has a new father now," Declan said. "And Ciaran is a good man. Old Brady's part in our niece's life is over. No one will miss him."

Maud started crying again. With all eyes on Annie, Bradley strained to reach into his left boot for his knife.

"Regardless of what he deserves," Annie said, with a voice that implied she was wondering if he did deserve what he was getting. "I can't let you kill him."

Fergus stepped next to Declan. Suddenly, both men had knives in their hands. They took a menacing step toward Annie. "You can only shoot one of us with that pistol," Declan said.

Abraham stepped in front of Annie while Maud stared down her brothers. "Stop," said Maud in an exhausted voice and tears streaming down her face. "You can't kill Brady. He isn't Fiona's father."

Declan's face reddened as he pointed to Bradley. "He—"

"Fiona is not his child," Maud said louder. She choked, trying to get her next words out. "I lied."

Declan and Fergus dropped their knives to their sides.

"What are you saying?" Fergus said.

"Brady is not the father. Fiona's real father is—"

"Conor Murphy," Bradley said, interrupting Maud. "I'm sorry that I lied too. Conor was a friend of mine who worked with me at the theater. Had red hair like Fiona. A real charmer. After he took advantage of Maud and found out she was with child, he—well, he ran. Asked me to tell her he wasn't the marrying kind. I felt so bad that I convinced her to tell everyone that the baby was mine."

"Why would you do that?" Declan said.

"She's beautiful," Bradley said. "What man wouldn't be lucky to marry her?" Bradley could see the brothers nodding in agreement. He also noticed a shadow passing over Annie's face. He pushed on. "After I met your lovely family, I knew I wasn't ready to be a father. I— I ran away too. I'm so sorry, Maud. I know I left you in a tough spot."

Declan looked confused and then disappointed. He needed

something to focus his rage on. "Where's this Conor Murphy now?"

"California, last I heard," Bradley said. "The coward took off the day he heard you and your brother were looking for me—and what you were telling people you were going to do when you found me. He knew you wouldn't give up searching. He also knew I would eventually rat him out."

Declan turned to Maud. "Is this true?"

Maud's eyes had gone wide. She stared at Bradley, who nodded in encouragement. "I-I was so ashamed," she said. "Brady was only trying to help." She continued crying while trying to comfort her daughter. Any remaining anger her brothers held faded away.

"Ah, now, come on," Fergus said, "you're upsetting the baby."

Declan backhanded Bradley once more. "That's for being a weak man and for being a rat. What kind of friend is that? You are lucky our mate Ciaran was more of a man than you. Stepped up and married Maud."

Declan untied Bradley. He pulled him up and pushed him toward Annie and Abraham. "He's all yours."

Bradley landed on his knees next to Abraham. Lack of sleep and a solid thrashing will drain a man. Abraham helped him to his feet. Bradley looked back and locked eyes with Maud. "Maud," he said, "have a good life." He heard a mumbled thank you as Abraham guided him out of the room. Annie backed out behind them, still pointing her derringer at the brothers.

As the door shut, they could hear Fergus's voice. "I told you Fiona didn't look anything like Brady."

Annie tucked the derringer into her pocket. Bradley could see her shaking. He put his hand on her shoulder. "You were amazing."

"Can you walk?" Abraham asked Bradley. "If so, I'm going to bring the wagon around to the front of the hotel."

Bradley nodded, and Abraham hurried away. Annie tucked her hair back into her hat and kept her head down as they walked through the lobby of the Fall Brook House. She didn't want anyone to recognize her. Bradley pulled his jacket closed, trying to hide the bloodstains on his shirt.

"How did you know I was here?" he asked as they passed through the lobby unnoticed and stepped out the front entrance into

NEW YORK THEATER

the daylight.

Annie looked distracted. Her eyes focused on something far away. "I recognized their carriage came from the Fall Brook's livery," she said. "I ran to Abraham's house and found him hitching Goldie to the wagon. We raced over and asked for the room number of the two big Irishmen. The towel delivery idea was all I could think of on short notice."

"Thank you," Bradley said, "you—"

"Was any of that true?" Annie asked, interrupting him. She looked at the bruises and cuts on his face, then held his eyes with hers.

"About the baby and Maud?" Bradley asked. "Mostly... no."

"Who is the real father?"

"Her husband, Ciaran is the real father."

"What? That doesn't make sense." A group of vacationers passed by, so Annie and Bradley stepped closer to the street, avoiding the flow of people.

"I promise I'll tell you the entire story later," Bradley said. His head was starting to feel fuzzy.

"Tell me now," Annie insisted.

Seeing the resolve in Annie's eyes, he nodded. "I lived in a theater in New York," he said. "I helped clean up and maintain the place for room and board. Maud was one of the dancers. After a show one night, I found her crying on the sidewalk. She had fallen in love with Declan's best friend, Ciaran, and one thing led to another. She had learned she was pregnant. But... Maud's brothers had already threatened Ciaran with death if he ever laid a hand on her. If Maud and Ciaran ran away, she would never see her family again. If they stayed, she would have a ruined reputation, and the love of her life and the father of her child would likely meet an untimely end. So, I offered a third choice. We pretended I was her new boyfriend, Brady Whelan. She brought me around to meet the family. After a week, I disappeared, and she told her family I had forced myself on her and left her pregnant. She was disgraced— soiled so no one would want to marry her. No one except Ciaran who was in on the plan. He stepped in and proposed, promising to raise the child as his own. It all worked out. Except I underestimated her brothers' commitment to seeking revenge."

"That's—" Annie started.

"Inspired?" Bradley offered.

"The most foolish thing I've ever heard," Annie finished. "So, there's no Conor?"

"No," Bradley admitted. "I made him up on the spot."

"So, you lied to everyone?"

Bradley bristled at the criticism. "I made sure," he said, "that little Fiona would grow up with her real father."

Annie leaned into the street, looking for Abraham's wagon. "Maud was very beautiful," she said, almost offhandedly.

Bradley started to agree, then caught himself. "I suppose," he said. "But she's not my type."

Annie looked into Bradley's eyes as if judging him.

"I would never lie to you," he said.

"That sounds like something you'd tell a woman after you've lied to her."

Before Bradley could respond, a large shadow loomed over them. Bradley stepped in front of Annie. The Walrus—Dewers—stood before them, smiling an evil smile.

"You look like shit," he said to Bradley. This pleased the Walrus very much. He leaned closer. "I told you I'd find out who you were." Bradley had a sinking feeling. "Miss Anderson, we haven't had the pleasure yet." Annie remained still. Her disguise hadn't fooled the Walrus. "Did your new friend tell you where the money came from for those fancy clothes of his? Someone paid him to murder a man in prison in New York a few weeks ago. Then he escaped." The Walrus's smile grew wider. "His real name is Bradford Whitey. I would be careful with this one if I were you." He tipped his hat toward Annie and laughed aloud as he continued down the sidewalk.

Annie turned to Bradley as Abraham pulled the wagon up in front of them. He wanted to explain, but he saw the look on her face. She had seen the truth in what the Walrus said. "Bradley? Brady? Bradford? Who are you?" Her voice had gotten small. She didn't wait for him to answer. "I believed in you, but now I realize I don't know you." She looked up into the sky and then back at Bradley. "We should part ways here." Annie jumped into the wagon, leaving Bradley on the sidewalk. "It's over. We've lost. There are no clues left to find." She turned away. "Good day, sir."

Abraham looked at Bradley in confusion. Bradley shrugged and waved Abraham along. As Goldie started in motion, Bradley heard Abraham's voice as the carriage gained momentum. "You just saved his life."

"Yes," came Annie's bitter reply. "And now we're even."

Bradley stood alone on the sidewalk, watching them drive away. The midmorning heat and the beatings left him lightheaded. Could his luck get any worse?

He heard a voice approaching. "Sir, do you need assistance?" He turned to see a beautiful girl with dimples smiling at him. It was the girl from the Montour House who had served him coffee.

CHAPTER XLIX

MELANCHOLY

Monday, July 27, 1874

A NNIE stayed locked in her house, where she'd remained hidden away since returning from Fall Brook House Saturday morning. Nana had been so relieved to see her, she'd forgotten to scold Annie for staying out all night dressed as a teenage boy. "When you didn't return," Nana said, "I had to send the messenger boy home with Roland's old suit. He was excited to have clothes to grow into, but he wants his boots back." Nana was surprised by the look of disappointment on Annie's face. "It's not like you will ever need to dress like a boy again."

Annie's grandmother would never understand the freedom she'd felt pretending to be someone else walking the canal with Bradley. Now, all Annie could do was wander through the house like a bird trapped in a gilded cage. She couldn't even enjoy the view from her favorite seat—a burgundy velvet upholstered armchair of carved walnut that looked down on the village and Seneca Lake through a sun-soaked parlor window. Annie had spent her youth looking out that window but now couldn't even peek around the curtain for fear of would-be murderers with moderate rifle skills.

Her only connection to the outside world now came midmornings when Abraham stopped to check on her.

Annie looked about the parlor and breathed in slowly, capturing the moment in her memory. The scent of wildflowers—brought in every few days by her grandmother—mixed with the faded smell of Glendon's pipe tobacco blend and the beeswax and linseed oil used to polish the furniture.

Across the room, Sheriff Swartwood's youngest deputy sat in her father's favorite armchair, waiting to catch her eye so he could politely strike up a conversation. Naïve but enthusiastic, Deputy Hodgkins was pleasant enough and probably didn't deserve the bitterness Annie harbored for his presence in the house. The deputy was only doing his job—waiting for Roland to die or recover enough to arrest him and send him to prison or the gallows. Hodgkins had found the leg irons Roland used on Bradley and bound the unconscious man to the bed. It made his job of watching Roland easier but did not endear the deputy to Annie.

"Lovely evening, isn't it, Miss Anderson?"

Annie tried to be polite, but the question annoyed her. Did he not notice she never went outside?

"Your grandmother is fixing rabbit stew for dinner this evening," he said, undeterred. "Will you be joining us?" The deputy had already gained a few pounds from Nana's cooking.

Annie shook her head as the sliding doors to the back parlor opened. Nana stepped through and closed the doors behind her. She had been watching over Roland. When Magee's caretaker and his men brought Roland home, they couldn't risk carrying him up the stairs to his bedroom. Instead, the back parlor became a makeshift hospital room.

"How is he?" Annie asked, fearful of the answer.

Nana shook her head. "Roland's breathing is more ragged, and his color... he is getting worse, Annie. I'm sorry," Nana said, "but we must prepare ourselves for the worst."

Annie's eyes watered, but the tears did not come. The deputy looked away, embarrassed to be present for such a personal family moment.

"I'll sit with him for a while," Annie said. She stood up and passed through the doors into the back parlor. Roland lay unmoving in a bed that filled the center of the room. As she stepped closer, she inhaled the sickly-sweet smell of carbolic acid—diligently applied to Roland's dressings to prevent the putrefaction of his wound. *At least he looked peaceful*, Annie thought. She took his hand and leaned forward to whisper encouraging words into his ear. When Annie heard the back parlor doors opening again, she squeezed Roland's hand and turned to see Deputy Hodgkins enter the room.

"Just making my rounds," he said apologetically.

Annie nodded. She laid Roland's hand back at his side and excused herself. Retreating from the parlor, she climbed the long staircase to the second floor. When she reached her bedroom, she closed the door and locked it behind her.

How many times would she climb the stairs and enter her bedroom before it was the last time? Not many now. Annie looked about her room, trying to memorize every detail. She had come to a decision. During the Firehouse Charity Auction at the opera house tomorrow night, Annie would flee Watkins. Everyone who is anyone had gotten an invitation and would be there. Nana was going, so Annie could give her grandmother the dress made to be donated and then slip away into the night. No long goodbyes. Annie couldn't bear the thought.

She picked the tin box off the bed, the worn metal cold in her hands. Her grandmother had been apologetic when she'd given it to Annie that morning. "I'm sorry I only remembered this today. Glendon wanted me to give this to you if anything happened to him." Nana paused as her voice caught in her throat. "I never expected to outlive him."

Glendon's tin box contained a note, a photographic print, and enough money for Annie to run away and invest in a dress shop in a new city. She opened the box and stared at the picture first. The card-mounted photograph bearing the name of a photographer's studio in Watkins was taken when Annie was a teenager. She had followed Glendon on a portrait appointment, and at the last second, he encouraged her to jump into the frame. She was thrilled, which explained her silly grin in the photo.

Annie read the note again and wiped the tears from her eyes. Her decision to seek the truth about the dead man in the cemetery, to "question everything," had led to Roland being wounded and clinging to life, Glendon missing or dead, and Annie about to run for her life. She would spend the rest of her life looking over her shoulder, not knowing who to trust or who might want to kill her. She would give anything now to reunite her family.

Annie returned the note and the photo to the box with the money and reluctantly sat down in front of her sewing machine. She needed to finish the dress to donate for the auction. The skirt was done, but the bodice remained. She picked up fabric for the bodice's sleeves and felt the smoothness of the silk taffeta between her fingertips. She set to her task and let herself get lost in the work. Sewing calmed her.

Hours later, Annie held up the finished bodice and set it aside. She would apply the remaining flourishes—the extra lace and ruffles—in the morning. Looking out the window, the darkness surprised her. She stood and raised her hands over her head, loosening her shoulders. She straightened her sewing area and headed downstairs to check on her grandmother and Roland.

Annie found Nana sleeping upright in her favorite chair in the parlor. She noticed the empty glass and the half-empty bottle of whisky on the table beside her grandmother. "Oh, Nana." The back parlor door remained open. Annie saw the deputy's feet. He was sound asleep on a sofa.

Annie checked on Roland and then roused her grandmother.

"Oh, dear," she said. "I must have dozed off." Nana looked at her granddaughter through blurry eyes. "Help me to my bed, won't you, dear?"

Annie helped Nana to her feet, and then her grandmother placed a hand on Annie's arm to steady herself. Together, they exited the parlor and reached the bottom of the long stairway. Nana looked up, annoyed. The climb personally offended her on nights she had been drinking.

"Will you be all right after I leave?" Annie asked as they started up the wooden stairs together. Nana knew Annie planned to leave, but not when. Annie worried that her grandmother would struggle without her help around the house.

"I'll be fine," Nana said. "Mrs. Casey will return in a week to take over the cooking and the housekeeping. She will be sorry she missed you." Nana paused to catch her breath halfway up the stairs. She turned her head to look at Annie. "Just promise me that wherever you end up, you will find yourself a man worth marrying. The sooner, the better."

"No," Annie said, surprising them both with the force of her reply. "If I ever get married, I'll do so when the time is right for me."

Nana looked away and then continued up the stairs. "When I

was your age," she said grumpily, "I was married with a two-year-old."

"Nana, why is it so important to you that I be married off?"

Nana paused a few steps from the top. "Your mother's death broke me," she said quietly. "But I had to be strong. For you." She reached into her pocket, retrieved a crumpled handkerchief, and dabbed her eyes. She put it away with shaking hands. "I had to raise a child when I only wanted to spoil you as your grandmother. I had no choice. I promised myself I would keep you safe and raise you to be a woman your mother would be proud of." Nana squeezed Annie's arm gently. "And you are that woman. But I cannot rest until you have a husband to care for you. Then my job will be done." Nana inhaled slowly and exhaled. "Now, help me up these damn stairs."

"I can take care of myself. You can stop worrying about me."

Her grandmother laughed. "It doesn't work that way, child. I'll never stop worrying about you." When they reached the top landing, Nana turned to Annie. "But Annie, I'm glad you are leaving."

"What!?"

Wisps of gray hair framed the deepening wrinkles on Nana's face. "My dear, you've talked about leaving since you were a teenager. You've wanted to go on adventures, and something has stopped you each time."

"I don't know what you mean."

"Why did you choose Elmira Female College? You could have chosen Vassar in Poughkeepsie or Oberlin in Ohio."

"To be closer to home..."

"And didn't you tell me Glendon offered to take you to Europe or India just a week ago?"

"Yes, but—"

"Annie, you want to go on adventures but are afraid to leave. Don't pretend that I'm the one who is holding you back."

They shuffled down the hallway and into Nana's bedroom. After lighting an oil lamp, Annie threw back the covers, and Nana collapsed onto the bed, groaning with pleasure. Annie covered her with a light blanket.

"Annie, you know I love you. I don't say it as much as I should."

Annie was sure now that her grandmother was drunk. Sober, she never shared her feelings so directly.

"I love you, too, Nana. Do you want your sleeping elixir?"

"No, dear. It is downstairs anyway." Annie dimmed the light and prepared to close the door. "The dress you are making," Nana said in the darkness, "it's your best yet. I'm sure Emma Magee will fight over it with that friend of hers."

What friend? "Who, Nana?"

"Elizabeth Sinclair."

Why would the Sinclairs still be in town? "Are you sure?"

"Yes," Nana said with a yawn. "Emma Magee mentioned it after church yesterday. The Sinclairs are helping organize the auction."

Before Annie could ask any more questions, Nana's breathing settled into a steady rhythm. There would be no waking her until morning.

Annie stood in the hallway, her mind racing. *If Alistair Sinclair had finished printing his counterfeit money, why stay in town? Why not take the money and run? Was something going to happen at the auction? Was the auction a front for disposing of the money? Or the plates?* Annie shook her head. That seemed unnecessarily complicated.

Whoever wanted her dead knew about Maurice Vance and the counterfeiting ring. And the only two people left in town involved in counterfeiting were Alistair Sinclair and his bodyguard, the Walrus. They had to know why someone was trying to kill her. What if she confronted them in a crowded place? Like an auction? Was it worth the risk? If Annie could figure out who wanted her dead and why, she could reclaim her life.

Annie headed back downstairs to sit with Roland. She had a lot to think about before sleep claimed her.

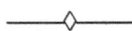

Annie woke after a short night. With a yawn, she forced herself out of bed and got to work putting the finishing touches on the charity auction dress. As she filled a new bobbin, she couldn't shake the feeling that she had overlooked some small but significant detail from the last two weeks. It nagged at her like a burr under a saddle. Something she had seen or perhaps heard? Annie sighed. Maybe the unsettled feeling came from realizing this was her last morning in Watkins.

Annie pressed down on the sewing machine treadle and focused on what she knew. This mystery started with Crawford's body in Glenwood Cemetery. Someone had lured him to Watkins with hints of found gold. Someone who knew the Southerner well enough to know that his greed would be his undoing. That person had to be a member of the Lucky Six or someone who knew one of the Lucky Six well. Had one of them survived? Or was it a spouse, a sibling, or a son or daughter? According to the journal, Annie's father was the only member of the group to have a child before the war ended ten years ago. Not a child, then.

There also had to be a Lucky Six link to the counterfeiting operation. Sinclair was up to his eyeballs in the counterfeiting ring, but was he the link to the Lucky Six? Could Sinclair be Corporal Taylor returning to punish Glendon for taking the gold? Had Glendon met Sinclair? Annie did not think so. She wondered how to check if Sinclair had a Lucky Six tattoo. Would Elizabeth have shared that information with her friend Emma Magee? That would be an awkward conversation to have.

Nana hollered from the bottom of the stairs. "Annie, come down for breakfast."

Annie set aside her sewing and finished dressing. As she passed Glendon's room, she felt doubts creeping back into her thoughts. Could she trust that Glendon wasn't lying to her? And what about George Magee? He and Sinclair knew each other through their wives. Was George involved with the counterfeiting and collaborating with the sheriff to suppress information related to the murder in the cemetery? Annie shook her head. Too many questions. Why was Elizabeth Sinclair sneaking around? What was her role in all this? And then there was Bradley. A man who wasn't who he pretended to be. A murderer, not a gentleman. He'd been lying to her all along.

"Good morning, dear!" Nana said with a smile as Annie entered the dining room. Regardless of how much her grandmother drank, Nana always arose early the next day, appearing none the worse for wear. Annie sat down to a plate of flapjacks and a bowl of fresh fruit. Before she could start eating, her grandmother dropped a package wrapped in brown paper and tied with string in front of her.

"What is this?"

"I don't know, dear, but it has your name on it."

Annie brushed off the cobwebs attached to the package and turned it over several times. Someone had written her name on one side in pencil with confident penmanship. There were no other markings.

"Where did you find it?" Annie asked.

"Taking up space on the side table right here in the dining room."

Annie frowned. She vaguely remembered either Bradley or Abraham holding a similar package. But why was her name on it? She untied the string and tugged at the brown paper, trying not to rip anything in case she had to rewrap the package later. She set the paper aside and looked at the box in her hands. Still confused, she opened the lid. Her eyes went wide, and her mouth opened involuntarily.

"What is it, Annie?"

Annie held up an attractive pair of front-laced women's boots. She set them aside and pulled out the note hidden beneath.

Dear Miss Anderson,

The clerk assured me these are the most fashionable and comfortable women's boots available outside of New York City. A small price to pay for your life-saving services.

Yours sincerely, Bradley Webster

Annie couldn't help herself. She kicked off her slippers and wiggled her feet into her new boots. They fit perfectly. She stood up and walked around the dining room table. Nana nodded in appreciation. Annie did another lap around the table and then looked back at the packaging… she paused and blinked three times. The small but significant detail that had eluded her dropped into her head.

"Is everything all right?" Nana asked. "You look like your flap-jacks are giving you indigestion."

"Yes," Annie said distractedly. "Yes, I—Nana, will you forgive me for not clearing the table? Something has come up."

Nana waved her off, freeing Annie to race back up the stairs to her room. Annie considered the implications this seemingly trivial detail created. Question everything. The more Annie thought about it, the more she realized she was on to something. But how to use the information to her advantage? Annie smiled. She would seek the truth and bluff with confidence.

As the plan formed in her mind, Annie sat at her writing desk and pulled out her stationery, ink, and dip pen. She filled the nib of her pen with black ink and held it above a piece of plain cream paper. If this worked, she could draw out her would-be killer into the open. Was she willing to take that risk? Annie started writing.

As Annie sealed the last letter in its matching cream envelope, she heard a muted knock on the front door. Abraham was earlier than usual for his daily visit. She placed the letter bearing Brad-ley Webster's name with the rest and hurried down the stairs. She was confident Abraham would be willing to deliver her letters by noon. Time was of the essence. As Annie reached the bottom of the stairs, she saw her grandmother standing in the doorway. It wasn't Abraham on the other side of the door.

Nana turned back to Annie, looking pale. "It's the sheriff," she said. "They've found a body in the lake."

CHAPTER L

Soldier's Heart

Tuesday, July 28, 1874

B RADLEY trailed Cornelius "the Walrus" Dewers through the
streets of Watkins in the afternoon sunshine. He had finally
found the Walrus alone. The large man sauntered along the waterfront, admiring the lake and every young lady he encountered.
After passing the train station and steamboat landing, the Walrus
turned south down Franklin Street by Frost's Foundry and Machine Shop and the Schuyler Marble Works. The Walrus looked
neither right nor left—unless there was an attractive woman to
admire—and strolled forward as if he had no care in the world.
The summer vacationers kept the streets busy, making it easier for
Bradley to stay out of sight. Still, with no disguise today, he hung
back, having enough experience not to tail the Walrus too closely,
especially after he caught the big man using the reflections in shop
windows to check the sidewalk behind him.

Bradley looked at his own reflection in a large store window as
he passed. He winced. Three days after the O'Donnell brothers had
bruised their knuckles on his face and body, he still ached everywhere. He kept the brim of his hat low, but passersby, noticing his
face, gave him a wide berth.

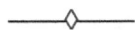

Bradley had little memory of what happened after leaving the
Fall Brook House. He recalled watching Abraham's wagon disap-
pearing around a corner. He had heard a woman's voice calling out.
Did he smile at the woman? Probably. Did he say anything to her?
He couldn't recall. The blows to his head and the sleepless night in
the Malthouse had drained him. He remembered wishing for the

safety of his Jefferson House room, only a block away, but his legs failed him.

He had woken up hours later in complete darkness, disoriented. When he reached into his pocket for a match, he remembered that Annie still had his match safe. Panic rose inside him until he realized he was in his hotel bed at the Jefferson House. He had no memory of how he had gotten there. His wounds had been bandaged, and a glass of water and fresh fruit had been placed at the side of his bed. Bradley sipped the water and devoured the fruit before falling back into a troubled sleep. His nightmares had returned.

When morning light came, he found a note from Otto Fuchs under his door. *Meet me for breakfast at eight.* Otto must have rescued him from the sidewalk and returned him to his hotel room.

He found Fuchs sitting in the Jefferson House's dining room, reading *The New York Times*. Fuchs's brown suit and hat matched the worn leather satchel at his feet. When he saw Bradley, he set the paper down and watched him approach. "You look horrible," Fuchs said.

"I feel worse than I look," Bradley said as he sat down heavily. It only hurt when he moved. Was breathing supposed to be painful? The heavy-handed O'Donnell brothers must have cracked one of his ribs.

Fuchs handed Bradley the hotel's bill of fare, but Bradley waved it away. He had eaten here many times. Fuchs motioned the server over, and after they'd ordered, he turned to Bradley. "When you are ready," he said, "I must hear what has happened." His English was precise, despite his heavy German accent.

Bradley took a shallow breath and explained how a clue led him to the *Ortus Solis* and then to the Malthouse. He left out Annie's involvement but described the Ballard brothers' secret printing room and his fight with the brothers. "Tom Ballard bragged about printing ten million dollars in one hundred and five-hundred-dollar bills," Bradley said. "He said Vance or Dewers took the money every few days. The Ballard brothers got away with all the counterfeiting equipment except the two printing presses. Those should still be in the hidden room."

"Your face," Otto asked. "The Ballard brothers' work?"

"No," Bradley said. "Old friends saying hello."

"You need better friends, Mister Webster. A story for another time, perhaps?" Fuchs asked additional questions about the Malthouse until their food arrived.

Bradley devoured his eggs and started on the ham. Otto chewed and swallowed a large piece of mutton.

"I'll search this Malthouse myself," Fuchs said, "and then alert the Pinkertons and the Secret Service to be on the lookout for the Ballard brothers. When we catch them, we might learn who was responsible for what happened here in Watkins."

Bradley paused mid-bite and set his fork down. "I saw Tom Ballard pull out ten thousand dollars of counterfeit bills from under the floorboards while I was tied to a printing press." It had happened while Annie slept. "The Ballard brothers did not leave empty-handed."

"Unfortunate. With that kind of money and a full day's head start, they can find many hiding places." Fuchs washed down the last of his brown bread with coffee. "Is there anything else you have to tell me?"

Bradley, his mouth full of dry toast, shook his head.

Fuchs sat back in his chair. He placed his cutlery on his plate and his linen napkin on the table. "It is finished."

Bradley thought he meant the meal, but then he realized Fuchs meant their investigation.

"I'm disappointed on your behalf," Otto said. "You did well to discover the counterfeiters' hideout, but without the counterfeit money, the currency plates, or any conspirators... We cannot stop the millions of dollars in counterfeit currency that will soon flood nearby cities."

Bradley's shoulders slumped. Had he reached a dead end? I've let you down, Mac, he thought to himself. With Smythe stabbed, Vance drowned, and the Ballard brothers in the wind, only Alistair Sinclair and the Walrus were left. "What about Sinclair and Dewers?" he asked. "If we can catch either of them with counterfeit money—"

Fuchs held up his hand. "Unless we have ironclad proof that can be used against him, Sinclair's wealth and status make him untouchable. And while Sinclair employs him, Dewers will also be untouchable. Do you have any proof?"

"The money has to be here somewhere...."

Fuchs shook his head. "Counterfeit money is usually 'shoved' as soon as it is printed. It is sold at one-tenth face value to people who never meet the actual counterfeiters. I suspect the money is long gone with no obvious trail to follow."

"So, the Butzemann gets away?" Bradley failed to keep the anger out of his voice.

Fuchs shrugged. "Without proof, his existence remains myth and conjecture."

Bradley used his fork to push aside the last few bites of his breakfast. His appetite had deserted him.

"You have one final lead," Otto said, leaning in. "Your secret note writer. That person could have more information to share."

Bradley felt confident that Nanny Kate had been his benefactor, but he had no proof. "I can't say for sure," he admitted, "and there have been no notes since I left the Lake View Hotel."

Fuchs sat back. "Then go home, Mister Webster. Leave now while you can. If you are correct about the Butzemann's involvement—and I think there is a strong possibility—then you, too, could be seen as a loose end needing closure."

"I have nothing to return to. I might as well stay here." A vision of Annie's smiling face came to Bradley's mind.

Fuchs read his mind. "You are thinking of the woman from the side of the cliff, perhaps? Did you know Miss Anderson was courted by George Magee's younger brother, John? A girl used to that position in society is not a girl for you."

Bradley failed to hide his shock. "How do you know that?"

"It is a small town, Mister Webster," Otto said. "I simply asked questions. That is what a detective does."

Bradley had no reply.

"One day soon," Fuchs said, "I will retire and write my memoirs. I have already started to add this story to my notes." Fuchs reached down and tapped his leather case. He looked at Bradley with sympathy. "Remember, one can learn as much from failures as successes. And do not worry, I will change your name in the book."

Bradley gave him a sour look. Fuchs laughed.

"You are an interesting man, Mister Webster," Fuchs said. He leaned forward again. "I have been asked to orchestrate the transportation of the steamship, *Bonnie Lynn*, back to New York City, where it will be taken apart and searched thoroughly. I suspect I will now be asked to bring the printing presses with me. This will take time to arrange. If you find any new leads in the next few days, bring them to me, and I will help you if I can. You should not harass Sinclair or Dewers, but you could follow them. Perhaps they will make a mistake and incriminate themselves."

"Thank you," Bradley said, even if Fuchs's gesture felt like pity.

Fuchs grasped the leather handle of his satchel and stood up. He paused when he saw the look on Bradley's face. "You are young," he said. "The future holds many possibilities. Be careful not to choose the wrong path."

Fuchs tipped his hat and departed.

Once again, the detective left without contributing to the bill.

Bradley grabbed *The New York Times* that Fuchs left behind and headed to his room. One hour later, Bradley exited the hotel dressed as an elderly man. He would follow Alistair Sinclair, as Fuchs suggested, but only until he caught the man alone and unaware. Then, with his revolver pressed against Sinclair's ribs, he would take the man to a quiet place and learn what he needed to know. He had two questions. Where is the money? Who is the Butzemann? Bradley Webster had nothing to lose.

He was foolish to think he'd had a chance to be with someone like Annie. The kiss had surprised him, and he couldn't stop thinking about it. He touched his lips, remembering. But he could not compete with a millionaire beau. Bradley swore to himself when he left New York with Pickens's money in his pocket that he would never be poor again, but he had spent much of that money keeping up appearances. If he managed to recover the counterfeit money, could things be different?

Even with money, what would Annie want with a broken man? The doctor had called it soldier's heart. Overstimulation of his heart's nervous system during the war caused the palpitations, shortness of breath, sweating, and chest pains he suffered at random times—like when he stared at the painting in James Hope's gallery. He was broke, broken... and a killer. A real prize. Bradley considered the lives he had taken. Did he regret ending any of those lives? Without hesitation. No. Not one.

Bradley found Alistair Sinclair with his family and followed him all day Sunday. The man did not venture off alone or stray far from his wife and the twins. Only one incident stood out to Bradley that day. He had followed Sinclair to church and waited outside until the service ended. When Sinclair and his family exited the church, George Magee pulled Alistair aside. Bradley timed his steps to pass the two men as they talked.

"...need payment by the charity auction," George said.

"It can't be later," Sinclair replied. "We are leaving for New York the next day."

Bradley wanted to know more but did not dare linger. Were they talking about charity finances, or did Sinclair and Magee have a business relationship? Was Magee counting on Sinclair to help him finance his new railroad? Bradley wondered how often Magee traveled to New York City. Bradley followed the family until they returned to the Lake View Hotel. He waited outside until after midnight with nothing to show for his efforts.

On Monday, Bradley followed the Sinclairs to Watkins Glen dressed as a working-class man with a large beard, ill-fitting suit, and weathered hat. The family entered the Glen near the southern Glen Mountain House. Bradley bought a ticket and followed at a safe distance as the family climbed the rocky trail, occasionally ascending wooden stairs to reach the next section of the gorge. Many vacationers crowded the trails, making it easy for Bradley to stay unseen. As they approached Rainbow Falls, the gorge narrowed considerably, and the trail crossed to the left side of the stream along a lovely series of cascades. An intersecting stream flowed down the cliff face and across the overhanging rocks, creating a spray of water that visitors walked under. If the sun hit the watery mist just right, rainbows formed.

Bradley watched the Sinclair family dash under Rainbow Falls and out the other side. The twins stomped through puddles with joyous laughter as they went. After the family climbed the wooden stairs beyond, Bradley joined the waiting line for his turn. He was so preoccupied with searching for a rainbow that he failed to notice the family had turned around and were coming back down the trail. He looked up as he reached the overhanging rocks just in time to catch Elizabeth's eye as she passed in the opposite direction. Despite his disguise, he saw recognition flash across her face.

Bradley cursed at his lapse of attention and bad luck and hurried up the wooden stairways beyond Rainbow Falls until he was out of sight. He didn't look back. He found a bench—they were placed at every landing for the weary—and waited until the Sinclair family had left the gorge. He had no choice but to abandon his surveillance of Alistair Sinclair. If Elizabeth's husband disappeared, she would know who to blame.

Time to move on to his next target, the Walrus. It would be a pleasure to stick a gun in the Walrus's ribs.

The Walrus favored the Jefferson House or the Lake View Hotel for dinner. Bradley might run into the Sinclairs at the Lake View, so he decided to have dinner in his disguise at the Jefferson House. He lingered over his meal as long as possible, but the Walrus never appeared. Before returning to his room, Bradley decided to try the hotel's billiard room. The space was dimly lit except for the bright lights illuminating two large billiard tables. Smoke hung in the air from men's pipes and cigars. A few smoked cigarettes. Bradley looked in, shocked to see the Walrus sitting at the bar in deep conversation with Sheriff Swartwood. Bradley found an inconspicuous spot to watch the men, but to his disappointment, the sheriff and the Walrus departed together soon after.

Frustrated, Bradley went back to his room. There was only one day left to corner either Alistair Sinclair or the Walrus before they returned to New York City. He began to shed his disguise, removing the wig and beard and washing his face. He'd taken off his shirt when a muffled knock came on the door. Bradley ignored it, but the knocking continued, quietly insistent. Picking up his revolver, he held it behind his back and opened the door. Elizabeth Sinclair slipped inside, shut the door, and locked it behind her.

Watkins Glen, Rainbow Falls

Her cheeks were flushed with excitement. Her long blonde curls were perfectly piled on her head as was the style. He tried not to notice her low-cut dress.

"Elizabeth—"

"Shh! No one can know I was here," she said. She looked up at his face and gasped. "What happened?"

"I look worse than I feel," he said. That was a lie.

Elizabeth looked concerned but did not ask for details. He wondered if she was reconsidering whatever had brought her to his room.

"It is lovely to see you," he said, "but why are you here?"

She stepped closer and placed her hand on his bare chest. The gesture had the desired effect—it focused all his attention on her. She looked up into his eyes. "Bradley Webster, I need something from you," she said. "And we don't have much time."

Bradley's eyes widened as she took a step back and started to unbutton her bodice.

Twenty minutes later, Elizabeth Sinclair slipped away as quietly as she had entered, leaving Bradley sitting on the edge of his bed, marveling at the turn of events. He had a lot to think about.

He finished dressing and slipped out the door for a walk in the night air. When he returned to his room, he slept nightmare-free.

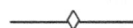

Earlier in the morning, the Walrus had joined the Sinclairs for another game of croquet. Bradley wore his old-man disguise but stayed far back to avoid being spotted. When the family had gone off to lunch, Bradley rushed back to the Jefferson to alter his disguise. He found a cream-colored envelope slipped under his door. From the feminine writing, he assumed it was from Elizabeth and tore the note from the envelope. The signature was not from Elizabeth Sinclair. The note was signed Annie Anderson. Bradley sat down on his bed and read the note three times. Each time, the frustration and anger grew inside him. Unbelievable. After the third read, he crumbled the note and threw it into the corner of the room. Not satisfied, he picked up the note and burned it in the room's fireplace. Bradley changed into his own clothes and left the hotel.

It was time for drastic measures.

A few hours later, Bradley had found the Walrus by the waterfront. Now, as he followed the big man along Franklin Street, Bradley had a confident guess of the Walrus's destination. The big man was a creature of habit.

Bradley watched the Walrus climb the steps of the Jefferson House, heading for the hotel's billiard room. Bradley followed close behind, no longer caring if the Walrus spotted him. When the Walrus sat at the bar, Bradley sat beside him.

"We need to talk," Bradley said.

Walrus turned and looked at Bradley's face. "You look like shit," he said. "Sorry, it wasn't me that gave you the beating."

"I'll keep you in mind for next time," Bradley said. Since Watkins was now a dry town and no longer served intoxicating liquor, he ordered two ginger ales from the bartender and pushed one in front of the Walrus.

The Walrus pulled a flask from his jacket pocket and added a healthy dose of whiskey into his drink. He did not offer Bradley any.

"I have something your boss wants," Bradley said.

"I doubt that."

Bradley looked around the room. He had reached the point of no return. Unfortunate that he needed money to win the girl, but the only way to get that kind of money was... to give up the girl. Bradley lowered his voice. "Annie Anderson is leaving Watkins tonight. She will not be returning."

The Walrus's face twitched, giving away his interest. He waited for Bradley to continue.

"I want fifty thousand dollars. Or Vance's share. Whichever is larger."

"You son of a—"

"For that money," Bradley said, "I'll deliver her to you tonight."

The Walrus glared at him, but something had changed in his eyes. Perhaps an understanding of the type of man he was dealing with.

"This is your boss's last chance before she disappears," Bradley said. "Leave word at the front desk by five this evening if we have a deal. And have the money tonight after the auction."

Bradley slipped off his barstool and walked out. The Walrus watched him leave with guarded eyes.

CHAPTER LI

FREER'S OPERA HOUSE

Tuesday, July 28, 1874

U NDER the glow of gas streetlights, the wealthy and influential descended on Freer's Opera House for the Watkins social event of the summer—the Firehouse Charity Auction. The exclusivity of the "by invitation only" auction—and the endorsement of the richest man in Watkins—guaranteed that few invited would stay home. Even the weather cooperated. Those walking to the event enjoyed a balmy summer evening under a nearly full moon. Steady breezes from the south kept the summer heat from spoiling the event.

From the safety of her darkened carriage, Annie observed the auction guests arriving at the corner of Franklin and Fourth Street and then disappearing through a doorway between the dry goods store on the left and the grocery store on the right.

Annie's plan this evening was straightforward. Confront Sinclair, determine what connected the auction to the counterfeiting ring, and avoid dying. As a realist, she understood every part of her plan could go horribly wrong, but she had to try. She had a packed travel bag hidden and waiting and could be out of the county before sunrise if necessary. She would leave knowing she had done her best to seek the truth.

"Would you look at that!" Nana said, leaning over Annie and sticking her head out the carriage window. "Who's that young woman hanging on Mister Wright's arm. Scandalous!"

"Shh!" Annie pulled Nana back inside the carriage.

"Don't shush me, young lady!"

"Nana, that's his daughter, Lydia."

"Oh…" Nana said. "Oh, dear. Have you seen my glasses?"

Mrs. Phelps, sitting across from Annie and her grandmother, stifled a giggle. It was nervous laughter. Mrs. Phelps was a last-minute addition to the guest list. Annie felt guilty for asking, but she needed another person she trusted near her. Mrs. Phelps understood the risk and volunteered willingly. "Glendon would want me to help you in any way I could," she said. It was painful to think of Glendon. The body pulled from the lake hadn't yet been identified.

Nana slid on her wire-rimmed glasses and returned to watching the arrivals. She had also insisted on helping her granddaughter. "I can't live forever," she said in response to potential danger.

Freer's Opera House, like most small-town opera houses, served as the social center for Watkins, hosting meetings, dances, and traveling performances of musicals, plays, lectures, and vaudeville shows. Over the last month, the opera house hosted the town's strawberry festival on the fourth of July, a vocal concert by three sisters billed as the Vescelius Trio, and a performance by the famous little person, General Tom Thumb and his traveling troupe. Annie had been looking forward to attending a play next month inspired by the frontiersman, Davy Crockett. Now, she'd settle for being alive when August arrived.

Tonight, the opera house was filled with successful business owners, wealthy farm patriarchs, and other town elites. Annie noticed Charles Frost, the owner of the town's Marble Works, enter the building wearing a top hat and tails. John J. Lytle, the new owner of the Glen and the Glen Mountain House, followed Frost inside. Annie was excited when she saw James Hope step down from a carriage with his wife and daughter. Jesse Hope looked stunning in the plum-colored dress Annie had made for her. Behind the Hopes, a group of hard-faced men that Annie did not recognize entered the building.

"There's George and Emma Magee," Mrs. Phelps said. The Magees and Sinclairs had arrived together. They greeted Judge George Freer, the opera house owner, and disappeared into the building. The Walrus followed in their wake.

"How long do we have to wait?" Nana asked.

"Not much longer," Annie said. More guests arrived, including Allen Hastings, the scoundrel who tried to have his way with her at

Glen Eldridge. He wore Josephine Knapp on his arm like a beautiful accessory. The sight of Hastings made Annie's blood boil. She only felt pity for Josephine.

The last group to enter the building were leaders from the Watkins Fire Department. They were the evening's honored guests. Funds raised by the auction benefited the town's hook and ladder company and its rescue fire patrol.

As Sheriff Swartwood and two of his deputies joined the firefighters, Annie leaned forward. Bradley appeared behind the sheriff and lingered near the men. Annie watched him exchange a few words with Deputy Cole. After the lawmen and firefighters entered the opera house, Bradley stepped off the curb and bumped into Otto Fuchs as the detective arrived. They exchanged a few words, and then only Bradley remained outside, nonchalantly leaning against the gray stone bricks of the opera house. Was he looking for me, Annie wondered? She waited. Eventually, Bradley removed his hat, ran his hands through his brown hair, and went inside. *He does have lovely hair*, she thought.

"It's time." Annie handed identical parasols to Nana and Mrs. Phelps. The parasols matched their bright-colored dresses. Annie knocked on the carriage roof, and Abraham maneuvered the carriage as close to the entrance as he could. Dressed alike, the three women stepped out of the carriage, lifted their parasols overhead, and moved quickly into the building. If an assassin with a rifle watched from above, he would have no obvious target.

Wooden stairs led to a second-story landing and then to the opera house's main room on the third floor. They each handed over an invitation and were waved through. Annie realized that "by invitation only" also meant anyone holding a printed invitation would be admitted, no questions asked.

The third floor offered a cavernous space with high ceilings. Seven tall windows provided a lovely view of Franklin Street. Another nine windows ran along the wall overlooking Fourth Street. The walls opposite were richly frescoed. A stage occupied the west end of the hall with rows of chairs awaiting an audience. For now, the guests gathered in the gallery on the east end, where they enjoyed complimentary hors d'oeuvres and a choice of sparkling grape juice or wine from the Seneca Lake Wine Company (donated for the event since selling alcohol was no longer permitted). Wine seemed the more popular choice, which must have pleased the organizers hoping to loosen up the bidding. After all, the rich didn't get that way by giving their money away.

Annie felt exposed by the large space and the crowds and struggled to steady her breathing. Was being here a mistake? She found a spot near the windows, away from the main crowd. Nana and Mrs. Phelps stayed close, forming a shield around her.

Annie watched Alistair and Elizabeth Sinclair chatting with C.S. Frost and Abraham Lawrence, an acquaintance of Glendon's who owned the land around Cayuta Lake. Annie tried to imagine how Sinclair could pull off an auction within an auction. Could he have hidden the counterfeit money and currency plates in an auction item? Annie had no idea how much space ten million dollars in counterfeit one hundred and five-hundred-dollar bills took up, but the currency plates, the size of large washboards, might fit in a chest of drawers or on the bottom of the hand-carved hope chest.

Still, the whole idea seemed unnecessarily complicated. How would the bidding work? Would a ten-dollar bid for a chest of drawers really mean a ten-thousand-dollar bid for currency plates hidden inside? How would the money transfer happen? And who would be bidding? Pushers willing to pay one-tenth of the face value or more for the nearly perfect fake money, or future counterfeiters anxious to buy flawless currency plates?

Annie scanned the crowd for unfamiliar faces. To pull this off, Sinclair needed a few interested parties bidding against each other and driving up the price. Since Annie knew almost everyone worth knowing in the area, the three groups of men—standing isolated from the Watkins elite and each other—were easy to spot. *Who do we have here?* Annie wondered. She bit her lip, leaned over, and whispered into Mrs. Phelps's ear. With a smile, Mrs. Phelps plumped up her decolletage and headed for the first group of men.

"There's your dress, Annie." Nana pointed toward the long tables lining the long, frescoed wall.

All the items the organizing committee had convinced residents to donate were on display. Annie's dress, fitted on a seamstress mannequin, stood at one end. An easel next to her dress held a donated painting by James Hope of Rainbow Falls. Woodward's bookstore offered enough rolls of their newest washable wallpaper pattern to cover a dining room. A.O. Whittemore, owner of the Havana pottery factory, donated three large stoneware crocks. Several boat captains donated excursions on their vessels. There were quilts, furniture, jewelry, and many more items from local vendors.

A hand grabbed Annie's forearm. Mr. Nichols, the clerk from the Glen Mountain House, appeared so quickly that he almost got clobbered by Nana's parasol before Annie called her off. Nichols leaned forward and whispered into Annie's ear. She looked about the room and discreetly pointed. Nichols took his time but eventually nodded.

"Are you sure?"

"Yes," he said. With a slight bow to Annie and her grandmother, Nichols headed over to pocket more free food before leaving.

A bell rang at the front of the room. The auction was about to start. Emma Magee, looking stunning in her understated dress, made her way to the stage as fellow organizers herded the crowd behind her. As everyone took a seat, Emma addressed her audience.

"Ladies and gentlemen, thank you for attending our first ever Watkins Firehouse Charity Auction. We are gathered here on this beautiful summer evening to raise funds for the Watkins Fire Department. I want to thank the tireless efforts of our organizers," she paused for the modest applause that followed, "and the generous contributions from so many members of our fine community." Emma looked over the audience. She smiled when she saw Annie standing in the back. "Before our auction begins, please welcome our guest of honor to the stage. Fire Chief George Norman."

Another round of polite applause followed as Chief Norman took the stage. He thanked the audience for their generosity in advance and then discussed the importance of a well-equipped fire station. As the chief recalled the cautionary tragedies of the Great Chicago Fire of '71 and the Great Boston Fire of '72, Mrs. Phelps returned with a half-empty glass of wine from her socializing.

"I can hold that for you," Nana offered, eyeing the wine.

As Mrs. Phelps extended the glass to Nana, Annie grabbed it and finished the wine in two gulps. She handed the empty glass to her grandmother, ignored the angry stare that followed, and turned to Mrs. Phelps. "What did you learn?"

"All three groups are from out of town." Mrs. Phelps said. Flushed with excitement from her clandestine mission, she kept her voice low. "The first two men were tight-lipped, but I believe they came from Washington, DC," she said. "The accents of the next group were definitely from the Philadelphia area. They proudly admitted it and invited me out for drinks in Havana after the auction."

Annie looked surprised.

"Well, of course, I said no!" Mrs. Phelps laughed.

"And the last group?"

"Three men from the South. Two from Georgia and one from Louisiana. They offered me the wine. They seemed like gentlemen, but from how they talked about negros, I'm glad your friend Abraham isn't in the room."

As Chief Norman finished his remarks, Emma returned to the stage with the auctioneer hired for the event. The first item up for bid was a complete set of stereographs of the Watkins Glen by local photographer G.F. Gates. Gates delivered his item to the stage, described it briefly, then returned to his seat. The bidding started slow but became heated until Mr. Hazlitt, a farm owner from Hector, triumphed.

A volunteer walked past carrying Annie's donated dress and the sewing mannequin. It was the next item up for bid. Annie walked confidently forward, and when she reached the stage, she turned to stand next to the dress and faced the crowd. *Whoever wants me dead, here I am*, she thought. Out in the crowd, George Magee sat near Elizabeth and Alistair Sinclair. Sheriff Swartwood and Deputy Cole lingered by the exits. There was no sign of Bradley or the Walrus. The crowd stayed silent, waiting for her to speak. She inhaled deeply, then pointed out the dress's Parisian styling and offered the winning bidder a custom fitting. Annie stepped off the stage and returned to Nana and Mrs. Phelps. She had put herself on display to set the hook and now she would wait to see which person was the hungriest trout in the room.

The bidding started at one dollar and quickly escalated. With

SMALL TOWN OPERA HOUSE

Emma's encouragement, George Magee triumphed as the highest bidder.

Annie watched and waited as several more auction items came and went. The out-of-town bidders sat on their hands, showing no interest. What had they come to bid on? Had she guessed wrong? It had to be more than a coincidence these unknown men had attended.

Emma swooped by to tell Annie she loved her new dress and was excited to have it tailored for a perfect fit. Annie was pleased but not surprised, as she'd had Emma in mind when she'd designed the dress.

At that moment, Josephine Knapp stood up and headed toward the rear stairwell with Allen Hastings close behind. Annie had seen that look on Hastings's face at Glen Eldridge and felt something snap inside her. "Excuse me, Emma," she said as she hurried after Hastings and Josephine.

"Annie?" Nana called to her in confusion, wondering if the plan had changed.

"I'll be right back."

Annie pushed through the crowd in time to see Hastings and Josephine descend to the second floor. Annie hurried to catch up. As she turned the corner in the dimly lit hallway on the second floor, she found Hastings pressing Josephine against a wall and whispering fiercely in her ear. All the color drained from Josephine's face.

Without hesitation, Annie grabbed a hatpin from her hair and marched up to Hastings. "Let. Her. Go!" Her sudden approach caught Hastings by surprise, forcing him back a step. Annie pulled Josephine from the wall and gently pushed the woman behind her.

"Are you all right?" Annie asked.

"Yes," Josephine mumbled, but Annie knew from experience that the answer was more a reflex than the truth.

Realizing Annie was unescorted, Hastings regained his bluster. "Annie Anderson," he sneered, "are you so obsessed with me that you're willing to attack my new paramour here at the opera house?"

Annie laughed in his face. "Is that the story you're going to tell everyone?" Annie took a step toward the large man. How dare he. Any lingering fear Annie had was replaced with righteous indignation. "You assaulted me at Glen Eldridge, and when I refused your advances, you threatened me into silence. Because I did not speak out, you have done the same thing to Josephine. Shame on me for being silent. And shame on you for being a cad, a womanizer, and a bully. I don't care about your job, your authority, or what lies you spread about me. I'll tell George Magee and anyone who will listen what type of man you really are, no matter the consequences." Annie stabbed the air in front of her with the hatpin, to emphasize her words.

Hastings looked around to make sure they were still alone. "Not only will I destroy your reputation," he said, leaning forward, "I will sue you for slander. My lawyers will take every dollar you and your family ever earned. George Magee will never believe your word over mine."

"George will believe my word."

All three of them turned to see Emma Magee step around the corner.

"Annie," Emma said. "Is it true? Did Mister Hastings assault you on our excursion?"

"She's lying!" Hastings blurted out.

Annie looked Emma in the eyes and nodded.

Emma appeared stricken. "He told us you left Glen Eldridge after he rejected your advances. I'm so sorry I believed him. I know you too well. Please forgive me."

Before Annie could reply, Emma turned to Mr. Hastings.

"It would be best to take your leave now," she said.

Hastings straightened his jacket. "Fine," he replied. "I'll go have a word with George." He maneuvered to get around the women to return to the auction.

Emma held up her hand, blocking his path. "You misunderstand me, sir. You are no longer welcome in this building. My husband makes the decisions at work, but I assure you he defers to my opinion at charitable events. And my opinion is that you should leave. Now."

Hastings's eyes flared. "This is outrageous!"

"Plead your case with my husband at work in the morning," Emma said, "but be assured he takes a very dim view of employing men who disrespect women. And if anything slanderous is said about either of these women, my family has much better lawyers at our disposal than you do."

Hastings muttered under his breath, turned, and stomped away.

The three women watched him leave, and then Emma turned to Annie and Josephine. "He will be out of a job before noon tomorrow. I guarantee it."

Josephine struggled to speak. "I—" She cleared her throat. "Thank you both."

Emma grabbed the girl's hand. "You poor dear. Let's get you something to drink, and you can tell me what happened before I talk to my husband." Emma turned to Annie. "Coming?"

"I'll be right there," Annie said. The rush of the confrontation had passed, and she felt jittery and suddenly exhausted. Emma and Josephine turned the corner and climbed the stairs as Annie breathed in and out to steady her nerves. She only needed a minute to compose herself, but it was a minute too long. A man dressed in black stepped out of the shadows, holding a knife.

The man was slender with a dark beard and large eyes that stared intently at her. Something about him looked familiar. Annie looked down at his boots, and her blood ran cold.

"You killed Smythe, didn't you?"

The man said nothing.

"I'll scream."

"You'll be dead, and I'll be gone before anyone arrives," the assassin said in a low voice.

Annie wondered if she could remove her derringer before he could reach her with his knife. Her hand moved toward her dress pocket.

"Don't."

Annie froze. She said, "What do you want?" She feared the answer but hoped to keep the man talking until someone came down the stairs. No one came. They remained alone.

"You know that someone wants you dead?" The assassin sounded curious.

Annie nodded her head, not breaking eye contact.

"And yet you exposed yourself to help that girl? Who is she to you?"

The question surprised Annie, but she answered it honestly. "We were friends once, but we aren't close now. I don't think she likes me very much." Annie laughed nervously and then shrugged. "What was happening was not her fault. Sometimes, we women need to watch out for one another."

The man stared at her and nodded slowly, making a decision. He reached up with his free hand and pulled the fake beard off his face. He was a woman. Annie saw hints of dimples at the corners of the assassin's cheeks. "Did you kill the man in Glenwood Cemetery?" the female assassin asked.

"No, of course not," Annie said, failing to hide the shock on her face. "Aren't you trying to kill me because I've been searching for the man's murderer?"

The assassin shook her head but did not answer Annie's question. She appeared agitated, but the moment was fleeting. "You don't belong on my list," she said. "You should go back to the auction."

Annie turned toward the stairs wistfully. When she looked back, the assassin had disappeared into the shadows.

"Thank you," Annie whispered into the darkness as she rushed back to the auction.

At the top of the stairs, Annie stumbled headlong into Alistair Sinclair. The man stepped back and apologized. Annie was shaken by her encounter with the assassin but realized that this was the moment she had been waiting for. The opportunity to confront Sinclair and find out why he wanted her dead. Alistair Sinclair gazed down at Annie with a blank expression. She stared back, waiting for him to speak first. A look of recognition crossed Sinclair's face. "You're the woman who made that lovely dress, right? Well done," he said, then excused himself and moved past her to the nearest water closet.

No one was that good of an actor, Annie decided. *He had no idea who I was.* She returned to Nana and Mrs. Phelps, struggling to understand what had happened. If Sinclair didn't know who she was and the assassin had spared her, was she safe now?

Annie looked up when she heard an unfamiliar voice call out, "Ten dollars." It was one of the men from Washington, DC.

"Whose item are they bidding on?" Annie asked her grandmother.

"A writing table donated by Elizabeth Sinclair," Nana said.

Was this it? Mr. Frost, the owner of the Marble Works, was raising the bid. Neither the Southerners nor the men from Philadelphia joined in. The bidding went back and forth until Mr. Frost won.

Annie watched Mr. Frost walk to the back of the room to pay for his new table. As he did, Sheriff Swartwood and Deputy Cole intercepted him. Annie looked over to Mrs. Phelps and nodded meaningfully toward the sheriff.

"I'm on it!" Mrs. Phelps said. She headed back to where the two men were talking.

Only a few more items were left before the auction ended. Captain Murphy offered a family excursion on his new steam yacht the *Lilly*, and then Mr. A.O. Whittemore brought three of his stoneware crocks to the stage. Each was decorated with lovely cobalt blue floral patterns. Mr. Whittemore explained the five-gallon crock had been packed with salted meat, the two-gallon crock with butter, and the three-gallon stoneware jug with whiskey.

Mrs. Phelps returned breathless. "The sheriff told Mister Frost that he'd been alerted that there was a hidden key and directions secured to the bottom of the desk's drawer. They are leaving now to search the carriage house on Third Street. The sheriff threatened to arrest Mister Frost and Mister and Mrs. Sinclair if he found anything illegal."

The first bid for the stoneware came from the Louisiana man, a handsome fellow with a square jaw and a faint scar across his right cheek. The second came from a stone-faced man from Washington, DC. The Philadelphia group quickly joined the bidding.

"It's not the desk," Annie realized. "The desk was misdirection." She rushed over to Mr. Whittemore, who had returned to his seat. "Mister Whittemore, who filled your stoneware containers?"

"Oh, hello, Miss Anderson," he said. "An auction committee

member suggested that filling my stoneware would fetch a higher price. I guess it's working!" The price continued to climb thanks to feverish bidding by the out-of-town visitors.

"Who from the committee?" Annie asked.

"What's the name?" Mr. Whittemore asked himself before remembering. "Sinclair. Mrs. Sinclair generously offered to fill the stoneware pieces."

Elizabeth hid something in the stoneware. Annie was sure of it. Something that would lead the highest bidder to the counterfeit money and the printing plates. She thanked Mr. Whittemore and turned to search for Elizabeth. *Why couldn't it be a woman?* Annie thought. Maybe Elizabeth's husband was only the figurehead of the counterfeiting ring, and she was the real mastermind. She was tall for a woman. Tall enough to be the person Bradley saw the night he followed Alistair Sinclair to his meeting with the shadowy figure in Lafayette Park?

Annie saw Elizabeth Sinclair standing with the two men from Washington, DC. Elizabeth stared back at Annie with a hostile expression. *She knows I know*, Annie realized. Elizabeth whispered to the men standing next to her. One started toward Annie.

"Time to go," Bradley whispered in Annie's ear. Surprised, Annie turned toward him. He smiled grimly. "Save the hellos for later. We have to run." Annie wanted to return to her grandmother and Mrs. Phelps, but they were on the other side of the approaching man. She let Bradley grab her hand and pull her to the stairs. They raced down with the DC man close behind. As they burst out the front door, Bradley headed for a waiting horse and carriage and helped her in. The man from DC was two steps too slow. Bradley snapped the reins, and the black horse leaped forward and raced down Franklin Street.

Bradley gave his horse free rein. Annie held on as the small carriage bounced and careened down Franklin Street at breakneck speed. Pulling on the reins, Bradley made a hard left onto Tenth Street. They crossed Decatur Street without slowing and turned left again on Porter Street, where Bradley brought the horse to a slow trot, allowing Annie and the horse to catch their breath.

"I don't think we were followed," Bradley said.

Annie did not know what to say. She had expected to see Bradley earlier in the evening, but everything happened too quickly. Was he a murderer and a scoundrel? Or was he the man who had risked his own life to save hers more than once? Annie looked at Bradley in the moonlight. She had decided to trust him when she wrote that letter.

Bradley turned left onto Fifth Street and pulled their carriage to a halt alongside Lafayette Park.

"Elizabeth Sinclair knows the location of the counterfeit money and the printing plates," Annie said.

Bradley stepped out of the carriage and tied the horse's reins to the nearest hitching post. "I know," he said.

"What—" Annie looked around. "LaFayette Park?" The moon was bright, but the park was filled with dark shadows.

"Yes," Bradley said. He held out his hand. Annie hesitated, but she grasped Bradley's hand and stepped down. Bradley nodded toward the park. "This way." As they walked, the wind picked up. For a moment, the moon disappeared behind a cloud.

He offered her his arm, and she took it. Bradley guided her toward the gazebo near the center of the park. As they approached, a shadow detached itself from the building.

The moon emerged from behind the cloud. It was Dewers. The Walrus.

"Bradley," Annie said, her voice trembling. "What is going on?"

"I had to choose," Bradley said, no expression in his voice.

The words sent a chill down Annie's spine. When Bradley refused to look at her, she reached for the derringer in her pocket. It was gone. Bradley held it up and then put it back in his pocket. He must have taken it when he helped her out of the carriage.

"I don't understand," Annie said, the panic rising in her voice. Bradley ignored her.

The Walrus threw a bulging sack at Bradley's feet. "Fifty thousand. As agreed."

"She's all yours," Bradley said. He took a step back.

"For money!?" Annie raised her voice. She let her anger take over. "You are doing this for money? They are going to kill me."

Tears streamed down her face.

"They promised not to hurt you," Bradley said, still refusing to look at her. He kept his eyes staring out into the darkness. "They only want the gold back from Glendon."

"You can't believe that!"

The Walrus's hands were empty, but he looked menacing as he stepped toward Annie.

"What have we here?"

The voice came from the center of the park. Detective Otto Fuchs stepped out of the shadows, pointing his revolver at the Walrus while keeping an eye on Bradley. "When I started following Mister Dewers, I didn't expect to end up here with you."

Annie was relieved to see the gun in Fuchs's hand. It was the same one he'd had on the cliff the night Glendon jumped.

Fuchs's aim shifted from the Walrus to Bradley. "I'm surprised by your choices, Mister Webster," he said. "You aren't the person I thought you were. You pretended to be a gentleman, but you are a survivor first, aren't you?" Fuchs stepped closer, keeping Bradley and the Walrus in his line of sight.

Bradley stared at Fuchs's revolver but said nothing.

"Miss Anderson, please come toward me," Fuchs said. "I'm afraid you can't trust Mister Webster any longer."

With a relieved look on her face, Annie walked toward Fuchs. The detective smiled as he swung his gun away from Bradley, aimed for Annie's heart, and pulled the trigger.

PART FOUR

Shadows Dance

CHAPTER LII

UNMASKED

Tuesday, July 28, 1874

BRADLEY watched as the hammer of Fuchs's revolver smashed down. Click. Fuchs's gun did not fire. Surprised by the misfire, Fuchs pulled the hammer back and squeezed the trigger again. Again, the gun did not fire. The detective did not get a third attempt. Bradley stepped in front of Annie and aimed an identical 1849 Colt pocket revolver at Fuchs's chest. Hard to miss at this distance in the bright moonlight. Behind Bradley, Annie exhaled. She had been holding her breath.

"All well, Abraham?" Bradley called out. He did not want to turn his head but was counting on Abraham to step out of his hiding place and level a polished shotgun at the Walrus's midsection. A handy way to discourage the big man from interfering.

"All's well," Abraham replied.

Bradley allowed himself a satisfied smile. It had been a risky plan, but it had worked.

"You swapped revolvers when you bumped into me in front of the auction house," Fuchs said.

Bradley shrugged, not wanting to brag. "This revolver," he said, referring to the one in his hand, "has working percussion caps." The 1849 Colt's Revolving Pocket Pistol was a cap-and-ball revolver. When the revolver's hammer struck the percussion cap, it detonated the cap's mercury fulminate and ignited the gunpowder in the chamber, which launched the .31-caliber ball toward its unfortunate target. Remove the mercury fulminate from the percussion cap—as Bradley did with the replacement gun he swapped with Fuchs—and the balls stayed in the gun.

Fuchs tossed his revolver into the grass. "Foolish of you, Miss

Anderson, to let a man like Bradley Webster put you in harm's way. If he failed to make the swap or if I had checked my weapon, you would be dead now."

Bradley had worried about the same thing, so he had not let Fuchs out of his sight since the swap. Not until he left the opera house with Annie. Then, he could only hope the time it took to get to Lafayette Park was too short for Fuchs to inspect or exchange his weapon.

"It was not his plan," Annie said. "It was mine. I knew this would force you into exposing yourself." Bradley appreciated her faith in him. He had swapped weapons with Fuchs before giving her the signal in front of the opera house. "Remove your hat and run your fingers through your hair" had been an odd choice for a signal, but he had complied.

"You were the bait in this snare," Fuchs said, addressing Annie. "Impressive. But I must know. What made you suspect me?"

Annie stepped forward and stood shoulder-to-shoulder with Bradley. "On the cliff, when I said, *'Ich glaub ich spinne,'* you told me I was a fly, not the spider."

Fuchs's brow wrinkled. "I think, I spider?"

"That is the literal translation," Annie said. "My German teacher used those words whenever our class's attention lapsed. To a true German, it expresses a feeling of disbelief. 'I think I'm going crazy.' A native speaker would have known that. You speak German, but you are not from Germany. Once I realized that, I started questioning everything."

Fuchs nodded and gave a slight bow. "Still," he said, "a Pinkerton agent has many disguises. Pretending to be German could have been one of mine. There must be more."

"I only suspected you. Mr. Nichols confirmed that you lied about when you arrived in Watkins."

"Nichols?"

"The clerk from the Glen Mountain House," Annie said. "Nichols never forgets a face. I arranged his attendance at the auction and pointed you out. He remembered you as a guest at the Glen Mountain House. You stayed at the hotel the night Lewis Crawford was killed."

"A simple miscommunication. Is that all you have?"

"You just tried to kill me," Annie said. "You are no detective."

"True," Fuchs admitted. "I stole the badge from a drunken Pinkerton."

Bradley hadn't wanted Annie to be right because that would mean she had seen something in Fuchs that he had missed. But he did not doubt her intelligence. After getting her note, he called on Mr. Buntz, the telegraph operator in Watkins. The man tried to deny it, but with some encouragement, he confessed that the Walrus had threatened his family to ensure none of Bradley's telegrams were delivered. If Bradley's telegrams had not gone out, how could Fuchs arrive from New York to meet him? Annie was right. Fuchs was not who he pretended to be.

Fuchs looked relaxed. Too relaxed. It worried Bradley.

"You lured Lewis Crawford to Watkins and killed him in the cemetery," Annie said. "You were Alistair Sinclair's silent partner in the counterfeiting ring. You are the one who wants me dead. Why?"

"You have your father's luck," Fuchs said, ignoring her question. "Perhaps you are the spider after all."

"Who are you, really?" Annie asked.

Bradley took a step closer. "He is the Butzemann." Bradley said, then addressed Fuchs directly. "You killed Mac McGregor."

Fuchs stared at Bradley. "The detective from New York? So that's your interest in all this. Are you the assistant who arrived too late for McGregor's dinner meeting? But, of course, the Butzemann couldn't have been involved. The Butzemann is myth. And I will remain a myth because of your overconfidence." Fuchs gave a sharp whistle as Bradley's finger tightened on the trigger.

The first bullet knocked the revolver out of Bradley's hands. The second landed at Abraham's feet, forcing the older man to throw himself behind a tree for cover. Annie grabbed Bradley and pulled him to the ground behind the gazebo while Fuchs and the Walrus sprinted in different directions. More bullets ricocheted off Abraham's tree and the edge of the gazebo.

Annie's eyes had gone wide. "How are we still alive?" she asked, sitting up and pressing her back against the wooden boards of the gazebo.

Bradley worried she might be in shock. He looked out at his revolver in the grass but then ignored it. There was no target to shoot at.

"If they are good enough to shoot a gun out of your hand," Annie said, her voice level and calm, "they could have killed us before we moved. This is a distraction."

Bradley glanced over, impressed with Annie's composure. He'd seen grown men piss themselves when bullets started flying in their direction. She was breathless and flushed but not terrified. "Fuchs's insurance policy," he said. "The shooter didn't need to kill us, just create a diversion to help Fuchs escape." And it worked. Fuchs and the Walrus had disappeared into the shadows. The bag with $50,000 had also disappeared. "My guess—someone is firing out of a second-floor window from one of these houses overlooking the park."

Another shot pinged off the ground a few feet away. That made six shots fired, but that told Bradley nothing. Three rounds a minute with an Enfield rifle was impressive during the war. Now, the newest Springfield rifle fired eight to ten shots a minute.

The wind picked up, rustling the leaves.

"Were you going to shoot Fuchs?" Annie asked.

Bradley glanced at her and then looked away. "The Butzemann killed a friend of mine."

"I'm sorry," Annie said. A bullet bounced off the ground near Abraham. "These shots will draw the attention of the neighborhood. We need to keep our heads down until—"

Another bullet ricocheted off the gazebo, and then the shooting stopped.

As the silence dragged on, Bradley wondered if this was a ruse to draw them out, or if the shooter stopped firing to take up a better position. Stay or run. Bradley was considering their options when a voice called out from the park's edge.

"Annie? Annie, are you safe?"

Annie jumped to her feet. "Glendon!" A sob of relief escaped her lips.

Bradley chanced a look around the corner of the gazebo. Glendon Robinson came out of the shadows and strode toward them. Annie ran to Glendon and let him wrap his arms around her in a bear hug. Then, she pulled away and punched him in the arm. "That's for making me think you were dead."

Behind Glendon came a giant bear of a man. Frank had survived the shooting near the Glen Mountain House. He carried a rifle in his left hand as he used his right to drag along a smaller man dressed in black by the scruff of his neck. The smaller man's hands and feet were bound with rope.

"You caught our sniper," Annie said.

Glendon shook his head. "We broke into the house he was shooting from, expecting a fight. He was waiting to surrender."

Frank handed the rifle to Glendon and then placed the smaller man, whose hands were bound behind him, on his knees in front of them. Bradley looked at their would-be assassin, and his mouth dropped open. The man's black wig had been knocked askew, exposing short golden hair. The shooter was the waitress from the Montour House, wearing men's clothing. "He's a she!"

Sanna looked up at Bradley and then looked away.

Abraham joined them after dusting himself off. "We should leave here," he said. "Now that the shooting has stopped, people will come to see what the commotion was about."

"Fuchs is getting away," Bradley said.

"If he gets out of town before we stop him...."

Bradley grabbed the two identical revolvers from the grass while Frank threw their captive over his shoulder. They headed for Abraham's wagon, a short distance from the park. Frank placed the Montour House waitress in the back of the wagon on her side and checked the ropes binding her. Annie kept her voice low as she told Glendon and Frank what had happened in the park.

"Fuchs is on foot for now," Bradley said.

Glendon rubbed his chin. "The trains aren't running this late, but if Fuchs found a fast horse, he could leave town in at least six directions. We can't cover all of them, but we can start at the nearest livery. Can the three of you watch our captive?"

Frank and Glendon left quickly, heading back toward Franklin Street.

Abraham checked on his horse Goldie, leaving Annie and Bradley to interrogate their captive. "Thank you for sparing my life at the opera house," Annie said. "What's your name?"

The woman hesitated, then shrugged. "Sanna."

"Sanna, if we don't find Fuchs, I'll spend the rest of my life looking over my shoulder. Where was he headed?"

The woman lay in shadow. She didn't reply.

Annie turned to Bradley. "Would Fuchs go to the Sinclairs for help?"

"No," Bradley said, "Fuchs was blackmailing Alistair Sinclair. Turns out Sinclair wasn't in the war. He was convalescing in a hotel in Switzerland from a carriage accident in Milan that killed another man's wife. A wife that shouldn't have been in the carriage with him. The scandal was covered up, but Fuchs learned of it and threatened to expose Sinclair if he didn't agree to run the counterfeiting ring." Bradley learned all this from Elizabeth Sinclair's visit to his room last night.

"But what about Elizabeth Sinclair?" Annie said. "She knows where the counterfeit money and plates are. I know she hid something in the stoneware. She could be working with Fuchs."

"The auction was a setup," Bradley said. "Fuchs had Dewers tip off the police. Sheriff Swartwood would have arrested the Sinclairs if the key in their donated desk led to a million dollars in counterfeit money and the missing currency plates. But Elizabeth suspected the double cross and had the plates and the money moved to a new location." Last night, Elizabeth had unbuttoned her bodice to hand him a key hidden there. Her life, she told him, depended on Bradley traveling to the Third Street carriage house with the two men from Washington, DC, picking the lock on the steamer trunk, and moving the money and plates.

A voice came from the back of the wagon. "Alistair Sinclair was on my list."

"What?" Bradley and Annie turned toward Sanna.

"Sinclair killed that woman in Milan," she said, "so he was on my list. I was the guarantee he wouldn't leave the Watkins's jail alive."

"The Butzemann tying up loose ends," Bradley said.

Annie looked at Sanna's black, dusty boots. "You killed Smythe, didn't you?"

"He was a bad man who liked young boys."

"Did you shoot Roland?"

"No. Fuchs disguised himself as Glendon and ambushed Roland on Magee's property."

"Why would Roland look for Glendon there?"

"Because I told Roland that's where Glendon was waiting for him."

"Roland's not a bad man."

"He was on my list."

"I'm on your list," Annie said. "Your list is flawed."

From the look on her face, Bradley suspected Sanna knew that now. Sanna looked at Bradley. "Did you kill the woman in the Glen?"

"No," Bradley said. "That was Maurice Vance. Is that why I was on your list?"

Sanna nodded. "Did you kill Vance?"

Bradley shrugged. "Self-defense. He was trying to kill Annie at the time."

"Sanna," Annie asked, "why work for Fuchs?"

Sanna defiantly held her chin up. "He told me he was a Pinkerton," she said. "My job was to make sure people on my list couldn't hurt anyone else. I stopped bad people from hurting innocent people." She looked away. "I believed that."

"Fuchs lied to you," Annie said. "He killed the man in the cemetery. For money. Or revenge. I don't know which. Both maybe. He is a person who hurts others. Help me stop him. Please tell us where Fuchs is going."

Sanna looked into Annie's eyes. Then, she repositioned herself and looked toward the lake. "He said that after today, it would be smooth sailing to New York. I was to meet him there."

"The steamer," Bradley said. "Fuchs planned on taking the *Bonnie Lynn* back through the Erie Canal to New York."

"You two go," Abraham said. "I'll take this one to the sheriff," he said, pointing with his thumb at Sanna, "and then meet you at the steamship landing."

Abraham gave Bradley his double-barreled shotgun and spare cartridges in return for the two Colt pistols. Annie and Bradley ran for the horse and carriage they'd left hitched next to the park. Sanna's voice called out from the darkness behind them. "Fuchs has another revolver on the steamship."

Bradley watched Otto Fuchs pilot the *Bonnie Lynn* away from the Malthouse and toward the open waters of Seneca Lake. The steamer was escaping with Annie on board, and Bradley could do nothing to prevent it.

Forty minutes earlier, Bradley had remembered the printing presses that Fuchs planned to load and assumed—correctly in this case—that the steamer would be lying at anchor behind the Malthouse. He and Annie had arrived to find the steamer empty, but with a fire lit under the boiler and pressure building up. Fuchs had to be nearby, preparing to depart.

There had been enough moonlight to see a large canvas covering several bulky items on the back half of the ship. "Tom Ballard told us they printed ten million dollars of counterfeit money," Annie said quietly. "If Elizabeth auctioned off one million, nine are left somewhere."

Bradley had looked toward the Malthouse. Fuchs was probably inside. Bradley wanted to keep Annie away from Fuchs. Killing the Butzemann to avenge McGregor's death was the reason he had come to Watkins. "You check the steamer," Bradley whispered in her ear. "I'll check the Malthouse."

"Be careful," Annie whispered back. Bradley hurried away as she nimbly crossed the gangplank onto the steamer.

He kept a firm grip on the shotgun as he cracked open the door to squeeze his body through. The bready smell of toasted malt rushed toward him. It must have been a kiln day. Inside was pitch black. It would take time for his eyes to adjust. Bradley wondered if Fuchs had left something else hidden in the secret room on the third floor. He took three steps into the Malthouse before the hair on the back of his neck stood up.

Bradley flung himself forward, hearing a whoosh near his ear as he did so. Fuchs had waited in the darkness to club him over the head quietly. Bradley forced himself into a tuck and rolled away as he hit the ground. Fuchs fired two bullets into the space he had just occupied. So much for the subtle approach, Bradley thought while changing his trajectory and jumping to his left. A third bullet zipped dangerously close to his head. This last maneuver knocked the shotgun from his hands, and it skittered away in the darkness. Bradley fell against one of the large storage tanks for soaking barley, hitting his head. He saw stars. Dazed, he rolled under one of the tanks, not wanting to be an easy target for Fuchs.

Bradley lay still, trying to control his breathing as he listened for movement. His ears were ringing from the three shots, and the muzzle flashes had destroyed what night vision he'd had. Was the Butzemann lurking in the shadows with his revolver at the ready? Bradley wasn't going to wait to be killed. He had to find the shotgun. He crawled forward quietly, feeling the ground before him with his hands.

From outside the Malthouse, he heard a subtle change in the sound of the steamship.

Annie!

Bradley scrambled forward until his hand gripped the barrel of the shotgun. He stood, wobbled momentarily, and then rushed out the door. Fuchs had made it to the *Bonnie Lynn*, kicked the gangplank away, and stood at the controls of his steamship heading for open water. There was no sign of Annie.

Bradley heard nothing except the wind rattling the trees and the chugging and hissing of Fuchs's steam engine growing fainter. For a moment, he held out hope that Annie had gotten off the ship. He called her name. "Annie?" No answer. She didn't pop out of any nearby hiding places.

No shots had been fired, and no screams had come from the boat. Fuchs wouldn't have had time to tie her up, so Bradley assumed she was hiding under the canvas at the back of the ship. What would she do next? Bradley reached into his pants pocket and cursed. He pulled out Annie's derringer. He had failed to return it to her in the park. Her next best option was to slip off the back of the steamer unnoticed and swim away. Somehow, Bradley knew she wouldn't do that. Fuchs getting away meant a life of fear, waiting for his return.

A gust of wind distracted Bradley. He checked the trees. The steady breeze blew south to north. It might be enough. He turned and ran toward the railroad tracks that paralleled the shore, heading toward the train depot and the steamboat landing. As he ran, two shadows appeared in the darkness before him. It was obvious from their sizes who they were. He ran past Glendon and Frank without slowing down.

"Where's Annie," Glendon yelled as the two men turned and ran after him.

"On that steamer," Bradley called over his shoulder, gesturing toward the water.

He heard cursing behind him but kept his focus forward.

There! He ran to a rowboat that had been pulled up on shore. He set the shotgun inside the boat and started to push it toward the water. Glendon, breathing heavily, ran up, placed his rifle next to the shotgun, and pushed as well. "What's the plan?" he said.

The rowboat reached the water before Bradley could answer. He climbed in and manned the oars as Glendon pushed off and hopped in. Frank jumped aboard at the last second, almost capsizing them. They settled the boat, and Bradley pulled hard on the oars. It did not take long to reach the racing sloop moored offshore. The one he had seen the day he'd left by train for Ithaca.

Bradley scrambled onto the sailing yacht. It was a beauty—nearly thirty feet long with a broad beam. He reached out as Frank and Glendon handed up the weapons before climbing on board. The empty rowboat drifted away in the darkness. Frank immediately curled up onto the deck near the mast. Bradley looked down at the big man in confusion. "Ignore him," Glendon said. "How can I help?"

"We need to unfurl the sails," Bradley said. They worked quickly in the moonlight. Once the mainsail was unfurled, the two men pulled hard on the halyard to raise the sail to the top of the mast. Bradley released the mooring lines and then moved to the back of the ship to pull on the sheets, trimming the sails. Bradley brought her about as the ship's sails caught the wind. They were

Sailboat on Seneca Lake

underway, but slowly. *This is taking too long*, Bradley thought.

"Glendon, I need you at the helm while I raise the jib." Bradley pointed toward the center of the lake. "Keep us in that direction." He stepped around Frank and raised the jib sail as quickly as possible. He kept an eye out for the *Bonnie Lynn* as he did so, but a cloud crossed in front of the moon, limiting visibility.

Bradley got the jib up and ran back to take over from Glendon. With the right encouragement, the sailing yacht, responsive and eager, leaped forward, gliding across the lake with full sails.

"How fast can we go?" Glendon asked. He stared out into the darkness. It was dangerous to sail at night in unfamiliar waters, but they had no choice. At least the lake was deep, with no submerged islands or shallows offshore.

"Seven to eight knots if the wind holds."

"How fast can that steamer go?"

"At full speed," Bradley said, considering, "maybe eight knots."

"Fuchs has a thirty-minute head start. We'll never catch him."

"Fuchs is not counting on being followed," Bradley said. "He won't be running at top speed." Bradley wanted that to be true. He tried to concentrate on finding the steamer first. The lake was one to two miles wide and almost forty miles long. He'd stay in the center for now and keep their ship running with the wind.

Bradley looked at Glendon. "They found a dead body in the lake. Annie thought it was you. How did you manage not dying from a hundred foot fall?"

"I overheard it was Vance's body that floated to the surface," Glendon said. "As for surviving my fall, I made sure I entered the water with my toes pointed and my arms at my sides and was really lucky. When I realized I hadn't died, I swam underwater back to shore until I was under the overhang and out of sight from above. I had a canoe hidden nearby that got me to Hector Falls where Frank was waiting with a carriage."

Frank hadn't moved or made a sound since stepping on board. He was nothing but a large, dark lump in the moonlight.

"What's his problem?" Bradley asked Glendon.

"Can't swim. Terrified of the water."

"Annie and I saw him get shot and fall near Glen Mountain

House. We thought he was dead."

Glendon chuckled. "It takes a lot to kill Frank. He had a pocket Bible in his jacket. It stopped the bullet. Barely. But enough."

"Lucky Six indeed," Bradley said. "Where were you two hiding out?"

"Frank had been living in the woods when he found me," Glendon said, "but I know a lot of people in town. The Gardners were away on vacation, so we made good use of their barn."

On a hunch, Bradley searched the steering area and found a pair of leather gloves, a compass, and a glass bottle. He held the bottle out to Glendon. "Give Frank this."

Glendon accepted the bottle and opened it, smelling the contents. "Rum?"

"Liquid courage. We may need Frank later."

Glendon sighed. "No reason why this might go badly," he said. He nudged Frank and handed him the bottle.

The night was quiet. Bradley strained but could not hear the steamer over the sounds of the wind and the waves.

"What's the plan?" Glendon asked.

Bradley pictured the steamer in his mind. "Steering and throttle control is just forward of the cabin in the middle of the *Bonnie Lynn*. If Annie is smart—and she is—she will stay hidden under the canvas at the back of the steamer. She will be safe enough until we get there." *Assuming Fuchs hadn't already found her.* Bradley pushed the negative thought aside. "It's too risky to take a shot at Fuchs in the dark from here. So I'll get us close, then you hold the tiller while I jump aboard the steamer and take Fuchs by surprise."

"You're the only one who can pilot this sailing yacht," Glendon said. "I should be the one to go."

Bradley gritted his teeth. He wanted Fuchs for himself. He stared ahead, searching the darkness.

Glendon noticed the look on Bradley's face. "You're not telling me something," Glendon said. "What is it? Why are you so involved with this counterfeiting ring in the first place?"

Bradley tried to ignore Glendon, but the older man waited him out. Bradley looked away. He inhaled, exhaled, and then shrugged. "I want to kill Otto Fuchs."

"Why?"

"He's the Butzemann."

"So?"

Bradley gathered his thoughts. "A detective in the city named Mac McGregor hired me as his apprentice and agreed to train me to be a detective. He'd been working for months to learn the identity of a crime boss named the Butzemann."

"I thought the Butzemann was a myth?"

Bradley shook his head. "Mac was meeting an informant the night he died. An informant who promised information that would expose the Butzemann. Mac asked me to be there to back him up, but I... I showed up late." Bradley's voice caught. "Only five minutes, because of a trolley accident.... When I got to the restaurant, I saw the back of a man fleeing the scene and found my boss dead— face down in his dinner with a knife in his heart."

Glendon let out a low whistle.

"Mac walked into a trap," Bradley said, "and I wasn't there to have his back."

Glendon rubbed his chin and looked out at the water. There was still no sign of the steamer. "Why come to Watkins?"

"Some of Mac's papers pointed to a connection between an engraver named Thomas Pickens and a counterfeiting ring that the Butzemann was setting up somewhere out of the city. I leveraged my boss's connections with the Secret Service and got placed in The Tombs with a friend of mine, pretending to be an assassin to get Pickens to turn state's evidence. My real goal was to find a clue to track down the Butzemann's location. I promised myself I would make him pay for what he did to Mac."

"I don't blame you," Glendon said, "for wanting to pull the trigger yourself. But if we don't do this right, my daughter dies and the Butzemann gets away. We both know it makes more sense for you to steer the ship and for me to go. So tell me how the hell you'll get me close enough."

Bradley thought of Annie huddled under the tarpaulin on the steamer. Glendon was right, as much as Bradley hated to admit it. "Okay. Okay. I plan to approach from behind the steamship," Bradley said. "Fuchs won't hear us until we're on him. I'll get close enough for you to jump. But then, you are on your own. It will be difficult to match his speed, so you have to stop the steamer's engines so I can circle and come alongside."

"Are you sure you can get close enough?"

Bradley laughed. "Have you ever heard of Sadie 'the Goat'?"

"Didn't she run the Charlton Street Gang for a time?"

"Yes," Bradley said. "A few summers ago, I was crewing on a sloop running goods up the Hudson when Sadie and her band of river pirates boarded us. Killed our captain and made the other two crew members walk the plank. They were about to do the same to me, so I told Sadie it would be a mistake because I was a better pilot than the man she had. She laughed but let me prove it. So I did. I spent three weeks as a river pirate sneaking up on other ships and dropping off boarding parties."

"What happened after three weeks?"

Bradley shrugged. "I got tired of their cruelty. They made an old man walk the gangplank with his hands tied. I couldn't stand the terrified look on his face, so I used an axe to cut the halyard, dropping the mainsail, and then grabbed a knife and jumped over the side to save him. I got to him before he drowned while Sadie and her gang drifted down the Hudson with the current."

"Well done," Glendon said. "A happy ending."

Bradley sighed. "I got the old man to shore, but his heart gave out. He didn't drown, but he stopped breathing. Scared to death."

"So, not always a happy ending."

"No, not always."

They were both surprised when Frank's voice barked from the center of the ship. "There!"

From off in the distance, the faint hiss of a steam engine drifted across the water toward them. Bradley turned the wheel. "The boom is coming around," he warned Glendon.

The chugging of the steam engine grew louder. A steady wind propelled the sailing yacht silently forward. Ahead in the darkness, an oil lamp glowed from the front of the steamer. Fuchs thinks he's alone on the water, Bradley realized. That will be his downfall.

Glendon held the shotgun in his hands. "Get me close."

They came in from behind as planned. The moon—partially

obscured by clouds—gave off enough light for Bradley to see the outline of the steamer. He timed it perfectly. Glendon jumped onto the long and narrow steamship, landing on his feet just behind the small, center cabin that held the steam engine.

Fuchs turned from his position closer to the bow with a revolver in his hand. His surprise at Glendon's arrival turned into a wolfish grin. "Hello, Harper. It's been a long time."

Glendon looked at Fuchs. "You look pretty healthy for a dead man, Ace."

They raised their weapons at the same time.

CHAPTER LIII

THE SURVIVOR

October 1864

Ace lay on his cot in the Elmira Prison Camp isolation ward as his fellow prisoners suffered around him. Overcrowding, poor rations, and the worsening weather accelerated the prison death toll. He gagged every time the sweet and pungent odor of decaying flesh drifted past him, but it was the relentless sounds of men crying, praying, and whimpering as they died that kept him awake through the long nights, exhausting him.

Ace's rash disappeared after a week in isolation, and a doctor gave him the good news. He'd had chicken pox all along, not smallpox—an unfortunate mistake that the overworked doctors should have noticed. He should've known better as he'd been vaccinated for smallpox, after all. The doctors kept him for a few more days to ensure he hadn't contracted any other deadly diseases in isolation, then released him to the main camp.

Ace held his breath as he passed stagnant and fetid Foster's Pond and walked enthusiastically toward his tent. He looked forward to having Harper, Frank, and Buck thump him on the back for his good luck in surviving isolation and then tell him the tunnel was ready for their escape. He would be out of Hellmira in a matter of days and on his way to Georgia and his fiancée.

When he reached his tent, he stuck his head inside and found two men he had never seen before looking at him with trepidation. Ace pulled his head back out and looked around in confusion. Somehow, he had miscounted the rows and gotten the wrong tent. He blamed his lack of sleep. He returned to a known starting point, counted carefully, and returned to the same location.

He stuck his head back in the same tent. "What are you doing in my tent?"

"Bugger off. It's ours now," the larger of the two prisoners said.

A gnawing feeling took hold inside Ace.

"How long? How long have you been in this tent?"

"Since last week," the smaller prisoner said defensively.

"And the men that were here before?"

The smaller prisoner leaned forward and lowered his voice. "Didn't you hear about the escape? Ten men got out through a tunnel. Guards and officers up in arms. Every tent searched after. I heard they only caught one. The rest got away."

Ace stumbled backward out of the tent. Harper, Frank, and Buck left without him. He checked the tents of the other tunnel diggers. Traweek and his Alabama cohorts were gone as well. Every man Ace knew since arriving in this godforsaken hellhole had gone through the tunnel and left him behind. He was overcome with anger. Anger that he would miss the birth of his child. Anger that he might be stuck in Hellmira until the war's end. Anger at the greed of the other members of the Lucky Six, who chose gold over friendship.

With tunnel digging no longer an option, Ace needed to find another way to escape. He stole a jacket from a distracted guard and tried to sneak out wearing it but only made it three steps out of the guardhouse before an alert guard noticed his muddy and worn prisoner boots. His next and best chance came when he bribed another Confederate soldier to nail him into a prisoner-made coffin to be transported to Woodlawn Cemetery in Elmira for burial—an easier place to escape from. The plan would have worked if the same prisoner that had nailed him in hadn't sold him out to the camp authorities for extra food rations. In desperation, Ace tried to scale the prison camp's twelve-foot stockade wall in the middle of the night, but hadn't reached the top before warning shots splintered the wood around him. Each failed attempt got him sentenced to increasingly longer stays in the dungeon, an old military barracks repurposed as a prisoner jail.

As each day passed, the weather worsened, more prisoners died, and Ace's anger and panicked urgency grew.

Ace wrote letters to his fiancée, Bonnie, whenever he was able to buy or steal paper and ink. Over the many months that passed, he received three replies. The first came in early November. Bonnie told him she missed him and that while food was scarce, her aunt was looking after her and the pregnancy was going well. The second letter arrived in late December. Tears streamed down his face as Bonnie's delicate handwriting confirmed he was the father of a healthy baby boy. Bonnie hadn't picked a name yet, but she begged him to hurry to her so he could help name his son and they could be together as a family.

It was early March, after his longest stay in the dungeon, that he received the third and final letter. He did not recognize the handwriting. Confused, he opened the envelope to see it had been written by Bonnie's aunt. Charleston had fallen to the Union Army. As Confederate soldiers evacuated the city, they'd left behind stockpiles of gunpowder at the Northeastern Railroad Depot. Children were playing with the black powder when an explosion occurred. More than one hundred and fifty people died in the blast, including Bonnie and their unnamed son.

Ace lost his will to live.

The temperature in the camp fell below minus eighteen degrees twice. Ace had never known such cold. But it did not kill him. As spring came, the Chemung River flooded from the melting snow and filled the tents and barracks with up to two feet of water with feces and other waste. He survived. He considered rushing an armed Yankee soldier to force his own death but refused to give the Union Army the satisfaction of taking his life.

Hellmira's death toll began to drop after his captors dug a canal to get fresh water from the Chemung River flowing through Foster's Pond, improving prisoner health. As the weather turned warmer, Ace's prayers for the reprieve of death went unanswered.

Ace's anger and bitter resentment turned into burning hatred for the Union Army and for the men who left him behind. Gold had meant more than friendship and brotherhood to the surviving members of the Lucky Six. He would not forget, nor would he ever forgive them for leaving him behind. It had cost him everything that mattered to him in this life.

On April 9, 1865, the Confederate Army surrendered at Appomattox Courthouse in Virginia. The war was over. To be released from the camp, the Union required each prisoner to take an oath of *allegiance to the United States. Ace refused at first, but with no alternatives, he took the cursed oath and was offered transportation to wherever he wanted to go. With no life to return to in the South, Ace headed for New York City.*

July 1, 1874 – Otto Fuchs did not smile often, but today was an exception. His nine years of scraping and clawing his way up from an impoverished Confederate soldier to a secretive crime boss were about to come to a fulfilling conclusion. From the roof of his building on the Lower East Side, he looked out at the notorious Five Points neighborhood, home to dance halls, bars, gambling houses, and prostitution. He had his fingers in many of those pies, but always as a shadowy figure behind the scenes.

He turned back to Sanna Virsunen, who patiently waited for his response in the early evening breeze.

"You're sure?" he asked her. An unnecessary question, he knew. She had never provided him with inaccurate information.

"Yes," she said with her neutral expression. "Roland Smith is wanted for murder in Georgia."

Fuchs nodded. This was good news. "Send an anonymous telegram to the sheriff down there with Smith's location. Make sure he sends out a bounty hunter. In the interest of public safety."

"He's a murderer," Sanna said. "Let me put him on my list."

"Let's give the law a chance first," Fuchs said. He would save her talents for more important targets. Besides, having Smith shamefully dragged away as a murderer was better than killing him.

"We leave for Watkins in three days. You know what needs to be prepared. I'll be unreachable until the morning of our departure."

Sanna nodded and left. She knew he was telling her that he was going undercover. She didn't know that being undercover for Fuchs meant returning to his real life. This beautiful and deadly woman had once been a small blonde guttersnipe – knee high to a bumble bee – picking his pocket outside a rum-hole only to find the Pinkerton badge he had recently acquired from a drunk Pinkerton. Young Sanna's eyes had grown wide when she realized what she held. He was ready to give her a good whipping when she apologized and returned the badge to him with her small hands. She called him sir. Her deference made him see himself differently.

Otto Fuchs was born that day using an accent borrowed from his late German grandfather. Creating Fuchs allowed Ace to thrive in his new dual life. To the city's underbelly, he was the whispered-about crime boss named the Butzemann—German for bogeyman— who never worked with the same crew twice and never left witnesses. To Sanna, he was the Pinkerton detective and her guardian who punished criminals—usually the Butzemann's rivals—when the police failed to bring down the full weight of justice.

Fuchs changed his clothes, donned a worn-out hat and fake beard, and became Ace again as he stepped out into the night. He moved confidently through the streets—to do otherwise invited the attention of predators—moving south and west past the county courthouse and city hall. When he reached Broadway, he headed south.

When he arrived in the city nine years ago as a penniless Confederate soldier full of hatred for the North, he found the place crawling with discharged Union soldiers with pockets full of greenbacks from recently paid back salaries. Slipping a dagger between the ribs of an occasional Yankee in a dark alley for their money kept food in Ace's belly. He felt no guilt—these men had been trying to kill him for the last four years. Former soldiers were such easy marks that Ace moved on to financial cons. He set up fake business opportunities and invited naïve Yankee soldiers to invest in a new railroad or gold mine. After they handed over their cash, he stepped into the back room to get their stock certificate and departed using a rear exit. For the more suspicious types, offering a drug-laced cigar before talking business worked just as well. He lightened the unconscious men's pockets and walked out the front door.

With money piling up, Ace found a ready supply of thieves, hustlers, and street thugs available for bigger jobs. He was careful to remain behind the scenes. Crime was rampant in Manhattan neighborhoods like Five Points, the Fourth Ward, Hell's Kitchen, and the Bowery, but large gangs laid claim to illicit activities in those areas. Ace learned to choose his targets carefully and en-

sured no one could identify him when the job ended.

This evening, as he worked his way down Broadway, he set his sights on Trinity Church. The church's Gothic Revival spire made it easy to find. It was the tallest building in the city. He slowed as he neared the church grounds and checked his pocket watch. He had intentionally arrived early to give himself twenty minutes to wander through the encircling cemetery, looking for anyone suspicious. When he was satisfied there were no threats, he returned to the front entrance, slipped through large wooden doors, and entered the cavernous sanctuary.

Maurice Vance sat in a wooden pew halfway up the left side. Ace took a seat directly behind him.

"The boss wants an update," he said in a low voice.

For each job, Ace picked a young and ambitious thug. Someone enthusiastic but not experienced enough to recognize the dangers of working for the Butzemann. Maurice Vance fit the role perfectly. He knew Ace only as a messenger.

"I thought I was going to meet the boss," Vance said testily. "It was a long trip down from Watkins."

"He's a busy man," Ace said. "What's your news?"

Vance had picked the team for the counterfeiting ring. Ace, the real boss, had provided the funding and the boxes of currency paper and insisted on Watkins as the location. He'd already identified Alistair Sinclair as the fall guy. Wealthy men with secrets should hide them better.

"We are back on track," Vance said. "Thomas Pickens turned us down, but the Ballard brothers can run the two printing presses with impressive results. We'll reach ten million dollars before the month is out."

"By July 28," Ace said. "The boss was very clear on that date." Pickens turning down their job offer wasn't a surprise but couldn't go unpunished. Ace would drop information into the right ears. Pickens would be in jail before the week was over. "And Smythe?"

"Can't beat a man sober." Vance shrugged. Smythe had been Vance's choice, but the man couldn't keep his hands off a whiskey bottle. He had started well enough but now couldn't be counted on to show up for work. "The Ballard brothers will get the job done."

Smythe would need to be taken care of, but Ace already had a

Trinity Church

plan. As the auction date approached, he'd get Smythe to kidnap Henry Sinclair. That would give Ace leverage over Alistair Sinclair to ensure he followed through with the auction. And after? Smythe liking young boys was information that would be mentioned to Sanna. List or no list, nothing would save Smythe from Sanna's vengeance after that.

Ace had one extra task for Vance. "The boss is offering you a well-paid side job if you're interested," Ace said.

"What is it?"

"Is killing a woman going to be a problem for you?" Ace said, mentioning the price.

"No," Vance said, shaking his head. "Especially for that price."

"There's a young woman in Watkins named Annie Anderson," Ace said. "Kill her and make it look accidental. The boss doesn't care how you do it or what liberties you take, but he wants the body to be found and recognizable."

"Consider it done."

Ace had chosen Vance well. "The boss has been impressed with your work," he told the younger man. "Go back to Watkins. He will meet you there when the job is finished."

Ace stood up, exited the church quickly, and watched from the shadows of the cemetery as Vance departed. As the younger man disappeared down Broadway, Ace allowed himself another smile. Killing the girl solved two problems. It would devastate Harper Thompson and put Vance on Sanna's list when the time came. Sanna had never failed him. Vance would be one less loose end to worry about.

Ace moved slowly through the cemetery, looking for a specific grave and thinking about the surviving members of the Lucky Six. Their greed deprived him of his fiancée and infant son, so he planned to take away what mattered most to each of them, and after they'd suffered, he'd take their lives. Ace tracked down Buck and hired men to burn the family mercantile store to the ground. A shame Buck's parents had been in the building at the time. Frank hadn't strayed far from home, having started a farm outside Asheville, North Carolina. He was now doing odd jobs in town after returning home one day to find every animal on the property slaughtered with no explanation. "An eye for an eye, a tooth for a tooth,"

Ace whispered to himself.

Ace found the grave he was looking for and pulled out a large knife hidden in the lining of his jacket. He bent down and started digging near the headstone.

In all his years of sending men out searching, no one had ever reported a sighting of Harper Thompson. This is why Ace was dumbstruck when he stumbled upon Harper strolling down Broadway without a care six months ago. Harper, wearing the fashionable attire of a gentleman, appeared to have been enjoying a prosperous life. Ace hated him even more at that moment. He followed Harper back to his hotel and then bribed the clerk to learn Harper's name was now Glendon Robinson, and he lived upstate in Watkins. Ace, disguised as Otto Fuchs, traveled to Watkins to look for Harper's weaknesses. He found her. Samantha Ann Anderson, named after her grandfather Samuel, looked just like the photo of her mother that Harper had shown him all those years ago on the battlefield. Ace would make sure Harper felt the same pain of loss he'd suffered.

The notes luring Frank and Buck to Watkins were already delivered. When the month was over, Ace expected to be on his way to Buenos Aires with ten million dollars as the last surviving member of the Lucky Six.

Ace unearthed a large clump of dirt from the grave. He wiped away the soil to reveal the golden nugget he'd buried nine years earlier. He'd found the cursed nugget hidden in the lining of Taylor's jacket after the train wreck and managed to hide it from the guards at Hellmira all those months. It had brought him nothing but bad luck in prison, so he'd buried it the moment he arrived in the city. Now, it would be useful in Watkins. Buck would find it irresistible. It would serve as a nice distraction when it came time to stab his old comrade through the heart.

CHAPTER LIV

Bloody Reunion

Tuesday, July 28, 1874

HARPER and Ace fired simultaneously as both threw themselves to the side. Harper felt Ace's bullet graze the fabric of his suit jacket as he landed and rolled behind the center cabin in the middle of the steamer. His shotgun blast wouldn't need a direct hit to wound Ace seriously. "Still alive?" Harper called out.

"Birdshot?" Ace's laugh came from the other side of the cabin. "You brought birdshot to a gunfight?"

Harper cursed. He had assumed the rifle was loaded with buckshot—larger pellets that could bring down a deer or a man. Birdshot's smaller pellets could be debilitating from a distance but rarely lethal except to birds or squirrels. He'd have to get extremely close to make the shot count. "We were friends once," Harper said. "I don't want to kill you."

"I don't feel the same."

Harper looked behind him but did not see Annie. He willed her to stay hidden. He focused on Ace, listening for movement, but the chugging of the steam engine's pistons drowned out other sounds. He stayed light on his feet as he tried to guess which way Ace would attack him when the oil lamp hanging from the front of the ship went out. Harper took a chance, stuck his head around the corner of the cabin, and pulled it back immediately. Wood splintered where his head had been. That had been close.

"You've lost a step, old man," Ace called.

Ace was as fast as Harper remembered. Having lost the element of surprise, he knew the outcome was now up in the air. Whose luck would give out first?

Harper hadn't known Ace was alive until he'd seen him coming out of the woods when he prepared to jump off the ledge. Harper knew then that Ace had been involved but couldn't understand his reasons. "Why kill Crawford?"

"Are you joking? You greedy bastards left me in Hellmira for the gold. You have no idea what that cost me."

"Buck told us you were dead." Harper pulled one of the spare cartridges from his pocket and reloaded the shotgun to have two shots at the ready.

"Buck? You ruined my life on Buck's word?" Ace spit out the words. "Did you check? No! You needed the gold to buy back your old love, so you left me behind. And because you did, my fiancée and infant son died. If I wasn't stuck in that hellhole, I could have prevented their deaths."

"I'm sorry." It was a stretch to place the blame at his feet, but there seemed little point in arguing.

"You don't get to be sorry."

Ace's revolver blasted three times. Harper ducked down, but Ace was not firing at him. Out of the darkness on the port side, the sailing yacht tacked away from the *Bonnie Lynn*. Bradley had tried to get close again. The sound of the steam engine changed, and the ship's speed increased. Ace was trying to outrun the sailing yacht. Harper moved quickly to the opposite side of the cabin, leaned out with his shotgun, and fired toward the ship's bow. He heard cursing.

"Nice try, Harper," Ace said, still alive. "You've used up your two shots. Hope you brought spare cartridges."

"Don't worry," Harper said, "I have plenty." He reached into his pocket. He had two more spares and loaded one. "How did you find me?"

Ace laughed. "You walked by me in New York City and didn't even know it. I had you followed for months and learned everything I could about your life. Figured out Annie was your daughter. I lured Buck and Frank to Watkins to kill them. I even told that useless bounty hunter where to find your friend Roland."

"Did you shoot Roland?"

"No, you did," Ace said. "Or at least the sheriff thinks you shot Roland. I dressed like you and stood in the shadows. The trusting fool walked right up to me. Amazing that he still managed to get a shot off, but his missed. Mine didn't. Framing you for murder was a welcome bonus."

Roland was near death because of Harper's Lucky Six past. And Harper had played into Ace's hands when he buried Crawford's body on his own property—stupid move. And then there was Annie. "Leave my daughter out of this, Ace," Harper said. "Annie has done nothing to you."

"You don't get it, do you? An eye for an eye, Harper. My child is dead because of you. I want you to know the pain of losing your only child." Ace's voice changed slightly. He was up to something. "You are going to die tonight," Ace said, his voice sounding farther away. "Then, I'll find your daughter, and—when she least expects it—I'll send her to join you."

The ship went quiet. Harper tried to block out the sound of the steam engine but heard nothing else except the ship's bow slicing through the waves. Ace would come around one side of the cabin or the other, giving Harper an even chance to guess correctly. He took a step back to cover both options. It was luck or perhaps the smallest of sounds that made Harper look up as Ace dropped from the cabin roof on top of him. He tried to bring his weapon around but was too slow. He managed to step to the side and keep his footing as Ace landed and grabbed for the shotgun.

Each man had two hands on the weapon as they fought for control. They were evenly matched. Ace was stronger, but Harper weighed more, giving him greater leverage. Ace sent a knee toward Harper's groin. Harper blocked it, but as his eyes glanced down, Ace headbutted him. Harper's head snapped back, and he saw stars but managed to hold on to the shotgun. Ace hooked his thumb inside the trigger guard. Two shotgun blasts in rapid succession shattered the air between them. Harper, with his ears ringing, pulled Ace close and headbutted his former friend in return. As Harper tried to free the shotgun, Ace let go and kicked out, sending Harper flying backward with an empty shotgun.

Harper scrambled to his feet while reaching into his pocket for his final cartridge. He froze when Ace pulled out a revolver and pointed it at the center of his chest. Ace wouldn't miss from ten feet away.

"My last bullet," Ace said with a satisfied smile. "You will soon be forgotten, Harper."

"I'll give you the gold. I still have most of it."

"I don't want your damn gold. What's it worth now? A few hundred thousand? After I kill you, I'll be on my way to South America with ten million dollars. Goodbye, Harper."

"No!" Both men turned toward the back of the boat. Annie stepped out from her hiding spot with gray smoke billowing around her body.

Annie was cramped and miserable under the tarpaulin as the *Bonnie Lynn* steamed north to an unknown destination with Otto Fuchs at the helm. She couldn't believe she was back on this damned ship with another man who wanted her dead.

When she had crossed the gangplank, she wanted to confirm the presence of the counterfeit money. Then came three gunshots. Annie had immediately ducked down when she saw Fuchs step out of the Malthouse into the moonlight carrying his leather satchel. Waiting in the shadows, her chest tightened, and her heart skipped a beat. *Bradley would not have let Fuchs get past him unless severely wounded. Or dead.* Annie shook her head to force out negative thoughts. For now, she had to focus on herself. Fuchs, the man who wants to kill her, is on his way to the ship. He would see her if she tried to cross the gangplank to escape.

She reached into her dress pocket and cursed silently. Bradley had taken her derringer in the park, and she hadn't thought to ask for it back. With nowhere to run and no way to defend herself, she could only stay hidden and pray Fuchs did not check his cargo before departing.

Sitting under the tarpaulin, Annie hugged her knees against her chest. She listened as Fuchs crossed the gangplank. He kicked at something, and she heard a loud splash. He had pushed the gangplank into the water. After a few anxious moments listening to his footfalls thumping across the deck, she heard louder hissing from the steam engine, and the *Bonnie Lynn* was underway.

Annie exhaled slowly. She thought of Glendon and Frank looking in the wrong places. Even if they saw the steamer heading north, they would not know she was on board or have a way to stop it. Where was Fuchs headed? Geneva and the passage that connected Seneca Lake to the Erie Canal were both almost forty miles away. At top speed, that distance would take at least four hours. Would Fuchs travel that far? Or did he have a horse and carriage waiting at one of the many landings along the lake?

She peeked out from her hiding place to see moonlight dancing on the tips of the waves and darkness beyond. *The darkness must be the shoreline*, she thought. She had few options, but the obvious choice was slipping off the steamer's stern and making for shore. She was a good swimmer, and Fuchs wasn't too far off the eastern side of the lake. He wouldn't see Annie go over the side with the wooden cabin between them. But if he heard a splash and realized what had made it, he could circle around and shoot her while swimming. Not ideal. For now, she would keep that as her backup plan. She had another reason to stay on board. If she abandoned ship, Fuchs would get away with murder.

It was dark under the tarpaulin, but Annie searched for something to defend herself with. *Finding a loaded weapon would be nice*, she thought. She reached out with her hands to feel around, ignoring the two large printing presses. Pushed up against the presses, she found a large steamer trunk and two smaller wooden crates. The lid of the steamer trunk was secured with a brass lock in the center and two latches on either side. The latches opened easily, but the lock stopped her. She moved on to the wooden crates. Kneeling in the darkness, she slid the wooden lid off the first crate. It contained tools and equipment for the printing presses. She pulled out a screwdriver—a poor weapon, but better than nothing.

The second crate started out promising. Her hands closed on a smaller wooden case inside the crate. It was about the right size to hold a revolver. Elated, she opened the case. It was a revolver case, but it was empty. She dug deeper, finding a second wooden case. With trembling hands, she opened it only to find that it was also empty. Annie slumped backward in the darkness and sat with the screwdriver in her lap.

As she fiddled with the screwdriver, a thought came to her. She pulled a second screwdriver out of the tool crate and then moved back to the wooden steamer trunk. The hinged hasp for the brass lock connected to a recess on the lid. She had once seen Roland open a trunk with a lost key using two screwdrivers. Surely, she could do it. After ten minutes of flailing in the darkness, she gave up. After two minutes of fuming, she tried again. When the lock popped opened, Annie grinned like the Cheshire cat in *Alice's Adventures in Wonderland*. She had to push against the tarpaulin, but she opened the lid.

Inside, she found folded suits which she pulled out and dropped on the deck. She kept pulling out garments until she had emptied a third of the trunk. When she touched paper, she reached in with both hands and pulled out a stack of currency. This must be the missing nine million dollars. She reached into her pocket and pulled out Bradley's match safe. It was a risk, but lighting one match would confirm what she had felt with her hands. She had a better idea. What if she used her match to set the money aflame? She could swim away while Fuchs tried to put out the fire. Best case, he couldn't put the fire out and went down with the ship. If she was lucky, he'd at least lose the money and be forced overboard to swim to shore with wet gunpowder. A reasonable risk, she decided.

Leaning into the trunk, Annie broke apart the top stacks of money, reasoning that loose bills burned faster. The fire needed to take hold quickly for her to get away. She lay down on the deck, wriggled out of her cotton drawers and the crinolette frame that gave volume to the back of her dress. Both were highly flammable. She placed them in the trunk on top of the money. After peering out from under the tarpaulin to check that the shore was close, Annie lit one of her matches.

She hesitated when she heard a large thump and felt vibrations through the deck board. Had someone jumped on board? She blew out the match as soon as she heard Glendon's voice. "You look pretty healthy for a dead man, Ace." Glendon had found her!

Annie started to crawl out from under the tarpaulin when a gunshot ricocheted off one of the printing presses, sending her scrambling back to her hiding place. She could hear Fuchs and

Glendon yelling back and forth. Fuchs was Ace from the Lucky Six! Annie wanted to signal Glendon to let him know where she was but worried that exposing herself to Fuchs—Ace—would put Glendon in more danger. Glendon would sacrifice himself for her if it came to that.

After more revolver and shotgun blasts, Annie saw the shore getting dangerously close. Was no one piloting the ship?

From Harper's account of the Battle of the Wilderness, Annie remembered that Ace was afraid of fire. It would distract him. Maybe enough to give Glendon an edge. When she heard Ace say he had one more bullet left and that Harper—Glendon—would be forgotten, she lit her last match and placed it gently in the crinoline where it flared to life. She crawled out from under the tarpaulin as Ace raised his revolver to shoot Glendon.

She stood up and yelled, "No!"

Both men turned toward her. The moon was free of the clouds, so she could see their faces clearly. Glendon had a stricken look on his face while Fuchs grinned at her. But the smile faltered when he saw the smoke rising from under the tarpaulin.

"You are full of surprises, Miss Anderson. Very convenient of you to spare me a return trip to kill you. Guess I haven't lost my luck after all."

As Fuchs spun the revolver toward Annie, a rifle shot slammed into the cabin inches from Fuchs's head, forcing him to crouch down. Glendon, ignoring the bullets, dropped his shotgun, dove forward, and tackled Fuchs.

Annie turned to see a sailing yacht keeping pace with the steamer off the port side. Frank—his back to the mast and a rifle in one hand—lowered his rifle and saluted her with what looked like a near-empty bottle of alcohol.

Annie turned back to the *Bonnie Lynn*. Fire had ignited the tarpaulin and was spreading fast. Fuchs and Glendon fought over the revolver. Annie reached down and picked up the shotgun and a spare cartridge that had fallen out of Glendon's pocket.

"Annie," Glendon yelled. "The shore. We're too close."

Annie raced around the other side of the cabin and sprinted to the steering. A wall of darkness rose up dangerously close on the starboard side. She wrenched the controls to turn to port, pulled back on the throttle to slow down the steamer, and then cracked open the shotgun to take out the empty cartridges.

The sound of a gunshot made her jump. She turned around to see Fuchs standing over Glendon. Glendon moaned and tried to reach up to Fuchs, but his hand fell away. Fuchs tossed the revolver aside, pulled a large knife from his jacket, and stepped toward Annie.

She snapped the shotgun closed and pointed it at him. "Drop the knife!" Annie yelled. "Or I swear I'll kill you." Tears formed in her eyes as she noticed Glendon had stopped moving.

"You're bluffing," Fuchs said. "We both know that the shotgun is empty."

"Please, stop. I'm not bluffing."

Fuchs glanced over his shoulder at the spreading fire, his eyes filling with fear and rage. His fortune in counterfeit bills was turning into embers and ash. "You did this." She saw his eyes narrow. "*Klappe zu, Affe tot*," he said, then raised his knife and lunged toward her.

Annie pulled the shotgun against her shoulder and pulled the trigger. A blast of birdshot caught Fuchs in the head and neck at close range, killing him instantly.

Fuchs fell to the deck, and Annie dropped the shotgun and rushed to Glendon who clung to life. His shirt was soaked with his blood. A wave of prickling heat advanced before the fire, now moving toward the wooden cabin. The ship would be fully engulfed in minutes.

Glendon's eyes opened. "Leave me. Swim to shore."

"I'm not leaving you." Annie ripped off the bottom of her dress, wadded it up into a ball, and pressed it into Glendon's wound to stop the bleeding. Glendon grimaced in pain.

She had to get him off the ship. Maybe she could roll him into the water and save him like she'd saved Bradley. She frantically looked for something that floated, but Fuchs hadn't replaced the life-preserver rings.

She heard Glendon mumble something.

"What? I can't hear you."

"Your mother would be proud of you," Glendon said, his voice weak. "I've always been proud of you." He closed his eyes. Annie tried to lift him. He made no noise this time. Tears streamed down her face, and her vision narrowed. She felt lightheaded and nauseous. Smoke billowed about them as the fire burned closer. With the steam engine idling, Annie could hear the fire and the gentle lapping of the waves against the ship. *Strange*, she thought, *to burn to death surrounded by so much water.*

She felt a jolt as something hard hit the steamer.

"Annie!" *That sounded like Bradley, but he was dead, wasn't he?* "Frank, I need your help. We've got to move quickly before the fire spreads to our sails."

Annie looked up to see Bradley's face emerge from the smoke. Her eyes widened as Frank towered over Bradley's left shoulder. She didn't resist as Bradley pulled her to her feet and guided her across the deck to a sailing yacht roped to the steamer. Frank, carrying Glendon, followed close behind. Annie slumped down on the sailboat's deck as Frank laid Glendon beside her. She cradled her father's head in her lap and continued to put pressure on the wound.

As Bradley scrambled to throw off the lines, Frank jumped back onto the steamer.

"Dammit, Frank. We have to leave. Now!" Bradley disappeared into the smoke after Frank.

Annie's brain was in a fog. When they returned, Frank carried Ace's bloody body, and Bradley carried a leather satchel. She looked at Ace's body, and her vision narrowed. She'd killed a man. Annie closed her eyes as the memory of Fuchs lunging for her and the boom of the shotgun kept repeating itself in her mind.

She heard Bradley push off from the steamer and rush to the helm to work the sheets. The sailing yacht came about and began an upwind journey back to Watkins.

"Here," a deep, rumbling voice said in Annie's ear. She opened her eyes as Frank pressed a bottle against her lips and tipped it up. She gulped down the last of the rum in the bottle and coughed as it burned her throat. "You're in shock," he said. "But you'll survive."

Frank sat back down. He had covered Ace's body with an extra sail.

"Why?" Annie asked. "Why bring him back?"

Frank shrugged. "Fire terrified him," he said, "and he was our friend once."

"Coming about," Bradley called as he prepared to tack. They would need to zigzag their way upwind. "I'll get us to Watkins as quick as possible, and we'll get Glendon to a doctor." He'd tried to sound confident.

Fuchs's last words echoed in Annie's head. *Klappe zu, Affe tot.* In German, it translated as "close the lid, the monkey is dead," but to a German it meant "It's the end." Fuchs had gotten the expression right this time.

CHAPTER LV

ANGEL OF DEATH

Wednesday, July 29, 1874

A BROWN-HAIRED young woman with glasses lifted the front of her brown cotton dress as she climbed aboard the 9:17 a.m. train in Havana, heading southbound to Elmira. Anyone watching might have guessed her profession as schoolmarm, or, uncharitably, future spinster. Moving down the aisle, the young woman kept her head down, but her eyes darted left and right until they settled on two chatty middle-aged ladies halfway down the train car.

"Is this seat taken?" she asked, referring to the bench beside the older ladies in a quiet voice. Both women shook their heads, so she sat down. As the train pulled out of the Havana station, she glanced at the woman beside her and cleared her throat. "Thank you. I'm a bit nervous to travel alone." Not a lie, exactly.

"Really? Well, you have nothing to fear, my dear. You are safe with us. I'm Rebecca and this is my good, good friend Netty." Netty smiled and waved from the other side of Rebecca.

"Thank you," the young woman said. "And please call me Lily."

"Where are you heading, Lily?" Netty asked. "We are on our way to Philadelphia."

"I'm traveling to Buffalo to care for a sick relative."

"Oh, dear," Rebecca said, turning around in her seat and looking back toward Havana. "Shouldn't you have taken the northbound train? You could have gotten to Buffalo much faster."

The young woman shrugged. "My uncle bought the tickets," she said and leaned in conspiratorially. "He's a bit of a tightwad. It was probably cheaper this way."

Before long, the older women resumed their conversation. Anyone watching would assume the three women traveled together.

Sanna smoothed out the plain brown dress and ignored the women's conversation as she scanned the train car for potential threats. She had kept a sharp eye out for anyone following her but had seen no one. She avoided going north through Watkins in case Abraham or the sheriff were looking for her. Easy enough to change trains in Elmira and head back north and west, reaching Niagara Falls by evening. Some of the tension left Sanna's body. The risks she'd taken had been acceptable.

Letting herself be captured by Glendon and Frank had been a risk. She wanted information and needed to get close to Bradley and Annie to get it. They confirmed what she feared—Annie did not stab the man in the cemetery, and Bradley hadn't killed the woman who fell to her death in the Glen. Fuchs had been lying to her and using her. With that knowledge, she had waited for Abraham to start his wagon in motion then cut through the ropes binding her with a knife hidden in her boot. She'd slipped off the back of the wagon and made her way through the darkness to the Montour House in Havana. She could not risk staying in her old room, so she gathered her belongings, picked the lock on an empty room at the end of the hall, and slept until first light.

Sanna watched the scenery pass by the train window. Her eyes followed the Chemung Canal's straight line and Catharine Creek's meandering journey beside it. She had been on the straight path until she realized it had all been a lie. Was it possible to change your destiny—to switch paths?

Fuchs would make his escape on the Bonnie Lynn and expect to meet her back in New York City. He would be disappointed. Using her left thumb to massage her right palm, she remembered Fuchs's Pinkerton badge, shiny and warm, that she had pulled from his pocket all those years ago. She had stared at the badge in awe and then at the lawman—a man who protected the weak—and had held the badge up to him with her small arms. "I'm sorry, sir," she'd said. She'd felt blessed when he took her off the streets and let her live in his house as his ward. He offered her no emotion and never touched her but praised her when she worked hard cleaning the house. She learned to crave his approval.

As she got stronger, Fuchs trained her to defend herself, and when she used those skills to beat up a man who struck a female garment worker, Fuchs praised her even more. He told her the time had come for her to help him punish guilty criminals who escaped justice. He added weapons training, fighting techniques, and the art of disguise to her lessons. He taught her how to read people—to look for their tells—and how to identify the strongest and weakest person in any room. Sanna embraced her mission and, when the time came, her list. She felt no guilt in dispatching those on the wrong side of the law—especially men who preyed on women or children.

All that time, she believed Otto Fuchs was a Pinkerton detective. All that time, he had only been playing a part and using her skills for his own nefarious reasons. Her list was a lie. She could not face the thought that she had killed innocent men or women at Fuchs's word.

Last night, she knew she had to leave behind everything she had known since she was a little girl. She'd saved some money so she would be fine for a while. She wondered if she would see Fuchs again, but hoped not, for his sake. Firing the rifle to create a diversion had been the last act of service he would receive from her. Any debt she owed had been repaid when she aided his escape from the park. She would take her life back.

In Elmira, she said goodbye to Rebecca and Netty and boarded a train heading through Corning, Bath, and Avon to Batavia. From there, the New York Central & Hudson Railroad would take her west to Niagara Falls.

Sanna was glad she had not killed Bradley Webster when she'd had the chance. Had he drunk from his poisoned coffee that first day she'd met him at the Montour House, he would have been dead before the next sunrise, but Fuchs had given her the signal—mentioning sugar—to stand down. She'd had to smack Bradley's coffee away to prolong his life. Fuchs chose to keep him alive to learn who the informer was inside the counterfeiting ring.

Cracks in Sanna's resolve to kill Bradley first appeared at the circus. As her carriage departed the Watkins fairgrounds, she heard a man shouting, "Driver! Driver! You dropped your coin purse." She recognized Bradley's voice and instructed her own driver to

Niagara Falls Cave of the Winds

pull over. From a distance, she watched Bradley rescue the Sinclair boy from his kidnapper. His were not the actions of a cold-blooded killer. Instead, Sanna made room on her list for the man who kidnapped boys. She followed Smythe back to the Glen Mountain House, knocked on his door, and took his life without remorse.

Then she'd missed her shot on purpose while aiming at Annie and Bradley in the wagon at Twelfth and Decatur. Fuchs had been furious, but she was already having doubts. She had another chance to kill Bradley a few days later. He'd smiled at her and collapsed at her feet outside the Fall Brook House. His friends had abandoned him, and he looked so pitiful that Sanna helped him back to his room at the Jefferson House and laid him on his bed. Killing him then would have been too easy. Why hadn't she? Perhaps because as she guided him to his room, he had whispered in her ear, "You are an angel." An angel of death, she thought of herself.

Bradley passed out immediately after collapsing on his bed. She'd bandaged his wounds, brought water and fresh fruit for when he woke and stared at him for a long time while he slept. Then she slipped out of his hotel room. She could kill him another time, she reasoned.

As she watched the greenness of upstate New York go by outside her window, Sanna decided she would like to see Bradley Webster again. But first, she had to visit Niagara Falls.

After her family had arrived in America from Finland, but before the tragedy that abandoned her to the streets, her father told bedtime stories to Sanna and her brother every night. Her favorite was listening to her father try to recreate the sound of water crashing over Niagara Falls. It always made her laugh. Her father promised that one day he would take their whole family to Niagara Falls so she could hear it for herself. Sanna was all that was left of her family now. She had read about a long set of wooden stairs that led to a natural cave behind the falls where rainbows formed an entire circle. She would go there. Her family would have liked that.

And after? She had a lot to atone for but had no idea how to begin.

CHAPTER LVI

A BEAUTIFUL FUNERAL

Friday, August 7, 1874

B RADLEY was the last mourner to arrive at Glenwood Cemetery for the small service in Watkins on a beautiful, summer morning with a sky filled with puffy white clouds. He passed carriages and wagons with patient horses lining the cemetery road and stood at the back of the assembled crowd. He resisted the urge to reach for his missing pocket watch but decided he wasn't too late when the minister raised his voice to start with a call to prayer. The town fathers had counseled against a full church funeral, deciding that a man accused of murder did not deserve more than a discreet gravesite burial. Still, a decent-sized crowd had formed from those who knew the deceased. There were only a few faces Bradley recognized. He caught Abraham's eye and tipped his hat to him. At the front, next to the minister and the grave, stood Annie and her grandmother. Annie looked beautiful in a formfitting black bodice and flowing black skirt.

She hadn't had time for Bradley in the week following the events on the *Bonnie Lynn*. He understood that she was grieving and had a funeral service to plan and that perhaps she still saw him as an escaped murderer from The Tombs. He had come to the funeral hoping to talk to her before leaving Watkins. As the days passed without communication, Bradley realized nothing kept him in this town. He decided to stay until the service—out of a sense of obligation—but would not linger afterward. He patted his jacket pocket, confirming the location of his late afternoon train ticket that would take him to Washington, DC, where he had unexpected business to attend to.

It was ironic that Fuchs—for all the evil he had done—unwittingly left Bradley a tremendous gift. Bradley had been ready to give up searching the Lost and Found section of *The New York Times*. But he found the copy that Fuchs had left after their Jefferson House breakfast. Bradley opened the paper and, following long years of habit, ran his fingers down the columns until reaching Lost and Found.

> *LOST – a poorly trained Cooper Hawk named Orion. The finder will be suitably rewarded if same returned unharmed to 3051 M Street, NW, Washington, DC.*

The breath left Bradley's body, and he had to read the notice three times before he'd let himself believe that his brother had finally reached out using a code they had come up with as young boys. Bradley had been waiting ten years for this message. His brother was alive and asking to meet in Washington, DC.

The day was growing warmer. Bradley tugged at the collar of his shirt as the minister preached about the importance of forgiveness. Appropriate, Bradley thought, considering the man they were burying. "Do not seek revenge or bear a grudge against anyone among your people," the minister intoned, "but love your neighbor as yourself."

Over the last four weeks, Bradley had sent multiple telegrams to his friend Nilsson, the bald, tattooed Swede he'd befriended working at the theater in New York. The Walrus suppressed the first one, the O'Donnell brothers stole the second, but a third finally reached its destination. Nilsson arrived at the Watkins train station three days ago. Spending time together at the Jefferson House billiards room had been the one bright spot in Bradley's week.

"Brother!" Nilsson had yelled when he caught sight of Bradley. The big man had wrapped him in a bear hug and squeezed his ribs hard enough for Bradley to groan. After the theater burned down, Bradley had gotten his detective job while Nilsson took work as a stevedore loading and unloading cargo on the docks along New York's harbor. He had only grown stronger.

"You're looking healthy for a dead man!" Bradley had replied, leading his friend down Franklin Street toward the Jefferson House.

BILLIARDS ROOM

"Ha, I could be a great actor, ja?"

"You made a perfect assassin. Very menacing. Pickens was shaking in his boots."

"Small man almost soiled himself in the yard," Nilsson said, laughing at the memory.

"How did it go with Pickens after I left?"

"As you planned. I paid guards like you asked to say you stabbed me in my cell." Nilsson waved a finger at Bradley "Not believable that I let you kill me."

Bradley smiled. "As long as Pickens believed it."

Nilsson grinned. "Warden very happy when he let me out. Pickens begged for protection. Promising all his secrets."

They entered the billiards room of the Jefferson House. A smoky haze from cigars and pipes filled the room. Bradley ordered two ginger ales and pulled a flask of whiskey from his jacket and topped off their glasses. The Walrus had had at least one good idea in his life.

"Skål!" both men said, lifting their glasses.

"I was happy to leave prison," Nilsson said. "I worried it was a bear favor."

"A what?"

"Bear favor?" Nilson scrunched up his face, translating the words in his head. "Do a favor for a bear. Good intentions but bad results. Like if Nilsson," he said, pointing to himself, "gets left in prison."

"Ah, I wouldn't let that happen, old friend."

Nilsson smiled. "I know this. That is why I let you fake kill me in prison." He thumped Bradley on the back, almost knocking him out of his chair. Nilsson found this hilarious and roared with laughter.

Bradley righted himself, exaggerated an injured back, and laughed along. Then he reached into his jacket, pulled out a large envelope, and placed it in front of his friend. Nilsson's eyes grew wide.

"This envelope is bigger than expected."

"Half of the money I got from Pickens," Bradley said. He was burning through his portion of the money with all his new clothes and expensive hotel rooms, but a deal was a deal. "What will you do with it?"

Nilsson felt the weight of the envelope, then shoved it into his pocket without bothering to count the money. "Return to Sweden, I think. Find a wife who can understand me," he said, grinning. They took another drink. Nilsson turned serious.

"You hoped to find good fortune. Did you?"

Bradley watched a billiard player miss an easy shot, the ivory billiard ball bouncing harmlessly off the bumper after avoiding every other ball. "No," he admitted with a shrug. "The counterfeit money burned up, and I'm out of work." He secretly hoped to catch the counterfeiters and get offered a job from the Secret Service or Pinkertons. Or both. But neither had come calling. His last hope, the leather satchel, had disappeared the night of the fire. When the sailboat finally reached Watkins, Abraham had been waiting for them. In a rush to get Glendon onto Abraham's wagon and then to fetch the doctor, Bradley forgot the satchel on the yacht. When he returned hours later, he found the yacht's owner screaming at the sheriff about vandals desecrating his vessel. There was no sign of the satchel, and Bradley was smart enough not to admit he was the one who took the man's ship for a sail. If the satchel had anything of value inside, the rich yacht owner would not advertise his new prize.

"And the murderer of your friend?" Nilsson asked, looking at him intently.

"My friend has been avenged."

"That is good," Nilsson had said, slapping the table. "Too bad your detective career is over before it started." He drained his glass and signaled the waiter. "Again!" he said. "Less ginger ale this time."

Nilsson joined Bradley that night for dinner with Abraham and his sister. Nilsson charmed Esther and bonded with Abraham over a love of horses and oily fish. Bradley was sorry to see his friend leave on the first train back to the city the next morning. He wished Nilsson could have met Annie. Selfishly, he wanted her to know he was not a murderer. Although he was, wasn't he? He killed in the war and drowned Maurice Vance in the lake, even if it was in self-defense.

After Nilsson's departure, Bradley went back to moping around Watkins, feeling obligated to stay in town until the burial service. Now, he listened as the minister droned on about life and loss while a gentle breeze rustled the trees on the cemetery's edge. Whoever was paying the minister was getting their money's worth.

Behind him, Bradley heard a thumping noise. He looked over his shoulder and scanned the trees until he spotted the redheaded woodpecker on the trunk of a dead pine. *Fitting*, he thought. *Hadn't he been hitting his head against a hard object while in Watkins, hoping to dislodge a tasty morsel?* Only in hindsight did he realize how little he'd known and how many mistakes he'd made—like focusing on engravers, sending telegrams that went nowhere, or confiding in the one man he was trying to bring to justice.

Elizabeth Sinclair had filled in the gaps in Bradley's knowledge when she visited him on her last morning in town. For her, she'd told him, it had started when Alistair began behaving oddly—moving their summer plans from Saratoga Springs to Watkins at the last minute, introducing her to questionable men like Maurice Vance and Cornelius "the Walrus" Dewers, and showing an uncharacteristic interest in Emma Magee's charity auction. When Alistair dismissed her concerns, Elizabeth hired private investigators. As they began to unravel the mystery, the Secret Service was brought in. Those were the men she had been sneaking out to meet at night.

Elizabeth had made a deal with the Secret Service. In exchange for the currency plates, a million in counterfeit money, and the arrest of anyone else involved in the counterfeiting ring, the government would choose to ignore Alistair Sinclair's involvement. But the auction set off alarm bells with her feminine intuition. It seemed an unnecessary and overly public way to unload the plates and fake money.

The "anonymous tip" to the sheriff—initiated by Otto Fuchs—was intended to disgrace Alistair at the auction and let him take the fall for the counterfeiting ring. When Bradley told Elizabeth an assassin had been prepared to murder Alistair in jail, the color drained from her face. She thanked him again for picking the lock and transferring the money and plates from the carriage house on Third Street to Charles Frost's Schuyler Iron and Agricultural Works building. Mr. Frost had been in on the sting and offered his building as a new location to hide the money and plates. He also bid on Sinclair's desk as a distraction. While the sheriff was on a wild goose chase with the key from the desk, the Secret Service—the two men from Washington, DC—arrested the auction winners from Philadelphia when they showed up with the key from the stoneware.

"In the end," Elizabeth said, "everything worked out. One day, I might tell Emma Magee the whole story, but for now, I'll let her enjoy the success of her record charity auction fundraiser."

"What made you trust me enough to send those notes to my room?" Bradley asked.

"Ah, you figured out that was me?"

"Not at first," he admitted. "I thought Nanny Kate had delivered them."

"She did, but at my request."

"Why?"

"The day you asked for a job, I saw Vance's face as he was leaving my husband's room. He was furious. You had made him that way. As they say, the enemy of my enemy... anyway, I trusted my gut and hired you. But I also had my investigators dig into your past. You have many secrets still hidden, don't you?"

Elizabeth laughed at Bradley's discomfort. "Don't worry, your past is your own. But my investigators learned you had been working for a detective in the city, so the notes were my way of helping your investigation along."

"And going to Ithaca? That wasn't my idea after all, was it?"

She laughed. "Let's just say you didn't disappoint me when you suggested it. I knew the note about *Cornell* and *Jacub Jagusiak* would make you want to travel there."

"And with me there, Dewers had someone else to follow, freeing you up to meet with the Secret Service."

Elizabeth cupped his chin with her hand and gave it a small shake. "Handsome and intelligent. So much to like about you."

Bradley got to skip stones again with Hannah and Henry before their train left later that day. They begged him to visit them in the city. Alistair, hearing this, only scowled. Bradley also said goodbye to Nanny Kate. The Ballard brothers were still on the loose, but the Walrus had been apprehended in Horseheads with $50,000 in cash. He would go to jail for his part in the counterfeiting ring. Nanny Kate admitted she had appreciated his attention, but, in the end, he was "a bad dog not worth whistling for."

The minister finally ran out of words and invited members of the crowd to step forward and place flowers on the casket. Annie dropped her flower into the open grave and then stepped away. Bradley remembered the softness of her lips on his. He didn't know why she kissed him, but he was glad she did. Not that it mattered, now. He had little to offer her without a job or prospects. Nana dropped her flower next. Then came Mrs. Phelps, supporting Glendon Robinson. They dropped their flowers and moved to stand near Annie. Glendon did not look well—his right arm in a sling—but in the words of Dr. Bennett, he was "one lucky bastard." The pressure Annie had applied to Glendon's wound on the sailing yacht had prolonged his life long enough for Dr. Bennett to save him.

Bradley stared at Annie and then sighed. He had wanted to talk to her before he left, but seeing her would have to be enough. What could he say to her that would change anything? There was no point staying any longer. As he turned to leave, Abraham grabbed him by the arm. "Just a few more minutes, if you don't mind?"

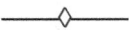

There was no large turnout for the graveside service, but Annie did not mind. Not everyone was willing to be associated with a suspected murderer. Even one as well-liked as Roland Smith had been.

Annie and Nana wore black, although they were not officially related to Roland. A typical mourning period when losing an aunt or uncle was three to six months. Out of respect, Annie would mourn for three. Nana, overly fond of traditions, would surely last six. Annie's grandmother had kept the curtains in their house closed all week to prevent the soul of the deceased from leaving before the funeral but also covered their mirrors to prevent that same soul from getting trapped in the house.

Annie glanced over at Glendon. She was thankful he was alive and standing beside her in the sunshine. If Otto Fuchs's bullet had been an inch to the left, Dr. Bennett said it would have hit an artery, and Glendon would have bled out. Glendon was still weak but insisted on attending Roland's funeral. Mrs. Phelps stayed by his side as his unofficial personal nurse, ensuring he did not rush his recovery. Annie could tell Glendon was enjoying the attention. They looked happy together.

Glendon leaned over and whispered in Annie's ear, "Roland wouldn't have cared to hear so many scripture readings over his grave."

"You paid the minister too much money," she whispered. Glendon had given the church a generous donation to ensure the minister showed up and said a few words. The man was overachieving. Annie shrugged. Perceptions mattered, and funerals were for the living, anyway. She looked sideways at Glendon. "I'm going to miss having Roland make me laugh," she whispered, fighting back tears.

"I know...."

They bowed their heads as the minister finished his closing prayer. After saying "Amen," the minister closed his Bible and those gathered lined up to file past Annie, Nana, and Glendon.

George and Emma Magee were the first to offer their condolences. George gave Glendon a healthy handshake that made Glendon wince, and then he took Annie's hand. "I had chosen Roland for the landscaping contract," George said, shaking his head. "He will be missed."

Emma hugged Annie. "Forgive my husband," she said. "He is always thinking about business. If you need anything, you will let us know?" Annie nodded and thanked her. Annie had finally admitted to Emma that she thought George blamed her for his brother's death. Emma was horrified. "Not at all," she had clarified. "He thought you were uncomfortable around him because he reminded you of John."

Josephine Knapp had come alone to the service. Annie hadn't seen her since the opera house.

"I'm sorry about Roland," Josephine said, "and thank you for what you did for me." Allen Hastings wouldn't bother either of them again. He'd lost his Fall Brook Coal Company job and left town to look for work in Philadelphia. Josephine looked down at her feet, took a deep breath, and then looked back at Annie as more words tumbled out. "I'm sorry if I treated you badly before. It's just—you made the most amazing dresses in school and had so much confidence. You never worried about what people thought of you. I was always so jealous...."

Annie was speechless. "Josephine, I—"

"Maybe we can meet for tea sometime," Josephine offered.

"Yes. Yes, I'd like that."

As Josephine stepped away, Mr. Nichols came forward. He offered his condolences and held Annie's hand for a heartbeat longer than was comfortable. He looked like he wanted to say more but, mercifully, he moved on. He ran to catch up with Josephine.

Jesse Hope and her family came next, followed by Esther Newby, her son Stephen, and a few more of Roland's friends. Near the end of the line waited the messenger who let Annie borrow his clothes. He stood in front of Annie, beaming in a tailored suit. "Thank you, Miss Anderson. I love my new clothes," he said. "And I'm sorry for your loss." He handed her a daisy and walked away. How dashing he looked, Annie thought. It was a shame he would outgrow this new suit within months.

Sheriff Swartwood was the last man in line. He presented himself to Glendon, Annie, Nana, and Mrs. Phelps with his hat in his hand. This, Annie realized, was her moment of victory. She had wanted to prove that the sheriff should have listened to her about the dead man on her mother's grave. That it wasn't a drunk who'd wandered away. The body found on Glendon's property proved the man had been dead. By choosing to ignore her, more people had been gravely injured. He was wrong. She was right. While all these thoughts flashed through her mind as he stepped forward, she realized that calling him out would not make him magically become a better person. He would not suddenly value her opinion because she had proven him wrong once. If anything, he would be resentful or embarrassed. What mattered—what had changed over the last four weeks—was the confidence Annie had found within herself.

"Sheriff," Annie said, "so kind of you to pay your respects to Roland... given the circumstances." She knew perfectly well that was not why he was standing before them.

"Sorry to disturb you," the sheriff said, "but there are still some unanswered questions to be cleared up. Glendon has been a difficult man to reach."

"Some nerve," Nana muttered, "interrupting a funeral." She excused herself and set out toward the Glen Mountain House for tea on the porch. Mrs. Phelps stayed by Glendon's side.

"I'm sure you appreciate," Annie said, "that Glendon is lucky to be alive and, until today, was in no condition to be interrogated."

"Yes, of course."

Glendon touched Annie on the arm. "It's okay, Annie," he said. "Ask your questions, Sheriff."

"Right." The sheriff held up the first of two pieces of paper. "In this written statement, you say that Roland Smith is dead because of you." The sheriff waved the paper at Glendon. "He was your friend. Do you expect me to believe this?"

"I stand by my statement," Glendon said. "When we returned home after the charity auction, we found your deputy unconscious and Roland shackled to his bed, brandishing the deputy's revolver. Roland was feverish. He threatened to kill all of us if we did not release him, so I grabbed the nearest weapon I could find—a shotgun used for hunting pheasant. I tried to talk sense into Roland, but he swore he'd rather die in Watkins than be forced back to Georgia to hang. Then he begged me to kill him. He said it would be a mercy. I refused, so he shot me. When he pointed the deputy's revolver at Annie, I had no choice. I pulled the trigger on the shotgun and fell unconscious from my wound." Glendon looked off into the distance. "I didn't know I'd killed him until I woke up three days later. It broke my heart."

The sheriff stared at Glendon and then shook his head. He held up the second piece of paper. "And this?"

Annie jumped in. "I found that by Roland's bedside after Doctor Bennett took his body away," Annie said. "As you can see, Roland confessed in writing to killing Lewis Crawford in Glenwood Cemetery and moving the body to Glendon's property on the east side of the lake. I'm sure George Magee could verify the signature matches Roland's recent landscaping bid."

The sheriff looked at Glendon. "Why would Roland move the Southerner's body to your property?"

"What idiot would hide a body on his own property?"

The sheriff nodded at the valid point. He did not ask why Roland would want to kill a Southerner like Crawford. Being wanted for murder in the South was enough of a connection.

The sheriff rubbed his chin. He folded up Roland's confession and put it in his pocket. He held up Glendon's written statement. "None of these details have been made public yet," he said. "I think this is a fairy tale." He ripped up the statement and dropped the pieces into the open grave. "Is there any other story you'd like to tell me?" He looked from Annie to Glendon. When they remained silent, he sighed. "Fine. Then, here is the official version of events going into my report. Roland attempted to take his own life on George Magee's property. When he woke, he realized the hangman's noose was still waiting for him. He was distraught and attacked my deputy, who valiantly fought back. As they battled, a bystander was injured but is expected to recover fully. Regrettably, my deputy had to use lethal force to subdue Roland Smith. Are we clear?"

Annie and Glendon looked at each other. Glendon cleared his throat. "I appreciate, Sheriff, that your version keeps my name out of the newspapers."

"And I appreciate," Annie offered, "that public confidence in our police force will increase just in time for the regatta."

The sheriff shot her a sour look but chose to move on. "One more thing," he said to Annie. "That one-armed man stormed into my office when he heard Roland had been killed. Demanded to see the body. He thought he could take what was left of Roland back to Georgia and still claim the reward. I didn't give him the time of day, so he threatened that I would be hearing from his lawyer. Swore he would appeal to the governor if need be."

"And?" Glendon asked.

"And several witnesses swear Miss Annie Anderson approached the one-armed man a short while later, and after their brief conversation, he departed on the next train." The sheriff turned curiously to Annie. "I wanted to know what you said to him."

"Oh, I just pointed out that if there were a reward for killing Roland, it would go to the man brave enough to pull the trigger," Annie said. "Not to him."

"You called him a coward to his face," the sheriff chuckled. "I'm impressed, Miss Anderson." The sheriff was satisfied. "Thank you for your cooperation," he said, tipping his hat and leaving the cemetery.

"What did you really say to the one-armed man?" Glendon asked.

Annie smiled. "I told him I knew that he was the bank robber who killed the civilian in Georgia and not Roland. I knew Roland shot him in the arm to stop him from shooting another bank customer. I told him I have evidence to prove he later framed Roland by hiding the money and bank bags in Roland's hotel room. I knew he'd been lying all this time, and if he didn't leave town and never return, I would deliver the evidence to the sheriff."

Glendon grinned. "There was no evidence."

"True, but I guess he was unwilling to take that chance. He was a coward, through and through." Annie looked down at the inscription on the gravestone. *Roland Smith.* "Where do you think Roland is now?"

Glendon considered. "Oh, I would guess about halfway to St. Louis by now."

It had been Roland's idea to swap places with Fuchs's body.

Roland had not been as close to death as Annie and her grandmother had led Deputy Hodgkins to believe. Roland had woken up three nights before the charity auction while Nana was watching over him. Nana and Annie had hatched a plan for his escape. During the day, Roland slept and appeared to be dying—helped by some white powder on his face, selling the illusion. In the evening, Nana spiked the deputy's drink with her sleeping elixir to ensure he slept through the night. After the deputy passed out, Annie and Nana took turns nursing Roland back to health and rebuilding his strength.

After the charity auction, Nana returned to the house and

spiked the deputy's drink as usual. With the deputy quietly snoring on the couch, Nana and Roland waited for Annie. They were growing frantic at her absence when, in the middle of the night, the front door burst open, and a blood-covered Annie came in, followed by Abraham and a large, burly man carrying a severely wounded Glendon. A few minutes later, Bradley arrived with a bleary-eyed Dr. Bennett.

At the sight of Annie's bloody hands and dress, Dr. Bennett marched straight for her. "Are you injured?" he asked.

"I'm fine, doctor. It's Glendon, he's been shot. Please save him."

"I'll do what I can," he said.

While Nana enlisted Bradley and Frank to boil water and gather towels, Roland guided Annie into the dining room and sat her at the table. "Annie, are you sure you aren't injured?"

"It's not my blood."

Roland breathed a sigh of relief and stepped out of the room. He returned a minute later with a basin of water and helped wash the blood from her hands and arms. "Tell me everything," he said.

An hour later, Dr. Bennett declared Glendon to be one lucky man. If he could avoid an infection, he would survive his wound. While the doctor cleaned up, Roland pulled him aside. They whispered furiously back and forth until the doctor nodded his head. "After all," Dr. Bennett grumbled, "I didn't save your life just to have some rebels string you up and end it."

Abraham drove Dr. Bennett home, and Roland gathered everyone else around the dining room table and shared his plan. With no evidence to prove otherwise, he would be sent to Georgia and hung for a crime he did not commit. So Roland Smith had to die. If they put Roland's clothes on Fuchs's dead body, who would be the wiser? The shotgun blast to Fuchs's face would make identification impossible. No one would question Dr. Bennett's word that it was Roland lying dead.

Roland needed to be on the road before the town woke up for the plan to work.

"I'll go with you," Annie said. They had planned to leave together before Fuchs's death.

Roland knelt before her. "Annie, you have to stay."

"What? Why!?"

"You must stay and mourn for Roland Smith. If you leave, too many questions will be asked about where you've gone and why."

Fresh tears formed in Annie's eyes.

"I loved your father," Roland said, taking Annie's hand. "After he died, I stayed in Watkins, knowing he would want me to watch over you. And I've done that. I have watched you grow into the beautiful, intelligent woman that you are. I'm so proud of you. And I love you. But it's time for me to leave. Your time will come. When it does, come visit me in St. Louis. I'll be using the name William Anderson."

No one objected to Roland's plan, so Frank brought in Fuchs's lifeless body—still wrapped in the extra sail. They moved quickly, knowing the deputy could wake up at any moment. Annie had run upstairs and brought back the money Glendon had left for her. She gave it to Roland. "For your new start," she said.

Roland was still weak, so Frank agreed to spirit him out of town. Frank promised to return to Watkins after Roland reached St. Louis. He wanted to escort Buck's body back to Rutherford-ton—after getting the body transferred from the steamer trunk into a proper coffin. Lewis "Buck" Crawford had his demons, but his wife deserved a chance to bury her husband in North Carolina soil.

Annie had mourned Roland for the week he'd been gone, but knowing he was living his life out in the world made her happy. She stepped away from the grave and waved the gravedigger over. The man had been patiently leaning on his shovel but was happy to finish the job and got to work filling in the grave. Annie would mourn Roland, but she would not be visiting Otto Fuchs's final resting place. She was glad his grave was nowhere near her parents.

Mrs. Phelps stepped forward and gripped Glendon by the arm. "It's time to get you back to bed. You need your rest to recover fully."

Glendon turned and hugged Annie. "Once the dust settles," he said, "we can discuss what is next for you. I support whatever direction you choose. Life is full of adventures, and it is time to start your next one."

She hugged him back. "Thank you, Father."

Glendon stiffened in surprise and then gave her a wistful smile.

"Careful," he said, "I could get used to hearing you call me that." Glendon hugged her again and then motioned to where Bradley and Abraham stood waiting. "Will you be okay?"

"Yes, I'll be fine."

As Annie watched Glendon and Mrs. Phelps climb into the remaining carriage and disappear down Cemetery Hill, a motion in the corner of her eye caught her attention. She watched as the brightly colored dragonfly zipped left and right and then hovered before her. Annie smiled. Dragonflies had always reminded her of her mother. Her mother had believed in heaven but had also promised to visit from time to time as a dragonfly to watch over Annie. Maybe this was her mother's way of checking on her from the next life. The dragonfly moved up and down and then darted away across the cemetery toward Bradley and Abraham.

Annie turned and watched the two men approach. She felt guilty for ever believing Abraham could have been Crawford's killer. He had not been the black man in Harper/Glendon's journal either. She also felt guilty for ignoring Bradley's requests to meet. She could claim she'd had her hands full with Roland's funeral preparations and Glendon's recovery, but the truth was she'd been afraid of her feelings. She could still feel Bradley's kiss on her lips.

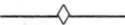

Abraham was nervous. He prided himself on being calm under pressure, but the outcome of this conversation with Annie and Bradley could change the rest of his life.

Annie offered a warm smile as he and Bradley approached. She was unbowed by all she had been through these last few weeks. Abraham was impressed. Wherever Abraham's daughter was—if she was still alive—Abraham hoped she had grown up as smart, resourceful, and resilient as Annie Anderson.

"Thank you for coming to Roland's service," Annie said.

"It was a beautiful funeral," Abraham said. "And it was nice to see Glendon on his feet."

"Doctor Bennett changed his bandages before the service and saw no sign of infection. He is optimistic about Glendon's full recovery."

Abraham lowered his voice, although no one was nearby. "Any word from Roland?"

Annie stepped closer—a co-conspirator sharing confidential information. "Frank returned yesterday and plans to leave tomorrow with Crawford's coffin," Annie said. "He told us Roland is safe in St. Louis and was getting stronger every day."

Abraham nodded.

"Did Frank ever say what brought him to Watkins?" Bradley asked.

"He told Glendon that he got the same letters as Crawford," Annie said, "but he ignored them. He never cared about the gold, and they sounded suspicious. It was only after Crawford visited him on his way north that Frank changed his mind. He worried Crawford was walking into a trap, so he followed a day later. He was a day too late to prevent Crawford's murder, but he didn't know it because the body had disappeared. Frank's only clue pointed to my mother's grave, so he watched over it until Roland and I visited. Then he followed me, hoping to be led to Crawford. Instead, I unknowingly led him to Glendon, whom he recognized as Harper."

"Frank really didn't want any of the gold?" Abraham asked.

Annie shrugged. "He said he didn't. And that was before the surviving members of the Lucky Six decided it was cursed and couldn't be spent. Glendon believes it can only be given away. Even Bradley thinks it's bad luck."

Abraham looked at Bradley, surprised.

"Well," Bradley said, kicking the dirt at his feet, "I'm not superstitious, but... after the O'Donnell brothers showed up out of nowhere and beat me up, I couldn't risk any more rotten luck. So when I swapped revolvers with Fuchs, I dropped the gold nugget Glendon gave me into one of Fuchs's jacket pockets."

"The nugget fell out of Fuchs's jacket when Roland and Frank dressed his body in Roland's clothes," Annie said. "I almost put it back in Fuchs's pocket, but, on Glendon's behalf, I took it to the bank and placed it back in one of the six satchels of gold stored in the vault. Not even Fuchs deserves an eternity of bad luck."

Abraham was relieved. Glendon wouldn't give cursed gold to Annie, so it made her more likely to agree to his plan. He opened his mouth to speak, but Annie was still focused on Bradley. She bent down and lifted her skirt to show Bradley her boots. "I didn't have a chance to thank you," she said. "These are even better than the ones I lost in the lake."

Bradley smiled. "I'm just glad they fit."

"And to return the thank you." Annie held out her hand to Bradley.

Confused, he extended his hand palm up. Their fingers touched as she placed his father's pocket watch in his hand. "My father's watch! I thought it was gone forever." He held it to his ear and listened to it ticking. "And it's working!"

"I know a good watchmaker in Elmira who repaired it," Annie said. "I'm sorry it took so long."

"Where did you find it?"

"It had fallen under the bed when you were—"

"Naked and bound to your bedframe?"

Abraham's eyes widened as Bradley laughed. Annie blushed.

"I was wondering," Annie said. "The initials on the watch are B.W. Are you named after your father?" She paused and then said what she was thinking. "I still don't know your real name."

Bradley stared at the watch, then tucked it into his pocket. "No," he said. "I'm not named after my father." He looked up at Annie. "And I haven't told anyone my real name since the war."

A shadow flashed across Annie's face, and Abraham stepped in to redirect the conversation. He needed both Annie and Bradley for his plan's success. "I have something I want to show both of you," he said. "It's in the wagon."

Annie and Bradley followed Abraham back to his wagon. Annie rubbed Goldie's neck as they passed. In the bed of the wagon was a tarp, and under the tarp, there was a small bulge. Abraham grabbed the tarp's edge as if to fling it off and reveal what was beneath but turned back to Annie and Bradley.

"I have a proposition," he said, "that I hope you will both consider." Abraham wanted to get the words right. "You make a great team," he said. "Neither of you gave up even when others would have run away. I need that type of determination." He paused. "I need help with something that means the world to me... something

I cannot do alone."

Before Annie or Bradley could reply, Abraham pulled the tarp away to reveal an alligator leather satchel sitting in the back of the wagon.

Bradley's mouth dropped. "Fuchs's satchel!"

"I saw it when you arrived on the sailboat," Abraham said. "Bradley, to your credit, you were so focused on saving Glendon's life that you left it behind. When I took Doctor Bennett home, I went back to the sailboat. It was still there, so I recovered it. For safekeeping."

"Do you know what's inside?" Annie asked.

"Yes, I do."

"Fuchs told me he was writing his memoirs," Bradley said.

Annie shook her head. "A Pinkerton writing his memoirs sounds plausible, but a master criminal? Fuchs is dead and has no known relatives so there is no one else to claim it, but if it's more counterfeit money, we would have to turn it over to the Secret Service."

"It's not counterfeit money," Abraham said.

"Is it valuable?" Bradley asked.

Annie looked at Abraham. "You recovered it," she said, "so whatever is inside belongs to you."

Bradley opened his mouth to argue but closed it again and nodded in agreement.

"Thank you, but no," Abraham said. He appreciated their generosity but could only imagine the questions asked of a colored man if he claimed what was in the satchel all for himself. "Let's agree to split the contents three ways evenly. Consider it compensation for the pain and suffering Fuchs put you both through."

Annie and Bradley agreed, Annie more reluctantly than Bradley.

"What is in the satchel, Abraham?" Annie asked.

Abraham hesitated. "First, my proposal," he said. "With my third of the money, I want to hire you both—if you are willing to work together—to help me find my wife and daughter. I searched for years with no answers, but you can go places I could never go. Talk to people who refused to talk to me. I know it is a long shot, but I have to try. I have to know what happened to them. Will you help me?"

Without waiting for an answer, he stepped forward and opened the leather satchel. "This is one million dollars of gold certificates in this satchel."

Bradley let out a low whistle. Gold certificates were as good as currency and could be redeemed for their equivalent value in gold.

"Fuchs said he was leaving for South America with ten million dollars," Annie said. "He only had nine million in counterfeit money left after the auction, so this must be the extra million." She looked at Abraham sadly. "But Abraham, we aren't detectives."

"I disagree," Abraham said. "I have watched you work together for weeks. Because of you, the counterfeiting ring was broken up. Because of you, the Butzemann will no longer terrorize New York City. Because of you, the mystery of the dead man in the cemetery has been solved."

Bradley shrugged. "It's been over ten years. The trail is cold... it could be a lot of work and a lot of traveling that amounts to nothing."

"I'm willing to take that chance," Abraham said.

Annie looked at Bradley, "We'd be crazy to do this, wouldn't we?"

He smiled at her. "Yes, I think we would have to be crazy."

"We would have to form a detective agency," Annie said.

Bradley nodded. "I've got just the name," Bradley said, "since you have inherited Glendon's good fortune."

"The Lucky Detective Agency?"

"Exactly," Bradley said. He reached out his hand. "Partner?"

Annie looked at Bradley's hand. She looked at Abraham. She smiled at him and then shook Bradley's hand. "Partner."

Abraham had been holding his breath. He let it out slowly. Now, he dared to believe that together they could find the answers to questions that had haunted him for years.

"Abraham," Annie said, "you've secured the services of the Lucky Detective Agency. When do we begin?"

LVII

A GOLDEN OFFERING

Monday, August 17, 1874

B RUCE Collingsworth looked up from his ledger as one of his
  orderlies entered his office in the National Home for Disabled
Volunteer Soldiers in Hampton, Virginia. "What is it now, Jenkins?" He was a busy man responsible for, among other things, the
home's financial recordkeeping. Ten years after the war, more and
more disabled veterans needed subsistence, quarters, and clothing.

"A shipment has arrived, sir."

"A shipment?" Collingsworth shuffled through more papers on
his desk, looking at outstanding invoices. "I'm not expecting any
shipments today. Did the blankets we ordered come in early?"

"It's not blankets, sir."

Collingsworth looked at the orderly with growing impatience.
"Am I supposed to guess?"

"Perhaps you should come outside, sir, and see for yourself."

Collingsworth huffed at the inconvenience, but he was a kind
man. If the orderly felt something of importance needed his attention, well, a short walk into the sunshine wasn't the worst thing.

He followed the orderly out the front entrance and down the
stairs. A horse-drawn wagon with no horse attached sat on the
gravel drive. A tarp covered a sizable mound in the center of the
wagon.

"How did this get here?" Collingsworth asked.

"A large man—as big as a bear—arrived no more than fifteen
minutes ago," Jenkins said. "He asked me if I worked here. When
I told him I did, he unhitched the horse from this wagon, mounted
the horse, and sauntered away."

"He left the wagon?" Collingsworth was confused. "Was that

all he said?"

"Well...."

"What did he say, Jenkins?"

"He didn't say anything else. He handed me this note." The orderly passed a folded piece of paper to Collingsworth.

Collingsworth unfolded the paper and read the handwritten message aloud. "Use wisely. *Bono malum superate.*" Collingsworth considered the words and then walked to the back of the wagon. With Jenkins's help, they flung the tarp aside. Sitting in the middle of the wagon was a wooden coffin.

Jenkins waited for Collingsworth's reaction, which confirmed that his orderly had already peeked under the tarp. "Sir," Jenkins said, "I can't read Latin. What does the note say?"

Collingsworth ignored the question and sent Jenkins in search of a crowbar. "Are you sure, sir?" Jenkins asked.

"Yes, yes, hurry now."

Jenkins returned, crowbar in hand. Reluctantly, he climbed onto the wagon and pried the lid off the coffin. Inside were six leather satchels filled with gold ore. Collingsworth smiled. A coffin was a clever way to transport something this valuable.

He turned to Jenkins. "*Bono malum superate* is Latin for 'overcome evil with good.'"

"Oh. But... What does that mean?"

"Mean?" Collingsworth chuckled. "It means that after you help me get these satchels in a safe place, we will put this gift to good use for our veterans. For starters, I'm going to double our blanket order."

Watkins Glen, The Cathedral

HISTORICAL NOTES

Real people depicted in *The Lucky Six* include George and Emma Magee, Sheriff John Swartwood, Thomas Ballard and his brothers, Washington Traweek, James Hope and his daughter Jesse, Big Mag, Dr. Bennett, Charles Frost, AO Whittemore, and Ruth Van Etten.

George Magee completed the Syracuse, Geneva and Corning Railroad as planned in 1877 on the western shore of Seneca Lake (including the trestle and a station at the top of the Glen). He moved the company headquarters to Corning, N.Y., that same year. Unable to compete with the railroads, the Chemung Canal closed in 1878.

Sheriff John S. Swartwood lost his reelection campaign in November 1874 to John Wood of Cayuta. With the new sheriff suffering from consumption, Swartwood continued to live in the sheriff's residence.

Thomas Ballard and his four brothers were all involved in counterfeiting. Thomas, the expert engraver, was arrested in October 1874 in Buffalo, N.Y., and sentenced to thirty years in Albany Penitentiary for possession of counterfeiting engravings, plates, paper, etc.

James Hope lived in the Glen and continued to paint until his death in 1892. His artwork was moved to a gallery near the Glen entrance, where many paintings were damaged in the flood of 1935.

Big Mag's establishment caught fire in 1875. No one rushed to put out the fire. The building was a loss and was not rebuilt.

Washington Traweek really did lead a prisoner escape of Elmira Prison Camp. Ten prisoners, mostly from Alabama, escaped through an undiscovered tunnel. You can find Traweek's story of his escape online.

Other real historical events portrayed in *The Lucky Six* include the Shohola Train Wreck, Ruth Van Etten's falling death in Watkins Glen on July 16, 1874, and The Great New York and New Orleans Zoological and Equestrian Exposition visit to Watkins in July 1874.

The legend of the missing gold was reported in the *Forest City (N.C.) Courier* in 1938. There is no record of the gold ever being found.

ACKNOWLEDGMENTS

Writing is a solitary activity, but *The Lucky Six* would not exist without the help and encouragement of many people. Which means I have many people to thank.

My sisters, Nancy Oliver and Diane Cooper, read every chapter as it came out and served both as cheerleaders to encourage my efforts and early warning detectors, making sure the book was logical and kept a consistent tone. I owe special thanks to Jeannie Gardner, who also provided feedback on each new chapter and served as my primary research partner/assistant. Jeannie has a talent and passion for tracking down historical information and could do it from Watkins Glen, allowing me to focus on writing this novel from my home in California. I cannot overstate the value of her support and commitment to the project.

Although I agonized over any deviations from the historical record in this novel, and there are a few (looking at you, charity auction, for being about twenty years too early), overall, I'm satisfied I got most of the history right. Thanks to Gary Emerson, the Schuyler County historian, for sharing his knowledge of the Chemung Canal, Elmira Prison Camp, and the steamer *Estelle*. Thanks to Andrew Tompkins, former director of the Schuyler County Historical Society, who provided invaluable help on my 2009 book, *Watkins Glen Tour Guide*, as well as information on steam yachts and his grandfather's 1849 Colt pistol. Thanks also to researchers from the History Center in Tompkins County, the Chemung Valley History Museum, the Genealogical Society of Old Tryon County, NC, the Burke County Public Library, and The History Museum of Burke County, NC.

Perhaps the most fun I had while writing the book was getting out and doing field research. Thanks to Nico and Emma Piacentini for a tour of their home, the A. F. Chapman House, which became the model for Annie's home in 1874. Thanks to Reverend Cara Milne and Ken Wilson for a guided tour of the Presbyterian

Church and its bell tower. Many years have passed since my sisters and I attended services there with our grandparents. Thanks to Bill Tague for a tour of the old Freer Opera House on the third floor above Jerlando's. Thanks to Mark Lembeck for sharing his family information and photos of the Lembeck Malt House. I also owe thanks to the owners of Stone Path Malt in Wareham, Massachusetts, for the personal tour of their malthouse.

I want to thank my childhood classmate, Shari Scaptura and her daughter Aran, who let me pilot them out to the middle of Seneca Lake on a lovely summer day and then jump over the side in the name of field research (I did make it back onto the boat). Also, I want to thank Jeannie Gardner and Barb Abbey for letting me join their swim across Cayuta Lake. I owe undying gratitude to their friend Tammy Vona and her kayak for making sure I didn't drown and could finish this novel.

I owe a big thanks to all my beta readers and ARC readers— you know who you are—whose efforts definitely made this book more readable. A special shout-out to Dave Domingo, Sandrine Chaumette, Rebecca Wilber, and Ken Ciocco who each, in their own way, provided feedback and encouragement in the early days. Thanks also to my editor, Rachel Santino. If I've managed to reinsert typos, the blame is mine, not hers.

Finally, thanks to my wife, Jill, and my sons, Evan and Alex, for their patience, support, and encouragement for this multi-year effort. Evan provided the most relatable feedback on the manuscript, and Alex helped me act out many of the action scenes and drew the Lucky Six's tattoo. I am extremely proud of this book, but that pales in comparison to how proud I am of the men my sons have become.

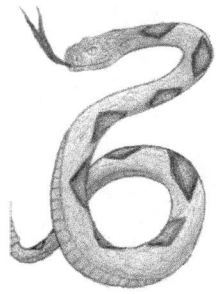

ABOUT THE AUTHOR

Gordon Cooper grew up in Watkins Glen, N.Y., and graduated from Watkins Glen High School before venturing off into the world to seek his fortune. Returning often to his hometown, he researched and wrote his first book, *Watkins Glen Tour Guide*, which received *Foreword Review's* GOLD Winner for Travel Guides in 2009. That effort produced a stack of research material on Watkins, N.Y., in the 1870s, which formed the background of his debut novel, *The Lucky Six.*

Gordon has spent most of his working career as an electrical engineer in Boston, Atlanta, and San Jose. He is also a retired Army Public Affairs officer who served on peacekeeping missions in Bosnia and Kosovo. He currently lives in California with his wife and sons.

Learn more at GordonCooper.com.